ROBOTICS

(Elective III)

For
FINAL YEAR (B.E.) MECHANICAL ENGINEERING GROUP

As Per Revised Syllabus

MANDAR T. PURANIK

M.E. (Mech.) Design Engineering
Dy. Manager, Training and Application,
SMC Pneumatics (India) Pvt. Ltd., Pune and
Formerly with Vishwakarma Institute of Technology,
PUNE – 411037.

RATNAKAR R. GHORPADE

M.E. (Mech.) Design Engineering,
Assistant Professor
Department of Mechanical Engineering
Maharashtra Institute of Technology (MIT)
Kothrud. **PUNE – 411 038.**

Dr. MANMOHAN M. BHOOMKAR

Ph.D., (Mech. Engg.)
Associate Professor,
Department of Mechanical Engineering,
Pune Vidyarthi Griha's College of Engineering and Technology,
Parvati, **PUNE – 09.**

N1398

ROBOTICS　　　　　　　　　　　　　　　　　　　　　**ISBN 978-93-81962-21-3**

Sixth Edition　:　January 2014

© 　　　　　:　**Author**

Published By :
NIRALI PRAKASHAN
Abhyudaya Pragati, 1312, Shivaji Nagar,
Off J.M. Road, PUNE – 411005
Tel - (020) 25512336/37/39, Fax - (020) 25511379
Email : niralipune@pragationline.com

DISTRIBUTION CENTRES

PUNE

Nirali Prakashan
119, Budhwar Peth, Jogeshwari Mandir Lane
Pune 411002, Maharashtra
Tel : (020) 2445 2044, 66022708, Fax : (020) 2445 1538
Email : bookorder@pragationline.com

Nirali Prakashan
S. No. 28/27, Dhyari,
Near Pari Company, Pune 411041
Tel : (022) 24690371
Email : dhyari@pragationline.com
bookorder@pragationline.com

MUMBAI
Nirali Prakashan
385, S.V.P. Road, Rasdhara Co-op. Hsg. Society Ltd.,
Girgaum, Mumbai 400004, Maharashtra
Tel : (022) 2385 6339 / 2386 9976, Fax : (022) 2386 9976
Email : niralimumbai@pragationline.com

DISTRIBUTION BRANCHES

NAGPUR
Pratibha Book Distributors
Above Maratha Mandir, Shop No. 3, First Floor,
Rani Jhanshi Square, Sitabuldi, Nagpur 440012,
Maharashtra, Tel : (0712) 254 7129

BENGALURU
Pragati Book House
House No. 1, Sanjeevappa Lane, Avenue Road Cross,
Opp. Rice Church, Bengaluru – 560002.
Tel : (080) 64513344, 64513355,
Mob : 9880582331, 9845021552
Email:bharatsavla@yahoo.com

JALGAON
Nirali Prakashan
34, V. V. Golani Market, Navi Peth, Jalgaon 425001,
Maharashtra, Tel : (0257) 222 0395
Mob : 94234 91860

KOLHAPUR
Nirali Prakashan
New Mahadvar Road,
Kedar Plaza, 1st Floor Opp. IDBI Bank
Kolhapur 416 012, Maharashtra. Mob : 9850046155

CHENNAI
Pragati Books
9/1, Montieth Road, Behind Taas Mahal, Egmore,
Chennai 600008 Tamil Nadu, Tel : (044) 6518 3535,
Mob : 94440 01782 / 98450 21552 / 98805 82331, Email : bharatsavla@yahoo.com

RETAIL OUTLETS

PUNE
Pragati Book Centre
157, Budhwar Peth, Opp. Ratan Talkies,
Pune 411002, Maharashtra
Tel : (020) 2445 8887 / 6602 2707, Fax : (020) 2445 8887
Pragati Book Centre
Amber Chamber, 28/A, Budhwar Peth,
Appa Balwant Chowk, Pune : 411002, Maharashtra,
Tel : (020) 20240335 / 66281669
Email : pbcpune@pragationline.com

Pragati Book Centre
676/B, Budhwar Peth, Opp. Jogeshwari Mandir,
Pune 411002, Maharashtra
Tel : (020) 6601 7784 / 6602 0855
PBC Book Sellers & Stationers
152, Budhwar Peth, Pune 411002, Maharashtra
Tel : (020) 2445 2254 / 6609 2463

MUMBAI
Pragati Book Corner
Indira Niwas, 111 - A, Bhavani Shankar Road, Dadar (W), Mumbai 400028, Maharashtra
Tel : (022) 2422 3526 / 6662 5254, Email : pbcmumbai@pragationline.com

www.pragationline.com　　　　　　　　　　　　　　　　info@pragationline.com

Unit I

Chapter 1: INTRODUCTION TO ROBOTICS

1.1 Brief History

The word "ROBOT" came into English language in 1923 from the translation of a play "Rossum's Universal Robot", originally a Czechoslovakian play written by Karel Capek in 1921. It is derived from the Czech word "robota" meaning "slave labourer" or "forced labourer". In the play robots are designed to replace human workers and are depicted as very efficient workers indistinguishable from humans except for their lack of emotions. In the play, the robots rebel against their human masters and destroy the entire human race, except one man, so that he can continue making robots.

1.2 Three Laws of Robotics   (W-11)

On the contrary, to avoid dangers of mechanization, a science fiction writer Issac Asimov[*] used word "robotics" to describe "study of robots" (in fact, robot ethics) in his story "Runaround" in 1942 and gave three laws of robotics, as below.

1. A robot may not injure a human being or allow a human to be harmed through in action.
2. A robot must obey orders given by humans, except when those conflicts with the First law.
3. A robot must protect its own existence unless that conflicts with the first or Second law.

Although the words "robot" and "robotics" came into existence after 1920s the actual robot-like machine were invented, built and used quite before. The documented evidence of use of human-sized mechanical dolls for playing music is found in mid of 18th century.

1.3 Definition and Basic Concepts

The robot in modern science is an automatic, servo-controlled, freely programmable, multi-purpose manipulator, with several areas, for handling of work pieces, tools or special devices.

---

[*]   The movie "I Robot" is picturised using collection of Issac Asimov's short stories written in 1950s.

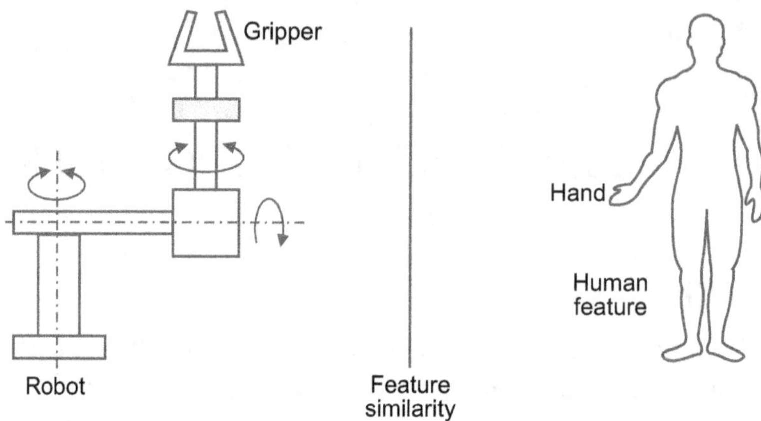

Fig. 1.1: Similarity in Robot and Human

Robot is a machine that looks and works like a human being. The industrial robots of today can replace human beings as regards to physical work and decision-making to some extent. All the research is directed to provide more and more anthropomorphic and human like features and super-human capabilities.

An industrial robot, also called as robotic manipulator or robotic arm is a general purpose computer-controlled manipulator, which consists of several rigid links connected in series by revolute or prismatic joints, one end of the kinematic chain is attached to a supporting base, while the other end is free and equipped with an end-effector, which may be a tool or gripper. The motion of the joint results in relative motion of the links. The links correspond to such features of the human anatomy as the chest, upper arm, and forearm, while the joints correspond to the shoulder, elbow and wrist.

There are numerous applications of robots, some of which are listed below,

1. They are commonly employed in hostile environment. e.g. in an atomic plant for handling radioactive materials.

2. They are being employed to construct and repair space stations and satellites.

3. They find applications in nursing aiding a patient.

4. Microrobots are being designed to do damage control inside human veins.

5. Robot like systems are used in heavy earth-moving equipments.

6. They are employed for basic manufacturing activities like assembly, welding, spray painting, coating and repetitive tasks like pick and place.

1.4 Robots and Robotic Mechanisms

According to a very generalised definition, the Webster dictionary "robot is a mechanism that can move automatically". Or its detailed definition is "an automatic device that performs functions normally ascribed to humans", in other words "machine in the form of human". If we **strictly** follow these definitions then today's robots cannot be called as robots at all, because they are not fully automatic or autonomous in the sense of making decisions. Further, there will not be any such robot into existence, if every robot manufacturer **strictly** adheres to the laws of robotics (i.e. robot ethics), written by Issac Asimov in his sciencefiction story "Runaround".

1.4.1 What is a Robot?

Later, in this chapter we will see definition of an industrial robot which includes reprogrammable, multi-functional manipulators designed to move materials parts, tools for performance of a variety of tasks. Thus, all industrial robots now fall under the category as "what is a robot?".

1.4.2 What is not a Robot?

Nevertheless, there are many mechanisms, in industry or otherwise, required to complete specified tasks but they fall under category "What is not a robot?" These mechanisms although look like industrial robots are neither automatic in any sense nor reprogrammable, but are designed to perform various tasks under a continuous human control. These robots like devices may be classified in four groups as under:

1. **Prosthesis:**

This is an artificial device used to replace a missing or removed part of human body, like arm, leg. These parts are not simply designed for appearance as part of human body, but for performing the tasks that would have been otherwise performed by the original part.

2. **Telecheric:**

This is a device that allows the robot operator to control the robot like mechanism situated at a distance. The word comes from the telerobotics technology. An example of telecheric may be a wearable dataglove with force sensors attached to it, which the operator can wear on his hand. The movements and forces exerted by the operator's fingers are sensed by the sensors and fed to the mechanism which may be located remotely, to grip or release an object. This may find applications in the hazardous areas where human cannot enter, such as handling of explosive chemicals, automatic fuel.

3.   Locomotive mechanisms:

These devices imitate human or animals. A person sitting inside it, controls the mechanism just like a vehicle. Any earth moving machine may be taken as an example of locomotive machine.

4.   Exoskeleton:

It is a device that may be worn by the operator to amplify human powers. For example, a soldier wearing a properly designed exoskeleton will be able to carry more weapons. Also will be able to remove obstacles from the path due to amplification of the strengths. Though the path is obstacles-filled and there is a lot of load to carry on human body, the soldier will be able to walk at a greater speed than normal, and in addition will be able to jump high as well as long with the help of properly designed exoskeleton worn on his body.

1.4.3 Examples of Robot like Devices in Science Fiction Movies

Possibly you must have seen some robot like devices in sciencefiction movies.

Following are some of the examples from such movies presented here for better understanding.

1.   Prosthesis:

In the Star Wars movies, the hero, Anakin Skywalker loses his hand in a battle and gets operated to put on an artificial hand. Afterwards in another battle, burns almost full of his body. But manages to remain alive and subsequently transforms himself into a powerful villain Darth Vader by putting prosthetic organs on his body and by wearing a prosthetic mask.

2.   Telecheric:

Arnold Schwarzenegger (Adam Gibson) in the movie "The 6th Day", operates and drives a helicopter from outside of it using a telecheric device that really operates the levers inside the helicopter and navigates it.

3.   Locomotive mechanisms:

In the last episode of the Star Wars Series of movies "Return of the Jedi", robot like the vehicles imitating a biped animal splitting fire shots through laser weapons looking like break fitted on it are used in the war. The vehicles are named AT-ST Walker (All Terrain Scout Transport) or Scout Walker and have two seats for the pilot and co-pilot.

In another movie "Wild Wild West" the villain Dr. Arliss Loveless uses a giant-spider-like walking machine for his transports.

4.   Exoskeleton:

Ripley, the lady in the central role in the movie "Aliens" fights with the beast wearing an exoskeleton, which is a mechanism like two legged robot, having a sufficient space for a human to stand inside it and operate.

1.5 Automation and Robotics

Automation and robotics are two closely related technologies. Both the terms are related by the use and control of production operations. Industrial automation can be defined as the technology that is concerned with the use of mechanical, electronic and computer-based systems to control production processes. e.g. transfer lines, mechanized assembly machines, feedback control systems, numerically controlled machine tools.

Robots are mechanical devices which assist industrial automation.

There are three broad categories of industrial automation.

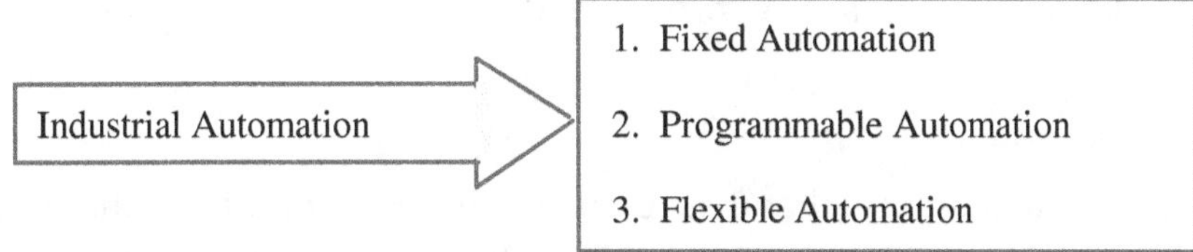

1.   Fixed Automation:

- It is used when the volume of production is very high and it is, thus appropriate to design specialised equipment to process products at high rates and low costs.

- Example, in the automobile industry, where highly integrated transfer lines are used to perform machining operations on engine and transmission components.

- The economics of fixed automation is such that the cost of the special equipment can be divided over a large number of units produced, so that the resulting unit cost can be lowered relative to alternative methods of production.

- **Disadvantages/Problems with Fixed Automation:**
    - ☛ The initial investment cost is high, and if the volume of production turns out to be lower than anticipated, then the unit cost becomes greater.

☛ The equipment is specially designed to produce only one product. After the life cycle of that product is finished, the equipment is likely to become obsolete.

☛ Thus, for products with short life cycles, fixed automation is not economical.

2. Programmable Automation:

- It is used when the volume of production is relatively low and there is a variety of products to be made.

- In this type of automation, the production equipment is designed to be adaptable to variations in a product configuration.

- This adaptability feature is accomplished by operating the equipment under the control of a 'program' of instructions that has been prepared especially for the given product.

- The program is read into the production equipment and the equipment performs the particular sequence of operations to make that product.

- In terms of economics, the cost of the programmable equipment can be spread over a large number of products even though the products are different.

- Due to the programming feature, and the resulting adaptability of the equipment, many different and unique products can be processed economically in small batches.

3. Flexible Automation:

- It is a third category that lies between fixed automation and programmable automation. It is also called as 'Flexible Manufacturing Systems' (FMS) and 'Computer-Integrated Manufacturing' (CIM).

- It has only developed within the past twenty or twenty five years. This type of automation is most suitable for the mid-volume production range as shown in Fig. 1.2.

- Flexible automation systems possess some of the features of both fixed and programmable automation.

- Flexible automation typically consists of a series of workstations that are interconnected by material handling and storage equipment to process different product configurations at the same time on the same manufacturing system.

- A central computer is used to control the various activities that occur in the system, routing the various parts to the appropriate stations and controlling the programmed operations at the different stations.

Difference between Programmable and Fixed Automation:

- With programmable automation the products are made in batches, when one batch is completed, the equipment is reprogrammed to process the next batch.

- With flexible automation, different products can be made at the same time on the same system. This feature allows a level of versatility that is not available in pure programmable automation, as we have defined it. This means that products can be produced on a flexible system in batches, if desirable, or that several products can be mixed on the same system. The computational power of the control computer is what makes this versatility possible.

Where Robotics fit?

- Robots coincide most closely with programmable automation. The 'official' definition of an industrial robot is provided by the 'Robotics Industries Association (RIA)', formerly 'Robotics Institute of America' (RIA) as:

  "An industrial robot is a programmable, multifunctional manipulator designed to move materials, parts, tools or special devices through variable programmed motions for the performance of a variety of tasks".

- An industrial robot possesses certain anthropomorphic or human like characteristics. The most typical human like characteristic of present day robots is their movable arm. The robot can be programmed to move its arm through a sequence of motions in order to perform some useful task. It will repeat that motion pattern over and over until reprogrammed to perform some other task.

- Though the robots themselves are examples of programmable automation, they are sometimes used in flexible automation and even fixed automation systems. These systems consist of several machines and/or robots working together and are typically controlled by a computer or a programmable controller.

  A production line that performs spot welding on automobile bodies is example of this kind of system. The welding line might consist of two dozens of robots or more, and is capable of accomplishing hundreds of separate spot welds on two or three different styles of automobile bodies. The robot programs are contained in the computer or programmable controller and are downloaded to each robot for the particular automobile body that is to be welded at each station, such a line might appropriately be considered a high-production flexible automation system.

- Today the robots are single armed machines which almost always operate from a fixed location on the factory floor.

- Future robots are likely to have a greater number of attributes similar to the attributes of humans. They are likely to have greater sensor capabilities, more intelligence, a higher level of manual dexterity and a limited degree of mobility.

Fig. 1.2 shows the relationship between automation, programmable automation and flexible automation as a function of production volume and product variety to cost-effective robots.

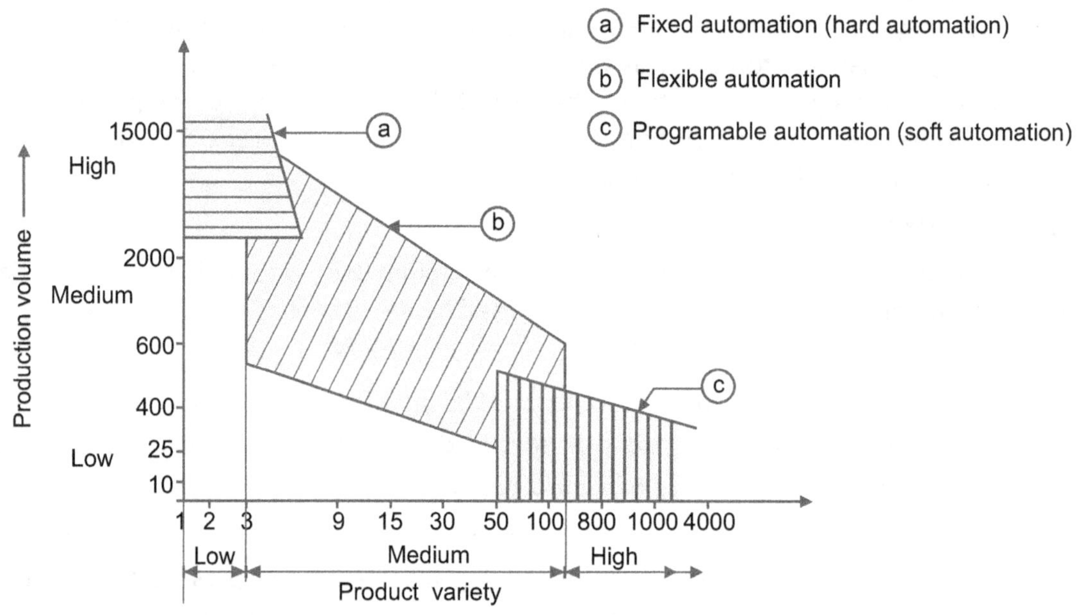

Fig. 1.2: Industrial Automation and Robotics

Relative cost effectiveness of Programmable/Soft automation:

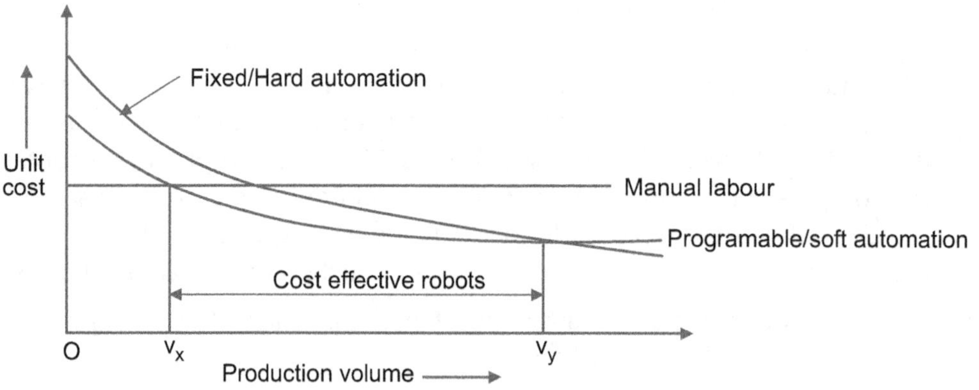

Fig. 1.3: Relative Cost-effectiveness of Soft Automation

- For very low production volumes, such as those occurring in small batch processing, manual labour is most cost effective.
- As the production volume increases, there comes a point V_x where robots become more cost-effective than manual labour.
- As the production volume increases still further, it eventually reaches a point V_y where hard automation surpasses both manual labour and robots in cost-effectiveness.
- The curves as shown in Fig. 1.3 are representative of general qualitative trends, with the exact data dependent upon the characteristics of the unit being produced.
- As the robots become more sophisticated and less expensive, the range of production volume (V_x, V_y), over which they are cost-effective continues to expand at both ends of the production spectrum.

1.6 Need for Industrial Robots

Robots are superior in many aspects as compared to human being. The features which can be taken for comparative study are as below:

1. Robots are capable of delivering a job of consistent quality, with reduction in rejection.
2. They can increase productivity, safety and efficiency of process.
3. They can work in hazardous environments without the need for life support, comfort or concern about safety.
4. They do not need environmental comfort e.g. lighting, air-conditioning, ventilation and noise protection.
5. They work continuously without experiencing fatigue or boredom, and do not have hangovers and do not demand for any incentives.
6. They have repeatable precision at all times unless something wrong happens to them.
7. They give better control over wastage.
8. Robots, their accessories and sensors can have capabilities beyond that of humans.
9. They can process multiple tasks simultaneously which is not possible for human.
10. Due to their high load lifting capacity, they are suitable where heavy material handling is required.

Disadvantages:

1. Robots replace human workers, creating individuals economic problems, such as lost salaries, and social problems.
2. Robots lack capability to respond in emergencies. Hence, safety measures are needed to ensure that they do not injure operators and other machines working with them.

3.   Robots have limited capabilities in:
     (i)   The degrees of freedom   (ii)   Dexterity
     (iii) Sensing   (iv)   Visioning
     (v)   Real-time response.
4.   Robots are costly due to:
     (i)   Higher initial cost of equipments. (ii) Higher installation costs.
     (iii) Need for peripherals.   (iv)   Need for training.
     (v)   Need for programming.

1.7 Robot Generations

In early 1960s, the growth rate in the capabilities of robots has been taking rapid strides since the introduction of robots in the industry. The growth of robots can be grouped into 'robot generations' based on characteristic break throughs in robots capabilities. The Japanese Government is known to be working on the fifth generation of electronic computers, in which thousands of microcomputers will work in parallel. Most of the US companies are also working on the fifth generation computers. Once, such computer designs come in reality will lead to more-intelligent robots, the fifth generation robots.

The five generations of robot controllers are described as follows:

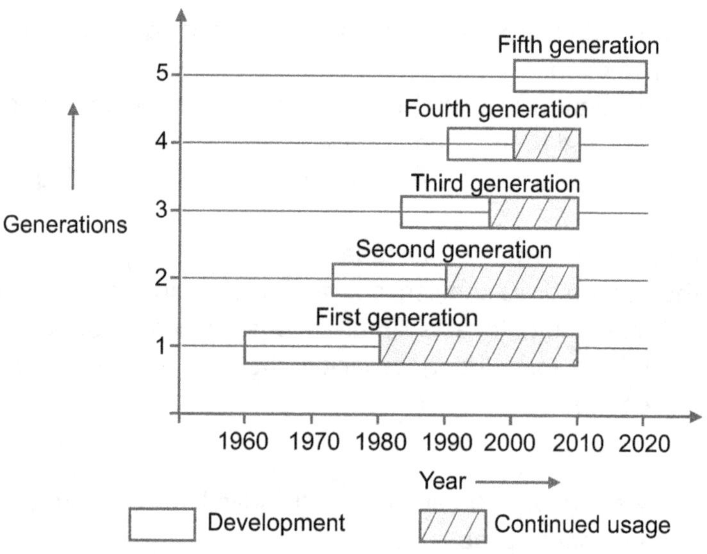

Fig. 1.4: Development of Robot Generations

1. First Generation:

The first generation robots are repeating robots, non-servo, pick and place or point-to-point, with mechanical sequences defining stop points. These robots were pneumatically powered. To reprogram the robot, a new precision CAM was installed. At this stage about 90% of early robots belong to this category. It is general prediction that these will continue to be in use for a long time.

2. Second Generation:

The second generation starts with the addition of sensing devices and enabling the robot to alter its movements in response to sensory feedback. Hardwired controllers provided the first programmable units. In 'pick and place' robots signals were derived from limit switches, proximity switches are similar devices.

These controllers were also applicable to servo control. These robots exhibit path-control capabilities.

3. Third Generation:

Development of robots having human-like intelligence marked the beginning of third generation. The growth in computers led to high-speed processing of information and thus, robots acquired artificial intelligence, self-learning. Programmable Logic Controllers (PLC), introduced into the industry, provided a microprocessor-based robotic controller that is easy to reprogram. The controller primarily serves to direct the sequence of robot motions, stop points, gripper actions and velocity.

4. Fourth Generation:

For the control beyond a PLC a microcomputer may control the entire system, including other programmable machinery in a robot *workcell. Whereas, PLCs are limited in their programming, minicomputer may use a special robot programming language or standard language for more advanced off-line programming or CAD/CAM and CIM interface. Minicomputer-type robots based on artificial intelligence became commercially available at the end of 1980. These controllers now allow integration with vision or tactile sensors.

5. Fifth Generation:

Prediction about its features is difficult, though not impossible. It may be a true android or an artificial biological robot or a super humanoid capable of producing its own clones. Robot controllers will involve complete 'Artificial Intelligence' (AI), miniaturized sensors, and decision-making capabilities. An artificial biological robot might provide the impetus for sixth and higher generation robots.

A pictorial visualization of these overlapping generations of robots is given in Fig. 1.4.

---

*   **Robot workcell:** The robot alongwith associated equipments like conveyors, production machines, fixtures and tools; is called as workcells. There are three basic workcell layouts –
1.   Robot-centered workcell.
2.   In-line robot cell.
3.   Mobile robot cell.

1.8 Robot Anatomy

Robot anatomy is the study of skeleton of robot i.e. the physical construction of the manipulator structure where the mechanical structure of a robot is like the skeleton in the human body.

Robot anatomy is concerned with the physical construction of body, arm and wrist of the machine. Most of the robots are mounted on a base which is fastened to the floor. In few cases, base is attached to mobile platform and so the robot is called as mobile robot. The body is attached to the base, and the arm assembly is attached to the body. Wrist is attached at the end of the arm. The wrist consists of many components that allow it to be oriented in a variety of positions. Relative movements between the various components of the body, arm and wrist are provided by a series of either sliding or rotating joints. The body, arm and wrist assembly is also called as manipulator. A detachable attachment, connected to the wrist is called as end effector, which may be a tool or gripper, as mentioned earlier. It is important to remember that, end effector is not considered to be a part of robot anatomy. Fig. 1.5 explains robot anatomy.

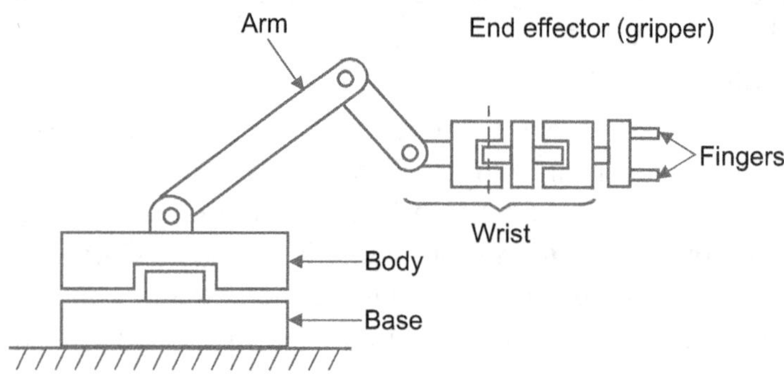

Fig. 1.5: Robot Anatomy

Robot is designed to reach a work piece within its work volume. Work volume is the term that refers to the space within which the robot can manipulate its wrist end. It is also called as work space. The surface of work space is termed as work envelop.

Robot anatomy can be explained with the following points:

    (a)   Links.

    (b)   Joints.

    (c)   Robot motion and physical configuration.
        (i)   Arm configuration and related work volume.
        (ii)   Wrist configuration and related work volume.
    (d)   Six-degrees of freedom.
        (i)   DoFs associated with arm and body motion.
        (ii)   DoFs associated with the robot wrist.
    (e)   Joint notation scheme.
    (f)   End effector.

(a) Links:

- The mechanical structure of a robotic manipulator is a mechanism, whose members are rigid links. And the link that can be connected, at most, with two other links is referred to as a binary link.

  Fig. 1.6 shows two rigid binary links with holes at their ends to join to other links.

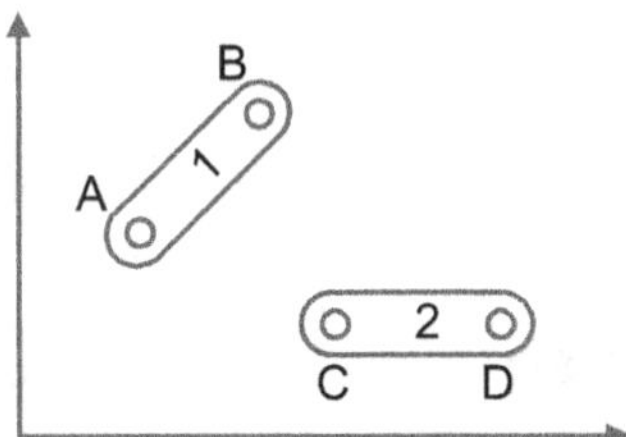

Fig. 1.6: Rigid Binary Links

(b) Joints: (S-11)

- Two links are connected together by a joint by using pin, if two links are joined by inserting pin through two joints, an open kinematic chain is formed and the corresponding joint formed is called pin joint or revolute or rotary joint.

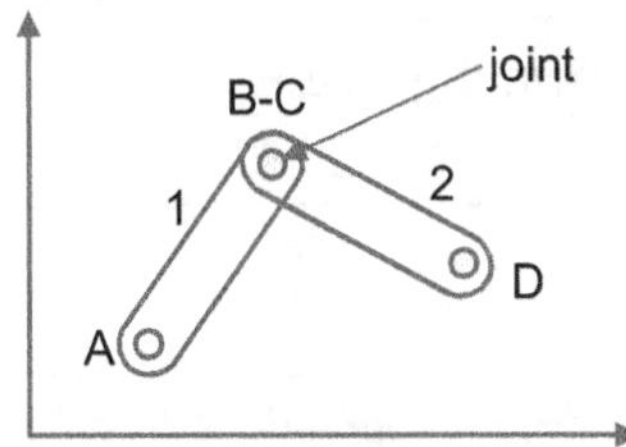

Fig. 1.7: An Open Kinematic Chain formed by joining Two Links

Links are represented by straight lines and rotary joint by a small circle.

Different types of joint can be made between two links. However, only two basic types are commonly used in industrial robots. These are:

    (I)   Linear or Prismatic Joint (L or P).

    (II)   Rotating joint.

        (i)   Type-R joint (R for rotational) or Rotary joint.

        (ii)   Type-T joint (T for twisting).

        (iii)   Type-V joint (V for revolving) or Revolute.

(I)   Linear or Prismatic Joint (L or P):

These joints involve a sliding or translational motion of connecting links. This type of motion can be achieved in a number of ways.

e.g. Screw and nut, rack and pinion, a piston and cylinder, telescopic mechanism.

Fig. 1.8: Linear or Prismatic joint

Thus, from above Fig. 1.8, it is clear that prismatic joint allows a pure translation of one link relative to the connecting link.

(II) Rotating Joint:

A rotating joint allows a pure rotation of one link relative to the connecting link. There are three types of rotating joint as:

    (i)   **Type-R or Rotary joint:** In this type of joint, the axis of rotation is perpendicular to the axes of the two connecting links. It is designated as Type-R joint where R for rotational motion. It is shown in Fig. 1.9.

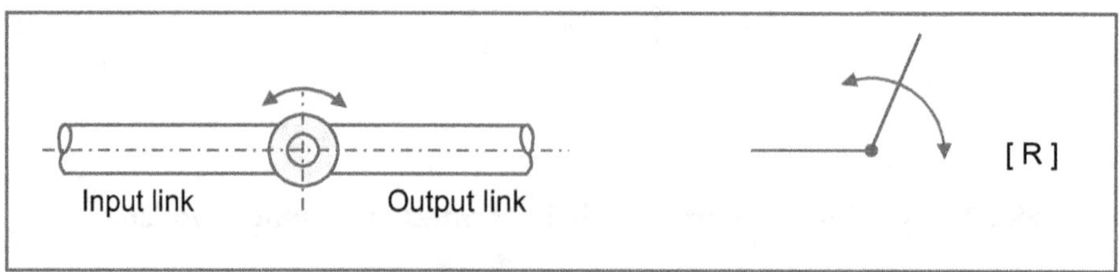

Fig. 1.9: Type-R or Rotary Joint

(ii) Type-T joint or Twist joint: In this type of joint, there is twisting motion between the input and output links. The axis of rotation of the twisting joint is parallel to the axes of both inks. Rather, they coincide with each other. It is designated as Type-T joint where T for twisting motion.

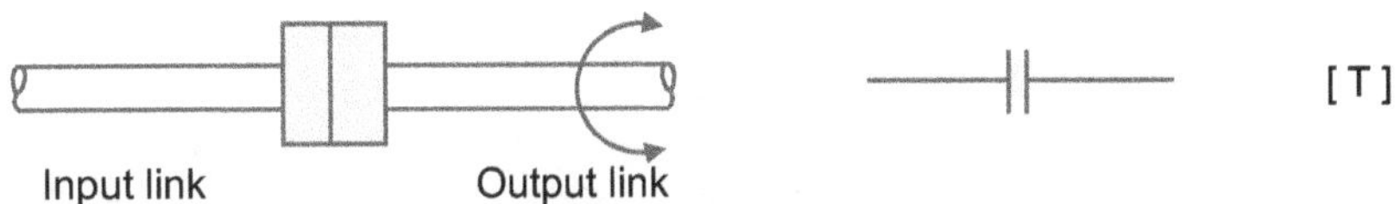

Fig. 1.10: Type-T Joint

(iii) Type-V joint or Revolving joint: In this type of joint, the input link is parallel to the axis of rotation and the output link is perpendicular to the axis of rotation. The output link revolves about input link. It is designated as a type V joint where V for revolving.

Fig. 1.11: Type-V Joint or Revolving Joint

(c) Robot motion:
- Industrial robots are designed to perform specific task. The work is accomplished by enabling the robot to move its body, arm and wrist through a series of motions and positions. End effector, attached to the wrist, is used by the robot to perform a specific work task. The robot's movements can be divided into two general categories:
  - (i) Arm and body motions.
  - (ii) Wrist motions.

(i) Arm and body motions and the configuration:
The arm mechanics with three degrees of freedom depends on the type of three joints employed and their arrangement. The purpose of the arm is to position the wrist in the 3D space. According to joint movements and arrangements of links, five distinguished structural configurations are possible for the arm which are:
- Cartesian (rectangular) configuration.
- Cylindrical (post-type) configuration.
- Spherical (polar) configuration.
- Jointed arm or revolute (articulated) configuration.
- Selective Compliance Assembly Robot Arm (SCARA).

- **Cartesian (Rectangular):**

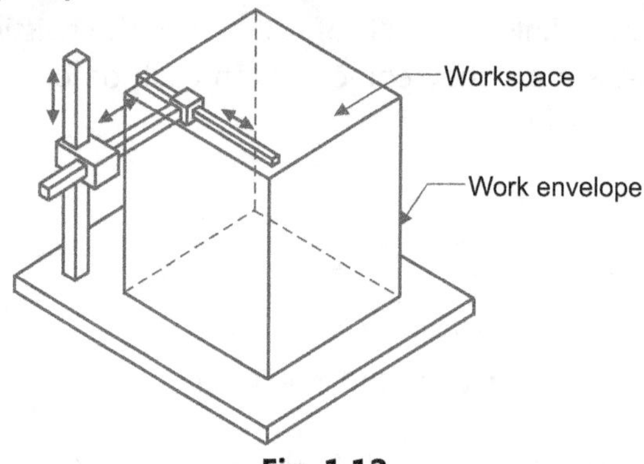

Fig. 1.12

Work envelope is cuboid as the arm is capable of operating in a cuboid space (Rectangular).
- This is simplest with all three linear or prismatic joints.
- It is constructed by three perpendicular slides to construct the x, y and z axes.
- Also called as xyz - robot or rectilinear robot or gantry-robot.
- It gives large work volume but has low dexterity.
- e.g., 1BM RS-1 (Model 7565).

- **Cylindrical (Post-type):**

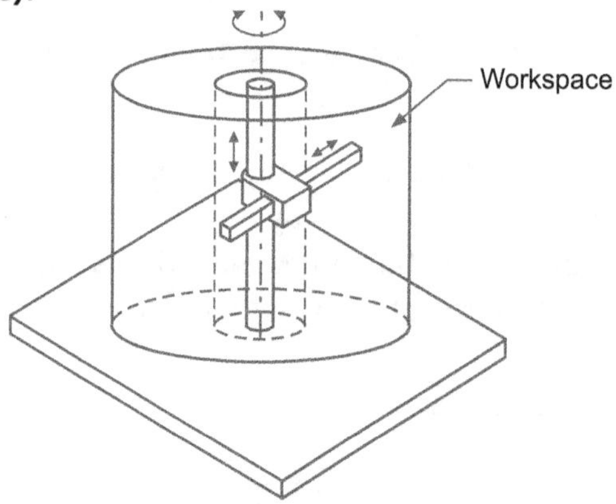

Fig. 1.13

By rotating the column, the robot is capable of achieving a cylindrical work envelop.
- It uses two perpendicular prismatic joints and a revolute joint.
- It uses a vertical column and a slide that can be moved up and down along the column.
- The robot arm is attached to the slide so that it can be moved radially with respect to the column.
- e.g. versatran 600 robot.
- It offers good mechanical stiffness and the wrist positioning accuracy decreases as the horizontal stroke increases.

- **Spherical (Polar):**

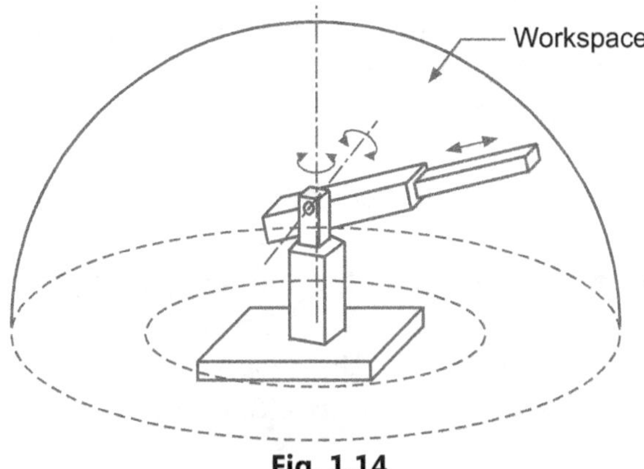

Fig. 1.14

RRP configuration gives the capability of moving the arm end-point within a partial spherical shell as work envelop.

- – The construction is slight complex.
- – It consists of a telescopic link (prismatic joint) that can be raised or lowered about a horizontal revolute joint. These two links are mounted on a rotating base. This arrangement of joints is known as RRP configuration.
- – This configuration allows manipulation of objects on the floor.
- – Its mechanical stiffness is lower than Cartesian and cylindrical configuration and the wrist positioning accuracy decreases with the increasing radial stroke.
- – These are employed for industrial applications as machining, spray painting.
  e.g. Unimate 2000 series, maker 110 (usa robots).

- **Joint arm or Revolute (Articulated):**

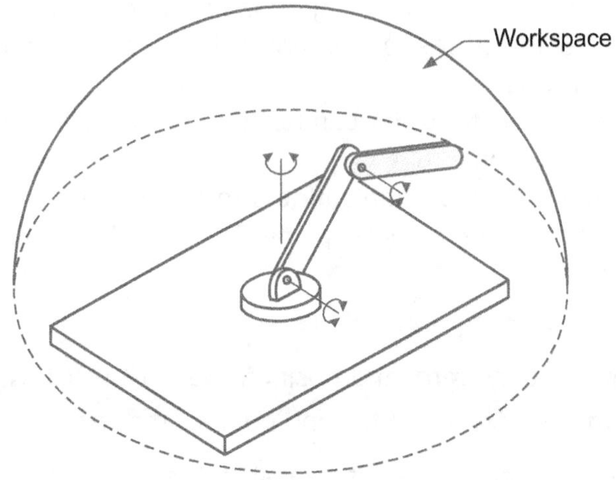

Fig. 1.15

The work volume is spherical shaped.

- – Its configuration is similar to that of the human arm, therefore termed as anthropomorphic manipulator.
- – It consists of two straight fore arm and upper arm, mounted on the vertical pedestal.
- – These components are connected by two rotary joints corresponding to the shoulder and elbow.
- – A wrist is attached to the end of the fore arm, thus providing several additional joints.
- – e.g., PUMA, Cincinnati Milacron of Unimation Inc.

- **Selective Compliance Assembly Robot Arm (SCARA):**

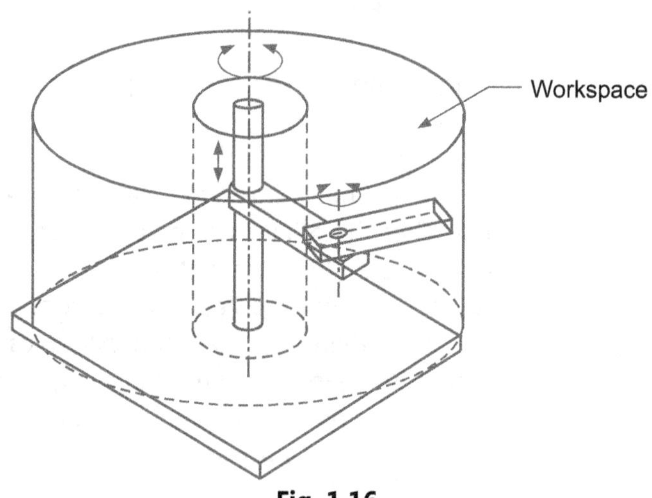

Fig. 1.16

The work envelope is cylindrical and much larger than all other configurations.

- – It is a special version of the jointed arm robot, whose shoulder and elbow joints rotate about vertical axes.
- – It can also be derived from the combination of characteristics of articulated and cylindrical configurations.
- – This configuration provides high stiffness to the arm in the vertical direction, and high compliance in the horizontal plane. Thus, SCARA is suitable for most of the assembly tasks.

(ii) Wrist motions and the configuration:

- • The arm configurations carry and position the wrist which is the second part of a manipulator that is attached to the end point of the arm.

- • The wrist subassembly movements enable the manipulator to orient the end-effector to perform the task properly.

- For arbitrary orientation in 3D space, the wrist must possess atleast 3 DoF to give three rotations about the three principal axes.

  (i)   Wrist roll i.e. motion in a plane perpendicular to the end of the arm.

  (ii)   Wrist pitch i.e. motion in a vertical plane passing through the arm.

  (iii) Wrist yaw i.e. motion in a horizontal plane that also passes through the arm.

- This type of unit is called roll-pitch-yaw or RPY wrist.

- A wrist with the highest dexterity is one where three rotary joint axes intersect at a point.

(d) Degrees of Freedom (DoF):

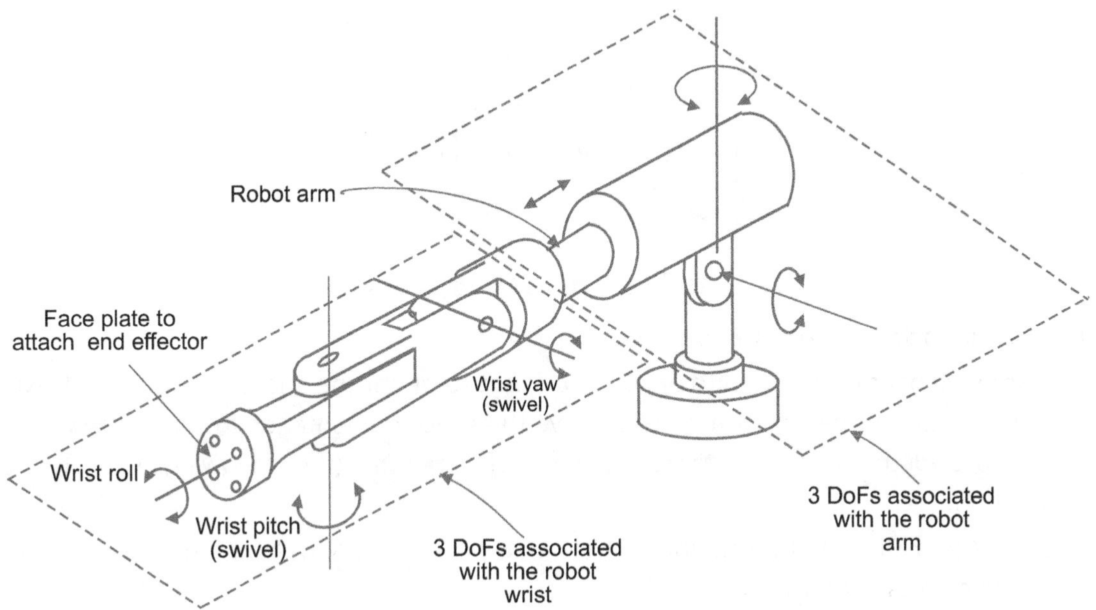

Fig. 1.17: Six degrees of freedom associated with arm body and robot wrist

- The number of independent movements that an object can perform in a 3D space is termed as the number of degrees of freedom (DoF). Thus, a rigid body free in space has six degrees of freedom - three for position and three for orientation.

- Six degrees of freedom can be categorised into:

  (i)   3 DoFs associated with arm and body of the robot.

  (ii)   3 DoFs associated with the robot wrist.

(i) 3 DoFs associated with arm and body of the robot:

The arm and body joints are designed to enable the robot to move its end affector to a desired position within the limits of the robots size and joint movements. For robots of polar, cylindrical or jointed arm configuration, the 3 DoF associated with the arm and body motions are:

(1) **Vertical traverse:** It is the movement of the arm in upward and downward direction about the horizontal axis to provide the desired vertical attitude.

(2) **Radial traverse:** It is the extension or retraction (in or out movement) of the arm from the vertical centre of the robot. Thus, it enables robot to move its arm in radial direction.

(3) **Rotational traverse:** It is the rotation of the arm about the vertical axis.

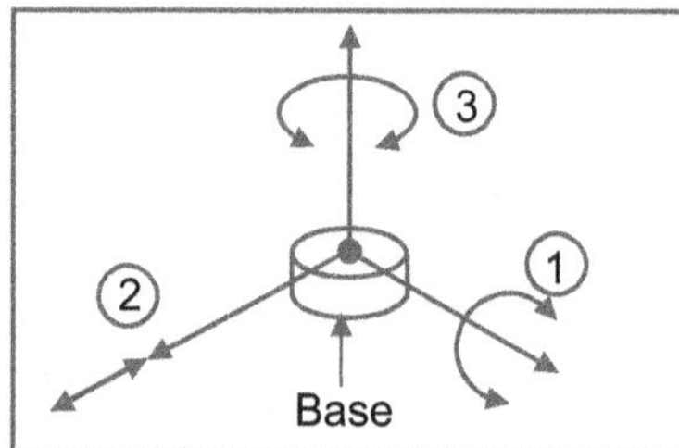

Fig. 1.18: Three DoF of Body and Arm

(ii) 3 DoF associated with the robot wrist:

The wrist movement is designed to enable the robot to orient the end effector properly with respect to the task to be performed. To achieve the specific orientation in space, the wrist is normally provided with upto three degrees of freedom (the following is a typical configuration).

1. **Wrist roll:** It is the rotation of the wrist mechanism about the arm axis. It is also known as wrist swivel.

2. **Wrist pitch:** It is the up and down rotation of the wrist. It is also known as wrist bend.

3. **Wrist yaw:** It is the right or left rotation of the wrist.

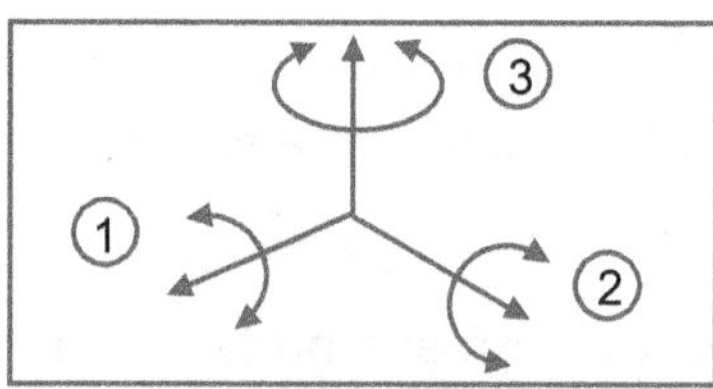

Fig. 1.19: Three DoF Wrist

(e) Joint Notation Scheme:

- The physical configuration of the robot manipulator can be described by means of a joint notation scheme.

- Considering the arm and body joints first, the letters can be used to designate the particular robot configuration starting with the joint closest to the base and proceeding to the joint that connects to the wrist.

- Thus, a jointed arm robot (excluding the wrist assembly) would have three rotational joints and would be designed as either TRR or VVR. Notations for the four basic configurations are given in Table 1.1.

- The rotation scheme can be expanded to include wrist motions by designating the two or three (or move) types of wrist joints.

- Wrist joints are predominantly rotating joints of type R and T. Hence, a typical wrist mechanism with three rotational joints would be indicated by TRR. This rotation is simply added to the rotation for the arm and the body configuration.

  e.g. A polar co-ordinate robot with a three-axis wrist might be designated as TRL: TRT.

- L-TRL: TRT: Means TRL: TRT robot fastened to a platform on wheels that can be driven along a track between several machine tools, where motion of robot is linear.

Table 1.1: Notation scheme for robot configuration

Robot Configuration	Symbol
I. Arm and body motion:	
(a) Polar configuration	TRL
(b) Cylindrical configuration	TLL, LTL, LVL
(c) Cartesian configuration	LLL
(d) Jointed arm configuration	TRR, VVR
II. Wrist motion:	
(a) Two-axis wrist	RT
(b) Three-axis wrist	TRT

(f) End Effector:

The term end-effector is used to describe the hand or tool that is attached to the wrist. The end effector represents the special tooling that permits the general purpose robot to perform a particular application. This special tooling must usually be designed specifically for the application.

End effectors can be categorised into:

    (i)   Grippers

    (ii)   Tools

(i) Grippers:

- Grippers are end effectors, utilized to grasp an object, usually the work part, and hold it during the robot work cycle.
- There are a variety of holding methods, i.e. the use of suction cups, magnets, hooks and scoops.
- The proper shape and size of the gripper and the method of holding are determined by the object to be grasped and the task to be performed.
- The applications include material handling, machine loading, unloading, palletizing, and other similar operations.

(ii) Tools:

- A tool would be used as an end effector in applications where the robot is required to perform some operation on the work part. The tool is usually directly attached to the end of the wrist.
- These applications include splot welding, arc welding, spray painting, and drilling.
- In each case, particular tool is attached to the robot's wrist to accomplish the application.

1.9 Classification of Robots   (S-11)

It is very difficult to classify robots, because of the variety of their sizes, technology involved, applications. Still they may be broadly classified by:

    1.   Basic configuration.   2. Drive systems.   3. Control systems.

1.9.1 Classification based on their basic configuration includes

- Cartesian configuration
- Cylindrical configuration
- Spherical configuration
- Jointed arm configuration

- After deciding the required number of degrees of freedom, a particular configuration of joints must be chosen to get those freedoms.
- For serial kinematic linkages, the number of joints equals the required number of DoF.
- Design of most of the manipulator is such that the last $(n - 3)$ joints orient the end-effector and have axes that intersect at the wrist point, and the first three joints position this wrist point.

This type of manipulator could be said to be composed to a positioning structure followed by an orienting structure or wrist. These manipulators always possess closed form kinematic solutions. Almost every industrial manipulator belongs to this **wrist partitioned** class of mechanisms.

- Also the positioning structure is designed to be kinematically simple, with link twists equal to 0° or 90°, and many of the link lengths and/or offsets equal to zero.
- Therefore, manipulators of the wrist partitioned, kinematically simple class can be classified according to the design of their first three joints (i.e. the positioning structure).

(i)	Cartesian manipulator	(ii)	Articulated manipulator
(iii)	SCARA manipulator	(iv)	Spherical configuration
(v)	Cylindrical configuration	(vi)	Wrist configuration

1.9.1 (i) Cartesian Manipulator

- It is most straight-forward configuration with prismatic joints.

  Fig. 1.20 shows joints 1 through 3 - (prismatic joints). They are mutually orthogonal, and correspond to $\hat{x}$, $\hat{y}$ and $\hat{z}$ cartesian directions.

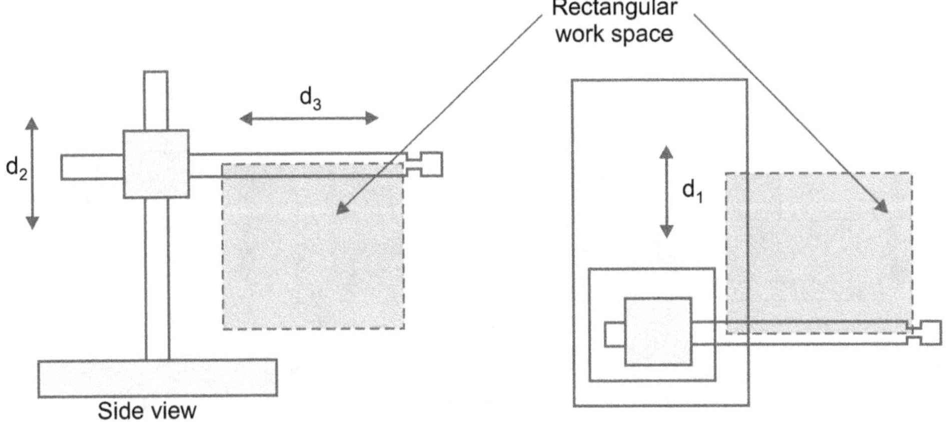

Fig. 1.20: Cartesian manipulator

- This configuration provides a rectangular work envelope. The three major axes of the manipulator are rectilinear and provide the movements along these axes. No rotational movement is available.
- The inverse kinematic solution for this configuration is **trivial**. This configuration produces robots with very **stiff structures.**
- These robot are of two categories:
  - **(a)** **Gantry robots :** It is the class of gantry cranes wherein the arm is suspended from a gantry moving with a rectangular frame and
  - **(b)** The sideways mounted arm.

– **Advantages :**
The first three joints are decoupled, that make them simpler to design.

- The size of the robots support structure limits the size and placement of fixtures and sensors. This can also make retrofitting cartesian robots into existing workcells too difficult.
- These are also applicable for assembly, palletizing and machine tool loading operations.

1.9.1 (ii) Articulated Manipulator

- It is also called as **jointed, elbow or anthropomorphic** manipulator.
- These types of manipulator consist of two **shoulder joints**, one for rotation about a vertical axis and one for elevation out of the horizontal plane, an **elbow joint**, axis of which is usually parallel to the shoulder elevation joint, and two or three wrist joints at the end of the manipulator.

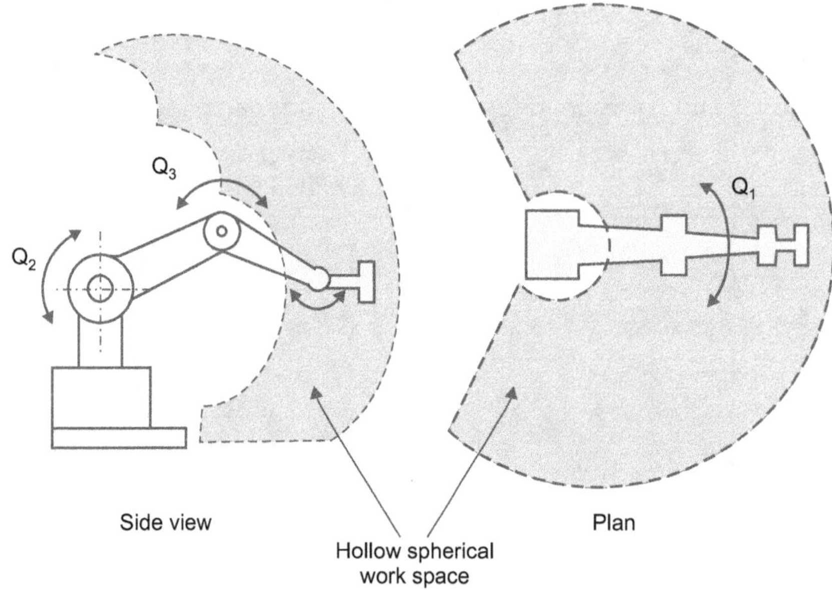

Fig. 1.21: Articulated configuration

- Articulated robots provide an ability to reach its manipulator into confined space easily. They require much less overall structure than cartesian robots, making them less expensive for applications needing smaller workspaces.

1.9.1 (iii) SCARA Manipulator

- It is selectively complaint assembly robot (SCARA) configuration.
- It is shown in Fig. 1.22, where it has **three parallel revolute joints** allow it to move and orient in a plane, and a **fourth prismatic joint** for moving the end-effector normal to the plane.

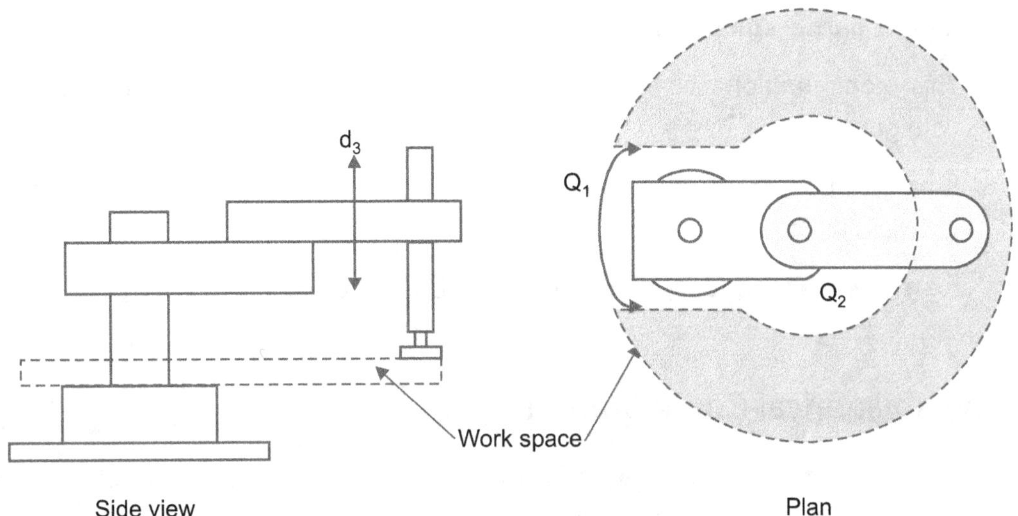

Fig. 1.22: SCARA configuration

– **Advantage :** The first three joints do not have to support any of the weight of the manipulator or the load.

Also base link can easily house the actuators for the first two joints.

The actuators can be made very large, so that robot can move very fast.

e.g. Adept-1 SCARA - moves 10 times faster than most articulated industrial robots. This configuration is best suitable for planar tasks.

1.9.1 (iv) Spherical Configuration

– It is almost similar to articulated configuration, but the elbow joint is replaced by a prismatic joint.

Fig. 1.23 shows spherical configuration.

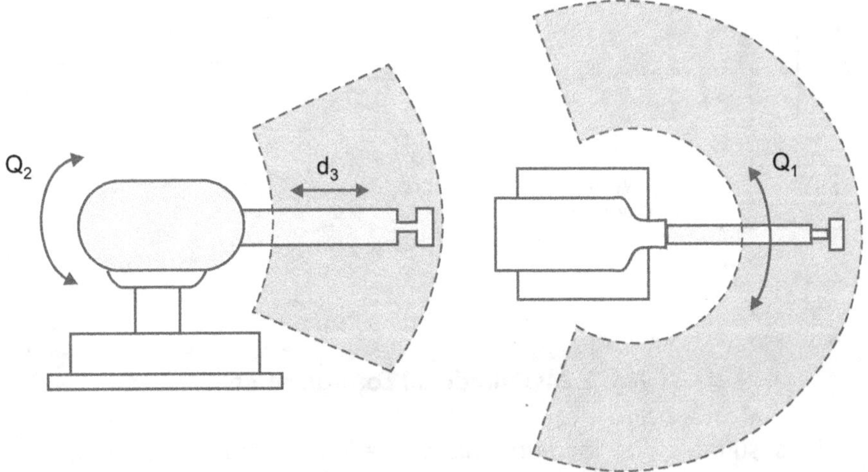

Fig. 1.23: Spherical configuration

–   It gives **partial sphere** as a work envelope.

–   This configuration is better suited to some applications than the elbow configuration.

–   It has rotation about horizontal as well as vertical axis and movement of arm along its axis is in linear manner.

–   e.g. these are used for spot welding, palletizing operations.

1.9.1 (v) Cylindrical Configuration

–   It consists of a **prismatic joint** for translating the arm vertically, a **revolute joint** with a vertical axis, another **prismatic joint** orthogonal to the revolute joint axis, followed by a wrist of some type.

–   This robot possesses a central pillar that can rotate about its axis on the base. This is the only rotational movement available along with two linear movements.

–   It gives **cylindrical** work envelope.

Fig. 1.24 shows cylindrical configuration.

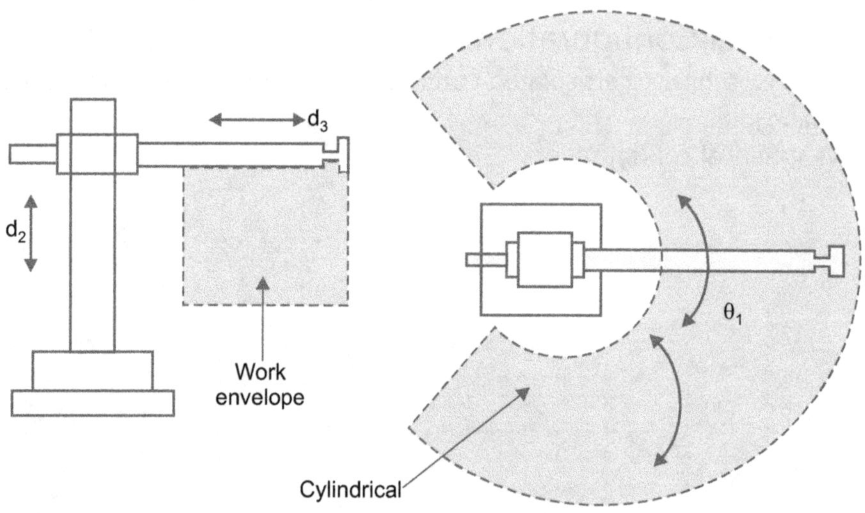

Fig. 1.24: Cylindrical configuration

–   e.g. it is suitable for loading and unloading operation on machine tools and palletizing.

1.9.1 (vi) Wrist Configuration

- The wrist configuration consists of either **two or three** revolute joints with orthogonal, intersecting axes.
  Fig. 1.25 shows an orthogonal configuration wrist driven by actuators via three concentric shafts. Any orientation can be achieved with this configuration. A three orthogonal axis wrist can be located at the end of the manipulator in any desired orientation. It consists of several sets of bevel gears to drive the mechanism from remotely located actuators.

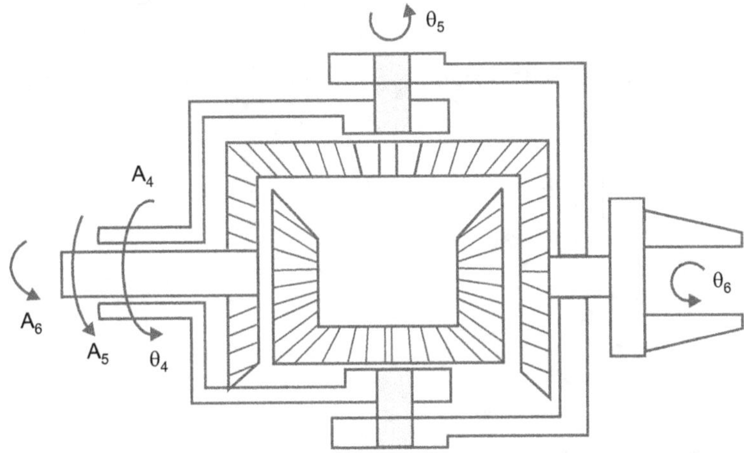

Fig. 1.25: An orthogonal axis wrist

- Most of the wrist employs three intersecting but non-orthogonal axes. Here, all three joints of the wrist can rotate continuously without limits. The non-orthogonality of the axes creates a set of orientations which are impossible to reach with this wrist. It is described by a cone which the third axis of the wrist cannot lie. It is shown in Fig. 1.26.

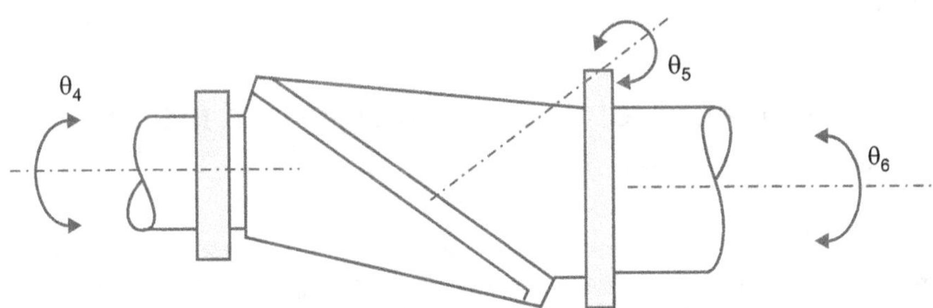

Fig. 1.26: Wrist with non-orthogonal axes

- Some industrial robots have wrists which do not have intersecting axes. It shows that a closed form kinematic solution may not exist.

The wrist is mounted on an articulated manipulator such that the joint 4 axis is parallel to the joint 2 and joint 3 axes. It is as shown in Fig. 1.27.

There will be a closed form kinematic solution.

A non-intersecting axis wrist mounted on a Cartesian robot also yields a closed form solvable manipulator.

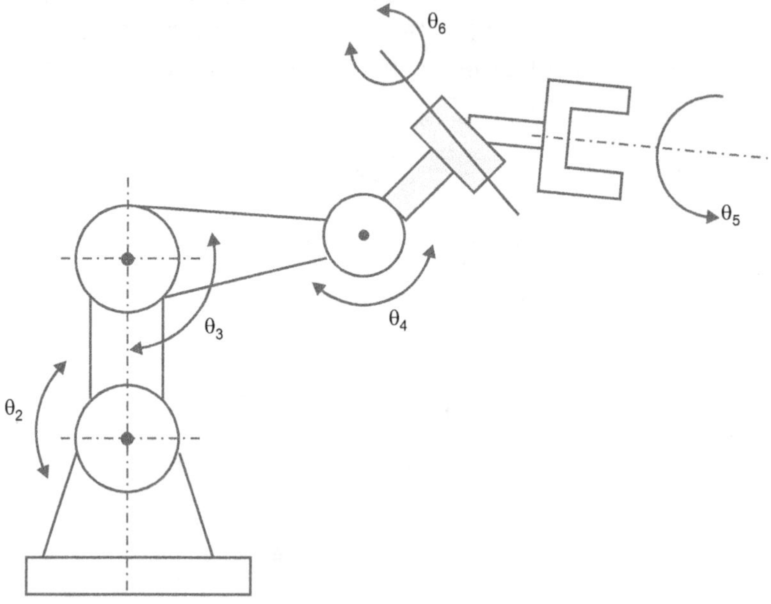

Fig. 1.27: Non-intersecting axes manipulator wrist

1.9.2 Classification based on their drive system includes

- Hydraulic drive
- Pneumatic drive
- Electric drive

1.9.3 Classification based on their control system includes

- Limited sequence robots
- Playback robots
- Intelligent robots

- **Limited sequence robots:** These robots do not use servo control to indicate relative positions of joint. Instead they use limit switches, and/or mechanical stops to establish end points of travel of each joint.

- **Playback robots:** These robots are trained by programme by actual walk through method, wherein relative positions of each joint are recorded and memorised. After completion of training, the robot is run for it's use. It is commanded by the recorded data of positions of each joint. It is just like recording a song or speech using tape recorder and play it back using a cassette player.

  Playback robots are further classified as:

  (a) Point-to-Point (PTP)   (b) Continuous Path (CP)

  Point-to-point robots are those which are normally used for pick-n-place applications.

  Continuous path robots are those which are generally used for welding, spray painting applications.

- **Intelligent robots:** These robots not only have playback capacity but also decision-making capacity to some extent. They have controlling unit consisting of digital computer or programmable controller. Unlike playback robots, they store multiple paths in the training mode. And in operation/execution, after interacting with environment take decision to select the path which is already stored and also most appropriate. Here it must be made clear that, they do not generate their paths at their own. If they can do so, they would be robots from fifth generation.

Modern Industrial Robots

For a non-engineering person, the popular concept of a robot is that it looks and acts like a human being. This humanoid concept has been inspired and encouraged by a number of sciencefiction stories. The modern industrial robot, as it first appeared, bore little resemblance to the sciencefiction inspired vision of a robot. In today's scenario too, most of the industrial robots simulate only human hand. Research is still going on for wheeled mobile robots, legged robots and humanoids. Although a robotic system is usually tailor-made for specified operations, there are some standard industrial robots in market like PUMA (Programmable Universal Machine for Assembly), Unimate 2000, SCARA (Selective Compliance Assembly Robot Arm), Stanford, Cincinatti Milacron T3 Robot (The Tomorrow's Tool), Yasukawa Motoman L-3.

1.10 Robot Performance   (W-11)

Robot's performance can be measured by its **Dynamic Properties.**

Following dynamic properties are used to define the positioning capability of their manipulators i.e. the capacity of a robot to position and orient the end of its wrist with accuracy and repeatability.

    (i)   Stability

    (ii)   Resolution –   (a)   Control resolution

                                (b)   Spatial resolution

    (iii) Accuracy –   (a)   Global accuracy

                                (b)   Local accuracy

    (iv) Repeatability –   (a)   Unidirectional repeatability

                                (b)   Bidirectional repeatability

    (v)   Compliance.

(i) Stability:

It is associated with the oscillations which occur in the motion of the robot tool i.e. end effector.

Less the number of oscillations in the system, more stable the operation of the robot. Following are some of the effects of oscillations:

- Additional wear is imposed on the robot systems as mechanical, hydraulic and other parts of the robot arm.
- The tool will follow different paths in space during successive repetitions of the same movement, thus, requiring more distance between the intended trajectory and surrounding objects.
- The time required for the tool to stop at a precise position will be increased.
- The tool may overshoot the intended stopping position, possibly causing a collision with some object in the system.

These oscillations may be damped or undamped.

Damped oscillations will degrade and cease with time while undamped oscillations may persist or may grow in magnitude and are most serious because of the potential damage they may cause to the surroundings or equipment.

Variations in inertial and gravitational loads on the individual joint servos results in oscillations during the operation of the robot. Sometimes, when the load accidentially slips out of the end effector. This causes a step change in the gravity loading on one or more joints and can cause oscillations. Motion of a joint can also exert various combinations of inertial, centrifugal, and coriolis forces on the other joint. The reactions of the other joints to these forces can exert force on the original joint, and this is another potential source of oscillation.

Finally, the gain of a controller also determines very important characteristics i.e. the type of damping or instability that the system displays in response to a disturbance. Four general conditions are shown in Fig. 1.28. As the gain of the controller is increased, the response changes in the following order:

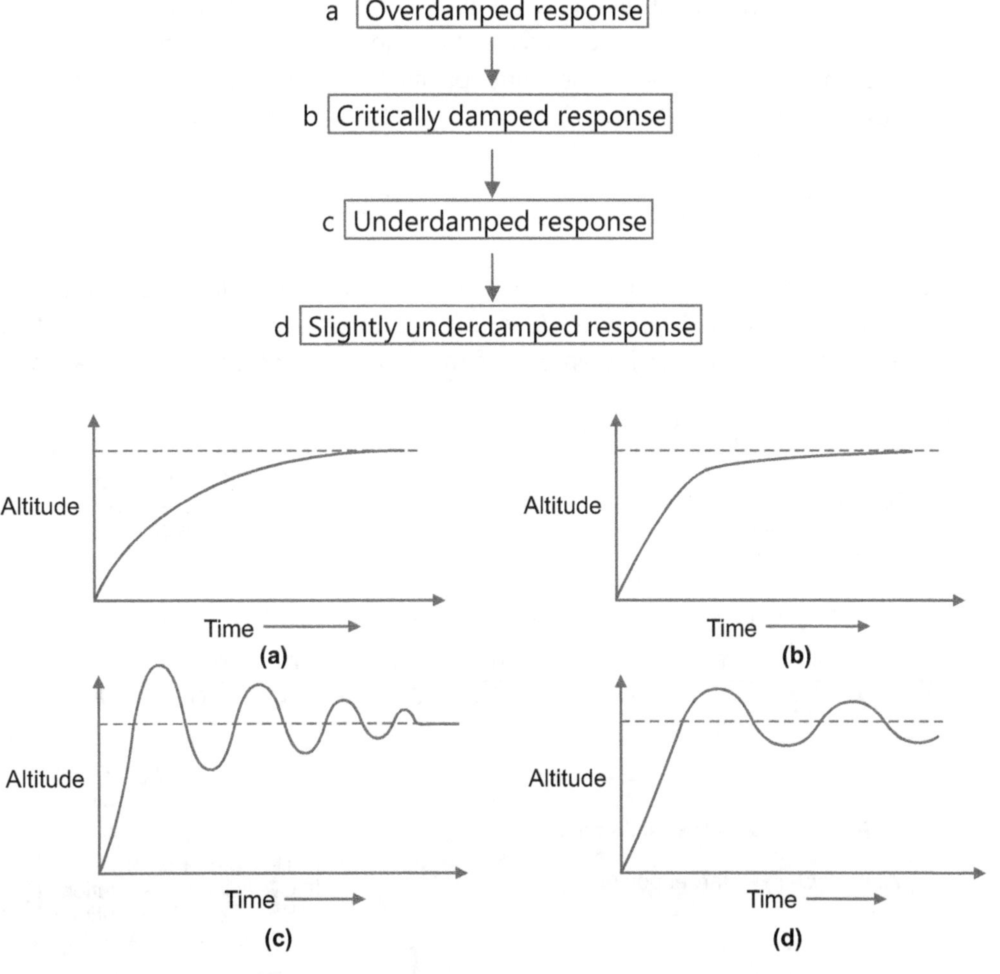

Fig. 1.28: Dynamic behaviours

Here, neither the underdamped response nor the overdamped satisfies the objective of minimizing error. Thus, the optimum response is either **critically damped** or **slightly underdamped.**

Two ways are suggested to eliminate oscillations.

(i)   By using joint servos which operate continuously e.g. some servo designs like in NC machines, oscillations are eliminated by avoiding start and stop motions regardless of the load carried.

(ii) By having the robot controller lock, each joint independently the first time it reaches its set point. The joint in this type of robot may lock in any order.

(ii) Resolution: (S-11)

It defines the ability of the manipulator to be able to reach positions close enough during initial training or it defines the smallest move that the robot can make which affects the ability of the manipulator to move in non-joint spaces such as cartesian co-ordinates. There are two kinds of resolution,

(a)   Control resolution.

(b)   Spatial resolution.

(a) Control resolution: Control resolution is defined as the smallest incremental change that the control system can distinguish. It is a function of the design of a robot control system and specifies the smallest increment of motion by which the system can divide its working space.

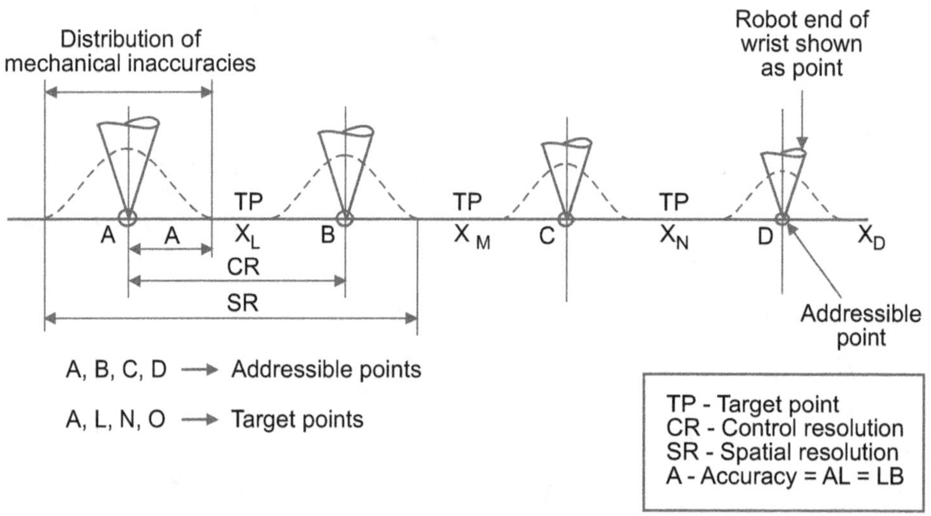

Fig. 1.29: Two kinds of resolution

Fig. 1.29 shows a series of equally spaced points representing where our mechanism may be commanded to go the distance between these points is the control resolution.

- The control resolution can be computed by dividing the total distance that can be travelled by the total number of discrete positions that the mechanism can resolve.
- Thus, the control resolution is determined by the robot's position control system and its feedback measurement system. It is the controller's ability to divide the total range of movement for the particular joint into individual increments that can be addressed in the controller. The increments are sometimes referred to as 'addressable points'.
- The ability to divide the joint range into increments depends on the bit storage capacity in the control memory.

$$\boxed{\text{Number of increments} = 2^n}$$

where, n = the number of bits in the control memory.

(b) Spatial resolution:

- The spatial resolution of a robot is the smallest increment of movement into which the robot can divide its work volume.
- Spatial resolution is the control resolution combined with mechanical inaccuracy, as shown in Fig. 1.29.
- In order to determine the spatial resolution, the range of each joint on the manipulator is divided by the number of control increments.
- Spatial resolution depends on following factors:
  (i)   The systems control resolution and
  (ii)   The robot's mechanical inaccuracies.

Mechanical inaccuracies come from elastic deflection in the structural members, gear back-lash, stretching of pulley cords, leakage of hydraulic fluids, and other imperfections in the mechanical system. Thus, the mechanical inaccuracies of the system become the dominant component in the spatial resolution conversely, the spatial resolution of the robot is the control resolution degraded by these mechanical inaccuracies.

(iii) Accuracy: (S-11)

- It is a measure of ability of robot to position and orient its wrist end at a desired target point within the work volume.
- In other words, accuracy of a robot is the difference between where its control point goes and where it is instructed or programmed to go.
- Thus, the accuracy of a robot can be defined in terms of spatial resolution because the ability to achieve a given target point depends on how closely the robot can define the control increments of reach of its joint motions.

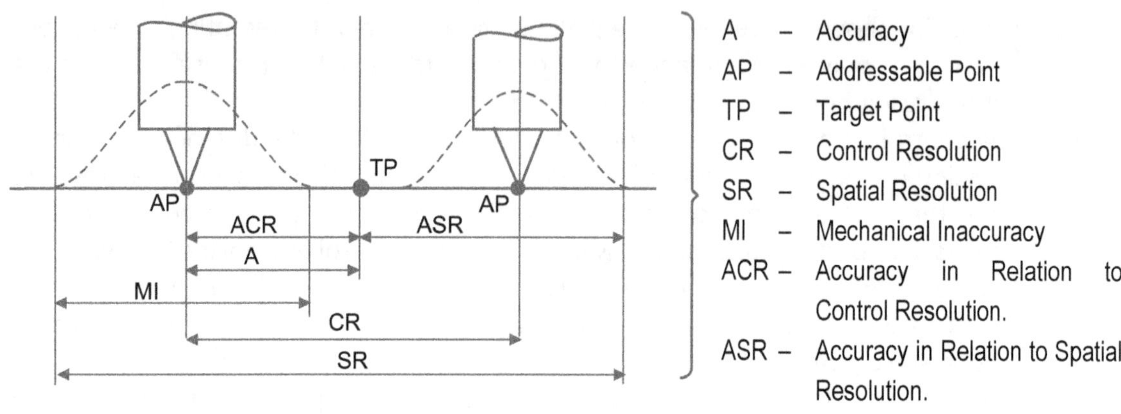

Fig. 1.30: Accuracy and Resolutions

- The mechanical inaccuracies would affect the ability to reach the target position. Our definition of accuracy applies to the worst case, where the target point is directly between two control points.

- **Factors affecting accuracy of a robot:**

(i) The accuracy varies within the work volume, tending to be worse when the arm is in the outer range of its work volume and better when the arm is closer to its base, because the mechanical inaccuracies are magnified with the robot's arm fully extended. The term 'error map' is used to characterize the level of accuracy possessed by the robot as a function of location in the work volume.

(ii) By restricting the motion cycle to a limited range, accuracy can be improved. The mechanical errors will tend to be reduced when the robot is exercised through a restricted range of motions.

   Local accuracy: The robot's ability to reach a particular reference point within the limited work space is sometimes called its local accuracy.

   Global accuracy: It is the accuracy assessed within the robot's full work volume.

(iii) The load being carried by the robot. Heavier workloads cause greater deflection of the mechanical links of the robot, resulting in lower accuracy.

(iv) Repeatability:

- Repeatability is defined as the ability of a robot to reposition itself to a position to which it was previously commanded or taught.

- Repeatability is affected by resolution and component inaccuracy.

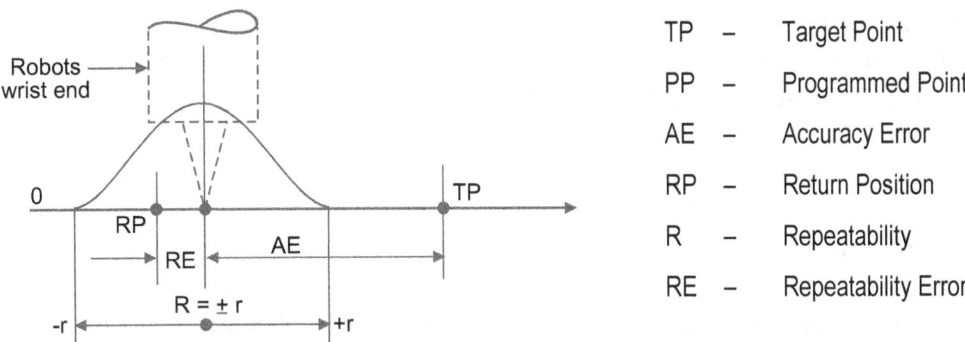

Fig. 1.31: Errors in accuracy and repeatability

- The desired target point is represented by 'TP'. During the teach procedure, the robot is commanded to move to point 'TP', but because of the limitations on its accuracy, the programmed position becomes point 'PP'.
- The distance between points 'TP' and 'PP' is a manifestation of the robot's accuracy in this case. Subsequently, the robot is instructed to return to the programmed point 'PP', however, it does not return to the exact same position. Instead, it returns to position 'RP'.
- The difference between 'PP" and 'RP' is a result of limitations on the robot's repeatability. The robot will not always return to the same position R on subsequent repetitions of the motion cycle. Instead, it will form a cluster of points on both sides of the position 'PP'.

Measurement of repeatability of manipulator system:

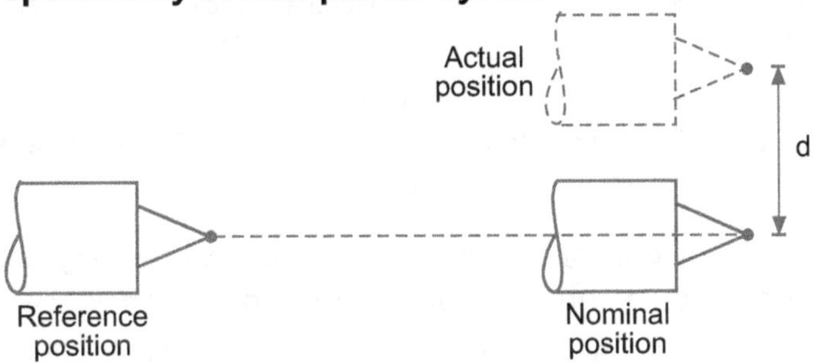

Fig. 1.32: Measurement of repeatability

The manipulator is moved by its control system from a reference position to a specified position, that may be the actual position or the position closer to actual position. This specified position is the nominal position. The distance of the actual position of the point of end effector from its nominal position is measured and recorded. This value is denoted by 'δ', as shown in Fig. 1.32. The experiment is repeated number of times and the largest value of δ i.e. δ_{max} is called as manufacturer's repeatability and usually given as $\pm\ \delta_{max}$.

Factors affecting repeatability of a robot manipulator:
  (i)   Ambient conditions e.g. temperature changes, operating conditions e.g. transient conditions between start up and shut down of the system.
  (ii) Rigidity of the structure and
  (iii) The tendency for the precision of the drive trains and transmissions to differ somewhat from one production model to the next.
  (iv) By decreasing the load rating below its true value, repeatability can be improved.

The difference between accuracy and repeatability can be well illustrated by Fig. 1.25, where Fig. 1.33 shows locations of five bullets hit by four different shooters on their targets. Naturally, they all were supposed to hit the target at centre.

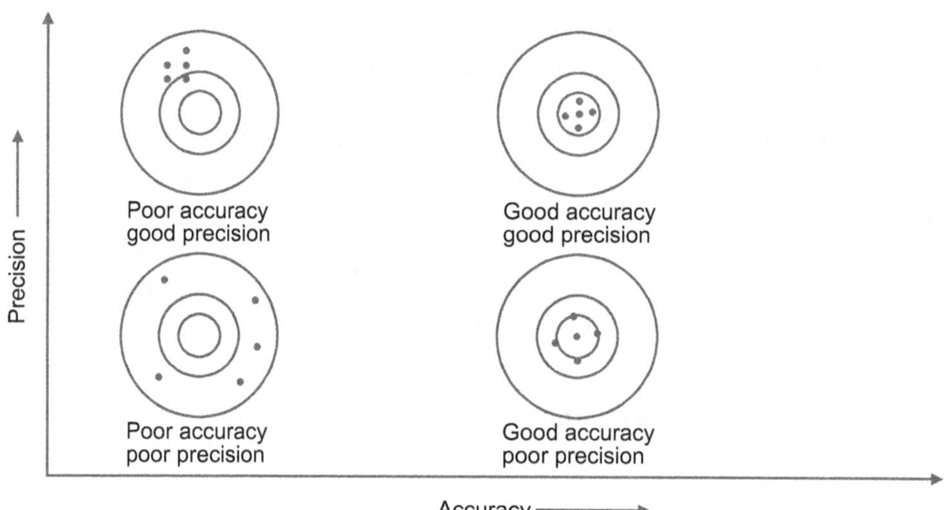

Fig. 1.33: Difference between Accuracy and Repeatability

(v) Compliance:
  - The compliance of the robot manipulator refers to the displacement of the wrist end in response to a force or torque exerted against it. Thus, compliance is a quality which gives a manipulator of a robot the ability to tolerate misalignment of mating parts.
  - Compliance prevents jamming, wedging and galling of the parts and therefore, it is essential for assembly of close-fitting parts.
  - Robot manipulator compliance is a directional feature i.e. compliance will be greater in certain directions because of the mechanical construction of the arm.
  - Compliance reduces the robot's precision of movement under load. If the robot is handling a heavy load, the weight of the load will cause the robot arm to deflect. If the robot is pressing a tool against a work part, the reactive force of the part may cause deflection of the manipulator. The robot's performance will be degraded because of compliance when it is operated under loaded situations.

- **High compliance** means the wrist is displaced a large amount by a relatively small force. The manipulator is said to be **'springy'** or **'spongy'** for a robot with high compliance. **Low compliance** means the manipulator is relatively stiff and is not displaced by a significant amount on application of same magnitude of force.
- Compliance is a complicated quantity to measure. Rather, one could find the **relationship between disturbances and displacements** which may be,
    - (i)   **Linear:** Wherein the displacement or rotation is proportional to force or torque.
    - (ii)   **Isotropic:** The displacement in this case is independent of the direction of the applied force.
    - (iii) **Diagonalised:** The displacement or rotation occurs only in the same direction as the force or torque.
    - (iv)   Constant with time and
    - (v)   Independent of tool position, orientation and velocity.
- In actual practice, a manipulator's compliance is a non-linear, anisotropic tensor quantity which varies with time and with the manipulator's posture and motion. It is a tensor because a force in one direction can result in displacements in other directions and even rotations. A torque can result in rotation about any axis and displacement in any direction.
- It is also found that:
    - (i)   Time can affect compliance through changes in temperature and subsequently viscosity in a hydraulic fluid.
    - (ii)   The compliance is a function of the frequency of the applied load or torque. e.g. A manipulator may be very compliant at frequencies around 2 Hz but very stiff in response to slower disturbances.

1.11 Socio-Economic Aspects of Robotisation

1.11.1 Sociological Aspects

Robotisation played a vital role in industrial growth but created lot of unemployment too. But still to certain extent it has raised the style of living today. Following points will depict some issues related to impact over social sector.

(i)   Ayres and Miller in their study conducted at Carnegie-Mellon University in 1980, predicted that by the year 2000, the class of non-sensor based robot would replace as many as 1 million manufacturing production workers, and the robots with some rudimentary tactile and vision sensing capabilities would replace about 3 millions of these workers. Also they predicted that by the year 2005, all the current manufacturing production workers could be expected to be replaced by highly sophisticated robots.

(ii)   Industry uses a thumb rule that one robot displaces three workers. Today robotisation puts lot of fear of displacement all over the world.

(iii) Conversely, James Albus of NBS (National Bureau of Standards) has said that "robots create profits, profits create expansion in industry and expanding industries hire more people". Also experts have suggested that these new jobs will require workers who are more skilled than before and those who are capable of building, repairing and maintaining the robots.

(iv) Few motivations for using robots are enlisted with their ranking.

Ranking	Motives
(a)	Reduction in labour costs.
(b)	Eliminate dangerous jobs.
(c)	Increase in output rate.
(d)	Improvement in product quality.
(e)	Increase in flexibility of product.
(f)	Material waste reduction.
(g)	Reduced labour turnover.
(h)	Reduced capital cost.

(v) In order to soften the inevitable impact of robotisation on the unemployment, following care should be taken:

(a) Industry should identify the class of jobs and workers well in advance, which will be adversely affected by robots.

(b) Industry, industry unions and government bodies should co-operate in long-range planning of employment needs.

(c) These groups must identify and publicize the new job skills that will be required in the future, this way it will alert young generation to the changing patterns in the job market and this will force them to acquire marketable skills.

(d) Job training and education facilities should be established to help retain those whose jobs will be lost.

(e) Government body and industry together should establish facilities to locate suitable jobs for displaced workers.

1.11.2 Economic Aspects

(i) Robots are meant to carry out

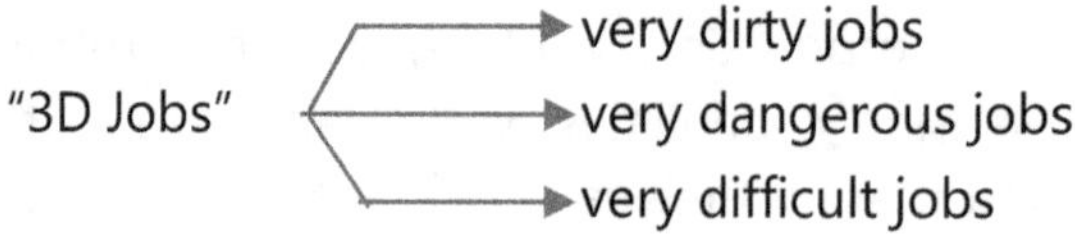

a survey conducted based on robot users and potential users, indicates that the primary reason for selecting a robot is to reduce labour costs.

(ii) It has been found that about –

55% of the overall system costs is for robot.

30% is for the additional tooling and fixturing along with engineering development cost.

15% is for installation.

But labour and operation cost is to be calculated in addition to above parts. This analysis does not include all the economic factors as the cost of money and the escalation of labour costs.

(iii) Above analysis can be refined by including factors like corporate tax rates, depreciation and the savings from using less material in a particular process.

Payback period 'Y' can be calculated from an equation

$$Y = \frac{X - C}{(Z)\,H\,(1 - TR) + D\,(TR)}$$

where,

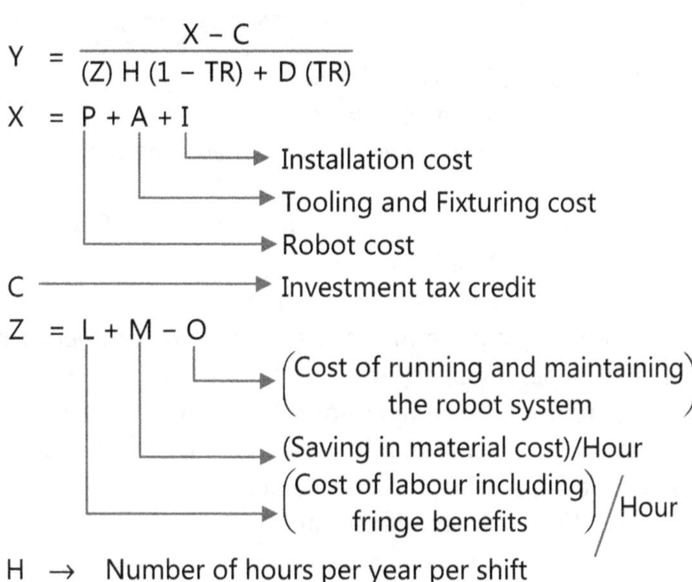

H → Number of hours per year per shift

TR → Corporate tax rate

D → Annual depreciation

This analysis does not take into account the time value of money.

(iv) **'Return on Investment'** is another economic measure used to determine whether a particular capital expenditure is warranted or not. It is defined as the ratio of the total annual savings realized from the equipment with the total investment.

It is expressed as percentage.

$$ROI = \frac{\text{Total annual savings}}{\text{Total investment}} \times 100\%$$

$$= \frac{(Z)\,H - D}{X - C} \times 100\%$$

(v) **'Internal rate of return'** is one of the important measures used to determine if the purchase of a robot is valid or not. It permit the time value of money to be included, and also the total cost of labour analysis.

(vi) The above quantitative measures do not take into account the economic benefits that can be derived from using a robot to produce a product that is of a consistently high quality.

All above considerations are extremely important when trying to justify the purchase of a robot.

EXERCISES

1. What are applications of robots?
2. Write a note on robot-like devices.
3. Explain the relation between industrial automation and robotics.
4. What are industrial applications of robots?
5. Explain various generations of robots, in brief. Also state the generation to which today's industrial robots be long.
6. Sketch and explain four types of joints in a robot.
7. Sketch and explain the motions a 3 DoF wrist can perform.
8. What is shape of work space in each of the following configurations.
    (i) Post-type, (ii) Polar, (iii) Gantry robot, (iv) Joint arm.
9. Sketch a 2 DoF planar manipulator and 2 DoF non-planar manipulator.
10. What is resolution? Is it related to accuracy?
11. Explain different types of resolutions.
12. Explain difference between accuracy and repeatability.
13. A robot is less accurate but has good repeatability. Another robot is accurate but poor in repeatability. Which robot will you select for –
    (i) Spray painting operation, (ii) Spot welding operation?
14. What are the factors affecting accuracy of a robot?
15. What are the factors affecting repeatability of a robot?
16. What is compliance? Explain.
17. Write a note on play back robots.
18. Discuss broad classification of robots.
19. State and explain robots performance parameters.
20. Explain socio-economic aspects of robotisation.

Unit II

Chapter 2: GRIPPERS

2.1 Introduction

- **End Effectors:**
  - Robots come in variety of sizes, shapes and capabilities. As discussed earlier robot have four basic components.
    - (i)   A manipulator.
    - (ii)   An end effect which is part of the manipulator.
    - (iii) A computer controller and
    - (iv)   A power supply.

  Robot with above components is as shown in Fig. 2.1 below.

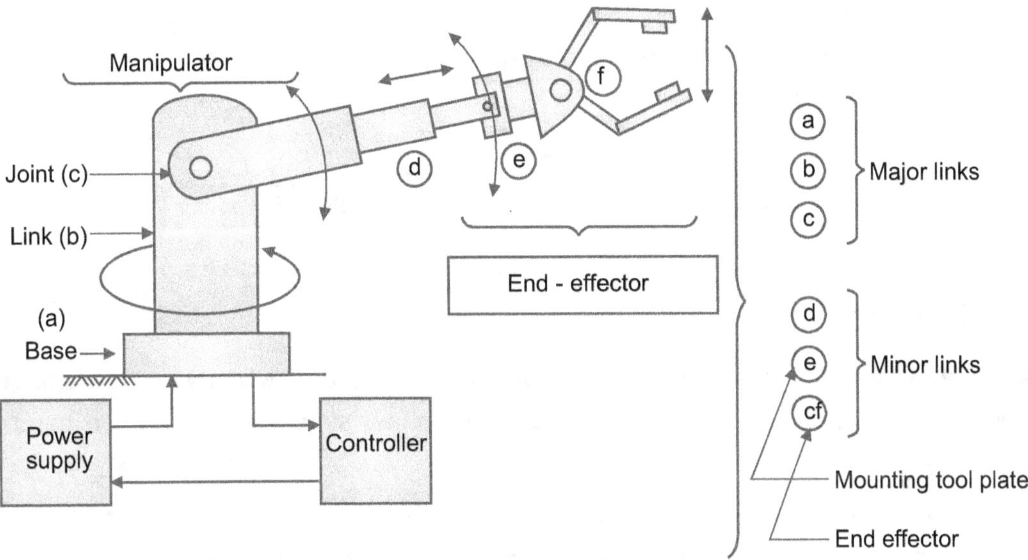

Fig. 2.1: A robot system components

  - The manipulator is a mechanism that consists of various segments or arms and composed of three sections:
    - (i)   The major linkages.
    - (ii)   The minor linkages.
    - (iii) The end effector (gripper or tool)

    –   The major linkages are the set of joint-link pairs that out-position the manipulator in space. They consist of the first three sets. The minor linkages are those joints and links associated with the fine positioning of the end-effector. They provide the ability to orient the tool mounting plate and subsequently the end-effector once the major linkages get it close to the desired position.

2.2 Types of End-Effector

Definition: *"A device, which is mounted on the tool plate, and used to make intentional contact with an object or to produce the robot's final effect on its surroundings by performing a particular task".*

Thus, it acts as the bridge between the robot arm and the environment around it. The actions of the gripper vary depending on the task.

    –   A robot end-effector which is attached to the wrist of the robot arm is a device that enables the general-purpose robot to grip materials, parts and tools to perform a specific task.

    –   The end-effectors are also called as grippers. End effectors can be broadly divided into two major categories.

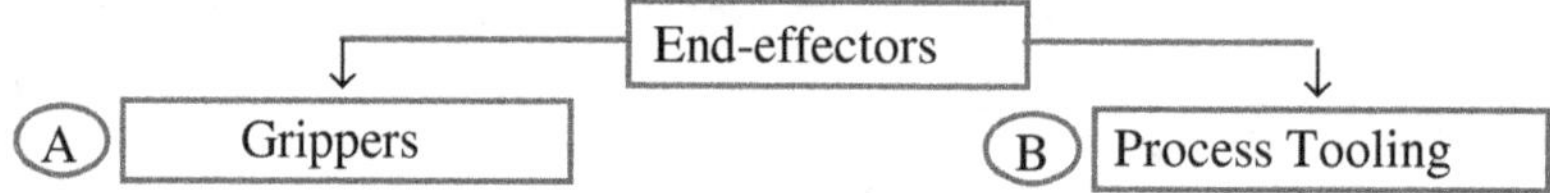

2.2.1 Grippers

These are end-effectors used to grasp and hold objects. There may be two or more fingered devices designed to grasp an object or tool in a manner similar to the human hand and finger.

    –   The gripper may be a simple pneumatically controlled device that opens and closes or a more complex servo-controlled unit capable of exerting specified forces or of measuring the part within its grasp.

    –   Grippers may be designed as physical constraints or as friction devices.

        (i)   A physical constraint device might work like a spatula that slides under an object to enable one to lift it.

        (ii)   A frictional device depends upon the frictional force between two materials to provide the gripping force.

2.2.2 Classification of Grippers

Grippers can be classified based on –

- (I) The number of gripping devices mounted on the robot's wrist.
    - (a) Single gripper and
    - (b) Double gripper
    - (c) Multiple gripper
- (II) The mode of gripping
    - (a) Internal gripper
    - (b) External gripper
- (III) The number of degrees of freedom (DoF)
    - – Incorporated in the gripper structure.
        - (a) 1 DoF
        - (b) 2 DoFs

(I) The number of gripping devices mounted on the robot's wrist:

(a) Single gripper: It is distinguished by the fact that only one grasping device is mounted on the robot's wrist and is used to handle single object.

(b) Double gripper: It has two gripping devices attached to the wrist and is used to handle two separate objects. It is useful in machine loading and unloading applications.

(c) Multiple gripper: If two or more grasping devices are fastened to the wrist, then it is a multiple gripper, where double grippers are a subset of multiple gripper. Multiple gripper systems enable effective simultaneous execution of more than two different jobs.

(II) Mode of gripping:

(a) Internal gripper: This kind of gripper grasps the part on its internal surface, therefore called as 'internal gripper'. It is as shown in Fig. 2.2.

(b) External gripper: This kind of gripper grasps the part on its external surface, therefore called as 'external gripper'. It is as shown in Fig. 2.3.

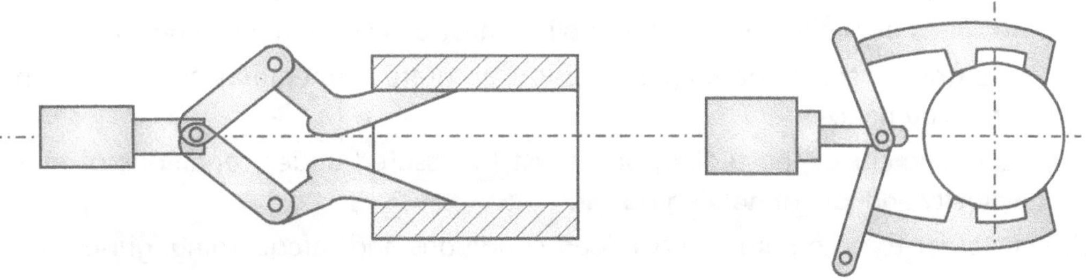

Fig. 2.2: Internal gripper   **Fig. 2.3: External gripper**

(III) The number of Degrees of Freedom (DoF):

(a) 1 DoF:

Some of the mechanical grippers belong

−   to the class of 1 DoF.

(b) 2 DoFs:

Few grippers belong to the class of 2 DoFs.

(IV) Special grippers:

The grippers of the robot may be specialized devices like Remote Centre Compliance (RCC) to insert an external mating component into an internal member like inserting a plug into a hole.

2.2.3 Process Tooling

−   It is an end-effector designed to perform work on the part rather than to merely grasp it.

−   Thus, process tooling may be any useful device such as

(i)	a spot-welding torch	(ii)	a spray-painting gun
(iii)	a vacuum cup	(iv)	drilling spindle
(v)	heating torches	(vi)	grinders
(vii)	wire brushes	(viii)	arc welding tools, etc.

2.2.4 Characteristics of Grippers   (W-11)

A gripper must satisfy the following characteristics:

(i)   Gripper must be capable of grasping, lifting and releasing the part as individual or family of parts required by the process.

(ii)   Some grippers sense the presence of the part with their gripping action.

(iii)   As far as possible weight of the tooling must be kept to a minimum value.

(iv)   The gripper should be simple in design, accurate in operation, economical and free of maintenance.

(v)   Containment of the tooling part must be assured under conditions of maximum velocity and loss of holding power.

(vi)   In order to accommodate overload conditions and safeguarding, gripper must be equipped with a collision sensor.

(vii)   The gripper for industrial robots, in a repetitive operation, requires minimum gripping dexterity.

2.3 Types of Grippers   (W-11)

There are various types of end-effectors to perform different work functions. The various types of grippers can be divided into the following major categories.

    (i)   Mechanical grippers
    (ii)   Vacuum grippers or vacuum cups.
    (iii)   Magnetic grippers.
    (iv)   Adhesive or electrostatic grippers.
    (v)   Expandable cuff.

2.3.1 Mechanical Grippers

- These are standard grippers that use mechanical fingers actuated by a mechanism to grasp an object.
- The fingers called the jaws, are the appendages of the grippers that actually make contact with the object.
- The fingers are either attached to the mechanism or are an integral part of the mechanism.

  The use of replaceable fingers allows for the wear and interchangeability. Replaceable fingers can also be designed to accommodate different part models.
- The gripper mechanism is used to translate some form of power input to the grasping action of the fingers against the part. The mechanism must be capable of opening and closing the fingers and to exert sufficient force against the part to hold it securely.
- The input power to the mechanism is supplied from the robot and can be pneumatic, hydraulic, electric or mechanical (i.e. spring activated).

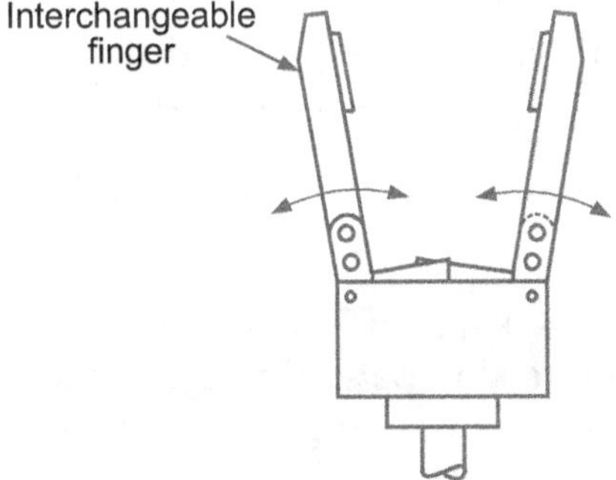

Fig. 2.4: Interchangeable fingers in mechanical gripper

–   There are two ways of constraining the part in the gripper.

(a) By physical constriction of the part within the fingers:

In this approach, the gripper fingers enclose the part to some extent, thus constraining the motion of the part. Therefore, it is required to design contacting surfaces of the fingers to be in the approximate shape of the part geometry.

It is as shown in Fig. 2.5.

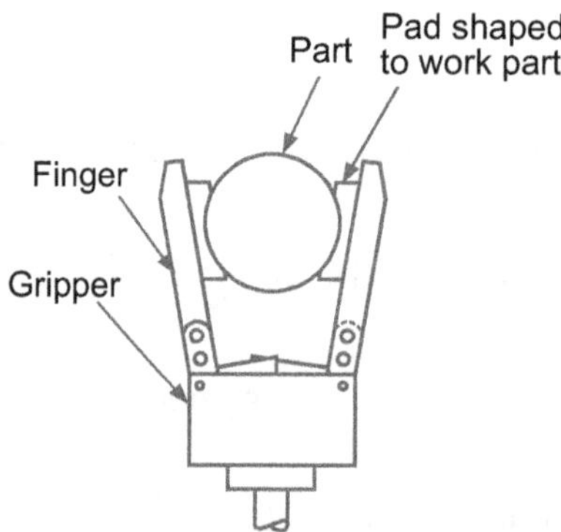

Fig. 2.5: Physical constriction of the part within the finger

(b) By friction between the fingers and the work part:

–   In this approach, the fingers must apply a force that is sufficient for friction to retain the part against gravity, acceleration and any other force that might arise during the holding portion of the work cycle.

–   The pads attached to the fingers that make contact with the part, are generally fabricated out of a material that is relative soft. This results in increase of the coefficient of friction between the part and the contacting finger surface. It also serves to protect the part surface from scratching or other kind of damages.

–   This approach results in less complicated and therefore less expensive gripper design.

–   Disadvantage with friction approach – If a force of sufficient magnitude is applied against the part in a direction parallel to the friction surfaces of the fingers, there might be slipping of part out of the gripper. In order to avoid this slippage, the gripper must be designed to exert a force that is greater than the weight of the part. It is illustrated in Fig. 2.6.

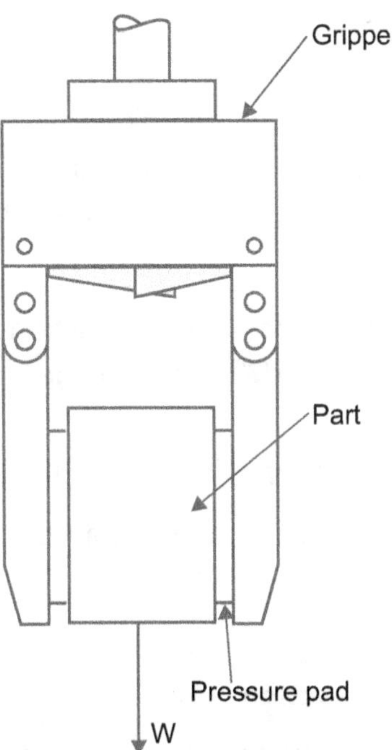

Fig. 2.6: Friction approach to hold a part in finger

2.3.2 Closing Motions of Mechanical Gripper

There are two closing motions of mechanical gripper:

    (i) Angular and (ii) Parallel.

In Angular motion, the jaws move in angular sense while in parallel motion, jaws move toward or away from each other. It is illustrated in Fig. 2.7 and Fig. 2.8.

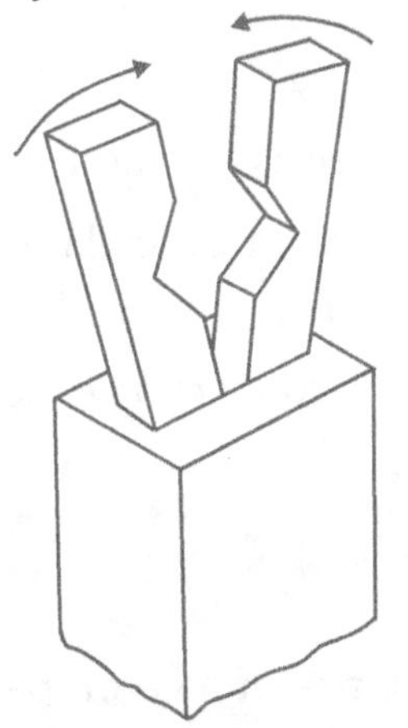

Fig. 2.7: Angular gripper

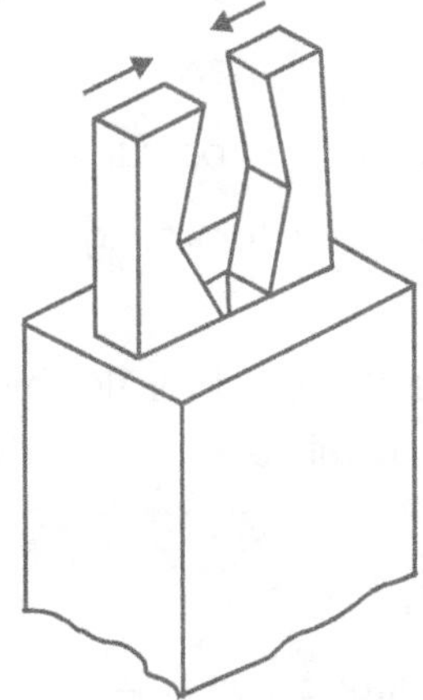

Fig. 2.8: Parallel gripper

2.3.3 Vacuum Grippers

Principle:

Vacuum is used as the gripping force. The lifting power is a function of the degree of vacuum achieved and the size of the area on the part where the vacuum is applied.

Vacuum grippers work on Bernoulli's principle where suction is created by using compressed air. The relative high vacuum is created by vacuum generator which is powered by an electric motor.

Vacuum cups or suction cups are used for lifting objects. They are made of neoprene or synthetic rubber.

Characteristics of vacuum cups or suction cups:

(i)   They are simple in construction and have extreme light weight.

(ii)   The number, size and type of cups used will depend on the weight, size, shape and type of material being handled.

(iii)   The diameter usually ranges between one to eight inches.

(iv)   They are round or oval in shape.

(v)   The workpiece to be handled be smooth and clean in order to form a satisfactory vacuum between the piece and the suction cup.

(vi)   Flexibility of the vacuum cup provides the robot with a certain amount of compliance.

Uses of vacuum gripper:

(i)   They can be used on curved and contoured surfaces as well as flat surfaces.

(ii)   They are ideal for lifting fragile parts such as glass, pans of glass, large lightweight boxes.

(iii)   They are also used for flexible soft materials, where the vacuum cup would be made of a hard substance.

Working:

    – The lifting power = f (Degree of vacuum achieved, size of area on part where the vacuum is applied.

–   Multiple-cup vacuum gripper increases the contact surface area and permit the size and weight of the workpiece to be increased.

–   The lift capacity of the suction depends on:

(i)   the effective area of the cup and

(ii)   the negative air pressure between the cup and the object to be lifted.

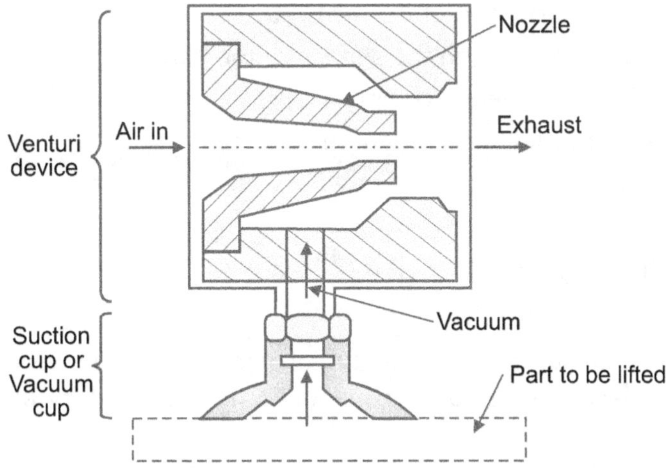

Fig. 2.9: Venturi device for flat surface gripping

The relationship can be given as under:

$$F = K \cdot P \cdot A_C$$

$$F = K \cdot A_C \, [P_A - P_{RES}]$$

where, F = The force or lift capacity, (N)

P = Negative pressure, (N/cm^2)

A_C = Total effective area of the suction cup(s) used to create the vacuum, (cm^2)

K = A coefficient depending on atmospheric pressure and sealing conditions

P_A = The atmospheric pressure

P_{RES} = Residual pressure in vacuum cup

–   The vacuum generator and venturi block (also known as miniature vacuum pump) and two common devices used to create suction by the use of compressed air.

–   The vacuum generator is a piston-operated or vane-driven device powered by an electric motor and is capable of creating a relative high vacuum.

–   The venturi is a simple device and can be operated by means of shop air pressure.

–   A single vacuum cup can produce 20 + inches of Hg vacuum from a 22 psi line. This enables the cup to support a weight of 10 to 100 *lb*, depending on the sealing capacity of the parts and the desired factor of safety used.

Advantages of vacuum cup grippers:

(i)   They require only one surface to grasp the part.

(ii)   They apply a uniform pressure on the surface of the part.

(iii) They need a relatively lightweight gripper.

(iv) They are suitable to a variety of different materials.

(v)   They have a very low cost.

2.3.4 Magnetic Grippers

Principle:

Magnetic grippers are similar in operation to vacuum grippers, however, instead of using vacuum to lift the object, they employ a magnetic field created by an electromagnet or permanent magnet.

–   Magnetic grippers are employed to handle ferromagnetic materials.

–   The material can be lifted in the form of a sheet or plate with an electromagnet mounted on the robot tool plate.

–   Fig. 2.10 (a) shows single magnetic and Fig. 2.10 (b) dual magnetic gripper.

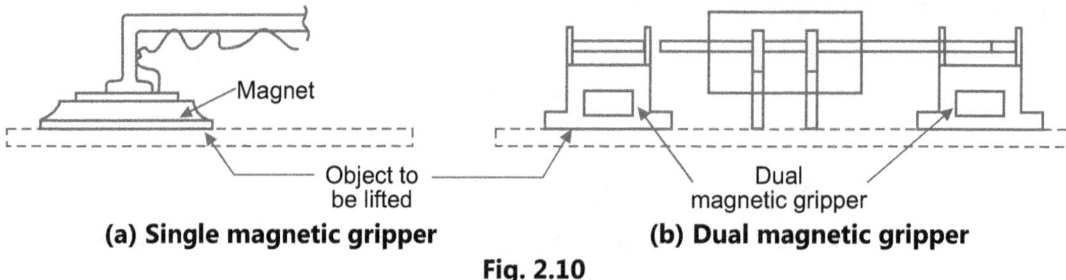

(a) Single magnetic gripper   **(b) Dual magnetic gripper**

Fig. 2.10

–   Magnetic grippers can be categorised into –
(i)   Electromagnets and
(ii)   Permanent magnets

(i)   Electromagnetic grippers:

They are easier to control, but require a source of dc power and an appropriate controller. When the part is to be released, the control unit reverses the polarity at a reduced power level before switching-off the electromagnet. This procedure acts to cancel the residual magnetism in the work piece ensuring a positive release of the part.

Using Maxwell's equation, the force of attraction of electromagnet can be given as,

$$P = \frac{(1N)^2}{2S \cdot A_C \cdot [R_A + R_M]}$$

where,

$$1N = \text{Number of amp-turns of coil}$$
$$A_C = \text{Area of contact of an object with magnet}$$
$$R_A = \text{Reluctance of magnetic paths through air metal}$$
$$R_M = \text{Reluctance of magnetic paths through air metal}$$
$$P \geq [a + g]\, m \cdot FoS$$

where,

$$a = \text{Gripper acceleration}$$
$$g = \text{Gravitational constant}$$
$$m = \text{Mass}$$
$$FoS = \text{Factory of safety}$$

(ii) Permanent magnets:

- They have the advantage of not requiring an external power source to operate the magnet.
- They require a device to remove the part from the magnet.
- It is possible to design the permanent magnet to penetrate only to a small depth in the part (i.e. as low as 0.0787 mm)
- Fig. 2.11 shows permanent magnet gripper.

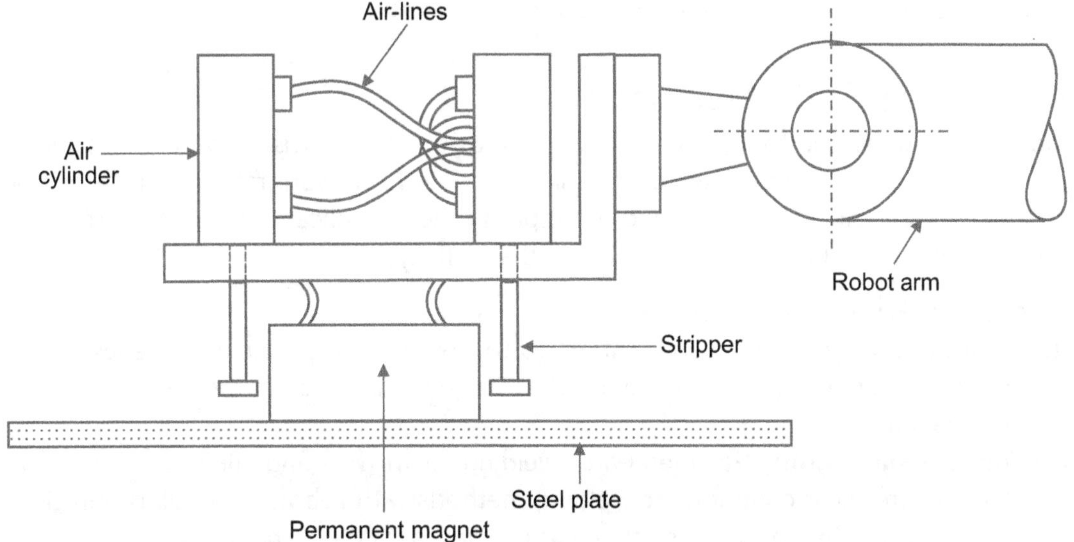

Fig. 2.11: Permanent magnet gripper with stripper device

Advantages of magnetic grippers:
(i)   In this type of grippers, pick-up times are very fast.
(ii)   Variations in part-size can be tolerated.
(iii)   They are capable to handle metal parts with holes.
(iv)   They need only one surface for gripping.
(v)   They can be used in hazardous and explosive environments, as there is no danger of sparks which might cause ignition in such environment.

Disadvantages:
(i)   The residual magnetism in the work piece may cause problems in subsequent handling.
(ii)   The magnetic attraction tends to penetrate beyond the top layer in the stack, which can cause more than a single part to be lifted by the magnet.

2.3.5 Adhesive Grippers

(i)   Adhesive grippers are useful for handling fabrics and lightweight materials.
(ii)   In this case, an adhesive material performs the grasping actions, as it is fed automatically to the robot wrist.
(iii)   The adhesive material is loaded in the form of a continuous ribbon into a feeding mechanism which is attached to the robot wrist.
(iv)   The requirements of the items to be handled are that they must be grasped on one side only.
(v)   The reliability of this gripping device is diminished with each successive operation cycle as the adhesive substances lose its tackiness on repeated use. To avoid this, the adhesive material can be loaded in the form of a continuous ribbon.

2.4 Tools as End Effectors

In most applications, the tool is fastened directly to the robot wrist and becomes the end effector. In this case, the end effector is designed to perform work rather than to pick and place a work part. The reason for using a gripper in these applications is that there may be more than one tool to be used by the robot in the work cycle.

Some of the tools used with robots are:
   (i) A spot-welding gun: It can be attached to the robot wrist to place a series of welds on flat or curved surfaces. A 3 DoF wrist is required because of the dexterity required for maneuvering the gun.
   (ii) Arc-welding gun: Gas-metal-arc welding (GMAW) and flux-core-arc-welding (FCAW) are most common arc-welding methods with robots. A welding gun can be attached to the robot wrist that carries gas and bar wire for GMAW or cored electrode filled with flux for FCAW. The robot can position the welding gun for a single straight or curved run or use a weaving pattern for wider welds.

(iii) Spray painting gun: These are also used by industrial robots. In some cases, only 2 DoFs may be required of the robot wrist for spray painting. The robot can spray parts with compound curved surfaces.

(iv) Grinders, routers, wire brushing or sanders: These are easily attached to the robot wrist for performing various tasks in foundary shop as well as for other fabrications.

(v) Liquid cement applicators, heating torches and waterjet cutting tools can also be incorporated in the robot wrist.

(vi) Variety of assembly tools such as drilling, screw drivers and wrenches, can be used by the robot. In certain cases, these tools are automatically interchangeable by the robot.

(vii) Multiple tools: A robot can handle several tools sequentially, with an automatic tool-changing operation programmed into the robot's memory. The tools can be of different types or sizes, permitting multiple operations on the same workplace. In order to remove tools, the robot lowers the tool into a cradle that retains the snap-in tool as the robot pulls its wrist away. The process is reversed to pick up another tool. It is shown in Fig. 2.12 and Fig. 2.13.

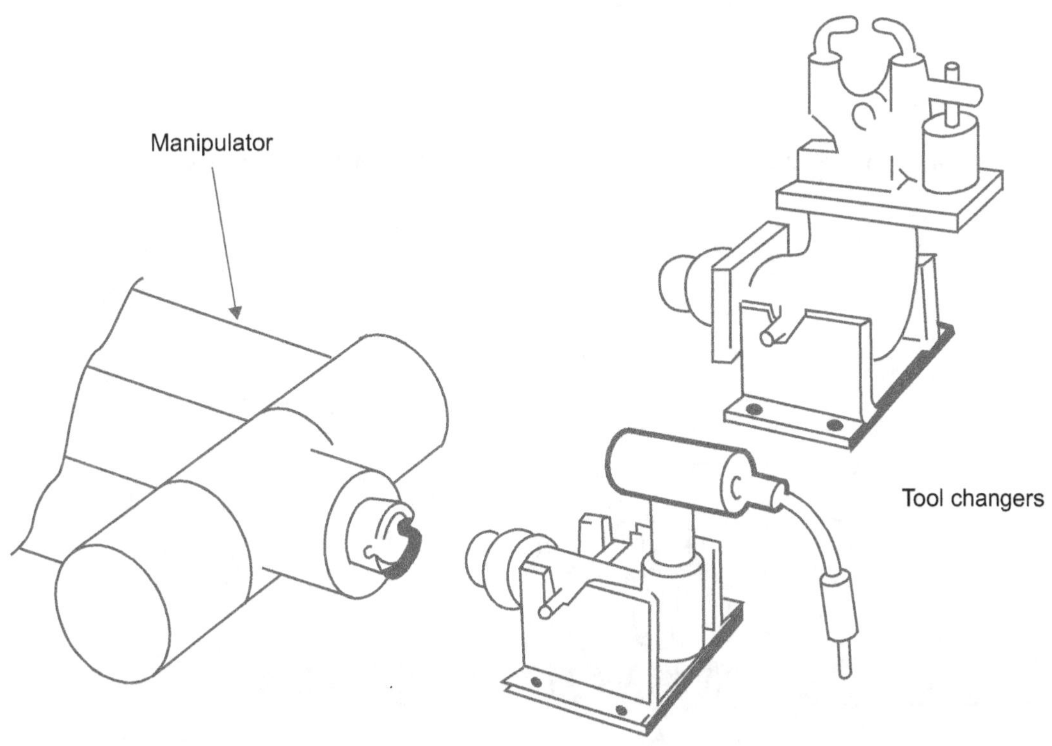

Fig. 2.12: Tool Changers

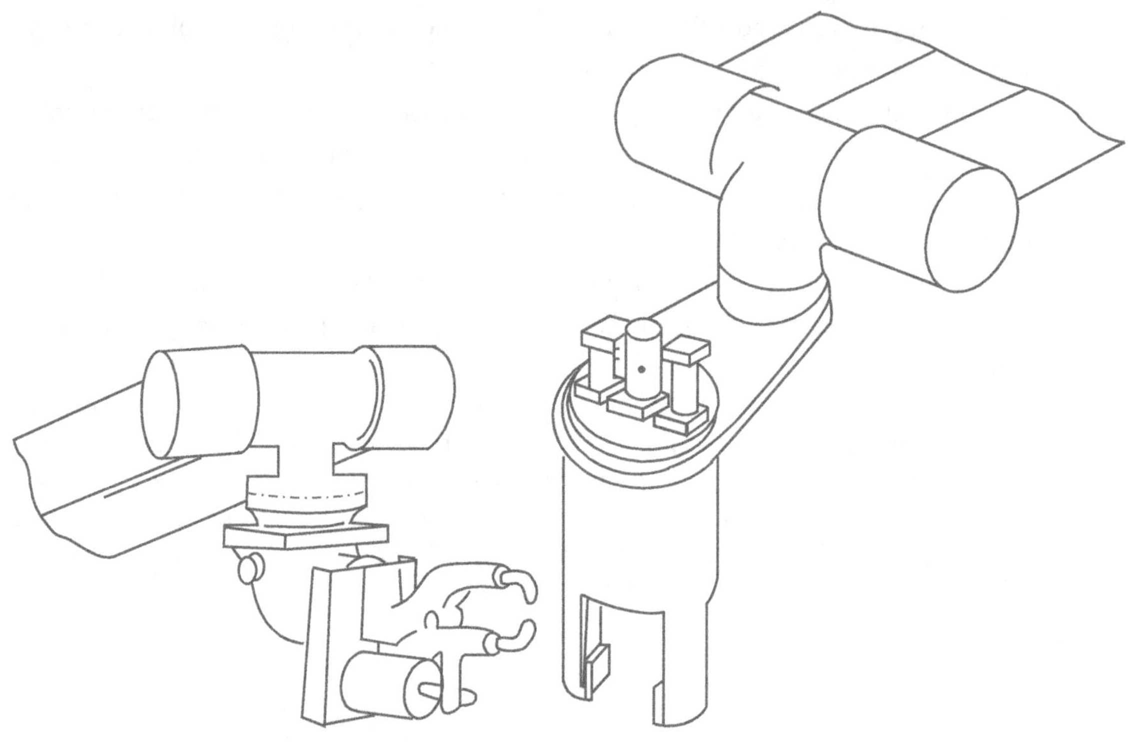

(a) Spot welding gun   **(b) Pneumatic nut-runners drills**

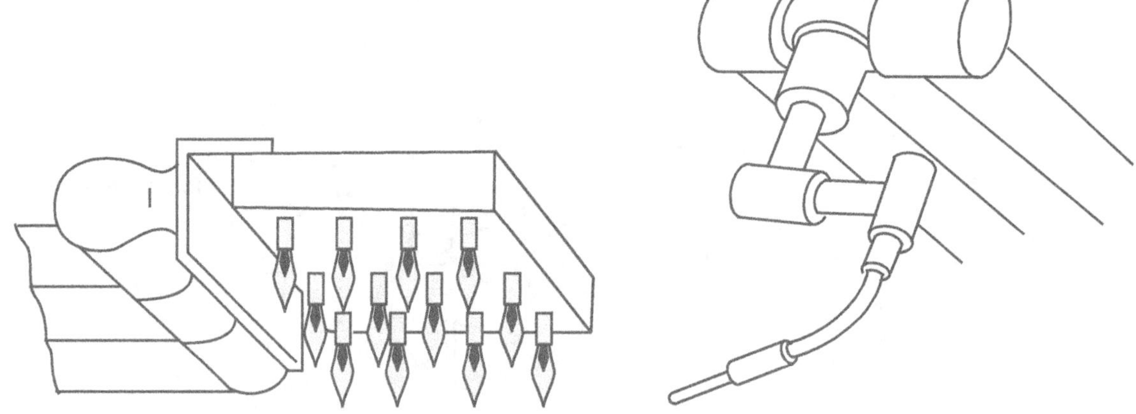

(c) Arc-welding torch   **(d) Routers, sanders**

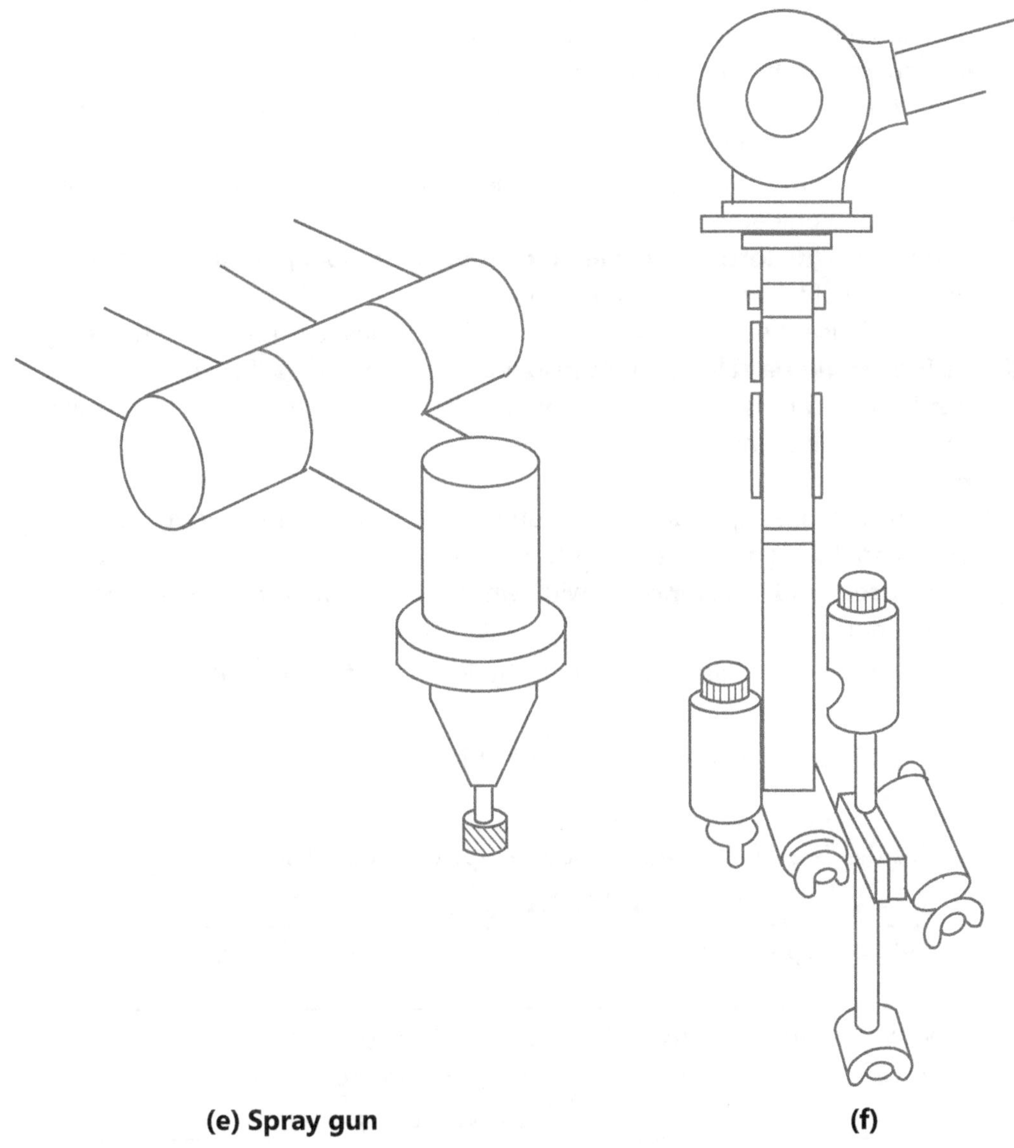

(e) Spray gun   **(f)**

Fig. 2.13: Types of Process Tool

2.5 Guidelines for Design of Robotic Grippers

It is an important aspect of the overall robot performance and the most demanding process in any robot system to match the need for the production requirement.

J. F. Engelberger, in his 'Robotics in Practice' defines various factors that are to be considered while selecting a gripper.

2.5.1 Considerations in Gripper Selection and Design

Following factors should be considered in assessing gripping requirement.

    (i)   The **part surface** to be grasped must be reachable.

    (ii)   The **variation in size** of the part must be accounted because this might affect the accuracy of locating the part.

    (iii)   The gripper design must accommodate **the change in size** that occurs between part loading and unloading.

    (iv)   **Scratching and distortion of the parts** during gripping must be taken into account as one of the major consideration.

    (v)   If there is choice between two different dimensions on the part, the **larger dimension should be selected** for grasping.

    (vi)   **Gripper fingers** can be designed **to conform to the part** shape by using resilient pads or self-aligning fingers.

    (vii)   **Gripping force:**

        Following factors are important that determine the required gripping force:

        (a)   The **overall weight** of the object to be grasped.

        (b)   The **speed and acceleration** with which the robot arm moves, and their orientation.

        (c)   The **method of constriction** either physical or by friction that is used to hold the part.

        (d)   The coefficient of friction between the object and the gripper fingers.

Following table gives the field of application and the type of gripper used.

Table 8.1

Sr. No.	Field of application	Type of gripper
1.	Handling parts of cylindrical, cuboidal or triangular.	(a) 3-finger gripper (b) Omnigripper (c) Vacuum gripper
2.	Handling part of complex configuration.	Multiple DoF gripper.
3.	Handling work parts of similar size and weight.	Notch gripper.
4.	For machine loading and unloading and handling light jobs.	Multiple gripper like double gripper
5.	For hollow workparts.	Internal gripper.
6.	For solid workparts	External gripper
7.	For ferrous work pieces.	Magnetic grippers.

2.5.2 Factors in the Selection and Design of Grippers

Following factors are taken into account while designing gripper.

(i)   Part to be handled:
- Weight of size of part.
- Shape of object and changes in shape during processing.
- Tolerance on the part size.
- Surface, condition, protection of delicate surfaces.

(ii) Actuation method:
- Mechanical grasping.
- Vacuum cup, magnetic grasping.
- Other methods - adhesive and scoopes etc.

(iii) Power and signal transmission:
- Pneumatic, electrical, hydraulic and mechanical.

(iv) Gripper force (mechanical gripper):
- Weight of object.
- Method of holding object.
- Coefficient of friction between fingers and object.
- Speed and acceleration during motion cycle.

(v) Positioning problems:
- Length of fingers.
- Inherent accuracy and repeatability of robot.
- Tolerance on the part size.

(vi) Service conditions:
- Number of actuations during lifetime of gripper.
- Replaceability of wear.
- Components.
- Maintenance and serviceability.

(vii) Operating environment:
- Heat and temperature.
- Humidity, moisture, dirt, chemicals etc.

(viii) Temperature problems:
- Heat shields.
- Long fingers, forced cooling and use of heat-resistant materials.

(ix) Fabrication materials:
- Strength, durability, rigidity, fatigue strength.
- Cost and ease of fabrication.
- Friction properties for finger surfaces.
- Compatibility with operating environment.

(x) Other conditions:
- Use of interchangeable fingers.
- Use of design standards.
- Risk of product changes and their effect on the gripper design.
- Lead time for design and fabrication.
- Tryout of gripper in production.

2.5.3 Gripper Design Criteria

(i)   They must be strong and durable.

(ii)   They must have light weight.

(iii) They must have dimensional stability and be able to hold the work piece orientation under height gravitational forces.

(iv)   They must have some built-in compliance or automatic alignment capability to accommodate positioning tolerances.

(v)   They must be fast acting.

(vi)   They must be maintainable.

2.5.4 Rules for Gripper Design

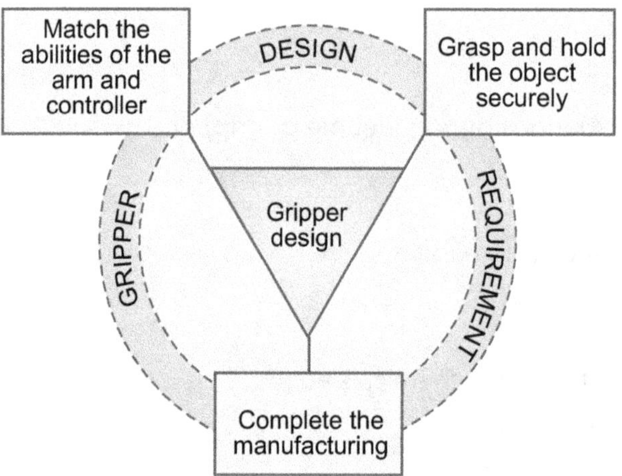

Fig. 2.14: Requirements for Gripper Design

(i)   Study the parts to be grasped and the task to be performed, and express the gripping requirements, keeping in view the types of material to be handled, shape and properties.

(ii)   Determine additional requirements if any (e.g. high temperature, presence of abrasive, dirt, chemical etc.).

(iii) Determine specific solutions and develop designs combining the modular solutions.

(iv)   Consider design with two or three grippers mounted together at the end of the arm.

(v)   Redesign the part, if it is feasible and necessary.

(vi)   Specify and design the particular gripper.

2.6   Force Analysis of Mechanical, Pneumatic and Hydraulic Grippers

2.6.1 Drive for Mechanical Gripper

1.   The robot controller supplies the electrical signals that result in the gripper's action. Most grippers are opened and closed with pneumatic actuator.

2.   For few applications, hydraulic or spring power is used.

3.   Less frequently, grippers are spring opened and power-closed.

4.   Electrical powered jaws are used in limited applications with solenoid or DC servomotor providing the opening and closing action.

A mechanical gripper comprises between 5 and 12 percent of the robot cost. For some specialized application this cost may exceed 20 percent of the total robot cost.

2.6.2 Gripper Force Analysis

–   Basic purpose of the gripper mechanism is to convert input power into the required motion and force to grasp and retain an object. Therefore, the first task is to evaluate the gripping force required. Once the gripping force is evaluated, the required actuator force or torque can be computed for a given gripper design.

–   Let us consider a rectangular block is to be lifted up. The gripping surface applies a force F_G along one axis that passes through the centre of gravity of the block. The force that must be applied to prevent slippage due to gravity depends on two parts:

(i)   The angle θ, subtended by gripping surface with horizontal, and

(ii) The coefficient of friction μ, between the gripping surface and the load surface.

It is illustrated in Fig. 2.15.

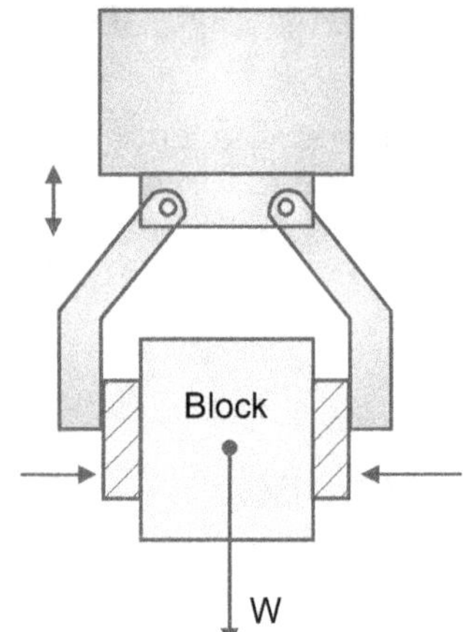

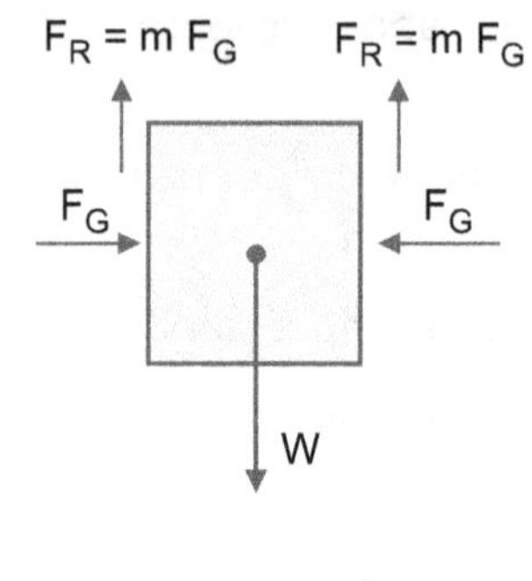

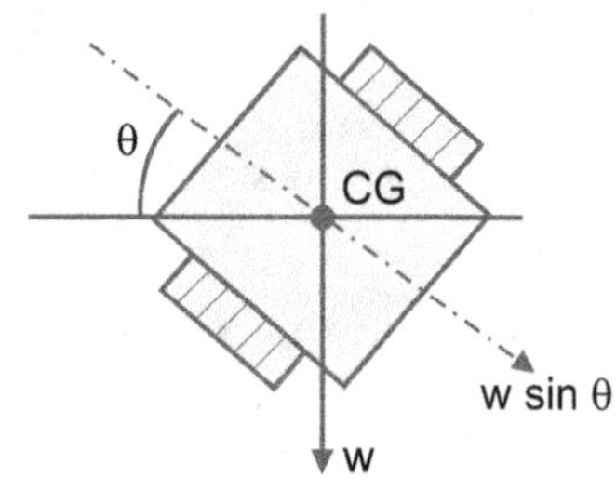

Fig. 2.15: Rectangular block in gripper   **Fig. 2.16: Free body diagram of block**   **Fig. 2.17: Block in different orientation**

The Gripping Force:

$$W \sin \theta = n \cdot \mu \cdot F_G$$

$$\therefore \quad F_G = \frac{W \sin \theta}{\mu \cdot n}$$

$$F_G = \frac{m \cdot g \cdot \sin \theta}{\mu \cdot n}$$

where, m = Mass (kg)

g = Acceleration due to gravity (m/s^2)

μ = Coefficient of friction

θ = Angle subtended with horizontal

n = Number of pairs of contact surfaces

This force evaluated represents only the static force, which is the minimum force that must be applied to the stationary object (load).

PROBLEMS

Problem 2.1:

A rectangular block weighing 10 kg is gripped in the middle and lifted vertically at a velocity of 1.2 m/s. If it accelerates to this velocity at 30 m/s² and the coefficient of friction between the gripping pads and the block is 0.45, calculate the gripping force required to prevent slippage.

Solution:

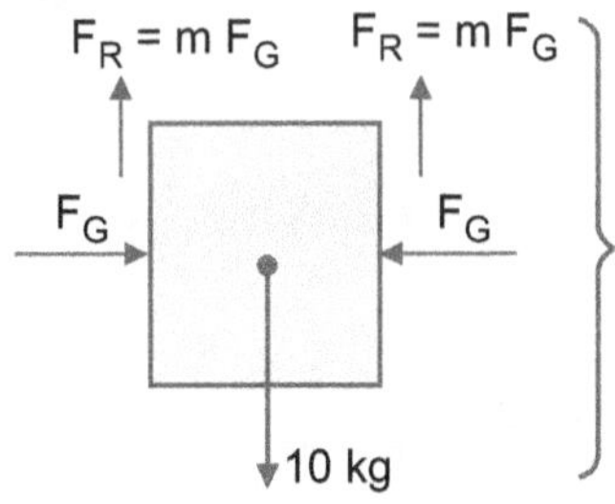

Fig. 2.18

Given:

$$W = 10 \text{ kg}$$
$$\theta = 90°$$
$$\mu = 0.45$$
$$n = 2 \text{ (considering two fingers)}$$

From free body diagram,

$$2\,F_R - m \cdot g = ma$$

$$2\,\mu \cdot F_G - m \cdot g = ma$$

$$F_G = \frac{m(a + g)}{2\,\mu}$$

$$F_G = \frac{10\,(30 + 9.81)}{2 \times 0.45}$$

$$F_G = 442.33 \text{ N}$$

Problem 2.2:

A simple pivot type gripper is used to hold rectangular box as shown in Fig. 2.19. The gripper is to be actuated by a piston device to apply a actuating force F_A. Gripping force F_G = 150 N. Evaluate the force F_A required to close the gripper.

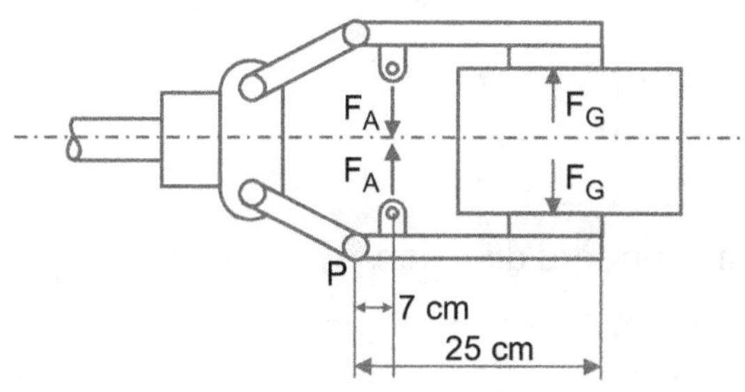

Fig. 2.19

Solution: For an equilibrium of forces, summation of moments due to the forces about pivot point is equal to zero.

i.e.
$$\sum M_p = 0$$
$$- F_G \cdot L_G + F_A \cdot l_A = 0$$

Sign convention
↻ ⇒ Clockwise moment negative
↺ ⇒ Anticlockwise moment positive

$$\therefore \qquad F_G \cdot L_A = F_A \cdot l_A$$
$$\therefore \qquad F_A = \frac{F_G \cdot L_G}{l_A}$$
$$F_A = \frac{150 \times 25}{7}$$
$$\boxed{F_A = 535.71 \text{ N}}$$

which is the actuating force provided by piston device to close the gripper.

Problem 2.3:

A box weighing 1 kN is to be gripped as shown in Fig. 2.20 using friction against two opposing fingers. Assume coefficient of friction $\mu = 0.22$. The centre of gripping does not coincide with the centre of gravity of box. Find clamping force assuming a factor of safety 1.6.

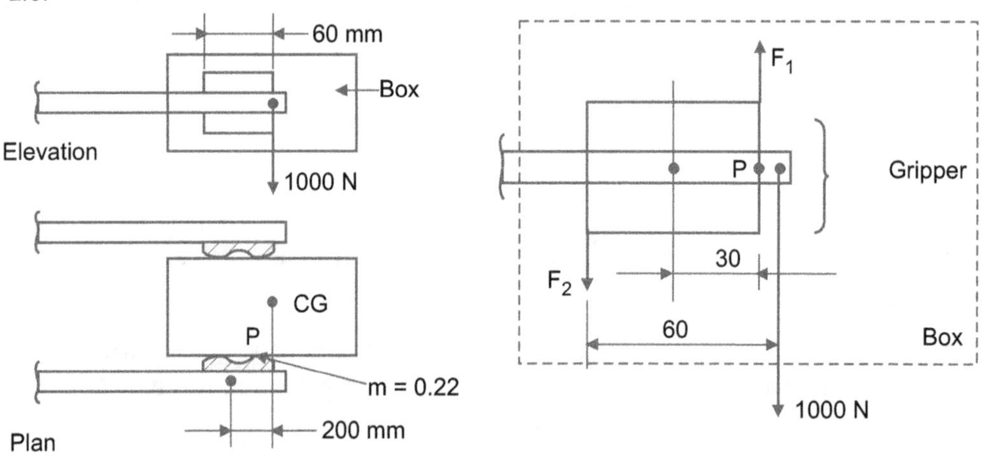

Fig. 2.20

Solution:

Given:
$$W = 1 \text{ kN}$$
$$\mu = 0.22$$
$$FoS = 1.6$$

Assume acceleration a in upward direction (↑)

Resolution of vertical forces gives

$$1000 + 2 F_2 + \frac{W \cdot a}{g} = 2 F_1 \qquad\qquad \text{... (2.1)}$$

Resolving moment of forces about P.

$$60\ F_2 + 60\ F_2 - 1000 \times (200 - 30) = 0$$

$$120\ F_2 - 1000 \times 170\ =\ 0$$

$$F_2\ =\ 1416.67\ N$$

Substituting in equation (2.1),

$$1000 + 2 \times 1416.67 + \frac{1000 \times 2.5\ g}{g}\ =\ 2 \times F_1 \qquad \text{... (Assuming } a = 2.5\ g)$$

$$F_1\ =\ 3166.67\ N$$

∴   Clamping force required,

$$F_1 + F_2\ =\ \frac{\mu \cdot F_C}{FoS}$$

where, F_C = Clamping force

FoS = Factor of safety

∴

$$F_C\ =\ \frac{(F_1 + F_2) \cdot FoS}{\mu}$$

$$=\ \frac{(3166.67 + 1416.67)\ 1.6}{0.22}$$

$$F_C\ =\ 33333.382\ N$$

which is required clamping force to grip the box. Gripping force will be small if the box is to be lifted by holding it at its C.G.

Problem 2.4:

Fig. 2.21 shows linkage mechanism and the gripper dimensions used to handle a workpart for a machining operation. The gripping factor is required to be 150 N. Calculate the required actuating force A_A applied to the plunger. P is pivot point in a mechanism.

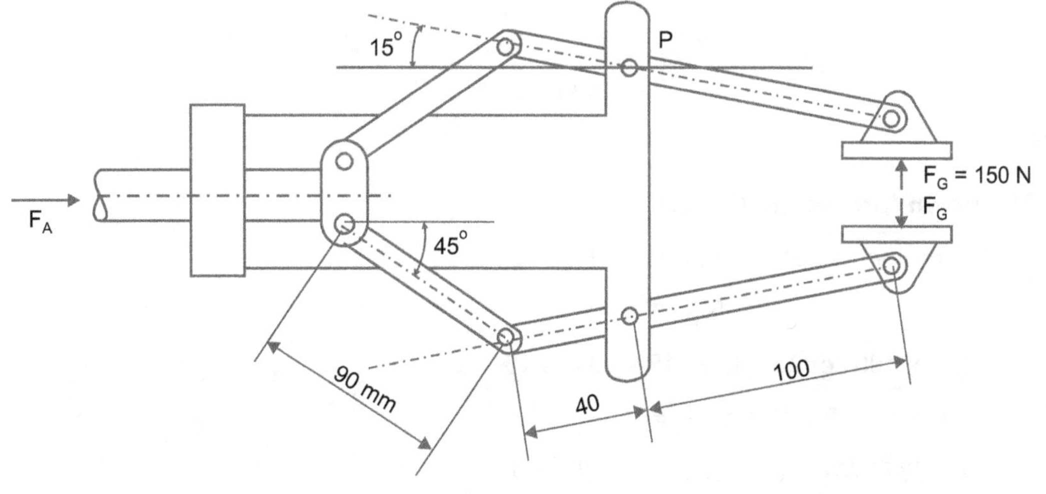

Fig. 2.21

Solution:

- Considering only half of the mechanism as it is symmetric about horizontal axis.

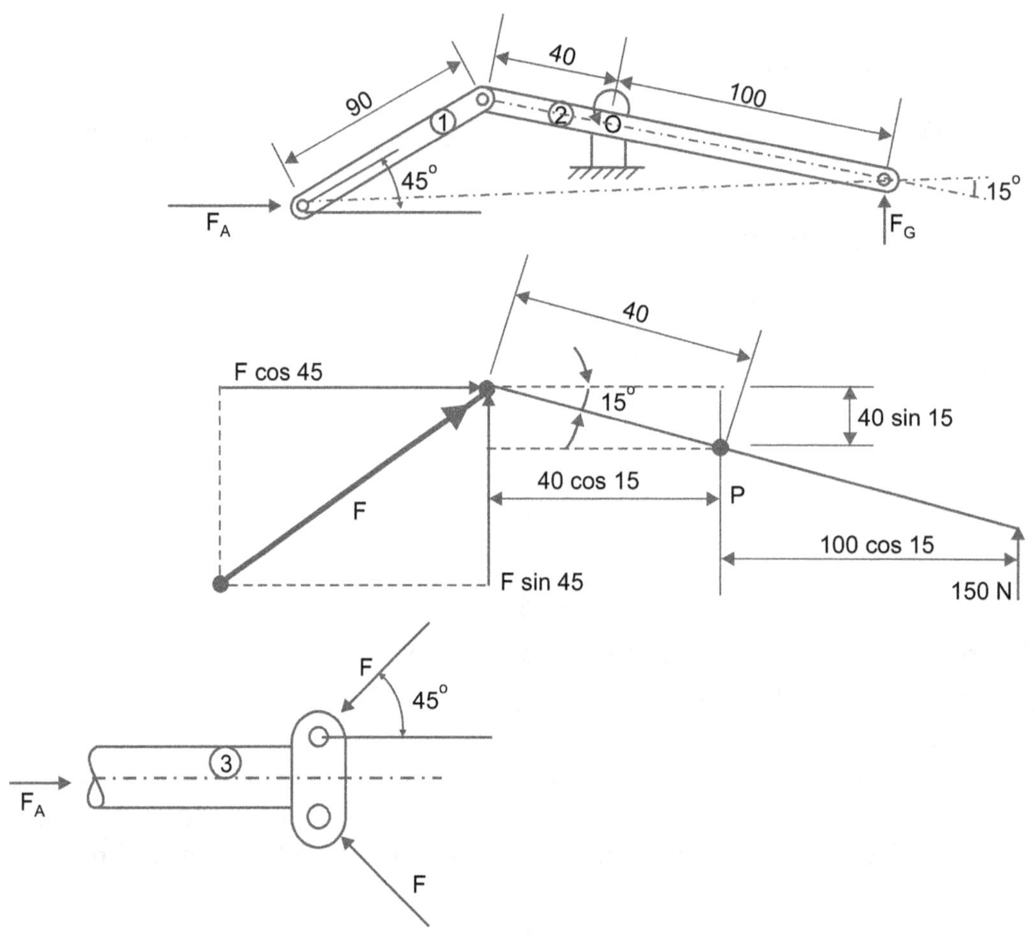

Fig. 2.22

- **Unknown force along link (1):**

Taking moments about pivot point 'P',

i.e. $\qquad\qquad \sum M_p = 0$

$$150 \times 100 \cos 15 - F \sin 45 \times 40 \cos 15$$

$$- F \cos 45 \times 40 \sin 15 = 0$$

$$14488.8874 - F (27.3205 + 7.3205) = 0$$

$$F = 418.258 \text{ N}$$

- **Force along link-3 i.e. force along the plunger:**

The actuating force applied to the plunger to deliver the force of 418.258 N to each finger can be calculated as,

$$F_A = F \cos 45 + F \cos 45$$
$$= 2 F \cos 45$$
$$= 2 \times 418.258 \cos 45$$
$$F_A = 591.506 \text{ N}$$

This actuating force is delivered by means of power input mechanism.

Problem 2.5:

A vacuum gripper is used to lift flat steel of dimensions 7 mm × 600 mm × 900 mm. The gripper uses two suction cups, 125 mm in diameter each, and they are located 450 mm apart for stability. Assume a factor of safety of 1.7 to allow for acceleration of the plate. Determine the negative pressure required to lift the plates if the density of steel is 8054.3×10^{-9} kg/mm^3.

Solution:

Given: Density of steel (ρ) = 8054.3×10^{-9} kg/mm^3

Plate size 7 mm × 600 mm × 900 mm.

Diameter of suction cup, d_c = 125 mm.

- **The weight of the steel plates:**

$$W = \rho \cdot A \cdot t$$
$$= (8054.3 \times 10^{-9}) (600 \times 900) (7)$$
$$\mathbf{W = 30.445 \text{ kg}}$$

- **The area of each suction cup:**

$$A_C = \frac{\pi \cdot d_c^2}{4}$$
$$= \frac{\pi \cdot (125)^2}{4}$$
$$\mathbf{A_C = 12271.846 \text{ mm}^2}$$

∴ The area of the two suction cups

$$A_{2C} = 2 A_C$$
$$= 2(12271.846)$$
$$\mathbf{A_{2C} = 24543.693 \text{ mm}^2}$$

- The weight of the plates to be lifted is equal to the force that must be applied by the two suction cups.

$$\text{Pressure required to lift the plates} = \frac{[\text{Weight of the plates}]}{[\text{Area of two suction cups}]}$$

$$= \frac{W}{A_{2c}}$$

$$= \frac{30.445}{24543.693}$$

$$P = 1.24044 \times 10^{-3} \, kg/mm^2$$

∴ **Total negative pressure required** to lift the plates considering factor of safety of 1.7.

$$P_T = (\text{FoS}) \, P$$

$$= 1.7 \times 1.24044 \times 10^{-3}$$

∴ $$P_T = 2.10875 \times 10^{-3} \, kg/mm^2$$

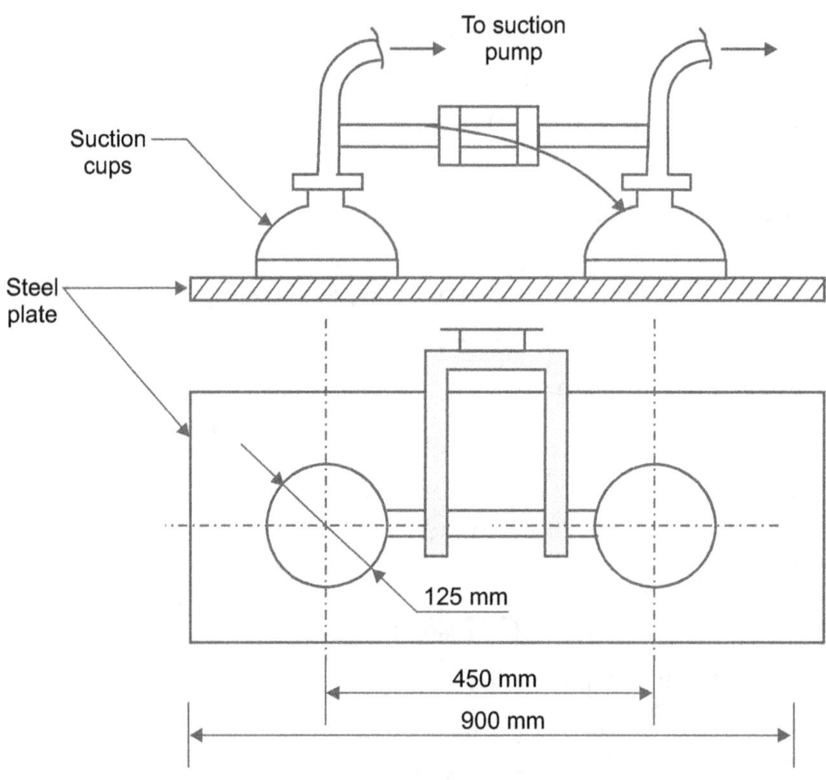

Fig. 2.23

EXERCISES

1. Define end-effector. What are two major categories of end-effectors?

2. Discuss a brief classification of grippers.

3. Give characteristics of grippers.

4. Explain in brief:
   (i)   Mechanical grippers   (ii) Vacuum grippers
   (iii) Magnetic grippers   (iv) Adhesive grippers

5. Explain mechanical grippers. What are two ways of constraining the part in the gripper?

6. Discuss gripper force analysis.

7. Explain vacuum grippers with reference to the principle, characteristics, use, and advantages.

8. Explain magnetic grippers. Give their advantages and disadvantages.

9. Explain adhesive grippers in brief.

10. Write a note on 'Tools as end-effectors'.

11. Discuss various consideration for selection of a gripper.

12. Explain different factors for design of a gripper.

13. Write a note on:
    (i)   Criteria for gripper design.
    (ii) Rules for gripper design.

EXAMPLES FOR PRACTICE

1. A rectangular block weighing 20 kg is gripped in the middle and lifted vertically at a velocity of 1.5 m/s. If it accelerates to this velocity at 25 m/s^2 and the coefficient of friction between the gripping pads and the block is 0.40, calculate the gripping force required to prevent slippage.

2. A rectangular block of weight 24 kg is gripped near its centre and lifted up at a velocity of 1.8 m/s. If it accelerates to this velocity at 20 m/s^2, and the gripping force required to prevent the slippage is 620 N, calculate the coefficient of friction between the gripping pads and the block.

3. A pivot type of gripper is used to hold an object as shown in Fig. 2.24. The gripper is to be actuated by a piston device to apply a actuating for F_A. Gripping force F_G = 220 N. Evaluate the force F_A required to close the gripper.

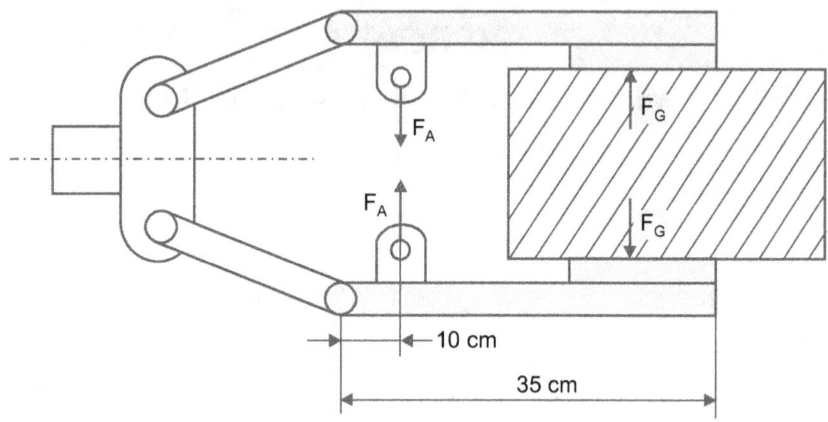

Fig. 2.24

4. A box having weight 1200 N is to be gripped as shown in Fig. 2.25 using friction against two opposing fingers. The coefficient of friction μ = 0.25. The centre of gripping does not coincide with the centre of gravity of box. Find the clamping force assuming a factor of safety 1.8.

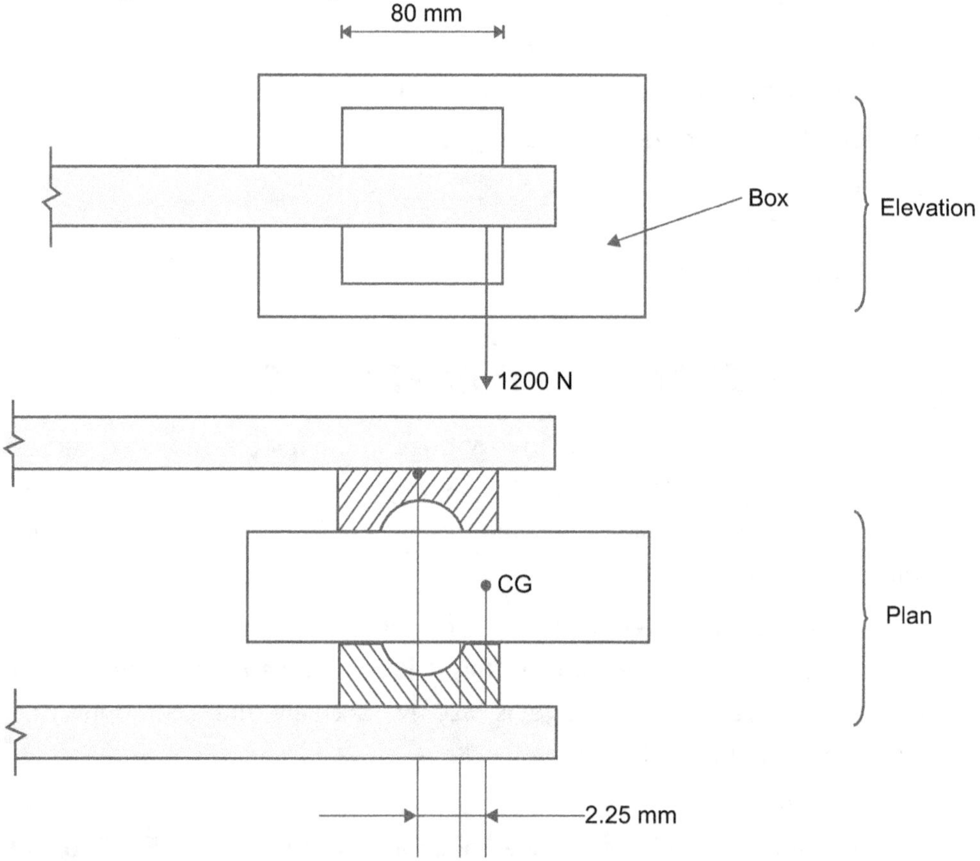

Fig. 2.25

5. The gripper shown in Fig. 2.26 is required to handle workpart. An actuating force of 520 N is acting along the plunger resulting in a gripping force F_G. Calculate the maximum gripping force that can be applied.

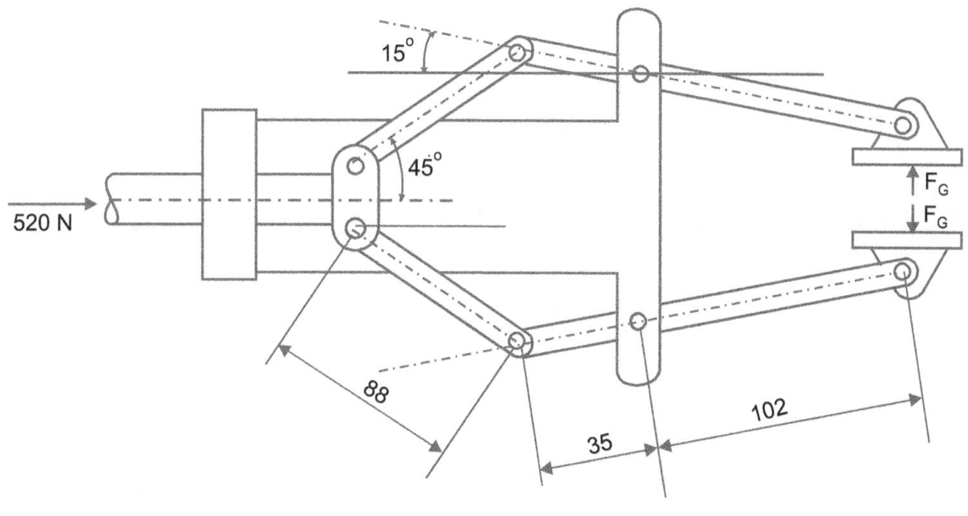

Fig. 2.26

6. A vacuum gripper is used to lift a weight of 150 N, with the help of a single suction cup having a diameter of 160 mm. Determine the negative pressure required to lift the weight.

7. A vacuum gripper is used to lift a plate of dimensions 300 mm × 800 mm having a net weight of 240 N. Assuming two suction cups engaged for lift the weight, determine the diameter of the suction cups. A pressure differential $(P_A - P_{RES})$ 2.8 N/cm² is maintained. Assume a factor of safety of 1.6.

8. A vacuum gripper is used to lift flat steel plates 8 mm × 650 mm × 950 mm. The gripper uses two suction cups, 140 mm in diameter each, and they are located 500 mm apart for stability. Assume a factor of safety of 1.8 to allow for acceleration of the plate. Determine the negative pressure required to lift the plates if the density of the steel is 8.0543×10^{-6} kg/mm³.

9. A mechanical gripper is shown in Fig. 2.27. Calculate the required actuating force F_A if the gripper force F_G is to be 120 N.

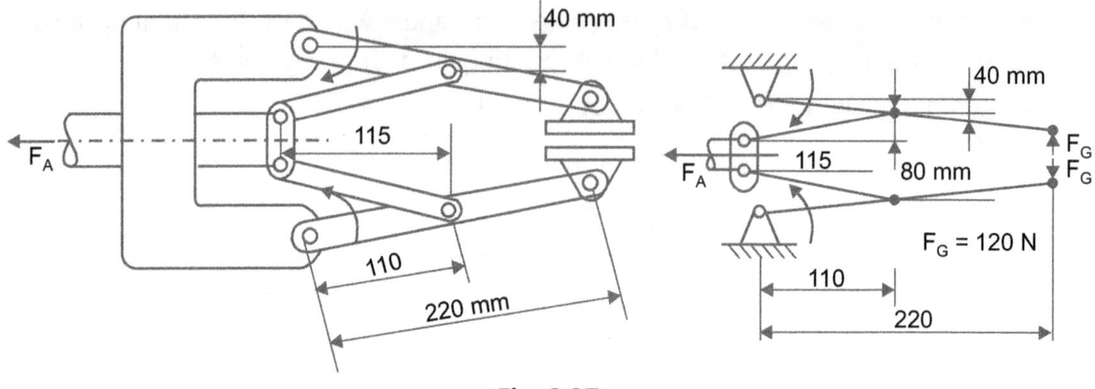

Fig. 2.27

***

Unit II

Chapter 3: SENSORS

3.1 Definition and Concept

'A robotic sensor is a device that detects information about the robot and its surroundings, and at the same time transmits it to the robot's controller'.

Human sensing (i.e. eyes to see, hands to physically feel, ears to hear voice), is considered as the best sensing and man-made sensors are still for inferior to human and other natural sensors in many aspect.

In order to function effectively, a robot has **to receive information from the environment** for necessary manipulation, **send signals** to various joints for necessary movement and interact with peripheral equipment. e.g. when a robot picks up an object and places it in a definite location, it has to initially get information about the **presence of the object.** As soon as it understands that the object is present, the arm approaches it with a controlled speed and acceleration. While approaching, it must **avoid collision** with any other obstacle. It may also **attempt to find the shape and orientation** of the object to be grasped. When the robot grips the object, it must identify the points **where it should grip** the object with specified force. The object should not be pressed hard or deformed, or slip. Sometimes, it is necessary to have prior knowledge about the shape of the object before it is gripped. Therefore, it is required to sense and measure all the important geometrical parameters of the object lying in an environment. Sensory feedback is thus more important for unstructured environment.

Therefore, some of the important steps to be done by a robot in a pick and place operation for which various sensors, internal as well as external are incorporated –

    (i)   Searching

    (ii)   Recognizing

    (iii)   Grasping and

    (iv)   Placing the object

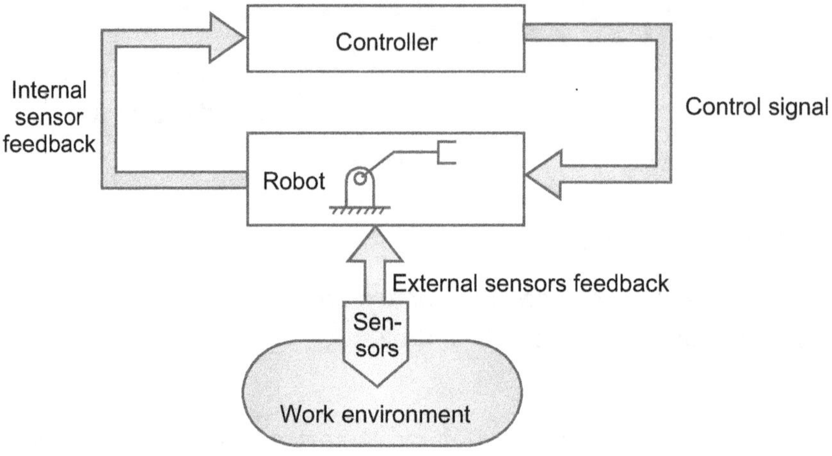

Fig. 3.1

3.2 Scheme of Robot Sensors

However, the signals or sensory data obtained through the sensors must be processed, interpreted and integrated properly in a robot controller so that the robot can effectively and reliably perform the task. Fig. 3.2 indicates a scheme of robot sensors.

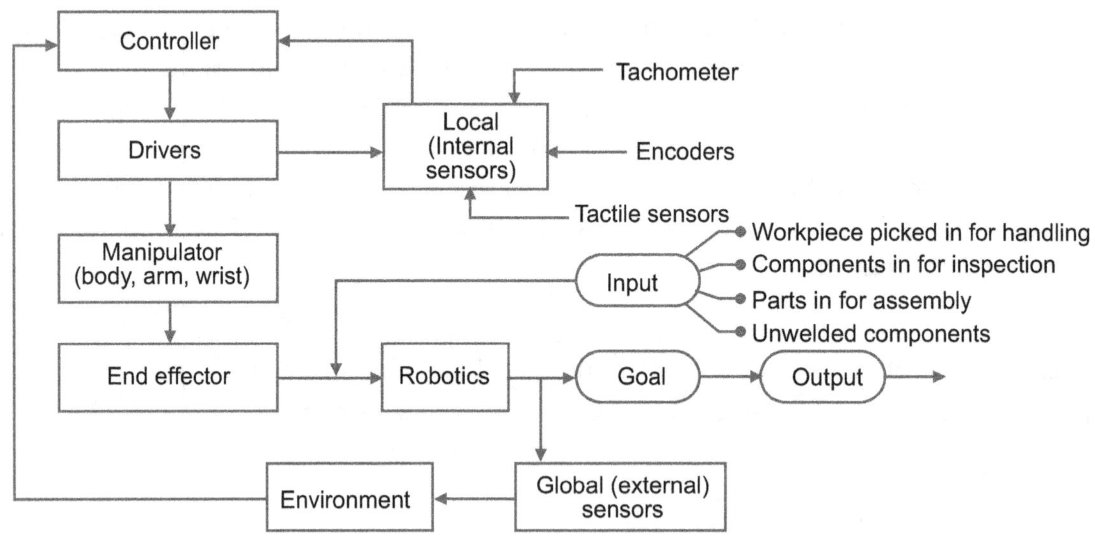

Fig. 3.2: Sensors in Robotics

3.3 Need of Sensors in a Robotic System

(i)   To perform various tasks without constant human supervision:
The human operator is capable of combining various types of sensory feedback to perform the most complex of tasks. If industrial robots are to be capable of performing the same types of tasks without constant human supervision, they too must be equipped with sensory feedback.

(ii)   Achieve a greater degree of intelligence in dealing with their environment:
The feedback from various sensors is analysed via. a digital computer and the associated software. The use of sensing technology to endow machines with greater degree of intelligence in dealing with their environment is an active area to concentrate. Therefore, for a robotic manipulator to operate effectively and intelligently and to enable it to work in unstructured environment, it must be equipped with sensors, which give information about itself and its environment.

(iii) Intelligent sensors to perform complex tasks:
A robot without intelligent sensors is handicapped and can only do very specific tasks, while a robot that is able to 'see' and 'feel' is easier to train to perform complex tasks.

(iv)   To provide positional and velocity information of elements of manipulator with the help of internal sensors
One of the reason for using sensory feedback in robots is to provide positional and velocity information concerning joint, arm and end-effector status, position, velocity and acceleration. This type of feedback is provided continuously and becomes an integral part of the physical robot control system. This category is called **'internal sensors'.**

(v)   To prevent damage to the robot itself, its surroundings and human operators:
Another reason for using sensory feedback is to prevent damage to the robot and its surroundings and human operators and to provide identification and real time information indicating the presence of different types of components and concerning the nature of tasks performed. These involve various sensory devices to suit the needs of the particular robot task being carried out and the characteristics of the working environment. This category of sensors is referred as **'external sensors'.**

3.4 Desirable Features of Sensors

The following are the desirable features of various sensors.

(i)   **Accuracy:** There should not be any error in the measurement i.e. it means no systematic positive or negative errors in the measurement.

(ii)   **Precision:** It means, there should not be random variability in the measurement.

(iii) **Operating range:** It means that the entire operating range is accurate and precise.

(iv) **Speed of response:** It means that it should be capable of responding in minimum time. Ideally, the speed of response should be instantaneous.

(v)   **Calibration:** It means it should be easy to calibrate.

(vi)   Reliability: It means it should possess a high reliability without failure.

(vii) Cost: It is the overall cost including costs to purchase, install and operate and it should be as flow as possible.

(viii) Ease of operation: It is easy to operate and it should be flexible to suit environment.

3.5 Sensor Characteristics

The various characteristics discussed below determine the performance, economy, ease of application, and applicabiity of the sensor. Therefore, they may be considered before a sensor is selected.

(i)   Cost of Sensor: It is an important consideration, for machine using many sensors. There should be well balance between the cost and the other factors.

(ii)   Size of Sensor: Size may be of primary concern. Example, in case of joint displacement sensors are used in design of joints and move with the robot's body elements. The space available around the joint may be limited. Also large sensor may limit joint ranges.

(iii) Weight of Sensor: A heavy sensor puts an inertia of the arm, also reduces its overall pay load.

(iv)   Type of Output: The out of sensor may be digital or of analog type. The output may be used directly or it may have to be converted. Example, the output of a potentiometer is analog and that of an encoder is digital. Thus, an appropriate type of output be used.

(v)   Interfacing: Sensors must be interfaced with other devices in system. Example, microprocessors and controllers. This is an important consideration.

(vi)   Resolution: It is the minimum step size within the range of measurement of the sensor. Example, in a digital device with 'n' bits, the resolution will be,

$$R = \frac{R_F}{2^n}$$

where,
R – Resolution
R_F – Full range
n – Bits

Example, for 4-bits encoder.

$$R = \frac{360}{12^4}$$

where, $R_F = 360°$.

$$R = 22.5°$$

(vii) Sensitivity: It is the ratio of a change in output in response to a change in input. Highly sensitive sensor shows larger fluctuations in output, due to the fluctuations in input combined with noise.

(viii) Linearity: It gives the relationship between input variations and output variations. The sensor with linear output shows that, the same change in input at any level within the range will produce the same change in output. But all devices behave in non-linear ways. Some devices can be assumed to be linear within a certain range of their operation. Some may be linearized through assumptions.

(ix) Range: It is the difference between the smallest and the largest outputs of the sensor can produce or the difference between the smallest and largest inputs with which it can operate properly.

(x) Response Time: It is the time that a sensor's output requires to reach a certain percentage of the total change. Generally, it is specified in percentage of total change i.e. 80%. Also it can be defined as the time required to observe the change in output as a result of a change in input.

Example, for a simple Hg-thermometer, a response time is long.

For a digital thermometer, a response time is short, that measures temperature based on radiated heat.

(xi) Frequency Response: The frequency is the range in which the systems ability to respond to the input remains relatively high. The larger the range of the frequency response, the better the ability of the system to respond to varying input. Thus, it is necessary to consider the frequency response of a sensor and determine whether the sensor's response is fast enough under all operating conditions.

(xii) Reliability: It is the ratio of the number of times a system operates properly to the number of times it is tried. Therefore, it is necessary to choose reliable sensors that lost a long time.

(xiii) Accuracy: It is defined as how close the output of the sensor is to be expected value. For a given input, the output is expected to be a certain value, the accuracy is related to how close the sensor's output is to this value.

(xiv) Repeatability: Repeatability is more important than accuracy in most cases. If the sensor's output is measured, a number of times in response to the same input, the output may be different each time.

Repeatability is a measure of how varied the different outputs are relative to each other. Repeatability is generally random and cannot be easily compensated.

3.6 Selection of Sensors

Selection of a sensor for a particular application depends on the following factors.

(i)   the **quantity** to be measured or sensed.

(ii)   the **interaction** of the sensor to be selected with other components in the system.

(iii)   **expected service life** of sensor.

(iv)   **level of sophistication** involved in the sensor to be selected for a particular application.

(v)   various **difficulties associated** with the use of sensors.

(vi)   **source of power** for the sensor.

(vii) **cost** factor associated with sensor.

(viii) **Environment** in which the sensors are to be used.

(ix)   **maintainability** of the sensors to be selected is one of the important factors.

(x)   **Ruggedness:** It is also an important factor for selecting a rigid sensor.

       e.g. Rugged sensors are being developed to withstand extremes of temperature, shock and vibration, humidity, corrosion, dust and various contaminants, fluids, electromagnetic radiation and other interferences.

(xi)   **Availability:** Sensor should be made easily available for given application. It is the secondary selection criterion.

3.7 Classification of Sensory Devices

Sensors are used for a variety of functions in robotic systems. The most common and minimal use of sensors is to provide information about the status of links and joints of the manipulator and about the working environment of the robot. In addition, sensors can help the robot

(i)   for detecting positions and orientation of parts.

(ii)   to ensure consistent product quality.

(iii)   to discover variations of shape and dimensions of parts.

(iv)   to identify unknown obstacles and

(v)   to determine system malfunctions and to analyze it.

3.7.1 Functional Classification of Robotic Sensors

The major functions of sensors in robots can be grouped into five basic categories which is the functional classification of robotic sensors.

(a)   Status sensors   (b)   Environmental sensors

(c)   Quality control sensors   (d)   Safety sensors and

(e)   Workcell control sensors.

Above functional categories are described below.

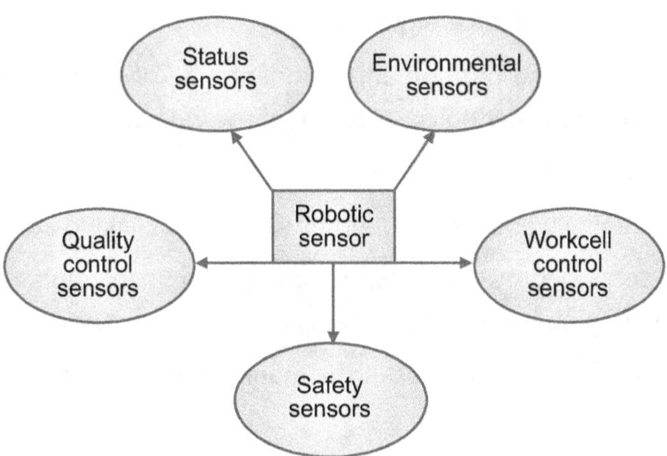

Fig. 3.3: Functional Classification of Sensors

(a)   Status Sensors:

- The primary aim of sensors on a robot is to sense position, velocity, acceleration and or torque or force at each joint of the manipulator for position and control of motion.

- As these sensors form an essential part of the basic or internal closed-loop control systems, they are called as 'internal sensors' or 'status sensors'. This is because the internal sensors give feedback on the status of the manipulator itself.

- The effectiveness and degree of accuracy that can be achieved by a manipulator depends on –

    (i)   the resolution and

    (ii) the accuracy of internal sensors

- Internal sensors must also be cost effective because they are required for each axis of the manipulator.

(b)   Environmental Sensors:

- Sensors are also used to extract features of the objects in the workcell or the surrounding environment of the robot. This data is utilized by the computer controller to modify to a given situation. e.g. if the robot has to process several types of different parts, each requiring a different sequence of actions by the robot, such as adjusting the gripper orientation or applying the exact gripping force, it must determine the required parameters for each part. These types of sensors are placed in the environment of the robot or are external to the manipulator and are called 'external' or 'environmental sensors'. Following are some of the uses of environmental sensors:

(i)   To detect the presence of workpiece.

(ii)   To determine the position and/or orientation of workpiece and objects to be articulated, or other objects present in the workcell.

(iii) To identify workpiece.

(iv)   To determine workpiece properties such as size, shape and so on.

(v)   To detect, identify obstacles in the environment, and provide the related information about their size, shape, location, speed and so on.

(vi)   To provide information about the manipulator environment interaction forces and torques.

(vii) To provide information about environmental variables such as temperature, humidity and so on.

(viii) To determine the position and orientation of the end-effector, joints, and links of the manipulator.

- The information from the external sensors would have to be processed by the computer in real-time to guide the manipulator in the execution of its programmed work cycle.

- Vision system is an important sensing method employed to determine the characteristics as –

(i)   the part location.

(ii)   orientation of part.

(iii) size and shape etc.

(c) Quality Control Sensors:

- Sensors are employed for some of the important functions as inspection and quality control.

- The use of sensors permits 100% inspection because sensors can be used to determine a variety of part quality characteristics.

- The external sensors used for environmental feedback can also be used for detecting faults and failures in the finished product.

- The inspection process can be made a part of the programmed work cycle and the sequence of operations performed by the manipulator may be linked to the result of inspection process.

  Following sensors can be used for inspection:

  (i)   **Computer vision system** that can provide a larger variety of information about the workpiece in addition to its position and orientation.

  (ii) Ultrasonic sensors.

  (iii) Sonic and other sensors.

(d) Safety Sensors:

- Safety and hazard monitoring is an important function of the sensors in robotics.

- The safety of the workers and other equipment in the work environment, and that of the manipulator itself are important aspects.

  e.g. safety in automation plant: If there is power failure, all the links of the manipulator may fall to zero-gravity position instantaneously. This may injure the human beings in the zone or may damage the equipment or the manipulator itself. A solution is to sense the power failure and apply breaks to prevent the uncontrolled falling of links due to gravity.

(e) Workcell Control Sensors:

- Implementation of interlocks in workcell is another important use of sensors in robotics.

- An **interlock** in the work-cycle is a situation that requires sequencing of tasks such that completion of a task must be ensured before proceeding to the next task.

  e.g. a part must arrive on the conveyor before the gripper of the manipulator can pick it. By incorporating the signals from a variety of sensors in the robot program, the verification of interlocked task can be done.

- Sensors may also be used to detect and resolve the interlocks in the workcell.

All above categories require sensors to be an integral part of robot control system to accomplish specific control functions.

3.7.2 Sensory Devices

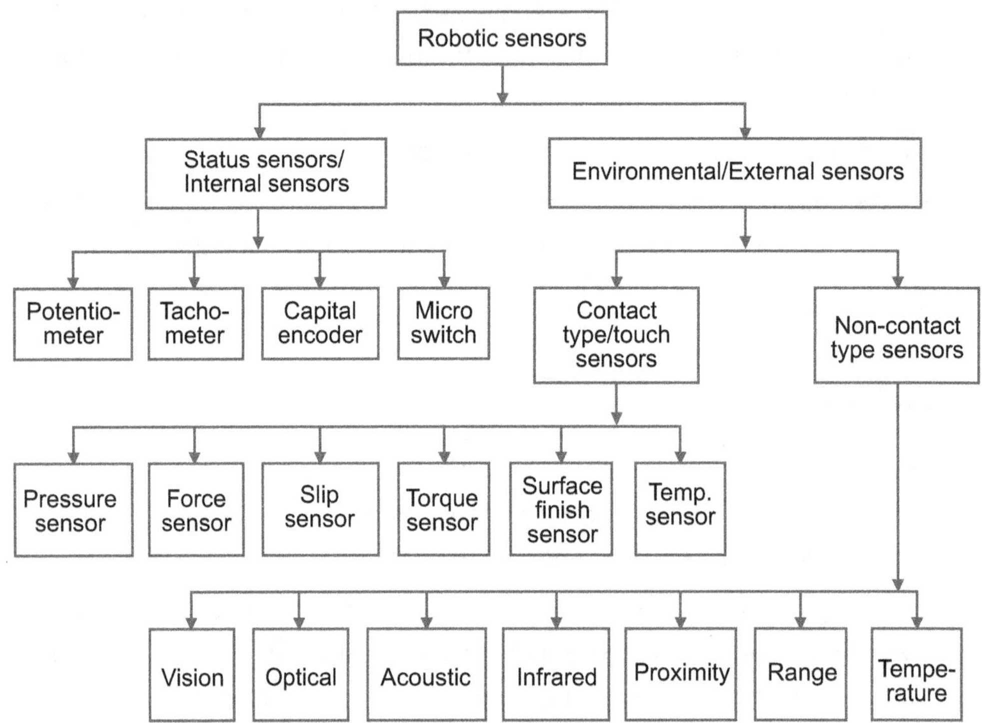

Fig. 3.4: Types of Sensors Based on Working Principle

3.7.3 Various Sensing Devices used in Robot Workcell

"A robotic workcell may be defined as a cluster of one or more robots and several machine tools or transfer lines that are interconnected in such a way that they work together in unison".

Based on the output, there are two main categories of sensor as –

(i)   Discrete sensors and

(ii) Complex sensors

(i)   Discrete sensors (Simple sensors):

- These are also known as simple or digital sensors whose output has only two states - on/off, yes/no, high/low, or 1 or 0 in which case it is frequently referred to as a **binary device.**

- Simple sensor interface is the process in which a device transmits signals from a simple sensor to a controller.

(ii) Complex sensors:

- The output from complex sensors has more than two state and can be of any value within the range values it measures.
- Complex sensors would include analog sensors and serial communication sensors.
- Complex sensors interface is the process that transmits a complex sensor's signal to a controller after converting them to digital signals or otherwise conditioning them.
- Above two categories of sensors used in interface with most manufacturing systems can be grouped in three categories –

  (i)   Contact sensors

  (ii) Non-contact sensors and

  (iii) Process control sensors

  Fig. 3.5 shows the different types of sensors used in robot workcells.

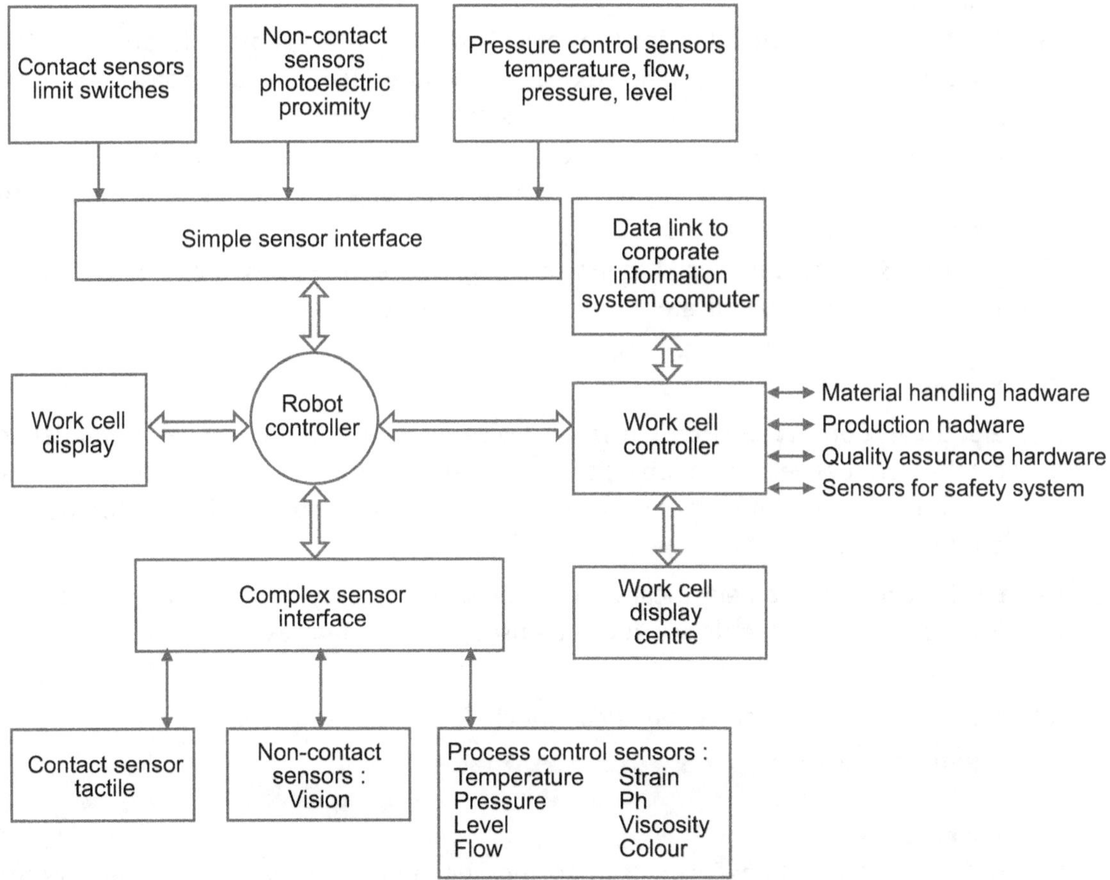

Fig. 3.5: Sensors in Robot Workcells

In following section, various sensors used in Robot workcells are discussed.

Sensors used in Robot Workcells:

Following types of sensors are generally used in robot workcells.

1. **Proximity Sensor:**
    (a) **Eddy Current Detectors:** It emits an alternating magnetic field at the tip of a proble, which induces eddy currents in any conductive object in the range of the device. It can be used to indicate presence or absence of a conductive object.
    (b) **Infrared Sensor:** It acts as a transducer that measures temperatures by the infrared light emitted from the surface of an object. It can be used to indicate presence or absence of a hot object.
    (c) **Optical Pyrometer:** It is used to measure high temperatures by sensing the brightness of an object's surface. It can be used to indicate presence or absence of a hot object.
    (d) **Photometric Sensors:** It is used to sense light. It includes photocells, photoelectric transducers, phototubes, photodiodes, phototransistors, and photoconductors. It can be used to indicate presence or absence of an object.
    (e) **Radiation Pyrometer:** It is used to measure high temperatures by sensing the thermal radiation emitting from the surface of an object. It can be used to indicate presence or absence or a hot object.
    (f) **Vacuum Switches:** It is used to indicate negative air pressures. It can be used with a vacuum gripper to indicate presence or absence of an object.

2. **Touch Sensors:**
    (a) **Electrical Contact Switch:** It is a device in which an electrical potential is established between two objects, and when the potential becomes zero, this indicates contact between the two objects. It can be used to indicate presence or absence of a conductive object.
    (b) **Limit Switch:** It is an electrical on-off switch actuated by depressing a mechanical lever or button on the device. It can be used to measure presence or absence of an object.
    (c) **Microswitch:** It is a small-electrical switch. It can be used to indicate presence or absence of an object.

3. **Force Sensor:**
    Strain Gauge: It is a transducer used to measure force, torque, pressure and other variables. It can be used to indicate force applied to grasp on object.

4. **Miscellaneous Sensors:**
    (a) **Ammeter:** It is an electrical meter used to measure electrical current.
    (b) **Linear Variable Differential Transformer:** It is an electromechanical used to measure linear or angular displacement.
    (c) **Ohmmeter:** It is a meter used to measure electrical resistance.
    (d) **Piezoelectric Accelerometer:** It is a type of sensor used to indicate or measure vibration.
    (e) **Potentiometer:** It is an electrical meter used to measure voltage.
    (f) **Pressure Transducer:** It is used to indicate air pressure and other fluid pressures.
    (g) **Thermistor:** It is used to measure temperature based on electrical resistance.
    (h) **Thermocuple:** It is used to measure temperatures. It is based on the physical principle that a junction of two dissimilar metals will emit an emf which can be related to temperature.

5. **Vision Sensors:**
    These are advanced sensors used in conjunction with pattern recognition and other techniques to view and interpret events that are occurring in the robot workplace.

6. **Voice Sensors:**
    These are advanced sensors used to communicate commands or information orally to the robot.

3.8 Different Types of Sensors

3.8.1 Photoelectric Sensors

- These are of non-contact type and used for position sensing and output of which responds to –
    (i) Interruption of a light beam by an objector.
    (ii) Reflection of a light beam back to its source by an object or part passing infront of the project beam.
- Photoelectric sensors are of four types as shown in block diagram below.

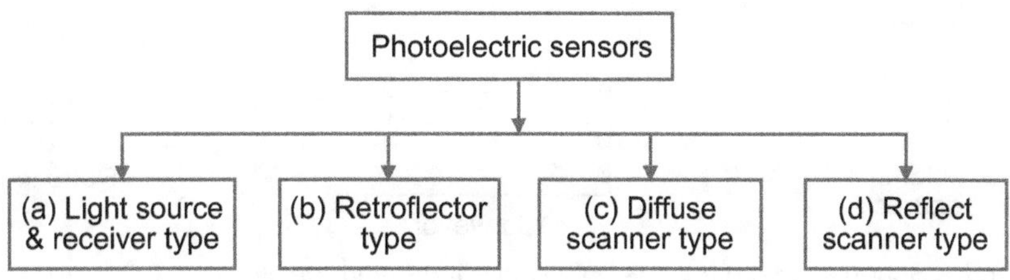

Fig. 3.6: Types of Photoelectric Sensors

(a) Light Source and Receiver Type Sensor:

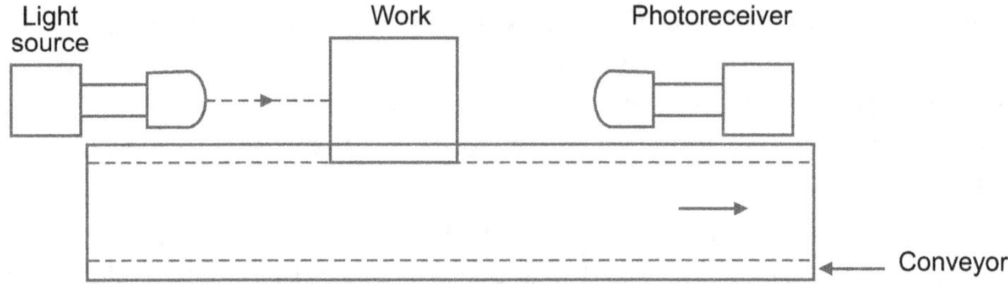

Fig. 3.7: Light Source and Receiver Type Sensor

- **Principle:** 'As the work moves between the light source and receiver, the light beam is interrupted, resulting in a switch closure' (or opening).
- The light source and receiver type consists of a light source and photoreceiver for a direct scan or through a scan photoelectric control system. The photoreceiver detects light from the source, amplifies it, and switches its output contacts when a change in nominal conditions occurs. A receiver can be energized on light or energized on dark depending on its intended applications. When the light path between source and receiver is interrupted, an output in the form of a switch closure is obtained. Output contacts of forms A, B and C are widely available with ratings of upto 10 amps.
- AC devices can switch circuit loads such as relays, solenoids, or small motors directly.
- DC devices are usually used for logic-level switching, the output switches are solid-state and switch DC currents on the order of 150 ma.
- Scanning arrangements can be used with source or receiver separation distances of over 30 m, although workcell applications rarely call for such a range.

(b) Retroflector Type:

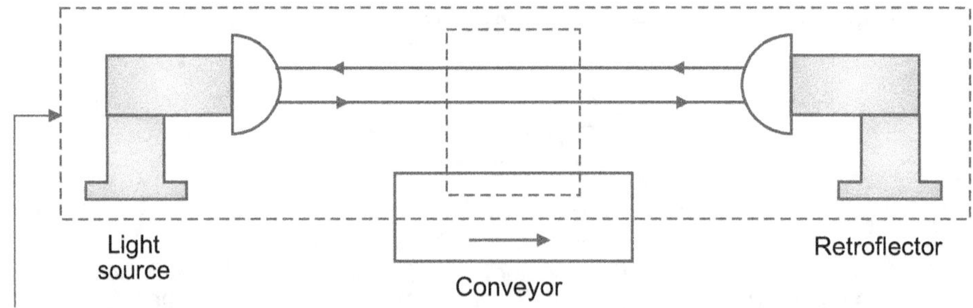

Fig. 3.8: Retroflective Type Sensor

- In this type of sensor, both light source and photoreceiver are packaged in the same housing, which is called as scanner.
- The retroreflective scanner can switch when the light beam from a fixed reflector is interrupted, or from a passing workpiece or machine element.
- This type of scanner has limited distance between target and light source.

(c) Diffuse Scanner Type:

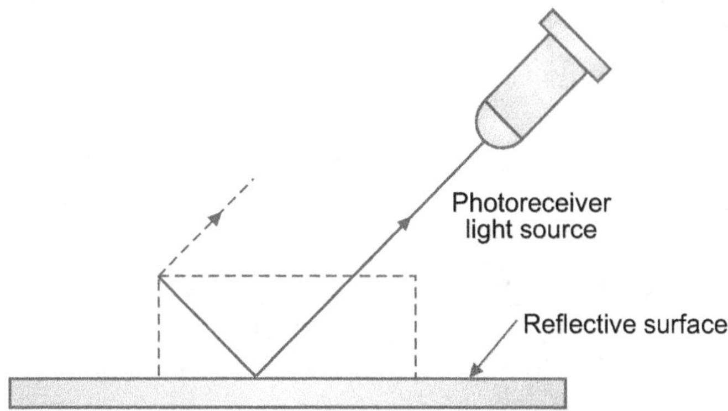

Fig. 3.9: Diffuse Scanner Type

- In this type of sensor arrangement, both light source and photoreceiver are built into the same housing.
- A workpiece (as a object placed on plane reflective surface) reflects the beam to the receiver when it moves into the sensing position.
- An output control signal results when the object passes this point. Here light beam is initially aligned to reflect from surface to receiver. Object interferes with beam, thereby initiating a control signal.

(d) Reflect Scanner Type:

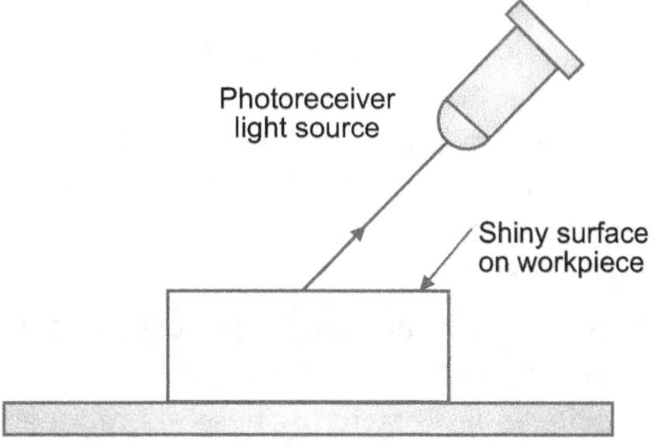

Fig. 3.10: Reflect Scanner Type Sensor

- In this arrangement, the sensor works like a combination of the retroflector and diffuse scanner type.
- The light source and receiver are both located in the same enclosure, and the beam uses the part's surface to reflect light back to the receiver.
- The light reflected must be a definitive beam because diffused light alone will not be sufficient to activate the receiver.
- The angle of the light projected by sensor is adjusted to improve sensitivity and establish a specific distance at detection.
- The light source is the light-emitting diode (LED), which generates light in the infrared (IR) spectrum.
- Most of the sensors use silicon photo-detectors, which are sensitive to IR light and are economical.
- Photoelectric devices should always be mounted so as to avoid or be protected from dirty environments. The devices should be selected with excess gain G appropriate to the environment.

Excess Gain	Element
1.0	Clean air
1.0-2.00	Low contamination
2.0-10.00	Moderate contamination
10.0-25.00	High contamination

- The closer the working distance, the higher the excess gain characteristics of photoelectric device.

3.8.2 Limit Switches

- It is a category of micro-switches, which are electromechanical devices actuated either by some part or motion of a robot or machine to alter the electrical circuit.
- Limit switches are the most common linear position sensors used in robots and work cells.
- Limit switch is designed to be mechanically actuated when a machine member or object reaches a particular position.
- The machine member physically contacts the limit switch actuator and switches the contacts, normally one to four poles.
- The limit switch can be used to control machine operation sequencing, or to provide machine protection functions by shutting down the machine when machine members or workers are at a prohibited location.

There are following types of switches:

(i) **Industrial limit switch:** These are usually enclosed in cases in order to protect the switch from dust, water and human abuse.

(ii) **Standard duty-enclosed limit switch:** These are rugged and enclosed in cases as similar to above case.

(iii) Heavy duty-limit switch: These are available as oil-tight, corrosion resistant, and are most rugged enclosures than above two cases. These switches should undergo 20 million cycles, without failure, under moderately severe industrial usage.

- NEMA-type of enclosures are commonly used for limit switches.
- **Limit switch actuators:**

These are used in workcells. Types of actuator are primarily selected on the basis of where the limit switch might be located with respect to the controlled machine member.

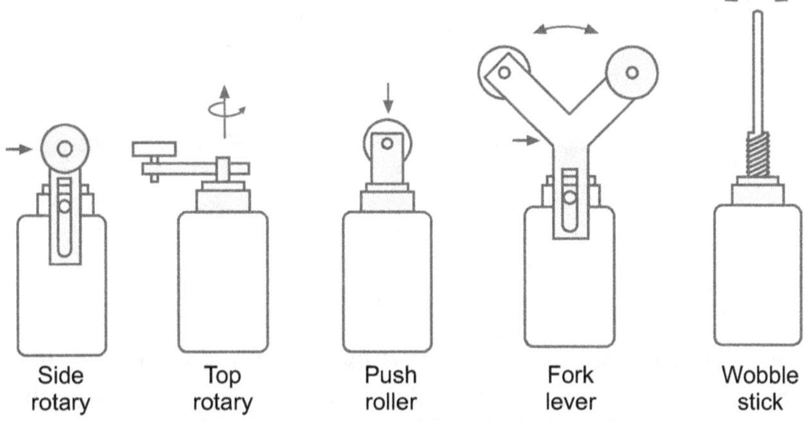

Fig. 3.11: Actuators for Limit Switch

It is important to install the limit switch in a location and position such that:
(i)   The moving member will not destroy the limit switch.
(ii) It should be easily accessible for maintenance.
(iii) It is protected from accidential actuation.
(iv) Chips, moisture, grease, or oil does not accumulate on the actuator.
It is illustrated in Fig. 3.11.

3.8.3 Range Sensors

- It is a non-contact type of sensor category and is used to sense and measure the distance between the objects and sensing device. Along they can be used to locate workpiece in the robot workcell.
- They may be located on the end-effector or wrist. For robot navigation and obstacle avoidance, range sensors are generally used.
- There are following range sensing techniques:
  (i)   Triangulation Technique.   (ii) Structured Lighting Approach
  (iii) Time-of-flight Range Finders.

(i)   Triangulation Technique:
- It is a simplest method of measuring range. It is explained with the help of Fig. 3.12.

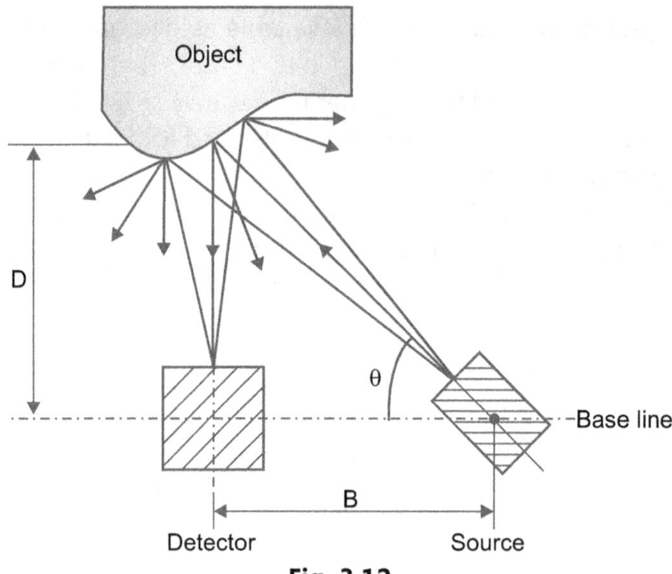

Fig. 3.12

- An object shown above is illuminated by a narrow beam of light which is swept over the surface. The sweeping motion is in the plane defined by the line from the object to the detector and the line from the detector to the source.
- If the detector is focussed on a small portion of the surface then, when the detector sees the light spot, its distance D to the illuminated portion of the surface can be calculated from the geometry of Fig. 3.12.

Since		θ – be the angle of the source with the baseline.

		B – be the distance of the source from the detector.

		D – be the distance of illuminated surface from the detector.

From geometry of Fig. 3.13,

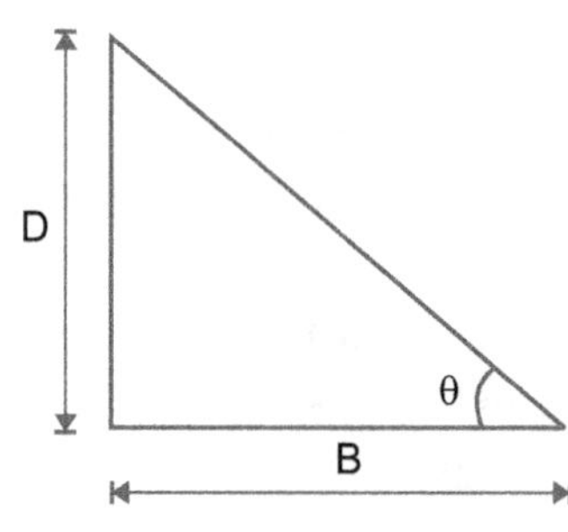

Fig. 3.13

$$\tan \theta = \frac{D}{B}$$

$\therefore$		$\boxed{D = B \cdot \tan \theta}$

This approach gives a point measurement.

- If the source-detector arrangement is moved in a fixed plane (i.e. up and down and sideways on a plane perpendicular to the paper and containing the baseline), then it is possible to obtain a set of points whose directions from the detector are known. These distances are easily transformed to the three-dimensional co-ordinates by keeping track of the location and orientation of the detector as the object are scanned.

(ii) Structured-Lighting Approach:

- In this approach, the light pattern is projected onto a set of objects and using the distortion of the pattern to calculate the range.
  The light pattern generally employed is a sheet of light generated through a cylindrical lens or a narrow slit.
  Fig. 3.14 shows measurement of range by structured lighting approach.

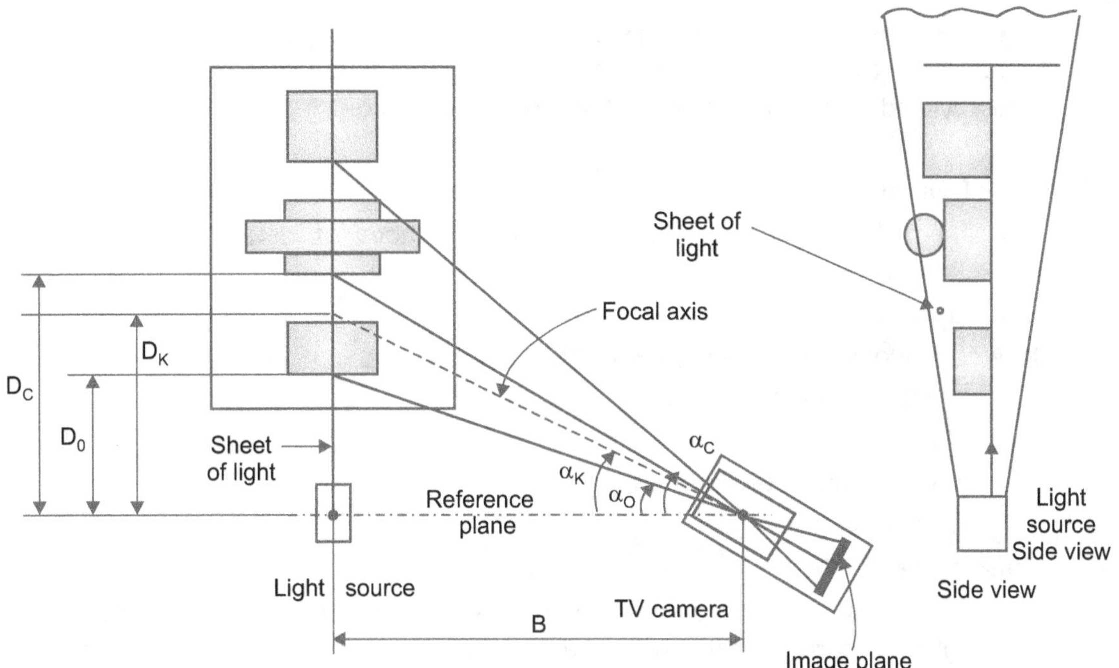

Fig. 3.14: Measurement of Range using Structured Lighting Approach

- The intersection of the sheet of light with objects in the workspace yields a light strip which is viewed through a television camera. It is placed at a distance of B from the light source.
- The strip pattern is easily analyzed by a computer to obtain necessary range information.
  e.g. an inflection indicates a change of surface, and a break corresponds to a gap between surfaces.

- Fig. 3.13 shows a top view of a set of objects and a line from light source which is a sheet of light. In this arrangement, the light source and camera are placed at the same height, and the sheet of light is perpendicular to the line joining the origin of the light sheet and the center of the camera lens. The vertical plane containing this line is called as the 'reference plane', which is perpendicular to the sheet of light.
- Any vertical flat surface that intersects the sheet of light will produce a vertical strip of light in which every point will have the same perpendicular distance to the reference plane.
- The basic objective of the arrangement is to position the camera so that every such vertical strip also appears vertical in the image plane. Thus, every point along the same column in the image will be known to have the same distance to the reference plane.
- **Calibration:** It consists of measuring the distance 'B' between the light source and the lens centre, and then determining the angles α_c and α_o.
- One of the advantages of this technique is that it results in a relatively simple range measuring technique. Once the calibration is completed, the distance associated with every column in the image is computed.

(iii) Time-of-Flight Range Finders:

Based on time-of-flight concept, there are three methods of determining the range, as under –

(a)   A pulsed-laser system;

(b)   A continuous-beam laser system; and

(c)   An ultrasonic range finder.

Above techniques are illustrated in following section.

(a)   A Pulsed-laser System:

- To determine range using a laser, is to measure the time it takes on emitted pulse of light to return coaxially from a reflecting surface. The distance to the reflecting surface is calculated using the relationship

$$D = \frac{c \cdot T}{2}$$

  where,   T is the pulse transit time.
  c is the speed of light.

- A pulsed-laser technique, produces a 2-dimensional array with values proportional to distance, and a 2-D scan is accomplished by deflecting the laser light via. a rotating mirror. So a 3D object is viewed and it's 2D scan (i.e. the corresponding sensed array displayed as an image) is achieved. In 2D scan the intensity at each point is proportional to the distance between the sensor and the reflecting surface at that point. Darker point is closer, and the bright areas around the object boundaries represent discontinuity in the range determined by post processing in a computer.

- The working range of this device is of the order of 1 to 4 m, with an accuracy of ± 0.25 cm.

(b) A Continuous-Beam Laser System:

- In this approach, a continuous-beam laser is used to measure the delay (i.e. phase-shift) between the outgoing and returning beams. This technique is as illustrated in Fig. 3.15.

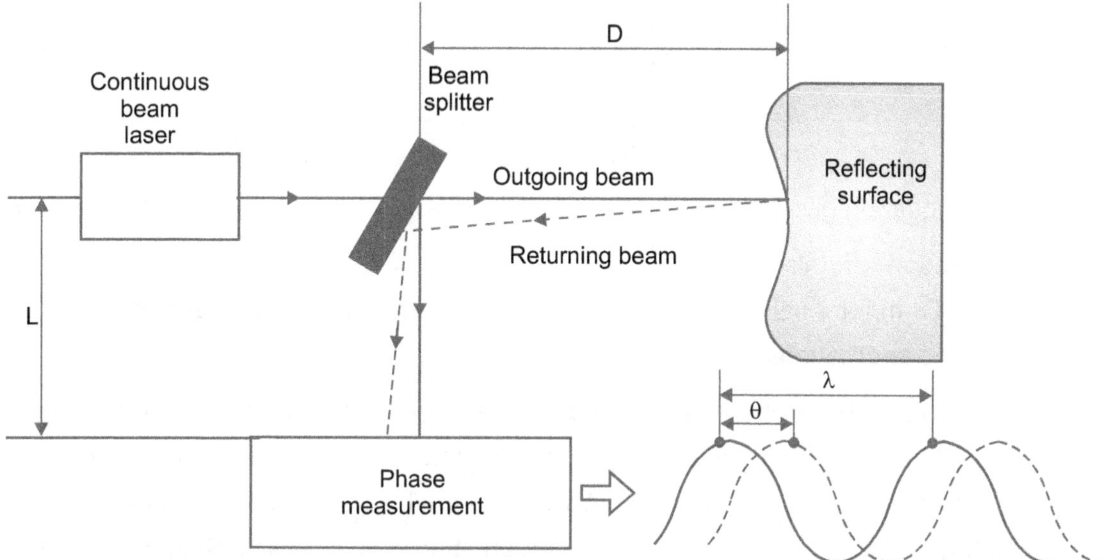

Fig. 3.15: Range Measurement by Phase-shift using Continuous Laser Beam

- Consider a beam of laser light of wavelength λ is split into two beams. One of these beams called as 'reference beam', travels a distance L to a phase measuring device, and the other travels a distance D out to a reflecting surface. Therefore, the total distance travelled by the reflected beam is,

$$D_T = L + 2D$$

where,   D = 0, under this condition

$$D_T = L$$

and both the reference and reflected beams arrive simultaneously at the phase measuring device.

- As D increases, the reflected beam travels a longer path and thus, a phase-shift is introduced between the two beams at the point of measurement as shown in Fig. 3.15.

  Therefore, total distance travelled by the reflected beam is,

  $$D_T \;=\; L + \left(\frac{\lambda}{360}\right)\lambda$$

  If $\theta = 360°$, the two waveforms are aligned and we cannot differentiate between $[D_T = L]$ and $[D_T = L + n\lambda]$.

  where n = 1, 2, ..., based on measurements of phase-shift alone.

  Thus, a unique solution can be achieved only when $\theta < 360°$ or $2D < \lambda$.

  Since, $D_T = L + 2D$

  where, $2D = \dfrac{\theta}{360}\,\lambda$

  $\therefore$ $D = \left(\dfrac{\lambda}{360}\right)\dfrac{\lambda}{2}$

  This equation gives the distance in terms of phase-shift if the wavelength is known.

- Limitation of this case that the wavelength of laser light is small (of order 632.80 nm for a helium-neon laser), therefore, the method becomes impractical for robotic applications.

- Solution to this problem is to modulate the amplitude of the laser light by using a waveform of much higher wavelength. In this case, the reference signal is the modulating function. The modulated laser signal is sent out to the target and the returning beam is stripped of the modulating signal, which is then compared against the reference to determine phase-shift.

- An advantage of the continuous beam laser technique vs. the pulse-light technique is that the former yields intensity as well as range information.

(c) An ultrasonic range finder:

- It is another major type of the time-of-flight concept.

- Basic principle is same as in previous case, an ultrasonic chip is transmitted over a short time period and since the speed of sound is known for a specified medium, a simple calculation involving the time interval between the outgoing pulse and the return echo yields an estimate of the distance to the reflecting surface.

- They are primarily used for navigation and obstacle avoidance, as it introduces severe limitations in resolution due to beam pattern which is around 30°.

3.8.4 Proximity Sensors

- Most of the proximity sensors do not require any physical contact at all in order to produce a signal that can be used by a robot to determine whether it is near an object or obstacle.
- The non-contact type of proximity devices depend on variety of operating principles in order to make the proximity determination. e.g. inductance, magnetic-effect, capacitance ultrasound, optical category etc. These categories are described in the following section.

  Thus, proximity sensors generally have a binary output which indicates the presence of an object within a specified distance interval.

- **Classification:**

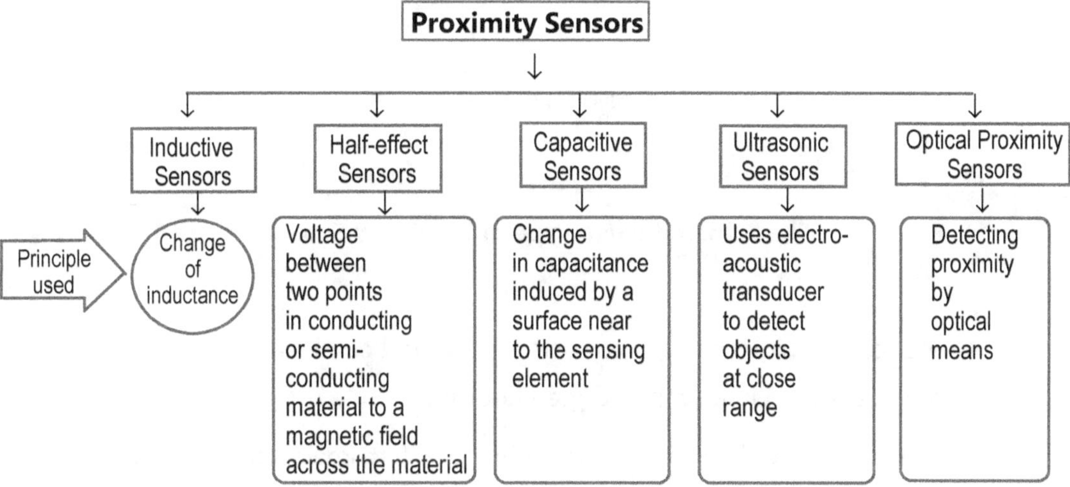

- Practical uses of a proximity sensor in robotics would be –

  (i)   To detect the presence or absence of a workpart or other object.

  (ii) To sense human beings in the robot workcell.

(i) Inductive Sensors:

- **Principle:** Sensors based on a change of inductance due to the presence of a metallic object.

Fig. 3.16 illustrates the operation of inductive sensor.

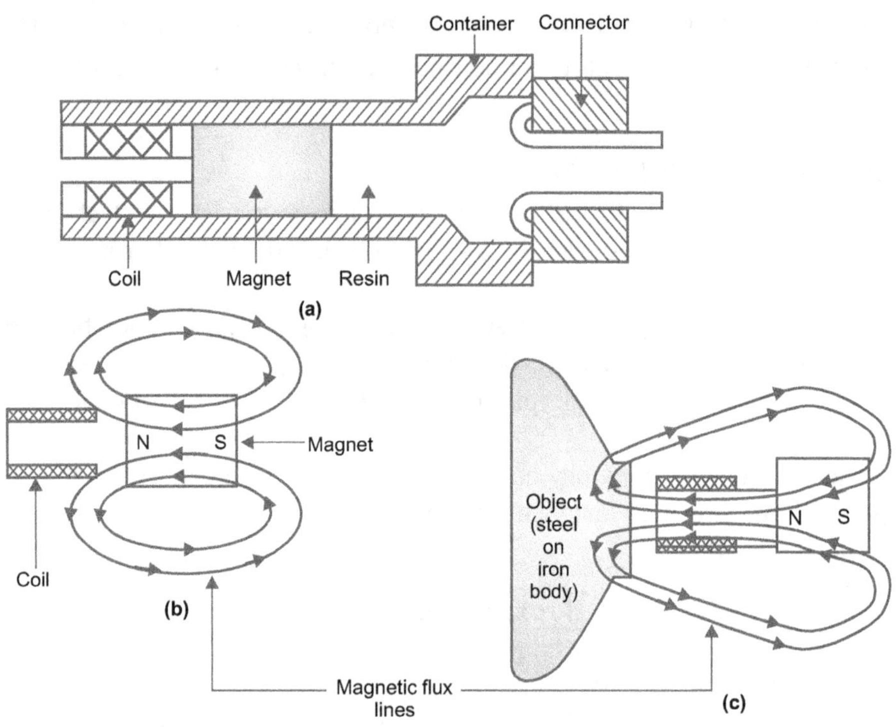

Fig. 3.16: Inductive Type of Proximity Sensor

- An inductive sensor basically consists of a wound coil located next to a permanent magnet packaged in a simple rugged housing.

- As sensor is brought in close proximity to a ferromagnetic material, it causes a change in the position of the flux lines of the permanent magnet as shown in Fig. 3.16 (b) and (c).

- For static conditions there is no movement of the flux lines and thus, no current is induced in the coil.

- But as a ferromagnetic material enters or leaves the magnetic field of the magnet, the resulting change in the flux lines induces a current pulse whose amplitude and shape are proportional to the rate of change of the flux.

- **The Voltage Waveform:**

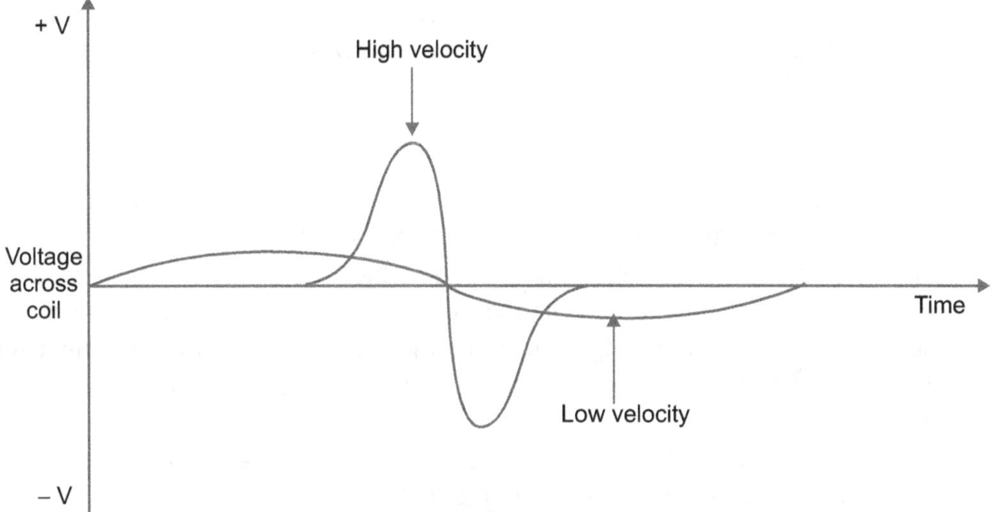

Fig. 3.17: Inductive Response as a Function of Speed

- The voltage waveform at the output of the coil provides an effective means for proximity sensing. Fig. 3.17 shows how the voltage measured across the coil varies as a function of the speed at which a ferromagnetic material is introduced in the field of the magnet.
- The polarity of the voltage out of the sensor depends on whether the object is entering or leaving the field.

- **Voltage Amplitude V/s Sensor-object Distance:**

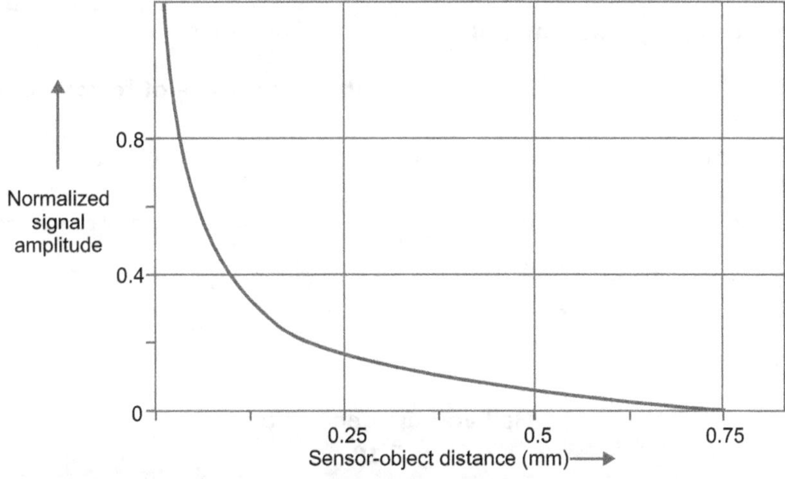

Fig. 3.18

The relationship between voltage amplitude and sensor-object distance is as shown in Fig. 3.18. It is noted that the sensitivity falls off rapidly with increasing distance, and that the sensor is effective only for fractions of a millimeter.

- The sensor requires motion to produce an output waveform, one approach for generating a binary signal is to integrate this waveform. The binary output remains low as along as the integral value remains below a specified threshold, and then switches to high when the threshold is exceeded.

(ii) Hall-effect Sensors:

- **Hall-effect:** It relates the voltage between two points in a conducting or semi-conducting material to a magnetic field across the material.
- Hall-effect sensors can detect magnetized objects only. However, when used in conjunction with a permanent magnet in a configuration as shown in Fig. 3.18 (a), they are capable of detecting all ferromagnetic materials and a Hall-effect sensors arrangement senses a strong magnetic field in the absence of a ferromagnetic metal in the near field.

  As shown in Fig. 3.19 (b), when a ferromagnetic material is brought in close proximity with the device, the magnetic field weakens at the sensor due to bending of the field lines through the material.

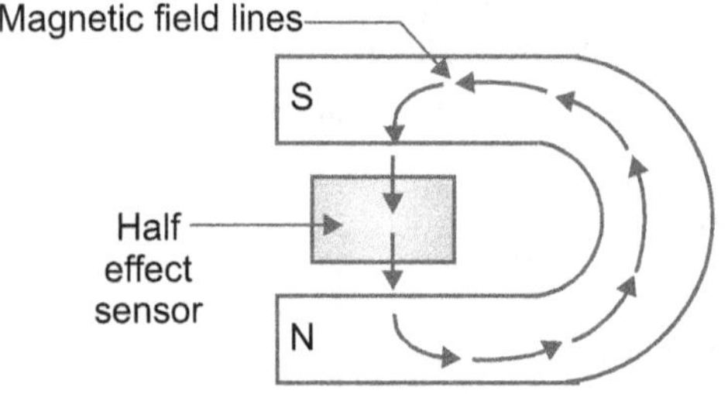

(a) Without ferromagnetic material

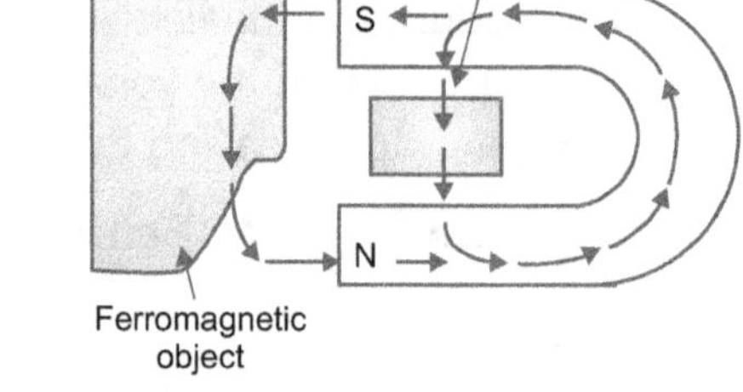

(b) In presence of ferromagnetic object

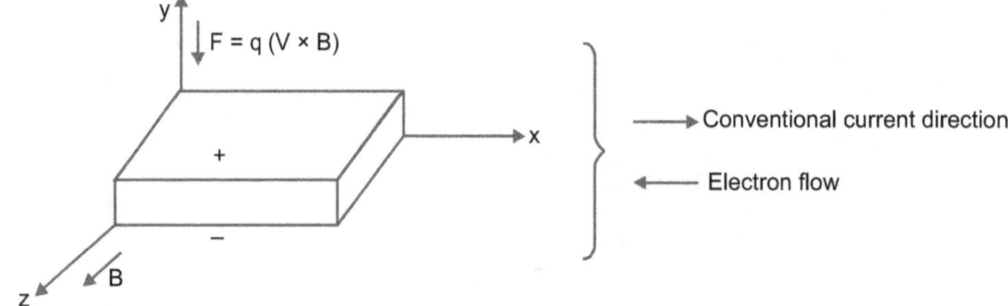

(c) Hall voltage generation

Fig. 3.19

- These sensors are based on the principle of Lorentz force which acts on a charged particle travelling through a magnetic field. The force acts on an axis perpendicular to the plane established by the direction of the motion of the charged particle and the direction of the field.

Lorentz force is given by,

$$F \ = \ q \, (v \times B)$$

where,   q is the charge, v is the velocity vector, B is the magnetic field vector, X is the vector cross product

- **Illustration:** A current flows through a doped n-type semiconductor which is immersed in a magnetic field as shown in Fig. 3.19 (c). As electrons are the majority carriers in n-type materials, and the conventional current flows opposite to electron current. The force acting on moving negatively charged particles have the direction as shown in Fig. 3.19 (c). This force would act on the electrons, which would tend to collect at the bottom of the material and thus produce a voltage across it, which is positive at the top. If we bring a ferromagnetic material close to the semiconductor-magnet device, the strength of the material field decreases, thus Lorentz force gets reduced and also the voltage across the semiconductor.

- The drop in voltage is the key for sensing proximity with Hall-effect sensors.

(iii) Capacitive Sensors:

- **Principle:** These sensors are based on detecting a change in capacitance induced by a surface that is brought near the sensing element.
- These sensors are capable of detecting all solid and liquid materials, unlike inductive and Hall-effect sensors.
  Constructional Features: Fig. 3.20 shows basic components of a capacitive sensor, as

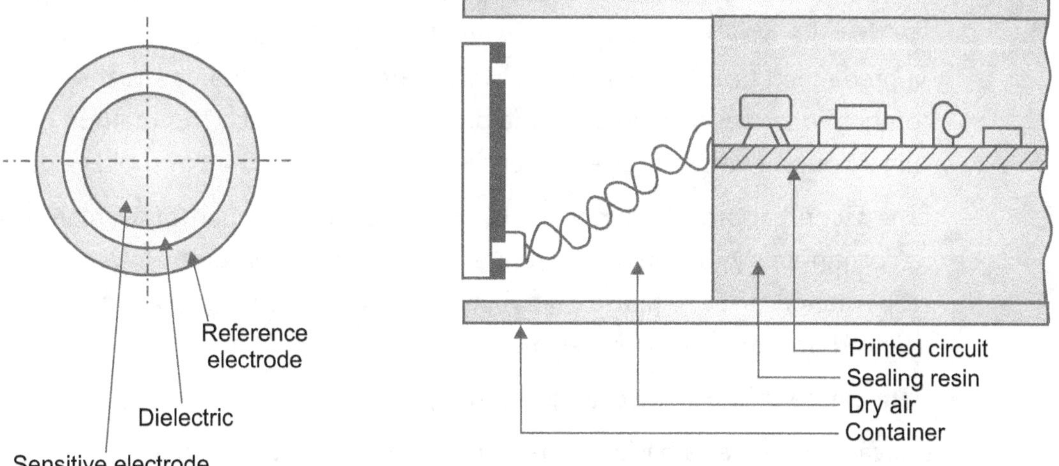

Fig. 3.20: A Capacitive Proximity Sensor

(a)   The Sensing Element

(b)   The Dielectric Material

(c)   The Dry Air-Gap

(d)   Electronic Circuit

(a) The Sensing Element:

It is basically a capacitor composed of a sensitive electrode and a reference electrode. A sensitive electrode in the form of a metallic disk and a reference electrode as a ring.

(b) The Dielectric Material:

A metallic disk (i.e. a sensitive electrode) and a ring (i.e. a reference electrode) are separated by a dielectric material medium.

(c) The Dry-Air Gap:

A cavity of dry-air is usually maintained behind the capacitive element to provide isolation.

(d) The Electronic Circuit:

The sensor is composed of electronic circuitry which can be included as an integral part of the unit, wherein it is normally embedded in a resin to provide seating and mechanical support.

- **Operation:**
  - There are varieties of electronic approaches for detecting proximity based on a change in capacitance:
    - First approach includes the capacitor as part of an oscillator circuit designed so that the oscillation starts only when the capacitance of the sensor exceeds a predefined threshold value. The start of oscillation is then translated into an output voltage which indicates the presence of an object. This method gives a binary output whose triggering sensitivity depends on the threshold value.
    - The second approach utilizes the capacitive element as part of a circuit which is continuously driven by a reference sinusoidal waveform. A change in capacitance gives a phase shift between the reference signal and a signal derived from the capacitive element.

      [The phase shift] $\propto$ [The change in capacitance]

      Thus, it can be used as a basic mechanism for proximity detection.

      Fig. 3.21 shows how capacitance varies as a function of distance for a proximity sensor based on the above concepts (i.e. approaches).
  - The sensitivity decreases sharply past a few millimeters, and that the slope of the response curve depends on the material being sensed.

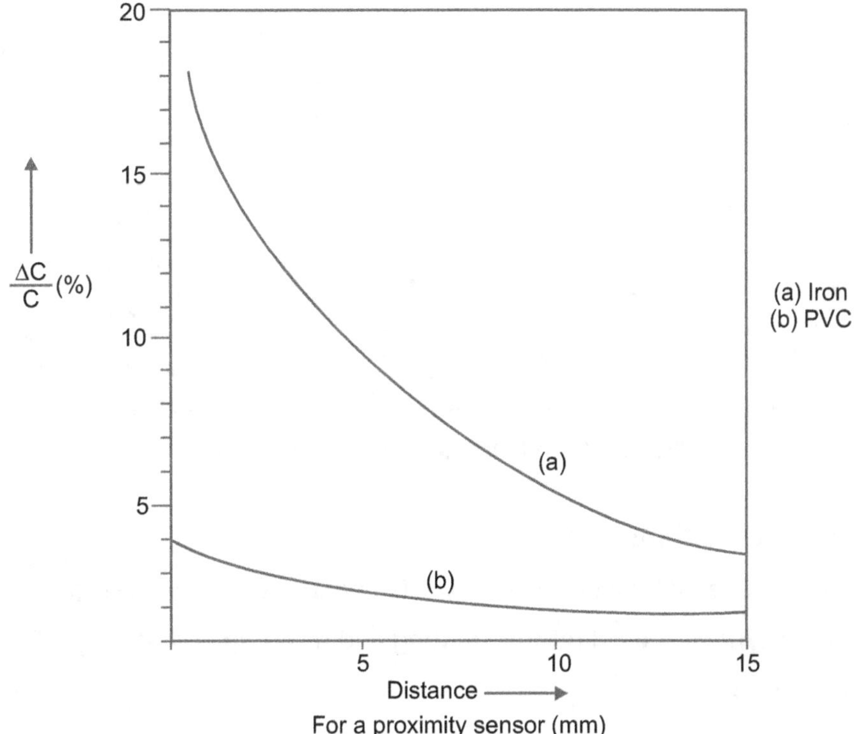

Fig. 3.21: % Change in Capacitance vs. Distance

- These sensors are operated in a binary mode so that a change in the capacitance greater than a preset threshold indicates the presence of an object, while changes below the threshold indicate the absence of an object with respect to detection limits established by the value of preset threshold.

(iv)   Ultrasonic Sensors:

- **Principle:** 'It operates on the principle of reflected ultrasound, wherein, the time between the signal output and return of the reflected signal is proportional to distance between the sensor and the target'.

- **Structure of a ultrasonic sensor:** A typical ultrasonic sensor used for proximity sensing consists of the following components:

  (a)   An Electroacoustic transducer;

  (b)   Resin layer;

  (c)   Acoustic absorber; and

  (d)   Housing
  - Sensor housing
  - Metallic housing

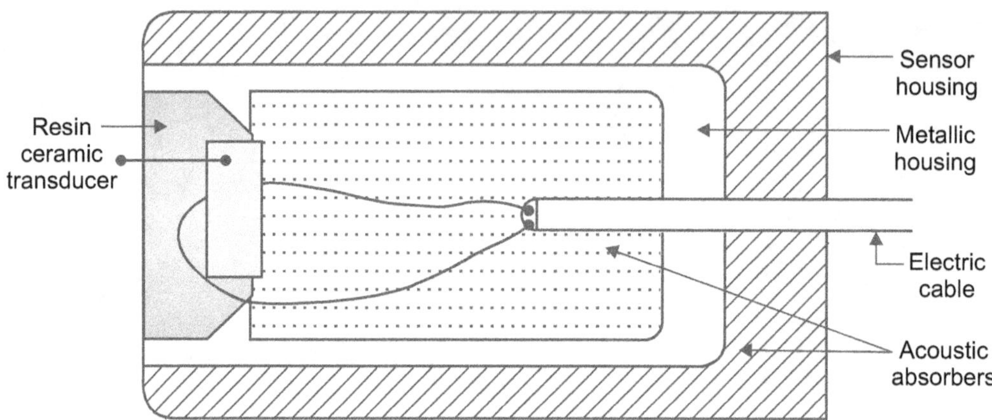

Fig. 3.22: An Ultrasonic Proximity Sensor

(a) An Electroacoustic Transducer:

It is a basic element of an ultrasonic proximity sensor and is of the piezoelectric –

- **Ceramic type:** It is used for transmitting and receiving acoustic signals.

(b) The Resin Layer:

- It protects the transducer against humidity, dust, and other environmental factors.

- It also acts as an acoustical impedance matcher.

(c) Acoustic Absorbers:

- In order to detect objects at close range, fast damping of the acoustic energy is necessary, which is accomplished by providing acoustic absorbers.

- One of the absorber is maintained at the ceramic transducer and the other acoustic absorber used around the metallic housing.

(d) The Housing:

- The housing is designed so that it produces a narrow acoustic beam for efficient energy transfer and signal-directionality.

- It is of two kinds, one is metallic housing which separates acoustic absorbers and other is sensor housing which gives mechanical support to sensor.

Operation:

- Different waveforms are analyzed, which are used for both transmission and detection of the acoustic energy signals.

  Fig. 3.23 shows typical set of waveforms used for the sensors.

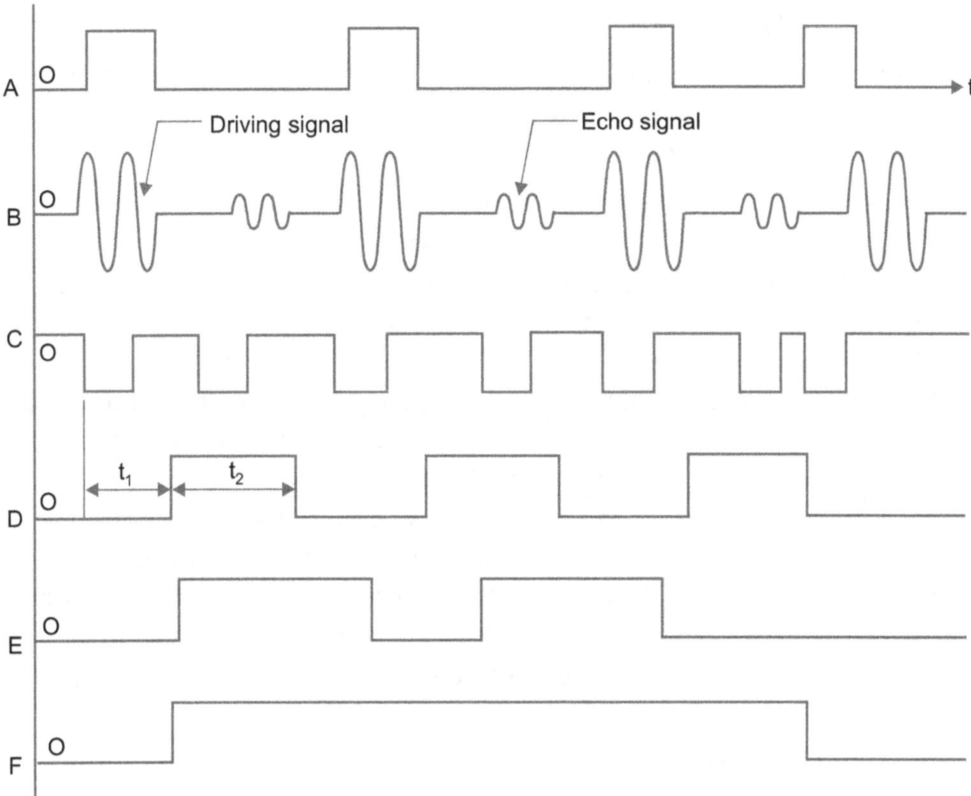

Fig. 3.23: Different Waveforms Related to an Ultrasonic Proximity Sensor

- **Waveform 'A':** It is the gating signal used to control transmission.
- **Waveform 'B':** It shows the output signal as well as the resulting echo signal.
- **Pulse 'C':** The pulse in 'C' result either upon transmission or reception.
- **Waveform 'D':** In order to differentiate between pulses corresponding to outgoing and returning energy, a time window is introduced, called as waveform 'D', which essentially establishes the detection capability of the sensor.

  i.e. time interval (Δt_1) is the minimum detection time, and $(\Delta t_1 + \Delta t_2)$ is the maximum detection time.

  It is noted that these time intervals are equivalent to specifying distances since the propagation velocity of an acoustic wave is known given the transmission medium.

- **Waveform 'E':** A echo received while signal 'D' is high produces the signal 'E', which is reset to low at the end of a transmission pulse in signal 'A'.
- **Waveform 'F':** Signal 'F' is set high on the positive edge of a pulse in 'E' and is reset to low when 'E' is low and a pulse occurs in 'A'.

  In this way, 'F' will be high whenever an object is present in the distance interval specified by the parameters of waveform 'D'. Thus, 'F' is the output of interest in an ultrasonic sensor operating in a binary mode.

(iv) Optical Proximity Sensors:

- **Principle:** 'Optical proximity sensors detect proximity of an object by its influence on a propagating wave as it travels from a transmitter to a receiver, as similar to that of an ultrasonic sensors'.

- Optical sensors can be designed using either visible or invisible light source. Invisible (i.e. infrared) sensors may be **active** or **passive.**

- The **active sensors** send out an infrared beam and respond to the reflection of the beam against a target. This kind of sensor can be used to indicate not only whether or nor a part is present, but also the position of the part.

- By timing the interval from when the signal is sent and the echo is received, a measurement of the distance between the object and the sensor can be made. This aspect is essentially useful for locomotion and guidance systems.

- Passive infrared sensors are simply devices which detect the presence of infrared radiation in the environment. These sensors often find application in security systems to detect the presence of bodies giving off heat within the range of the sensor.

  Fig. 3.24 shows one approach for detecting proximity by optical means.

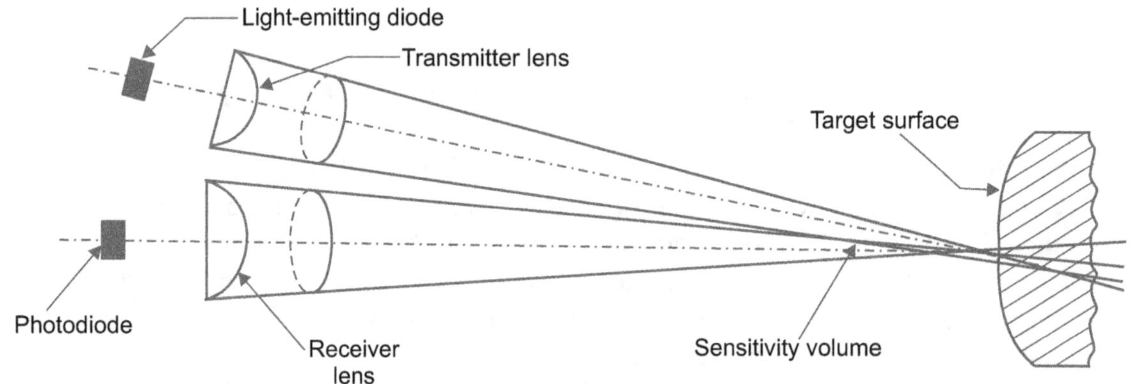

Fig. 3.24: Optical Proximity Sensor

- This sensor consists of a solid-state light emitting diode (LED), which acts as a transmitter of infrared light and a solid-state photodiode which acts as the receiver.

- The cones of the light formed by focussing the source and detector on the same plane intersect in a long, pencil-like volume. This volume defines the field of operation of the sensor since a reflective surface which intersects the volume is illuminated by the source and simultaneously 'seen' by the receiver.

- It is important to note that the detection volume shown in Fig. 3.24, does not yield a point measurement (i.e. a surface located anywhere in the volume will produce a reading) while it is possible to calibrate the intensity of these readings as a function of distance for known object orientations and reflective characteristics.

3.8.5 Touch Sensors

- Touch sensors are used to obtain information associated with the contact between a manipulator hand and objects in workspace.
- The touch information can be used for –
    - object location and recognition, and
    - to control the force exerted by a manipulator on a given object.
- Touch sensors are categorized into –
    (a) Binary sensors; and
    (b) Analog sensors.

(a) Binary Sensors:
- Binary sensors are basically switches which respond to the presence or absence of an object.
- Binary touch sensors are contact sensors such as micro-switched.
- As shown in Fig. 3.25, a switch is placed on the inner surface of each finger of a manipulator hand.

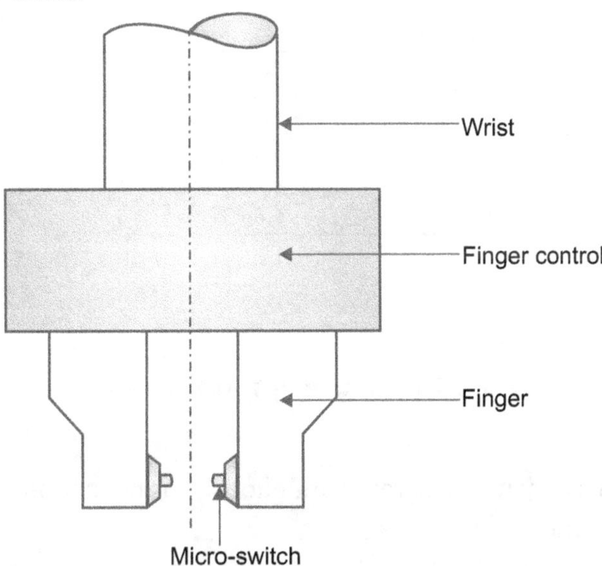

Fig. 3.25: Robot Hand with Binary Touch Sensor

- This type of sensing is used for determining if a part is present between the fingers. It is also possible to center the hand over the object for grasping and manipulation, by moving the hand over an object and sequentially making contact with its surface.
- In order to provide further tactile information multiple binary touch sensors can be used on the inner surface of each finger.
- Also they are often mounted on the external surfaces of a manipulator hand to provide control signals useful for guiding the hand throughout the workspace.

(b) Analog Sensors:

- An analog sensor is a compliant device whose output is proportional to a local force.

  Fig. 3.26 shows simple arrangement of an analog device consisting of a spring-loaded rod, which is mechanically linked to a rotating shaft in such a way that the displacement of the rod due to a lateral force results in a proportional rotation of the shaft.

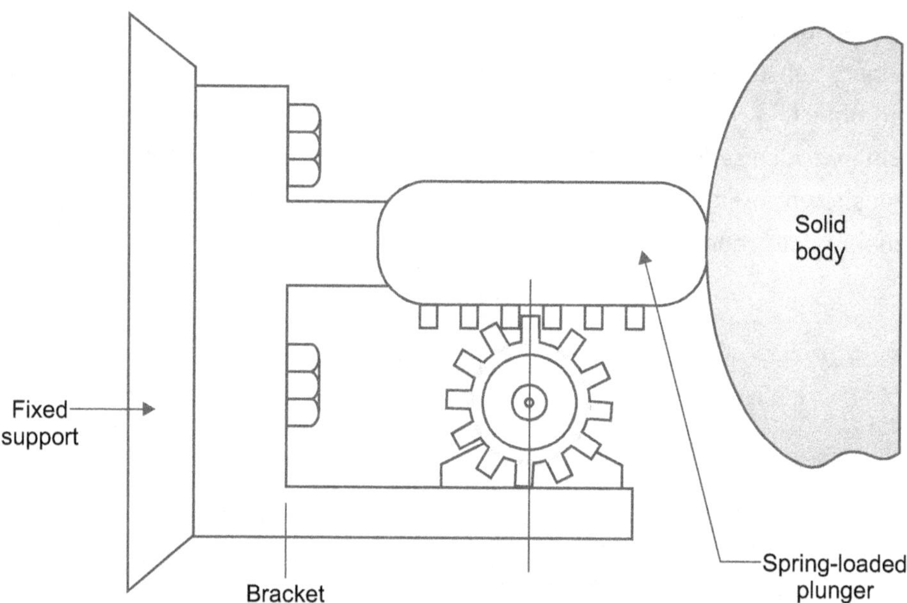

Fig. 3.26: An Analog Touch Sensor

- The rotation is then measured continuously using a potentiometer or digitally using a code wheel.

- Further based on the spring constant, it yields the force corresponding to a given displacement.

- **Tactile Sensing Array:**

  - Tactile sensing arrays capable of yielding touch information over a wider area that afforded by a single sensor.

  - Fig. 3.27 shows use of these devices, with a robot hand in which the inner surface of each finger has been covered with a tactile sensing array.

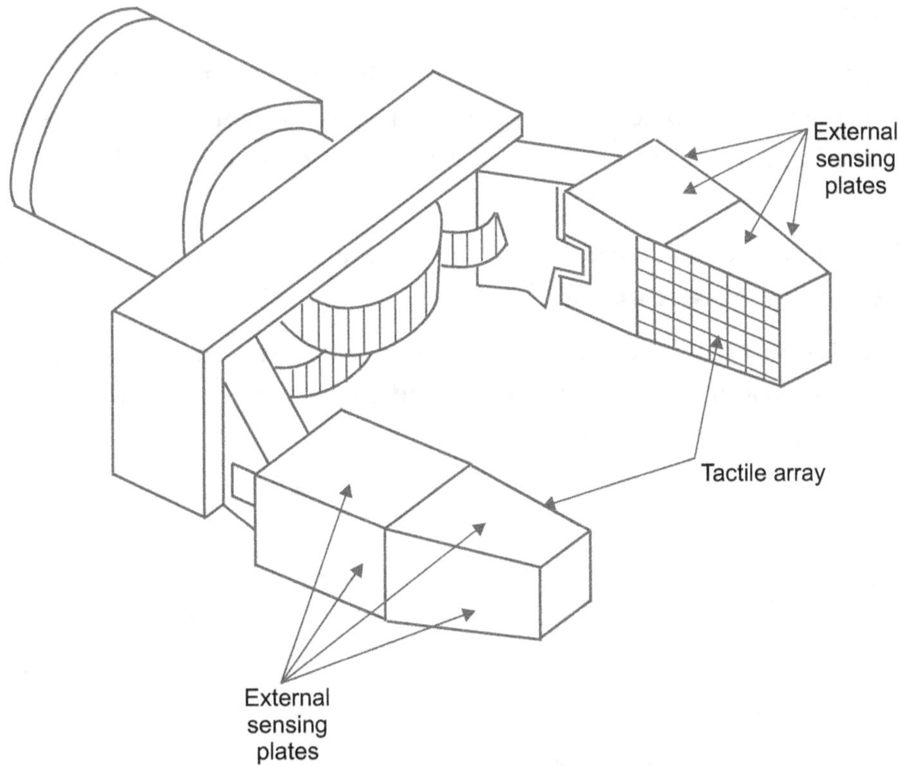

Fig. 3.27: A Robot Hand with Tactile Sensing Array

  - The external sensing plates are binary devices and have the function as discussed in previous section.

3.8.6 Remote Center Compliance (RCC) Device

- **Compliance** is a special end-effector feature i.e. a sensor or device that fits between the robot wrist and end-effector for special assembly applications. Therefore, a compliant robot system is one that complies with externally generated forces to modify its motion for the purpose of alignment between mating parts.

- The term **active compliance** is used, where a robot uses a force sensor and modifies its control strategy based on that sensor's output and the term **passive compliance** is used, where the robot's gripper is constructed in such a way that the mechanical structure deforms to comply with those forces.

  Thus, the problems with mating-part alignment in assembly and other applications are resolved using active and passive compliance techniques.

- **RCC Device:**

  - In passive compliance technique, it allows the robots wrist to deform in such a way that the external forces are minimized. Thus, passive compliance is using a spring-loaded wrist to provide the deformation. The concept of this principle applies to a RCC device.

  - This device was developed at the **Charles Stark Draper Laboratories of Cambridge, Massachusetts.**

  - The RCC-device is a unique device that compensates for position errors due to machine inaccuracy, parts vibration, and fixturing tolerance. This minimizes the assembly forces and the possibility of parts jamming.

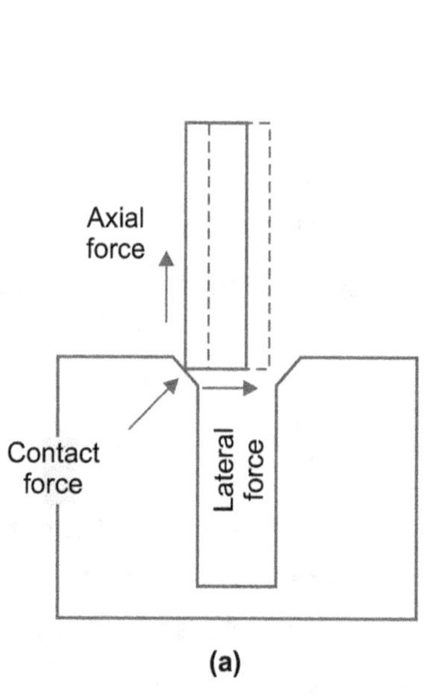

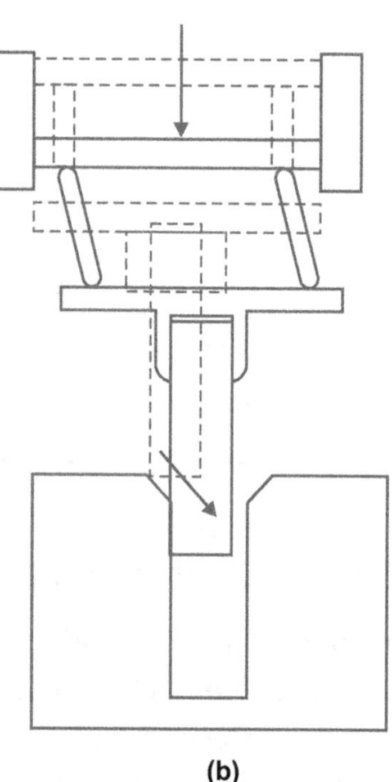

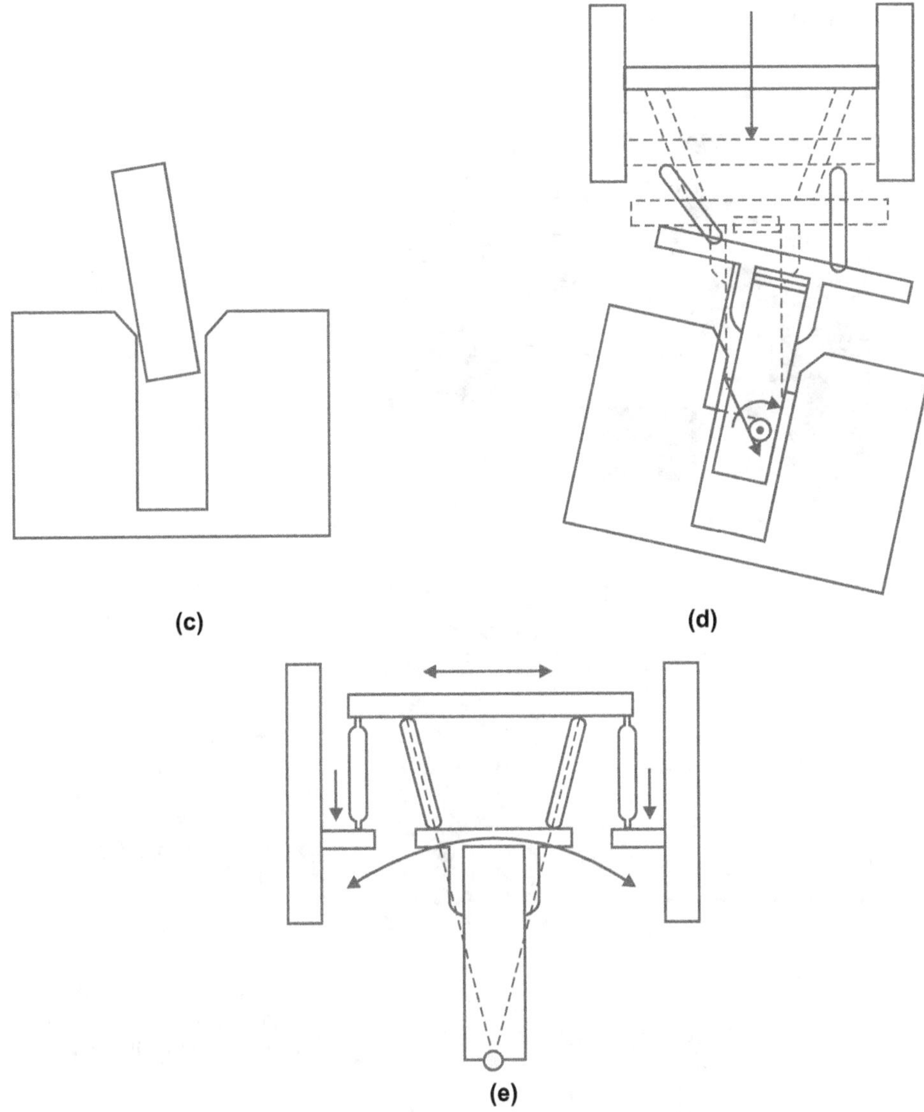

Fig. 3.28: Operation of RCC-Device

(a) The Original RCC device consists of three plates:

- The center plate is connected to the top plate with four rods and to the bottom plate with four additional rods.

- During actual operation, four rods, one on each corner, are used for **lateral compliance** and four angled rods, one on each corner, are used for **rotational compliance.** The flexible rods allow the plates to move relative to each other and provide a **combination of lateral and rotational compliance,** and this device is rigid in **axial direction** with no compliance provided.

(b) Modern RCC-devices, which is as shown in Fig. 3.29 below.

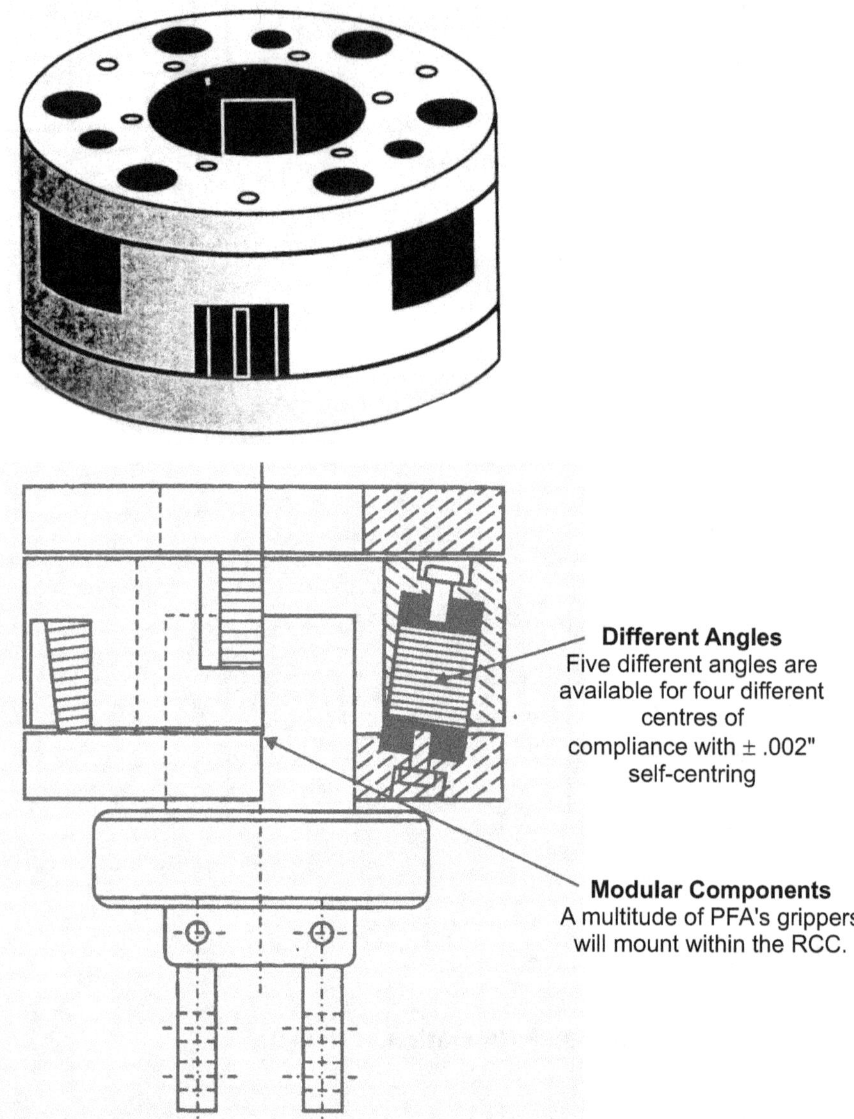

Fig. 3.29: Modern RCC-device (Automated Assembly Compliance Device Model ASP-85)

- It consists of a set of six elastomertic shear pads sandwiched between two plates, and mechanical stops protect against overload movements in all directions.

- The shear pads are stiff in the axial direction but highly compliant in the lateral and rotational directions.

- The upper plate is attached to the robot tool plate and the lower plate is attached to the gripper.

- This device can also be furnished with a lockout feature. It is locked during movement and unlocked immediately before part insertions to allow the RCC to compensate for misalignment during assembly. This capability reduces assembly cycle time and increases the operation life of the shear pads.

- In operation, the center of compliance is the point in space about which rotational and translation motion occurs.

- Positioning the center of compliance as the part-mating surface allows the part being inserted to translate laterally and rotate around the center of compliance, which reduces assembly forces and the possibility of parts jamming. This compensation for lateral and rotational misalignment reduces wear on the gripper as well as the need for high-accuracy machines and fixturing.

EXERCISES

1. Define a robot sensor. Explain the basic function of sensor.

2. Explain basic need of sensors in a robotic system.

3. Give a functional classification of robotic sensors.

4. Write a short note on –

   (i)   Status sensors

   (ii) Environmental sensors

   (iii) Quality control sensors

   (iv) Safety sensors

   (v)   Workcell Control Sensors

5. What are the different types of sensors based on working principle?

6. Discuss a broad classification of sensors based on working principle.

7. Discuss various desirable features of sensors.

8. State various sensing devices used in Robot workcell.

9. Explain in brief various sensing devices used in Robot workcell.

10. Discuss various sensor characteristics.

11. Discuss the following terms in the light of robotic sensors:

    (i)   Range   (vii) Accuracy

    (ii) Resolution   (viii) Cost

    (iii) Sensitivity   (ix) Size and weight

    (iv) Linearity   (x) Interfacing

    (v)   Reliability   (xi) Response time

    (vi) Repeatability   (xii) Frequency response   (xiii) Type of output

12. Discuss different factors considered for selection of sensors.

13. State the principle of photoelectric sensors. Explain different types of photoelectric sensors.

14. What is the function of a microswitch? Explain Limit Switch Actuators.

15. What is the function of a range sensor in the robot workcell? Explain various range sensing techniques.

16. State different types of proximity sensors with the principle of operation of each sensor.

17. Give a brief classification of proximity sensors.

18. Explain the following types of proximity sensors.

    (i)   Inductive sensors   (ii) Hall-effect sensors

    (iii) Capacitive sensors   (iv) Ultrasonic sensors

    (v)   Optical proximity sensors

19. Describe how touch sensors operate.

20. What is compliance? Explain active and passive compliance in brief.

21. Explain Remote Center Compliance (RCC) Device.

✳✳✳

Unit III

Chapter 4: ROBOT DRIVES

4.1 Introduction to Drives

Actuators are the devices which give the actual motive force for the robotic joints. Generally, power is supplied by compressed air, pressurized fluid or electricity.

Depending upon the type of power input to actuator, they are called as pneumatic actuators with compressed air as input power, hydraulic actuators with pressurized fluid as input power and electric actuators with electric input.

4.2 Classification of Drives

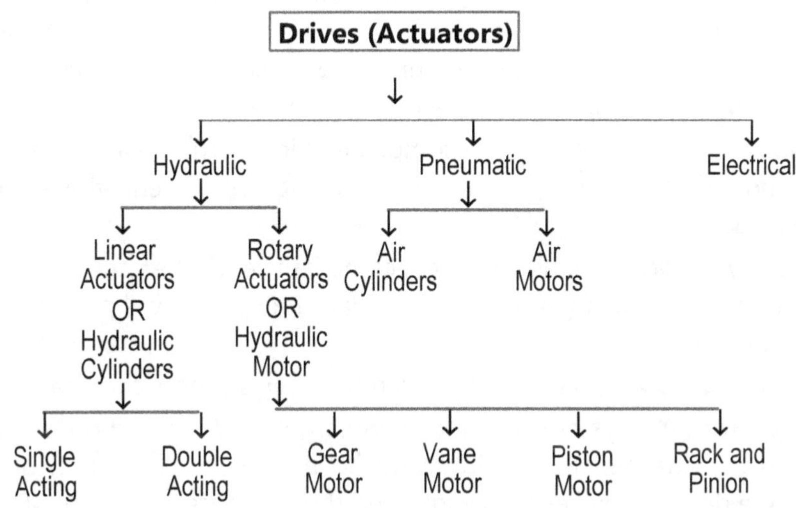

The drives are chosen based on –

(i)   The power consumption

(ii)   Positional accuracy

(iii) Repeatability

(iv)   Speed of operation

(v)   Stability

(vi)   Reliability

(vii) Cost.

4.3 Characteristics of Drives

(i)   **Weight:** It is an important characteristics of any actuating system. It plays important role while selecting actuating system for a particular application.

(ii)   **Power to Weight Ratio:** It shows the type of actuation system which will be best suited for given application and higher the power to weight ratio, better is suited for given application.

- Power to weight ratio of electric systems is average.
- Stepper motors are generally heavier than servomotors for the same power and thus have a lower power to weight ratio.
- Pneumatic cylinders deliver the lowest power to weight ratio.
- Hydraulic systems have the highest power to weight ratio.

(iii) **Operating Pressure:** Hydraulic system delivers high power, due to high operating pressures ranging from 55 psi to 5000 psi, whereas pneumatic system has low operating pressure as compared to hydraulic system that may range between 100 to 120 psi.

(iv) **Stiffness:** It is the resistance offered by a material against deformation. Stiffness is directly related to the modulus of elasticity of the material. Modulus of elasticity of fluids is very high, therefore, hydraulic systems are very stiff. Stiff systems have a rapid response to changing loads and pressures and these are more accurate also. But stiff system will not prevent damage to the robot or the part.

(v)   **Compliance:** A system is said to be compliant, if it deforms easily under changing load or changing driving force. Thus, the more compliant system, the easier it deforms under the load.

Therefore, hydraulic systems are non-compliant and the pneumatic systems are compliant. Also a compliant system will be inaccurate, but it will prevent damage to the robot or the part.

Therefore, good working balance is needed between stiffness and the compliance.

(vi) **Reliability:** Hydraulic systems produce very large forces with short strokes, thus they can be directly attached to the links and do not require reduction gear trains. This simplifies the design, reduces the weight and thus increases reliability of the system.

(vii) **Resolution:** The electric motors rotate at high speeds and they must be used in conjunction with the reduction gears to increase the torque and to decrease their speed. This increases the cost, and also the number of parts, thus results in decrease of reliability and increase the resolution of the system, as it is possible to rotate the link at very small angle.

(viii) Uses of Reduction Gears:

- Hydraulic systems do not need reduction gears for the power transmission.
- Electric systems use reduction gears which reduce the inertia on the motor.

4.4 Different Types of Drives

4.4.1 Hydraulic Actuators

- Hydraulic actuators are powered by pressurized oil (i.e. at 1,000 to 3,000 lb/in^2).

- They extract energy from the fluid and convert it to mechanical energy to perform useful work.

- Depending upon the motion they transmit, the hydraulic actuators are classified as –

4.4.1 (i) Linear Actuators or Hydraulic Cylinders

- They convert hydraulic energy into straight line motion, thus actuating a linear joint by means of a moving piston.

- Simplest form of hydraulic cylinder is the single acting design, as shown in Fig. 4.1.

It consists of a piston inside a cylindrical 'barrel'. Attached to one end of the piston is a rod, which extends outside one end of the cylinder. At the other end is a part for the entrance and exit of oil. These cylinders can exert a force in only the extending direction. Retraction is accomplished by using gravity or by the inclusion of compression spring in the rod end.

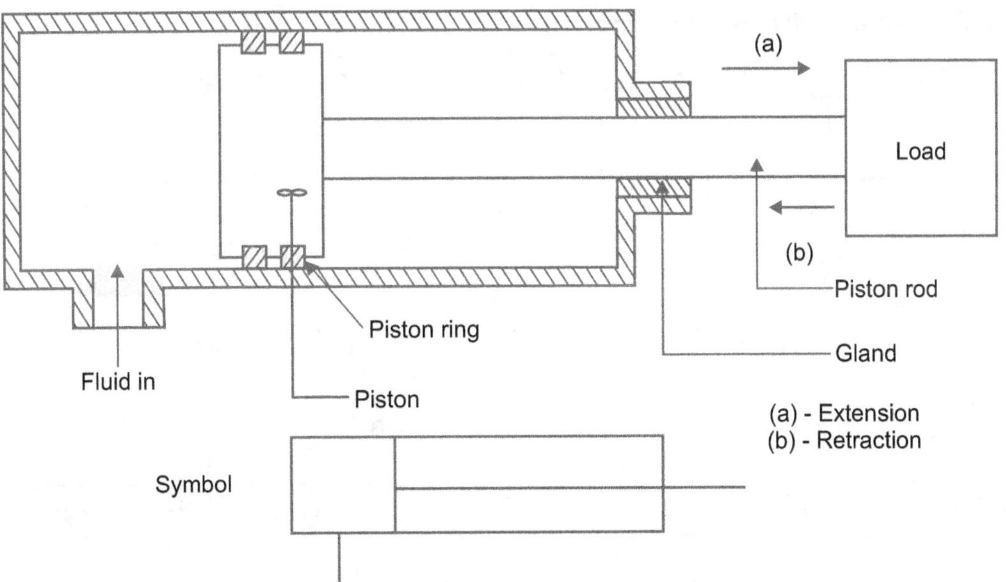

Fig. 4.1: Single acting hydraulic cylinder

(a) Double-acting cylinder with single piston rod:

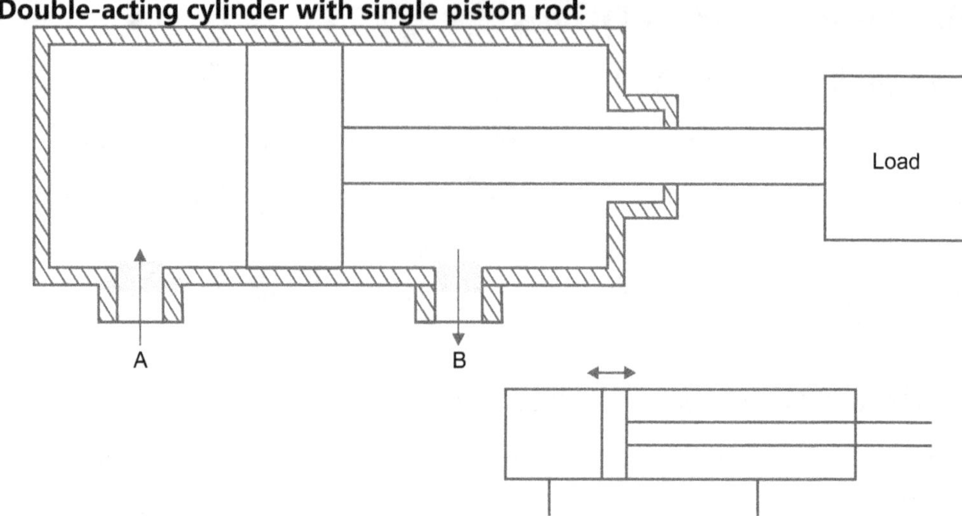

Fig. 4.2: Double acting cylinder with single piston

- In this arrangement, the fluid may enter through either the blank end (i.e. A) or the rod end (i.e. B). Extension of the piston rod occurs when the fluid is pumped into the blind end. Retraction of the piston occurs when the fluid is pumped into the rod end of the cylinder.

  Due to differential area, the retraction stroke is faster than the extension stroke as well, force obtained in extension stroke is more than that of in retraction stroke.

(b) Double acting with double piston rod:

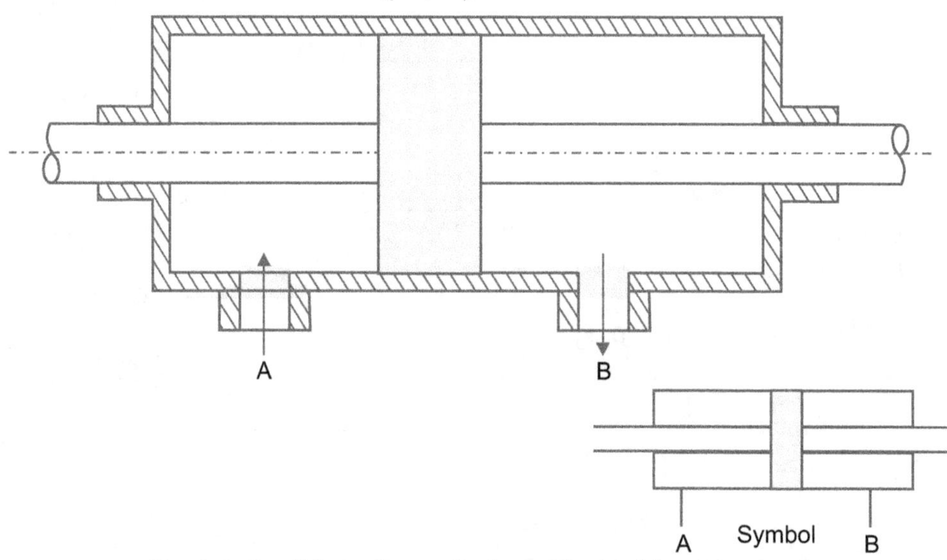

Fig. 4.3: Double acting cylinder with double piston rod

- The piston rod is extended due to the fluid pressure exposed on the blind end of the piston.
  The area exposed to the fluid towards the rod end (i.e. B) of the cylinder reduces due to the presence of the piston rod and so the extending force is greater than the force of retraction.
  But the speed of retraction is larger as compared to the speed of extension.
- Force and speed are equal in both the directions due to the extension of piston rods on both sides of the piston inside the cylinder.

Design considerations for hydraulic cylinder:
Following are the design considerations for hydraulic cylinder.

(a)	Thrust required	(b)	Operating pressure
(c)	Speed	(d)	Stroke length
(e)	Type of construction	(f)	Type of mounting
(g)	Expected service life	(h)	Operating environment
(i)	Lateral loads and buckling failure		

4.4.1 (ii) Hydraulic Rotary Actuators or Hydraulic Motors

- Rotor actuator is a device that converts hydraulic energy into rotational motion, it may be limited rotation or continuous full rotation.
- The continuous full rotation type of rotary actuator is sometimes called as hydraulic motor.

Classification of Hydraulic Motors

- Rotary actuators are mainly of three types:

  (a) Gear motors   (b) Vane motors and   (c) Piston motors

(a) Gear motors:

- These devices work opposite to that of gear pumps and develop torque and rotary motion when they are acted upon by the fluid.
- Fluid enters the inlet port and is carried around the outside of the casing and finally flows out of the outlet port.
- The direction of rotation of gears can be reversed by changing the direction of inlet and outlet flows.
- The volumetric displacement of a gear motor is fixed. Side thrust occurs due to difference in pressure between inlet and outlet ports.
- The shaft drives the load, when it gets power from one of the gears in the gear motor.

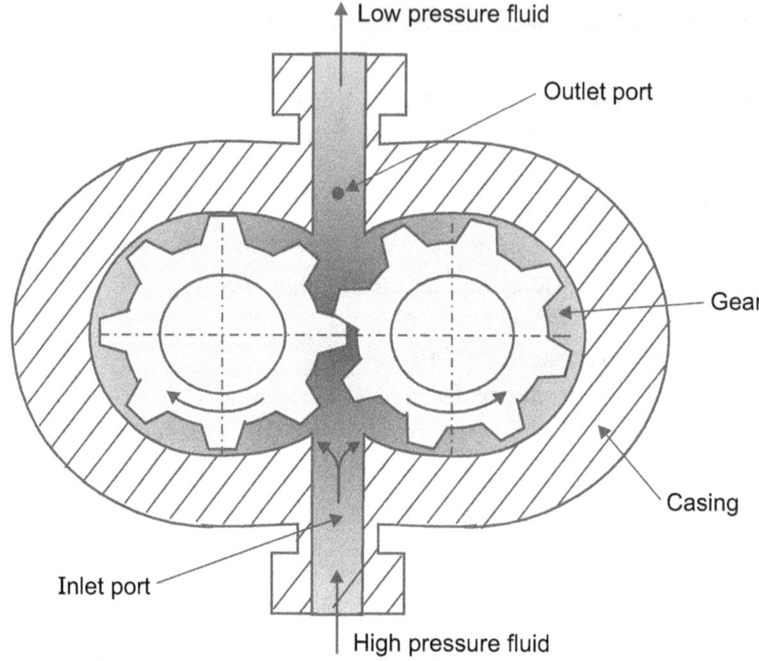

Fig. 4.4: Gear motor

- Gear motor develops torque due to hydraulic pressure acting on the surfaces of the gear teeth.

- Gear motors are normally limited to 2000 psi operating pressures and 2400 rpm operating speeds.

- Gear motors are available with a maximum flow capacity of 150 gpm.

Advantages:

(a) It is simple in design.

(b) Cost of gear motor is low.

(c) In case of internal gearing arrangement insteady of external gearing, it can operate at higher pressures and speeds and also has greater displacements than the external gear motor.

(b) Vane motors:

Principle: 'Vane motors develop torque by the hydraulic pressure acting on the exposed surfaces of the vanes, which slide in and out of the rotor connected to the drive shaft'.

Fig. 4.5 shows constructional details of vane motor.

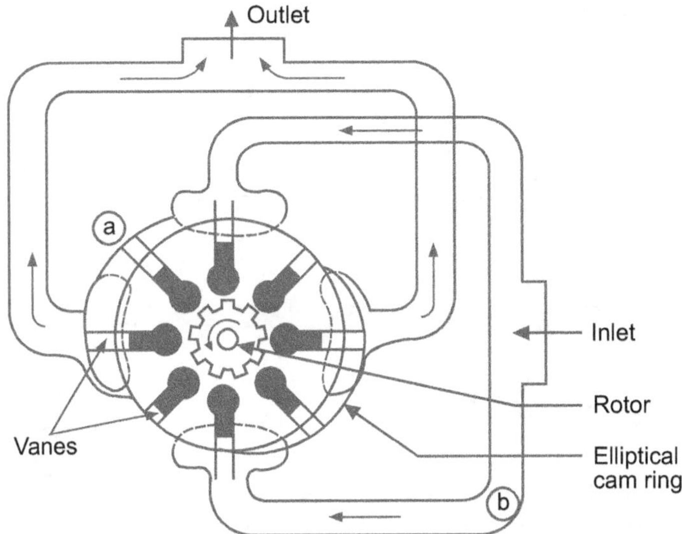

(a)   Vane subjected to high pressure at inlet side and low pressure opposite.

(b)   The inlet connecting two opposing pressure passages to balance side loads on the rotor.

Fig. 4.5: A Vane motor

- As rotor revolves, the vanes follow the surface of the cam ring because springs are used to force the vanes radially outward.
- There is no centrifugal force until the rotor starts to revolve.
- The sliding action of the vanes forms sealed chambers, which carry the fluid from the inlet to the outlet.
- Balanced design of vane motors is usually followed in practise. In this design, pressure build up at either port is directed to two interconnected cavities located 180° apart.
- The side loads that are created are therefore cancelled out. As the vane motors are hydraulically balanced, they are fixed displacement units.

Advantages:
(a)   Compared to gear motors, vane motors have less leakage tendency.
(b)   Vane motors can be used at lower speeds due to less leakage tendency.
(c)   As side loading occurs on the shaft of a single vane motor, these are commonly used.

(c) Piston motors:
- Piston motors can be either fixed or variable displacement motors.

-     Piston motors are classified as –
  (a)   In-line piston motor
  (b)   Radial piston motor.

(a)   In-line piston motor:

- They generate torque by pressure acting on the ends of pistons reciprocating inside a cylinder block.
- Fig. 4.6 shows the in-line piston motor in which the motor drive shaft and cylinder block are centered on the same axis.

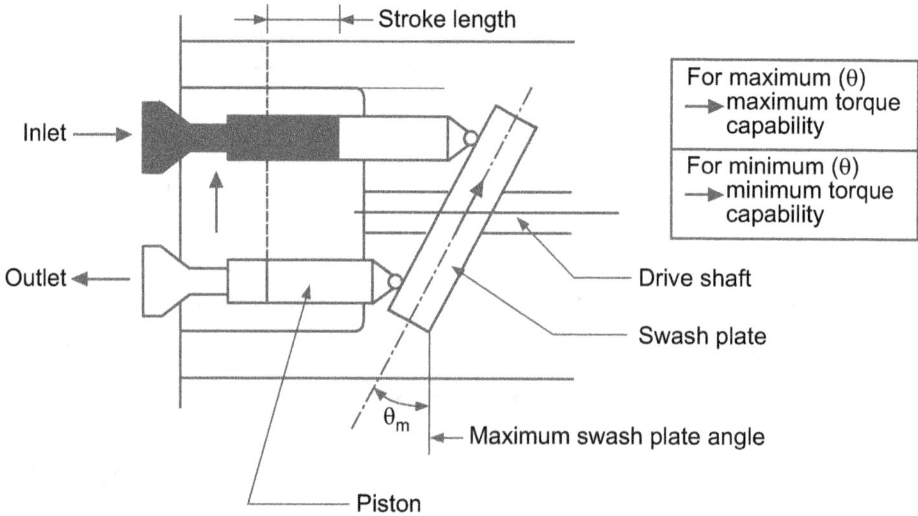

Fig. 4.6: Piston motor

- Pressure acting on the ends of the pistons generates a force against an angled swash plate, this causes the cylinder block to rotate with a torque that is proportional to the area of the pistons.

- The torque capability is also a function of the swash plate angle.

       i.e. $T = f(\theta)$

- The swash plate angle gives the volumetric displacement.

(b)   Radial piston motor:

- Radial piston motor is most commonly used motor. It operates in reverse of the radial piston pump.

- In this type, fluid is forced into the cylinders and drives the piston outward.

- Fig. 4.7 shows the constructional details and operation of radial piston motor.

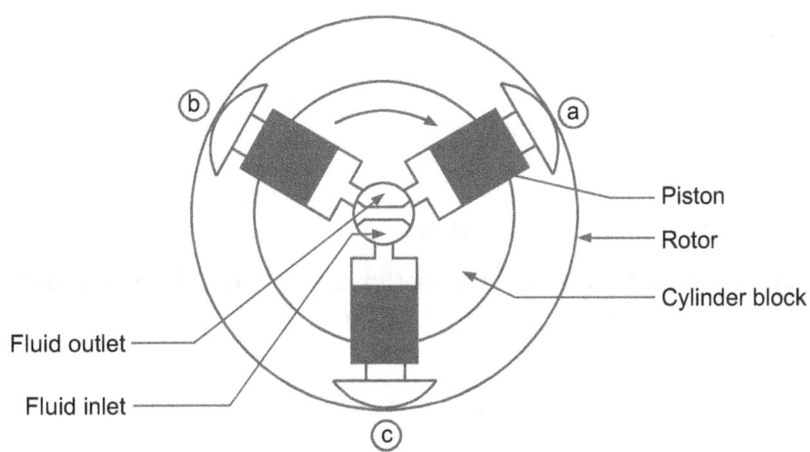

Fig. 4.7: Radial piston motor

- The piston pushing against the rotor causes the cylinder block to rotate. Usually, the motor contains seven or nine pistons, but for simplicity we have considered three pistons.
- When fluid is forced into the cylinder bore containing piston (a), the piston moves outward, as the fluid cannot be compressed. This causes the cylinder to rotate in a clockwise direction.
- As the force acting on piston (a) causes the cylinder block to rotate, piston (b) starts to rotate and approach the piston of piston (c).
- As piston (b) rotates, it is forced inward and thus, forces the fluid out of the cylinder.
- As there is little or no pressure on this side of the valve, the piston is moved easily in by its contact with the reaction ring of the rotor, the fluid is easily forced out of the cylinder block and back to the reservoir.
- The action continues as long as fluid under pressure enters the cylinders.

Advantages of Hydraulic Motors

(a) Compact in size: It has highest power to weight ratio, as it is compact in size.

(b) Wide range of speed: It has speed range from zero to maximum, which can be obtained from the maximum flow provided by pumping system.

(c) Frequent use: Frequent starting, stopping, reversing can be possible with the use of control valves.

(d) Provision of variable torque: It can provide variable torque by use of pressure control valves.

(e) Explosive proof: These are generally proof in nature.

(f) Ruggedness: These actuators can be operated in dirty, abrasive wet and mildly corrosive environments.

(g) Safety: These are safe in operation.

Hydraulic Motor Performance Characteristics

(i) Theoretical Torque: Due to frictional losses, a hydraulic motor delivers a torque which is less than its theoretical value. Theoretical torque is the torque that a frictionless hydraulic motor would deliver.

It can be given by following equation –

$$T_{TH} = \frac{V_d \cdot p}{2\pi}$$

where, T_{TH} – Theoretical torque in (N · m)

V_d – Volumetric displacement in (m³/rev)

p – Pressure in (Pa)

Thus, the theoretical torque is proportional to pressure and volumetric displacement.

(ii) Theoretical power: Theoretical power is the power a frictionless hydraulic motor would develop, can be expressed as,

$$P_{TH} = \frac{V_d \ p \cdot N}{2\pi}$$

where, V – Theoretical power in (W)

V_d – Volumetric displacement of fluid in (m³/rev)

p – Pressure in (Pa)

N – Speed in (rad/sec)

(iii) Theoretical flow rate: The theoretical flow rate is the flow rate a hydraulic motor would consume if there were no leakage, it can be expressed as,

$$Q_{TH} = V_d \cdot N$$

where, Q_{TH} – Theoretical flow rate in (m³/s)

V_d – Volumetric displacement in (m³/rev)

N – Speed in (rev/sec)

(iv) Volumetric efficiency: It is denoted by η_v and can be defined as the ratio of the theoretical flow rate, that motor should consume to the actual flow rate consumed by motor,

i.e.
$$\eta_v = \frac{Q_{TH}}{Q_A}$$

where, Q_{TH} – is theoretical flow rate (m^3/s)

           Q_A – is actual flow rate (m^3/s)

(v) Mechanical efficiency: It is denoted by η_m, and can be defined as the ratio of the actual torque delivered by motor to the torque that motor should theoretically deliver.

i.e.
$$\eta_m = \frac{T_A}{T_{TH}}$$

where, T_A – is the actual torque (N-m)

           T_{TH} – is the theoretical torque (N-m)

$$\eta_m = \frac{\left[\dfrac{\text{Actual wattage delivered by motor}}{N}\right]}{\left(\dfrac{V_d \cdot p}{2\pi}\right)}$$

(vi) Overall efficiency: Overall efficiency can be defined as the ratio of the actual power delivered by motor to the actual power delivered to the motor.

It is denoted by η_0.

i.e.
$$\eta_0 = \frac{\text{Actual power delivered by motor}}{\text{Actual power delivered to motor}}$$

$$\eta_0 = \frac{T_A \cdot N}{p \cdot Q_A}$$

where, T_A –   Actual torque (N-m)

           N –   Speed (rps)

           p –   Pressure in (Pa)

           Q_A –   Actual flow rate (m^3/s)

Here, actual power delivered to a motor by the fluid is called **hydraulic power** and the actual power delivered to a load by a motor through a rotating shaft is called as **brake power.**

4.4.2 Pneumatic Actuators

– Pneumatic devices make use of a fluid medium that is highly compressible. Fluid is usually air and it is both readily available and non-flammable.

– Pneumatic actuators are of lighter construction.

These are of two types:

(a)   Linear actuators – Pneumatic cylinders and

(b)   Rotary actuators – Piston motor or vane motor.

4.4.2 (i) Linear Actuators

These actuators are the means of converting the air pressure delivered by the air circuit into applied force and straight line motion. Most often used configurations are a linear single or a double-acting piston actuator.

Classification:

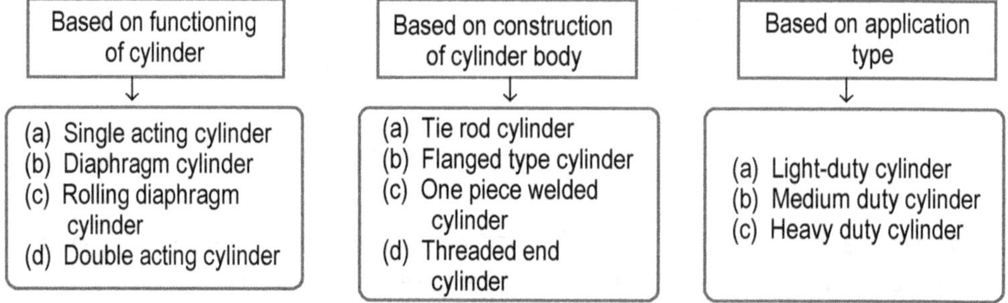

Following Fig. 4.8 shows constructional details and working of linear actuator.

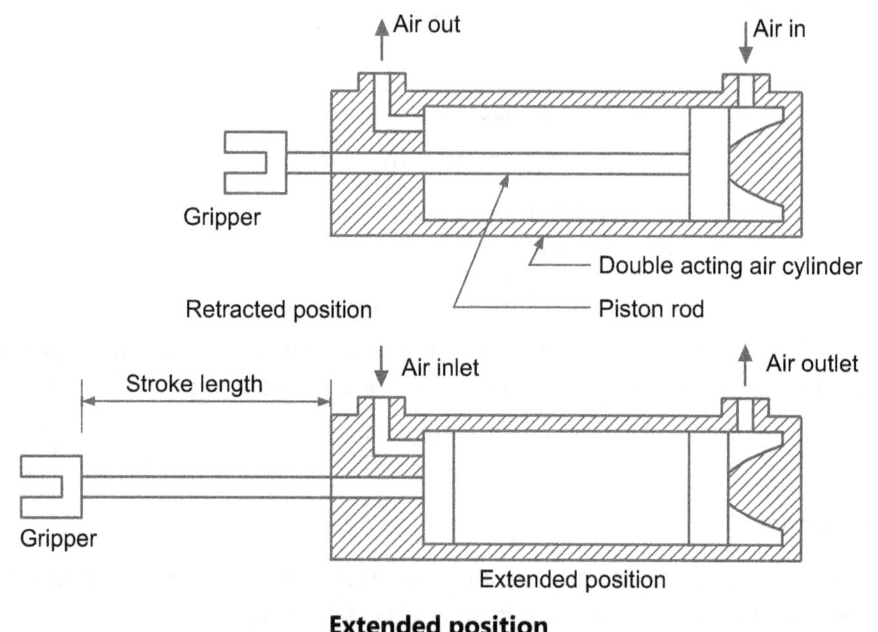

Extended position

Fig. 4.8: Linear Actuator

–   In this case, fluid is compressed air and they typically operate with pressure at about one hundred pounds per square inch.
–   There is linear motion of gripper attached to piston rod during retraction stroke. And stroke length is shown in extended position.

There are two relationships i.e. the piston velocity of the actuator and the force output of the actuator with respect to the input power. They are different for extension and retraction strokes.

For **Extension stroke:**

$$(\text{Force})_e \;=\; \text{Pressure} \times \text{Piston area}$$

$$(\text{Velocity})_e \;=\; \frac{\text{Input flow rate}}{\text{Piston area}}$$

For **Retraction stroke:**

$$(\text{Force})_r \;=\; \text{Pressure} \times [\text{Piston area} - \text{Rod area}]$$

$$(\text{Velocity})_r \;=\; \frac{\text{Input flow rate}}{\text{Piston area} - \text{Rod area}}$$

4.4.2 (ii) Rotary Actuator

Usually, air motors are the rotary actuators in pneumatic system.
They convert the power supplied by pressurized air into rotary motion. Pneumatic motors can deliver very high rotational speed upto 9000 rpm or even more.
There are two types of rotary actuators:
(i)   Low speed piston motor and
(ii)   Variable speed vane motor.

(i)   Low speed piston motor: Fig. 4.9 shows working of piston motors.

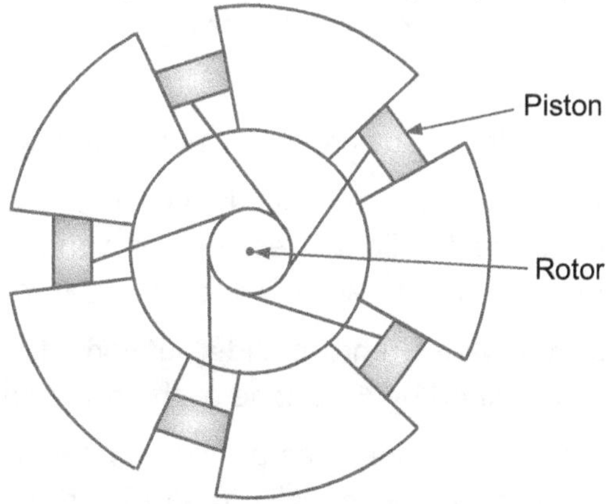

Fig. 4.9: Piston motor

- These motors can be used to provide a smooth source of power. They are not susceptible to overload damage. They can be started and stopped very quickly and with pressure regulation and metering of flow can provide infinitely variable torque and speed.

- The fire-cylinder piston design provides even torque at all speeds due to overlap of the fire power impulses occurring during each revolution of the motor. At least two pistons are on the power stroke at all times.

- The smooth power flow and accurate balancing make these motors vibrationless at all speeds.

- The piston motor has relatively little exhaust noise, and this can be further reduced by use of an exhaust muffler.

- It is suitable for continuous operation using 100 psi air pressure and can deliver upto 15 HP.

(ii) Variable speed vane motor:

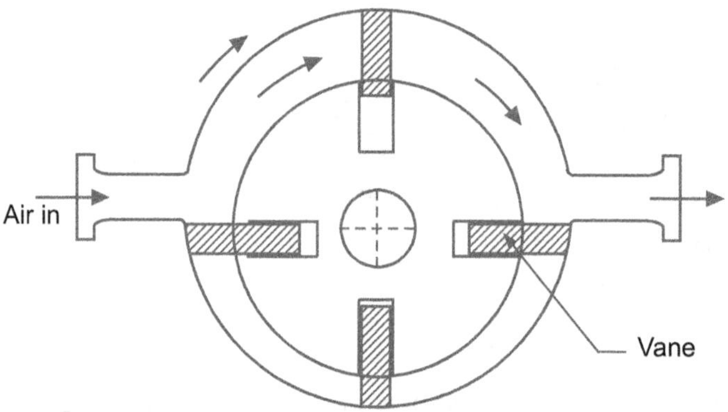

Fig. 4.10: Vane motor

- It consists of four vanes and it provides rotation in one direction only.

- The rotating element is a slotted rotor, which is mounted on a drive shaft. Each slot of the rotor is fitted with a freely sliding rectangular vane. The rotor and vanes are enclosed in the housing, the inner surface of which is offset from the drive shaft axis.

- When the rotor rotates, the vanes tend to slide outward due to centrifugal force. The distance the vane slides, is limited by the shape of the rotor housing.

- The motor operates on the differential area principle. When compressed air enters into the inlet port, its pressure is exerted equally in all directions. Each vane in turn takes positions and the rotor turns continuously.

– The pressure energy of the compressed air is thus converted into kinetic energy in the form of rotary motion and force.

– Finally, the air at reduced pressure is exhausted to the atmosphere.

– The shaft of the motor is connected to the unit to be actuated.

Applications:

– Due to cool running operations, these motors can be used in ambient temperature upto 250°F.

– Also these are used for mixing equipment, conveyor drives, food packaging, hoists, tension devices and turn tables etc.

4.4.2 (iii) Advantages and Disadvantages

Advantages:

(i) Low power to weight ratio: Rotary actuators are employed where lightness and compactness is required and develop more power per kg weight as compared to other actuators.

(ii) Shock and explosion proof: Rotary actuators are shock and explosion proof. As compared to electric actuators which need very special and costlier construction, these actuators provide better performance.

(iii) Less heating: These actuators can be overloaded or stalled without burning on the other hand the harder the rotary actuator works, the cooler it runs. This is due to fact that air creates a cooling effect while it expands in motor.

(iv) Acceleration and deceleration is fast: Due to low inertial of rotary actuators, it can accelerate and decelerate faster. As compared to the electric actuator, the rotary actuator does not have the loads on the shaft.

(v) Clean operation: As compared to hydraulic actuators, the leaks from motor can result in damage to material, which is being processed. It is not there with rotary actuators, thus these actuators are found widely applicable in food processing industry. Also rotary actuators are easy to maintain due to cleanliness.

(vi) Variable speed: Using a simple flow control valve, rotary air motor speed can be varied over a wide range from 100 rpm to 10,000 rpm.

Disadvantages:

(i) Noise in operation: The air exhaust from the motor creates noise, unless it is absorbed by use of mufflers.

(ii) Non-precision motion: In certain applications, where high precision motion is needed, rotary actuators are not suitable due to compressibility of air.

Thus, air actuated systems are highly compliant because of the compressibility of air.

4.4.3 Electrical Actuators

- Electrical actuators become more popular due to their excellent controllability with a minimum of maintenance required.
- There are variety of motors in use for robotic applications, the most commonly used motors are –
  - (a) DC servomotors
  - (b) Stepper motors and
  - (c) AC servomotors
  - (d) Brushless DC motors (BDCM)

4.4.3 (i) DC Servomotors

- DC servomotors convert electrical energy into mechanical energy by developing suitable torque on the motor shaft.
- They have high torque to volume ratios. Using closed loop servo controls, DC motors can be made suitable for high precision.
- They provide clean drives as compared to hydraulic and pneumatic actuators.
- There are two kinds of motors:
  - (i) Permanent magnet motors.
  - (ii) Motors with wound field coils.
- Fig. 4.11 shows DC servomotors with wound field coils.

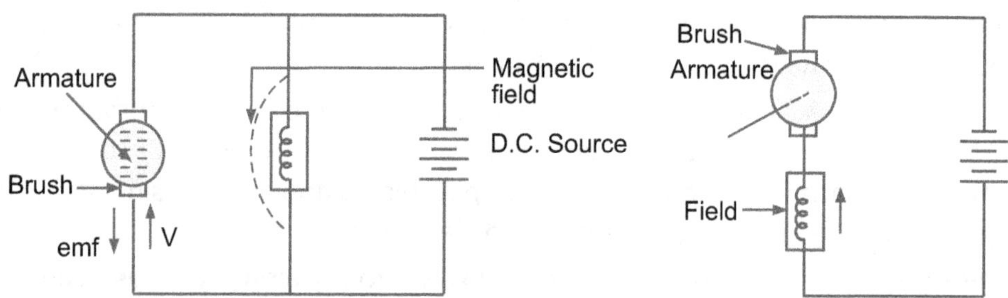

Fig. 4.11: Shunt wound DC servomotor   **Fig. 4.12: Series wound motor**

- The main components of the dc servomotor are the rotor and the stator.
- The rotor includes the armature and the commutator assembly and the stator includes the permanent magnet and brush assemblies.
- When current flows through the windings of the armature, it sets up a magnetic field opposing the field set up by the magnets. This results a torque on the rotor.

–   As the rotor rotates, the brush and commutator assemblies switch the current to the armature so that the field remains opposed to the one set up by the magnets. Thus, the torque produced by the rotor is constant throughout the rotation.

–   As field strength of the rotor is a function of the current through it,

Then, for a DC servomotor,

$$T_M(t) \;=\; K_M \cdot I_A(t)$$

where, T_M – is the torque on the motor

I_A – is the current flowing through the armature

K_M – is the motor's torque constant.

–   **Back-emf:**

A DC motor with armature spinning in the presence of a magnetic field produces a voltage across the armature terminals. This voltage is proportional to the angular velocity of the rotor.

i.e. $e_B \cdot (t) \;=\; K_B \cdot \omega t$

where, e_B – is the back-emf

K_B – is the voltage constant of the motor

ω – is the angular velocity

The effect of the back-emf is to act as viscous damping for the motor i.e. as the velocity increases the damping increases proportionately.

Illustration:

V_{in} – a voltage supplied across the motor terminals

R_A – resistance of the armature

$\therefore$ The current through the armature

$$I_A \;=\; \frac{V_{in}}{R_A}$$

This current produces a torque on the rotor and causes the motor to spin.

Due to spinning of the armature, it generates back-emf equal to,

$$e_B(t) \;=\; K_B \cdot \omega(t)$$

This voltage need to be subtracted from V_{in} in order to evaluate the armature current.

∴   The actual armature current

$$I_A (t) = \frac{V_{in}(t) - e_B \cdot (t)}{R_A}$$

Characteristics:

–   As the motor speed increases, the back-emf voltage increases, and the current available to the armature decreases.

–   This decrease in current reduces the torque generated by the rotor.

–   Also as the torque decreases, the acceleration of the rotor decreases.

–   **Speed torque characteristics of a shunt wound motor:**

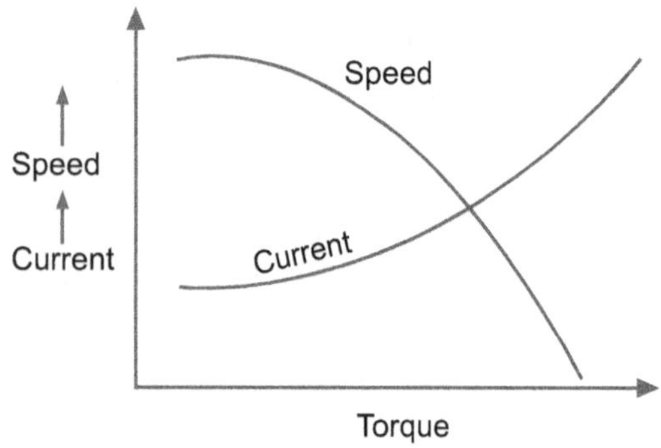

Fig. 4.13

–   **Speed torque characteristics of series wound motor:**

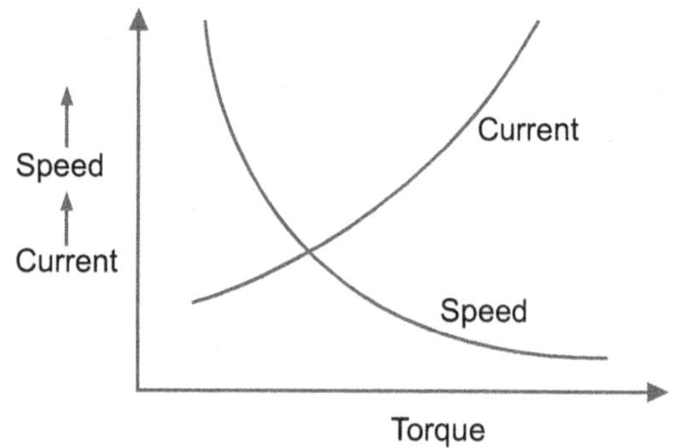

Fig. 4.14

–   **Speed torque characteristics of a compound DC motor:**

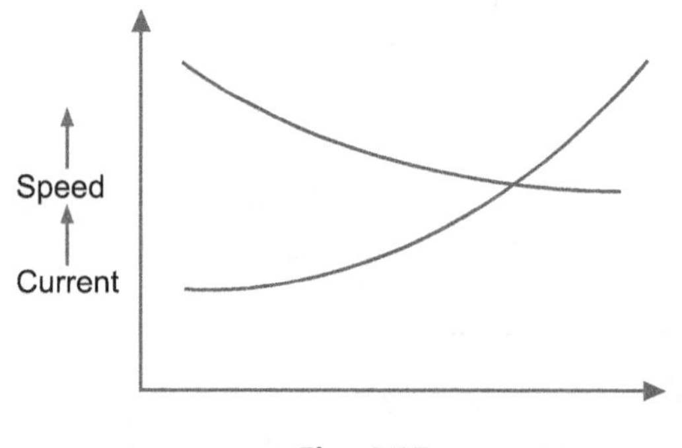

Fig. 4.15

–   **Speed torque characteristics of a permanent magnet DC motor:**

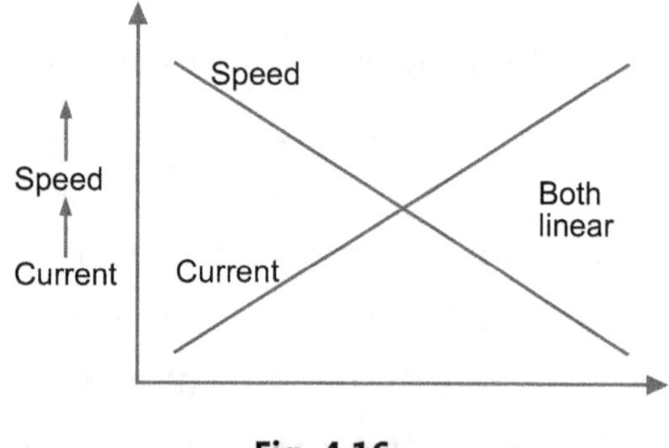

Fig. 4.16

Undesirable effects of brushes:

- They have limited life time and require periodic inspection and replacement.
- There can be problem of arcing at brushes in an explosive environment.
- Cost of motor with brushes is higher.
- Brushes cause electrical transients that are a source of electromagnetic interference.

4.4.3 (ii) Stepper Motors

- These are also called as 'stepping motors'. It can be considered as a digital device that provides output in the form of discrete angular motion increments.
- It is actuated by a series of discrete electrical pulses. For every electrical impulse there is a single-step rotation of the motor shaft.
- Stepper motors are usually employed for light duty robotic applications.
- Also these motors are used in open-loop system rather than the closed-loop system.
- A typical application is positioning a work table in two dimensions for automatic drilling.
- Fig. 4.17 shows a schematic representation of one type of stepper motor.
- It consists of a stator and a rotator. The stator is made up of four electromagnetic poles and the rotor is a two-pole permanent magnet.
- If the electromagnetic stator poles are activated in such a way that pole 'C' is N (i.e. magnetic north) and pole 'A' is S then rotor is aligned as shown.
- If the stator is excited so that pole 'D' is N and pole 'B' is S, the rotor makes a 90° turn in the clockwise sense.

  Thus, by rapidly switching the current to the stator electronically, it is possible to make the motion of the rotor appear continuous.

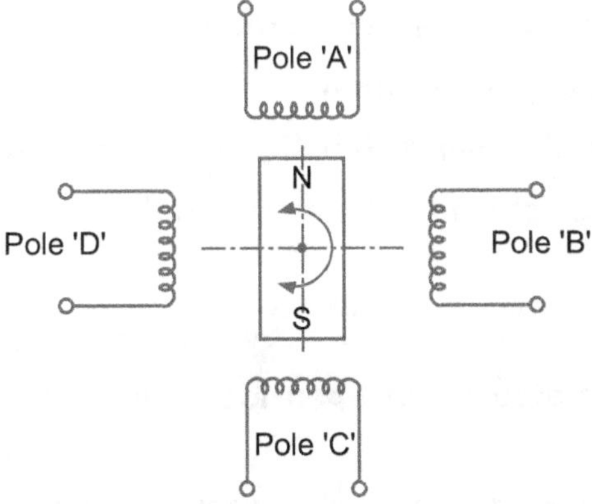

Fig. 4.17: Stepper motor representation

– By determining the number of poles in the stator and rotor, the resolution of a stepper motor can be fount out.

   The relation between a stepper motor's resolution and its step angle is given by,

$$R = \frac{\theta}{360°}$$

where,   R – is the resolution

and θ – is the step angle

– The relation between a stepper motor's speed and torque is not a straight-line.

– The torque is a 'function of the angle between the stator and the rotor poles. The torque is maximum when the poles are aligned, and this value of torque is termed as the **holding torque** of the motor.

– **Half stepping or micro-stepping:**

   It is technique to increase the resolution of a stepper motor, thus reducing the holding torque value.

   – In case of some motors, the speed-torque relation degrades at certain frequencies of operation and at these frequencies the operation of the motors must be avoided.

Advantages:

(i)   These motors can be **directly compatible with digital control techniques** or it can be interfaced with digital controllers.

(ii) It gives **excellent positioning accuracy.**

(iii) **Errors** associated with these motors are **non-cumulative** in nature.

(iv) As open-loop control can be used with motor, it is not required to use a tachometer and encoder. It results in considerable **cost reduction.**

(v)   Motor **construction is simple** and **rugged.**

(vi) Motor has a **long and maintenance-free life.** Therefore, it is a **cost-effective actuator.**

(vii) The stepper motor **can be stalled** without causing damage.

Characteristics:

(i)   The motor can be **operated in an open-loop** way with a **positioning accuracy of ± 1 step.**

(ii) The motor **exhibits high torque** at small angular velocities.

(iii) The motor also **exhibits a large holding torque** with a dc excitation. Thus, it acts as a 'self-locking' device, when the rotor is stationary.

(iv) A **dc holding characteristic** of stepper motor make it an extremely attractive choice in the actuation of a robot joint.

(v) Under the supply of full voltage, the motor will move one step and hold, thus no runaway condition will exist, and the stepper is seen to be safer under this type of failure.

Disadvantages:

(i) Position errors can be caused when one attempts to move the rotor too rapidly, which is called as phenomenon of 'dropped steps', and it will cause the robot arm to reach a final position that is in error.

(ii) The stepwise motion can excite significant manipulator oscillation. As there is no velocity feedback used, the only way to improve the response is to employ a much more elaborate controller that is capable of **microstepping.** It will raise the cost of the equipment.

4.4.3 (iii) AC Servomotors

– These are cheaper to manufacture.

– They have no brushes and they possess a high power output.

– With a proper provision of electronics package, the performance of AC servomotors can be made similar to that of DC servomotors.

4.4.3 (iv) Brushless DC Motors

– Brushless DC motors can be viewed as an **"inside-out"** version of standard dc servomotor.

– Rotor of brushless dc motor contains the permanent magnets, whereas the stator consists of the coil segments and iron.

– There is no **mechanical commutation** of the coils in BDCM due to elimination of the brushes and commutator bars. A provision of properly energizing the stator coil segments must be provided. It is accomplished by placing inside the motor itself solid-state devices i.e. Hall-effect bipolar sensors that will determine the actual position of the magnets as the rotor turns.

– A simple electronic logic circuit then processes the information provided by these sensors, thus, enabling the appropriate stator coil to be excited.

–   Fig. 4.18 shows constructional details of brushless DC motor.

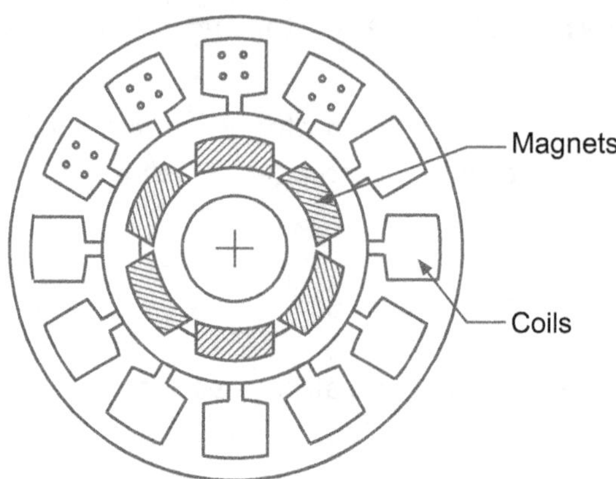

Fig. 4.18: Brushless DC Motor (BDCM)

Advantages:

*   They require reduced maintenance.

*   Brush arcing is eliminated.

Disadvantages:

*   They are more expensive.

*   Rotor inertia is greater than other motors due to the mass of permanent magnets.

4.5 Comparison of Driver Systems   (W-11)

Type of Actuators	Advantages	Disadvantages
(a) Hydraulic actuators	• Long life with moderate speed. • Offers accurate control with fluid. • These are stable system since temperature resistance is absent. • Provides the robot with greater speed and strength.	• Systems are expensive. • Pollute the workspace with fluids and mix, as leaking of oil. • Not suitable for high speed cycling. • Overall set up is complicated, that disturb the comfort. • Large floor space required.

Type of Actuators	Advantages	Disadvantages
(b) Pneumatic actuators	• It is reserved for small capacity robots with fewer DoFs. • High speed is possible. • These are relatively inexpensive, but can be used in laboratory work. • Give minimum output errors.	• Air compressibility limits the accuracy. • Noise pollution. • Leakage of air filtering system and drying system is needed. • Increased maintenance. • Chatter in operation affects robot accuracy.
(c) Electric actuators	• Easy availability. • Better accuracy and repeatability. • Less floor space required. • Suitable for more precise work e.g. assembly. • Simple to use. • Sophisticated control techniques can be applied. • Compact and can be easily incorporated.	• Require links or gear trains for transmission. • Gear backlash limits the precision. • There is limitation on output power. • Problem of electric arcing is expensive. • Difficulty in replacement of damaged parts.

EXERCISES

1. Define actuator. Classify them.

2. Discuss various characteristics of actuators.

3. What are the types of hydraulic actuators used in robotics ? Explain them in brief.

4. Explain:

    (i) Gear motors

    (ii) Vane motors

    (iii) Piston motors

    (iv) Linear actuators

5. Discuss advantages of hydraulic motors in brief.

6. Explain various performance characteristics of hydraulic motors.

7. Give a classification of Pneumatic actuators.

8. Explain different types of Pneumatic actuators.

9. Discuss advantages and disadvantages of Pneumatic actuators.

10. What are the different types of electrical actuators ? State working principle of each type.

11. Write a short note on:

    (i)   DC Servomotors

    (ii)   Stepper motors

    (iii) AC Servomotors

    (iv)   Brushless DC Motors (BDCM)

12. Discuss advantages, disadvantages and characteristics of stepper motors.

13. Compare hydraulic, pneumatic and electrical actuators with reference to their relative merits and demerits.

14. Compare various actuating systems in brief.

15. Compare hydraulic, pneumatic and electrical actuators with reference to following points:

    (i)   Weight   (v)   Compliance

    (ii)   Power to weight ratio   (vi)   Resolution

    (iii) Operating pressure   (vii) Cost

    (iv)   Stiffness   (viii) Ease of operation

✳✳✳

Unit III

Chapter 5: TRAJECTORY PLANNING AND MANIPULATOR CONTROL

5.1 Introduction

To accomplish a specified task, the end effector of the robotic system is required to move in a particular fashion, so as to follow a predetermined path. Thus, path and trajectory planning relates to the way, a robot (either a joint or end effector) is moved from one location to another in a controlled manner. Path and trajectory though looking similar are different terms by definition. Path is independent of time on the other hand trajectory is function of time.

Path is defined as a sequence of robot configurations in a particular order without regard to the timing of these configurations.

Trajectory is defined as time history of position, velocity and acceleration of either actuated joint or the end effector of the robot.

Basic objective of trajectory planning is to take the joint or end effector from one location to another in specified time; additionally with certain magnitudes of velocity and/or accelerations, furthermore, through certain intermediate points; and lastly with certain orientations.

In the above process of trajectory planning the known points where the trajectory starts and ends are called as "start point" and "end point" ("goal point"). If there are any pre-determined points through which trajectory must pass, then such points are called as "via points" or "knot points". All the via points, start point and end point, together are called as *path points*.

Depending on user's (robot operator's) requirement there may be multiple trajectories between given two points as shown in Fig. 5.1.

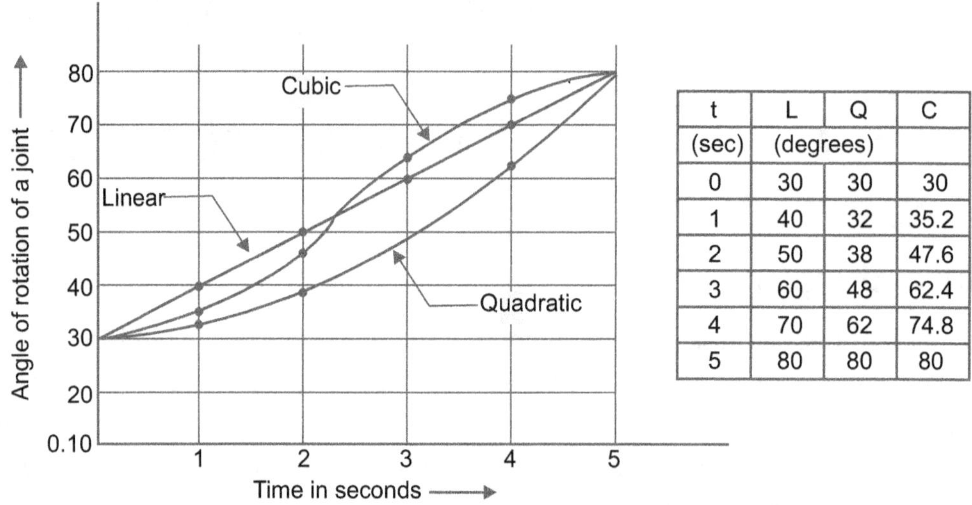

t	L	Q	C
(sec)	(degrees)		
0	30	30	30
1	40	32	35.2
2	50	38	47.6
3	60	48	62.4
4	70	62	74.8
5	80	80	80

Fig. 5.1

5.2 Consideration in Path Description and Generation

Consider positions of manipulator as shown in Fig. 5.2.

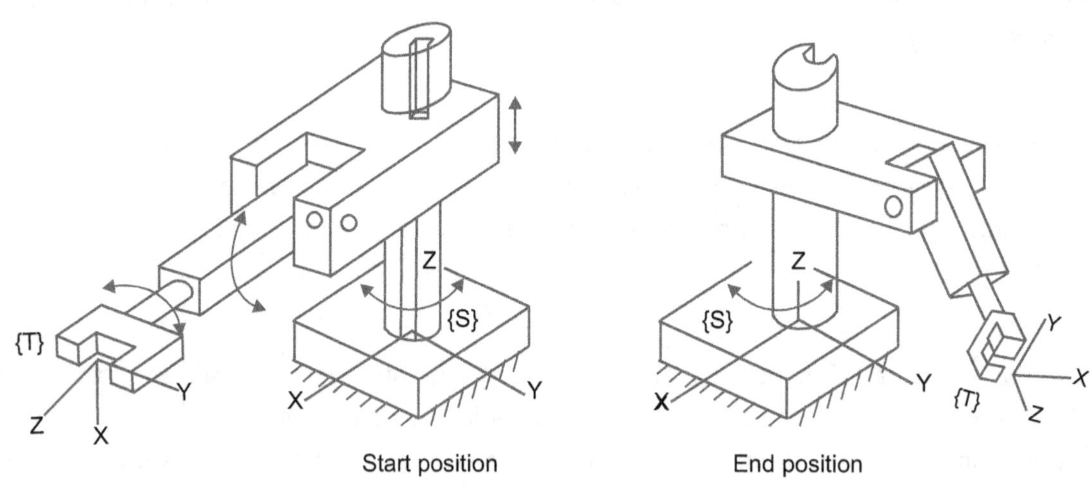

Fig. 5.2

If co-ordinate frames {T} and {S} are attached to the end effector (assuming that it is holding a tool) and to the stationary base, trajectory generation would be simply description of position and orientation of frame {T} with respect to frame {S} from start position to end position. Naturally, time duration and various positions and orientations of {T} between the start and end positions are also important while describing or generating the trajectory.

It may be understood now, that if tool size is changed, in turn if the end effector is opened widely or shrunk, that should not make any difference in the earlier trajectory. Similarly, one can design a totally different configuration of manipulator to follow the same trajectory.

Already, it has been mentioned that there may be multiple trajectories between given two points. Similarly, there may be multiple configurations to trace a given trajectory.

5.3 How to Plan a Trajectory ?

Consider a 2 DoF RR planar manipulator as shown in Fig. 5.3.

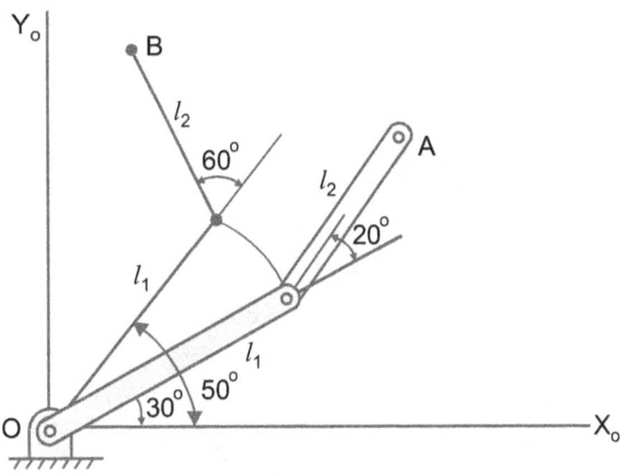

Fig. 5.3

The end effector of the manipulator is initially at point A, located by having inclinations of links as $\alpha = 30°$ and $\beta = 20°$ while the end position of the end effector that is point B may be located by $\alpha = 50°$ and $\beta = 60°$ as shown.

To move end effector of manipulator from A to B, one may plan trajectory as increase in α and β both by same increment say 5°.

So the step-by-step movement of manipulator may be tabulated as:

α	30	35	40	45	50	50	50	50	50
β	20	25	30	35	40	45	50	55	60

And the same is shown in Fig. 5.4.

It is observed that the movements of the two links do not have any specific relation existing between them. Also there is no predicted or predetermined motion of end effector between two given points. Hence, this kind of trajectory planning is called as "Non-normalised movement in Joint Space".

For normalising the movement, one may arithmetically relate movement of the second link with that of the first link. Net change in α is $\Delta\alpha = 20°$ and that in β is $\Delta\beta = 40°$. So one may plan trajectory in such a way that change in β is twice the change in α.

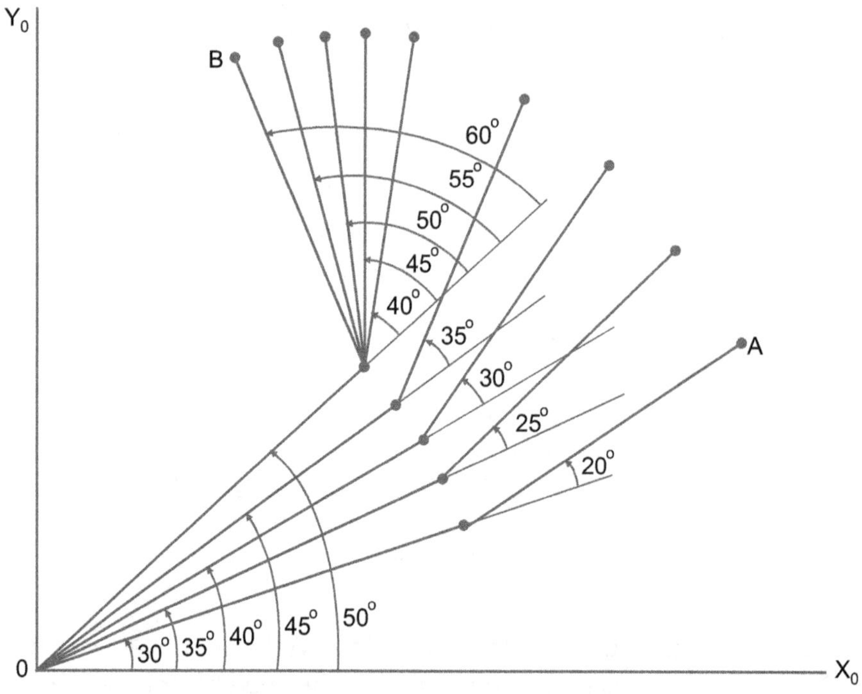

Fig. 5.4

So, the step-by-step movement of manipulator may be tabulated as,

α	30	35	40	45	50
β	20	30	40	50	60

The movement is as shown in Fig. 5.5. Now the link movements have certain relation between them but again there is no predicted or pre-determined motion of end effector between given two points. That means, the end effector movement is still not expressed as a function of time. This kind of planning of trajectory is called as "Normalised movement in Joint Space".

The term "Joint Space" refers to the description of movements of individual joints (or the end effector) with respect to the prior joint. That is movement of ith joint with respect to $(i-1)^{th}$ joint.

Usually, robot operator does not specify movement of joints but is interested in movement of the end effector with respect to X and Y axis drawn at the base of the manipulator. Let us say, the operator wishes to have linear movement of the end effector between A and B. Now to plan this movement, the trajectory planner cannot define any relation between change of angles of links. Thus, this becomes trajectory planning in Cartesian Space.

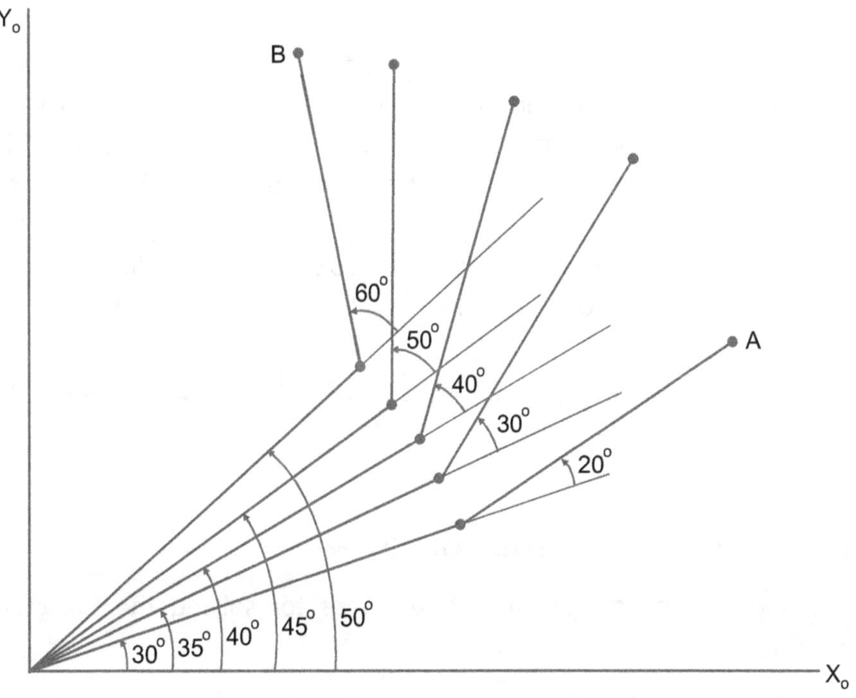

Fig. 5.5

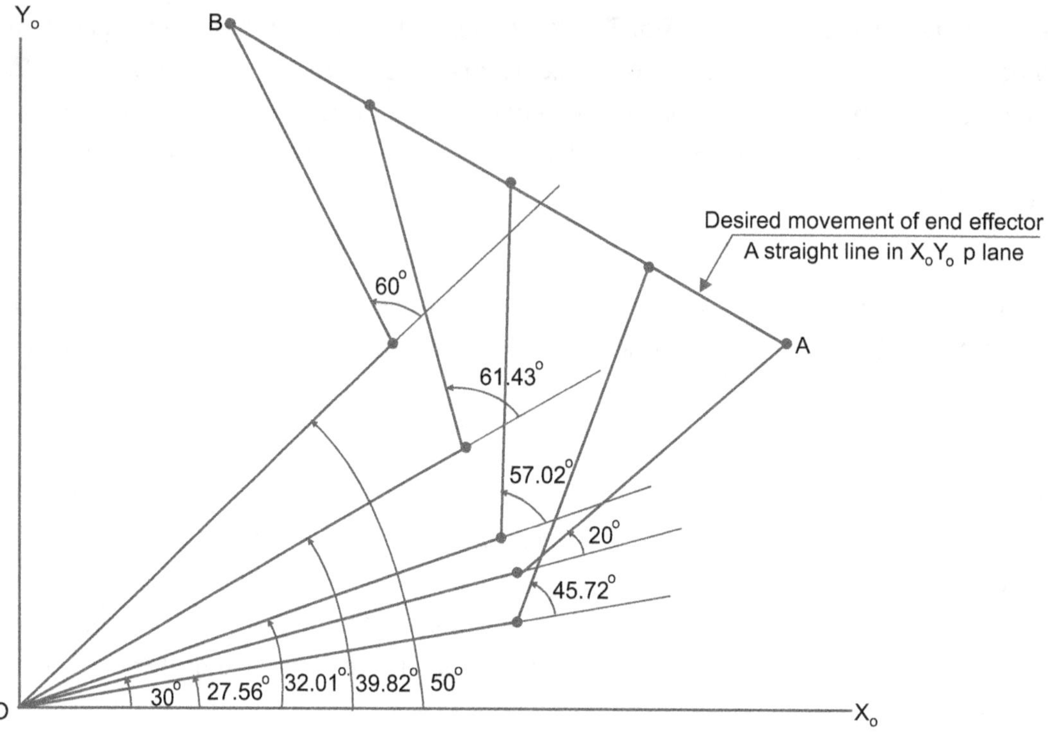

Fig. 5.6

The trajectory planner, in this kind of planning called as "Movement in Cartesian Space", will have to select some via points between the goal points at equal distances. Then will have to find α and β individually for every via point by performing inverse kinematics. The values of α and β found by inverse kinematics are listed below in a table and the movement is shown in Fig. 5.6.

α	30	27.56	32.01	39.82	50
β	20	45.72	57.02	61.43	60

This kind of trajectory planning in Cartesian Space is discussed in detail, later in this chapter.

5.4 Steps in Trajectory Planning

Trajectory planning may be divided into three steps for solving the trajectory planning problem as follows.

1.   Task description: The first step in planning is to identify kind of motion required. The tasks can be classified mainly into three categories.

(a) **Pick and place:** Here task is specified by only initial and final locations of end effector. This is also called as point-to-point motion. Trajectory planner is free to choose any convenient path between the two locations.

(b) **Continuous path:** In addition to start and end locations, if certain series of points is to be traced, as in case of pen of the plotter or continuous arc welding or spray painting, the trajectory planner looses freedom of selecting a path and has to generate algorithm to compute almost all intermediate positions between given two points.

(c) **Pick and place with obstructions:** Due to obstructions at some specific locations, either robot operator or the trajectory planner has to identify intermediate knot points (via points) so that obstruction is avoided. Here, the planner may select a path that passes smoothly through all the points or may select various paths between two consecutive points and blend them with some patches of curves for overall smoothness in motion.

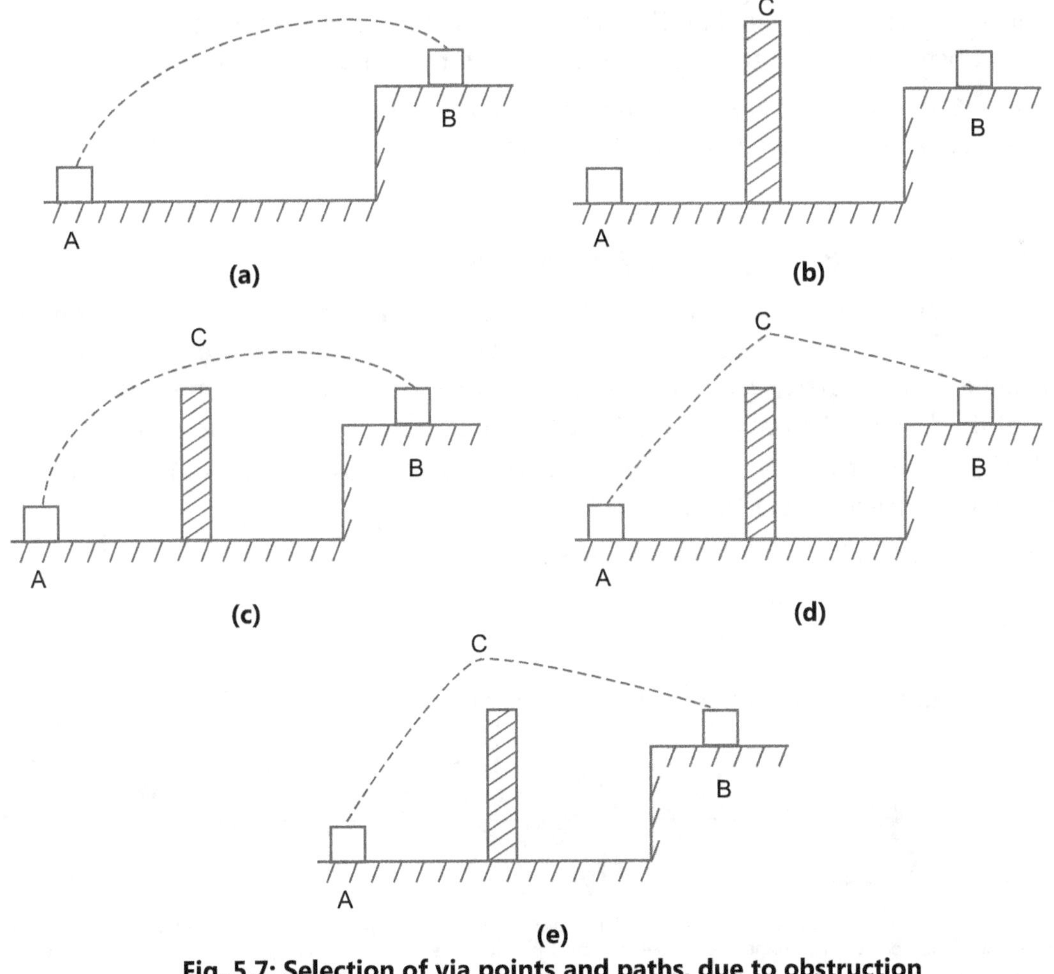

Fig. 5.7: Selection of via points and paths, due to obstruction

This is illustrated by Fig. 5.7. Say an object is to be picked from point A and placed at point B. The planner decides certain path as shown in Fig. 5.7 (a). But the operator reports an obstacle in the path. Hence, a third point C is selected by the planner as in Fig. 5.7 (b). The planner may select single smooth curve passing through A, B and C as shown in Fig. 5.7 (c). The disadvantage here, is the path is too long. So, to reduce length of travel the planner may select two different curves as shown in Fig. 5.7 (d). Here, the path is shortened but the motion of end effector is no longer smooth at point C. To avoid discontinuity, which may result in jerky motion, blending of curves may be done as shown in Fig. 5.7 (e).

The "blending of path" may be more clear after reading the related text, given at the end of this chapter under section "Further Study in Trajectory Planning".

2. Selecting and employing trajectory planning technique: As discussed earlier, two techniques are used to plan the trajectory, namely Joint space trajectory planning and Cartesian space trajectory planning. The first one is used in point-to-point applications, with or without obstructions. And the second one is used for continuous path tasks.

3. Computing the trajectory: Setting up the algorithm and to compute time sequence of the value attained by the parameters of the manipulator.

5.5 Joint Space Trajectory Planning

Consider the task of actuating a joint of robot, so that the end effector will move from one point to other. The joint parameter θ is its orientation with respect to its own X-axis. Let us say magnitude of θ at start i.e. at time $t = t_0$ is known and is θ_0. Similarly, magnitude of θ at end i.e. at time $t = t_f$ is known and is θ_f. Now task of trajectory planner is to select a smooth curve between these two points, which is also known as interpolation curve[*]. The curve to be selected may be linear, circular, polynomials etc.

For simplicity, let the curve initially be linear.

Thus,
$$\frac{\theta_t - \theta_0}{\theta_f - \theta_0} = \frac{t - t_0}{t_f - t_0}$$

Hence, magnitude of joint parameter 'θ_t' at any time 't' may be calculated as,

$$\theta_t = \theta_0 + (\theta_f - \theta_0)\frac{t - t_0}{t_f - t_0} \qquad \dots (5.1)$$

---

[*] Interpolation curve is a curve plotted on 'θ' versus 't'. Thus, trajectory is $\theta = f(t)$ and path is $y = f(x)$. Path traced by the end effector (or a joint) is curve plotted in x-y plane. Hence, linear trajectory in Joint Space, that is, linear interpolation between θ_0 and θ_f will not generate straight line motion of the end effector (or the joint).

Problem 5.1:

The first joint of a 3R robot is to rotate from 30° to 75° in 5 seconds. Determine the linear trajectory and its rotation after 2 seconds.

Solution:

$\theta_0 = 30°$, $\theta_f = 75°$, $t_0 = 0$ seconds, $t_f = 5$ seconds, $t = 2$ seconds.

From equation (6.1),

$$\theta_t = 30 + (75 - 30)\frac{t - 0}{5 - 0}$$

∴ Trajectory is,

$$\boxed{\theta_t = 30 + 9t}$$ **... Ans.**

And at t = 2 seconds, $\theta_{t=2} = 30 + 18 = 48°$ **... Ans.**

In linear trajectory the planner cannot control velocity and/or acceleration because by default the velocity is constant. In above example, velocity of joint, $\dot{\theta}_t = 9°/\text{second}$.

Obviously, if the trajectory planner wishes to have variation in speed, the planner must go for higher order polynomials.

Problem 5.2:

It is desired to have a joint of six-axis robot go from initial angle of 20° to a final angle of 80° in 5 seconds. Using a third degree polynomial, calculate the joint angles at interval of 1 second.

Solution:

$\theta_0 = 20°$, $\theta_f = 80°$, $t_0 = 0$ second, $t_f = 5$ seconds. Find θ at t = 1, 2, 3 and 4 seconds.

Assumption: Initial and final velocities, $\dot{\theta}_i$, $\dot{\theta}_f$ are zero and

$$\theta_t = a_0 + a_1t + a_2t^2 + a_3t^3$$

where a_0, a_1 a_2, a_3 are coefficients in the required polynomial.

$$\text{Velocity, } \dot{\theta}_t = a_1 + 2a_2t + 3a_3t^2$$

At t = 0,

$$\theta_0 = a_0 = 20°$$

and

$$\dot{\theta}_0 = a_1 = 0$$

Similarly, at t = 5,

$$\theta_5 = a_0 + 5a_1 + 25a_2 + 125a_3 = 80$$

$$\Rightarrow 20 + 0 + 25a_2 + 125a_3 = 80$$

∴ $$5a_2 + 25a_3 = 12$$ **... (5.2)**

And
$$\dot{\theta}_5 = a_1 + 10a_2 + 75a_3 = 0$$
$$\Rightarrow 0 + 10a_2 + 75a_3 = 0$$

$\therefore$
$$a_2 = -7.5a_3 \qquad \text{... (5.3)}$$

Substituting for a_2 from equation (5.3) into equation (5.2),
$$5 \times (-7.5a_3) + 25a_3 = 12$$

$\therefore \qquad -37.5a_3 + 25a_3 = 12$

$\therefore \quad a_3 = -0.96$ and from equation (5.3), $a_2 = 7.2$

$\therefore \quad$ Trajectory is,

$$\theta_t = 20 + 7.2t^2 - 0.96t^3$$

$\therefore \quad$ At $\quad t = 1 \qquad \theta_1 = 20 + 7.2 - 0.96 \qquad\qquad = 26.24°$

$\qquad\qquad\quad t = 2 \qquad \theta_2 = 20 + 7.2 \times 2 - 0.96 \times 4 \quad = 41.12°$

$\qquad\qquad\quad t = 3 \qquad \theta_3 = 20 + 7.2 \times 3 - 0.96 \times 9 \quad = 58.88°$

$\qquad\qquad\quad t = 4 \qquad \theta_4 = 20 + 7.2 \times 4 - 0.96 \times 16 = 73.76°$

As further observations with the same problem, we may calculate joint velocities and accelerations as follows:

$$\dot{\theta}_t = 14.4t - 2.88t^2$$

and
$$\ddot{\theta}_t = 14.4 - 5.76\,t$$

Joint velocities

at $\qquad\quad t = 0 \qquad \dot{\theta}_1 = 0°/sec$

$\qquad\qquad\quad t = 1 \qquad \dot{\theta}_1 = 11.52°/sec$

$\qquad\qquad\quad t = 2 \qquad \dot{\theta}_2 = 17.28°/sec$

$\qquad\qquad\quad t = 3 \qquad \dot{\theta}_3 = 17.28°/sec$

$\qquad\qquad\quad t = 4 \qquad \dot{\theta}_4 = 11.52°/sec$

$\qquad\qquad\quad t = 5 \qquad \dot{\theta}_5 = 0°/sec$

Joint accelerations

at $\qquad\quad t = 0 \qquad \ddot{\theta}_0 = 14.4°/sec^2$

$\qquad\qquad\quad t = 1 \qquad \ddot{\theta}_1 = 8.64°/sec^2$

$\qquad\qquad\quad t = 2 \qquad \ddot{\theta}_2 = 2.88°/sec^2$

$$t = 3 \qquad \ddot{\theta}_3 = -2.88°/\text{sec}^2$$

$$t = 4 \qquad \ddot{\theta}_4 = -8.64°/\text{sec}^2$$

$$t = 5 \qquad \ddot{\theta}_5 = -14.4°/\text{sec}^2$$

Fig. 5.8 gives time history plot of the joint from 0 seconds to 5 seconds.

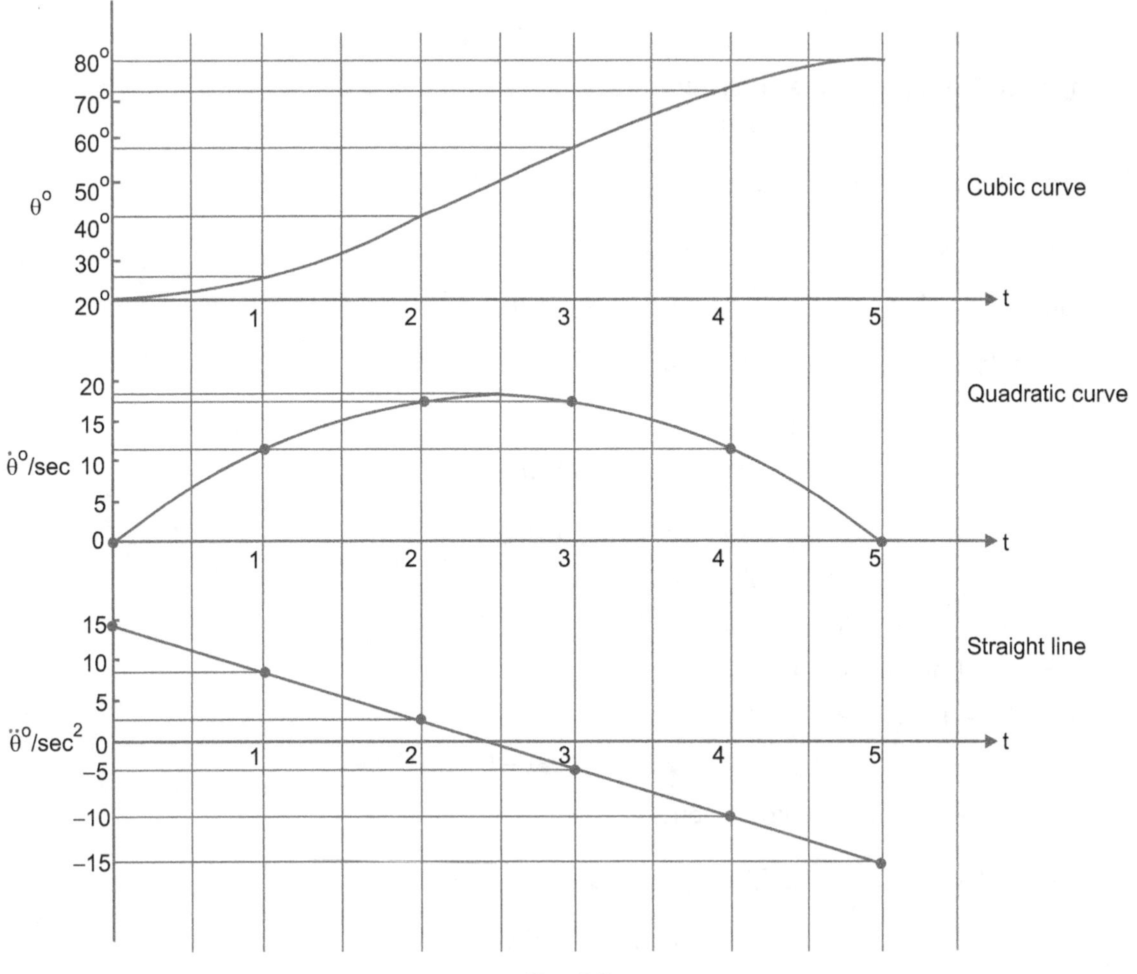

Fig. 5.8

The above example of a cubic polynomial demonstrates variation in joint parameters. In practice, many times it may be required to have certain value of certain parameter at certain time. Following example illustrates planning of such trajectory where position and velocity must have certain values at certain time in movement of the actuated joint.

Problem 5.3:

Determine trajectory for the joint of previous problem, so that, in addition to previous data, joint will have position of 53° and joint velocity 20°/sec. at t = 3 sec.

Solution:

In this situation, it is quite obvious that the trajectory will have discontinuity[*] at t = 3 seconds and the trajectory will be a set of two expressions, one from t = 0 to t = 3 and other from t = 3 to t = 5.

The first segment of trajectory may be written as,

$$\theta_{t_1} = b_0 + b_1 t + b_2 t^2 + b_3 t^3 \qquad \text{for } 0 \le t \le 3$$

and the second segment may be written as,

$$\theta_{t_2} = c_0 + c_1 t + c_2 t^2 + c_3 t^3 \qquad \text{for } 3 \le t \le 5$$

To determine the b-coefficients

$$\theta_0 = 20°,\ \theta_3 = 53°,\ \dot{\theta}_0 = 0°/sec,\ \dot{\theta}_3 = 20°/sec$$

and
$$\dot{\theta}_{t_1} = b_1 + 2b_2 t + 3b_3 t^2$$

At t = 0,
$$\theta_0 = 20° = b_0$$

$$\dot{\theta}_0 = 0 = b_1$$

And at t = 3,
$$\theta_3 = 53° = b_0 + 3b_1 + 9b_2 + 27b_3$$

$$\dot{\theta}_3 = 20 = b_1 + 6b_2 + 27b_3$$

∴
$$3b_2 + 9b_3 = 11$$

$$6b_2 + 27b_3 = 20$$

Solving above equations,

$$b_2 = 4.3333,\ b_3 = -0.2222$$

∴
$$\theta_{t_1} = 20 + 4.3333t^2 - 0.2222t^3 \qquad\qquad \text{... (5.4)}$$

Now to determine all c-coefficients,

$$\theta_3 = 53°,\ \theta_5 = 80°,\ \dot{\theta}_3 = 20°/sec,\ \dot{\theta}_5 = 0°/sec.$$

and
$$\dot{\theta}_{t_2} = c_1 + 2c_2 t + 3c_3 t^2$$

At t = 3,
$$\theta_3 = 53 = c_0 + 3c_1 + 9c_2 + 27c_3$$

$$\dot{\theta}_3 = 20 = c_1 + 6c_2 + 27c_3$$

---

[*]   Discontinuity of curve does not necessarily be a physical gap, it is a point where curve will have two tangents in different directions, in other words, it is a corner created by intersection of two smooth curves.

Thus, for 4 unknowns we have 4 linear simultaneous equations as follows:

$$c_0 + 3c_1 + 9c_2 + 27c_3 = 53$$
$$c_1 + 6c_2 + 27c_3 = 20$$
$$c_0 + 5c_1 + 25c_2 + 125c_3 = 80$$
$$c_1 + 10c_2 + 75c_3 = 0$$

Solving above equations, we get,

$c_0 = 42.5$, $c_1 = -28.75$, $c_2 = 16$, $c_3 = -1.75$.

$$\therefore \qquad \theta_{t_2} = 42.5 - 28.75t + 16t^2 - 1.75t^3 \qquad \text{... (5.5)}$$

Equations (5.4) and (5.5) put together will define the required trajectory. Thus,

$$\theta_{t_1} = 20 + 4.3333t^2 - 0.222t^3 \qquad \text{for } 0 \le t \le 3$$

$$\theta_{t_2} = 42.5 - 28.75t + 16t^2 - 1.75t^3 \qquad \text{for } 3 \le t \le 5$$

For further observations, let us get expressions for velocity and acceleration.
Velocity is given by,

$$\dot{\theta}_{t_1} = 8.6667t - 0.6667t^2 \qquad \text{for } 0 \le t \le 3$$

$$\dot{\theta}_{t_2} = -28.75 + 32t - 5.25t^2 \qquad \text{for } 3 \le t \le 5$$

and acceleration is given by,

$$\ddot{\theta}_{t_1} = 8.6667 - 1.333t \qquad \text{for } 0 \le t \le 3$$

$$\ddot{\theta}_{t_2} = 32 - 10.5t \qquad \text{for } 3 \le t \le 5$$

Fig. 5.9 shows variation in all the above parameters. As expected, every curve has discontinuity at the via point reached at $t = 3$ seconds. The position, velocity and acceleration at various timings are tabulated below.

t (sec)	θ (deg)	$\dot{\theta}$ (°/sec)	$\ddot{\theta}$ (°/sec^2)
0.0	20.00	0.00	8.67
0.5	21.06	4.17	8.00
1.0	24.11	8.00	7.33
1.5	29.00	11.50	6.67
2.0	35.56	14.67	6.00
2.5	43.61	17.50	5.33
3.0	53.00	20.00	4.66 & 0.50
3.5	62.84	18.94	−4.75
4.0	71.50	15.25	−10.00
4.5	77.66	8.94	−15.25
5.0	80.00	0.00	−20.50

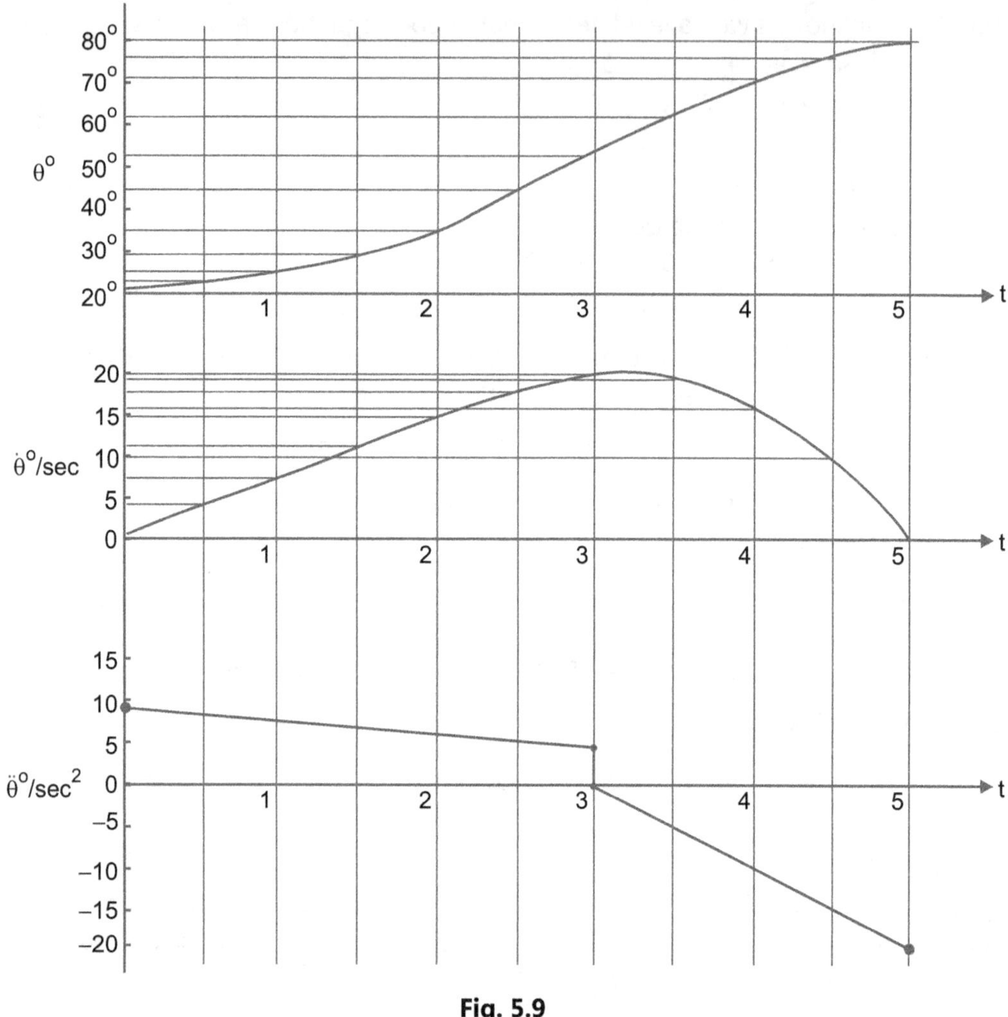

Fig. 5.9

5.6 Geometric Problems with Cartesian Path

There are basically three types of problems while planning trajectory in Cartesian space. The problems are due to limitations of workspace and singularities.

What is a Singularity ?

Singularity is that configuration of a given manipulator where the joint velocities of the configuration are mathematically indeterminate.

If it is required to know the velocity of end effector with respect to the base co-ordinate frame, we obtain time derivative of the kinematic equation of the manipulator. This process is also known as mapping the velocity of end effector from Joint Space to Cartesian Space. We have studied this mapping of velocity already in "LE formulation requirements of spatial manipulator" in "Chapter 5: Dynamics", where we observe that, many of the elements of differential matrix of the joint under study, become zero. Thus, the matrix looses its rank. Eventually, the magnitude of matrix, that is its determinant, may become equal to zero, and the inverse of matrix will not exist. Such a matrix is called Singular matrix and corresponding manipulator configuration (position) is called as a singular configuration or a Singularity.

Usually, any manipulator when reaches a point at its work envelop (the boundary of the workspace), it stretches all of its links and becomes kinematically unstable. In a physical sense, for very small velocity of the end effector, the joints must have very high velocities. For example, consider a slider-crank mechanism which is constrained 2R planar manipulator. When it reaches TDC or BDC position the slider velocity becomes zero, for any angular speed of the crank. That, at the location, inverse kinematics fails to determine joint velocities for given magnitude of the end effector velocity. Such a configuration is called as Singularity.

1. Problems of type 1: Intermediate points unreachable:

Consider a 2R manipulator as shown in Fig. 5.10. Its workspace is an annulus having inside radius $(l_1 - l_2)$ and outside $(l_1 + l_2)$. Due to lack of knowledge of these limitations of workspace if robot operator forces the end effector to move along straight line joining A and B, the end effector will move correctly till point C and will start automatically tracing points along the inner circumference till it reaches point D, then will continue its path as a straight line between D and B. The trajectory planner must understand this problem and plan the trajectory in two segments, as discussed earlier in "Steps in Trajectory Planning".

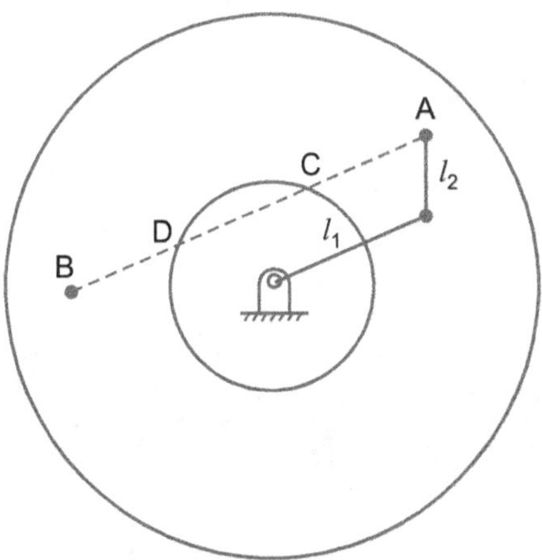

Fig. 5.10

2. Problems of Type 2: High joint velocity near singularity:

It is already known that near singularity, for very small movements of end effector, the joints are required to have high velocities. And, when the end effector approaches the location of singularity, the requirement of joint speed may reach infinite magnitudes. Hence, trajectory planner must avoid not only singularities but the neighbouring positions of singularities, too.

3. Problems of Type 3: Start and goal points reachable in different solutions:

Mainly, these problems arise due to joint limitations. Consider a physical structure of revolute joint made of a slotted end link as shown in Fig. 5.11.

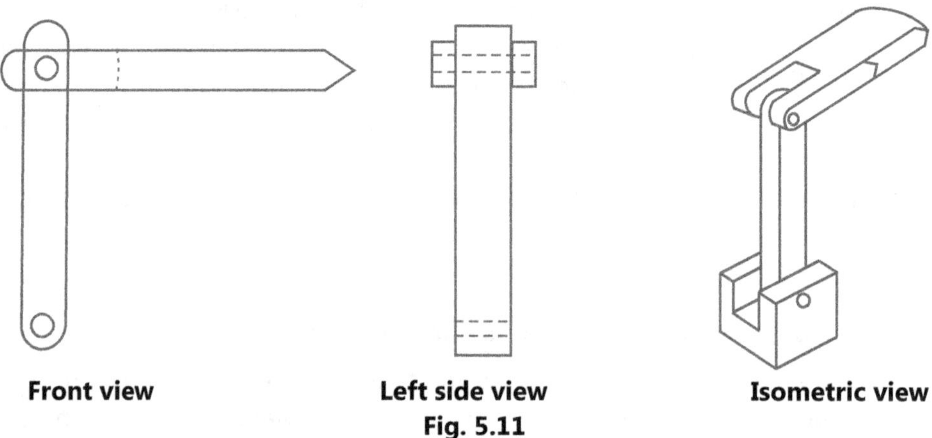

Fig. 5.11

Now, looking at line diagram of this mechanism, as shown in Fig. 5.12 a trajectory planner may plan a straight linear trajectory between the start point A and goal point B. It is quite obvious that both the points A and B will be reached as shown. But due to physical limitation of the joint the second link must be turned almost 270° in anticlockwise direction to reach point B. Thus, tracing a straight line trajectory is not possible, although the end points are reachable.

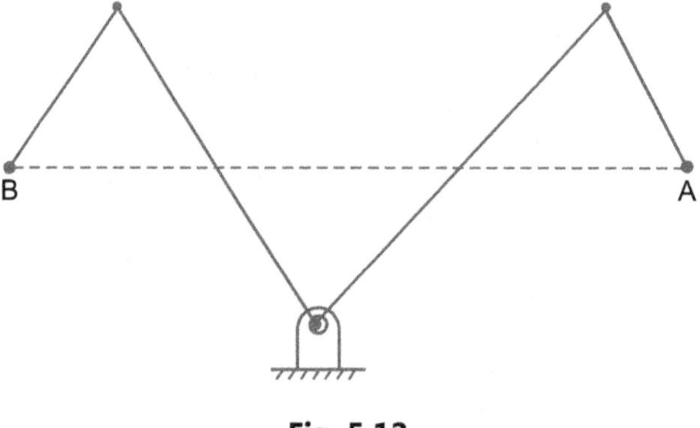

Fig. 5.12

5.7 Cartesian Space Trajectory Planning

As discussed earlier and as shown in Fig. 5.7, usually in practice, the trajectory planner has to plan the trajectory according to robot operators requirement. The requirement of robot operator will never be a description of joint movement in Joint Space but the description of end effector movement in Cartesian Space. This movement may be as simple as linear or it may be an arc of circle or any other complex movement. We will restrict ourselves to understand solution of linear trajectory planning in Cartesian Space.

Problem 5.4:

A two degree-of-freedom RR manipulator having link lengths l_1 = 100 mm and l_2 = 75 mm is shown in Fig. 5.13.

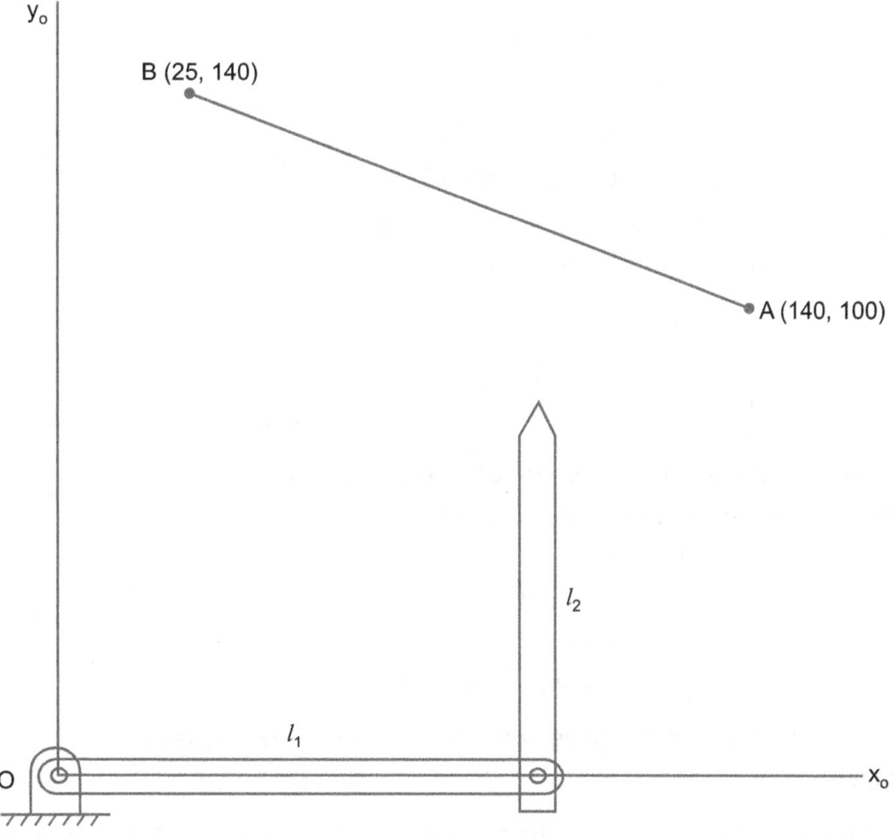

Fig. 5.13

It is required to move its end effector from point A (140, 100) to B (25, 140) along a linear path. Determine configurations of the manipulator from A to B with three intermediate points at equal distances.

Solution:

In such cases, the trajectory planner has to calculate link angles by inverse kinematics. Hence, let us first prepare expressions for solving the inverse kinematics and getting link angles.*

$$x = l_1\, c\theta_1 + l_2\, c\theta_2 \;\Rightarrow\; c\theta_2 = (x - l_1\, c\theta_1)/l_2$$
$$y = l_1\, s\theta_1 + l_2\, s\theta_2 \;\Rightarrow\; s\theta_2 = (y - l_1\, s\theta_1)/l_2 \qquad \text{... (5.6)}$$
$$c\theta_2 = \sqrt{1 - s^2\theta_2}$$

$$\therefore \qquad \frac{(x - l_1\, c\theta_1)^2}{l_2^2} = 1 - \frac{(y - l_1\, s\theta_1)^2}{l_2^2}$$

$$\therefore \qquad x^2 - 2xl_1\, c\theta_1 + l_1^2\, c^2\theta_1 = l_2^2 - y^2 + 2yl_1\, s\theta_1 - l_1^2\, s^2\theta_1$$

$$\therefore \qquad x^2 + y^2 + l_1^2 - l_2^2 = 2yl_1\, s\theta_1 + 2xl_1 c\theta_1$$

Substituting $x^2 + y^2 + l_1^2 - l_2^2 = C$, a constant

and
$$c\theta_1 = \sqrt{1 - s^2\theta_1}$$

$$\therefore \qquad C = 2yl_1\, s\theta_1 + 2xl_1 \sqrt{1 - s^2\theta_1}$$

$$\therefore \qquad C^2 - 4Cyl_1 s\theta_1 + 4y^2 l_1^2\, s^2\theta_1 = 4x^2 l_1^2 - 4x^2 l_1^2\, s^2\theta_1$$

$\therefore$ The quadratic equation of $s\theta_1$ will be

$$4l_1^2\,(x^2 + y^2)\, s^2\theta_1 - 4Cyl_1 s\theta_1 + (C^2 - 4x^2 l_1^2) = 0$$

$$\therefore \qquad s\theta_1 = \frac{4Cyl_1 \pm \sqrt{16C^2 y^2 l_1^2 - 16 l_1^2\,(x^2 + y^2)\,(C^2 - 4x^2 l_1^2)}}{8 l_1^2\,(x^2 + y^2)} \qquad \text{... (5.7)}$$

Equations (5.6) and (5.7) are solution of inverse kinematics.

For determining link angles to locate point A, we have
$l_1 = 100$, $l_2 = 75$, $x = 140$, $y = 100$.

$$\therefore \qquad C = 33975$$

$$\therefore \qquad s\theta_1 = 0.70278 \Rightarrow \theta_1 = 44.65° \text{ and } \theta_2 = 23.35°$$

$$\text{or} \qquad s\theta_1 = 0.44502 \Rightarrow \theta_1 = 26.42° \text{ and } \theta_2 = 47.73°$$

Any one orientation out of above two may be selected. Let us select
$\theta_1 = 26.4245$ and $\theta_2 = 47.72873$

Now to determine link angles, so that correct word end effector is located at point B,
We have, $l_1 = 100$, $l_2 = 75$, $x = 25$, $y = 140$

$$\theta_1 = 110.01° \qquad \text{and} \qquad \theta_2 = 37.86°$$

$$\text{or} \qquad \theta_1 = 49.75° \qquad \text{and} \qquad \theta_2 = 121.89°$$

---

*   Link angles θ_1 and θ_2 are measured with respect to X_0.

For the obvious reason, that the orientation of links will be abruptly changed due to the first pair of answers ($\theta_1 = 110$, $\theta_2 = 37.86$) the pair is rejected. Refer Fig. 5.14.

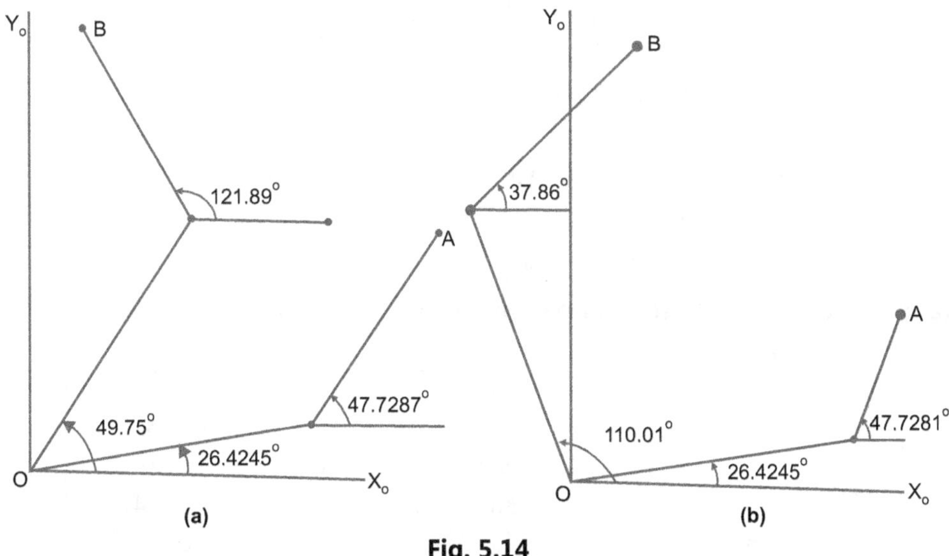

Fig. 5.14

Now let us divide the straight line joining A and B into three equal parts as shown in Fig. 5.15.

The via points V_1, V_2, V_3 are ends of equal length segments.

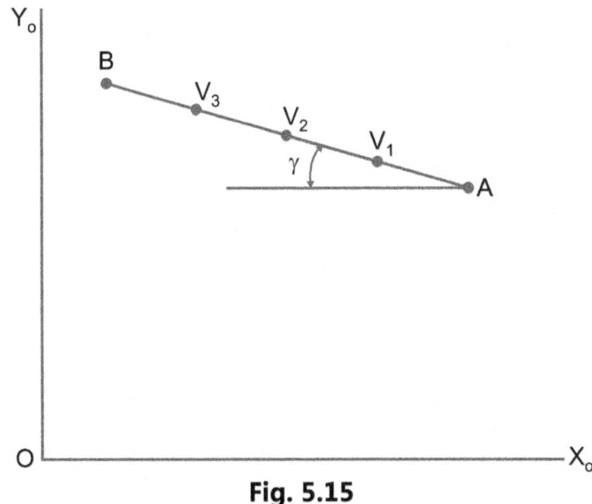

Fig. 5.15

The X and Y co-ordinates of these points may be obtained by following procedure.

$$\text{Distance (AB)} = \sqrt{(x_B - x_A)^2 + (y_B - y_A)^2} = 121.75796$$

$$\text{Angle (AB)} = \gamma^{-1} = \tan^{-1}\frac{|y_B - y_A|}{|x_B - x_A|} = 19.18°$$

$$\text{Distance (AV}_1) = \text{Distance (AB)}/4 = 30.43949$$

$$\text{X co-ordinate of } V_1 = x_A - \text{Distance } (AV_1) \cos \gamma = 111.25$$
$$\text{Y co-ordinate of } V_1 = y_A + \text{Distance } (AV_1) \sin \gamma = 110$$
$$\text{Distance } (AV_2) = \text{Distance } (AB)/2 = 60.87898$$
$$\text{X co-ordinate of } V_2 = x_A - \text{Distance } (AV_2) \cos \gamma = 82.5$$
$$\text{Y co-ordinate of } V_2 = y_A + \text{Distance } (AV_2) \sin \gamma = 120$$
$$\text{Distance } (AV_3) = 3 * \text{Distance } (AB)/4 = 91.31847$$
$$\text{X co-ordinate of } V_3 = x_A - \text{Distance } (AV_3) \cos \gamma = 53.75$$
$$\text{Y co-ordinate of } V_3 = y_A + \text{Distance } (AV_3) \sin \gamma = 130$$

Using equations (5.6) and (5.7) for inverse kinematics, angles θ_1 and θ_2 for every configuration to locate end effector at path points A_1, V_1, V_2, V_3 and B.

Via point	θ_1	θ_2
A	26.42485	47.72873
V_1	21.90698	75.74258
V_2	26.93355	95.08939
V_3	36.72671	110.60944
B	49.74547	121.887

Fig. 5.16 shows the sequence of configurations for linear movement of the end effector in Cartesian space.

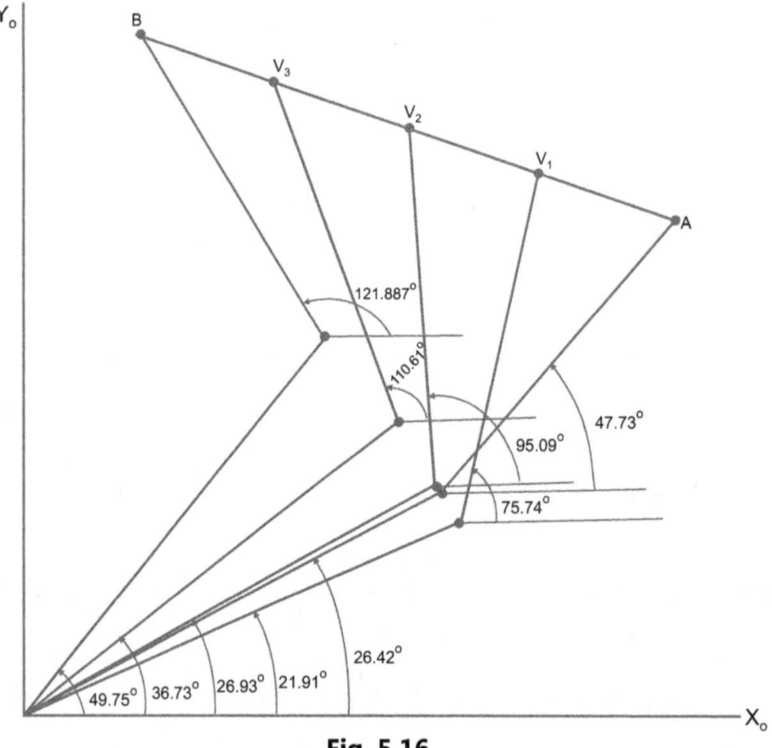

Fig. 5.16

5.8 Further Study in Trajectory Planning

5.8.1 Joint Parameter as a Function of Time

In the process of trajectory planning in the Cartesian space, the trajectory planner calculates the combinations of various joint parameters. This data is not sufficient to actuate the joint. Hence, the trajectory planning will be completed only when the results of Cartesian space trajectory planning are converted to Joint Space and every joint parameter is expressed as a function of time. These time functions will help the trajectory planner to decide the velocity and acceleration to each joint to perform the particular task.

For example, let it be required to move the end effector of the 2 DoF plannar manipulator given in Problem 6.4 from point A (140, 100) to point B (25, 140) in 5 seconds duration. Now, the trajectory planner may select a function either as linear, or quadratic or cubic or any other polynomial equation for individual joint actuations and get the solution as discussed in "Joint Space Trajectory Planning", by assuming suitable additional intermediate points and suitable velocities at various points.

5.8.2   Intermediate Points due to

Variable Speeds and Variable Accelerations

In case of the manipulator and its motion given in Problem 5.4, it is observed that the joint angle of the first joint initially decreases and then increases. Thus, it will have a certain minimum value where velocity of the joint will be zero. Also, before reaching that orientation, the joint will be decelerated and instantaneously, will be accelerated to avoid dead stop of the manipulator. Simultaneously, the other joint must be instantaneously accelerated with a large magnitude, so that a large joint angle is turned in the initial stage. Therefore, the robot must have actuators strong enough to provide large forces necessary to accelerate and decelerate the joints as needed.

To reduce the requirement of large accelerations, the trajectory planner may introduce the intermediate points in such a way that the critical point, where speed of the first joint becomes zero is identified and also the variation in rotation angle and the speed is minimized. In other words, instead of dividing straight line into equal segments, it may be divided in such a way that the variations at the start of actuation and at the end of actuation are lowered. Therefore, the straight line path may be divided with smaller segments at start and end; and with bigger segments at middle portion as shown in Fig. 5.17. Comparing Fig. 5.16 with Fig. 5.17, one may realise the reduction in variation of joint angles.

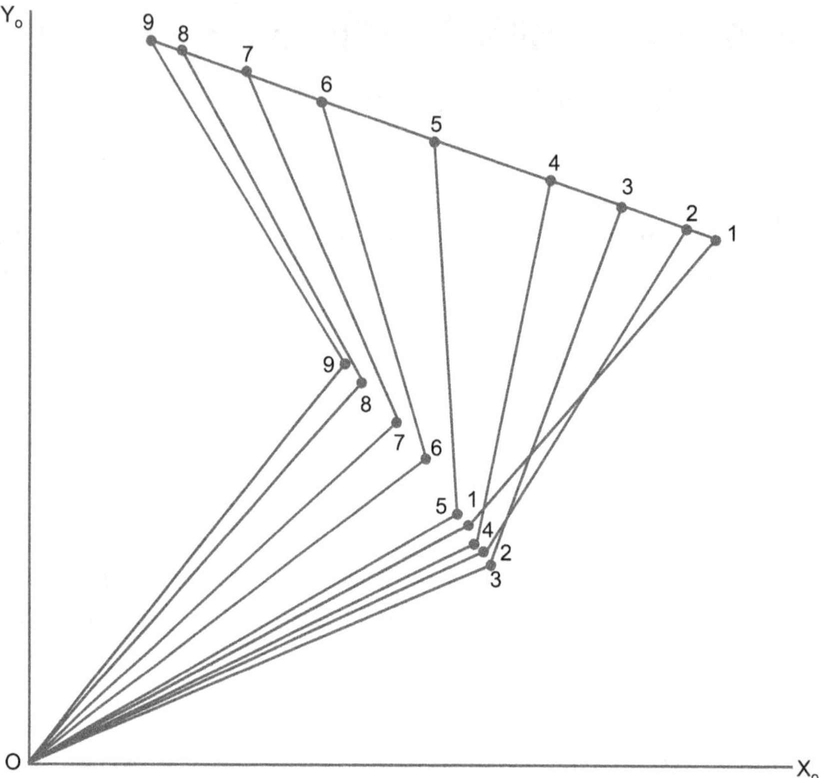

Fig. 5.17: Unequal segments of the path

5.8.3 Non-linear Cartesian Path

Another variation to this trajectory planning is to plan a path that is not straight, but some other path like quadratic. To do this, the co-ordinates of each segment are calculated based on the desired path equation. Interested students may solve Exercise No. 10 for quadratic path of the end effector in Cartesian Space.

In the cases mentioned in 5.8.2 and 5.8.3, the trajectory planner needs to solve the inverse kinematic equations of the manipulator at each point, as it is done in the Solved Problem 5.4.

5.8.4 Blending of Paths

The next level of trajectory planning is to plan it not only between two points but between multiple points and eventually for continuous movements. Assume that the end effector is to move from point A to B and then to C as shown in Fig. 5.18.

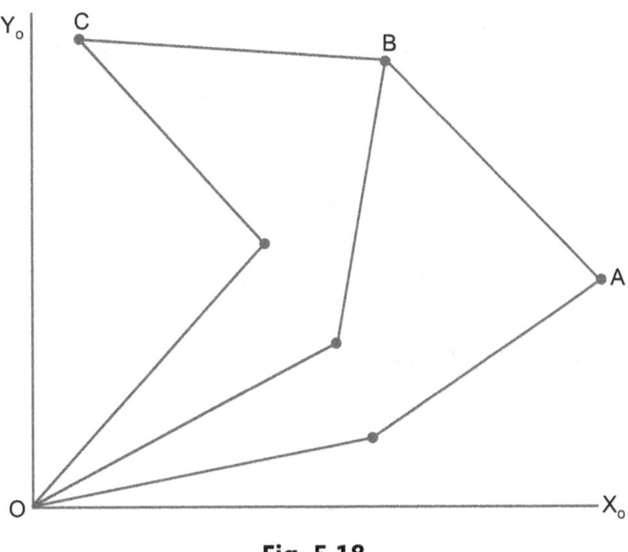

Fig. 5.18

One way to run the manipulator is to accelerate from point A towards B, maintain the speed then decelerate so that it stops at B. Again accelerate from B towards C, Cruise and decelerate to stop at C. This stop-and-go motion will create jerks with unnecessary stops. An alternative way is to blend two portions of motion at point B, so that the end effector will approach point B, decelerate if necessary follow the blended path and accelerate towards C and eventually stop at C. This creates a smooth motion and also reduces stresses on the robot and requires comparatively less energy. Due to blending of the segments the end effector may go through a different point B' and not the desired point B. If it is most importantly necessary to pass end effector exactly through point B, then the trajectory planner must identify another point B" before blending, in such a way that point B is not skipped. Both of these blended paths are shown in Fig. 5.19 (a) and (b).

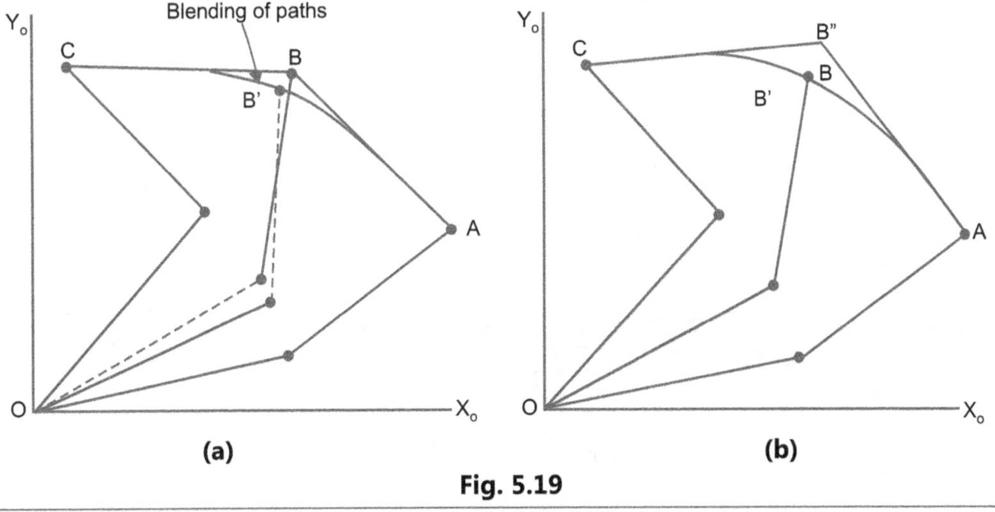

Fig. 5.19

5.9 Trajectory Planning for Spatial Manipulators

In practice, the trajectory planner may require to plan the trajectories that must be traced by spatial manipulators. Although steps in trajectory planning are same, due to complexity in inverse kinematics of spatial manipulators, a huge amount of computations are required to get the joint parameters for each intermediate point location. After obtaining the values of the joint parameters, time function for variation of each joint parameter may be selected and the task of trajectory planning may be completed.

Problem 5.5:

Plan a trajectory for Cartesian configuration as shown in Fig. 5.5 having link parameters L_2, L_5, L_6 as below.

$$L_2 = 300 \text{ mm}$$
$$L_5 = 80 \text{ mm}$$
$$L_6 = 100 \text{ mm}$$

To trace a straight line path from point A (400, 100, 250) to point B (560, 300, 150) so that end effector will have initial and final velocities equal to zero and will have constant acceleration of 5 mm/s^2. While tracing three quarters of the path and then constant deceleration till it reaches the goal point B, without changing orientation of the end effector.

Solution:

Let the total path be divided into three equal segments, by introducing three via points v_1, v_2, v_3.

The via point v_2 is mid point of the line AB. Therefore, its co-ordinates are,

$$x_{V_2} = \frac{x_A + x_B}{2}$$
$$= \frac{400 + 560}{2}$$

$$\therefore \quad x_{V_2} = 480$$

and

$$y_{V_2} = \frac{y_A + y_B}{2}$$
$$= \frac{100 + 300}{2}$$

$$\therefore \quad y_{V_2} = 200$$

Similarly,

$$z_{V_2} = \frac{z_A + z_B}{2}$$
$$= \frac{250 + 150}{2}$$

$$\therefore \quad z_{V_2} = 200$$

The via points V_1 and V_3 are mid points of segments AV_2 and V_2B respectively. So, after finding co-ordinates, all the path points may be tabulated as below.

Point	x-co-ordinate	y-co-ordinate	z-co-ordinate
A	400	100	250
V_1	440	150	225
V_2	480	200	200
V_3	520	250	175
B	560	300	150

As discussed in Problem 5.7, joint parameters L_1, L_3, L_4 may be evaluated for given end effector location by following equations:

$$L_2 + L_4 + L_5 = x$$
$$L_3 = y$$
$$L_1 - L_6 = z$$

The magnitude of joint parameters for each of the path point may be evaluated using above equations. Following table shows joint parameters for each location as the path.

Point	L_1	L_3	L_4
A	350	100	20
V_1	325	150	60
V_2	300	200	100
V_3	275	250	140
B	250	300	180

The end effector has a constant acceleration of 5 mm/s^2 for the first three quarters of the total path, that is between point A and point V_3. This acceleration vector may be written as,

$$\bar{a}_1 = \text{Magnitude (direction vector)}$$

$$= 5 \left[\frac{(x_{V_3} - x_A)\, i_x + (y_{V_3} - y_A)\, j_y + (z_{V_3} - z_A)\, k_z}{\sqrt{(x_{V_3} - x_A)^2 + (y_{V_3} - y_A)^2 + (z_{V_3} - z_A)^2}} \right]$$

$$= 5 \left[\frac{120\, i_x + 150\, j_y - 75\, k_z}{\sqrt{120^2 + 150^2 + 75^2}} \right]$$

$$= 5\, (0.5819\, i_x + 0.7274\, j_y - 0.3637\, k_z)$$

$$\therefore \qquad \bar{a}_1 = 2.9095\, i_x + 3.637\, j_y - 1.8185\, k_z \qquad \qquad \dots (5.8)$$

Therefore, accelerations of various joints are,

$$\text{Acceleration of joint 1} = \ddot{L}_1 = 2.9095 \text{ mm/s}^2$$

$$\text{Acceleration of joint 2} = \ddot{L}_3 = 3.637 \text{ mm/s}^2$$

$$\text{Acceleration of joint 3} = \ddot{L}_4 = -1.8185 \text{ mm/s}^2$$

The time functions for actuations of these joints between point A and point V_3 may be assumed as,

Joint 1: $L_1(t) = b_0 + b_1 t + b_2 t^2 + b_3 t^3 + \ldots$ ... (5.9)

Joint 2: $L_3(t) = c_0 + c_1 t + c_2 t^2 + c_3 t^3 + \ldots$ ... (5.10)

Joint 3: $L_4(t) = d_0 + d_1 t + d_2 t^2 + d_3 t^3 + \ldots$ ... (5.11)

The boundary conditions are –

$$L_1(0) = b_0 = 350 \text{ mm}$$
$$L_3(0) = c_0 = 100 \text{ mm}$$
$$L_4(0) = d_0 = 20 \text{ mm}$$

Differentiating the above three equations with respect to time and using boundary conditions for velocity of joints at initial point.

$$\dot{L}_1(0) = b_1 = 0$$

$$\dot{L}_3(0) = c_1 = 0$$

$$\dot{L}_4(0) = d_1 = 0$$

The next derivative will give acceleration,

$$\therefore \quad \ddot{L}_1(0) = 2b_2 = 2.9095 \text{ mm/s}^2$$

$$\ddot{L}_3(0) = 2c_2 = 3.637 \text{ mm/s}^2$$

$$\ddot{L}_4(0) = 2d_2 = -1.8185 \text{ mm/s}^2$$

As the acceleration is constant, all next derivatives will be equal to zero. That means every time function between point A and point V_3 is a quadratic polynomial. These time functions are listed below.

$$L_1(t) = 350 + 1.45475\, t^2 \qquad \ldots (5.12)$$
$$L_3(t) = 100 + 1.8185\, t^2 \qquad \ldots (5.13)$$
$$L_4(t) = 20 - 0.90925\, t^2 \qquad \ldots (5.14)$$

To obtain time function of the joints for tracing path between point V_3 and point B, we will require the boundary conditions. To get the boundary conditions we need to determine total working time of manipulator, that is, total time of travel from point A to point B.

Let the conditions reach point V_3 in t_1 seconds.

Applying Newton's Law of motion,

$$s = ut + \frac{1}{2}at^2 \qquad \qquad ... (5.15)$$

where, s = Distance travelled

$$= \sqrt{120^2 + 150^2 + 75^2}$$

$\therefore$
$$s = 206.2159 \text{ mm}$$
$$u = \text{Initial velocity}$$
$$= 0 \text{ mm/s}$$
$$a = \text{Acceleration}$$
$$= a_1 = 5 \text{ mm/s}^2$$
$$t = \text{time of travel}$$
$$= t_1 \text{ seconds}$$

$\therefore$
$$206.2159 = 0 + \frac{5}{2} \times t_1^2$$

$\therefore$ Time of travel from point A to point V_3 is,

$$t_1 = 9.0822 \text{ seconds}$$

Also, velocity of end effector at point V_3,

$$V = u + a_1t_1$$
$$= 0 + 5 \times 9.0822$$

$\therefore$
$$V = 45.411 \text{ mm/s}$$

For the second part of travel, this velocity is the initial velocity.

Final velocity at point B has to be equal to zero.

Using another law of motion, we will determine the magnitude of deceleration.

$$V_2 = u^2 + 2as$$

where,

$$v = \text{Final velocity between point } V_3 \text{ and point B}$$
$$= 0 \text{ m/s}$$
$$u = \text{Initial velocity between point } V_3 \text{ and point B}$$
$$= 45.411 \text{ m/s}$$
$$s = \text{Distance between point } V_3 \text{ and point B}$$
$$= \sqrt{40^2 + 50^2 + 25^2}$$
$$= 68.7386 \text{ mm}$$
$$a = \text{Acceleration} = a_2$$

$\therefore$ Acceleration of the end effector (deceleration in true sense) between point V_3 and point B is,

$$a_2 = -15 \text{ mm/s}^2$$

The acceleration a_2 may be written in vector form as,

$$\bar{a}_2 = \text{Magnitude (direction vector)}$$

The direction vector is same for segment AV_3 and segment V_3B.

$\therefore$
$$\bar{a}_2 = -15\,(0.5819\,i_x + 0.7274\,j_y - 0.3637\,k_z)$$

$\therefore$
$$\bar{a}_2 = -8.8365\,i_x - 10.911\,j_y + 5.4555\,k_z \qquad \text{... (5.16)}$$

Therefore, accelerations of various joints are,

$$\text{Acceleration of joint 1} = \ddot{L}_1 = -8.8365 \text{ mm/s}^2$$

$$\text{Acceleration of joint 2} = \ddot{L}_3 = -10.911 \text{ mm/s}^2$$

$$\text{Acceleration of joint 3} = \ddot{L}_4 = 5.4555 \text{ mm/s}^2$$

Let time of travel from point V_3 to point B be t_2 seconds.

$\therefore$
$$t_2 = \frac{V - u}{a}$$

$$= \frac{0 - 45.411}{-15}$$

$\therefore \qquad t_2 = 3.0274 \text{ seconds}$

$\therefore \qquad \text{Total time of travel} = t_1 + t_2 = 12.1096 \text{ seconds}$

That means the end effector will reach the goal point B in 12.1096 seconds.

The time functions for actuations of various joints between point V_3 and point B may be assumed to be quadratic functions, because of constant acceleration; they are listed as below.

Joint 1:	$L_1(t) = e_0 + e_1 t + e_2 t^2$	... (5.17)
Joint 2:	$L_3(t) = f_0 + f_1 t + f_2 t^2$	... (5.18)
Joint 3:	$L_4(t) = g_0 + g_1 t + g_2 t^2$	... (5.19)

The boundary conditions based on displacements are

$$L_1 (9.0822) = 275 = e_0 + 9.0822\, e_1 + 82.4864\, e_2 \qquad \text{... (5.20)}$$
$$L_3 (9.0822) = 250 = f_0 + 9.0822\, f_1 + 82.4864\, f_2 \qquad \text{... (5.21)}$$
$$L_4 (9.0822) = 140 = g_0 + 9.0822\, g_1 + 82.4864\, g_2 \qquad \text{... (5.22)}$$
$$L_1 (12.1096) = 250 = e_0 + 12.1096\, e_1 + 146.6424\, e_2 \qquad \text{... (5.23)}$$
$$L_3 (12.1096) = 300 = f_0 + 12.1096\, f_1 + 146.6424\, f_2 \qquad \text{... (5.24)}$$
$$L_4 (12.1096) = 180 = g_0 + 12.1096\, g_1 + 146.6424\, g_2 \qquad \text{... (5.25)}$$

Boundary conditions based on velocity are

$$\dot{L}_1 (12.1096) = 0 = e_1 + 24.2192\, e_2 \qquad \text{... (5.26)}$$

$$\dot{L}_3 (12.1096) = 0 = f_1 + 24.2192\, f_2 \qquad \text{... (5.27)}$$

$$\dot{L}_4 (12.1096) = 0 = g_1 + 24.2192\, g_2 \qquad \text{... (5.28)}$$

From equations (5.20), (5.23) and (5.26), we get,

$e_0 = 650$, $e_1 = -66.0627$, $e_2 = 2.7277$

From equations (5.21), (5.24) and (5.27), we get,

$f_0 = -500$, $f_1 = 132.1254$, $f_2 = -5.4554$

From equations (5.22), (5.25) and (5.28), we get,

$g_0 = -460$, $g_1 = 105.7$, $g_2 = -4.3643$

$\therefore$ The joint functions (5.17), (5.18) and (5.19) may be rewritten as,

$$L_1(t) = 650 - 66.0627\, t + 2.7277\, t^2 \qquad \text{... (5.29)}$$
$$L_3(t) = -500 + 132.1254\, t - 5.4554\, t^2 \qquad \text{... (5.30)}$$
$$L_4(t) = -460 + 105.7\, t - 4.3643\, t^2 \qquad \text{... (5.31)}$$

Thus, equations (5.12), (5.13), (5.14), (5.29), (5.30) and (5.31) are solutions of the desired trajectory planning.

The velocities and acceleration of the joints may be obtained by differentiating the above six equations with respect to time. The velocities of the joints between point A and point V_3 will be,

$$\dot{L}_1 = 2.9095\, t$$

$$\dot{L}_3 = 3.637\, t$$

$$\dot{L}_4 = -1.8185\, t$$

and between point V_3 and point B,

$$\dot{L}_1 = -66.0627 + 5.4554\, t$$

$$\dot{L}_3 = 132.1254 - 10.9108\, t$$

$$\dot{L}_4 = 105.7 - 8.7286\, t$$

The accelerations will be constant between point A and point V_3 as,

$$\ddot{L}_1 = 2.9095$$

$$\ddot{L}_3 = 3.637$$

$$\ddot{L}_4 = -1.8185$$

and between point V_3 and point B as,

$$\ddot{L}_1 = 5.4554$$

$$\ddot{L}_3 = -10.9108$$

$$\ddot{L}_4 = -8.7286$$

5.10 Introduction to Manipulator Control

The purpose of robot arm control is to maintain the dynamic response of the manipulator in accordance with some prespecified performance criterion. The control requires the knowledge of the mathematical model and some sort of intelligence to act on the model. The mathematical model is obtained from basic physical laws governing robot dynamics and associated devices. The intelligence requires sensory capabilities. The prespecified task of the robot may be divided in two classes, "Contact type task" and "Non-contact type task". Contact type task is one in which force or torque interaction is involved. For example, a robot arm used for spray painting operation, has to grip the spray bottle at start and then keep it moving along a prespecified trajectory. Thus, force interaction is not involved in its operation. On the other hand, if it is required to scrap the paint from a glass panel and wipe it clean the end effector, the scrapping tool in this case, is not to be simply moved along the trajectory, but it must apply a calculated force against the glass panel. Thus in this case end effector interacts with the environment. It continuously applies a constant force against the glass while maintaining its trajectory.

Fig. 5.20 (a) and (b) show both the tasks listed above.

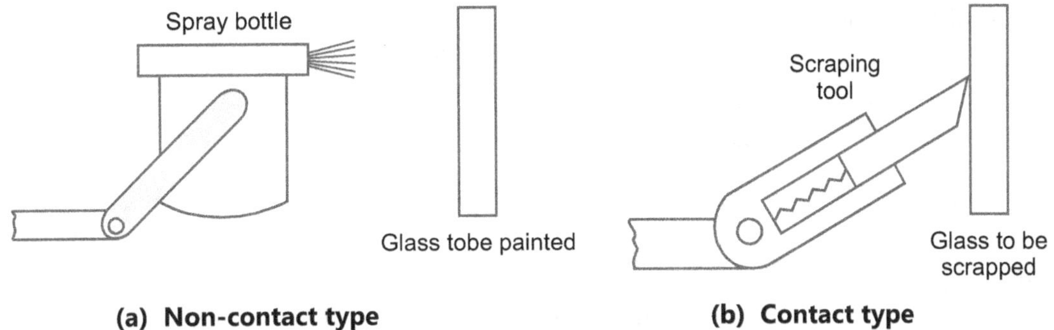

(a) Non-contact type   **(b) Contact type**

Fig. 5.20: Types of tasks

What is control ?

To control means to regulate, to direct or to command. Hence, a control system is an arrangement of different physical elements connected in such a manner so as to regulate to direct or to command the robotic system to perform the prespecified task.

Linearity and Non-linearity of Math Functions and Controls:

There are two types of control systems, namely "Linear control system" and "Non-linear control system". Here, it is important to note that Linear control system is not to be confused with straight line equation or a linear trajectory. Further every straight line equation is not mathematically a linear function. A mathematical function is said to be linear if superimposition principle applies to it. That is,

$$\text{if} \qquad f(a + b) = f(a) + f(b)$$

$$\text{and} \qquad f(\alpha a) = \alpha \cdot f(a)$$

Let us take the function

$$f(x) = 3x$$

$$\text{For } x = 3 \qquad\qquad f(x) = 9$$

$$\text{For } x = 5 \qquad\qquad f(x) = 15$$

Now, $f(3 + 5) = f(8) = 24$

and also $f(3) + f(5) = 24$

Thus, $f(3 + 5) = f(3) + f(5)$

Also, $f(2 \cdot 3) = f(6) = 18$

and $2 \cdot f(3) = 2 \cdot 9 = 18$

Thus, $f(2 \cdot 3) = 2 \cdot f(3)$

Hence, the function $f(x) = 3x$ is linear.

Now, let us change the function slightly as,

$$f(x) = 3x - 2$$

	For x = 3	f(x) = 7
	For x = 5	f(x) = 13
and	For x = 8	f(8) = 22

But
$$f(3) + f(5) = 20$$

Thus,
$$f(3 + 5) \neq f(3) + f(5)$$

and also
$$f(2 \cdot 3) = f(6) = 16$$
$$2 \cdot f(3) = 2 \times 7 = 14$$
$$f(2 \cdot 3) \neq 2f(3)$$

Hence, the function $f(x) = 3x - 2$ is non-linear.

In practice most of the functions are non-linear in nature. Furthermore, for control systems, if the system under study can be modelled by a linear differential equation, for example a spring-mass system shown in Fig. 5.21, then it is said to be a linear control.

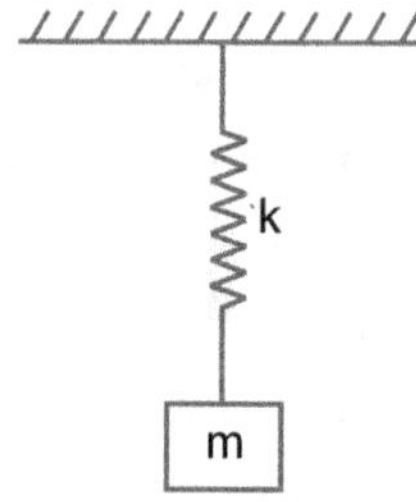

Fig. 5.21: Spring mass system

$$m\ddot{x} + kx = 0$$

We will go into detail of such system later in this chapter.

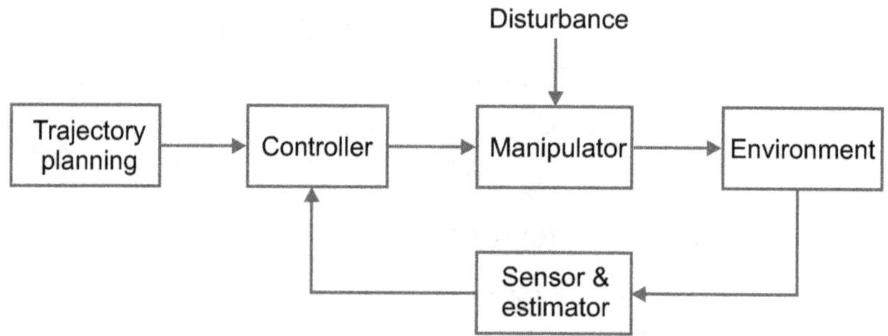

Fig. 5.22: Basic control block diagram for robot manipulator

5.11 Controller Systems

The function of controller is to examine the error between set point and measured value of physical parameter and then determine the action to reduce that error. Thus input to the controller is an error signal. This error between set point value (expected) and measured value (present) is detected by the error detector. The output of error detector is an error signal which is then applied to the controller. Note that error detector finds error only when set point value (s_p) and measured value (m_v) are in same form. Let us see some important terminologies that are required in further discussion.

5.11.1 Error

The error or deviation of the controlled variable from set point is given by,

$$e = r - b \qquad \qquad \text{... (5.32)}$$

where,

$$e = \text{Error in absolute value}$$
$$b = \text{Measured value of variable}$$
$$r = \text{Setpoint value of variable (reference)}$$

Generally, error is expressed in percentage of span of measured value.

$$e_p = \frac{r - b}{(b_{max} - b_{min})} \times 100 \qquad \qquad \text{... (5.33)}$$

5.11.2 Control Parameter Range

This range is associated with the controller output. The controller output as a percent of full scale is given as :

$$P = \frac{u - u_{min}}{u_{max} - u_{min}} \times 100 \qquad \qquad \text{... (5.34)}$$

where,

$$P = \text{Controller output as percent of full scale}$$
$$u = \text{Value of output}$$
$$u_{max} = \text{Maximum value of controlling parameter}$$
$$u_{min} = \text{Minimum value of controlling parameter.}$$

5.11.3 Controller Modes

The controller produces a output (i.e. control signal) to final control element based on input error signal (i.e. set point – measured variable). The objectives of controller are,

(a) Minimum deviation/error and

(b) Minimum duration/time.

The measured value should reach to the set point value within a small time. How it is achieved by the controller ? The answer is : Controller solves some mathematical equations to calculate its output (i.e. control signal). These mathematical equations are called "controller modes" or "controller actions".

There are many mathematical equations available to calculate controller output. All these equations are not required every time. Which equation is suitable for our application ? Selection of mathematical equation (i.e. controller mode) depends upon process characteristics. The process characteristics are well explained in chapter 4.

These are :
(a) Process equation   (b) Process load
(c) Process lag   (d) Self regulation
(e) Capacity of the process.

Controller modes show how controller responds to the error signal. These equations are also called 'control strategies'. To solve these mathematical equations, we need some hardware. According to the hardware used, the controllers are classified as follows.

5.11.4 Types of Controllers

The controllers are broadly classified according to system used as :
1. Pneumatic controllers   2. Hydraulic controllers
3. Electronic controllers

The flapper-nozzle system is building block in pneumatic controller to solve some mathematical equations. Hydraulic controller uses jet valves and pistion-cylinder arrangement for the same.

Electronic controllers are classified into :

(a) Analog controllers : Operational amplifier (op-amps) is the main component.

(b) Digital controllers : Above equations are solved using software in computers, programmable logic controllers, microprocessors, etc.

The purpose of above different types of controller is to solve only mathematical equations (control actions). Type of controller is important specification of a controller. But which equation is suitable for application does not depend upon :
(a) Type of controllers.   (b) Type of processes.

Selection of suitable control action depends only upon process characteristics.

Types of Controller Modes

Fig. 5.23 shows different controller modes.

In discontinuous control mode, the controller output changes in discontinuous manner with the error input. There is a certain controller output for some band of error. If an error occur is more than this band, then only controller output is changed stepwise. These controllers are simplest, cheapest and form the basis of continuous control mode.

There are three types of discontinuous control mode namely : Two position (ON-OFF), Three position (multiposition) and time proportionating (Floating) control mode.

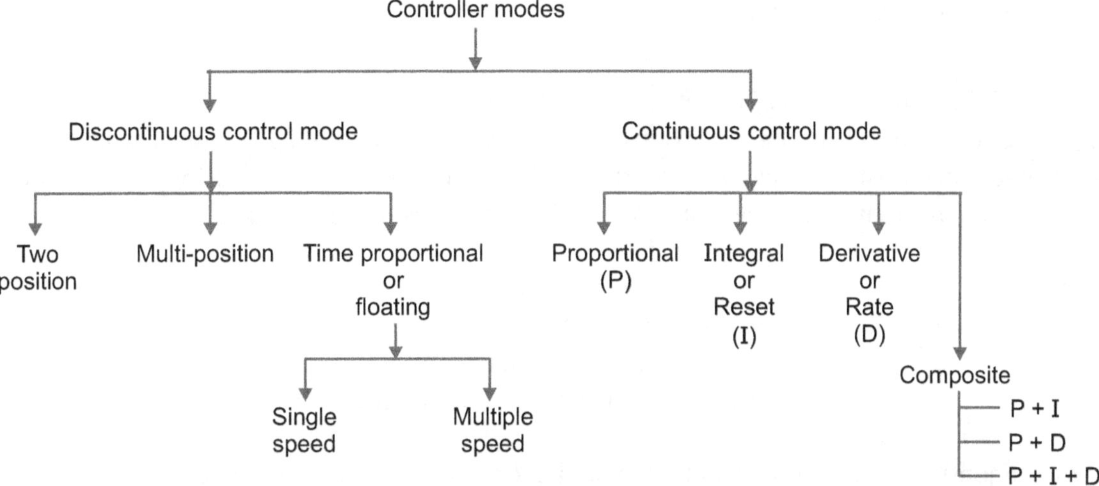

Fig. 5.23: Types of Controller modes

In continuous control mode, the controller output changes in smooth manner (continuously) with the error input. They are more accurate, reliable, effective on disturbances and suitable for complex process. For every value of error, there is certain controller output. There is one-to-one relationship between error and controller output.

According to relationship between error and controller output the different types of continuous control modes are : Proportional (P), Integral (I) or Reset, Derivative or Rate (D). Each mode having some advantages and drawbacks. To collect the advantages of individual mode and to eliminate its drawbacks, these modes are combined together which is called "combinational or composite control mode". It includes Proportional Integral (P + I), Proportional – Derivative (P + D) and Proportional Integral – Derivative (P + I + D) controller mode.

Continuous Controller Mode

In these modes, the controller output changes continuously with the error input. They are more accurate, reliable and effective on disturbances and suitable for complex processes. The types of continuous control modes are according to relationship between controller output and error input. They are :

(a) Proportional (P) control

(b) Integral (I) or Reset control

(c) Derivative (D) or Rate or Anticipatory control

(d) Combinational or Composite control mode

    (i) Proportional + Integral (P+I)

    (ii) Proportional + Derivative (P+D)

    (iii) Proportional + Integral + Derivative (P+I+D)

Let us see every mode in detail.

5.11.5 Proportional Control (P)

In proportional control mode, the controller output (P) changes linearly with the error input (e_p). Linear relationship is given by a straight line equation $y = mx + c$ for x input and y output. Similarly, mathematically, proportional controller is represented as :

$$P = K_p\, e_p + P_o \qquad \qquad \text{... (5.35)}$$

where,
$$P = \text{controller output .... (\%)}$$
$$e_p = \text{error input .... (\%)}$$
$$K_p = \text{proportional gain .... (\%/\%)}$$
$$P_o = \text{controller output when error} = 0 \text{ .... (\%)}$$

Above equation (5.35) represents reverse action of controller, in which when error is negative, controller output is decreasing.

For direct action,

$$P = -K_p e_p + P_o \qquad \qquad \text{... (5.36)}$$

5.11.6 Integral Control Mode [I]

It is also called 'Reset controller' because it resets the offset (error), which is produced in proportional control mode when a disturbance occurs. Integral mode produced zero-error output eventhough a disturbance occurs. In this mode, measured value approaches to setpoint value with no error.

In floating control mode, the controller output changes with some fixed or multiple speed depends upon error zero. But in integral control mode, the controller output changes continuously with the error. It is defined as, "Rate of change of controller output is proportional to the error". Mathematically, it is given by equation (5.37),

$$\frac{dp}{dt} \propto e_p \qquad \qquad \text{... (5.37)}$$

where,

$$\frac{dp}{dt} = \text{Rate of change of controller output ... (\%/sec)}$$

$$e_p = \text{Error ... \%}$$

The equation (5.37) shows that there is continuously change in rate of output until error becomes zero. Thus it resets the error. If the error is large controller output changes with large rate and when error is less, the output changes with small rate.

Conclusion of P, I and D actions : Table 5.1 shows response of P, I and D controller for standard input signal.

Table 5.1: Response of P, I, D actions for test signals

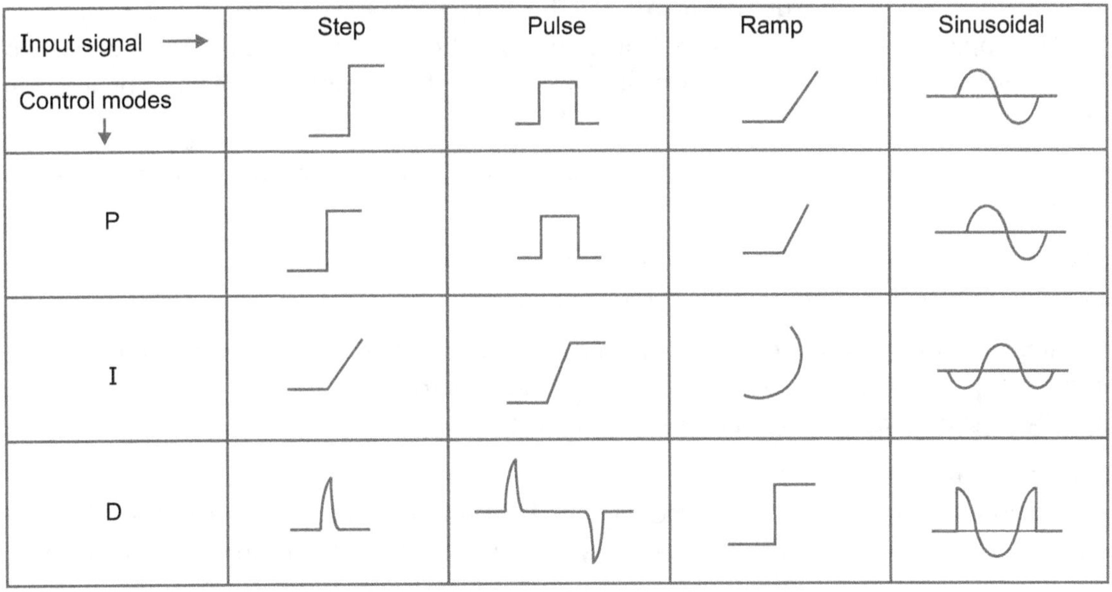

5.11.7 Composite Control Modes

The control modes discussed up till now are not generally used alone because they have certain limitations as shown in Table 5.1. So to collect advantages of each mode and eliminate its drawbacks, these modes are combined together which are called 'composite control modes'. They are :

(a) Proportional – Integral Control Mode (P-I).

(b) Proportional – Derivative Control Mode (P-D).

(c) Proportional – Integral – Derivative Control Mode (P-I-D).

Let us see each mode in detail.

5.11.7.1 *Proportional – Integral Control Mode (P-I)*

This mode is formed by the combination of proportional and integral control modes. Mathematically, it is written as :

$$P = K_p \cdot e_p + K_p \cdot K_I \int_0^t e_p \cdot dt + P_o \qquad \ldots (5.38)$$

where, K_p = Proportional gain

K_I = Integral gain

P_o = Integral term value at $t = 0$

This mode collects advantages as :

(a) One-to-one correspondence between P and e_p.

(b) Eliminates offset produced by P-mode.

It may have drawback of sluggish response. This is very popular control in industry. More than 95% applications required P-I controller. In proportional mode, offset is produced when a load change (disturbance) occurs, offset is fixed error state which is eliminated by integral term.

In PI controller, when error is zero, the controller output is fixed at the value that the integral term had, when error went to zero. Then $P = P_o$.

If the error is not zero, the proportional term contributes a correction and integral term begins to increase or decrease the accumulated value.

The integral term cannot be negative. Thus, it will saturate to zero. This controller has settings of K_p, I_I and P_o. For better control, K_p should be large (small P_B), K_I should be large (small T_I) and $P_o = 50\%$.

Repeats per minute :

This terminology is related to integral term of PI controller. The gain K_I has the effect of causing the controller output to change every unit time by the proportional mode amount.

Taking derivative of equation (5.38),

$$\Delta P = K_I K_p e_p \cdot \Delta t \qquad \ldots (5.39)$$

Here, $K_p e_p$ = Proportional contribution

Δt = Unit time interval

and K_I = Repeats the proportional gain per minute

If e_p = 0.5%

and K_p = 10%

then $K_p e_p$ = 5%

If K_I = 10% / %-min then for every minute the output is increased by 5% times 10%/%-min or 50% or 10 repeats per minute.

It repeats the proportional amount 10 times per minute. The number of minutes I term take to repeat action of p-term.

- **When to select P-I controller :**

  P-I control mode is selected for the processes having following characteristics :
  (a) Frequent or large load changes (disturbances)
  (b) Moderate process lags
  (c) Fast reaction rate
  (d) Any capacity process

5.11.7.2 Proportional-Derivative Control Mode (P-D)

This control mode is result of combination of proportional and derivative control modes. Mathematically, it is written as :

$$P = K_p\, e_p + K_p\, K_D\, \frac{de_p}{dt} + P_o \qquad \text{... (5.40)}$$

where, $\quad K_p$ = Proportional gain ..... %

$\quad K_D$ = Derivative gain ..... $\dfrac{\% \text{ - sec}}{\%}$

$\quad P_o$ = Controller output with no error ...... %

Advantages of these nodes are :
(a) One-to-one correspondence between P and e_p.
(b) Rapid initial response, which handles fast load changes.

But as there is no integral action, the drawback is, it cannot eliminate the offset of proportional action. This controller is used where offset error is acceptable. Because of derivative action, overshoots and undershoots are reduced and it takes less time to get steady-state response. Let us see some problems.

Problem 5.6:

Draw the controller response for given error graph as shown in Fig. 5.24. $K_p = 5$, $K_D = 0.5$ s and $P_o = 20\%$.

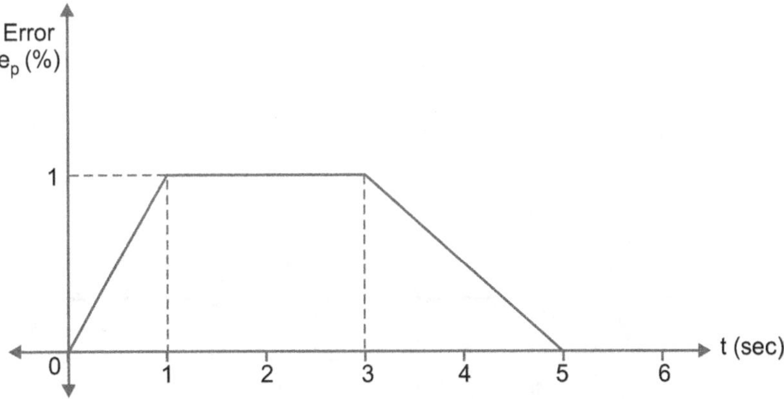

Fig. 5.24: Error input to controller for Problem 5.6

Solution: The proportional-derivative controller output is given by

$$P = K_p\, e_p + K_p\, K_D\, \frac{de_p}{dt} + P_o$$

Over three ranges of error : 0 to 1 sec., 1 to 3 sec. and 3 to 5 sec.

(a) For error range 0 to 1 second,

$$e_p = at$$
$$P_1 = K_p \cdot at + K_p\, K_D \cdot a + P_o$$

Here a = 1%

$$\therefore \qquad P_1 = 5t + 2.5 + 20$$
At t = 0, $\qquad P_1 = 22.5\%$
At t = 1, $\qquad P_1 = 27.5\%$

(b) For error range 1 to 3 seconds $e_p = 1$, $\dfrac{de_p}{dt} = 0$.

$$P_2 = 5 + 5\,(0.5) \times 0 + 20$$
$$P_2 = 25\%$$

From t = 1 to t = 3, controller output = 25%.

(c) For error range 3 to 5 seconds,

$$e_p = -0.5\,t + 2.5$$
Then $\qquad P_3 = 5\,(-0.5\,t + 2.5) + 5(0.5)\,(-0.5) + 20$
$$= -2.5t + 12.5 - 12.5 + 20$$
$$= -2.5t + 31.25$$

These outputs w.r.t. time plotted are as shown in Fig. 5.25.

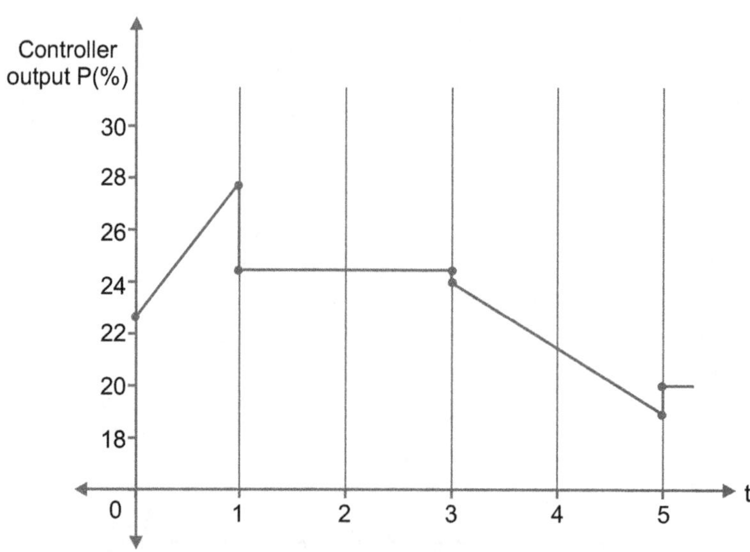

Fig. 5.25: Controller response for Problem 5.6

Problem 5.7:

Draw the P-D controller response for given error graph as shown in Fig. 5.26.

Solution:

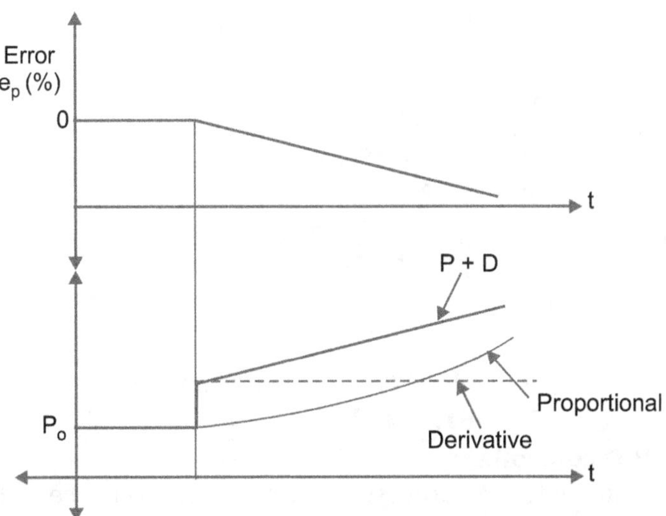

Fig. 5.26 : P + D controller response for Problem 5.7

Problem 5.8:

Draw the PD controller response for given error graph as shown in Fig. 5.27.

Solution:

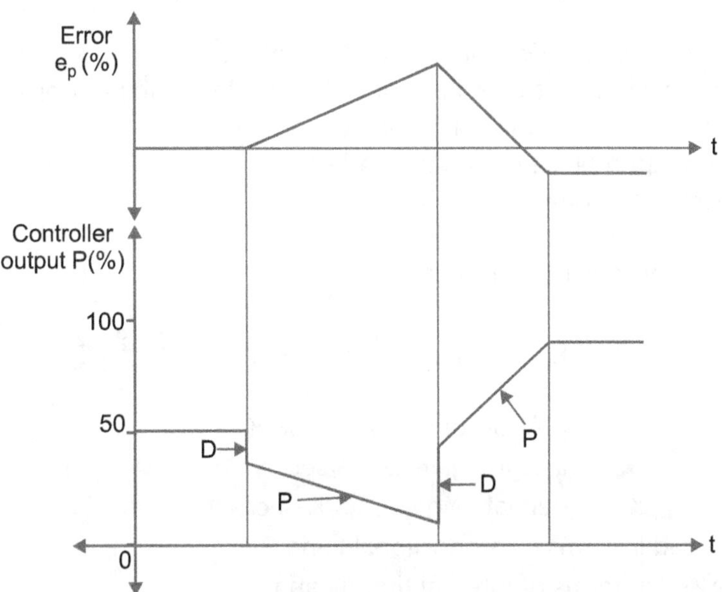

Fig. 5.27: P + D controller response for Problem 5.8

Problem 5.9:

What is the P+D controller output (a) initially, (b) after 2 seconds, if error begins to change from zero at the rate of 1.2%/sec.? The controller has $P_o = 50\%$, $K_p = 4$ and $K_D = 0.4\%–s/\%$.

Solution: The P-D controller has output,

$$P = K_p\, e_p + K_p\, K_D \cdot \frac{de_p}{dt} + P_o$$

(a) Initially, $\qquad e_p = 0, \quad \dfrac{de_p}{dt} = 1.2\%/\text{sec.}$

So $\qquad P = 0 + (4 \times 0.4 \times 1.2) + 50$

$\qquad \mathbf{P = 51.9\%}$ ... **Ans.**

(b) After 2 seconds,

$$e_p = 1.2 + 1.2 = 2.4\%$$

$$\frac{de_p}{dt} = 1.2\%/\text{sec.}$$

So, $\qquad P = (4 \times 2.4) + (4 \times 0.4 \times 1.2) + 50$

$\qquad \mathbf{P = 61.56\%}$ ... **Ans.**

- **When to select P-D controller :**
  P-D controller is suitable for the processes having following process characteristics :
  (a) For fast load changes.
  (b) For large process lags.
  (c) For small or large capacity process.
  (d) For the process where offset generated by the proportional control mode is tolerable.
  (e) For process having large process equation.

5.11.7.3 Proportional-Integral – Derivative (PID) Control Mode

This is one of the powerful but complex controller mode combining proportional, integral and derivative control modes. It has following advantages :

(a) One-to-one correspondence between P and e_p.
(b) Eliminates offset of P-mode.
(c) Provides fast response.

Mathematically, PID controller is written as :

$$P = K_p \cdot e_p + K_p \cdot K_I \int_0^t e_p\, dt + K_p \cdot K_D \cdot \frac{de_p}{dt} + P_I(0) \qquad \text{... (5.41)}$$

where, $\qquad K_p$ = proportional gain ...... %/%

$\qquad K_I$ = integral gain ...... %/sec/%

$\qquad K_D$ = derivative gain .... %-sec/%

K_p is expressed in terms of proportional band P_B,

K_I is expressed in terms of integral time T_I, and

K_D is expressed in terms of derivative time T_D.

For better control P_B should be less, T_I should be less and T_D should be high.

PID controller can be used as P controller by removing I and D actions. Integral action can be removed by using T_I = maximum. Derivative action can be removed by using T_D = 0. Similarly PID controller can be used as PI and PD controller, by removing D-action (T_d = 0) and I-action (T_I = maximum) respectively.

- **When to select PID controller :**
  PID controller is suitable for the processes having following characteristics :
  (a) Large process load changes
  (b) Large process equation
  (c) Large process lags e.g. Temperature process
  (d) Any capacity process

Let us see the changes in transient responses by adding I and D action in P-controller.

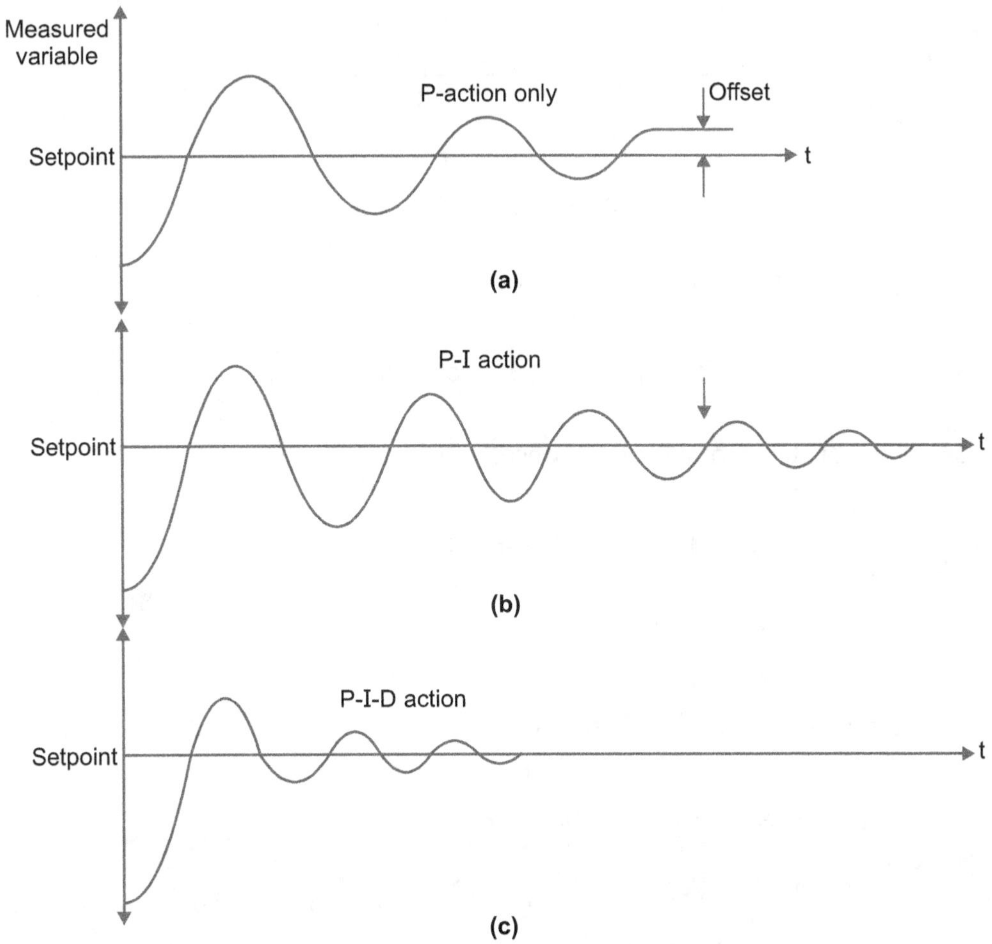

Fig. 5.28: Controller response (a) p-action, (b) P-I action, (c) P-I-D action

Problem 5.10:

What will be the PID output having $K_p = 4$, $K_I = 0.6$, $K_D = 0.5$, $P_o = 50\%$ and subject to error change as shown in Fig. 5.29.

(a) initially

(b) after 2 seconds

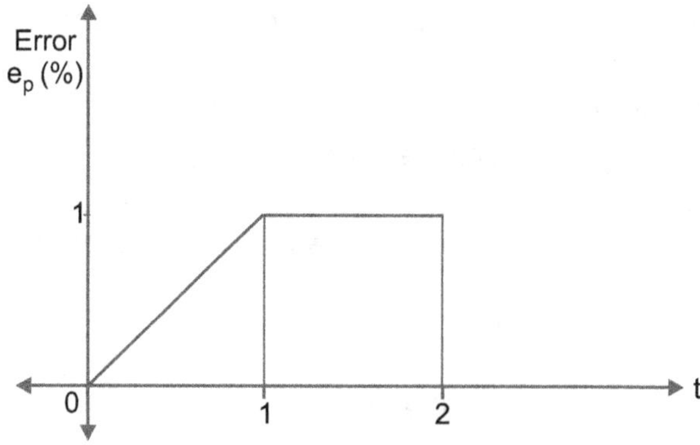

Fig. 5.29: Error graph for Problem 5.10

Solution: The PID controller output is given by

$$P = K_p \cdot e_p + K_p \cdot K_I \int_0^t e_p \, dt + K_p \cdot K_D \cdot \frac{de_p}{dt} + P_o$$

(a) Initially or at start, from error response,

$$e_p = 0, \quad \frac{de_p}{dt} = 1\%/\text{sec}, \quad \int_0^t e_p \cdot dt = 0$$

So,
$$P = 4 \times 0 + 4 \times 0.6 \times 0 + 4 \times 0.5 \times 1 + 50$$

$$\mathbf{P = 52\%} \qquad\qquad \textbf{... Ans.}$$

(b) After 2 seconds, from error response,

$$e_p = 1\%, \quad \frac{de_p}{dt} = 0, \quad \int_0^t e_p \cdot dt = 1.5$$

So,
$$P = (4 \times 1) + (4 \times 0.6 \times 1.5) + (4 \times 0.6 \times 0) + 50$$

$$P = 4 + 3.6 + 0 + 50$$

$$\mathbf{P = 57.6\%} \qquad\qquad \textbf{... Ans.}$$

5.12 Second Order Control System

For a second order control system, relationship between input parameter x and output parameter y is described by a differential equation of the form

$$a_0 y + a_1 \frac{dy}{dx} + a_2 \frac{d^2 y}{dx^2} = b_0 x$$

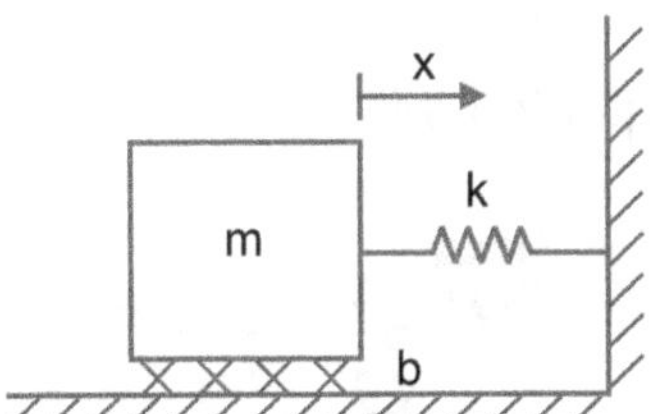

Fig. 5.30: Spring mass system with surface friction

Let us take an example of simple mechanical system, spring-mass system shown in Fig. 5.30.

A block of mass 'm' is attached to a rigid support through a spring having stiffness 'k'. Frictional resistance to the movement of the block is assumed to be proportional to the velocity of block.

There are in all three forces acting on the block one is due to acceleration, other due to spring stiffness and the last due to friction.

A block of mass 'm' is attached to a rigid support through a spring having stiffiness 'k'. Frictional resistance to the movement of the block is assumed to be proportional to the velocity of block.

There are in all three forces acting on the block one is due to acceleration, other due to spring stiffness and the last due to friction.

Hence, the equation of motion becomes,

$$m\ddot{x} + b\dot{x} + kx = 0 \qquad\qquad\qquad \dots (5.42)$$

As the coefficients are constant and degree of the equation is 1 the differential equation is linear. If any one or more of the three characteristics are non-linear the differential equation would become non-linear. For example, if spring has non-linear stiffness characteristic as Force $= qx^3$ instead of Force $= kx$; (where, q and k are constants of proportionality) the equation's degree will change and it will become a non-linear differential equation. Here, we will restrict our scope to discuss solution of linear differential equation only. The solution of above equation is a time function x(t) which describes motion of the block. One must remember that x(0) and $\dot{x}$(0) both cannot be equal to zero. One of the two parameters or both must be non-zero, to disturb the system and set it into motion. Thus, the system is set in motion because of initial displacement and/or initial velocity. If the spring has very less stiffness but surface has greater friction the block would return to its resting position in a very slow, sluggish manner. But if the spring is very stiff and the surface is very smooth, the block would oscillate several times before attaining the state of rest. Thus, different possibilities arise because of the characteristic values of m, b and k. Hence, the equation of motion may be rewritten as characteristic equation

$$ms^2 + bs + k = 0 \qquad \qquad \text{... (5.43)}$$

So that roots of this quadratic equation will help us in getting solution to the differential equation.

The two roots of the quadratic equation will be,

$$s_1 = \frac{-b + \sqrt{b^2 - 4mk}}{2m}$$

$$\text{and} \qquad s_2 = \frac{-b - \sqrt{b^2 - 4mk}}{2m} \qquad \qquad \text{... (5.44)}$$

Due to discriminant $b^2 - 4mk$, there are three possibilities as follows:

1. **The real and unequal roots:** If $b^2 > 4mk$, s_1 and s_2 will be real but not equal to each other. Physical significance of this case is that the friction is dominating characteristic, hence the motion is slow and sluggish and system is said to be **overdamped**. The time function for the motion of block then becomes,

$$x(t) = C_1 e^{s_1 t} + C_2 e^{s_2 t} \qquad \qquad \text{... (5.45)}$$

2. **Complex roots:** If $b^2 < 4mk$, roots s_1 and s_2 will have real and imaginary parts and they will be complex conjugates. The solution of differential equation in this case although same as in previous case, is difficult to use directly since it involves imaginary numbers explicitly. Hence, the solution is manipulated using Euler's formula given below.

$$e^{A+iB} = e^A e^{iB}$$

$$= e^A (\cos B + i \sin B)$$

This manipulation of the solution will be more clear after studying a solved example given at end of this section.

Physically, the block oscillates before it reaches a steady, rest position, due to dominating stiffness characteristic, and the system is said to be **underdamped**.

3. **Real and equal roots:** This is a special case when $b^2 = 4mk$, that is friction and stiffness are "balanced" yielding the fastest possible non-oscillatory motion of the block. The system is said to be **critically damped**.

In this case form of the time function for motion of the block is,

$$x(t) = C_1 e^{s_1 t} + C_2 t e^{s_2 t}$$

$$\text{As} \qquad s_1 = s_2 = s$$

$$x(t) = (C_1 + C_2 t) e^{st} \qquad \qquad \text{... (5.46)}$$

Problem 5.11:

The parameters m, b and k of spring mass system with friction as shown in Fig. 5.30 have values as given below,

$$m = 1, b = 7, k = 10$$

Determine the motion of system if the block is initially at rest and is released from position x = 1.5.

Solution:

As discussed in previous section, characteristic equation is,

$$s^2 + 7s + 10 = 0$$

$$\therefore \quad s_1 = \frac{-7 + \sqrt{49 - 40}}{2} = -2$$

$$\text{and} \quad s_2 = \frac{-7 - \sqrt{49 - 40}}{2} = -5$$

$$\therefore \quad x(t) = C_1 e^{-2t} + C_2 e^{-5t}$$

$$\text{and} \quad \dot{x}(t) = -2C_1 e^{-2t} - 5C_2 e^{-5t}$$

Using boundary conditions as,

$$x(0) = 1.5$$

$$\text{and} \quad \dot{x}(0) = 0$$

$$C_1 + C_2 = 1.5$$

$$\text{and} \quad 2C_1 + 5C_2 = 0$$

$$\therefore \quad C_1 = 2.5$$

$$\text{and} \quad C_2 = -1$$

Hence,

$$x(t) = 2.5 e^{-2t} - e^{-5t}$$

The response of the system is plotted in Fig. 5.31.

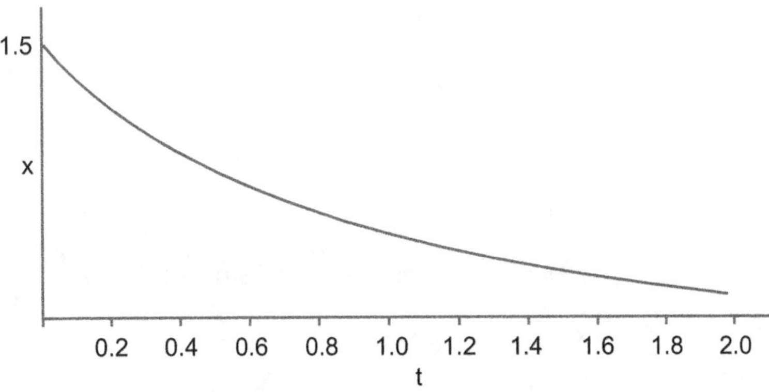

Fig. 5.31: Response of overdamped system

Problem 5.12:

Determine motion for above problem if m = 1, b = 2, k = 2.

Solution:

Characteristic equation becomes,

$$s^2 + 2s + 2 = 0$$

$$\therefore \qquad s_1 = \frac{-2 + \sqrt{4 - 8}}{2} = -1 + i$$

$$\text{and} \qquad s_2 = \frac{-2 - \sqrt{4 - 8}}{2} = -1 - i$$

$$\therefore \qquad x(t) = C_1\, e^{(-1+i)t} + C_2\, e^{-(1+i)t}$$

$$x(t) = C_1\, e^{-t}\, e^{it} + C_2\, e^{-t}\, e^{-it}$$

According to Euler formula

Substituting $\qquad e^{it} = \cos t + i \sin t$

and $\qquad e^{-it} = \cos t - i \sin t$

$$x(t) = C_1\, e^{-t}\,(\cos t + i \sin t) + C_2\, e^{-t}\,(\cos t - i \sin t)$$

$$= C_1\, e^{-t} \cos t + C_1\, i\, e^{-t} \sin t + C_2\, e^{-t} \cos t - C_2\, i\, e^{-t} \sin t$$

$$= (C_1 + C_2)\, e^{-t} \cos t + (C_1 - C_2)\, i\, e^{-t} \sin t$$

$$= C_3\, e^{-t} \cos t + C_4\, i\, e^{-t} \sin t$$

C_3 and C_4 are another constants.

Now substituting

$$C_3 = r \cos \theta$$

and $\qquad C_4 = r \sin \theta$

where, $\qquad r = \sqrt{C_3^2 + C_4^2}$

and $\qquad \theta = \tan^{-1}(C_3/C_4)$

$$x(t) = r\, e^{-t}\, [\cos t \cos \theta + i \sin t \sin \theta]$$

$$x(t) = r\, e^{-t} \cos(t - \theta)$$

and $\qquad \dot{x}(t) = -[r\, e^{-t} \cos(t - \theta) + r\, e^{-t} \sin(t - \theta)]$

To determine the new two unknown constants namely r and θ;

Using initial conditions as $x(0) = 1.5$ and $\dot{x}(0) = 0$

$$1.5 = r \cos \theta$$

and

$$0 = -[r \cos \theta - r \sin \theta]$$

$\therefore \qquad r \cos \theta = r \sin \theta = 1.5$

Thus, $\qquad r^2 \cos^2 \theta + r^2 \sin^2 \theta = 1.5^2 + 1.5^2 = 4.5$

$\therefore \qquad r = \sqrt{4.5}$

and $\qquad \dfrac{r \sin \theta}{r \cos \theta} = \dfrac{1.5}{1.5} = 1 \qquad \theta = 45° = \pi/4$ radians

$\therefore \qquad x(t) = \sqrt{4.5}\ e^{-t} \cos (t - \pi/4)$

The response of the system is plotted in Fig. 5.32.

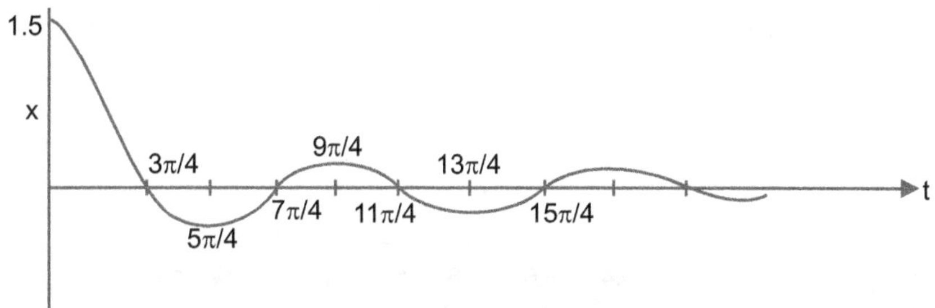

Fig. 5.32: Response of underdamped system

Problem 5.13:

For the system used in previous problems, determine motion if m = 1, b = 6, k = 9.

Solution:

The characteristic equation, in this case is,

$$s^2 + 6s + 9 = 0$$

$\therefore \qquad s_1 = \dfrac{-6 + \sqrt{36 - 36}}{2} = -3$

and $\qquad s_2 = \dfrac{-6 - \sqrt{36 - 36}}{2} = -3$

Thus, $\qquad s_1 = s_2 = s = -3$

$\therefore \qquad x(t) = (C_1 + C_2 t)\ e^{-3t}$

and $\qquad \dot{x}(t) = -3\ C_1 e^{-3t} - 3\ C_2\ t\ e^{-3t} + C_2\ e^{-3t}$

Using the initial conditions,

$$x(0) = 1.5$$

and
$$\dot{x}(0) = 0$$

$$C_1 = 1.5$$

and
$$-3 \times 1.5 + C_2 = 0$$

$$C_2 = 4.5$$

$$\therefore \quad C_2 = 4.5$$

Thus,
$$x(t) = (1.5 + 4.5\,t)\,e^{-3t}$$

The response of the system is plotted in Fig. 5.33.

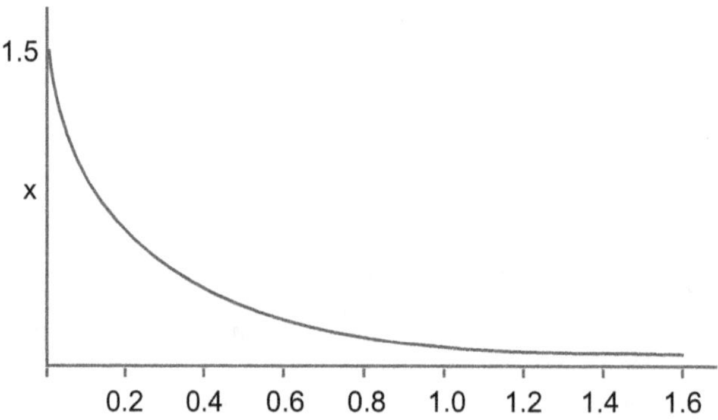

Fig. 5.33: Response of critically damped system

5.12.1 Control Law for the Second-Order System

If the natural response of the system shown in Fig. 5.30 is not as per our requirement, then an external force may be applied on the block so that the system will respond as we wish. That is when the system has certain values of parameters m, b and k, as seen in previous three solved problems the system will have certain fixed natures of response namely overdamped, underdamped and critically damped. If, for given values of m, b and k system has underdamped response but we wish to bring it to the rest as fast as possible by critical damping, then without actually changing the spring and without having control over the actual frictional force offered by the surface, we can apply a calculated external force on the block, so that it will respond like a critically damped system.

To understand this process, let us take a general example which is familiar to us and will make the concept clear.

Imagine a bicycle moving on a horizontal road with initial velocity 'v'. If we do not pedal the wheels, the bicycle will come to a halt, automatically, after certain time 't'. Lets say that this is natural response of the system. Now, if we wish to bring the bicycle to a halt in 't/2' time period, then physically we cannot change the frictional resistance offered by the road, but we can provide equivalent frictional force externally by applying brakes. In other words, we are gaining a frictional force separately, which adds to the frictional resistance offered by the road. Determining this "Gain" in frictional resistance is known as establishing a "control law".

Now, coming back to the spring mass system, if we wish the system to respond in certain manner then determining the modified values of parameters b and/or k is known as establishing the "control law". In other words, we will calculate "Gain" in b and k, which are characteristics of velocity control and position control respectively.

The spring mass system may be provided with an actuator to control its behaviour by applying predetermined force 'f' as shown in Fig. 5.34. Now, we will discuss the procedure for getting mathematical expression of 'f'.

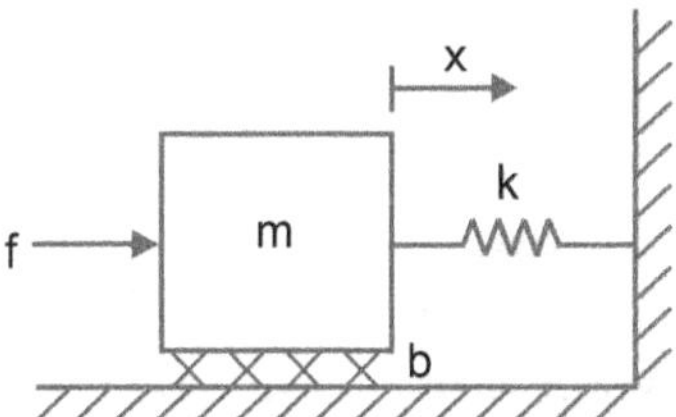

Fig. 5.34: Spring mass system with actuator

The differential equation for motion will be,

$$m\ddot{x} + b\dot{x} + kx = f \qquad \text{... (5.47)}$$

We wish to find modification in b and k such that the equation will become,

$$m\ddot{x} + b'\dot{x} + k'x = 0 \qquad \text{... (5.48)}$$

and b' and k' will have values such that systems response is as per our wish, say critically damped. For that purpose force 'f' should be,

$$f = -k_p x - k_v \dot{x} \qquad \text{... (5.49)}$$

where, k_p is gain in position control or in other words additional stiffness characteristics and k_v is gain in velocity control or in other words additional friction characteristics.

The differential equation becomes,

$$m\ddot{x} + (b + k_v)\dot{x} + (k + k_p)x = 0 \qquad \text{... (5.50)}$$

The expression (5.49) is the "control law" for achieving certain behaviour of the system. Fig. 5.35 is a block diagram to explain how feedback is taken from system and how modified inputs are fed to the system. (Fig. 5.35) Let us look back to the Problem 5.12 and Problem 5.13 which are solved before this section. The system in Problem 5.12 is underdamped because m = 1, b = 2, k = 2. We know, it would become critically damped if b = 6 and k = 9 as seen in Problem 5.3. Thus, we require gain of k_v = 4 and k_p = 7 to modify the values of parameters b and k. Thus, control law for controlling the systems behaviour is application of external force.

$$f \; = \; -4\dot{x} \, - 7x$$

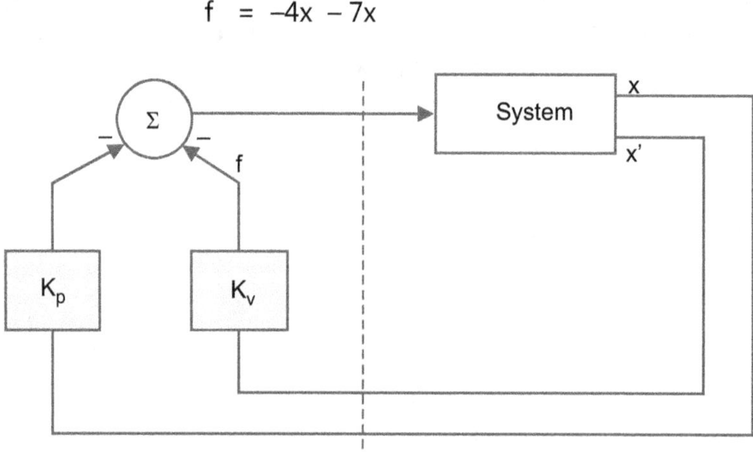

Fig. 5.35: Closed loop system with control law given by expression (5.49)

The differential equation of the system without control law is,

$$\ddot{x} + 2\dot{x} + 2x = 0$$

Hence, characteristic equation is,

$$s^2 + 2s + 2 = 0$$

After applying control law, the differential equation will become,

$$\ddot{x} + 2\dot{x} + 2x = -4\dot{x} - 7x$$

Thus, $\qquad \ddot{x} + 6\dot{x} + 9x = 0$

Hence, characteristic equation becomes $s^2 + 6s + 9 = 0$ and the system will become critically damped.

The modified values of friction characteristic (b') and stiffness characteristic (k') are also called as closed loop friction characteristic and closed loop stiffness because they are determined after getting feedback of original behaviour of the system. Thus, the original "open loop" system becomes a "closed loop" system, due to the feedback control.

Problem 5.14:

A spring mass system has $m = 2$, $b = 4$ and $k = 7$. What is the natural response of the system ? Determine the gains in position and velocity controls, so that the system will be critically damped with a closed loop stiffness as 8.

Solution:

The differential equation of the system is,

$$2\ddot{x} + 4\dot{x} + 7 = 0$$

Hence, characteristic equation is,

$$2s^2 + 4s + 7 = 0$$

The discriminant is,

$$b^2 - 4mk = 16 - 56 = -40$$

As the discriminant is negative that is, $b^2 < 4mk$ the system is underdamped.

To control the system and make it critically damped, it is required that,

$$(b')^2 = 4mk'$$

where,

$$k' = 8$$

$$\therefore \qquad b' = \sqrt{4 \times 2 \times 8} = 8$$

Hence, the gains in position control and velocity control are,

$$k_p = -k' - k = 8 - 7 = 1$$

and

$$k_v = b' - b = 8 - 4 = 4$$

Problem 5.15:

A spring mass system has $m = 3$, $b = 7$, $k = 4$. Determine the control law to make the system critically damped with the gain in velocity control as 3.

Solution:

Currently, $m = 3$, $b = 7$, $k = 4$.

and

$$k_v = 3$$

So

$$b' = 10$$

For critically damping $(b')^2 = 4\,mk'$

$$\therefore \qquad 100 = 4 \times 3 \times k'$$

Thus,

$$k' = \frac{100}{12}$$

$$= 8.3333$$

And gain in position control

$$k_p = 4.3333$$

Thus, control law must be,

$$f = -3\dot{x} - 4.3333$$

5.12.2 Control Law Partitioning

While designing control laws for more complicated systems (including non-linear systems) it becomes difficult to have total control on the system by simply additional gains in position control and velocity control because these gains are individually dependent on system parameters.

Hence, the controller, in turn the control law is partitioned in two parts as model-based portion and servo-portion.

As discussed earlier the open loop equation of motion for the system shown in Fig. 5.34, is given by expression (5.47) that is,

$$m\ddot{x} + b\dot{x} + kx = f \qquad \text{... (5.47)}$$

We call it "open loop" because still feedback was not introduced in the system.

Now one part of the control law, that is, model-based portion will make use of parameters m, b, k and will reduce the system so that it appears to be a unit mass system as follows.

$$\text{Let} \qquad f = \alpha f' + \beta \qquad \text{... (5.51)}$$

where, α and β are either functions or constants chosen in such a way that if f' is taken as the new input to the system, the system appears to be a unit mass.

By equating expressions (5.47) and (5.51)

$$m\ddot{x} + b\dot{x} + kx = 2f' + \beta$$

It is clear that, $\qquad \alpha = m$

and $\qquad \beta = b\dot{x} + kx$

so that system appears to be a unit mass, and the system equation becomes,

$$\ddot{x} = f' \qquad \text{... (5.52)}$$

Now, as the other part of control law, that is, servo position we may have,

$$f' = -k_v\dot{x} - k_p x \qquad \text{... (5.53)}$$

as we did earlier in expression (5.49).

Now, combining expressions (5.52) and (5.53), we get,

$$\ddot{x} + k_v\dot{x} + k_p x = 0 \qquad \text{... (5.54)}$$

Expression (5.54) leads to the characteristic equation as,

$$s^2 + k_v s + k_p = 0 \qquad \qquad \text{... (5.55)}$$

which has the two roots,

$$s_1 = \frac{-k_v + \sqrt{k_v^2 - 4k_p}}{2}$$

and

$$s_2 = \frac{-k_v - \sqrt{k_v^2 - 4k_p}}{2}$$

For achieving behaviour of the system to be critically damped the discriminant $k_v^2 - 4k_p$ must be zero. That means,

$$k_v = 2\sqrt{k_p} \qquad \qquad \text{... (5.56)}$$

Expression (5.56) makes the gains independent of the system parameters. Thus, the control law is partitioned to modify the system parameters α, β and the gains k_p, k_v separately. Fig. 5.36 explains the method of control law partioning.

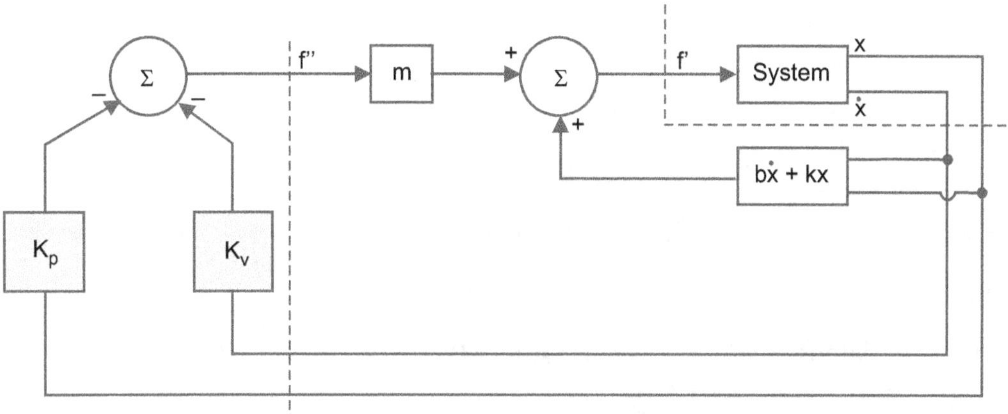

Fig. 5.36: Control law partitioning given by expressions (5.51) and (5.53)

Problem 5.16:

Determine α, β and k_p, k_v for the system given in Problem 5.14.

Solution:

As m = 2, b = 4, k = 7; we choose,

$$\alpha = 2$$

$$\beta = 4\dot{x} + 7x$$

∴   According to expressions (5.47) and (5.51),

$$2\ddot{x} + 4\dot{x} + 7x = 2f' + 4\dot{x} + 7x$$

Hence, $$\ddot{x} = f'$$

This makes system to appear as unit mass on input of force f'.

From expressions (5.54),

$$\ddot{x} + k_v\dot{x} + k_p x = 0$$

where, closed loop stiffness is given to be 8.

Hence, $$k_p = 8$$

Now, for the system to be critically damped from expression (5.56),

$$k_v = 2\sqrt{k_p} = 4\sqrt{2}$$

5.12.3 Additional Observations on Partitioning of Control Law

If we do not use partitioning methodology, we get differential equation of the system as,

$$2\ddot{x} + 8\dot{x} + 8x = 0$$

which reduces to

$$\ddot{x} + 4\dot{x} + 4x = 0$$

and the characteristic equation becomes,

$$s^2 + 4s + 4 = 0$$

The equal roots are,

$$s_1 = s_2 = -2$$

Hence, $$x(t) = (C_1 + C_2 t)\, e^{-2t}$$

and $$\dot{x}(t) = -2\, C_1\, e^{-2t} + C_2\, e^{-2t} - 2\, C_2\, t\, e^{-2t}$$

Using initial conditions as $x(0) = 2$, say and $\dot{x}(0) = 0$

$$C_1 = 2 \text{ and } C_2 = 4$$

Thus, $$x(t) = (2 + 4t)\, e^{-2t}$$

Now with the method of partitioning the control law, the differential equation becomes,

$$\ddot{x} + 4\sqrt{2}\,\dot{x} + 8x = 0$$

Hence, characteristic equation is,

$$s^2 + 4\sqrt{2}\,s + 8 = 0$$

The equal roots will be,

$$s_1 = s_2 = -2\sqrt{2}$$

$\therefore \qquad\qquad x(t) = (C_1 + C_2 t)\, e^{-2\sqrt{2}\,t}$

and $\qquad\quad \dot{x}(t) = -2\sqrt{2}\, C_1\, e^{-2\sqrt{2}\,t} + C_2\, e^{-2\sqrt{2}\,t} - 2\sqrt{2}\, C_2\, t\, e^{-2\sqrt{2}\,t} \qquad \text{... (5.57)}$

Using the same initial conditions, as $x(0) = 2$, $\dot{x}(0) = 0$

$\qquad C_1 = 2$ and $C_2 = 4\sqrt{2}$

Thus, $\qquad\qquad\qquad x(t) = (2 + 4\sqrt{2}t)\, e^{-2\sqrt{2}\,t} \qquad\qquad\qquad\qquad \text{... (5.58)}$

Let us now compare expressions (5.57) and (5.58) as below.

Time, t	x(t) without partitioning	x(t) with partitioning
0	2.0000	2.0000
0.2	1.8769	1.7785
0.4	1.6176	1.3751
0.6	1.3253	0.9883
0.8	1.0499	0.6791
1.0	0.8120	0.4526
1.5	0.3983	0.1507
2.0	0.1832	0.0465
2.5	0.0809	0.0137
3.0	0.0347	0.0039
3.5	0.0146	0.0011
4.0	0.0060	0.0003
4.5	0.0025	0.0001

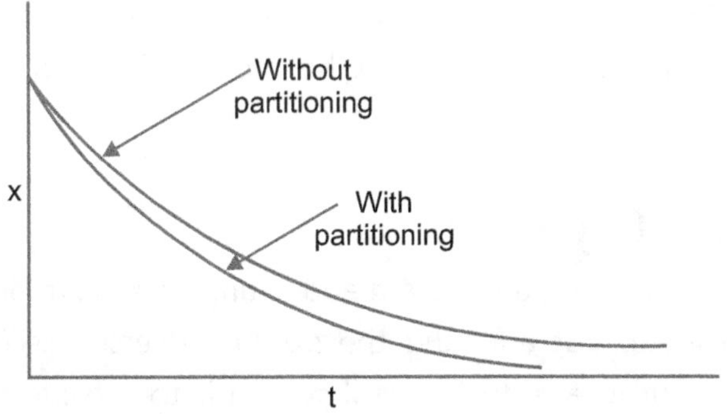

Fig. 5.37: Response of the system without and with control law partitioning

The sole objective of controlling the system is to bring it to the state of rest as fast as possible. From the above table and Fig. 5.37, it is clear that the methodology of control law partitioning is beneficial in this sense too.

5.13 Trajectory Following Control

Till now, we have discussed how the system can be brought back to the state of rest as its original position, if disturbed. Now lets understand what is disturbance with reference to the end effector movement. The end effector is supposed to follow the trajectory planned by the planner. Thus, the end effector is supposed to be positioned at particular predetermined location at given instant of time. At that instant, if the end effector is not located at the desired position, the difference between the two locations is known as error or the disturbance. The sole objective of the control system is to minimize this error (or reduce it to zero) as quickly as possible. Thus, the function x(t) discussed earlier may now be treated as equation written in "error space" or equation of motion to minimize error. Therefore, expression (5.54) may be rewritten as,

$$\ddot{e} + k_v \dot{e} + k_p e \ = \ 0 \qquad \qquad \text{... (5.59)}$$

where, e = Error or disturbance in the desired position

= Desired position – Actual position

= $x_d - x$

x is the time function of end effector's actual position and x_d is the time function of end effector's desired position.

If the parameters m, b, k are perfectly known and if there is no initial error, the end effector will follow the desired trajectory exactly. And if there is initial error, then it will be suppressed according to expression (5.59) and thereafter the end effector will follow the trajectory exactly. The expression (5.59) must be modified only if there is any external disturbance.

5.14 Disturbance Rejection

The disturbance generated outside the system and acting as an extra input to the system in addition to its normal input, but affecting the output adversely is called as an external disturbance. Hence, one purpose of the control system is to provide disturbance rejection. If the external disturbance is equivalent to a force f_{dist} expression (5.59) will be rewritten as,

$$\ddot{e} + k_v \dot{e} + k_p e \ = \ f_{dist} \qquad \qquad \text{... (5.60)}$$

The disturbance may be of any nature like varying with respect to time which may be modelled with certain time function, or it may be constant.

To understand the methodology of disturbance rejection, let us consider a simplest kind of disturbance, obviously, a constant disturbance, that is,

$$f_{dist} = \text{constant}$$

which means error in locating end effector at desired position.

$$e = \text{constant}$$

Naturally, first and second derivatives of 'e' with respect to time 't' $\dot{e}$ and $\ddot{e}$ are equal to zero.

Hence, from the expression (5.60),

$$k_p\, e = f_{dist}$$

and

$$e = \frac{f_{dist}}{k_p}$$

That implies, higher the position control gain (k_p), smaller the error. As error 'e' is not zero, the disturbance is not completely rejected.

Hence, for disturbance rejection, the control law expression (5.60) may be modified by an additional integral term as follows.

$$\ddot{e} + k_v\, \dot{e} + k_p\, e + k_i \int e\, dt = f_{dist} \qquad\qquad \text{... (5.61)}$$

The integral term is added so that error is not steady although f_{dist} is constant.

On further differentiation of expression (5.61), we get,

$$\dddot{e} + k_v\, \ddot{e} + k_p\, \dot{e} + k_i\, e = 0 \qquad\qquad \text{... (5.62)}$$

With this control law the system becomes third order system. To reject the disturbance completely, solution of differential equation given by expression (5.62) may be determined. It is obvious to keep integral control gain (k_i) as small as possible to bring the third order system almost close to second order system. The control law given by expression (5.61) is Proportional-Integral-Derivative (PID) control as it includes all the above mathematical terms.

5.15 Modeling and Control of a Single Joint

5.15.1 Modeling of a Single Joint

Usually, DC motor is used as an actuator in many industrial robots. The motor works on the principle of electromagnetism. It has non-rotating part that is stator consisting housing, bearings and permanent or electromagnets. The rotor consists of shaft and windings through which current flows, so that tangential force is generated with the robot which in turn generates torque. The tangential force is expressed as,

$$F = q\,v\,B$$

where,

q = Charge
v = Speed with the charge moves through the windings
B = Magnetic field set up by the magnets in stator

But, this equation won't lead us to model the system by a differential equation.

So, considering torque capacity of motor which is proportional to current flowing through the armature, it may be stated that,

$$T_m = k_m\,i_a \qquad \qquad \text{... (5.63)}$$

where,　　　T_m = Torque capacity of motor
k_m = Motor torque constant
i_a = Armature current

Further, when the rotor rotates, it generates a small amount of electromotive force across the armature, as it rotates in the magnetic field. This electromotive force (emf) or the voltage is proportional to motor speed. Hence,

$$V = k_e\,\dot{\theta}_m \qquad \qquad \text{... (5.64)}$$

where,

V = Voltage generated
k_e = Back emf constant

$\dot{\theta}_m$ = Rotational speed of motor

The armature circuit of DC torque motor is as shown in Fig. 5.38.

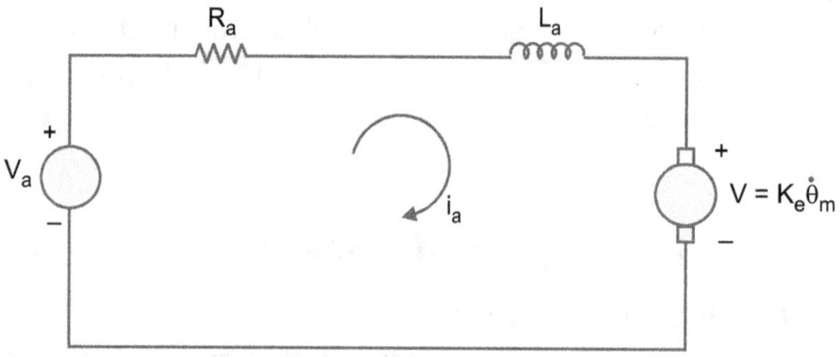

Fig. 5.38: Armature circuit of DC torque motor

where,

V_a = Armature source voltage

i_a = Armature current

V = Voltage generated due to rotation

R_a = Armature resistance

L_a = Armature inductance

Practically, it is observed that inductance of motor is negligible, hence the circuit may be represented by equation

$$V_a - V = i_a R_a$$

$$\therefore \quad V_a = \frac{T_m}{k_m} R_a + k_e \dot{\theta}_m \qquad \qquad ... (5.65)$$

This is first order differential equation of the system.

Control of a Single Joint

Fig. 5.39 shows mechanical model of the single joint actuated by a DC torque motor.

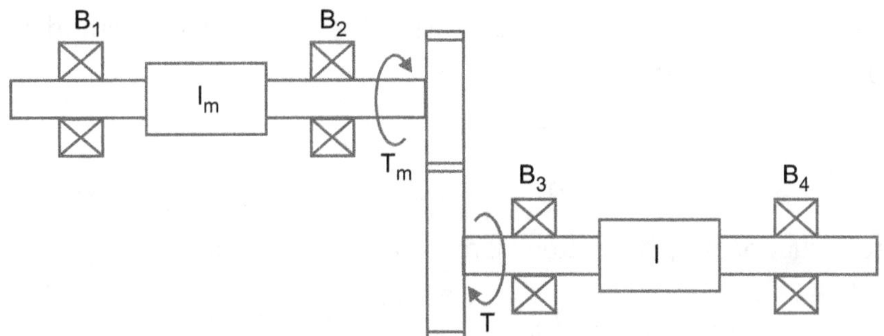

Fig. 5.39: Mechanical model of single joint

I_m = Inertia of motor rotor

I = Inertia of load

B_1, B_2 = Motor shaft bearings which give rise to viscous coefficient of friction b_m

B_3, B_4 = Load shaft bearings which give rise to viscous coefficient of friction b

$\dot{\theta}_m$ = Speed of rotation of motor shaft

$\dot{\theta}$ = Speed of rotation of load shaft

T_m = Motor shaft torque

T = Load shaft torque

Assuming efficiency of power transmission to be 100%.

$$T_m \, \dot{\theta}_m = T \, \dot{\theta}$$

$$\therefore \qquad \text{Gear ratio, } z = \frac{\dot{\theta}}{\dot{\theta}_m} = \frac{T_m}{T}$$

Torque balance in terms of motor variables is,

$$T_m = \left(I_m + \frac{I}{z^2} \right) \ddot{\theta}_m + \left(b_m + \frac{b}{z^2} \right) \dot{\theta}_m \qquad \text{... (5.66)}$$

and in terms of load variables it is,

$$T = (I + z^2 \, I_m) \, \ddot{\theta} + (b + z^2 \, b_m) \, \dot{\theta}$$

The term $(I + z^2 \, I_m)$ is called as effective inertia and $(b + z^2 \, b_m)$ is called as effective damping. These two terms are used in controlling the joint. Under method of control law partitioning, α and β are set as follows:

$$\alpha = I + z^2 \, I_m$$

$$\text{and} \qquad \beta = b + z^2 \, b_m$$

and the control equation may be written from expression (5.60) as,

$$\ddot{e} + k_v \, \dot{e} + k_p \, e = T_{dist} \qquad \text{... (5.67)}$$

where, T_{dist} is disturbance in the torque.

5.16 Introduction to Force Control

If the end effector needs to interact with the environment, as discussed earlier at the beginning of this chapter, it is very important to have knowledge about the environment to avoid damages. For example, if it is required to hold a glass flask which is a fragile material, that may get damaged due to grip of the end effector, if its stiffness is not set properly. Thus, knowledge of environment, force sensing and then force control these three activities are important in the same sequence.

Force sensing is usually achieved by force sensing wrist shown in Fig. 5.40.

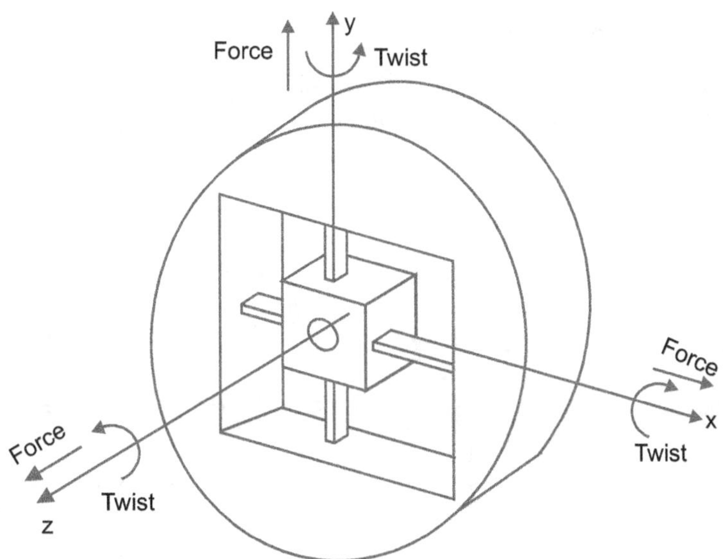

Fig. 5.40: Force sensing wrist

The wrist is fitted with eight pairs of semiconductor strain gauges bonded to the surfaces of cross bars connected to the core.

It is important to remember that the environment and the force requirement i.e. stiffness of end effector keeps on changing dynamically in any task. For example, consider a task of picking a peg and assembling it with a perfectly sized hole. The task may be divided in some subtasks as shown in Fig. 5.41.

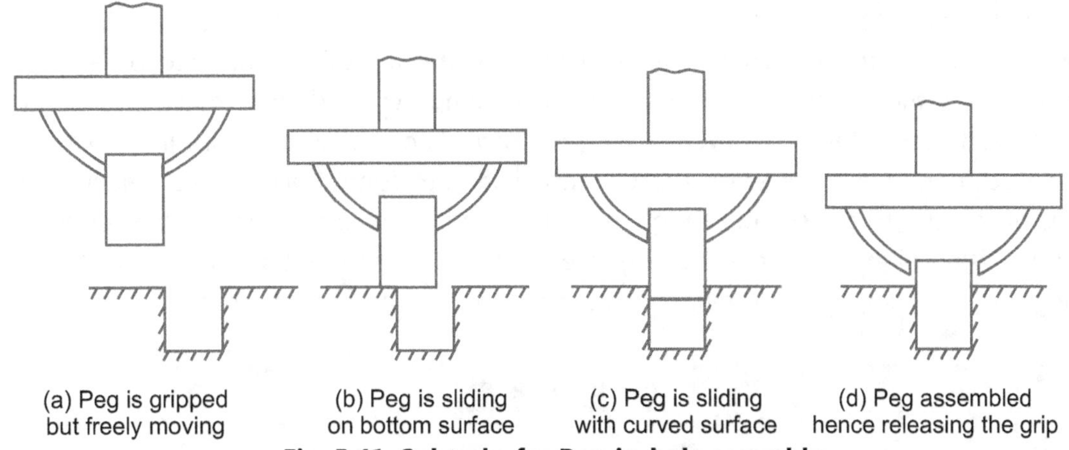

(a) Peg is gripped but freely moving   (b) Peg is sliding on bottom surface   (c) Peg is sliding with curved surface   (d) Peg assembled hence releasing the grip

Fig. 5.41: Subtasks for Peg-in-hole assembly

Thus, required force for gripping keeps on changing dynamically. That gives rise to broadly two categories of force control strategies, namely, pure force control and impedance control. In pure force control, the contact force is directly tracked to the desired force by controlling stiffness in only one direction. In impedance control, the stiffness is altered in various directions as desired.

Industrial Robot Control System

For industrial robots, it is necessary to control all the joints simultaneously so that the desired task is performed accurately within given time limit. Hence, the control system will have hardware architecture with two-level hierarchy as shown in Fig. 5.42.

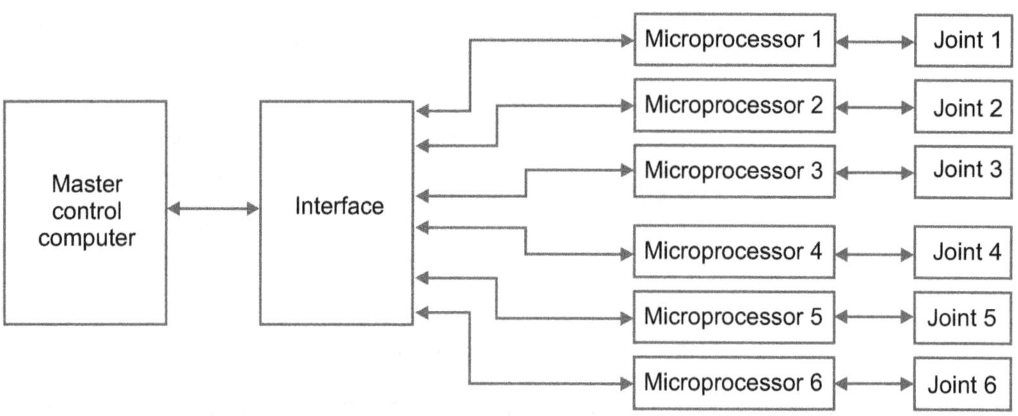

Fig. 5.42: Hierarchical computer architecture of a 6 DoF robot control system

Every individual joint is controlled by an individual microprocessor which interacts with and commanded by a Master Control Computer through an interface. Usually, the existing positions and joint velocities are obtained by motion counters and servo cycles. In order to command torques to the DC torque motors the microprocessor is interfaced to a Digital-to-Analog converter, and the current flowing through the motor is controlled by adjusting voltage across the armature. The master control computer sends new position command after a fixed time interval, to every microprocessor. The microprocessors interpolate the desired position, determine error, subsequently compute control law and command a new values of torques to the motors. Frequency of getting commands from the master control computer is so high, and simultaneously the duration of computation of control laws and setting torque values is so less that working of the robot appears to be continuous.

EXERCISES

1. Discuss various types of controllers.

2. Explain: (i) PD, (ii) Feedback controller, (iii) PID.

3. A 2R manipulator has links having lengths 75 mm and 50 mm. The longer link is joined to the base at one end and to the second link at other end. The other end of the second link is free to move in the work space. A trajectory is to be planned in Cartesian

space so that the free end will move from start point (60, 80) to goal point (–55, 20) in a straight linear path assuming origin of co-ordinate system to be at fixed end of the first-link. Analyse possibility of successful planning of this trajectory without any geometrical problems. State the types of problems, if unsuccessful.

4. The manipulator in above example is to be used for straight line motion from the same start point to a goal point at (–55, –20). Check the possibility of tracing the trajectory and state the types of problems, if impossible.

5. Can the trajectory of exercise be planned without any problems if both links are 75 mm long ?

6. An actuated joint of a six axis robot is to be rotated from 30° to 80° in 5 seconds. Determine linear, quadratic and cubic trajectories for the joint.

$$\textbf{(Ans.} \quad \text{Linear } \theta_t = 30 + 10t$$
$$\text{Quadratic } \theta_t = 30 + 2t^2$$
$$\text{Cubic} = 30 + 6t^2 - 0.8t^3\textbf{)}$$

7. A rotary arm of a manipulator is to rotate from 23° to 117° in 9 seconds. Determine coefficients of a cubic polynomial to interpolate a smooth trajectory. Plot the position, velocity and acceleration variation against time.

8. The first joint of a 3R robot is to rotate from 30° to 60° in 3 seconds. It is also required that the joint is at 55° after 2 seconds. The initial and final velocities are + 10°/sec and –30°/sec. The velocity at the intermediate via point is – 10°/sec. Draw the time history of the joint for position, velocity and acceleration.

9. A 2DoF manipulator has a translatory and a rotary joint as shown in Fig. 5.43. Determine magnitudes of parameters of the joints to move the end effector from P(65, 25), Q(65, 100).

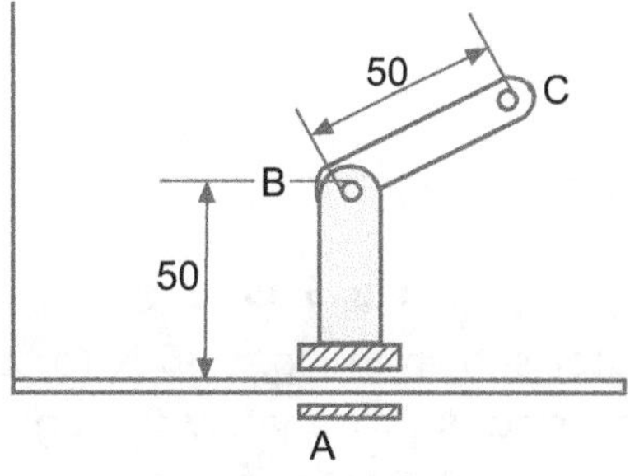

Fig. 5.43

10. A manipulator has a rotary and a linear joint as shown in Fig. 5.44.

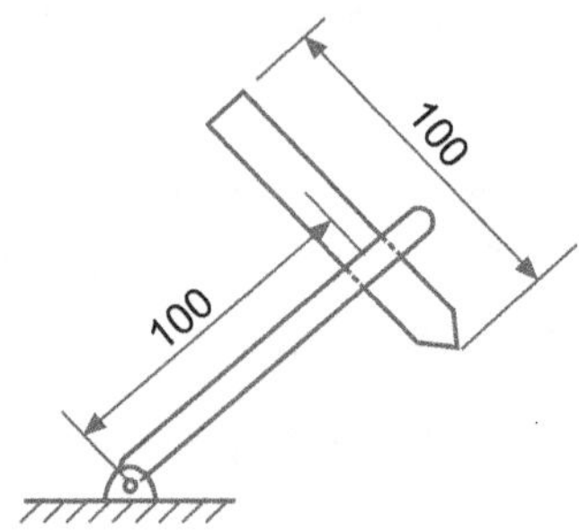

Fig. 5.44

It is required to plan a trajectory, so that end effector will move in a straight line between points (75, 70) and (55, 115). List the magnitudes of parameters for minimum five path points.

11. It is required to plan a linear trajectory for a 2-degree-of-freedom manipulator shown in Fig. 5.45. Divide the line joining start point and end point into four equal segments and calculate all the configurations.

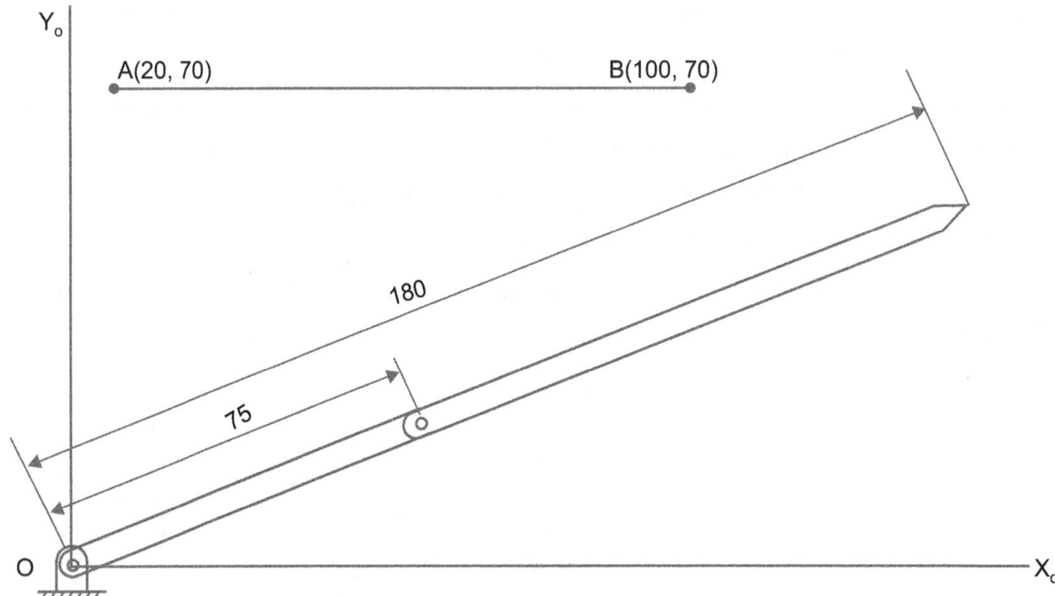

Fig. 5.45

12. End effector of a manipulator shown in Fig. 5.46 is to start its motion at A(10, 5) and end it at B(40, 101) while passing approximately through pseudo via points C(20, 10.5), D(30, 43.5). Determine the quadratic path for the above points. Locate any three via points on that path and determine configurations for all path points.

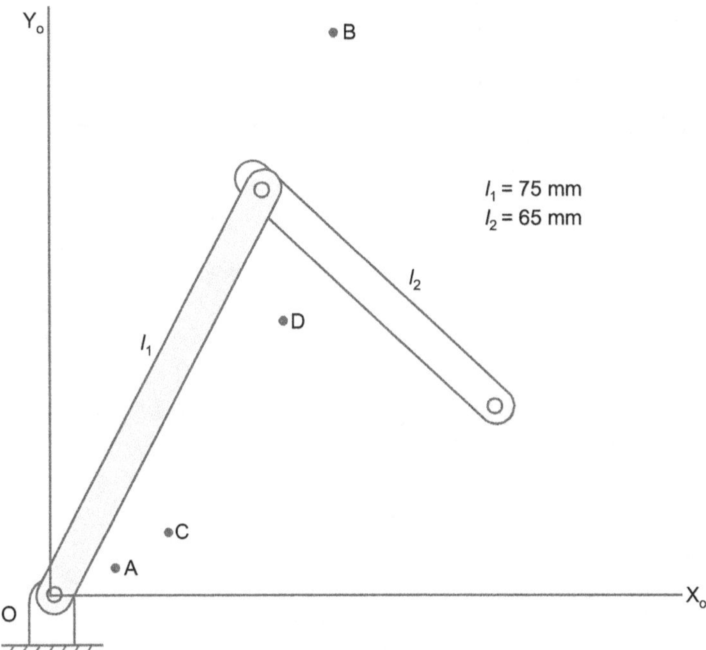

Fig. 5.46

13. Comment on behaviour of the spring mass system having m = 1, b = k = 2, if the initial velocity and position are zero.

14. Spring mass system as shown in Fig. 5.30 has m = 2, b = 4 and k = 7. Determine the motion of system if the block is initially at rest and released from x = 2.5.

15. Spring mass system as above has m = 2, b = 9, k = 8. Sketch the behaviour of system if the block is released from x = –1.5 with initial velocity equal to zero.

16. Determine the behaviour of the system given in Problem 5.13, if the block is released from x = 2 with initial velocity of 2.

17. Plot displacement versus time diagram for spring mass system whose block is located at x = 0 but has initial velocity of 1.5. Assume m = 1, b = 7, k = 10.

18. Determine gains in position and velocity controls, so that the spring mass system is critically damped with a closed loop stiffness of 9. The system has m = 1.5, b = 3 and k = 5.5.

19. A spring mass system has m = 2.2, b = 7.5, k = 3.5. If the gain in velocity control is 2.5, determine the control law to make the system critically damped. Compare the

behaviour of the system without gains to that with gains by plotting the graph, assuming $x(0) = 2.5$ and $\dot{x}(0) = 1.2$.

20. Compare behaviour of a spring mass system without any gains to that with position control gain 3.5 and also the behaviour if it is controlled by control law partitioning assuming $m = 2.5$, $b = 12$, $k = 3.2$ with $x(0) = 3$ and $\dot{x}(0) = -2$.

Unit IV

Chapter 6: KINEMATICS

6.1 Introduction

The robot consists of several rigid links connected to each other by joints. The joints are actuated to have relative motions of links, so that they occupy specific positions with certain orientations. A systematic and generalised approach for mathematical modeling of the positions and orientations of the links in space is needed for describing geometry of the manipulator and also to establish its relation with the object in workspace. Through this chapter, we will study such approaches to establish relation of position and orientation of the end effector with respect to the base of robot.

6.2 Rotations and Transformations

6.2.1 Co-ordinate Frames

To locate any point in space, a set of three orthogonal axes fixed at the origin is required. Hence, to locate any point on the rigid link under consideration, analyst needs to attach a co-ordinate frame to one end of the link. Naturally, as the other end is used for connection between the two links, one more frame will be attached to the other end of link and so on. Fig. 6.1 illustrates the notations for co-ordinate frames.

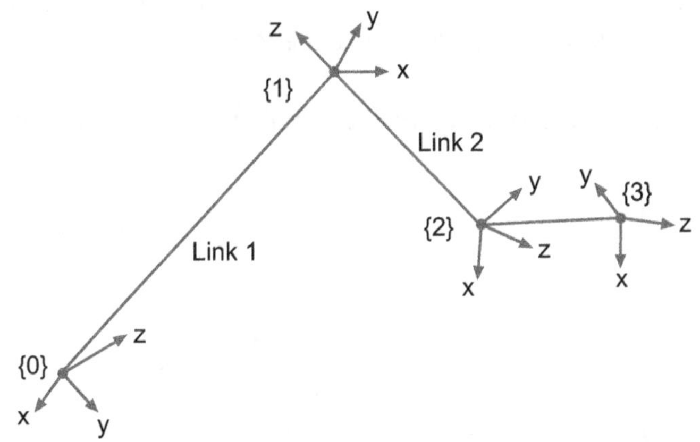

Fig. 6.1: Co-ordinate Frames at Base, Joint and End Point

The link 1 has ends 0 and 1. The link 2 has ends 1 and 2 and so on. Hence, frames {0} and {1} are attached at the respective ends of link 1. Similarly, frame {2} is attached at end 2 of link 2. Frame {3} is attached at the other end of link 3. Frame {0} may be used to locate any point on link 1, including the end points. Similarly, frames {1} and {2} may be used to locate any point on link 2 and link 3 including the end points. Further, frame {3} may be used to locate any point in space, possibly a location where object is located.

6.2.2 Rotation Matrix

Now, orientation of link 2 is changed, keeping position and orientation of link 3 unchanged, then end 3 will have new (x, y) co-ordinates assigned due to rotated frame {2}. Here, we need to have a generalised systematic mathematical method to identify new co-ordinates.

For simplicity, let us consider the links in a plane rather than in 3D space as shown in Fig. 6.2.

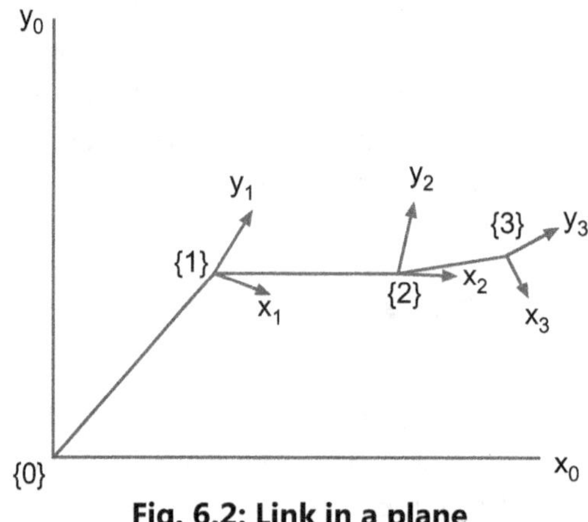

Fig. 6.2: Link in a plane

Consider that the links are rotated in such a way that links 1 and 2 occupy new positions but link 3 returns back to its original position. Thus, although point 3 is at its original location, its position with respect to frame {2} is definitely changed.

Fig. 6.3 shows the points 2 and 3 of link 3 and original and new orientations of frame {2}.

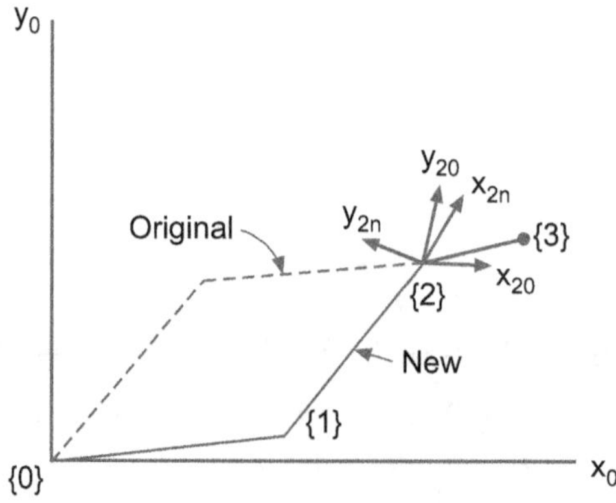

Fig. 6.3: Frame {2} rotates

Fig. 6.4 is equivalent to the original frame {2}, rotated frame {2} and the location of point 3.

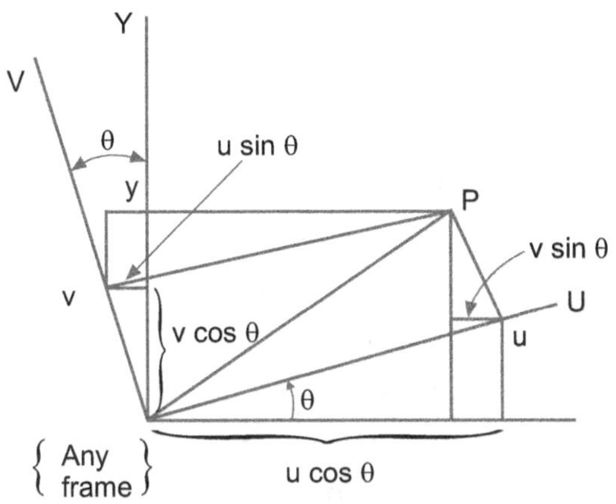

Fig. 6.4: Same point located with respect to two different systems

Let us name X_{20} and Y_{20} the original axes as X and Y. And X_{2n} and Y_{2n} the new axes as U and V, so that the mathematical procedure will become irrespective of joint numbers. Also rename point 3 as point P.

Now, the point P has (x, y) co-ordinates in {XY} frame whereas (u, v) co-ordinates in (UV) frame. And we are interested in finding relation between (x, y) and (u, v) when the frame {XY} is rotated through angle θ in anticlockwise direction to occupy new position as frame {UV}.

$$\left.\begin{array}{l} x = u \cos θ - v \sin θ \\ y = u \sin θ + v \cos θ \end{array}\right\} \qquad \dots (6.1)$$

which may be written in the form of matrix multiplication as,

$$\begin{bmatrix} x \\ y \end{bmatrix} = \begin{bmatrix} \cos θ & -\sin θ \\ \sin θ & \cos θ \end{bmatrix} \begin{bmatrix} u \\ v \end{bmatrix}$$

Thus, conclusion may be drawn as, if {XY} frame rotates about its origin through angle θ in anticlockwise direction to occupy new position as frame {UV} and locates an arbitrary point P(u, v) then co-ordinates of the point P with respect to the original frame {XY} may be given as,

$$^{XY}P = {}^{XY}R_{UV}\ {}^{UV}P$$

where,

^{XY}P — Location of point P in {XY}

^{UV}P — Location of point P in {UV}

$^{XY}R_{UV}$ — Matrix indicating rotation of {XY} to {UV}.

This process of identifying co-ordinates of a point with respect to another frame when it is completely described in one frame, is known as "mapping".

Similarly, if the point P is already located in {XY} then its location in {UV} will be given by,

$$^{UV}P = {}^{UV}R_{XY}\,{}^{XY}P$$

where, rotation matrix $^{UV}R_{XY}$ may be found from equations (6.1) as,

$$u = x \cos\theta + y \sin\theta$$
$$v = -x \sin\theta + y \cos\theta \qquad\qquad \ldots (6.2)$$

$$\therefore \quad \begin{bmatrix} u \\ v \end{bmatrix} = \begin{bmatrix} \cos\theta & \sin\theta \\ -\sin\theta & \cos\theta \end{bmatrix} \begin{bmatrix} x \\ y \end{bmatrix}$$

Thus, $$^{UV}R_{XY} = \begin{bmatrix} \cos\theta & \sin\theta \\ -\sin\theta & \cos\theta \end{bmatrix}$$

The frames may have third axis as Z in {XY} and W in {UV} which will remain unaffected due to planar rotation. Naturally, distance of point, if any, in that direction that is Z-coordinate or W-coordinate will remain unaffected by the rotation shown in Fig. 6.4. Hence, the rotation matrix may be treated as 3×3 matrix of rotation about Z-axis or W-axis, and may be written as,

$$^{XYZ}R_{UVW} = R_Z = \begin{bmatrix} \cos\theta & -\sin\theta & 0 \\ \sin\theta & \cos\theta & 0 \\ 0 & 0 & 1 \end{bmatrix} \qquad\qquad \ldots (6.3)$$

And $$^{UVW}R_{XYZ} = R_W = \begin{bmatrix} \cos\theta & \sin\theta & 0 \\ -\sin\theta & \cos\theta & 0 \\ 0 & 0 & 1 \end{bmatrix} \qquad\qquad \ldots (6.4)$$

The same, logical discussion and geometrical procedure may be applied to find R_X, R_Y consequently, R_U, R_V, which are directly given below.

If {XYZ} is rotated about X-axis through angle ϕ in positive sense then.

$$^{XYZ}R_{UVW} = R_X = \begin{bmatrix} 1 & 0 & 0 \\ 0 & \cos\theta & -\sin\theta \\ 0 & \sin\theta & \cos\theta \end{bmatrix} \qquad\qquad \ldots (6.5)$$

And $$^{UVW}R_{XYZ} = R_U = \begin{bmatrix} 1 & 0 & 0 \\ 0 & \cos\theta & \sin\theta \\ 0 & -\sin\theta & \cos\theta \end{bmatrix} \qquad\qquad \ldots (6.6)$$

If {XYZ} is rotated about Y-axis through positive angle ψ then,

$$^{XYZ}R_{UVW} = R_Y = \begin{bmatrix} \cos\theta & 0 & \sin\theta \\ 0 & 1 & 0 \\ -\sin\theta & 0 & \cos\theta \end{bmatrix} \qquad \text{... (6.7)}$$

And

$$^{UVW}R_{XYZ} = R_V = \begin{bmatrix} \cos\theta & 0 & -\sin\theta \\ 0 & 1 & 0 \\ \sin\theta & 0 & \cos\theta \end{bmatrix} \qquad \text{... (6.8)}$$

In general,

$$^{XYZ}P = {}^{XYZ}R_{UVW}\,{}^{UVW}P \qquad \text{... (6.9)}$$

And

$$^{UVW}P = {}^{UVW}R_{XYZ}\,{}^{XYZ}P \qquad \text{... (6.10)}$$

where, $^{XYZ}R_{UVW}$ or $^{UVW}R_{XYZ}$ is one of the above mentioned 3×3 rotation matrices

and

$$^{XYZ}P = \begin{bmatrix} x \\ y \\ z \end{bmatrix} = [x\ y\ z]^T \qquad \text{... T – Transpose}$$

$$^{UVW}P = \begin{bmatrix} u \\ v \\ w \end{bmatrix} = [u\ v\ w]^T$$

The above discussion has given us, rotation matrix for particular cases as rotation either about X or Y or Z. Hence, for total generalization, assume that {XYZ} and {UVW} were exactly matching at start, but now, {UVW} is arbitrarily rotated as shown in Fig. 6.5.

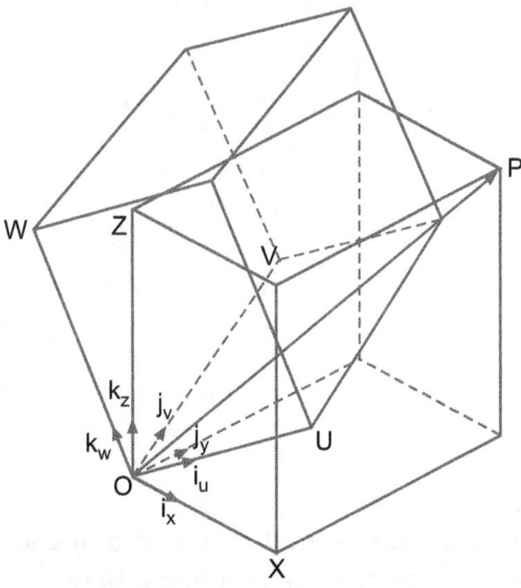

Fig. 6.5: Frames {UVW} and {XYZ} at arbitrary orientations

Focus on the X, Y, Z, U, V and W axes. The box and the tilted box are shown only for better visualisation of rotation of {XYZ} to {UVW}.

Lets have direction vectors of unit magnitudes i_x, j_y, k_z along X, Y, Z axes and i_u, j_v, k_w along U, V, W axes. Let an arbitrary point P be located, conveniently at opposite corner of untitled box which will have (x, y, z) co-ordinates in {XYZ} and (u, v, w} co-ordinates in {UVW}. The vector joining points O and P is position vector of point P and will have magnitude.

$$|\overline{OP}| = \sqrt{x^2 + y^2 + z^2} = \sqrt{u^2 + v^2 + w^2} \qquad \text{... (6.11)}$$

in vector form it may be written as,

$$\overline{OP} = x\, i_x + y\, j_y + z\, k_z = u\, i_u + v\, j_v + w\, k_w \qquad \text{... (6.12)}$$

It is known from vector algebra, that the magnitude of component of any vector along particular direction may be obtained by taking dot product (scalar product) of that vector with unit vector in the desired direction.

Thus, $\quad$ co-ordinate, $x = i_x \cdot \overline{OP} = i_x \cdot (u\, i_u + v\, j_v + w\, k_w)$

$\therefore \qquad x = (i_x \cdot i_u)\, u + (i_x \cdot j_v)\, v + (i_x \cdot k_w)\, w$

Similarly, $\qquad y = (j_y \cdot i_u)\, u + (j_y \cdot j_v)\, v + (j_y \cdot k_w)\, w \qquad \text{... (6.13)}$

and $\qquad z = (k_z \cdot i_u)\, u + (k_z \cdot j_v)\, v + (k_z \cdot k_w)\, w$

Writing equation (6.2) in matrix form we get,

$$\begin{bmatrix} x \\ y \\ z \end{bmatrix} = \begin{bmatrix} i_x \cdot i_u & i_x \cdot j_v & i_x \cdot k_w \\ j_y \cdot i_u & j_y \cdot j_v & j_y \cdot k_w \\ k_z \cdot i_u & k_z \cdot j_v & k_z \cdot k_w \end{bmatrix} \begin{bmatrix} u \\ v \\ w \end{bmatrix}$$

Thus, $\qquad {}^{XYZ}R_{UVW} = \begin{bmatrix} i_x \cdot i_u & i_x \cdot j_v & i_x \cdot k_w \\ j_y \cdot i_u & j_y \cdot j_v & j_y \cdot k_w \\ k_z \cdot i_u & k_z \cdot j_v & k_z \cdot k_w \end{bmatrix} \qquad \text{... (6.14)}$

And $\qquad {}^{UVW}R_{XYZ} = \begin{bmatrix} i_x \cdot i_u & j_y \cdot i_u & k_z \cdot i_u \\ i_x \cdot j_v & j_y \cdot j_v & k_z \cdot j_v \\ i_x \cdot k_w & j_y \cdot k_w & k_z \cdot k_w \end{bmatrix} \qquad \text{... (6.15)}$

Going back to the particular cases, for example rotation of θ angle about Z-axis, which may be conveniently denoted as R_{Z,θ_i} ; we observe that angle between i_x and i_u will be θ and that between j_y and j_v also will be θ but the angle between k_z and k_w will be equal to zero because W-axis coincides with Z-axis. All these angles are shown in Fig. 6.6.

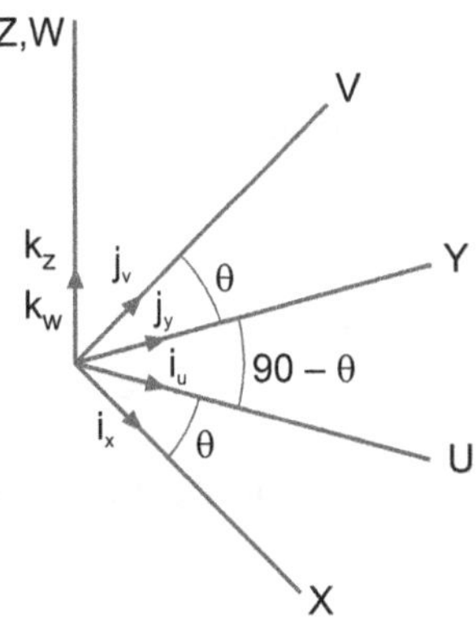

Fig. 6.6: Rotation $R_{Z,\theta}$

Hence,

$$i_x \cdot i_u = 1 \cdot 1 \cdot \cos\theta = \cos\theta$$
$$i_x \cdot j_v = 1 \cdot 1 \cdot \cos(90 + \theta) = -\sin\theta$$
$$i_x \cdot k_w = 1 \cdot 1 \cdot \cos 90 = 0$$
$$j_y \cdot i_u = 1 \cdot 1 \cdot \cos(90 - \theta) = \sin\theta$$
$$j_y \cdot j_v = 1 \cdot 1 \cdot \cos\theta = \cos\theta$$
$$j_y \cdot k_w = 1 \cdot 1 \cdot \cos 90 = 0$$
$$k_z \cdot i_u = 1 \cdot 1 \cdot \cos 90 = 0$$
$$k_z \cdot j_v = 1 \cdot 1 \cdot \cos 90 = 0$$
$$k_z \cdot k_w = 1 \cdot 1 \cdot \cos 0 = 1$$

$$\therefore \quad {}^{XYZ}R_{UVW} = \begin{bmatrix} \cos\theta & -\sin\theta & 0 \\ \sin\theta & \cos\theta & 0 \\ 0 & 0 & 1 \end{bmatrix}$$

and

$$\quad {}^{UVW}R_{XYZ} = \begin{bmatrix} \cos\theta & \sin\theta & 0 \\ -\sin\theta & \cos\theta & 0 \\ 0 & 0 & 1 \end{bmatrix}$$

The students are advised to verify other rotation matrices at their own.

6.2.3 Composite Rotation Matrix

If {UVW} has emerged out from {XYZ} by series of rotations then product of all rotation matrices for the corresponding rotations is known as Composite Rotation Matrix.

Let there be two integers a and b. Product c of a and b is,

$$c = a * b$$

or

$$c = b * a$$

Now, let there be two square matrices [A] and [B]. Products of the two matrices as,

$$[C] \; = \; [A]\,[B]$$

and

$$[D] \; = \; [B]\,[A]$$

will have different matrices generated. That means product of matrix is not commutative.

$$[C] \; \neq \; [D]$$

Thus, sequence of rotation matrices is important while getting composite rotation matrix.

Lets take a simple example as,

Example 1:

{UVW} is obtained from {XYZ} by rotation of 90° about Z-axis followed by rotation of 90° about X-axis. Then, {UVW} locates a point P at u = 10, v = 20, w = 30. Determine its co-ordinates with respect to {XYZ}.

Solution:

The two rotations are $R_{Z,90°}$ and $R_{X,90°}$. Therefore, the composite rotation matrix will be,

  either $R_1 \; = \; R_{Z,90°},\, R_{X,90°}$

  or $R_2 \; = \; R_{X,90°},\, R_{Z,90°}.$

Let us get both the composite matrices and find the correct answer graphically.

$$\therefore \qquad R_1 \; = \; R_{Z,90°}\, R_{X,90°} \; = \; \begin{bmatrix} \cos 90 & -\sin 90 & 0 \\ \sin 90 & \cos 90 & 0 \\ 0 & 0 & 1 \end{bmatrix} \begin{bmatrix} 1 & 0 & 0 \\ 0 & \cos 90 & -\sin 90 \\ 0 & \sin 90 & \cos 90 \end{bmatrix}$$

$$= \; \begin{bmatrix} 0 & -1 & 0 \\ 1 & 0 & 0 \\ 0 & 0 & 1 \end{bmatrix} \begin{bmatrix} 1 & 0 & 0 \\ 0 & 0 & -1 \\ 0 & 1 & 0 \end{bmatrix}$$

$$\therefore \qquad R_1 \; = \; \begin{bmatrix} 0 & 0 & 1 \\ 1 & 0 & 0 \\ 0 & 1 & 0 \end{bmatrix}$$

$$\text{And} \qquad R_2 \; = \; R_{X,90°}\, R_{Z,90°} \; = \; \begin{bmatrix} 1 & 0 & 0 \\ 0 & 0 & -1 \\ 0 & 1 & 0 \end{bmatrix} \begin{bmatrix} 0 & -1 & 0 \\ 1 & 0 & 0 \\ 0 & 0 & 1 \end{bmatrix}$$

$$R_2 \; = \; \begin{bmatrix} 0 & -1 & 0 \\ 0 & 0 & -1 \\ 1 & 0 & 0 \end{bmatrix}$$

Due to R_1,

$$^{XYZ}P = \begin{bmatrix} 0 & 0 & 1 \\ 1 & 0 & 0 \\ 0 & 1 & 0 \end{bmatrix} \begin{bmatrix} 10 \\ 20 \\ 30 \end{bmatrix} = \begin{bmatrix} 30 \\ 10 \\ 20 \end{bmatrix} \qquad \ldots (6.16)$$

and due to R_2,

$$^{XYZ}P = \begin{bmatrix} 0 & -1 & 0 \\ 0 & 0 & -1 \\ 1 & 0 & 0 \end{bmatrix} \begin{bmatrix} 10 \\ 20 \\ 30 \end{bmatrix} = \begin{bmatrix} -20 \\ -30 \\ 10 \end{bmatrix} \qquad \ldots (6.17)$$

That P may have co-ordinates with respect to the original frame {XYZ} as,

$$x = 30, y = 10, z = 20$$
$$\text{or} \quad x = -20, y = -30, z = 10$$

To identify the correct answer, we will do it graphically as below.

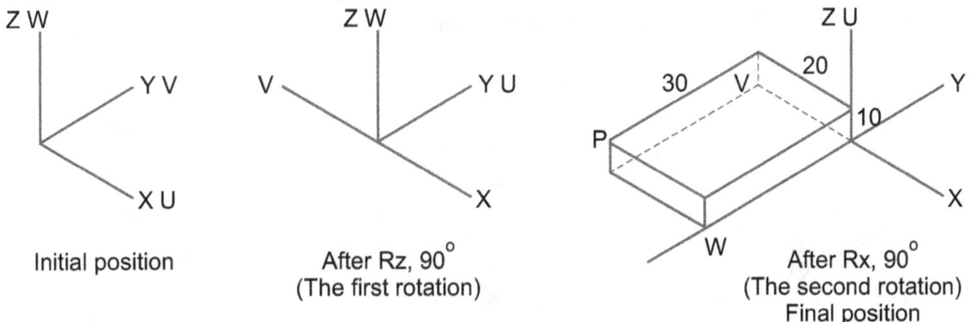

Fig. 6.7

Graphically, it is very clear that point P will have co-ordinates

$$x = -20, y = -30, z = 10.$$

Thus, results given by rotation matrix R_2 in equation (6.17) are correct.

Conclusion: As a conclusion of this example, we will say that if the second **rotation** (or any further rotation) is **about** either **X, Y, or Z** then, corresponding rotation matrix must be placed before the earlier one. That is corresponding rotation will be a **pre-multiplier** to find the composite rotation matrix.

Example 2:

{UVW} is obtained from {XYZ} by rotation of 90° about Z-axis followed by rotation of 90° about U-axis. Then, {UVW} locates a point Q at u = 10, v = 20, w = 30. Determine its co-ordinates with respect to {XYZ}.

Solution:

Before we start any procedure of calculations, it is important to note that rotation matrix about U-axis will **not** be used for mapping Q(x, y, z) into frame {UVW}. It will be used for mapping Q(u, v, w) into {XYZ}. Hence, R_U will be just like R_X, that is in this case,

$$R_U = R_X = \begin{bmatrix} 1 & 0 & 0 \\ 0 & \cos\theta & -\sin\theta \\ 0 & \sin\theta & \cos\theta \end{bmatrix}$$

and $\quad R_U$ is **not** $= \begin{bmatrix} 1 & 0 & 0 \\ 0 & \cos\theta & \sin\theta \\ 0 & -\sin\theta & \cos\theta \end{bmatrix}$

Thus, again the two rotations are $R_{Z,\ 90°}$ and $R_{U,90°}$ (that is mathematically $R_{X,90°}$). So R_1 and R_2 the two possibilities of composite rotation matrix will be as those in previous example and given by equations (6.16) and (6.17).

So, for finding correct possibility again going graphically,

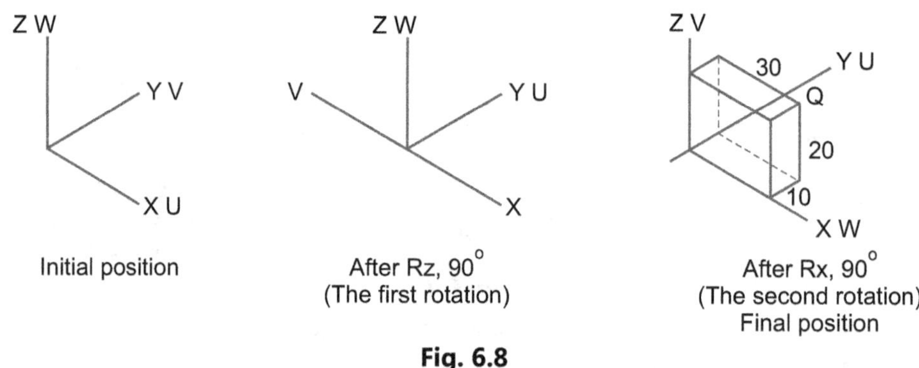

Fig. 6.8

It is very clear that point Q will have co-ordinates
$\quad$ x = 30, y = 10, z = 20.

Thus, results given by rotation matrix R_1 in equation (6.16) are correct.

Conclusion:

As a conclusion, if the second **rotation** (or any further rotation) is **about** either **U, V, or W,** then the corresponding rotation matrix must be written either as R_X, R_Y, R_Z and must be placed after the earlier one. That means the **corresponding R_X, R_Y or R_Z** matrix will be a **post-multiplier** to find the composite rotation matrix.

Problem 6.1:

Write expression in terms of R, to get composite rotation matrix if {UVW} is rotated about Y-axis by α, then rotated about W-axis by β, then rotated about X-axis by θ, then rotated about Z-axis by γ and finally rotated about U-axis by ϕ.

Solution:

The sequence of rotations using notations of axis is as,

1. Rotation about Y-axis by $\alpha = R_{Y,\alpha}$
2. Rotation about W-axis by $\beta = R_{W,\beta}$
3. Rotation about X-axis by $\theta = R_{X,\theta}$
4. Rotation about Z-axis by $\gamma = R_{Z,\gamma}$
5. Rotation about U-axis by $\phi = R_{U,\phi}$

While writing the expression there will be only R_X, R_Y, R_Z. The first rotation matrix is written at mid position then, depending on, whether it is rotation about X or Y or Z or U or V or W all the matrices will be placed at pre-multiplier or post-multiplier positions. This is illustrated below.

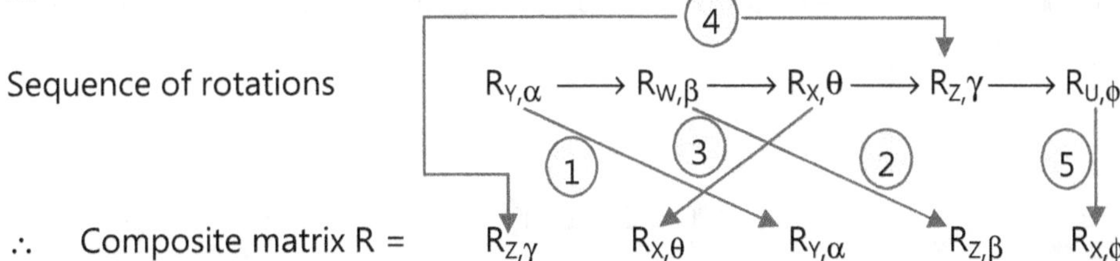

Problem 6.2:

A moving frame is rotated about a fixed frame in the following manner.

1. Rotation of 90° about U.
2. Rotation of 180° about Z.
3. Rotation of 90° about Y.
4. Rotation of –90° about X.
5. Rotation of 90° about V.
6. Rotation of –90° about U.

A point has co-ordinates (15, –27, 38) with respect to the moving frame. Map the point in the fixed frame.

Solution:

Rotation sequence is,

1.	$R_{U,90°}$	2.	$R_{Z,180°}$
3.	$R_{Y,90°}$	4.	$R_{X,-90°}$
5.	$R_{V,90°}$	6.	$R_{U,-90°}$

Therefore, replacing suffixes from U, V, W to X, Y, Z respectively and placing the terms at pre or post multiplier positions, according to the axis of rotation,

$$R = R_{X,-90°} \; R_{Y,90°} \; R_{Z,180°} \; R_{X,90°} \; R_{Y,90°} \; R_{X,-90°}$$
$$\quad\quad (4) \quad\quad (3) \quad\quad (2) \quad\quad (1) \quad\quad (5) \quad\quad (6)$$

We will use c to indicate cos and s to indicate sin, so that writing length of matrices is reduced without loss of clarity in understanding.

$$\therefore \quad R = \begin{bmatrix} 1 & 0 & 0 \\ 0 & c(-90) & -s(-90) \\ 0 & s(-90) & c(-90) \end{bmatrix} \begin{bmatrix} c(90) & 0 & s90 \\ 0 & 1 & 0 \\ -s90 & 0 & c90 \end{bmatrix} \begin{bmatrix} c180 & -s180 & 0 \\ s180 & c180 & 0 \\ 0 & 0 & 1 \end{bmatrix}$$

$$\begin{bmatrix} 1 & 0 & 0 \\ 0 & c90 & -s90 \\ 0 & s90 & c90 \end{bmatrix} \begin{bmatrix} c90 & 0 & s90 \\ 0 & 1 & 0 \\ -s90 & 0 & c90 \end{bmatrix} \begin{bmatrix} 1 & 0 & 0 \\ 0 & c(-90) & -s(-90) \\ 0 & s(-90) & c(-90) \end{bmatrix}$$

$$= \begin{bmatrix} 1 & 0 & 0 \\ 0 & 0 & 1 \\ 0 & -1 & 0 \end{bmatrix} \begin{bmatrix} 0 & 0 & 1 \\ 0 & 1 & 0 \\ -1 & 0 & 0 \end{bmatrix} \begin{bmatrix} -1 & 0 & 0 \\ 0 & -1 & 0 \\ 0 & 0 & 1 \end{bmatrix} \begin{bmatrix} 1 & 0 & 0 \\ 0 & 0 & -1 \\ 0 & 1 & 0 \end{bmatrix} \begin{bmatrix} 0 & 0 & 1 \\ 0 & 1 & 0 \\ -1 & 0 & 0 \end{bmatrix}$$

$$\begin{bmatrix} 1 & 0 & 0 \\ 0 & 0 & 1 \\ 0 & -1 & 0 \end{bmatrix}$$

$$\therefore \quad R = \begin{bmatrix} 0 & 0 & 1 \\ 0 & -1 & 0 \\ 1 & 0 & 0 \end{bmatrix}$$

Now for mapping point Q,

$$^{XYZ}Q = {}^{XYZ}R_{UVW} \; {}^{UVW}Q$$

$$\therefore \quad \begin{bmatrix} x \\ y \\ z \end{bmatrix} = \begin{bmatrix} 0 & 0 & 1 \\ 0 & -1 & 0 \\ 1 & 0 & 0 \end{bmatrix} \begin{bmatrix} 15 \\ -27 \\ 38 \end{bmatrix} = \begin{bmatrix} 38 \\ 27 \\ 15 \end{bmatrix}$$

Problem 6.3:

An object tracking system identifies a flying object at (800 m, 500 m, 1500 m) in its current co-ordinate system, which is oriented by 30° of rotation about the X-axis, then 25° of rotation about the Y-axis and finally –35° of rotation about the Z-axis of the Universal co-ordinate system. Map the object in Universal co-ordination system.

Solution:

Lets say Universal co-ordinate system be frame {XYZ} and current co-ordinate system of the tracking system be {UVW}.

$$\therefore \quad R = R_{Z,-35°}, R_{Y,25°}, R_{X,30°}$$

$$= \begin{bmatrix} c(-35) & -s(-35) & 0 \\ s(-35) & c(35) & 0 \\ 0 & 0 & 1 \end{bmatrix} \begin{bmatrix} c25 & 0 & s25 \\ 0 & 1 & 0 \\ -s25 & 0 & c25 \end{bmatrix} \begin{bmatrix} 1 & 0 & 0 \\ 0 & c30 & -s30 \\ 0 & s30 & c30 \end{bmatrix}$$

$$\therefore \quad R = \begin{bmatrix} 0.7424 & 0.6699 & 0.0130 \\ -0.5198 & 0.5882 & -0.6195 \\ -0.4226 & 0.4532 & 0.7849 \end{bmatrix} \qquad \text{... (6.18)}$$

For mapping the point,

$$^{XYZ}P = {}^{XYZ}R_{UVW} \; {}^{UVW}P$$

$$\therefore \quad \begin{bmatrix} x \\ y \\ z \end{bmatrix} = \begin{bmatrix} 0.7424 & 0.6699 & 0.0130 \\ -0.5198 & 0.5882 & -0.6195 \\ -0.4226 & 0.4532 & 0.7849 \end{bmatrix} \begin{bmatrix} 800 \\ 500 \\ 1500 \end{bmatrix} = \begin{bmatrix} 948.37 \\ -1050.99 \\ 1065.87 \end{bmatrix}$$

6.2.4 Properties of the Generalised Composite Rotation Matrix

There are some useful observations regarding an arbitrarily taken composite rotation matrix. These observations are useful in

1. Verifying whether a given 3×3 matrix is rotation matrix or simply collection of nine numbers.
2. Identify an element of matrix which is incorrect and rectify.
3. Inverse mapping of a point. That is if point is already known in original frame then locating it with respect to the rotated frame.
4. Visualising orientation of each axis of one frame with respect to each axis of the other frame.

All the observations are generalised without exception, therefore, they are treated as properties of the composite rotation matrix. These properties are as follows:

1. Magnitude of the matrix, that is its determinant is always unity.
   It will be +1 if {XYZ} and {UVW} have same hand. That is {XYZ} and {UVW} both are right handed or both are left handed co-ordinate systems.
   It will be −1 if {XYZ} and {UVW} have opposite hands.
2. Magnitude of every column and row vectors is +1.
3. Dot product of any two column vectors is equal to zero.
4. Dot product of any two row vectors is equal to zero.
5. The inverse of the matrix is same as transpose of the matrix.
   That is, $\left({}^{XYZ}R_{UVW}\right)^{-1} = {}^{UVW}R_{XYZ} = \left({}^{XYZ}R_{UVW}\right)^{T}$

** Let us verify all the above properties for composite rotation matrix of Problem 6.3 given by equation (6.18).

Property 1: Determinant of $^{XYZ}R_{UVW}$,

$$|^{XYZ}R_{UVW}| = \begin{vmatrix} 0.7424 & 0.6699 & 0.0130 \\ -0.5198 & 0.5882 & -0.6195 \\ -0.4226 & 0.4532 & 0.7849 \end{vmatrix}$$

$$= 0.7424\,(0.5882 \times 0.7849 + 0.4532 \times 0.6195)$$
$$+ 0.6699\,(0.5198 \times 0.7849 + 0.4226 \times 0.6195)$$
$$+ 0.0130\,(0.4226 \times 0.5882 - 0.5198 \times 0.4532)$$
$$= 1.00358$$
$$\doteq 1$$

Property 2: Magnitude of every column and every row.

$$\text{Magnitude of column 1} = \sqrt{0.7424^2 + 0.5198^2 + 0.4226^2} = 0.99997 \doteq 1$$
$$\text{Magnitude of column 2} = \sqrt{0.6699^2 + 0.5882^2 + 0.4532^2} = 1.00007 \doteq 1$$
$$\text{Magnitude of column 3} = \sqrt{0.0130^2 + 0.6195^2 + 0.7849^2} = 1.00354 \doteq 1$$
$$\text{Magnitude of row 1} = \sqrt{0.7424^2 + 0.6699^2 + 0.0130^2} = 1.00005 \doteq 1$$
$$\text{Magnitude of row 2} = \sqrt{0.5198^2 + 0.5882^2 + 0.6195^2} = 0.99998 \doteq 1$$
$$\text{Magnitude of row 3} = \sqrt{0.4226^2 + 0.4532^2 + 0.7849^2} = 1.00356 \doteq 1$$

Property 3: Dot product of two column vectors

$$\text{Column vector 1} = 0.7424i - 0.5199j - 0.4226k$$
$$\text{Column vector 2} = 0.6699i + 0.5882j + 0.4532k$$
$$\text{Column vector 3} = 0.0130i - 0.6195j + 0.7849k$$

Dot product of column vectors 1 and 2

$$= 0.7424 \times 0.6699 - 0.5198 \times 0.5882 - 0.4226 \times 0.4532$$
$$= 6.508 \times 10^{-5}$$
$$\doteq 0$$

Dot product of column vectors 2 and 3

$$= 0.6699 \times 0.0130 - 0.5882 \times 0.6195 + 0.4532 \times 0.7849$$
$$= 2.07488 \times 10^{-3}$$
$$\doteq 0$$

** You may find answers of these calculations to be approximately zero or one etc. That is because of rounding error introduced while calculating sin and cos of 25°, 30° and 35°.

Dot product of column vectors 1 and 3

$$= 0.7424 \times 0.0130 + 0.5198 \times 0.6195 - 0.4226 \times 0.7849$$

$$= -1.93314 \times 10^{-3} \doteq 0$$

Property 4: Dot product of two row vectors

$$\text{Row vector 1} = 0.7424i + 0.6699j + 0.0130k$$
$$\text{Row vector 2} = -0.5198i + 0.5882j - 0.6195k$$
$$\text{Row vector 3} = -0.4226i + 0.4532j + 0.7849k$$

Dot product of row vectors 1 and 2

$$= -0.7424 \times 0.5198 + 0.6699 \times 0.5882 - 0.0130 \times 0.6195$$

$$= 8.216 \times 10^{-5} \doteq 0$$

Dot product of row vectors 2 and 3

$$= 0.5198 \times 0.4226 + 0.5882 \times 0.4532 - 0.6195 \times 0.7849$$

$$= -5.83 \times 10^{-6} \doteq 0$$

Dot product of row vectors 1 and 3

$$= -0.7424 \times 0.4226 + 0.6699 \times 0.4532 + 0.0130 \times 0.7849$$

$$= 6.414 \times 10^{-5} \doteq 0$$

Property 5: Inverse of matrix

$$\text{Inverse} = \frac{1}{\text{Determinant}} \text{ Transpose of cofactor matrix}$$

$\therefore$

$$\text{Cofactor of 1, 1} = (-1)^{1+1} (0.5882 \times 0.7849 + 0.4532 \times 0.6195)$$
$$\doteq 0.7424$$

$$\text{Cofactor 1, 2} = (-1)^{1+2} (-0.5198 \times 0.7849 - 0.4226 \times 0.6195)$$
$$\doteq 0.6699$$

$$\text{Cofactor of 1, 3} = (-1)^{1+3} (0.4226 \times 0.5882 - 0.5198 \times 0.4532)$$
$$\doteq 0.0130$$

$$\text{Cofactor of 2, 1} = (-1)^{2+1} (0.6699 \times 0.7849 - 0.4532 \times 0.0130)$$
$$\doteq -0.5198$$

$$\text{Cofactor of 2, 2} = (-1)^{2+2} (0.7424 \times 0.7849 + 0.4226 \times 0.0130)$$
$$\doteq 0.5882$$

$$\text{Cofactor of 2, 3} = (-1)^{2+3} (0.7424 \times 0.4532 + 0.4226 \times 0.6699)$$
$$\doteq -0.6195$$

$$\text{Cofactor of 3, 1} = (-1)^{3+1} (-0.6699 \times 0.6195 - 0.5882 \times 0.0130)$$
$$\doteq -0.4226$$

$$\text{Cofactor of 3, 2} = (-1)^{3+2} (0.5198 \times 0.0130 - 0.7424 \times 0.6195)$$
$$\doteq 0.4532$$

$$\text{Cofactor of 3, 3} = (-1)^{3+3} (0.7424 \times 0.5882 + 0.5198 \times 0.6699)$$
$$\doteq 0.7849$$

$$\therefore \quad \text{Inverse} = \begin{bmatrix} 0.7424 & -0.5198 & -0.4226 \\ 0.6699 & 0.5882 & 0.4532 \\ 0.0130 & -0.6195 & 0.7849 \end{bmatrix}$$

Thus, inverse of the rotation matrix is its transpose.

A useful conclusion from these properties is that the columns of $^{XYZ}R_{UVW}$ represent the direction vectors along U, V, W axes and the rows represent the direction vectors along X, Y, Z axes.

This will be more clear from rotation matrices R_1 and R_2 obtained in Example 1 and Example 2, shown in Fig. 6.7 and Fig. 6.8.

Looking at R_1, we can observe U-axis is aligned with Y-axis because the first column which represent U-axis has X and Z components zero but a full Y-component. Similarly, second column indicates that V-axis is aligned with Z-axis and W-axis is aligned with X-axis. This description can be verified with "Final position" shown in Fig. 6.8.

Similarly, looking at R_2 we can describe that its U-axis is aligned with Z-axis, V-axis is opposite to X-axis, W-axis is opposite to Y-axis. This can be verified with "Final position" shown in Fig. 6.7.

Problem 6.4:

Find whether following matrix is a rotation matrix.

$$\begin{bmatrix} 0.5687 & 0.7141 & 0.4082 \\ 0.7462 & 0.6567 & 0.1094 \\ 0.3462 & 0.2424 & 0.7063 \end{bmatrix}$$

Solution:

To check whether it is a rotation matrix, we can test its first property. That is its determinant must be +1 or −1.

$$\therefore \quad \begin{vmatrix} 0.5687 & 0.7141 & 0.4082 \\ 0.7462 & 0.6567 & 0.1094 \\ 0.3462 & 0.2424 & 0.7063 \end{vmatrix}$$

$$= 0.5687\,(0.6567 \times 0.7063 - 0.2424 \times 0.1094)$$
$$- 0.7141\,(0.7462 \times 0.7063 - 0.3462 \times 0.1094)$$
$$+ 0.4082\,(0.7462 \times 0.2424 - 0.3462 \times 0.6567)$$
$$= -0.1196$$

Hence, given matrix is not a rotation matrix.

Problem 6.5:

For the matrix given in Problem 6.4, identify an element which may be modified to convert the matrix to rotation matrix.

Solution:

We may go on verifying every column and then every row for its magnitude. Let us take columns first.

$$\text{Magnitude of column 1} = \sqrt{0.5687^2 + 0.7462^2 + 0.3462^2} = 1.000044$$
$$\text{Magnitude of column 2} = \sqrt{0.7141^2 + 0.6567^2 + 0.2424^2} = 0.999976$$
$$\text{Magnitude of column 3} = \sqrt{0.4082^2 + 0.1094^2 + 0.7063^2} = 0.823077$$

Magnitudes of columns 1 and 2 are almost equal to 1 (neglect error which must be rounding error). But surely there is atleast one element incorrect in column 3, so its magnitude is considerably deviated from 1.

Let us take rows now.

$$\text{Magnitude of row 1} = \sqrt{0.5687^2 + 0.7141^2 + 0.4082^2} = 0.999993$$
$$\text{Magnitude of row 2} = \sqrt{0.7462^2 + 0.6567^2 + 1094^2} = 1.000019$$
$$\text{Magnitude of row 3} = \sqrt{0.3462^2 + 0.2424^2 + 0.7063^2} = 0.823087$$

Again, row 1 and row 2 seem to have all elements correct. But there is incorrect element in row 3.

Thus, incorrect element is in column 3 and row 3 i.e. the element 0.7063 is in correct.

The elements correct value must be 0.9063 so that column 3 and row 3 will have magnitude equal to 1.

Problem 6.6:

Following is a rotation matrix with some unknown elements marked with XXXX. Determine numeric values at XXXX.

$$R = \begin{bmatrix} XXXX & 0.1385 & 0.7162 \\ 0.4721 & XXXX & 0.2718 \\ XXXX & XXXX & 0.6428 \end{bmatrix}$$

Solution:

For row 2, $1 = 0.4721^2 + XXXX^2 + 0.2718^2$

Hence,   element (2, 2) = 0.8386

For column 2, $1 = 0.1385^2 + 0.8386^2 + XXXX^2$

Hence,   element (3, 2) = 0.5268

for row 1, $1 = XXXX^2 + 0.1385^2 + 0.7162^2$

Hence,   element (1, 1) = 0.6840

For row 3, $1 = 0.6840^2 + 0.4721^2 + XXXX^2$

Hence,   element (3, 1) = 0.5561

$$\therefore \quad R = \begin{bmatrix} 0.6840 & 0.1385 & 0.7162 \\ 0.4721 & 0.8386 & 0.2718 \\ 0.5561 & 0.5268 & 0.6428 \end{bmatrix}$$

Problem 6.7:

Write rotation matrix if V-axis is aligned with Z-axis, and W-axis is opposite to X-axis, so that both frames are right handed.

Solution:

Let us draw {XYZ} frame and align the V and W axes as given.

Fig. 6.9 indicates U-axis must be opposite to Y-axis, so that {UVW} will be a right handed frame.

$$\therefore \quad R = \begin{bmatrix} 0 & 0 & -1 \\ -1 & 0 & 0 \\ 0 & 1 & 0 \end{bmatrix}$$

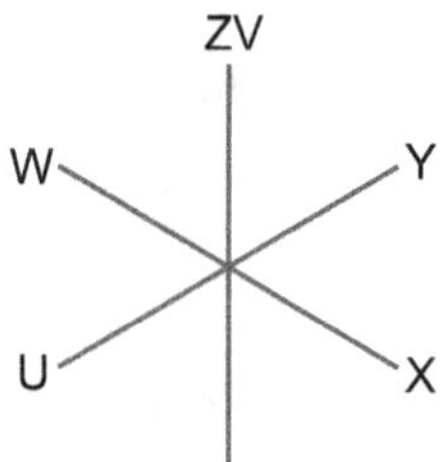

Fig. 6.9

6.2.5 Rotation of Frame about an Arbitrary Vector

In practical cases, frames do not follow certain sequence of rotation or also they do not always rotate about the six axes viz. X, Y, Z, U, V and W. As seen in Problem 6.3, an object tracking system, a radar system are examples where {UVW} is rotated about an arbitrarily selected axis through angle θ. This case may be solved in step-by-step manner to obtain composite rotation matrix as follows:

Let {UVW} be rotated through angle θ about an arbitrary vector, which is conveniently selected as position vector for point P having co-ordinates x, y, z with respect to frame {XYZ} as shown in Fig. 6.10.

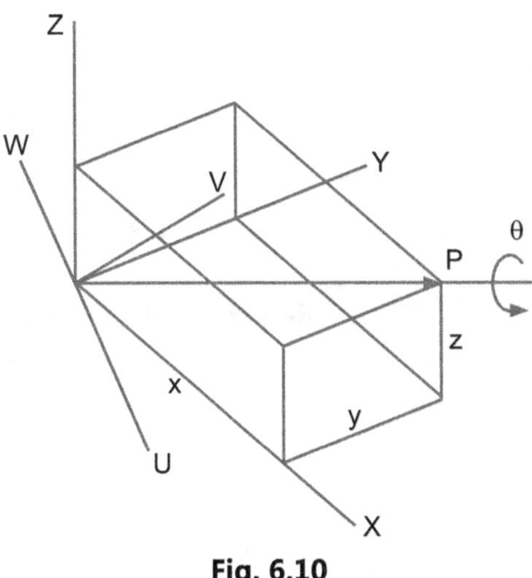

Fig. 6.10

Now, to get the rotation matrix, we will take some steps for our convenience, then a step for actual rotation through θ, finally compensatory steps to nullify effect of steps taken for convenience. All these steps are illustrated in sequence in Fig. 6.11.

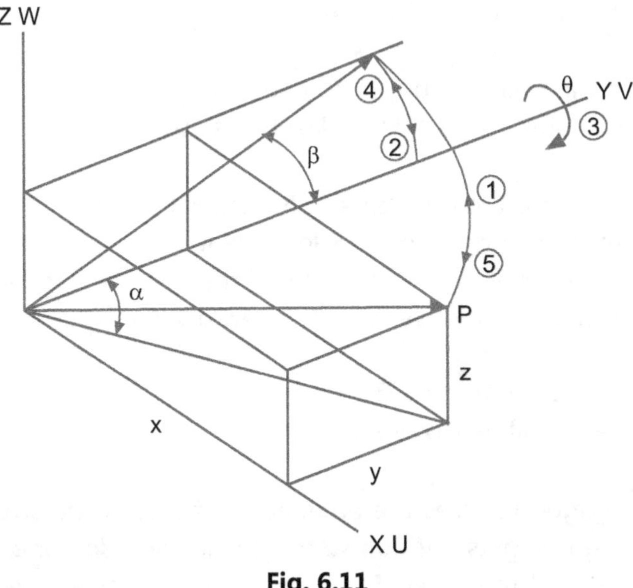

Fig. 6.11

Initially, {UVW} has to be aligned with {XYZ}.

Now steps taken are

rotation of {UVW} and $\overline{OP}$

1. By angle α about Z-axis.
2. By angle $-\beta$ about X-axis.
3. By angle θ about Y-axis.
4. By angle β about X-axis.
5. By angle $-\alpha$ about Z-axis.

The first two steps which were taken for convenience are compensated by the last two steps. Now, composite rotation matrix will be,

$$R = R_{Z,-\alpha} \ R_{X,\beta} \ R_{Y,\theta} \ R_{X,-\beta} \ R_{Z,\alpha} \qquad \qquad \text{... (6.18)}$$

where, θ is known angle through which {UVW} is turned and α and β are angles dependent on position of point P.

$$\therefore \qquad \sin\alpha \ = \ \frac{x}{\sqrt{x^2 + y^2}} \qquad\qquad \cos\alpha \ = \ \frac{y}{\sqrt{x^2 + y^2}} \qquad\qquad \text{... (6.19)}$$

$$\text{and} \qquad \sin\beta \ = \ \frac{z}{\sqrt{x^2 + y^2 + z^2}} \qquad\qquad \cos\beta \ = \ \frac{\sqrt{x^2 + y^2}}{\sqrt{x^2 + y^2 + z^2}}$$

where, x, y, z are co-ordinates of point P, hence are known.

It is important to note here, that first two steps are taken as per convenience, so one may take first rotation about Z-axis but in opposite direction to that shown in Fig. 6.11 or one may think of first rotation about X-axis or Y-axis.

The numeric values in the final composite rotation matrix will match as long as, whatever first two steps taken are compensated by the last two steps accordingly.

Problem 6.8

A screw driver 20 cm long has a co-ordinate frame attached to its gripping end as shown in Fig. 6.12. The mid point of the driving edge is located at a point having x and y co-ordinates 100 mm and 115 m respectively with reference to the base co-ordinate frame. There is a slotted head screw, which is to be driven by the screw driver. The screw is located at a point having

$$x = 75 \text{ mm}, y = 137 \text{ mm}, z = 125 \text{ mm}$$

The axis of screw is parallel to the axis of screw driver.

A robot (not shown in figure) senses the orientation of slot of the screw, then rotates the screw driver without disturbing its position so that its driving edge orientation matches with the orientation of the slot of the screw. Then translates the screw driver in such a way that the driving edge fits in the slot of the screw. In the above process, the robot sensed the orientation and rotates the screw driver along with the co-ordinate frame by $-30°$. As the frame is rotated the screw will have new co-ordinates with respect to the rotated frame. Determine the new co-ordinates, so that the robot can translate screw driver accordingly.

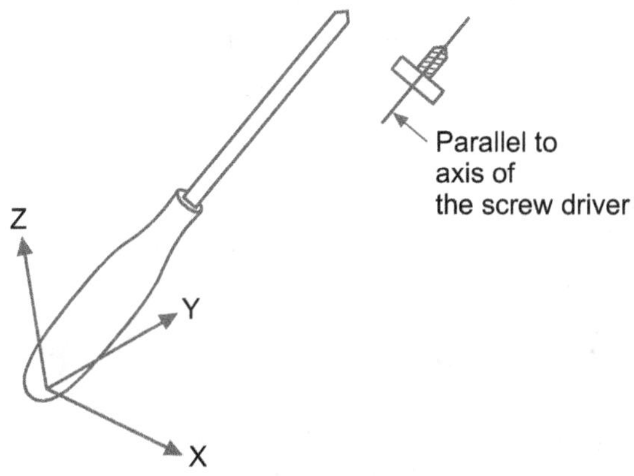

Fig. 6.12

Solution:

It is required to find $^{UVW}R_{XYZ}$, so that the screw location which is given with respect to {XYZ} will be mapped with respect to {UVW}. Further, the information is rotation of {UVW} about axis of the screw driver by −30°. The sequence of rotations about either X or Y or Z may be shown as in Fig. 6.13.

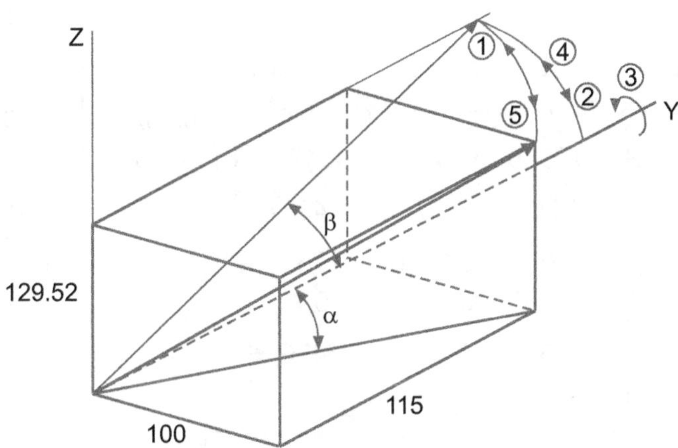

Fig. 6.13

Thus, composite rotation matrix may be obtained by equation (6.18) as,

$$^{XYZ}R_{UVW} = R_{Z,-\alpha}\ R_{X,\beta}\ R_{Y,\theta}\ R_{X,-\beta}\ R_{Z,\alpha}$$

where, $\theta = -30°$
where, $\theta = -30°$

∴ $\sin\theta = -0.5,\ \cos\theta = 0.866$

The x, y, z co-ordinates of the mid point of the driving edge are

$$x = 100$$

$$y = 115$$

$$z = \sqrt{200^2 - 100^2 - 115^2} = 129.52$$

where, $\theta = -30°$, $\sin\theta = -0.5$ and $\cos\theta = 0.866$.

And from equation (6.19)

$$\sin\alpha = \frac{100}{\sqrt{100^2 + 115^2}} = 0.6562$$

$$\cos\alpha = \frac{115}{\sqrt{100^2 + 115^2}} = 0.7546$$

$$\sin\beta = \frac{129.52}{200} = 0.6476$$

$$\cos\beta = \frac{\sqrt{100^2 + 115^2}}{200} = 0.762$$

$$\therefore \quad {}^{XYZ}R_{UVW} = \begin{bmatrix} 0.7546 & 0.6562 & 0 \\ -0.6562 & 0.7546 & 0 \\ 0 & 0 & 1 \end{bmatrix} \begin{bmatrix} 1 & 0 & 0 \\ 0 & 0.762 & -0.6476 \\ 0 & 0.6476 & 0.762 \end{bmatrix}$$

$$\begin{bmatrix} 0.866 & 0 & -0.5 \\ 0 & 1 & 0 \\ 0.5 & 0 & 0.866 \end{bmatrix} \begin{bmatrix} 1 & 0 & 0 \\ 0 & 0.762 & 0.6476 \\ 0 & -0.6476 & 0.762 \end{bmatrix} \begin{bmatrix} 0.7546 & -0.6562 & 0 \\ 0.6562 & 0.7546 & 0 \\ 0 & 0 & 1 \end{bmatrix}$$

$$= \begin{bmatrix} 0.7546 & 0.5 & -0.425 \\ -0.6562 & 0.575 & -0.4887 \\ 0 & 0.6476 & 0.762 \end{bmatrix} \begin{bmatrix} 0.866 & 0 & -0.5 \\ 0 & 1 & 0 \\ 0.5 & 0 & 0.866 \end{bmatrix}$$

$$\begin{bmatrix} 0.7546 & -0.6562 & 0 \\ 0.5 & 0.575 & 0.6476 \\ -0.425 & -0.4887 & 0.762 \end{bmatrix}$$

$$\therefore \quad {}^{XYZ}R_{UVW} = \begin{bmatrix} 0.8995 & 0.3623 & -0.2441 \\ -0.2853 & 0.9103 & 0.299887 \\ 0.3309 & -0.2001 & 0.9222 \end{bmatrix}$$

To determine new location of screw with respect to rotated frame,

$$^{UVW}Screw = {}^{UVW}R_{XYZ} \; {}^{XYZ}Screw$$

$$= ({}^{XYZ}R_{UVW})^T \; {}^{XYZ}Screw$$

$$= \begin{bmatrix} 0.8995 & -0.2853 & 0.3309 \\ 0.3623 & 0.9103 & -0.2001 \\ -0.2441 & 0.299887 & 0.9222 \end{bmatrix} \begin{bmatrix} 75 \\ 137 \\ 125 \end{bmatrix}$$

$$\therefore \quad {}^{UVW}Screw = \begin{bmatrix} u \\ v \\ w \end{bmatrix} = \begin{bmatrix} 69.7389 \\ 126.8711 \\ 138.052 \end{bmatrix}$$

To verify the answer, we may check distance of screw from the origin of the frame.

$$\therefore \quad \text{Distance of screw before rotation} = \sqrt{75^2 + 137^2 + 125^2}$$
$$= 200.0475 \text{ mm}$$

and distance after rotation

$$= \sqrt{69.7389^2 + 126.8711^2 + 138.052^2} = 200.0454 \text{ mm}$$

Thus, the new location of the screw with respect to the rotated frame is verified.

Problem 6.9:

Solve Problem 6.8 with following sequence:

Rotation of {UVW} and $\overline{OP}$

1. By angle γ about X-axis.
2. By angle $-\psi$ about Y-axis.
3. By angle θ about Z-axis.
4. By angle ψ about Y-axis.
5. By angle $-\gamma$ about X-axis.

The sequence is shown in Fig. 6.14.

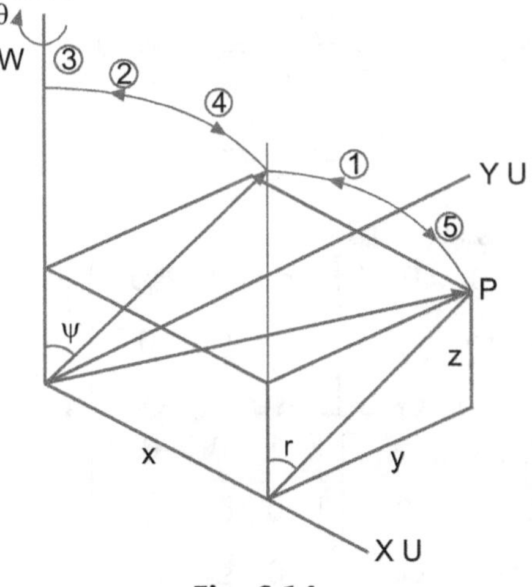

Fig. 6.14

Compare the answers with Problem 6.8.

Solution:

$$^{XYZ}R_{UVW} = R_{X,-\gamma}\ R_{Y,\psi}\ R_{Z,\theta}\ R_{Y,-\psi}\ R_{X,\gamma}$$

where,

$$\theta = -30°$$

$\therefore$

$$\sin\theta = -0.5$$
$$\cos\theta = 0.866$$

As x, y, z co-ordinates of the midpoint of the driving edge are

$$x = 100$$
$$y = 115$$
$$z = 129.52$$

$$\sin\gamma = \frac{y}{\sqrt{y^2 + z^2}} = \frac{115}{\sqrt{115^2 + 129.52^2}}$$

$\therefore$

$$\sin\gamma = 0.663948$$

$$\cos\gamma = \frac{z}{\sqrt{y^2 + z^2}}$$

$$= \frac{129.52}{\sqrt{115^2 + 129.52^2}}$$

$\therefore$

$$\cos\gamma = 0.747779$$

$$\sin\psi = \frac{x}{\sqrt{x^2 + y^2 + z^2}}$$

$$= \frac{100}{200}$$

$\therefore$

$$\sin\psi = 0.5$$

$$\cos\psi = \frac{\sqrt{y^2 + z^2}}{\sqrt{x^2 + y^2 + z^2}}$$

$$= \frac{\sqrt{115^2 + 129.52^2}}{200}$$

$\therefore$

$$\cos\psi = 0.866$$

$\therefore$

$$^{XYZ}R_{UVW} = \begin{bmatrix} 1 & 0 & 0 \\ 0 & c\gamma & s\gamma \\ 0 & -s\gamma & c\gamma \end{bmatrix} \begin{bmatrix} c\psi & 0 & s\psi \\ 0 & 1 & 0 \\ -s\psi & 0 & c\psi \end{bmatrix} \begin{bmatrix} c\theta & -s\theta & 0 \\ s\theta & c\theta & 0 \\ 0 & 0 & 1 \end{bmatrix}$$
$$\begin{bmatrix} c\psi & 0 & -s\psi \\ 0 & 1 & 0 \\ s\psi & 0 & c\psi \end{bmatrix} \begin{bmatrix} 1 & 0 & 0 \\ 0 & c\gamma & -s\gamma \\ 0 & s\gamma & c\gamma \end{bmatrix}$$

$$= \begin{bmatrix} c\psi & 0 & s\psi \\ -s\gamma s\psi & c\gamma & s\gamma c\psi \\ -c\gamma s\psi & -s\gamma & c\gamma c\psi \end{bmatrix} \begin{bmatrix} c\theta & -s\theta & 0 \\ s\theta & c\theta & 0 \\ 0 & 0 & 1 \end{bmatrix} \begin{bmatrix} c\psi & -s\gamma s\psi & -c\gamma s\psi \\ 0 & c\gamma & -s\gamma \\ s\psi & s\gamma c\psi & c\gamma c\psi \end{bmatrix}$$

$$= \begin{bmatrix} 0.866 & 0 & 0.5 \\ -0.663948 \times 0.5 & 0.747779 & 0.663948 \times 0.866 \\ -0.747779 \times 0.5 & -0.663948 & 0.747779 \times 0.866 \end{bmatrix}$$

$$\begin{bmatrix} 0.866 & 0.5 & 0 \\ -0.5 & 0.866 & 0 \\ 0 & 0 & 1 \end{bmatrix} \begin{bmatrix} 0.866 & -0.663948 \times 0.5 & -0.747779 \times 0.5 \\ 0 & 0.747779 & -0.663948 \\ 0.5 & 0.663948 \times 0.866 & 0.747779 \times 0.866 \end{bmatrix}$$

$$= \begin{bmatrix} 0.866 & 0 & 0.5 \\ -0.331974 & 0.747779 & 0.574979 \\ -0.3738895 & -0.663948 & 0.647577 \end{bmatrix} \begin{bmatrix} 0.866 & 0.5 & 0 \\ -0.5 & 0.866 & 0 \\ 0 & 0 & 1 \end{bmatrix}$$

$$\begin{bmatrix} 0.866 & -0.331974 & -0.3738895 \\ 0 & 0.747779 & -0.663948 \\ 0.5 & 0.574979 & 0.647577 \end{bmatrix}$$

$$= \begin{bmatrix} 0.749956 & 0.433 & 0.5 \\ -0.661379 & 0.48159 & 0.574979 \\ 0.008186 & -0.761924 & 0.647577 \end{bmatrix}$$

$$\begin{bmatrix} 0.866 & -0.331974 & -0.3738895 \\ 0 & 0.747779 & -0.663948 \\ 0.5 & 0.574979 & 0.647577 \end{bmatrix}$$

$$\therefore \quad {}^{XYZ}R_{UVW} = \begin{bmatrix} 0.8995 & 0.3623 & -0.2441 \\ -0.2853 & 0.9103 & 0.299887 \\ 0.3309 & -0.2001 & 0.9222 \end{bmatrix}$$

Now, $\quad {}^{UVW}Screw = {}^{UVW}R_{XYZ}\ {}^{XYZ}Screw$

$$= ({}^{XYZ}R_{UVW})^T\ {}^{XYZ}Screw$$

$$= \begin{bmatrix} 0.8995 & -0.2853 & 0.3309 \\ 0.3623 & 0.9103 & -0.2001 \\ -0.2441 & 0.299887 & 0.9222 \end{bmatrix} \begin{bmatrix} 75 \\ 137 \\ 125 \end{bmatrix}$$

$$\therefore \quad {}^{UVW}Screw = \begin{bmatrix} u \\ v \\ w \end{bmatrix} = \begin{bmatrix} 69.7389 \\ 126.8711 \\ 138.052 \end{bmatrix}$$

Thus, answers of Problem 6.8 and Problem 6.9 are exactly matching. Hence, it is verified that the final transformation matrix between frame {XYZ} and frame {UVW} is purely dependent on the vector $\overline{OP}$ and angle of rotation about that vector, only.

6.2.6 Fixed Angle and Euler Angle Representation

In previous section, we saw that {UVW} frame may be completely oriented by rotation of θ angle about any arbitrary axis. Similarly, for complete orientation it may be rotated by certain angles about each of X, Y, and Z axes. For example, let {UVW} be rotated by angle θ about X-axis, then by angle ϕ about Y-axis and finally by angle ψ about Z-axis. Hence, the composite rotation matrix becomes,

$$^{XYZ}R_{UVW} = R_{Z,\psi}\ R_{Y,\phi}\ R_{X,\theta}$$

$$= \begin{bmatrix} c\psi & -s\psi & 0 \\ s\psi & c\psi & 0 \\ 0 & 0 & 1 \end{bmatrix} \begin{bmatrix} c\phi & 0 & s\phi \\ 0 & 1 & 0 \\ -s\phi & 0 & c\phi \end{bmatrix} \begin{bmatrix} 1 & 0 & 0 \\ 0 & c\theta & -s\theta \\ 0 & s\theta & c\theta \end{bmatrix}$$

$$= \begin{bmatrix} c\psi c\phi & -s\psi & c\psi s\phi \\ s\psi c\phi & c\psi & s\psi s\phi \\ -s\phi & 0 & c\phi \end{bmatrix} \begin{bmatrix} 1 & 0 & 0 \\ 0 & c\theta & -s\theta \\ 0 & s\theta & c\theta \end{bmatrix}$$

$$= \begin{bmatrix} c\psi c\phi & c\psi s\phi s\theta - s\psi c\theta & c\psi s\phi c\theta + s\psi s\theta \\ s\psi c\phi & s\psi s\phi s\theta + c\psi c\theta & s\psi s\phi c\theta - c\psi s\theta \\ -s\phi & c\phi s\theta & c\phi c\theta \end{bmatrix} \qquad ...\,(6.20)$$

Thus, we get a matrix with all non-zero elements meaning that each of the moving frame axes is certainly inclined to each of the fixed frame axes. This orientation is known as Fixed angle representation.

Now, if we consider all the rotations about moving frame axes i.e. U, V, W such that rotation by angle ψ about W-axis followed by rotation of ϕ about V-axis and finally rotation by angle θ about U-axis then the composite rotation matrix will be built by post-multiplications and,

$$^{XYZ}R_{UVW} = R_{Z,\psi}\ R_{Y,\phi}\ R_{X,\theta} \text{ meaning that,}$$

$$^{XYZ}R_{UVW} = \begin{bmatrix} C\psi C\phi & C\psi S\phi S\theta - S\psi C\theta & C\psi S\phi C\theta + S\psi S\theta \\ S\psi C\phi & S\psi S\phi S\theta + C\psi C\theta & S\psi S\phi C\theta - C\psi S\theta \\ -S\phi & C\phi S\theta & C\phi C\theta \end{bmatrix} \qquad ...\,(6.21)$$

As none of these rotations is described about fixed axis, this orientation is known as Euler angle representation.

Here, this observation is noteworthy, that the Fixed angle representation and Euler angle representation of the completely oriented frame match exactly.

Euler observed that, although axes are selected from moving frame the resulting orientation matrix (that is composite rotation matrix) will match with that obtained by rotation about certain fixed axes. Further, for complete orientation all the three or any two out of three axes of particular frame may be used and three rotations may be performed. Students may verify the match of the composite matrices obtained in Fixed angle and Euler angle representation listed below.

Fixed angle representation	**Euler angle representation**
1. Rotation of θ about X then Rotation of ϕ and Z then Rotation of ψ and Y.	1. Rotation of ψ about V then Rotation of ϕ about W then Rotation of θ about U.
2. Rotation of α and Y then Rotation of β about X then Rotation of γ and Y	2. Rotation of γ about V then Rotation of β about U then Rotation of α about V.

6.2.7 Transformation Matrix

Consider {XYZ} and {UVW} frames as shown in Fig. 6.15, where orientation of axes is not changed but the origin of {UVW} is displaced by 10 units, 15 units and 20 units in X, Y and Z directions, so that its origin is located at point A.

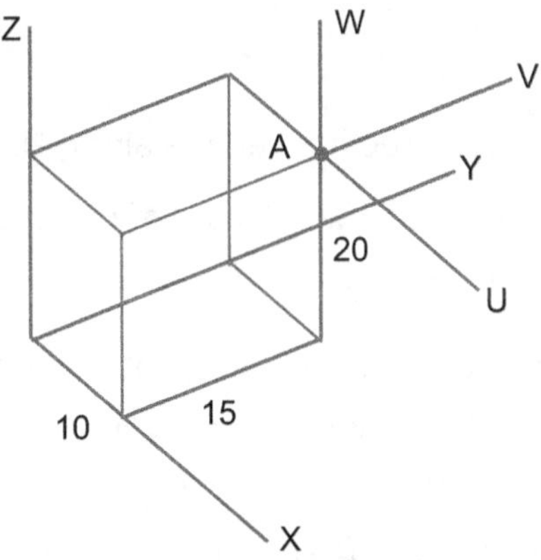

Fig. 6.15

Now, if {UVW} has located a point at (20, 10, 15) then one can imagine that its co-ordinates with respect to {XYZ} will be (30, 25, 35).

To get the co-ordinates by mathematical procedure we construct a 4×4 matrix which will have orientation part and translation part of the frames, as below.

$$^{XYZ}T_{UVW} = \left[\begin{array}{ccc:c} & ^{XYZ}R_{UVW} & & ^{XYZ} \\ \hdashline 0 & 0 & 0 & A \end{array}\right]$$

where,

$^{XYZ}R_{UVW}$ – Composite rotation matrix of order 3×3

^{XYZ}A – Position vector (column) of point A with respect to {XYZ}, so it contains x, y, z co-ordinates of A.

The last row is added to keep the transformation matrix as a square matrix.

The 4×4 matrix has rotation and translation, the two different kinds of motions put together, hence it is called as Homogeneous Transformation Matrix. The four parts of the matrix have names as given below.

$$^{XYZ}T_{UVW} = \left[\begin{array}{c:c} \begin{matrix} 3 \times 3 \text{ Rotation} \\ \text{matrix} \end{matrix} & \begin{matrix} 3 \times 1 \text{ Translation} \\ \text{matrix} \end{matrix} \\ \hdashline \begin{matrix} 1 \times 3 \text{ Perspective} \\ \text{matrix} \end{matrix} & \begin{matrix} 1 \times 1 \text{ Scaling} \\ \text{matrix} \end{matrix} \end{array}\right]$$

It can also be written as,

$$^{XYZ}T_{UVW} = \begin{bmatrix} u & v & w & p \\ 0 & 0 & 0 & 1 \end{bmatrix} \qquad \text{... (6.22)}$$

where,   u, v, w – Indicate direction vectors along U, V, W-axes

and   p – Indicates position vector of origin of {UVW} with respect to {XYZ}

Transformation matrix is unaffected by sequence of rotation and translation, with respect to the given axis. For example, if {UVW} rotates by 90° about X-axis and then translated by 10 units along X-axis, it produces transformation matrix as,

$$^{XYZ}R_{UVW} = \begin{bmatrix} 1 & 0 & 0 & 10 \\ 0 & 1 & 0 & 0 \\ 0 & 0 & 1 & 0 \\ 0 & 0 & 0 & 1 \end{bmatrix} \begin{bmatrix} 1 & 0 & 0 & 0 \\ 0 & c90 & -s90 & 0 \\ 0 & s90 & c90 & 0 \\ 0 & 0 & 0 & 1 \end{bmatrix}$$

$$\therefore \quad {}^{XYZ}T_{UVW} = \begin{bmatrix} 1 & 0 & 0 & 10 \\ 0 & 0 & -1 & 0 \\ 0 & 1 & 0 & 0 \\ 0 & 0 & 0 & 1 \end{bmatrix}$$

But, if it is translated by 10 units along X-axis and then rotated by 90° about X-axis, it produces transformation matrix as,

$${}^{XYZ}T_{UVW} = \begin{bmatrix} 1 & 0 & 0 & 0 \\ 0 & c90 & -s90 & 0 \\ 0 & s90 & c90 & 0 \\ 0 & 0 & 0 & 1 \end{bmatrix} \begin{bmatrix} 1 & 0 & 0 & 10 \\ 0 & 1 & 0 & 0 \\ 0 & 0 & 1 & 0 \\ 0 & 0 & 0 & 1 \end{bmatrix}$$

$$\therefore \quad {}^{XYZ}T_{UVW} = \begin{bmatrix} 1 & 0 & 0 & 10 \\ 0 & 0 & -1 & 0 \\ 0 & 1 & 0 & 0 \\ 0 & 0 & 0 & 1 \end{bmatrix}$$

Thus, in both the cases same transformation matrix is obtained. Therefore, transformation matrix for rotation and translation about a certain axis is denoted as,

$$T_{\text{axis, angle distance}}$$

6.2.8 Composite Homogeneous Transformation Matrix

Composite homogeneous transformation matrix is obtained by multiplication of various homogeneous transforms which correspond to various rotations and translations performed by {UVW} with respect to {XYZ}. The rule for placing a matrix in pre-multiplier or post-multiplier position is same as that for composite rotation matrix.

Problem 6.10:

Get expression for the composite homogeneous transformation matrix, in terms of T if {UVW} is translated by 'a' units along X, then rotated by angle θ about W, then translated by 'b' units and rotated by angle ϕ with respect to Y-axis and finally translated by 'C' units and rotated by angle ψ with respect to U-axis.

Solution:

The sequence of transformation is,

1. $T_{X,0,a}$
2. $T_{W,\theta,0}$

3. $T_{Y,\phi,b}$

4. $T_{U,\psi,c}$

$\therefore$ $T = T_{Y,\phi,b} \qquad T_{X,0,a} \qquad T_{Z,\theta,0} \qquad T_{X,\psi,c}$

                                                       (3)   (1)   (2)   (4)

Problem 6.11:

Write transformation matrix $^{XYZ}T_{UVW}$ for frames {XYZ} and {UVW} located at the corners of an L-shaped block, as shown in Fig. 6.16.

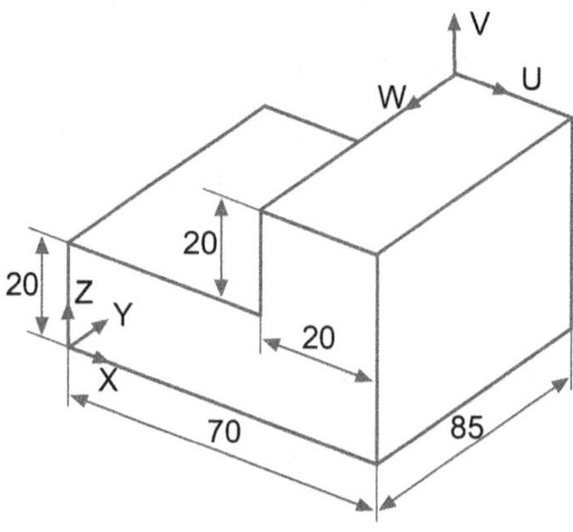

Fig. 6.16

Solution:

x, y, z co-ordinates of the origin of {UVW} are

$$x = 70 - 20 = 50$$

$$y = 85$$

$$z = 20 + 20 = 40$$

Seeing the arrangement of axes, as U is parallel to X, V is parallel to Z and W opposite to Y, the transformation matrix is,

$$^{XYZ}T_{UVW} = \begin{bmatrix} 1 & 0 & 0 & 50 \\ 0 & 0 & -1 & 85 \\ 0 & 1 & 0 & 40 \\ 0 & 0 & 0 & 1 \end{bmatrix}$$

6.2.9 Inverse of Homogeneous Transformation Matrix

For finding inverse of matrix we may use mathematical methods of identity matrix, or cofactors methods. But here we will see a practical approach.

Normally, we write equation for mapping as,

$$^{XYZ}P = {}^{XYZ}T_{UVW}\ {}^{UVW}P$$

but if point P is described in {XYZ} and is to be mapped with respect to {UVW} then, we write

$$^{UVW}P = {}^{UVW}T_{XYZ}\ {}^{XYZ}P$$

where, $^{UVW}T_{XYZ}$ is inverse of $^{XYZ}T_{UVW}$

Let us take an example to get a simple way of obtaining inverse of T.

Example 3:

Let there be a frame {UVW} located at point P (15, 20, 10) with respect to {XYZ} having axis U-opposite to Z-axis, and axis X parallel to V-axis. Let both frames be right handed. Determine location of point Q which is ^{XYZ}Q = (5, 15, 25).

Solution:

Let us do this problem graphically, the arrangements of axes are as shown in Fig. 6.17.

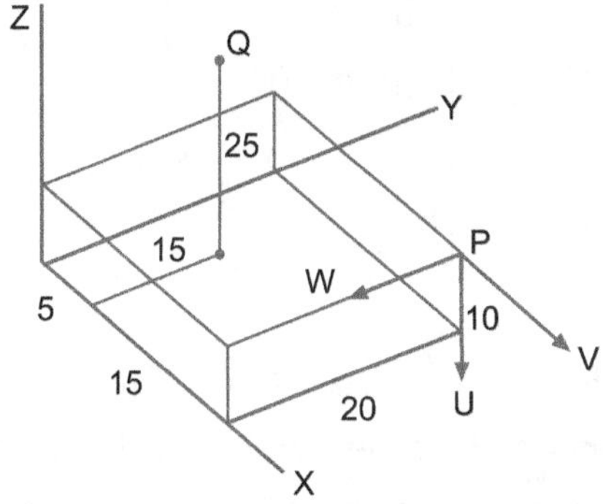

Fig. 6.17

Point Q will have co-ordinates,

$$u = 10 - 25 = -15$$

$$v = -15 + 5 = -10$$

$$w = 20 - 15 = 5$$

Thus, $^{UVW}Q = (-15, -10, 5)$ **... (Ans)**

Simultaneously, we can write $^{XYZ}T_{UVW}$ and $^{UVW}T_{XYZ}$

$$^{XYZ}T_{UVW} = \begin{bmatrix} 0 & 1 & 0 & 15 \\ 0 & 0 & -1 & 20 \\ -1 & 0 & 0 & 10 \\ 0 & 0 & 0 & 1 \end{bmatrix}$$

Similarly,
$$^{UVW}T_{XYZ} = \begin{bmatrix} 0 & 0 & -1 & 10 \\ 1 & 0 & 0 & -15 \\ 0 & -1 & 0 & 20 \\ 0 & 0 & 0 & 1 \end{bmatrix}$$

To verify correctness of $^{UVW}T_{XYZ}$ let us perform mapping as,
$$^{UVW}Q = {}^{UVW}T_{XYZ}\ {}^{XYZ}Q$$

$$\therefore \begin{bmatrix} u \\ v \\ w \\ 1 \end{bmatrix} = \begin{bmatrix} 0 & 0 & -1 & 10 \\ 1 & 0 & 0 & -15 \\ 0 & -1 & 0 & 20 \\ 0 & 0 & 0 & 1 \end{bmatrix} \begin{bmatrix} 5 \\ 15 \\ 25 \\ 1 \end{bmatrix} = \begin{bmatrix} -15 \\ -10 \\ 5 \\ 1 \end{bmatrix} \qquad \textbf{... (Ans)}$$

which matches with the graphical result.

Now, a keen observation will show that,

If
$$^{XYZ}T_{UVW} = \begin{bmatrix} u & v & w & p \\ 0 & 0 & 0 & 1 \end{bmatrix}$$

then,
$$(^{XYZ}T_{UVW})^{-1} = {}^{UVW}T_{XYZ} = \begin{bmatrix} ^{UVW}R_{XYZ} & \vdots & -u^Tp \\ & \vdots & -v^Tp \\ & \vdots & -w^Tp \\ \cdots & \cdots & \cdots \\ 0 \ \ 0 \ \ 0 & \vdots & 1 \end{bmatrix} \qquad \text{... (6.23)}$$

where,
$$^{UVW}R_{XYZ} = (^{XYZ}R_{UVW})^{-1} = (^{XYZ}R_{UVW})^T$$

and u^Tp is sum of products of first elements of columns 1 and 4, second elements of columns 1 and 4 and third elements of columns 1 and 4.

Similarly, v^Tp and w^Tp are sums of products of corresponding elements of columns 2 and 4 and columns 3 and 4 respectively.

Problem 6.12:

Find T^{-1} where,

$$T = \begin{bmatrix} 0.5687 & -0.7141 & 0.4082 & 10 \\ 0.7462 & 0.6567 & 0.1094 & 20 \\ -0.3462 & 0.2424 & 0.9063 & 30 \\ 0 & 0 & 0 & 1 \end{bmatrix}$$

Solution:

The rotation part will be simply transposed and the translation part will be evaluated as,
$$u^Tp = 0.5687 \times 10 + 0.7462 \times 20 - 0.3462 \times 30 = 10.225$$
$$v^Tp = -0.7141 \times 10 + 0.6567 \times 20 + 0.2424 \times 30 = 13.265$$
$$w^Tp = 0.4082 \times 10 + 0.1094 \times 20 + 0.9063 \times 30 = 33.459$$

$$\therefore \quad T^{-1} = \begin{bmatrix} 0.5687 & 0.7462 & -0.3462 & -10.225 \\ -0.7141 & 0.6567 & 0.2424 & -13.265 \\ 0.4082 & 0.1094 & 0.9063 & -33.459 \\ 0 & 0 & 0 & 1 \end{bmatrix}$$

Let us verify the inverse given by equation (6.23) with the cofactors method of determining inverse of matrix.

$$\text{Cofactor of } 1, 1 = (-1)^{1+1} \begin{vmatrix} 0.6567 & 0.1094 & 20 \\ 0.2424 & 0.9063 & 30 \\ 0 & 0 & 1 \end{vmatrix}$$

$$= 0.6567\,(0.9063 \times 1 - 30 \times 0) - 0.1094\,(0.2424 \times 1 - 30 \times 0)$$
$$+ 20\,(0.2424 \times 0 - 0.9063 \times 0)$$

$$\doteq 0.5687$$

$$\text{Cofactor of } 1, 2 = (-1)^{1+2} \begin{vmatrix} 0.7462 & 0.1094 & 20 \\ -0.3462 & 0.9063 & 30 \\ 0 & 0 & 1 \end{vmatrix}$$

$$= -1 \times [0.7462\,(0.9063 \times 1 - 30 \times 0) - 0.1094\,(-0.3462 \times 1 - 30$$
$$\times 0) + 20\,(-0.3462 \times 0 - 0.9063 \times 0)]$$

$$\doteq 0.7141$$

$$\text{Cofactor of } 1, 3 = (-1)^{1+3} \begin{vmatrix} 0.7462 & 0.6567 & 20 \\ -0.3462 & 0.2424 & 30 \\ 0 & 0 & 1 \end{vmatrix}$$

$$= 0.7462\,(0.2424 \times 1 - 30 \times 0) - 0.6567\,(-0.3462 \times 1 - 30 \times 0) +$$
$$20\,(-0.3462 \times 0 - 0.2424 \times 0)$$

$$\doteq 0.4082$$

$$\text{Cofactor of } 1, 4 = (-1)^{1+4} \begin{vmatrix} 0.7462 & 0.6567 & 0.1094 \\ -0.3462 & 0.2424 & 0.9063 \\ 0 & 0 & 0 \end{vmatrix}$$

$$= 0$$

$$\text{Cofactor of 2, 1} = (-1)^{2+1} \begin{vmatrix} -0.7141 & 0.4082 & 10 \\ 0.2424 & 0.9063 & 30 \\ 0 & 0 & 1 \end{vmatrix}$$

$$= -1 \times [-0.7141\,(0.9063 \times 1 - 30 \times 0)$$
$$- 0.4082\,(0.2424 \times 1 - 30 \times 0) + 10\,(0.2424 \times 0 - 0.9063 \times 0)]$$

$$\doteq 0.7462$$

$$\text{Cofactor of 2, 2} = (-1)^{2+2} \begin{vmatrix} 0.5687 & 0.4082 & 10 \\ -0.3462 & 0.9063 & 30 \\ 0 & 0 & 1 \end{vmatrix}$$

$$= 0.5687\,(0.9063 \times 1 - 30 \times 0) - 0.4082\,(-0.3462 \times 1 - 30 \times 0)$$
$$+ 10\,(-0.3462 \times 0 - 0.9063 \times 0)$$

$$\doteq 0.6567$$

$$\text{Cofactor of 2, 3} = (-1)^{2+3} \begin{vmatrix} 0.5687 & -0.7141 & 10 \\ -0.3462 & 0.2424 & 30 \\ 0 & 0 & 1 \end{vmatrix}$$

$$= -1 \times [0.5687\,(0.2424 \times 1 - 30 \times 0) +$$
$$0.7141\,(-0.3462 \times 1 - 30 \times 0) + 10\,(-0.3462 \times 0 - 0.2424 \times 0)]$$

$$\doteq 0.1094$$

$$\text{Cofactor of 2, 4} = (-1)^{2+4} \begin{vmatrix} 0.5687 & -0.7141 & 0.4082 \\ -0.3462 & 0.2424 & 0.9063 \\ 0 & 0 & 0 \end{vmatrix}$$

$$= 0$$

$$\text{Cofactor of 3, 1} = (-1)^{3+1} \begin{vmatrix} -0.7141 & 0.4082 & 10 \\ 0.6567 & 0.1094 & 20 \\ 0 & 0 & 1 \end{vmatrix}$$

$$= -0.7141\,(0.1094 \times 1 - 20 \times 0) - 0.4082\,(0.6567 \times 1 - 20 \times 0)$$
$$+ 10\,(0.6567 \times 0 - 0.1094 \times 0)$$

$$\doteq -0.3462$$

$$\text{Cofactor of 3, 2} = (-1)^{3+2} \begin{vmatrix} 0.5687 & 0.4082 & 10 \\ 0.7462 & 0.1094 & 20 \\ 0 & 0 & 1 \end{vmatrix}$$

$$= -1 \times [0.5687 \, (0.1094 \times 1 - 20 \times 0) -$$
$$0.4082 \, (0.7462 \times 1 - 20 \times 0) + 10 \, (0.7462 \times 0 - 0.1094 \times 0)]$$
$$\doteq 0.2424$$

$$\text{Cofactor of 3, 3} \; = (-1)^{3+3} \begin{vmatrix} 0.5687 & -0.7141 & 10 \\ 0.7462 & 0.6567 & 20 \\ 0 & 0 & 1 \end{vmatrix}$$

$$= 0.5687 \, (0.6567 \times 1 - 20 \times 0) + 0.7141 \, (0.7462 \times 1 - 20 \times 0)$$
$$+ 10 \, (0.7462 \times 0 - 0.6567 \times 0)$$
$$\doteq 0.9063$$

$$\text{Cofactor of 3, 4} \; = (-1)^{3+4} \begin{vmatrix} 0.5687 & -0.7141 & 0.4082 \\ 0.7462 & 0.6567 & 0.1094 \\ 0 & 0 & 0 \end{vmatrix}$$

$$= 0$$

$$\text{Cofactor of 4, 1} \; = (-1)^{4+1} \begin{vmatrix} -0.7141 & 0.4082 & 10 \\ 0.6567 & 0.1094 & 20 \\ 0.2424 & 0.9063 & 30 \end{vmatrix}$$

$$= -1 \times [-0.7141 \, (0.1094 \times 30 - 0.9063 \times 20) - 0.4082 \, (0.6567 \times 30$$
$$- 0.2424 \times 20) + 10 \, (0.6567 \times 0.9063 - 0.2424 \times 0.1094)]$$
$$= -10.225$$

$$\text{Cofactor of 4, 2} \; = (-1)^{4+2} \begin{vmatrix} 0.5687 & 0.4082 & 10 \\ 0.7462 & 0.1094 & 20 \\ -0.3462 & 0.9063 & 30 \end{vmatrix}$$

$$= 0.5687 \, (0.1094 \times 30 - 0.9063 \times 20) - 0.4082 \, (0.7462 \times 30 +$$
$$0.3462 \times 20) + 10 \, (0.7462 \times 0.9063 + 0.3462 \times 0.1094)$$
$$= -13.265$$

$$\text{Cofactor of 4, 3} \; = (-1)^{4+3} \begin{vmatrix} 0.5687 & -0.7141 & 10 \\ 0.7462 & 0.6567 & 20 \\ -0.3462 & 0.2424 & 30 \end{vmatrix}$$

$$= -1 \times [0.5687 \, (0.6567 \times 30 - 0.2424 \times 20)$$
$$+ 0.7141 \, (0.7462 \times 30 + 0.3462 \times 20)$$
$$+ 10 \, (0.7462 \times 0.2424 + 0.3462 \times 0.6567)]$$
$$= -33.459$$

$$\text{Cofactor of 4, 4} = (-1)^{4+4} \begin{vmatrix} 0.5687 & -0.7141 & 0.4082 \\ 0.7462 & 0.6567 & 0.1094 \\ -0.3462 & 0.2424 & 0.9063 \end{vmatrix}$$

$$= 0.5687\,(0.6567 \times 0.9063 - 0.2424 \times 0.1094)$$
$$+ 0.7141\,(0.7462 \times 0.9063 + 0.3462 \times 0.1094)$$
$$+ 0.4082\,(0.7462 \times 0.2424 + 0.3462 \times 0.6567)$$
$$\doteqdot 1$$

Now, $\text{Inverse} = \dfrac{1}{\text{Determinant}}\ \text{Transpose of cofactors matrix}$

where,   Determinant = Element 1, 1 × Cofactor of 1, 1

+ Element 1, 2 × Cofactor of 1, 2

+ Element 1, 3 × Cofactor of 1, 3

+ Element 1, 4 × Cofactor of 1, 4

∴   Determinant = $0.5687 \times 0.5687 + 0.7141 \times 0.7141$

$+ 0.4082 \times 0.4082 + 10 \times 0$

$= 0.99998754 \doteqdot 1$

$$\therefore \quad \text{Inverse} = \begin{bmatrix} 0.5687 & 0.7462 & -0.3462 & -10.225 \\ -0.7141 & 0.6567 & 0.2424 & -13.265 \\ 0.4082 & 0.1094 & 0.9063 & -33.459 \\ 0 & 0 & 0 & 1 \end{bmatrix}$$

6.2.10 Purposes of Transformations

The purpose of studying transformations is to map a fixed point between the frames. Now exactly where in robotics this mapping is required?

The end effector of the robot may be at a distance from the base of the robot. The orientation and location of end effector may be described with respect to the wrist which is adjoining part of robot from its anatomy. Also, there may be a work piece in the work space of the robot. The location and orientation of the object may be described by co-ordinate system of viewing camera which is totally a foreign body for the robot. Now, a controller at robot base has to move the end effector towards the work piece for performing certain task. Thus, the controller needs to have knowledge of orientation and position of the end effector as well as the work piece. If relationship between base co-ordinate system and camera system is known, mapping of work piece will be possible. Similarly, if relationship between base co-ordinate system and wrist co-ordinate system is established, mapping of end effector also will be possible. The later part i.e. establishing relationship between the base frame and wrist frame depends on robot configuration parameters such as link length, joint angle. Denavit and Hartenberg proposed a scheme of establishing relation between frames attached to the ends of links using two joint parameters and two link parameters, thus only four parameters in all. The scheme or the method may be extended beyond one or two links to the whole robot from its base to end effector to establish relationship between the fixed frame and the last out of all moving frames.

6.3 The Denavit-Hartenberg Parameters (D-H Parameters)

(W-11)

6.3.1 D-H Notation   (W-11)

- Robot can be described kinematically by giving the values of four quantities for each link. Out of which two of them describe link itself and remaining two describe the link's connection (i.e. joint) to a neighbouring link. The definition of mechanisms by means of these quantities is a convention usually called as **Denavit-Hartenberg notation.**

  Also a systematic procedure for assigning right-handed orthonormal co-ordinate frames, one to each link in an open kinematic chain, was proposed by Denavit and Hartenberg in 1955.

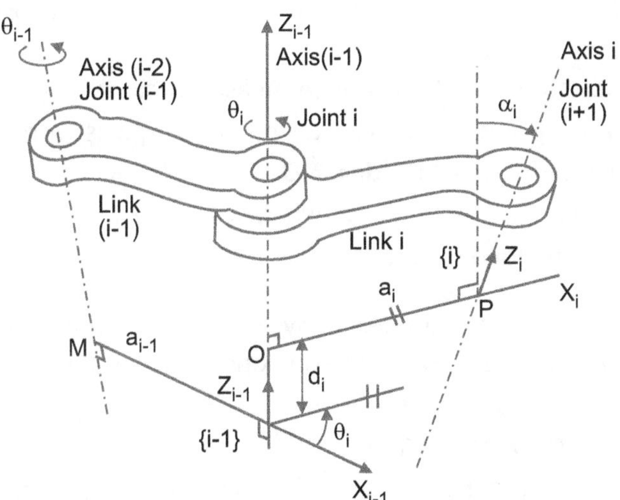

**Fig. 6.18: D-H parameters for Assigning Frames
to Links and Identifying Joint-link Parameters**

- A frame {i} is rigidly attached to end of link i. An n-DoF manipulator will have (n + 1) frames with the frame {0} or base frame acting as the 'reference inertial frame' and frame {n} being the 'tool frame'.

- Fig. 6.18 shows a pair of adjacent links, link (i – 1) and link i, their associated joints, joint (i – 1), joint i and joint (i + 1), and axes (i – 2), (i – 1) and i respectively. Line MN is the common normal to (i – 2) and (i – 1) axes and line OP is the common normal to (i – 1) and i axes.

A frame {i} is assigned to link i as follows:

(i)   The **z_i-axis** is aligned with axis i, its direction being arbitrary. The choice of direction defines the positive sense of joint variable θ_i.

(ii) The **x_i-axis** is perpendicular to axis z_{i-1} and z_i and points away from axis z_{i-1}, i.e. x_i-axis is directed along the common normal OP.

(iii) The origin of the ith co-ordinate frame, frame {i}, is located at the intersection of axis of joint (i + 1), i.e. axis i and the common normal OP between axes (i – 1) and i.

(iv) **y_i-axis** completes the right-handed orthonormal co-ordinate frame {i}.

The frame {i} is at the end of link i and moves with the link.

- The four D-H parameters with respect to frame {i – 1} and frame {i} (two link parameters (a_i, α_i) and two joint parameters (d_i, θ_i) are defined as:

    (i)   Link length (a_i): It is the distance measured along x_i-axis from the point of intersection of x_i-axis and z_{i-1} axis to the origin of frame {i}, i.e. distance OP.

    (ii) Link twist (α_i): It is the angle between z_{i-1} and z_i-axes measured about x_i-axis in the right-handed sense.

    (iii) Joint distance (d_i): It is the distance measured along z_{i-1} axis from the origin of frame {i – 1} (i.e. point N) to the intersection of x_i axis with z_{i-1} axis (i.e. point O), which is equal to distance **NO. d_i = NO**.

    (iv) Joint angle (θ_i): It is the angle between x_{i-1} and x_i axes measured about the z_{i-1} axis in the right-handed sense.

The above description of D-H parameters may look very complicated to understand, for beginners. Hence, we will discuss D-H parameters once again in the following section.

6.3.2 Understanding D-H Parameters   (W-11)

For understanding D-H Parameters, refer Fig. 6.19. Let frame {0} be the reference frame to list D-H Parameters of frame {1}. Frames {0} and {1} are arranged at corners of a rectangular box. D-H Parameters, in simple words are as follows:

θ_1 is angle from X_0 to X_1 looking through Z_0.

α_1 is angle from Z_0 to Z_1 when looking through X_1.

d_1 is distance between origins along Z_0.

a_1 is distance between origins along X_1.

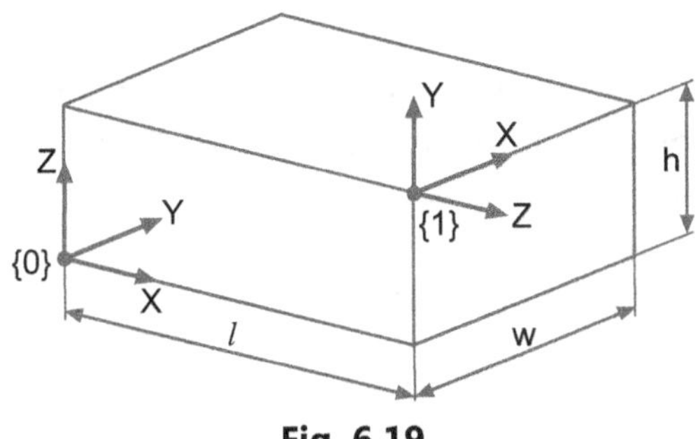

Fig. 6.19

To determine sign of angle θ_1 curl right hand fingers from X_0 to X_1 if thumb points in the direction of Z_0, then θ_1 is positive, otherwise it is negative. Similarly, curl right hand fingers from Z_0 to Z_1 if thumb points in the direction of X_1, then α_1 is positive, otherwise it is negative.

To determine sign of distance d_1, imagine a vector joining origin of {0} to origin of {1}. If component of this vector projected on axis Z_0 is in the direction of Z_0, then distance d_1 is positive, otherwise it is negative. Similarly, if component of the same vector projected on axis X_1 is in the direction of X_1, then distance a_1 is positive, otherwise it is negative.

$$\theta_1 = +90°$$
$$\alpha_1 = +90°$$
$$d_1 = +h$$
$$a_1 = 0$$

6.3.3 Limitations of D-H Parameters   (W-11)

If the co-ordinate frames are not arranged properly, D-H Parameters will not provide all possible information.

Case 1: One of the two distances or both may be equal to zero. For example, {0} and {1} shown in Fig. 6.18 are separated by distances l and h. But the distance l is not listed by D-H Parameters.

Case 2: Both the angles are not measurable. Refer Fig. 6.20. You cannot have thumb opposite to or in the direction of Z_0 when other fingers are curled from X_0 to X_1.

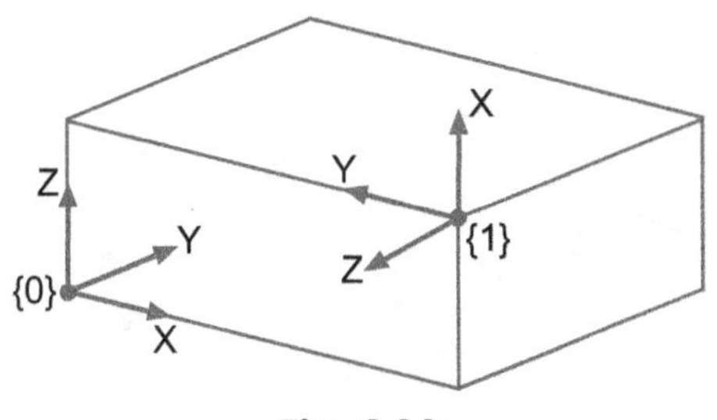

Fig. 6.20

Lastly, one more major limitation is that D-H Parameter cannot list information related to two frames if they are separated three dimensionally. For example, consider the frames {0} and {1} attached to the ends of solid diagonal of the rectangular box as shown in Fig. 6.21. Surely, origins are separated by distances l, w and h in three different directions. But there are only two distance parameters, in the list of D-H Parameters. Hence, maximum two distances will be considered and one will surely be skipped by D-H Parameter scheme.

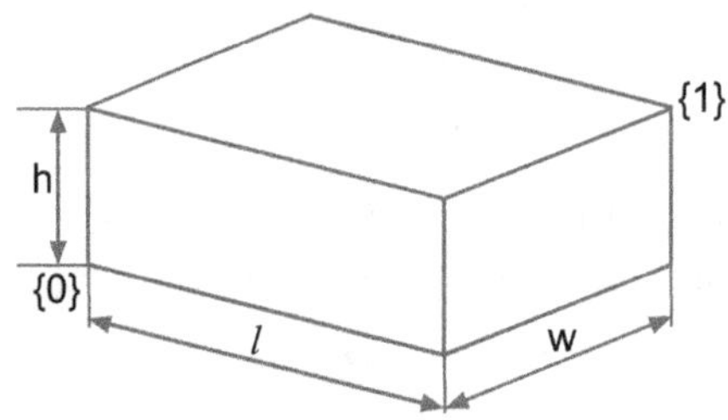

Fig. 6.21

6.3.4 Overcoming the Limitations

To overcome the first two limitations, frames may be arranged properly so that X_i will be perpendicular to Z_{i-1}.

In general, when joint movement is known, arrange frames in the following steps:
1.   Align Z_{i-1}, Z_i, etc. along the movement of joint.

     That means the Z-axis must be in the direction of translation if the joint is linear and in the direction of axis if the joint is rotary.

     That is, in the same direction if joint is linear and in the direction of axis if it is rotating.
2.   Arrange X_i perpendicular to both, Z_{i-1} and Z_i.
3.   Arrange Y_{i-1}, Y_i so that the frames are right handed.

To overcome the major limitation of 3D separation, user may arrange series of frames between the two frames, which are to be related to each other. Fig. 6.22 shows frames {S} and {E} for a start and an end point. To list complete information regarding the position and orientation of {E} with respect to {S}, an intermediate frame {I} is introduced so that all the three distances are listed.

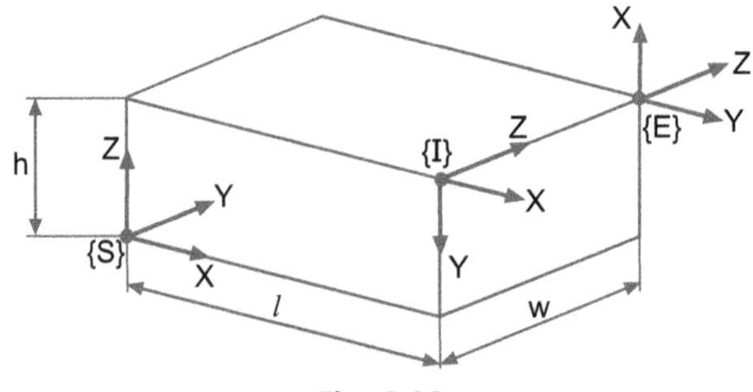

Fig. 6.22

D-H Parameters

Point	θ	d	a	α
I	0°	h	l	−90°
E	90°	w	0	0°

Note: D-H Parameters of {I} are listed with respect to {S} and for {E} with respect to {I}.

6.3.5 Use of D-H Parameters

D-H Parameters are useful in determing 4×4 homogeneous transformation matrix between the two frames. This matrix helps in mapping position of a point between the frames. That means, if a point is located with respect to frame {1} and it is required to locate it with respect to frame {0}, then 4×4 homogeneous transformation matrix between {0} and {1} multiplied by position matrix of the point with respect to {1} will produce position matrix of the point with respect to {0}.

Mathematically, for given point P,

$$^{0}P = {}^{0}T_1 \, {}^{1}P \qquad\qquad\qquad \text{... (6.24)}$$

where, ^{1}P is list of x, y, z co-ordinates of point P with respect to {1} in a column matrix form.

^{0}P is list of x, y, z co-ordinates of point P with respect to {0} in a column matrix form.

and $^{0}T_1$ is 4×4 homogeneous transformation matrix between {0} and {1}.

6.3.6 Physical Significance of D-H Parameters

A keen observation shows that D-H Parameters list rotation and translation about Z_{i-1}, and rotation translation about X_i. Physical significance of these rotations and translations will be understood if frame {i} is initially located at {i − 1} with the same orientation. Then, apply rotations and translations in sequence as follows:

1.   Rotation of {i} by θ_i about Z_{i-1}.
2.   Translation of {i} by d_i along Z_{i-1}.
3.   Rotation of {i} by α_i along X_i.
4.   Translation of {i} by a_i along X_i.

For understanding this sequence take example of frames {S} and {I} shown in Fig. 6.22 where the D-H Parameters are already listed as,

$\theta = 0, d = h, a = l, \alpha = -90°$

The sequence is explained step-by-step in Fig. 6.23 (a) to (e).

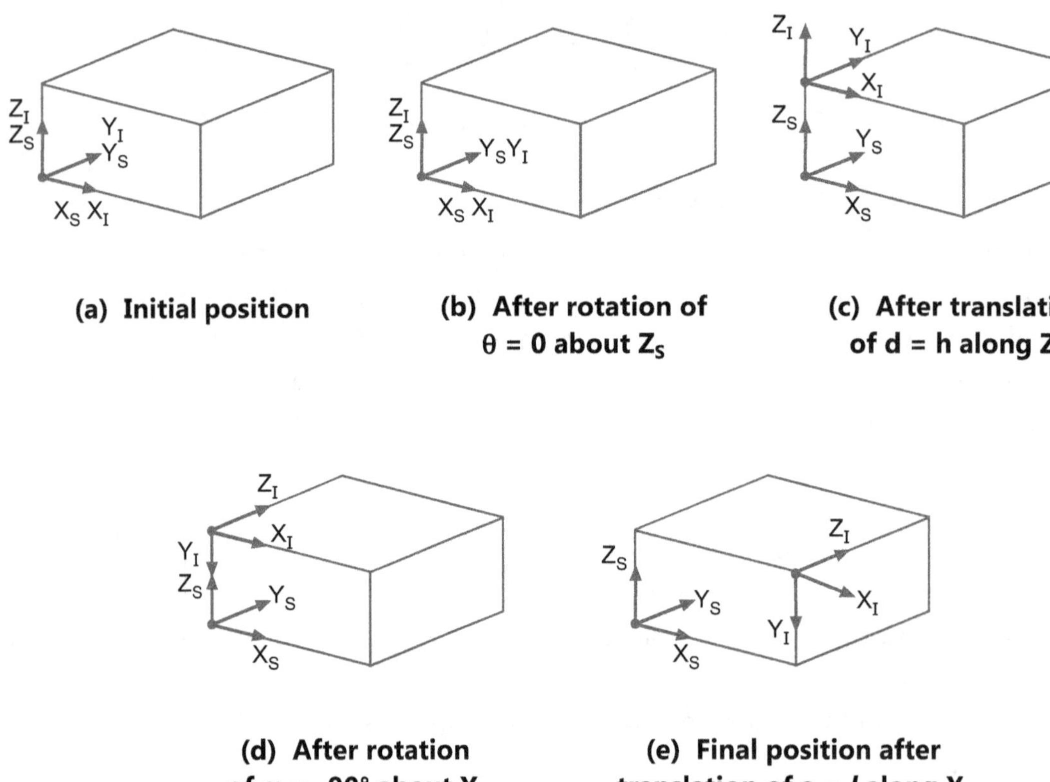

(a) Initial position   **(b) After rotation of**   **(c) After translation**
                                $\theta = 0$ about Z_S   **of $d = h$ along Z_S**

(d) After rotation   **(e) Final position after**
of $\alpha = -90°$ about X_I **translation of $a = l$ along X_I**

Fig. 6.23: Rotations and translations of the frame using DH Parameters

The rotations and translations shown in Fig. 6.23 may be written mathematically as,

$$^{S}T_I = T_{z_S}, \theta, d \quad T_{X_I}, \alpha, a$$

$$= \begin{bmatrix} c\theta & -s\theta & 0 & 0 \\ s\theta & c\theta & 0 & 0 \\ 0 & 0 & 1 & d \\ 0 & 0 & 0 & 1 \end{bmatrix} \begin{bmatrix} 1 & 0 & 0 & a \\ 0 & c\alpha & -s\alpha & 0 \\ 0 & s\alpha & c\alpha & 0 \\ 0 & 0 & 0 & 1 \end{bmatrix}$$

$$\therefore \qquad ^{S}T_I = \begin{bmatrix} c\theta & -s\theta c\alpha & s\theta s\alpha & ac\theta \\ s\theta & c\theta c\alpha & -c\theta s\alpha & as\theta \\ 0 & s\alpha & c\alpha & d \\ 0 & 0 & 0 & 1 \end{bmatrix} \qquad \qquad ... (6.25)$$

6.4 Mapping Revisited

If point P is located in frame {E}, then it would be mapped in frame {I} as,

$$^{I}P = {}^{I}T_{E}\ {}^{E}P \qquad\qquad ...\,(6.26)$$

where, $^{I}T_{E}$ may be found by equation (6.26).

Further, the point P which is now described in frame {I} as ^{I}P may be mapped in frame {S} as,

$$^{S}P = {}^{S}T_{I}\ {}^{I}P \qquad\qquad ...\,(6.27)$$

Substituting for ^{I}P from equation (6.25),

$$^{S}P = {}^{S}T_{I}\ {}^{I}T_{E}\ {}^{E}P$$

Thus,
$$^{S}P = {}^{S}T_{E}\ {}^{E}P \qquad\qquad ...\,(6.28)$$

where,
$$^{S}T_{E} = {}^{S}T_{I}\ {}^{I}T_{E} \qquad\qquad ...\,(6.29)$$

This logic may be extended to a six degrees-of-freedom robot that is a six-joint-robot, where co-ordinate frame {0} is attached to the fixed base and frames {1}, {2}, {3}, {4}, {5} and {6} are attached to the joints in sequence. Finally, gripper has its own co-ordinate frame {7}. Here, gripper co-ordinate frame locates an object which will be mapped in base frame as,

$$^{0}P = {}^{0}T_{1}\ {}^{1}T_{2}\ {}^{2}T_{3}\ {}^{3}T_{4}\ {}^{4}T_{5}\ {}^{5}T_{6}\ {}^{6}T_{7}\ {}^{7}P \qquad\qquad ...\,(6.30)$$

All the above transformation matrices may be obtained conveniently using D-H Parameters scheme.

6.5 Forward Kinematics

6.5.1 Introduction

In this Section, we will apply knowledge of Denavit Hartenberg Parameters to various manipulator configurations and will study method of establishing relationship of orientation and position of end effector with the base frame.

In the type of problems, we are going to solve in this section, the link and joint parameters will be available to us. And we will find out location of the free end. This is typically a forward kinematics problem, also known as direct kinematics problem.

If the position of the free end or the end effector is known and we are determining the configuration parameters to locate end effector to that position, the problem by its nature is called as inverse kinematics problem.

The comparison of forward and inverse kinematics may be better visualised by a table given below.

Table 6.1

	Configuration parameters like link length, joint angles	Desired location of end effector
Forward kinematics	Known	Not known
Inverse kinematics	Not known	Known

6.5.2 Reviewing the Transformations

As mentioned in the last section, there may be practical situations when relations between (that is transformations between) robot base and object, object and camera etc. are known. The study till last section will help us getting solutions to those problems.

Problem 6.13:

A camera is used to locate an object and the robot base. The three co-ordinate frames are as shown in Fig. 6.24. The homogeneous transformation matrix between camera and robot base and that between camera and object are as below.

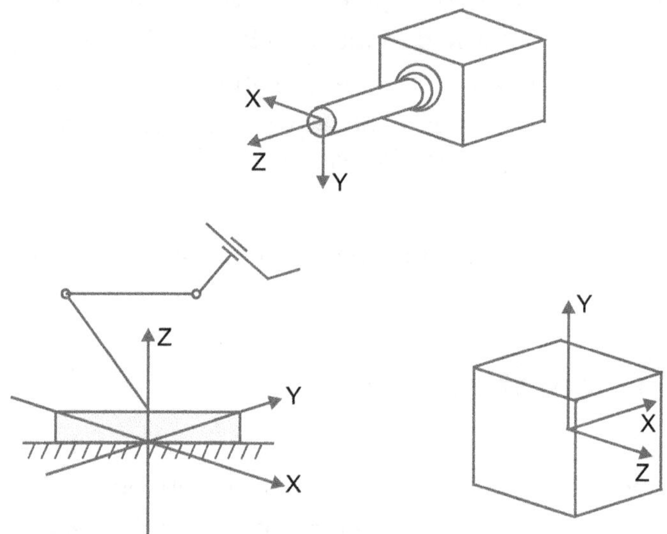

Fig. 6.24

$$^{camera}T_{robot} = \begin{bmatrix} -1 & 0 & 0 & 25 \\ 0 & 0 & -1 & 55 \\ 0 & -1 & 0 & 125 \\ 0 & 0 & 0 & 1 \end{bmatrix} \qquad ^{camera}T_{object} = \begin{bmatrix} 0 & 0 & -1 & -20 \\ 0 & -1 & 0 & 45 \\ -1 & 0 & 0 & 30 \\ 0 & 0 & 0 & 1 \end{bmatrix}$$

The work volume of the robot is hemisphere of radius 100 units. State whether the object can be reached by the end effector.

Solution:

To check whether the object can be reached, we require the true distance of the object from base of the robot. If this distance is smaller than the radius of hemispherical work volume, the object will be in reach of the robot, otherwise out of reach of the robot.

To know true distance between the base of the robot and the object, let us find relation i.e. transformation matrix between them.

Therefore, using equation (6.29),

$$^{robot}T_{object} = {}^{robot}T_{camera} \; {}^{camera}T_{object}$$

And

$$^{robot}T_{camera} = ({}^{camera}T_{robot})^{-1}$$

Using equation (6.23),

$$^{robot}T_{camera} = \begin{bmatrix} -1 & 0 & 0 & 25 \\ 0 & 0 & -1 & 125 \\ 0 & -1 & 0 & 55 \\ 0 & 0 & 0 & 1 \end{bmatrix}$$

$$\therefore \quad {}^{robot}T_{object} = \begin{bmatrix} -1 & 0 & 0 & 25 \\ 0 & 0 & -1 & 125 \\ 0 & -1 & 0 & 55 \\ 0 & 0 & 0 & 1 \end{bmatrix} \begin{bmatrix} 0 & 0 & -1 & -20 \\ 0 & -1 & 0 & 45 \\ -1 & 0 & 0 & 30 \\ 0 & 0 & 0 & 1 \end{bmatrix}$$

$$^{robot}T_{object} = \begin{bmatrix} 0 & 0 & 1 & 45 \\ 1 & 0 & 0 & 95 \\ 0 & 1 & 0 & 10 \\ 0 & 0 & 0 & 1 \end{bmatrix}$$

The translation matrix of this transform is position vector of the object with respect to the robot base co-ordinate frame.

$$\therefore \quad \text{Magnitude of the position vector} = \sqrt{45^2 + 95^2 + 10^2} = 105.5936 \text{ units}$$

Hence, the object is out of reach of the robot.

Problem 6.14:

A camera locates an object by,

$$^{camera}T_{object} = \begin{bmatrix} 0 & -1 & 0 & 50 \\ 1 & 0 & 0 & -75 \\ 0 & 0 & 1 & 20 \\ 0 & 0 & 0 & 1 \end{bmatrix}$$

The camera is then translated by 15 units along Z-axis of the object, then rotated about its own X-axis by −90°. Determine the new relation between camera and object.

Solution:

It is seen that the object is not moving, hence temporarily considering it to be a reference frame.

Using equation (6.23),

$$^{object}T_{camera} = \begin{bmatrix} 0 & 1 & 0 & 75 \\ -1 & 0 & 0 & 50 \\ 0 & 0 & 1 & -20 \\ 0 & 0 & 0 & 1 \end{bmatrix}$$

Now, translation is along axis of the object and rotation is about axis of the camera. Hence, composite homogeneous transformation matrix.

Using conclusions derived from the Example 1 and Example 2 solved in earlier section under Section 6.4, will be,

$$^{object}T_{camera_{New}} = T_{z,0°,15} \; {}^{object}T_{camera} \; T_{x,-90°,0}$$

$$= \begin{bmatrix} 1 & 0 & 0 & 0 \\ 0 & 1 & 0 & 0 \\ 0 & 0 & 1 & 15 \\ 0 & 0 & 0 & 1 \end{bmatrix} \begin{bmatrix} 0 & 1 & 0 & 75 \\ -1 & 0 & 0 & 50 \\ 0 & 0 & 1 & -20 \\ 0 & 0 & 0 & 1 \end{bmatrix} \begin{bmatrix} 1 & 0 & 0 & 0 \\ 0 & c(-90) & -s(-90) & 0 \\ 0 & s(-90) & c(-90) & 0 \\ 0 & 0 & 0 & 1 \end{bmatrix}$$

$$= \begin{bmatrix} 0 & 1 & 0 & 75 \\ -1 & 0 & 0 & 50 \\ 0 & 0 & 1 & -5 \\ 0 & 0 & 0 & 1 \end{bmatrix} \begin{bmatrix} 1 & 0 & 0 & 0 \\ 0 & 0 & 1 & 0 \\ 0 & -1 & 0 & 0 \\ 0 & 0 & 0 & 1 \end{bmatrix} = \begin{bmatrix} 0 & 0 & 1 & 75 \\ -1 & 0 & 0 & 50 \\ 0 & -1 & 0 & -5 \\ 0 & 0 & 0 & 1 \end{bmatrix}$$

Let us get back to the style of writing the relation i.e. $^{camera}T_{object}$.

Then the new relation between camera and object is,

$$^{camera}T_{object} = (^{object}T_{camera_{New}})^{-1}$$

$$= \begin{bmatrix} 0 & -1 & 0 & 50 \\ 0 & 0 & -1 & -5 \\ 1 & 0 & 0 & -75 \\ 0 & 0 & 0 & 1 \end{bmatrix}$$

6.5.3 Orientation of Gripper

The gripper will also have its co-ordinate frame which must be properly aligned with the frame of the object (or workpiece) so that gripping will be possible. Usually, gripper is oriented in such a way that its Z-axis is aligned in the direction of movement for gripping the object. In other words, it is the direction in which gripper approaches the object. Hence, Z-axis of gripper is also called as 'Approach vector'. The gripper usually has fingers which slide in and out for holding and releasing the object. Y-axis is normally kept parallel to this movement, so Y-axis of gripper is called as 'Sliding vector'. Finally, X-axis is placed in perpendicular (normal) direction, simultaneously with Y-axis and Z-axis, making the frame right handed. So the X-axis of gripper may be termed as 'Normal vector'. Fig. 6.25 shows all the three vectors for a 2-finger gripper.

Y-axis may be taken in downward direction. That will naturally change orientation of X-axis by 180°.

The gripper is normally related with robot base frame or for convenience sometimes it may be related with object's co-ordinate frame.

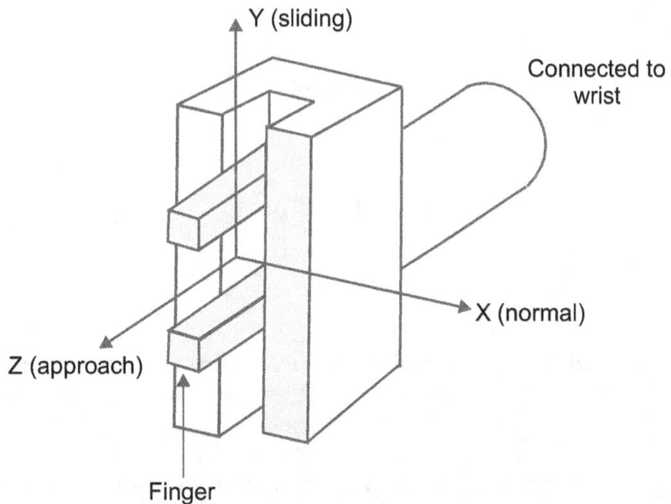

Fig. 6.25: Co-ordinate frame of a gripper

With whichever {XYZ} frame it is related to, the homogeneous transform will be written as,

$$^{XYZ}T_{Gripper} = \begin{bmatrix} n & s & a & p \\ 0 & 0 & 0 & 1 \end{bmatrix} \qquad \dots (3.1)$$

where,
  n – normal vector (X-axis of gripper)
  s – sliding vector (Y-axis of gripper)
  a – approach vector (Z-axis of gripper)
  p – position vector

Problem 6.15:

A robot shown in Fig. 6.26 is used to grip a cubical object so that the gripper moves towards centre of the object in the opposite direction to that of X-axis of the object. The fingers of the gripper move parallel to X-axis of the robot base. Determine orientation of gripper with respect to the base co-ordinate frame of the robot and also with respect to the object's co-ordinate frame. Also determine orientation and position of object with respect to the base of robot.

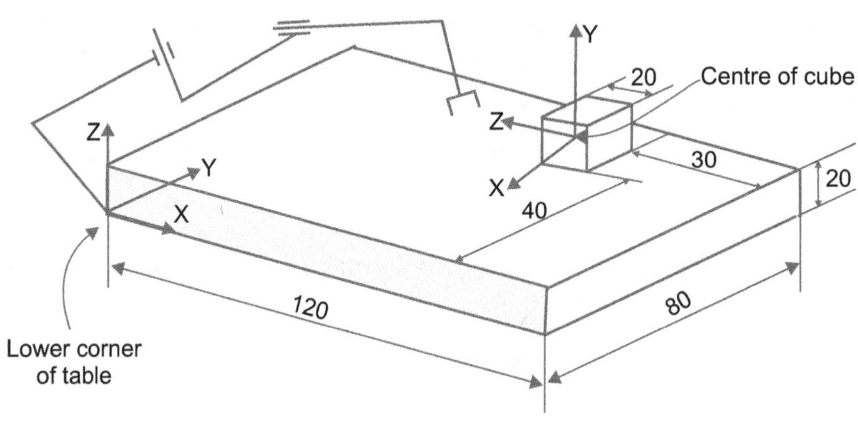

Fig. 6.26

Solution:

The gripper approach is opposite to X_{object} that is parallel to Y_{base}.

Similarly, sliding parallel to X_{base} that is parallel to Z_{object}.

Let us take direction of sliding vector pointing away from base that is parallel to X_{base} and opposite to Z_{object}.

Thus, relation of gripper co-ordinate system with other two may be shown as in Fig. 6.27 (a) and (b).

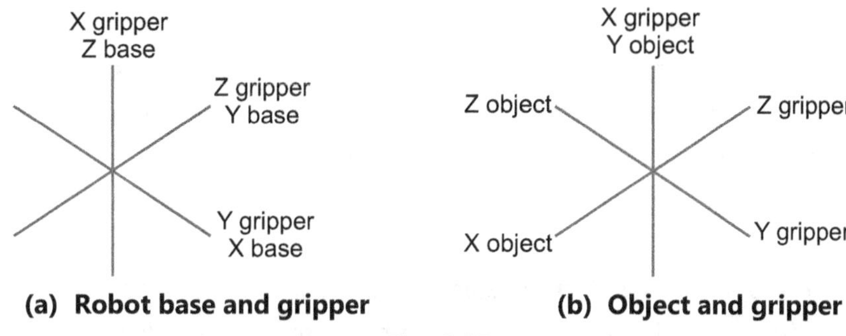

(a) Robot base and gripper   **(b) Object and gripper**

Fig. 6.27

$$\therefore \qquad {}^{base}R_{gripper} = \begin{bmatrix} 0 & 1 & 0 \\ 0 & 0 & 1 \\ 1 & 0 & 0 \end{bmatrix}$$

$$\text{and} \qquad {}^{object}R_{gripper} = \begin{bmatrix} 0 & 0 & -1 \\ 1 & 0 & 0 \\ 0 & -1 & 0 \end{bmatrix}$$

The two rotation matrices give required orientations of gripper.

From the orientations and dimensions given in the figure, orientation and position of object with respect to the base frame of the robot may be given by ${}^{base}T_{object}$ as,

$$ {}^{base}T_{object} = \begin{bmatrix} 0 & 0 & -1 & 80 \\ -1 & 0 & 0 & 50 \\ 0 & 1 & 0 & 30 \\ 0 & 0 & 0 & 1 \end{bmatrix}$$

6.5.4 Forward Kinematics applied to Various Manipulators

The main aim of forward kinematics is to determine orientation and position of end point (that is end effector) of the robot with respect to the co-ordinate frame attached to the base. We already have seen that Denavit Hartenberg parameters may be sequentially listed for all the joints starting from the base to the end effector. A row in the DH Parameters table helps us to determine relation between that joint and its previous joint, in the form of 4×4 homogeneous transformation matrix. If all such matrices are obtained and multiplied, in sequence, then we get a composite homogeneous transformation matrix which is the desired orientation and position of the end effector with respect to the co-ordinate frame attached to the base of robot. In this section, we will see variety of such examples.

One can take differently oriented co-ordinate frames than those shown in this book. As long as rules, regarding selection of the directions for axes, mentioned in "Overcoming limitations" from earlier section: "Rotations and Transformations" are strictly followed user is going to get correct orientation and position according to what that user has fixed at the base and the end effector.

If one maintains the orientations of frames at the base and the end effector as shown in this book, but takes differently oriented frames at intermediate joints and/or left handed systems at those joints, then also the final composite homogeneous transformation matrix, the user gets will exactly be same as that printed in this book.

This is because composite transformation matrix does not depend on intermediate frames or intermediate transformation matrices, it purely depends on the two co-ordinate frames between which the transform (transformation matrix) is written.

It is important to note that the DH parameters are listed when the robot is standstill and not moving. If it starts moving, the homogeneous transform will vary with respect to time. Hence, differentiation of the transformation matrix may lead to the study of differential motions like velocity, acceleration. The differential motions are not in the scope of undergraduate studies.

Another point worth mentioning is that, DH Parameters look constant as they are listed when the configuration is not moving. It does not mean that all the parameters will vary once the robot starts moving. It is quite interesting and useful to identify the nature of each parameter as either fixed or variable parameters. In the following examples, the fixed and variable natures of parameters are also listed.

Sometimes, it is necessary to have additional co-ordinate frame at the same joint. The additional co-ordinate frame is needed when the one (original) co-ordinate frame at a particular joint is incapable of listing DH parameters properly. In such cases, homogeneous transformation matrix is just an orientation matrix, which may be directly written without DH Parameters. Hence, listing DH Parameters between the two coinciding frames (which may be impossible in some cases) may be skipped, and that transformation matrix may directly be written. In the examples presented in this book, wherever additional frames are attached they are oriented in such a way that listing of DH Parameters is not impossible. Hence, the DH parameters are listed for those frames, too.

6.5.4 (i) Cartesian Configuration

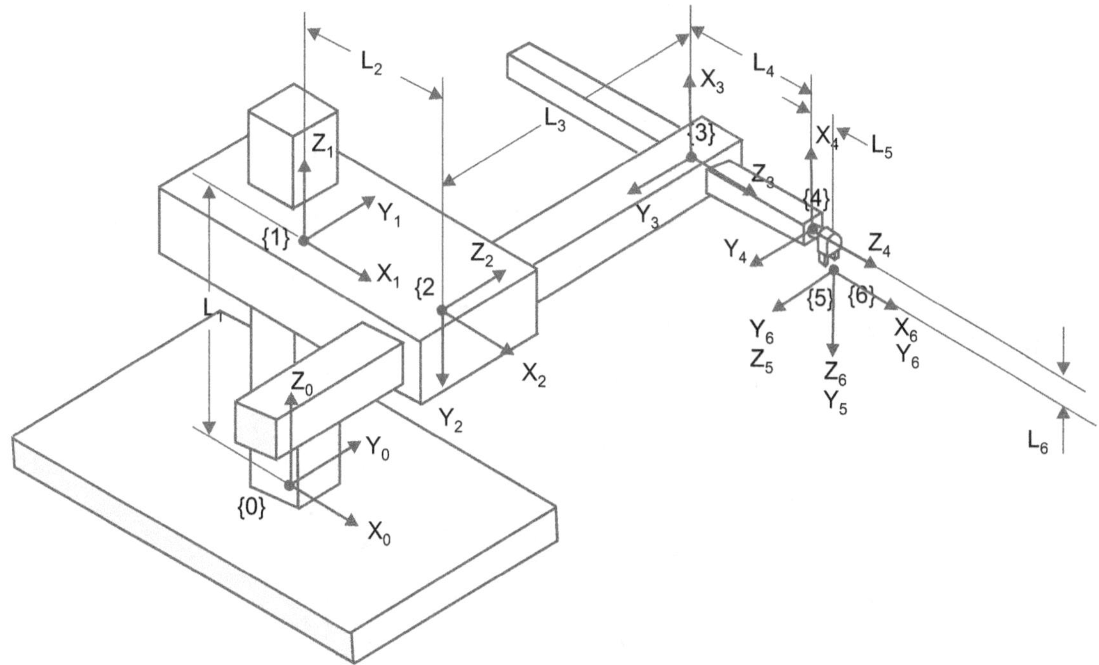

Fig. 6.28: Cartesian Configuration

Fig. 6.28 shows the Cartesian configuration with co-ordinate frames assigned at various joints, at the base and at the end effector. Frame {0} is assigned to the base and frame {6} is assigned to the end effector. Hence, we intend to find transformation between frame {0} and frame {6}. Additional frame {5} is attached at the end effector. This is because, {6} is attached considering approach, sliding and normal vectors of the gripper. And that frame is incapable of listing DH parameters with respect to prior joint i.e. frame {4}, because X_6 is not perpendicular to Z_4. Hence, frame {5} is being attached in such a way that X_5 is perpendicular to Z_4. Fortunately, X_6 is perpendicular to Z_5 so we can list DH parameters for {6} with respect to {5}. Otherwise we would have directly written $^5T_6$ by observing the alignments of axes.

Transformation matrix without DH Parameters:

In the case shown in Fig. 6.28, as X, Y, Z axes of frame {0} and frame {6} are either at 0°, 90°, 180° or 270° with each other, one may directly write $^0T_6$ by observing the alignments of axes and co-ordinates of origin of frame {6} with respect to frame {0}, as below.

Axis X_6 is parallel to and in the same direction of axis X_0.

Axis Y_6 is parallel to and in the opposite direction of axis Y_0.

Axis Z_6 is parallel to and in the opposite direction of axis Z_0.

Further, x, y, z co-ordinates origin of frame {6} with respect to frame {0} are:

$$x = L_2 + L_4 + L_5$$
$$y = L_3$$
$$z = L_1 - L_6$$

$$\therefore \quad {}^0T_6 = \begin{bmatrix} 1 & 0 & 0 & L_2 + L_4 + L_5 \\ 0 & -1 & 0 & L_3 \\ 0 & 0 & -1 & L_1 - L_6 \\ 0 & 0 & 0 & 1 \end{bmatrix}$$

DH Parameters:

Frame	θ_i	d_i	a_i	α_i
1	0	L_1	0	0
2	0	0	L_2	$-90°$
3	$-90°$	L_3	0	$-90°$
4	0	L_4	0	0
5	$180°$	L_5	L_6	$90°$
6	$90°$	0	0	$90°$

Composite Homogeneous Matrix:

$${}^0T_6 = {}^0T_1 \, {}^1T_2 \, {}^2T_3 \, {}^3T_4 \, {}^4T_5 \, {}^5T_6$$

Using equation (6.25),

$${}^0T_6 = \begin{bmatrix} 1 & 0 & 0 & 0 \\ 0 & 1 & 0 & 0 \\ 0 & 0 & 1 & L_1 \\ 0 & 0 & 0 & 1 \end{bmatrix} \begin{bmatrix} 1 & 0 & 0 & L_2 \\ 0 & 0 & 1 & 0 \\ 0 & -1 & 0 & 0 \\ 0 & 0 & 0 & 1 \end{bmatrix} \begin{bmatrix} 0 & 0 & 1 & 0 \\ -1 & 0 & 0 & 0 \\ 0 & -1 & 0 & L_3 \\ 0 & 0 & 0 & 1 \end{bmatrix}$$

$$\begin{bmatrix} 1 & 0 & 0 & 0 \\ 0 & 1 & 0 & 0 \\ 0 & 0 & 1 & L_4 \\ 0 & 0 & 0 & 1 \end{bmatrix} \begin{bmatrix} -1 & 0 & 0 & -L_6 \\ 0 & 0 & 1 & 0 \\ 0 & 1 & 0 & L_5 \\ 0 & 0 & 0 & 1 \end{bmatrix} \begin{bmatrix} 0 & 0 & 1 & 0 \\ 1 & 0 & 0 & 0 \\ 0 & 1 & 0 & 0 \\ 0 & 0 & 0 & 1 \end{bmatrix}$$

$$= \begin{bmatrix} 1 & 0 & 0 & L_2 + L_4 + L_5 \\ 0 & -1 & 0 & L_3 \\ 0 & 0 & -1 & L_1 - L_6 \\ 0 & 0 & 0 & 1 \end{bmatrix}$$

Fixed and Variable Parameters:
All angle parameters except θ_5, which is now 180°, are fixed. This is because, all joints except joint 4, are prismatic, and joint 4 is a rotating joint.
In addition to the angles, lengths L_2, L_5 and L_6 are also fixed.
As the lengths L_1, L_3, L_4 are variables, DH parameters dependent on L_1, L_3, L_4 along with θ_5 are also varying in nature.
Thus, in all d_1, d_3, d_4 and θ_5 these four DH Parameters out of 24 parameters listed in table are varying.

6.5.4 (ii) Cylindrical Configuration
The cylindrical configuration with frames attached is shown in Fig. 6.29.

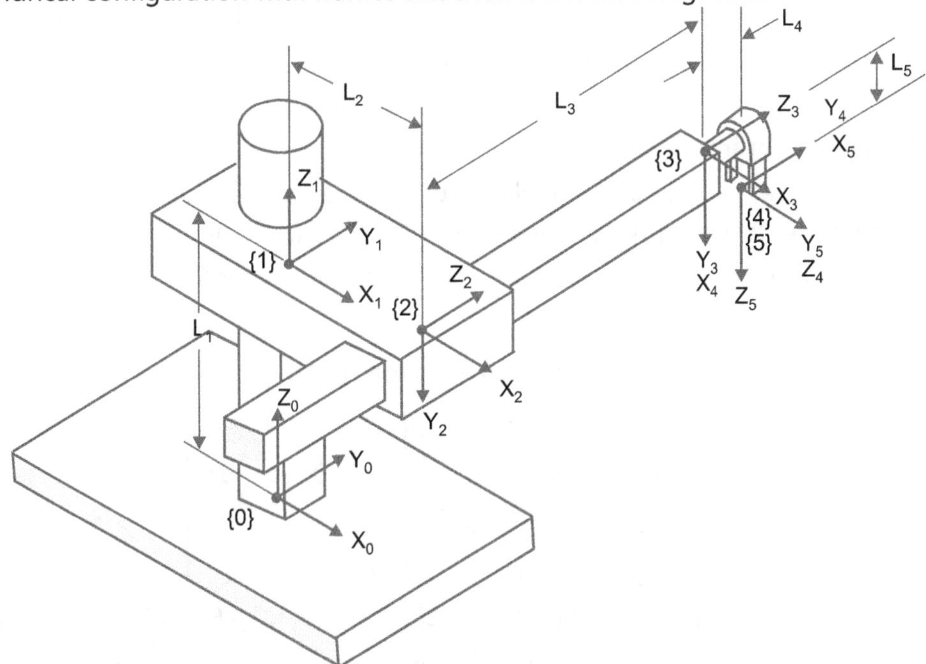

Fig. 6.29: Cylindrical Configuration

For the same reason as that mentioned in description for the Cartesian configuration, frame {4} is attached as an additional frame coinciding with {5}.
DH Parameters:

Frame	θ_i	d_i	a_i	α_i
1	0	L_1	0	0
2	0	0	L_2	−90°
3	0	L_3	0	0
4	90°	L_4	L_5	90°
5	90°	0	0	90°

Composite Homogeneous Transformation Matrix:

$$^0T_5 = \ ^0T_1 \ ^1T_2 \ ^2T_3 \ ^3T_4 \ ^4T_5$$

Using equation (6.25),

$$
^0T_5 =
\begin{bmatrix}
1 & 0 & 0 & 0 \\
0 & 1 & 0 & 0 \\
0 & 0 & 1 & L_1 \\
0 & 0 & 0 & 1
\end{bmatrix}
\begin{bmatrix}
1 & 0 & 0 & L_2 \\
0 & 0 & 1 & 0 \\
0 & -1 & 0 & 0 \\
0 & 0 & 0 & 1
\end{bmatrix}
\begin{bmatrix}
1 & 0 & 0 & 0 \\
0 & 1 & 0 & 0 \\
0 & 0 & 1 & L_3 \\
0 & 0 & 0 & 1
\end{bmatrix}
$$

$$
\begin{bmatrix}
0 & 0 & 1 & 0 \\
1 & 0 & 0 & L_5 \\
0 & 1 & 0 & L_4 \\
0 & 0 & 0 & 1
\end{bmatrix}
\begin{bmatrix}
0 & 0 & 1 & 0 \\
1 & 0 & 0 & 0 \\
0 & 1 & 0 & 0 \\
0 & 0 & 0 & 1
\end{bmatrix}
=
\begin{bmatrix}
0 & 1 & 0 & L_2 \\
1 & 0 & 0 & L_3 + L_4 \\
0 & 0 & -1 & L_1 - L_5 \\
0 & 0 & 0 & 1
\end{bmatrix}
$$

Fixed and Variable Parameters:

It is clear that lengths L_1 and L_3 are variable. Also frame {1} rotates about {0} and {4} rotates about {3}. Therefore, θ_1 which is now listed as 0° and θ_4 which is now listed as 90°, and distances d_1, d_3 are variable otherwise remaining 16 parameters are fixed.

Modified Composite Homogeneous Transformation Matrix:

$$
^0T_5 =
\begin{bmatrix}
c\theta_1 & -s\theta_1 & 0 & 0 \\
s\theta_1 & c\theta_1 & 0 & 0 \\
0 & 0 & 1 & L_1 \\
0 & 0 & 0 & 1
\end{bmatrix}
\begin{bmatrix}
1 & 0 & 0 & L_2 \\
0 & 0 & 1 & 0 \\
0 & -1 & 0 & 0 \\
0 & 0 & 0 & 1
\end{bmatrix}
$$

$$
\begin{bmatrix}
1 & 0 & 0 & 0 \\
0 & 1 & 0 & 0 \\
0 & 0 & 1 & L_3 \\
0 & 0 & 0 & 1
\end{bmatrix}
\begin{bmatrix}
c\theta_4 & 0 & s\theta_4 & L_5c\theta_4 \\
s\theta_4 & 0 & -c\theta_4 & L_5s\theta_4 \\
0 & 1 & 0 & L_4 \\
0 & 0 & 0 & 1
\end{bmatrix}
\begin{bmatrix}
0 & 0 & 1 & 0 \\
1 & 0 & 0 & 0 \\
0 & 1 & 0 & 0 \\
0 & 0 & 0 & 1
\end{bmatrix}
$$

To reduce length of writing the expressions, we will replace $c\theta_1$ by c_1, $s\theta_1$ by s_1, $c\theta_4$ by c_4 and $s\theta_4$ by s_4.

$$
\therefore \quad ^0T_5 =
\begin{bmatrix}
c_1 & -s_1 & 0 & 0 \\
s_1 & c_1 & 0 & 0 \\
0 & 0 & 1 & L_1 \\
0 & 0 & 0 & 1
\end{bmatrix}
\begin{bmatrix}
1 & 0 & 0 & L_2 \\
0 & 0 & 1 & L_3 \\
0 & -1 & 0 & 0 \\
0 & 0 & 0 & 1
\end{bmatrix}
\begin{bmatrix}
0 & s_4 & c_4 & L_5c_4 \\
0 & -c_4 & s_4 & L_5s_4 \\
1 & 0 & 0 & L_4 \\
0 & 0 & 0 & 1
\end{bmatrix}
$$

$$= \begin{bmatrix} c_1 & 0 & -s_1 & L_2c_1 - L_3s_1 \\ s_1 & 0 & c_1 & L_2s_1 + L_3c_1 \\ 0 & -1 & 0 & L_1 \\ 0 & 0 & 0 & 1 \end{bmatrix} \begin{bmatrix} 0 & s_4 & c_4 & L_5c_4 \\ 0 & -c_4 & s_4 & L_5s_4 \\ 1 & 0 & 0 & L_4 \\ 0 & 0 & 0 & 1 \end{bmatrix}$$

$\therefore$ The real and useful transformation matrix for any arbitrary position of cylindrical configuration is,

$$^0T_5 = \begin{bmatrix} -s_1 & c_1s_4 & c_1c_4 & L_5c_1c_4 - L_4s_1 + L_2c_1 - L_3s_1 \\ c_1 & s_1s_4 & s_1c_4 & L_5s_1c_4 + L_4c_1 + L_2s_1 + L_3c_1 \\ 0 & c_4 & -s_4 & L_1 - L_5s_4 \\ 0 & 0 & 0 & 1 \end{bmatrix}$$

where, θ_1 and θ_4 both can have any value from 0° to 360°, separately.

6.5.4 (iii) Spherical Configuration

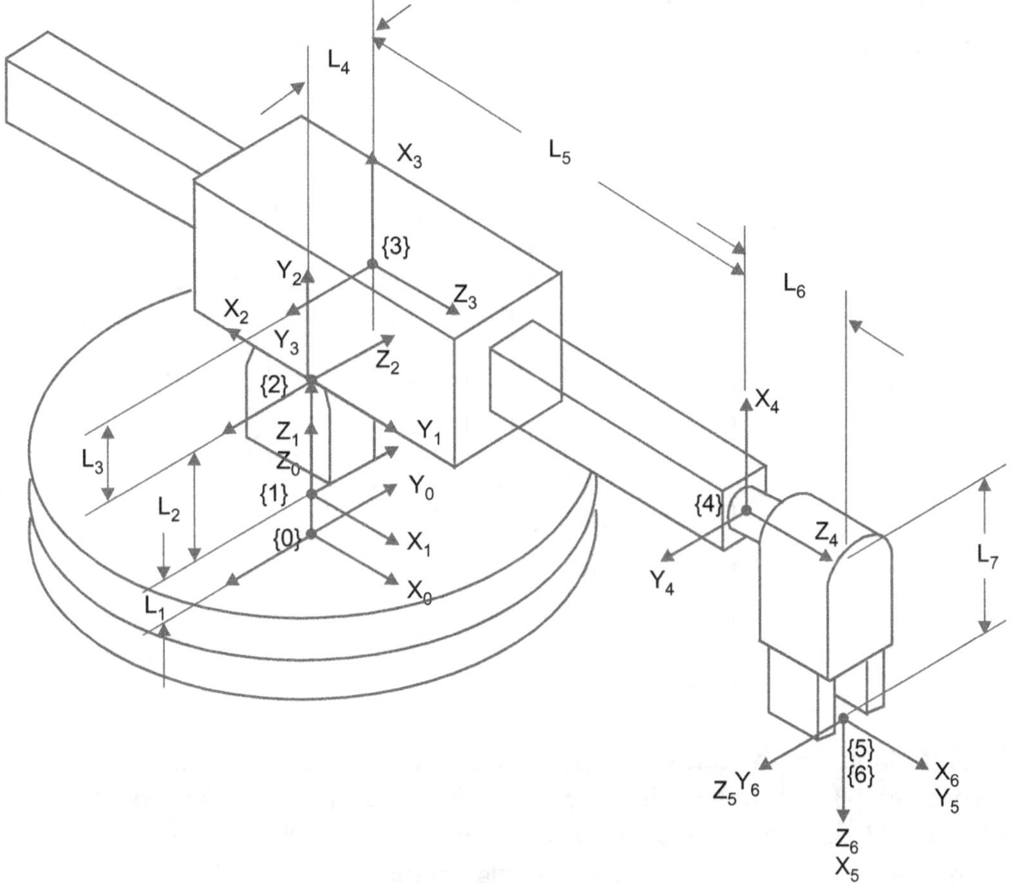

Fig. 6.30: Spherical Configuration

Fig. 6.30 shows the spherical configuration with the co-ordinate frames {1}, {2}, {3} and {4} attached to the joints. Frame {0} attached to the base and frames {5} and {6} attached to the end effector.

DH Parameters:

Frame	θ_i	d_i	a_i	α_i
1	0	L_1	0	0
2	180°	L_2	0	90°
3	90°	L_4	L_3	−90°
4	0	L_5	0	0
5	180°	L_6	L_7	90°
6	90°	0	0	90°

Composite Homogeneous Transformation Matrix:

Using equation (6.25),

$$^0T_6 = {}^0T_1\,{}^1T_2\,{}^2T_3\,{}^3T_4\,{}^4T_5\,{}^5T_6$$

$$^0T_6 = \begin{bmatrix} 1 & 0 & 0 & 0 \\ 0 & 1 & 0 & 0 \\ 0 & 0 & 1 & L_1 \\ 0 & 0 & 0 & 1 \end{bmatrix} \begin{bmatrix} -1 & 0 & 0 & 0 \\ 0 & 0 & 1 & 0 \\ 0 & 1 & 0 & L_2 \\ 0 & 0 & 0 & 1 \end{bmatrix} \begin{bmatrix} 0 & 0 & -1 & 0 \\ 1 & 0 & 0 & L_3 \\ 0 & -1 & 0 & L_4 \\ 0 & 0 & 0 & 1 \end{bmatrix}$$

$$\begin{bmatrix} 1 & 0 & 0 & 0 \\ 0 & 1 & 0 & 0 \\ 0 & 0 & 1 & L_5 \\ 0 & 0 & 0 & 1 \end{bmatrix} \begin{bmatrix} -1 & 0 & 0 & -L_7 \\ 0 & 0 & 1 & 0 \\ 0 & 1 & 0 & L_6 \\ 0 & 0 & 0 & 1 \end{bmatrix} \begin{bmatrix} 0 & 0 & 1 & 0 \\ 1 & 0 & 0 & 0 \\ 0 & 1 & 0 & 0 \\ 0 & 0 & 0 & 1 \end{bmatrix}$$

$$= \begin{bmatrix} 1 & 0 & 0 & L_5 + L_6 \\ 0 & -1 & 0 & L_4 \\ 0 & 0 & -1 & L_1 + L_2 + L_3 - L_7 \\ 0 & 0 & 0 & 1 \end{bmatrix}$$

Fixed and Variable Parameter: Frame {1} can rotate with respect to {0}, frame {3} can rotate with respect to {2} and frame {5} can rotate with respect to {4}. Due to sliding in the prismatic joint {3}, length L_5 can vary. Hence, θ_1, θ_3 and θ_5 which are currently 0°, 90°, 180° respectively and the distance d_4 are the variable parameters. Remaining 20 parameters are fixed.

Modified Composite Homogeneous Transformation Matrix:

$${}^{0}T_6 = \begin{bmatrix} c_1 & -s_1 & 0 & 0 \\ s_1 & c_1 & 0 & 0 \\ 0 & 0 & 1 & L_1 \\ 0 & 0 & 0 & 1 \end{bmatrix} \begin{bmatrix} -1 & 0 & 0 & 0 \\ 0 & 0 & 1 & 0 \\ 0 & 1 & 0 & L_2 \\ 0 & 0 & 0 & 1 \end{bmatrix} \begin{bmatrix} c_3 & 0 & -s_3 & L_3c_3 \\ s_3 & 0 & c_3 & L_3s_3 \\ 0 & -1 & 0 & L_4 \\ 0 & 0 & 0 & 1 \end{bmatrix}$$

$$\begin{bmatrix} 1 & 0 & 0 & 0 \\ 0 & 1 & 0 & 0 \\ 0 & 0 & 1 & L_5 \\ 0 & 0 & 0 & 1 \end{bmatrix} \begin{bmatrix} c_5 & 0 & s_5 & L_7c_5 \\ s_5 & 0 & -c_5 & L_7s_5 \\ 0 & 1 & 0 & L_6 \\ 0 & 0 & 0 & 1 \end{bmatrix} \begin{bmatrix} 0 & 0 & 1 & 0 \\ 1 & 0 & 0 & 0 \\ 0 & 1 & 0 & 0 \\ 0 & 0 & 0 & 1 \end{bmatrix}$$

$$= \begin{bmatrix} -c_1 & 0 & -s_1 & 0 \\ -s_1 & 0 & c_1 & 0 \\ 0 & 1 & 0 & L_1+L_2 \\ 0 & 0 & 0 & 1 \end{bmatrix} \begin{bmatrix} c_3 & 0 & -s_3 & L_3c_3- L_5s_3 \\ s_3 & 0 & c_3 & L_3s_3 + L_5c_3 \\ 0 & -1 & 0 & L_4 \\ 0 & 0 & 0 & 1 \end{bmatrix}$$

$$\begin{bmatrix} 0 & s_5 & c_5 & L_7c_5 \\ 0 & -c_5 & s_5 & L_7s_5 \\ 1 & 0 & 0 & L_6 \\ 0 & 0 & 0 & 1 \end{bmatrix}$$

$$= \begin{bmatrix} -c_1c_3 & s_1 & c_1s_3 & L_5c_1s_3 - L_3c_1c_3 -L_4s_1 \\ -s_1c_3 & -c_1 & s_1s_3 & L_5s_1s_3 - L_3s_1c_3 + L_4c_1 \\ s_3 & 0 & c_3 & L_1 + L_2 + L_3s_3 + L_5c_3 \\ 0 & 0 & 0 & 1 \end{bmatrix} \begin{bmatrix} 0 & s_5 & c_5 & L_7c_5 \\ 0 & -c_5 & s_5 & L_7s_5 \\ 1 & 0 & 0 & L_6 \\ 0 & 0 & 0 & 1 \end{bmatrix}$$

$$= \begin{bmatrix} c_1s_3 & -c_1c_3s_5 - s_1c_5 & s_1s_5 - c_1c_3c_5 & (L_5c_1s_3 - L_3c_1c_3 -L_4s_1 + L_6c_1s_3 + L_7s_1s_5 - L_7c_1c_2c_3) \\ s_1s_3 & c_1c_5 - s_1c_3s_5 & -s_1c_3c_5 - c_1s_5 & (L_5s_1s_3 - L_3s_1c_3 + L_4c_1 + L_6s_1s_3 - L_7c_1s_5 - L_7s_1c_3c_5) \\ c_3 & s_3s_5 & s_3c_5 & (L_1 + L_2 +L_3s_3 + L_5c_3 + L_6c_3 + L_7s_3c_5) \\ 0 & 0 & 0 & 1 \end{bmatrix}$$

where, θ_1 and θ_5 may have any value between 0° and 360°. Angle θ_3 will have limited range of variation due to physical limitations of the joint.

6.5.4 (iv) Jointed Arm Configuration

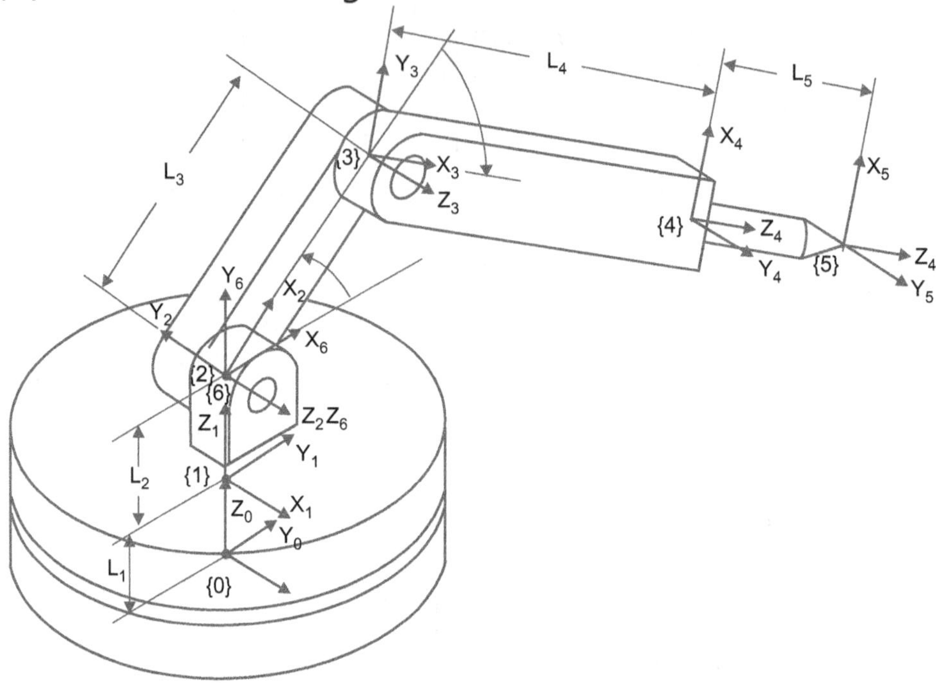

Fig. 6.31: Joint Arm Configuration

Fig. 6.31 is intentionally shown with arbitrary inclinations of the links. Hence, we will have to list varying dimensions right at the start of analysis. It may be observed that frame {1} rotates with respect to {0}, frame {3} rotates with respect to {2}, and frame {4} rotates with respect to {3}. Due to the pointer attached at {4} as an end effector, there is no need that frame {5} will rotate with {4}. If a gripper with fingers is attached then rotation of {5} with respect to {4} will be meaningful. There is no prismatic joint provided, so all lengths are constants, hence all d_i and a_i are fixed. Except θ_1, θ_2, θ_3 all other θ_i and α_i will also be fixed. Due to rotation of frame {3} about {2}, X_2 is rotating and the distance between origins of {1} and {2} along X_2 will mathematically vary. But as mentioned earlier, all the distances are fixed. Hence, introduction of frame {6} at the location of {2} as a frame between {1} and {2} with axis Z_6 along Z_2 and X_6 always horizontal, will solve that problem.

DH Parameters:

Frame	With respect to	θ_i	d_i	a_i	α_i
1	0	θ_1	L_1	0	0
6	1	90°	L_2	0	90°
2	6	θ_2	0	0	0
3	2	$-\theta_3$	0	L_3	0
4	3	90°	0	L_4	90°
5	4	0	L_5	0	0

Composite Homogeneous Transformation Matrix:

$$^{0}T_5 = {}^{0}T_1\ {}^{1}T_6\ {}^{6}T_2\ {}^{2}T_3\ {}^{3}T_4\ {}^{4}T_5$$

Using equation (6.25),

$$^{0}T_5 = \begin{bmatrix} c_1 & -s_1 & 0 & 0 \\ s_1 & c_1 & 0 & 0 \\ 0 & 0 & 1 & L_1 \\ 0 & 0 & 0 & 1 \end{bmatrix} \begin{bmatrix} 0 & 0 & 1 & 0 \\ 1 & 0 & 0 & 0 \\ 0 & 1 & 0 & L_2 \\ 0 & 0 & 0 & 1 \end{bmatrix} \begin{bmatrix} c_2 & -s_2 & 0 & 0 \\ s_2 & c_2 & 0 & 0 \\ 0 & 0 & 1 & 0 \\ 0 & 0 & 0 & 1 \end{bmatrix}$$

$$\begin{bmatrix} c_3 & s_3 & 0 & L_3 c_3 \\ -s_3 & c_3 & 0 & -L_3 s_3 \\ 0 & 0 & 1 & 0 \\ 0 & 0 & 0 & 1 \end{bmatrix} \begin{bmatrix} 0 & 0 & 1 & L_4 \\ 1 & 0 & 0 & 0 \\ 0 & 1 & 0 & 0 \\ 0 & 0 & 0 & 1 \end{bmatrix} \begin{bmatrix} 1 & 0 & 0 & 0 \\ 0 & 1 & 0 & 0 \\ 0 & 0 & 1 & L_5 \\ 0 & 0 & 0 & 1 \end{bmatrix}$$

$$= \begin{bmatrix} -s_1 & 0 & c_1 & 0 \\ c_1 & 0 & s_1 & 0 \\ 0 & 1 & 0 & L_1 + L_2 \\ 0 & 0 & 0 & 1 \end{bmatrix} \begin{bmatrix} c_2 c_3 + s_2 s_3 & c_2 s_3 - s_2 c_3 & 0 & L_3 c_2 c_3 + L_3 s_2 s_3 \\ s_2 c_3 - c_2 s_3 & s_2 s_3 + c_2 c_3 & 0 & L_3 s_2 c_3 - L_3 c_2 s_3 \\ 0 & 0 & 1 & 0 \\ 0 & 0 & 0 & 1 \end{bmatrix}$$

$$\begin{bmatrix} 0 & 0 & 1 & L_4 + L_5 \\ 1 & 0 & 0 & 0 \\ 0 & 1 & 0 & 0 \\ 0 & 0 & 0 & 1 \end{bmatrix}$$

$$= \begin{bmatrix} -s_1 c_2 c_3 - s_1 s_2 s_3 & s_1 s_2 c_3 - s_1 c_2 s_3 & c_1 & -L_3 s_1 c_2 c_3 - L_3 s_1 s_2 s_3 \\ c_1 c_2 c_3 + c_1 s_2 s_3 & c_1 c_2 s_3 - c_1 s_2 c_3 & s_1 & L_3 c_1 c_2 c_3 + L_1 c_1 s_2 s_3 \\ s_2 c_3 - c_2 s_3 & s_2 s_3 + c_2 c_3 & 0 & L_1 + L_2 + L_3 s_2 c_3 - L_3 c_1 s_3 \\ 0 & 0 & 0 & 1 \end{bmatrix} \begin{bmatrix} 0 & 0 & 1 & L_4 + L_5 \\ 1 & 0 & 0 & 0 \\ 0 & 1 & 0 & 0 \\ 0 & 0 & 0 & 1 \end{bmatrix}$$

$$= \begin{bmatrix} s_1 s_2 c_3 - s_1 c_2 c_3 & c_1 & -s_1 c_2 c_3 - s_1 s_2 s_3 & -(L_3 + L_4 + L_5)(s_1 c_2 c_3 + s_1 s_2 s_3) \\ c_1 c_2 s_3 - c_1 s_2 c_3 & s_1 & c_1 c_2 c_3 + c_1 s_2 s_3 & (L_3 + L_4 + L_5)(c_1 c_2 c_3 + c_1 s_2 s_3) \\ s_2 s_3 + c_2 c_3 & 0 & s_2 c_3 - c_2 s_3 & L_1 + L_2 + (L_3 + L_4 + L_5)(s_2 c_3 - c_2 s_3) \\ 0 & 0 & 0 & 1 \end{bmatrix}$$

where, θ_1 may take any value from 0° to 360°; θ_2 and θ_3 may take values from their respective ranges. It is quite interesting to note that not only θ_3 but the range of θ_3 also is variable, that means range of magnitude for θ_3 depends on the orientation of link between frames {2} and {3}. This is illustrated in Fig. 6.32.

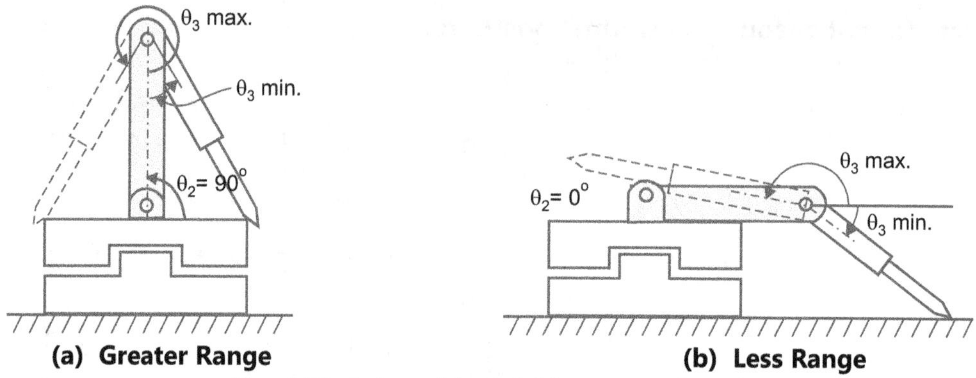

Fig. 6.32: Joint with variable range of angle

6.5.4 (v) SCARA Robot

Before analysis, we need to know the configuration of SCARA robot. It is basically an RR manipulator in the horizontal plane having a fixed supporting column with rotating joint at one end of the manipulator and one end effector attached to a sliding link at the other end of the manipulator. This description will help us to decide the fixed and variable parameters. Fig. 6.33 shows schematic representation of SCARA robot with co-ordinate frames attached.

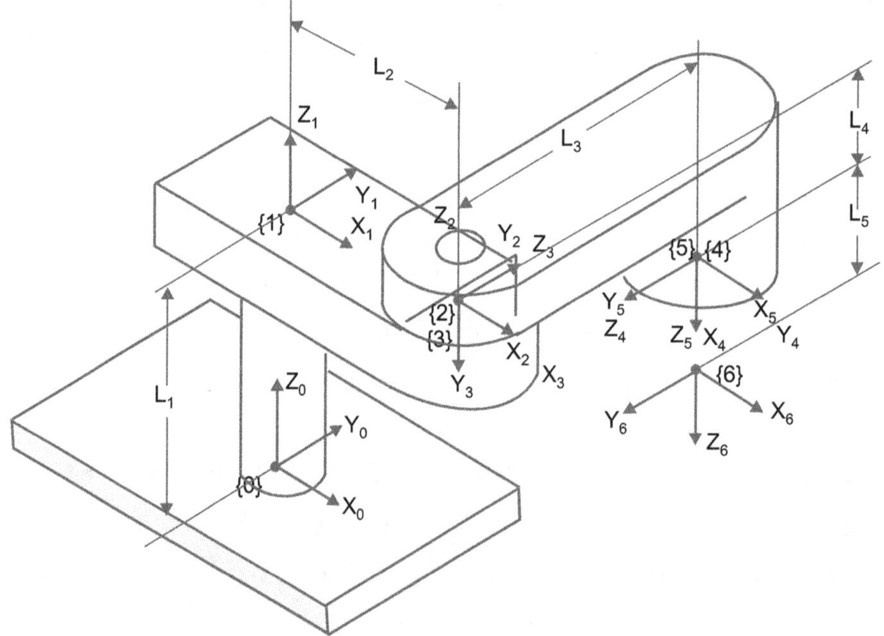

Fig. 6.33: SCARA Robot

It is observed that distance L_3 goes along Y_2 axis and if not properly taken may get skipped from the mathematical expressions. Hence, additional frame {3} is introduced at {2}. Similarly, to take care of distance L_4 additional co-ordinate frame {4} is introduced at {5}. The additional frames are numbered in such a way that they give sequence of frames in forward direction.

All distances except L_5 are constants, as all the joints except that at {5} are rotary. Further frame {1} rotates relative to {0}. Although frames {2} and {3} are coinciding, assuming that frame {2} is attached to the first horizontal link and frame {3} is attached to the second horizontal link, frame {3} rotates with respect to frame {2}. Thus, θ_1 and θ_2, now looking 0° are variables in actual sense.

DH Parameters:

Frame	θ_i	d_i	a_i	α_i
1	θ_i	L_1	0	0
2	0	0	L_2	0
3	θ_3	0	0	−90°
4	90°	L_3	L_4	180°
5	90°	0	0	90°
6	90°	L_5	0	0

Composite Homogeneous Transformation Matrix:

$$^0T_6 = {}^0T_1\,{}^1T_2\,{}^2T_3\,{}^3T_4\,{}^4T_5\,{}^5T_6$$

Using equation (6.25),

$$^0T_6 = \begin{bmatrix} c_1 & -s_1 & 0 & 0 \\ s_1 & c_1 & 0 & 0 \\ 0 & 0 & 1 & L_1 \\ 0 & 0 & 0 & 1 \end{bmatrix} \begin{bmatrix} 1 & 0 & 0 & L_2 \\ 0 & 1 & 0 & 0 \\ 0 & 0 & 1 & 0 \\ 0 & 0 & 0 & 1 \end{bmatrix} \begin{bmatrix} c_3 & 0 & -s_3 & 0 \\ s_3 & 0 & c_3 & 0 \\ 0 & -1 & 0 & 0 \\ 0 & 0 & 0 & 1 \end{bmatrix}$$

$$\begin{bmatrix} 0 & 1 & 0 & 0 \\ 1 & 0 & 0 & L_4 \\ 0 & 0 & -1 & L_3 \\ 0 & 0 & 0 & 1 \end{bmatrix} \begin{bmatrix} 0 & 0 & 1 & 0 \\ 1 & 0 & 0 & 0 \\ 0 & 1 & 0 & 0 \\ 0 & 0 & 0 & 1 \end{bmatrix} \begin{bmatrix} 1 & 0 & 0 & 0 \\ 0 & 1 & 0 & 0 \\ 0 & 0 & 1 & L_5 \\ 0 & 0 & 0 & 1 \end{bmatrix}$$

$$= \begin{bmatrix} c_1 & -s_1 & 0 & L_2c_1 \\ s_1 & c_1 & 0 & L_2s_1 \\ 0 & 0 & 1 & L_1 \\ 0 & 0 & 0 & 1 \end{bmatrix} \begin{bmatrix} 0 & c_3 & s_3 & -L_3s_3 \\ 0 & s_3 & -c_3 & L_3c_3 \\ -1 & 0 & 0 & -L_4 \\ 0 & 0 & 0 & 1 \end{bmatrix} \begin{bmatrix} 0 & 0 & 1 & L_5 \\ 1 & 0 & 0 & 0 \\ 0 & 1 & 0 & 0 \\ 0 & 0 & 0 & 1 \end{bmatrix}$$

$$= \begin{bmatrix} 0 & c_1c_3 - s_1s_3 & c_1s_3 + s_1c_3 & L_2c_1 - L_3c_1s_3 - L_3s_1c_3 \\ 0 & s_1c_3 + c_1s_3 & s_1s_3 - c_1c_3 & L_2s_1 - L_3s_1s_3 + L_3c_1c_3 \\ -1 & 0 & 0 & L_1 - L_4 \\ 0 & 0 & 0 & 1 \end{bmatrix} \begin{bmatrix} 0 & 0 & 1 & L_5 \\ 1 & 0 & 0 & 0 \\ 0 & 1 & 0 & 0 \\ 0 & 0 & 0 & 1 \end{bmatrix}$$

$$\therefore \quad {}^{0}T_{6} = \begin{bmatrix} c_1c_3 - s_1s_3 & c_1s_3 + s_1c_3 & 0 & L_2c_1 - L_3c_1s_3 - L_3s_1c_3 \\ s_1c_3 + c_1s_3 & s_1s_3 - c_1c_3 & 0 & L_2s_1 - L_3s_1s_3 + L_3c_1c_3 \\ 0 & 0 & -1 & L_1 - L_4 - L_5 \\ 0 & 0 & 0 & 1 \end{bmatrix}$$

6.5.4 (vi) PUMA Robot

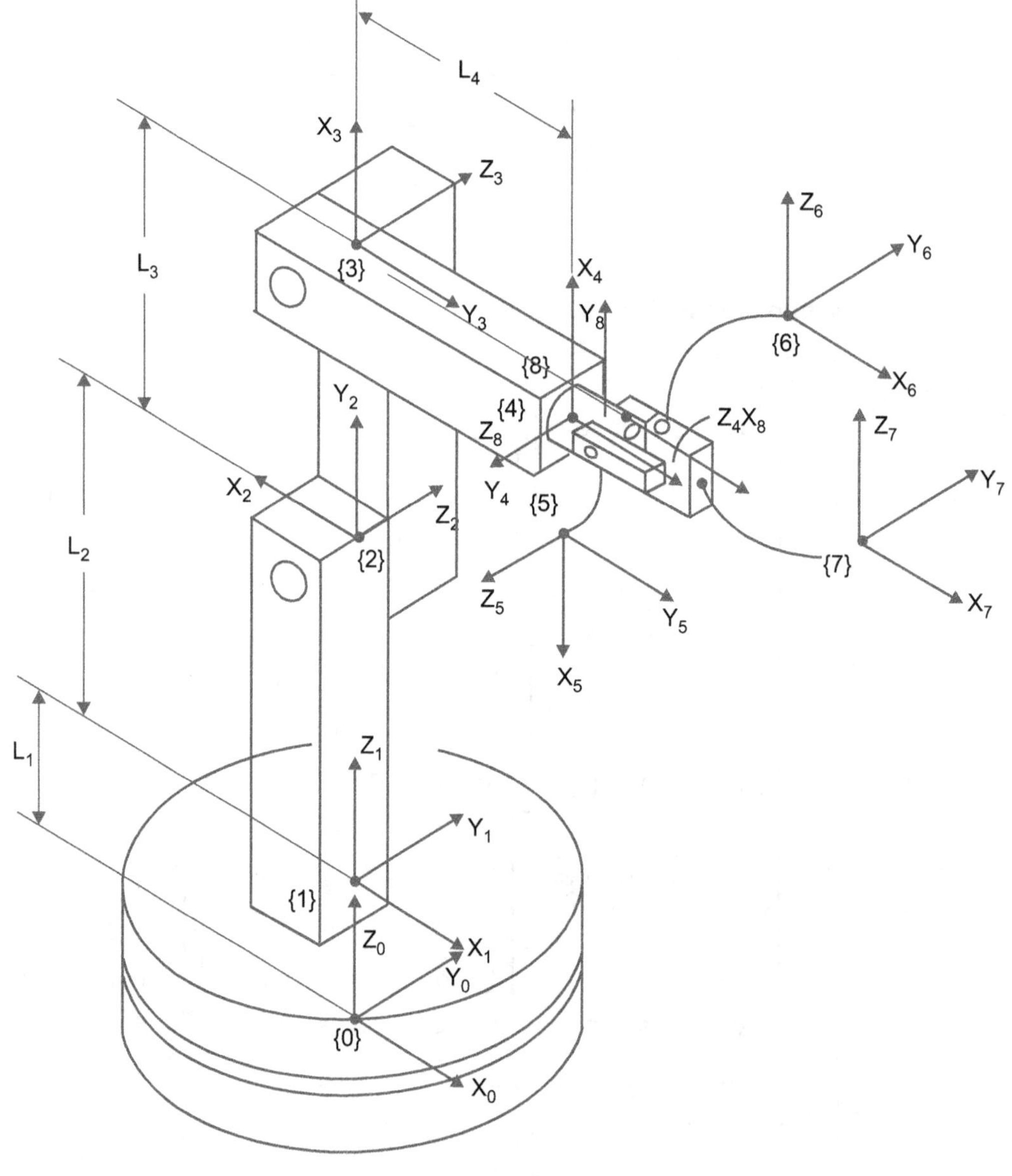

Fig. 6.34: PUMA Robot

This is a robot configuration having six degrees of freedom with all rotary joints. Naturally, six link lengths are fixed and six joint angles are variables. Individual element size, in the final transformation matrix grows to its maximum extent. Fig. 6.34 shows schematic diagram of a PUMA robot, where all the links are conveniently taken in horizontal or vertical orientations. Hence, all θ's and α's are 0°, 90° or 180°. But in true sense all θ's are variables and α's are constants. Frame {7} is a location where end effector will be attached with its own co-ordinate frame, hence will always have fixed orientation relative to {6}. For the reasons mentioned before as a dimension may get skipped (distance L_4) additional frame {8} is introduced sequentially between {3} and {4} at the location of {4}.

Now, there is another problem. When frame {4} rotates with respect to {3}, the variable angle of rotation could have been listed as angle θ_4 if DH parameters of {4} are written with respect to {3}. But to take care of distance L_4 frame {8} is introduced, which results in loss of θ_4, because θ_4, now becomes angle from X_8-axis to X_4-axis about Z_8-axis. Let the frame {4} be rotated by 90° and X_4-axis be aligned with Z_8-axis. Now θ_4 will become an angle between a point and a line, which is meaningless. To overcome this problem, one more frame {9} is introduced between {8} and {4} at the same location as that of {8} and {4} with orientations of X_9, Y_9, Z_9 same as X_4, Y_4, Z_4 respectively. Assume that frame {9} is fixed to the link joining frames {3} and {8}. Now if the frame {4} is rotated about its own Z_4-axis, angle between X_9 and X_4 will vary from 0° to 360° without any geometric problems, to measure it along Z_9-axis. Thus, θ_4 will now be a DH parameter listed for frame {4} with respect to {9}.

(**Please note:** Frame {9} is not shown in Fig. 6.34 to avoid crowding of frames. One can imagine existence of {9} just by replacing suffix 4 by 9 for all axes of frame {4} because, the orientation and location of {9} is same as {4}. Also the small distances 15, 16, 17 at the wrist joints are not shown in the figure.)

DH Parameters:

Frame	θ	d	a	α
1	θ_1	L_1	0	0
2	θ_2	L_2	0	90°
3	θ_3	0	L_3	0
8	90°	0	L_4	180°
9	90°	0	0	90°
4	θ_4	0	0	0
5	θ_5	L_5	0	90°
6	θ_6	0	L_6	−90°
7	0	0	L_7	0

Please note the sequence of frame numbers listed above. The DH parameters are listed for every frame, with respect to the earlier frame, in the same sequence.

Composite Homogeneous Transformation Matrix:

$$^{0}T_{7} = {}^{0}T_{1}\,{}^{1}T_{2}\,{}^{2}T_{3}\,{}^{3}T_{8}\,{}^{8}T_{9}\,{}^{9}T_{4}\,{}^{4}T_{5}\,{}^{5}T_{6}\,{}^{6}T_{7}$$

Let's do this by parts as,

$$^{0}T_{7} = T_{A}\,T_{B}$$

where, $\qquad T_{A} = {}^{0}T_{1}\,{}^{1}T_{2}\,{}^{2}T_{3}\,{}^{3}T_{8}\,{}^{8}T_{9}$

$$T_{B} = {}^{9}T_{4}\,{}^{4}T_{5}\,{}^{5}T_{6}\,{}^{6}T_{7}$$

Using equation (6.25),

$$T_{A} = \begin{bmatrix} c_1 & -s_1 & 0 & 0 \\ s_1 & c_1 & 0 & 0 \\ 0 & 0 & 1 & L_1 \\ 0 & 0 & 0 & 1 \end{bmatrix} \begin{bmatrix} c_2 & 0 & s_2 & 0 \\ s_2 & 0 & -c_2 & 0 \\ 0 & 1 & 0 & L_2 \\ 0 & 0 & 0 & 1 \end{bmatrix} \begin{bmatrix} c_3 & -s & 0 & L_3c_3 \\ s_3 & c_3 & 0 & L_3s_3 \\ 0 & 0 & 1 & 0 \\ 0 & 0 & 0 & 1 \end{bmatrix}$$

$$\begin{bmatrix} 0 & 1 & 0 & 0 \\ 1 & 0 & 0 & L_4 \\ 0 & 0 & -1 & 0 \\ 0 & 0 & 0 & 1 \end{bmatrix} \begin{bmatrix} 0 & 0 & 1 & 0 \\ 1 & 0 & 0 & 0 \\ 0 & 1 & 0 & 0 \\ 0 & 0 & 0 & 1 \end{bmatrix}$$

$$= \begin{bmatrix} c_1c_2 - s_1s_2 & 0 & c_1s_2 + s_1c_2 & 0 \\ s_1c_2 + c_1s_2 & 0 & s_1s_2 - c_1c_2 & 0 \\ 0 & 1 & 0 & L_1 + L_2 \\ 0 & 0 & 0 & 1 \end{bmatrix} \begin{bmatrix} c_3 & s_3 & 0 & L_3c_3 \\ s_3 & c_3 & 0 & L_3s_3 \\ 0 & 0 & 1 & 0 \\ 0 & 0 & 0 & 1 \end{bmatrix}$$

$$\begin{bmatrix} 1 & 0 & 0 & 0 \\ 0 & 0 & 1 & L_4 \\ 0 & -1 & 0 & 0 \\ 0 & 0 & 0 & 1 \end{bmatrix}$$

$$= \begin{bmatrix} c_1c_2c_3 - s_1s_2c_3 & c_1c_2s_3 - s_1s_2c_3 & c_1s_2 + s_1c_2 & L_3c_1c_2c_3 - L_3s_1s_2c_3 \\ s_1c_2c_3 + c_1s_2c_3 & s_1c_2s_3 + c_1s_2s_3 & s_1s_2 - c_1c_2 & L_3s_{11}c_2c_3 + L_3c_1s_2c_3 \\ s_3 & c_3 & 0 & L_1 + L_2 + L_3s_3 \\ 0 & 0 & 0 & 1 \end{bmatrix}$$

$$\begin{bmatrix} 1 & 0 & 0 & 0 \\ 0 & 0 & 1 & L_4 \\ 0 & -1 & 0 & 0 \\ 0 & 0 & 0 & 1 \end{bmatrix}$$

$$\therefore \quad T_A = \begin{bmatrix} c_1c_2c_3 - s_1s_2s_3 & -c_1s_2 - s_1c_2 & c_1c_2s_3 - s_1s_3c_3 & \begin{aligned}(L_3c_1c_2c_3 - L_3s_1s_2c_3 \\ + L_4c_1c_2s_3 - L_4s_1s_2c_3)\end{aligned} \\ s_1c_2c_3 + c_1s_2c_3 & c_1c_2 - s_1s_2 & s_1c_2c_3 + c_1s_2s_3 & \begin{aligned}(L_3s_1c_2c_3 + L_3c_1s_2c_3 \\ + L_4s_1c_2s_3 + L_4c_1s_2s_3)\end{aligned} \\ s_3 & 0 & c_3 & L_1 + L_2 + L_3s_3 + L_4c_3 \\ 0 & 0 & 0 & 1 \end{bmatrix}$$

Similarly, by using equation (6.25),

$$T_B = \begin{bmatrix} c_4 & -s_4 & 0 & 0 \\ s_4 & c_4 & 0 & 0 \\ 0 & 0 & 1 & 0 \\ 0 & 0 & 0 & 1 \end{bmatrix} \begin{bmatrix} c_5 & 0 & s_5 & 0 \\ s_5 & 0 & -c_5 & 0 \\ 0 & 1 & 0 & L_5 \\ 0 & 0 & 0 & 1 \end{bmatrix} \begin{bmatrix} c_6 & 0 & -s_6 & L_6c_6 \\ s_6 & 0 & c_6 & L_6s_6 \\ 0 & -1 & 0 & 0 \\ 0 & 0 & 0 & 1 \end{bmatrix}$$

$$\begin{bmatrix} 1 & 0 & 0 & L_7 \\ 0 & 1 & 0 & 0 \\ 0 & 0 & 1 & 0 \\ 0 & 0 & 0 & 1 \end{bmatrix}$$

$$\therefore \quad T_B = \begin{bmatrix} c_4c_5 - s_4s_5 & 0 & c_4s_5 + s_4c_5 & 0 \\ s_4c_5 + c_4s_5 & 0 & s_4s_5 - c_4c_5 & 0 \\ 0 & 1 & 0 & L_5 \\ 0 & 0 & 0 & 1 \end{bmatrix} \begin{bmatrix} c_6 & 0 & -s_6 & L_6c_6 + L_7c_6 \\ s_6 & 0 & c_6 & L_6s_6 + L_7s_6 \\ 0 & -1 & 0 & 0 \\ 0 & 0 & 0 & 1 \end{bmatrix}$$

$$\therefore \quad T_B = \begin{bmatrix} c_4c_5c_6 - s_4s_5c_6 & -c_4s_5 - s_4c_5 & s_4s_5s_6 - c_4c_5s_6 & (L_6 + L_7)(c_4c_5c_6 - s_4s_5c_6) \\ s_4c_5c_6 + c_4s_5c_6 & c_4c_5 - s_4s_5 & -s_4c_5s_6 - c_4s_5s_6 & (L_6 + L_7)(s_4c_5c_6 + c_4s_5c_6) \\ s_6 & 0 & c_6 & L_5 + (L_6 + L_7)s_6 \\ 0 & 0 & 0 & 1 \end{bmatrix}$$

Finally,

$$^0T_7 = \begin{bmatrix} A & D & G & J \\ B & E & H & K \\ C & F & I & L \\ 0 & 0 & 0 & 1 \end{bmatrix}$$

where,

$$A = c_1c_2c_3c_4c_5c_6 - c_1c_2c_3s_4s_5c_6 - s_1s_2s_3c_4c_5c_6 + s_1s_2s_3s_4s_5c_6 - c_1s_2s_4c_5c_6$$
$$- c_1s_2c_4s_5c_6 - s_1c_2s_4c_5c_6 - s_1c_2c_4s_5c_6 + c_1c_2s_3s_6 - s_1s_2c_3s_6$$

$$B = S_1C_2C_3C_4C_5C_6 - S_1C_2C_3S_4S_5C_6 + C_1S_2C_3C_4C_5C_6 - C_1S_2C_3S_4S_5C_6 +$$
$$C_1C_2S_4C_5C_6 + C_1C_2C_4S_5C_6 - S_1S_2S_4C_5C_6 - S_1S_2C_4S_5C_6 + S_1C_2S_3S_6 + C_1S_2S_3S_6$$

$$C = S_2C_4C_5C_6 - S_3S_4S_5C_6 + C_3S_6$$

$$D = S_1S_2S_3C_4S_5 + S_1S_2S_3S_4C_5 - C_1C_2C_3C_4C_5 - C_1C_2C_3S_4C_5 - C_1S_2C_4C_5 + C_1S_2S_4S_5$$
$$- S_1C_2C_4C_5 + S_1C_2S_4S_5$$

$$E = C_1C_2C_4C_5 - C_1C_2S_4S_5 - S_1S_2C_4C_5 + S_1S_2S_4S_5 - S_1C_2C_3C_4S_5 - S_1C_2C_3S_4C_5 - C_1S_2C_3C_4S_5$$
$$- C_1S_2C_3S_4C_5$$

$$F = -S_3C_4S_5 - S_3S_4S_5$$

$$G = C_1C_2C_3S_5S_6 - C_1C_2C_3C_4C_5S_6 - S_1S_2S_3S_4S_5S_6 + S_1S_2S_3C_4C_5S_6 + C_1S_2S_4C_5C_6 + C_1S_2C_4S_5S_6$$
$$+ S_1C_2S_4C_5S_6 + S_1C_2C_4S_5S_6 + C_1C_2S_3C_6 - S_1S_2C_3C_6$$

$$H = S_1C_2C_3S_4S_5S_6 - S_1C_2C_3C_4C_5S_6 + C_1S_2C_3S_4S_5S_6 - C_1S_2C_3C_4C_5S_6 - C_1C_2S_4C_5S_6 - C_1C_2C_4S_5S_6$$
$$+ S_1S_2S_4C_5S_6 + S_1S_2C_4S_5S_6 + S_1C_2S_3C_6 + C_1S_2S_3C_6$$

$$I = S_3S_4S_5S_6 - S_3C_4C_5S_6 + C_3C_6$$

$$J = (L_6 + L_7)(C_4C_5C_6 - S_4S_5C_6)(C_1C_2C_3 - S_1S_2S_3) - (L_6 + L_7)(S_4C_5C_6 + C_4S_5C_6)(C_1S_2 + S_1C_2)$$
$$+ (L_5 + L_6S_6 + L_7S_6)(C_1C_2S_3 - S_1S_2C_3) + L_3(C_1C_2C_3 - S_1S_2C_3) + L_4(C_1C_2S_3 - S_1S_2C_3)$$

$$K = (L_6 + L_7)(C_4C_5C_6 - S_4S_5C_6)(S_1C_2C_3 + C_1S_2C_3) + (L_6 + L_7)(S_4C_5C_6 + C_4S_5C_6)(C_1C_2 - S_1S_2)$$
$$+ (L_5 + L_6S_6 + L_7S_6)(S_1C_2S_3 + C_1S_2S_3) + L_3(S_1C_2C_3 + C_1S_2C_3) + L_4(S_1C_2S_3 + C_1S_2S_3)$$

$$L = (L_6 + L_7)(S_3C_4C_5C_6 - S_3S_4S_5C_6) + L_5C_3 + (L_6 + L_7)C_3S_6 + L_1 + L_2 + L_3S_3 + L_4C_3$$

The last three terms J K, L may be further developed by opening some of the brackets, but it is not going to reduce size of the element, so we will keep it as it is.

6.5.5 Steps in Forward Kinematic Analysis

At the end, after studying various manipulators' analyses, we may summarise the process of forward kinematic analysis as,

1. Draw sketch of the configuration, taken for analysis.
2. Attach co-ordinate frames at the base, at the end effector and at all the joints.
3. Check whether the frames are properly oriented to produce DH parameters, if not introduce additional frames.
4. Identify the fixed lengths, variable lengths, fixed angles, variable angles.
5. Check whether DH parameters are capable of including all these variables in the listing, if not introduce additional frames.
6. List all DH parameters.
7. Obtain transformation matrix for each row of DH parameters table.
8. Multiply all the transformation matrices in sequence to get the final Composite Homogeneous Transformation Matrix.

6.6 Inverse Kinematics

6.6.1 Introduction

Before going to inverse kinematics problems, let us understand meaning of a solution of problem in forward sense and that in the inverse sense, by taking a simple example in daily life.

6.6.2 Examples

6.6.2 (i) Example in General

A book seller wants to stock multiple copies of three different books, say book A, book B and book C. Let the prices be ₹ 50/-, ₹ 60/- and ₹ 70/- respectively.

If the book seller decides to purchase 25, 37 and 13 copies of books A, B, C respectively total price he will have to pay will be ₹ 4,380/-.

Thus, number of copies of each book and their prices are parameters of the problem. Total price is solution. The solution is directly obtained as all the parameters were known. This is called Forward approach to the problem.

Now, if the book seller knows the prices but has not decided number of copies to be purchased for individual books, but has decided that the total price should be exactly ₹ 4,380/-, then he may come to conclusion that he will purchase

       1.   25 copies of A, 37 copies of B, 13 copies of C.
or   2.   20 copies of A, 40 copies of B, 14 copies of C.
or   3.   30 copies of A, 20 copies of B, 24 copies of C.
or   4.   22 copies of A, 22 copies of B, 28 copies of C.
and so on.

Thus, solution to this problem is bit difficult to calculate because we do it in the reverse manner. But due to the nature of problem itself, we get multiple solutions. This kind of approach to the solution of problem is called Inverse approach.

6.6.2 (ii) Example in Robotics

Here, we will take a very simple example of RR planar manipulator having link lengths 100 mm and 75 mm as shown in Fig. 6.35.

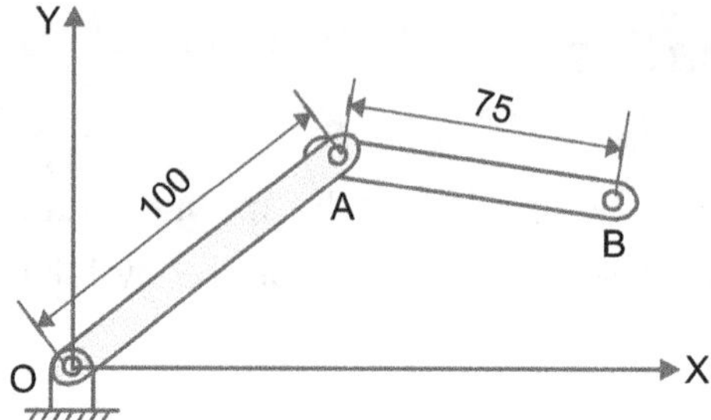

Fig. 6.35

If the operator of this manipulator wishes to locate the end effector (i.e. point B) at point having x, y co-ordinates (100, 75), then quite logically, one can instruct the operator to maintain first link horizontal and second link vertical as shown in Fig. 6.36.

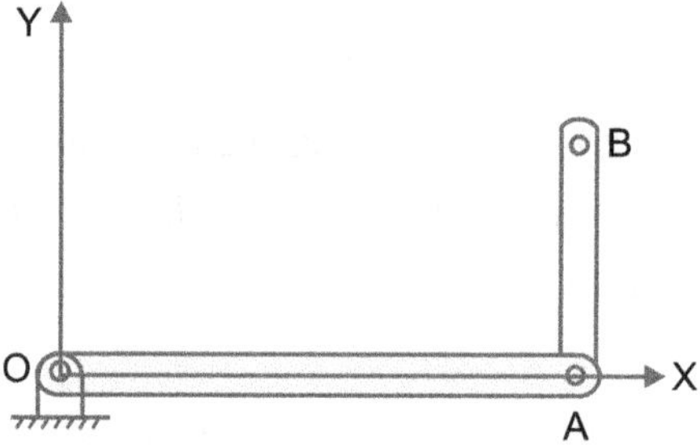

Fig. 6.36

Simultaneously, one can imagine that the mirror image of linkages if the mirror line is passing through origin (0, 0) and desired position (100, 75), also will have the end effector, located at the desired position. This is shown in Fig. 6.37.

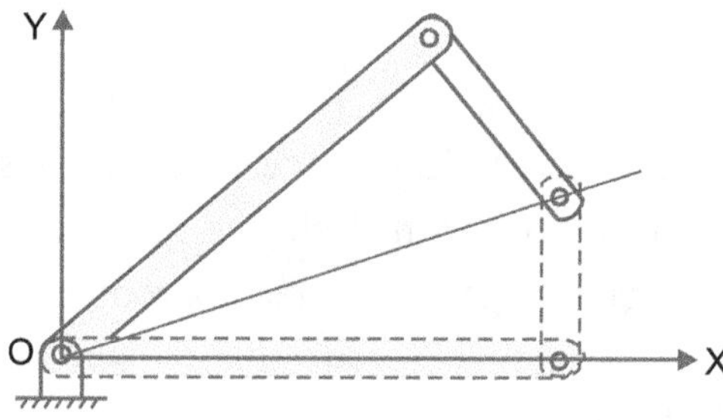

Fig. 6.37

6.6.3 Approaches for the Solution

The mathematical expressions may be obtained by geometrical relation or algebraic relations. Hence, there are two approaches to any inverse kinematic solutions, namely,

6.6.3 (i) Geometric Approach

Logically and graphically we see that there are two solutions, in other words two different arrangements by which a particular point can be reached by the manipulator. These arrangements and method of getting these arrangements must be presented mathematically, so that it will become a generalised procedure and may be used for finding arrangements of the same manipulator to locate different points.

For the simple problems, as above for finding inclinations of links we may use the simple geometrical relations as,

$$x = l_1 \cos \theta_1 + l_2 \cos \theta_2$$

and

$$y = l_1 \sin \theta_1 + l_2 \sin \theta_2$$

where,

x is x co-ordinate of the desired position.

y is y co-ordinate of the desired position.

l_1 is length of link 1.

l_2 is length of link 2.

θ_1 is angle made by link 1 with positive X-axis.

θ_2 is angle made by link 2 with positive X-axis.

As there are two equations and two unknowns, we will get solution of the problem. This procedure is discussed later in this chapter.

6.6.3 (ii) Algebraic Approach

In earlier approach, if the manipulator has three dimensional geometry, then it is necessary to decompose the geometry into several plane geometry problems, which is quite complicated and time consuming.

In such cases, for getting the inverse kinematic solution, one can develop the transformation matrix between the required frames, using procedures discussed in earlier section. The transformation matrix is 4×4 matrix where last row i.e. the fourth row is always [0 0 0 1], hence it is of no use in forming mathematical equations. Remaining 12 elements of the matrix may be non-zero elements and may contain the "fixed and variable Denavit

Hartenberg parameters". Thus, if certain location of end effector is desired, then x, y, z co-ordinates of that position can be equated to the first three elements of the fourth column, which is a position vector of end effector. Here, we get three equations. In many practical cases, these three equations are sufficient to get the inverse kinematic solutions, as the number of unknowns are less than or equal to three.

Thus, in this approach, for obtaining the basic equations, instead of decomposing geometry, we write expression for elements of transformation matrix in terms of variables, and then substitute for those variables. Hence, this approach is called as Algebraic approach.

It is important to note that, use of Geometric approach or Algebraic approach will not produce different solutions. So, one can use either Geometric approach or Algebraic approach, for solution of any problem, depending on the complexity involved. In general, for planar manipulators, Geometric approach is simple and for spatial manipulators, Algebraic approach is easy to get the solutions.

6.6.4 Assurance of the Inverse Kinematic Solution
6.6.4 (i) Existence of Solution

The manipulator whose solution may be obtained just be equating the expressions to the desired x, y, z co-ordinates is a 3 DoF manipulator. If a manipulator has more than 3 DoF, then naturally number of unknowns will increase and we will have to get some more expressions. A manipulator may have maximum 6 DoF as 3 rotations and 3 translations with respect to the co-ordinate frame axes. In that case, first three columns of composite homogeneous transformation matrix may be used to equate them with the desired directions of normal vector, sliding vector and approach vector. Thus, we get another three independent expressions. Summing up them, we may have six unknowns and six equations, and the kinematic problem becomes solvable. Surely, the six equations obtained are not linear simultaneous equations, as they ought to contain trignometric terms. Hence getting solution may be difficult but it is sure that there exists a solution. This statement is made, based on assumption that the desired locations of the end effector lies well inside the workspace or at the work envelope. The non-existence of solution is addressed at the end of "Inverse kinematics for a planar 2 DoF RR manipulator".

6.6.4 (ii) Multiple Solutions

As the set of six equations contains non-linear equations, it will produce more than one value for every unknown. Hence, inverse kinematics will always produce more than one solution. That is, it will have multiple solutions. The same is observed with the 2R manipulator considered in the example taken under "Example in Robotics".

6.6.5 Selection of Correct Solution

There may be cases when some of the solutions obtained mathematically, must be rejected to select a best suitable solution. The cases may be as under. This always happens with a manipulator shown in Fig. 6.38.

6.6.5 (i) Mathematical but not a Physical Solution

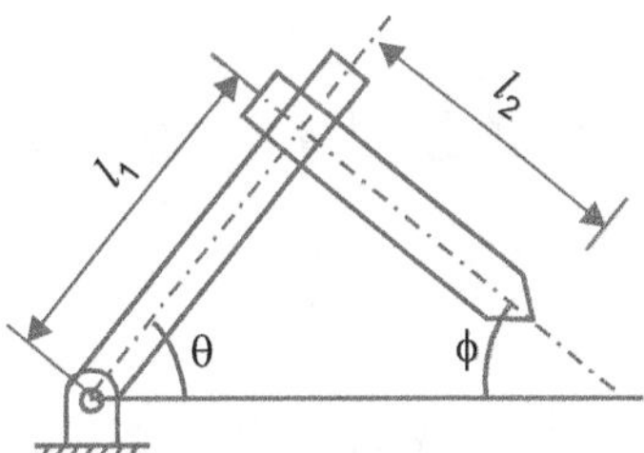

Fig. 6.38

Here, total numbers of parameters for the configuration is 4; 2 angles and 2 lengths. Out of these four only two are variables. They are θ and l_2. After solving the simultaneous equations, usually, we get two values of θ and corresponding values of l_2, where the two values of l_2 are numerically equal, but one positive and the other negative. The solution with the negative l_2 may be shown as in Fig. 6.39.

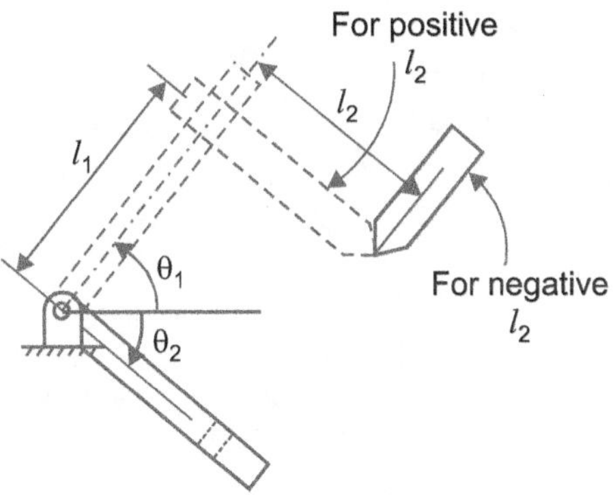

Fig. 6.39

The solution is mathematically correct, but physically there is loss of the joint. Hence, that particular solution must be rejected.

6.6.5 (ii) Obstruction in the Path

If a manipulator is required to move an object from location P to location Q as shown in Fig. 6.40, then a solution must be selected in such a way that there is no obstruction to the movement.

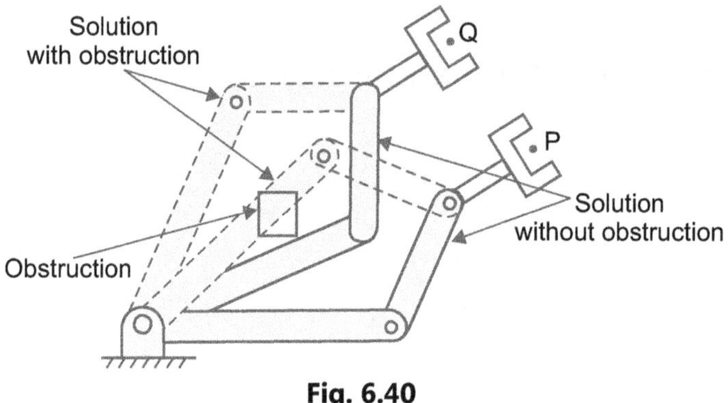

Fig. 6.40

6.6.5 (iii) Physical Limitations of the Joints

All the rotary joints may not work for rotation from 0° to 360°. A link can mathematically be located in particular position without loss of joint, but the position of link may require an angle which is not in range of the joint. Fig. 6.41 illustrates this situation.

It is quite obvious, that the first link will have limited range as approximately from 0° to 180°. Hence, the solution where the first link angle is required to be negative, although mathematically possible, rejected due to physical limitations of the joint.

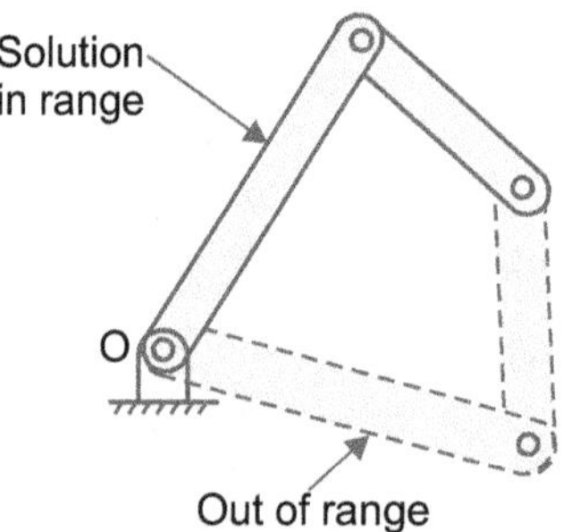

Fig. 6.41

6.6.6 Workspace

The term "workspace" has already been used in this book. It is the space where end effector of the manipulator can reach. Consider a planar 2R manipulator having link lengths l_1 and l_2.

It is quite logical that the free end of the second link can reach any point in circular area or annular area depending on relation between l_1 and l_2. Hence, workspace for this particular manipulator is either a circle or an annular ring, as shown in Fig. 6.42.

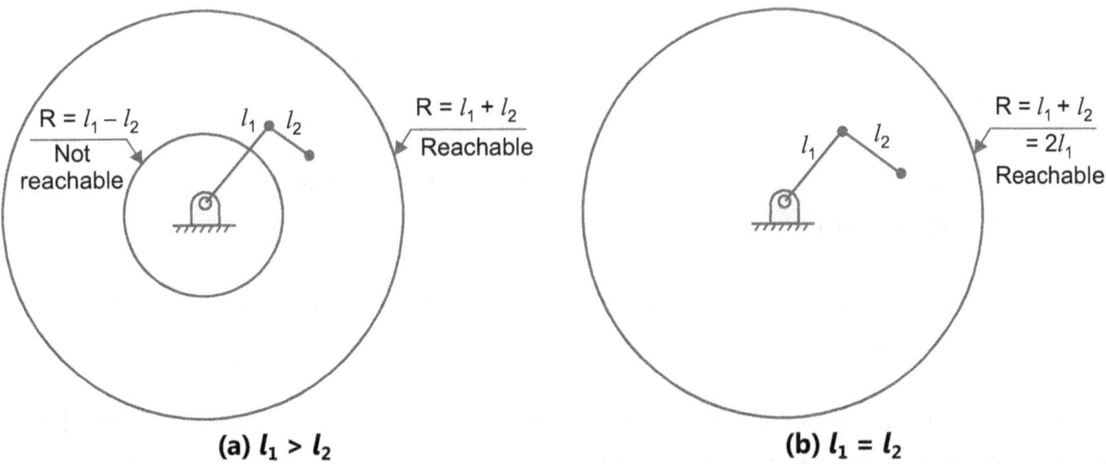

(a) $l_1 > l_2$

Workspace - Annular ring having inside radius (l_1 – l_2) and outside radius (l_1 + l_2)

(b) $l_1 = l_2$

Workspace - circle having radius (l_1 + l_2)

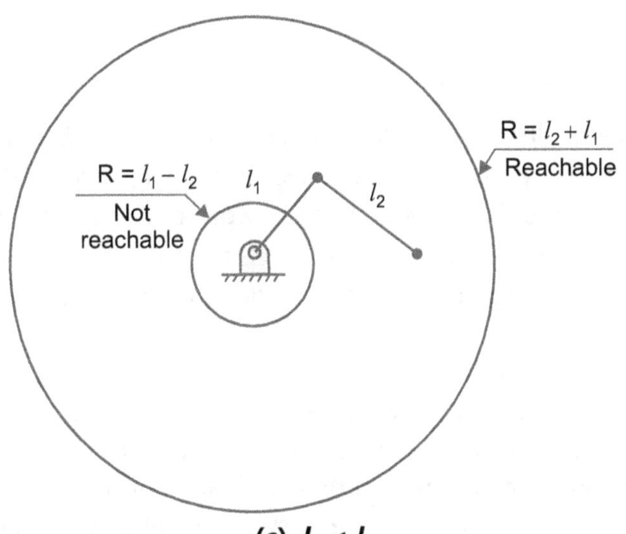

(c) $l_1 < l_2$

Workspace - Annular ring having inside radius (l_2 – l_1) and outside radius (l_2 + l_1)

Fig. 6.42

Flexibility or freedom of robot to locate its end effector at a reachable point with different orientations is termed as "Manipulability" of the robot. This is also known as "Dexterity" of the robot. The manipulator shown in Fig. 6.38 can reach any point in its workspace with only one particular orientation, hence, it has poor dexterity. The manipulator shown in Fig. 6.35 can reach every point in its workspace (except at the boundary) with two different orientations. So it has better dexterity than the earlier.

Due to dexterity, there are two terms related to workspace viz. Reachable Workspace and Dexterous Workspace (DWS).

Reachable workspace is that volume of space, where end effector of the robot can reach with **atleast one orientation**.

Dexterous workspace is that volume of space, where end effector of the robot can reach with **all orientations**.

In Fig. 6.42, it may be observed that the circle or the circular rings are the Reachable workspaces, but for case (a) and case (c) there cannot exist any dexterous workspace. In case (b) where link lengths are same, the fixed point of manipulator can be reached by free end in every orientation. Hence, case (b) includes Dexterous workspace equivalent to a point at centre of the circle.

6.6.7 Redundant Degree of Freedom

In case of RR manipulator discussed earlier and shown in Fig. 6.42, two degrees of freedom are sufficient to reach every point in the RWS. But to improve dexterity i.e. number of orientations in which every point (except those at work envelop), may be reached, an extra degree of freedom may be introduced by splitting the longer link in two parts, by introducing one more rotating joint. This new degree of freedom is called Redundant degree of freedom.

Another advantage of redundant degree of freedom is, it introduces and enhances Dexterous Workspace. It is already mentioned that 2R manipulator having unequal link lengths will not have DWS but on the contrary will have non-reachable space bounded by circle having radius $|l_1 - l_2|$. If the longer link is split in two parts having either equal or unequal lengths the space which was not reachable will directly be converted into Dexterous Workspace.

In other words, if a 3R manipulator has links of lengths l_1, l_2 and l_3 then RWS will be a complete circle of radius $(l_1 + l_2 + l_3)$ and DWS will be a concentric circle of radius equal to (sum of the two smaller link lengths – length of the longest link).

If this number is negative then the circle with that radius represents non-reachable workspace. If the number is zero, it represents DWS equal to a point and at centre of the RWS. If the number is positive, DWS is circular area with that radius.

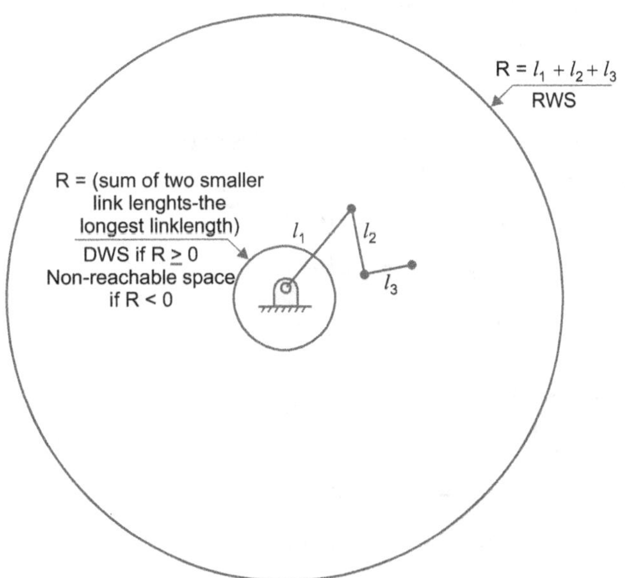

Fig. 6.43: RWS and DWS for 3R planar manipulator

In practice, we may find 7 DoF robot or further greater DoF, whereas 6 DoF are sufficient to locate a point in 3D workspace. The additional DoFs help in improving dexterity and increasing sufficient DWS in case of the spatial manipulators also.

6.6.8 Inverse Kinematics for various Manipulators
6.6.8 (i) Planar 2 DoF RR Manipulator

Consider a manipulator as shown in Fig. 6.44. It is required to determine orientations of the links to locate free end of the second link at a given position having known numeric values of x and y.

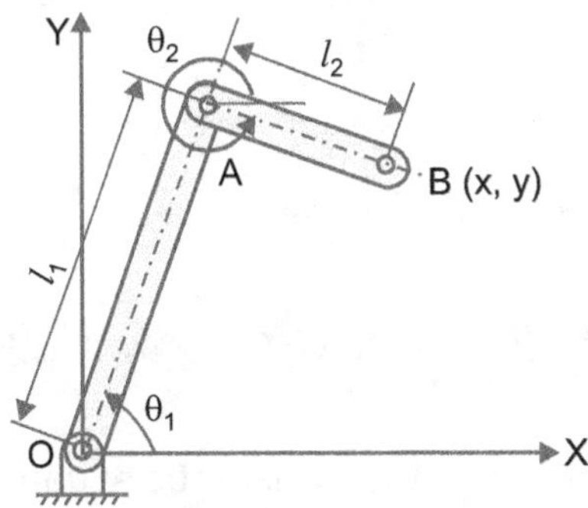

Fig. 6.44: Geometric approach for 2R planar manipulator

Using **Geometric approach**

$$x = l_1\,c\theta_1 + l_2\,c\theta_2 \qquad \text{... (6.32)}$$
$$y = l_1\,s\theta_1 + l_2\,s\theta_2 \qquad \text{... (6.33)}$$

where, x, y co-ordinates and the link lengths l_1, l_2 are known parameters and the joint angles θ_1, θ_2 unknown parameters.

We start with elimination of one of the angles. Hence, rearranging the terms the above equations may be rewritten as,

$$c\theta_2 = (x - l_1\,c\theta_1)/l_2 \qquad \text{... (6.34)}$$

and
$$s\theta_2 = (y - l_1\,s\theta_1)/l_2 \qquad \text{... (6.35)}$$

Also,
$$c\theta_2 = \sqrt{1 - s^2\theta_2}$$

Substituting for $c\theta_2$ in equation (6.34) and squaring both sides of equation (6.34) and equation (6.35),

$$(1 - s^2\theta_2) = (x - l_1\,c\theta_1)^2/l_2^2 \qquad \text{... (6.36)}$$
$$s^2\theta_2 = (y - l_1\,s\theta_1)^2/l_2^2 \qquad \text{... (6.37)}$$

Equating $s^2\theta_2$ from equation (6.36) and equation (6.37),

$$1 - (x - l_1\,c\theta_1)^2/l_2^2 = (y - l_1\,s\theta_1)^2/l_2^2$$
$$\therefore\ l_2^2 - (x^2 - 2xl_1\,c\theta_1 + l_1^2\,c^2\theta_2) = (y_2 - 2yl_1\,s\theta_1 + l_1^2\,s^2\theta_1)$$
$$\therefore\ l_2^2 = x^2 + y^2 + l_1^2 - 2xl_1 C\theta_1 - 2yl_1\,S\theta_1$$

Now, substituting $C\,\theta_1 = \sqrt{1 - s^2\theta_1}$ and rearranging the terms,

$$2xl_1\sqrt{1 - s^2\theta_1} + 2yl_1\,s\theta_1 = x^2 + y^2 + l_1^2 - l_2^2$$

As x, y, l_1 and l_2 are the known constant values, the right side may be replaced by a constant term C, where,

$$C = x^2 + y^2 + l_1^2 - l_2^2 \qquad \text{... (6.38)}$$
$$\therefore\qquad 2\,x\,l_1\sqrt{1 - S^2\theta_1} = C - 2yl_1\,S\theta_1$$

$\therefore$ Squaring both the sides,

$$4x^2l_1^2 - 4x^2l_1^2\,S^2\theta_1 = C^2 - 4C\,yl_1\,S\theta_1 + 4y^2l_1^2\,S^2\theta_1$$

Rearranging the terms, we will find that it is a quadratic equation of a variable term $s\theta_1$ as,

$$[4l_1^2\,(x^2 + y^2)]\,s^2\theta_1 - [4C\,yl_1]\,s\theta_1 + [C^2 - 4x^2l_1^2] = 0$$

$$\text{Therefore,} \quad s\theta_1 = \frac{4C\,y\,l_1 \pm \sqrt{16\,C^2\,y^2 l_1^2 - 16\,l_1^2\,(x^2 + y^2)\,(C^2 - 4x^2 l_1^2)}}{8l_1^2\,(x^2 + y^2)} \qquad \ldots (6.39)$$

Thus, we get two different values of $s\theta_1$, in turn two different values of joint angle θ_1 and subsequently using equation (6.34) or (6.35) two different values of θ_2 corresponding to those of θ_1.

This way, as a solution of inverse kinematics we get two pairs of θ_1 and θ_2. We may plot these two positions and observe that they are mirror images of each other as illustrated in Fig. 6.37, earlier in section "Example in Robotics in this chapter".

Let us solve the inverse kinematics of the same manipulator with **Algebraic approach**. Here, we need to get D-H parameters of the manipulator.

Hence, it is required to attach co-ordinate frames to each point.

Fig. 6.45 shows the frames, having Z-axis perpendicular to plane of paper and pointing towards us, attached to the points O, A and B.

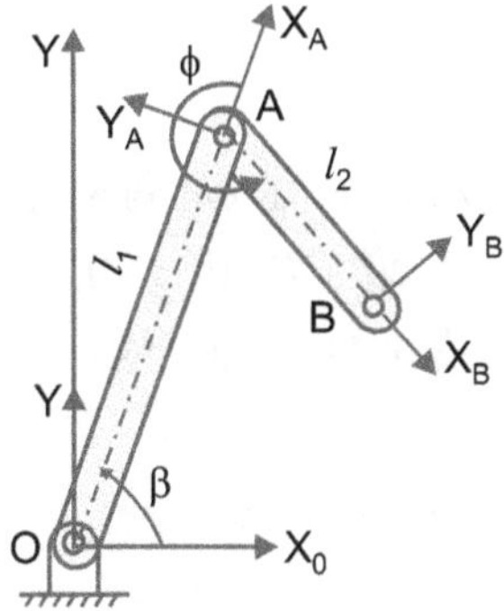

Fig. 6.45: Algebraic approach for 2R planar manipulator

X_A is in the direction of line joining points O and A.
X_B is in the direction of line joining points A and B.
Y_A and Y_B are perpendicular to X_A and X_B respectively.

D-H Parameters:

Frame	θ	d	a	α
A	β	0	l_1	0
B	ϕ	0	l_2	0

Symbols for joint angle are intentionally changed to avoid confusions. The joint angles are measured with respect to X_0 and X_A, and not with respect to the horizontal line.

The Composite homogeneous transformation matrix between {0} and {B} will be,

$$^0T_B = {}^0T_A\,{}^AT_B$$

$$= \begin{bmatrix} c\beta & -s\beta & 0 & l_1 c\beta \\ s\beta & c\beta & 0 & l_1 s\beta \\ 0 & 0 & 1 & 0 \\ 0 & 0 & 0 & 1 \end{bmatrix} \begin{bmatrix} c\phi & -s\phi & 0 & l_2 c\phi \\ s\phi & c\phi & 0 & l_2 s\phi \\ 0 & 0 & 1 & 0 \\ 0 & 0 & 0 & 1 \end{bmatrix}$$

$$= \begin{bmatrix} c\beta\,c\phi - s\beta\,s\phi & -(c\beta\,s\phi + s\beta\,c\phi) & 0 & l_1 c\beta + l_2\,(c\beta\,c\phi - s\beta\,c\phi) \\ s\beta\,c\phi + c\beta\,s\phi & c\beta\,c\phi - s\beta\,s\phi & 0 & l_1 s\beta + l_2\,(s\beta\,c\phi + c\beta\,s\phi) \\ 0 & 0 & 1 & 0 \\ 0 & 0 & 0 & 1 \end{bmatrix}$$

$$^0T_B = \begin{bmatrix} c(\beta + \phi) & -s(\beta + \phi) & 0 & l_1 c\beta + l_2 c(\beta + \phi) \\ s(\beta + \phi) & c(\beta + \phi) & 0 & l_1 s\beta + l_2 s(\beta + \phi) \\ 0 & 0 & 1 & 0 \\ 0 & 0 & 0 & 1 \end{bmatrix}$$

The fourth column is position vector of point B with respect to point O. Therefore,

$$x = l_1\,c\beta + l_2\,c(\beta + \phi)$$
$$y = l_1\,s\beta + l_2\,s(\beta + \phi)$$

For simplicity, $\qquad\qquad$ let $\gamma = \beta + \phi$ $\qquad\qquad\qquad\qquad$ ... (6.40)

Therefore, above equations become,

$$x = l_1\,c\beta + l_2\,c\gamma \qquad\qquad\qquad \text{... (6.41)}$$
$$y = l_1\,s\beta + l_2\,s\gamma \qquad\qquad\qquad \text{... (6.42)}$$

which are similar to equations (6.32) and (6.33) where θ_1 is replaced with β and θ_2 is replaced with γ. Hence, following the procedure described in geometric approach finally we will get,

$$S\beta = \frac{4Cy l_1 \pm \sqrt{16C^2 y^2 l_1^2 - 16 l_1^2\,(x^2 + y^2)\,(C^2 - 4x^2 l_1^2)}}{8 l_1^2\,(x^2 + y^2)} \qquad \text{... (6.43)}$$

which has right hand side exactly same as that in equation (6.39).

Thus, we will get two values of $s\beta$, in turn, two values of β. Two corresponding values of γ, will be found by equations (6.41) or (6.42). Subsequently, two corresponding values of ϕ from equation (6.40).

This way, we get two pairs of β and ϕ as a solution of inverse kinematics. On plotting the configurations, we will observe that the configurations of solution obtained by geometric approach and that obtained by algebraic approach are exactly same. This will be more clear after solutions of "Problem 6.16 and 6.17".

Before solving any numeric problem, it is important to note that surety of **existence of solution** is based on assumption that the desired location of end effector is within the workspace of the manipulator. If the desired location of end effector is outside the workspace, the mathematical model developed by inverse kinematics will automatically reject the solution. For example, for the 2 DoF planar 2R manipulator, we get mathematical model.

1.   Using Geometric approach as equation (6.38) and any one equation out of equations (6.34) and (6.35).
2.   Using Algebraic approach as equations (6.42) and (6.39), and any one equation out of equations (6.40) and (6.41).

In both the approaches, we have the discriminant term of quadratic equation as,

$$\Delta = 16C^2y^2l_1^2 - 16l_1^2\,(x^2 + y^2)\,(C^2 - 4x^2l_1^2)$$

This term will automatically be evaluated as a negative number, if the desired location of end effector is out of the workspace. As square root of negative number is imaginary part of a complex number, solution will not exist in real sense, and we may say that the solution is rejected by mathematical model. This will be more clear after solution of "Problem 6.18".

Problem 6.16:

A 2 DoF planar RR manipulator has $l_1 = 120$ mm, and $l_2 = 75$ mm. Determine joint angles using Geometric approach, so that the free end is located at (100, 70).

Solution:

Here link lengths are

$l_1 = 120, l_2 = 75$

and end effector location is,

$x = 100, y = 70.$

$\therefore$ The constant $C = x^2 + y^2 + l_1^2 - l_2^2 = 23675$.

From equations (6.38),

$$s\theta_1 = 0.945959 \qquad \Rightarrow \qquad \theta_1 = 71.0776°$$

or

$$s\theta_1 = -0.019085 \qquad \Rightarrow \qquad \theta_1 = -1.0936°$$

and correspondingly, from equation (6.35),

$$\theta_2 = -35.4646° \qquad \text{For } \theta_1 = 71.0776°$$

and

$$\theta_2 = 74.5516° \qquad \text{For } \theta_1 = -1.0936°$$

Problem 6.17:

Find solution of previous problem using Algebraic approach.

Solution:

All the known parameters are same, hence, constant term C also is unchanged.

Therefore, looking at equation (6.42), we find that,

β must be numerically same as θ_1.

$$\therefore \qquad \beta = 71.0776° \qquad \text{or} \qquad \beta = -1.0936°$$

From equation (6.41),

$$\gamma = -35.4646° \qquad \text{For } \beta = 71.0776°$$

and

$$\gamma = 74.5516° \qquad \text{For } \beta = -1.0936°$$

which are nothing but two values of θ_2, in previous problem.

But, here we are having angle ϕ for the second link, therefore using equation (6.39),

$$\phi = \gamma - \beta = -105.5422° \qquad \text{For } \beta = 71.0776°$$

and

$$\phi = \gamma - \beta = 75.6452° \qquad \text{For } \beta = -1.0936°$$

Arranging the first link at any of the above values of β and second link at corresponding value of ϕ is going to result in the same arrangement that was given in previous problem's solution.

Problem 6.18:

A planar RR manipulator has first link of 100 mm length and second link of length 70 mm. State whether the manipulator can reach points P, Q, R separately where P is at (15, 15), Q is at (15, 70) and R is at (15, 170).

Solution:

Looking at the data, one can understand that workspace of the manipulator is circular ring having inner radius 30 mm and outer radius 170 mm. If distance of the point from origin is greater or equal to 30 mm and less than or equal to 170, the point lies in the workspace and hence this manipulator can reach the point.

For point P distance from the origin is $= \sqrt{15^2 + 15^2} = 21.2132$

Less than 30, hence point P cannot be reached.

For point Q distance from the origin is $= \sqrt{15^2 + 70^2} = 71.5891$

Between 30 and 170, hence point Q can be reached.

For point R distance from origin is $= \sqrt{15^2 + 170^2} = 170.66$

The distance is slightly greater than 170. But surely, the point is not on the boundary of workspace. Hence, point is not reachable.

To check it in mathematical model, calculate value of the discriminant.

where,   discriminant, $\Delta = 16C^2 y^2 l_1^2 - 16 l_1^2 (x^2 + y^2)(C^2 - 4x^2 l_1^2)$

For point P,

$\qquad l_1 = 100,\ l_2 = 70,\ x = 15,\ y = 15.$

$\therefore \qquad\qquad\qquad\qquad C = 5550$

$\therefore \qquad\qquad\qquad$ Discriminant $= -4.6089 \times 10^{14}$ ... a negative number

Hence, solution is not possible and the point is not reachable.

For point Q,

$\qquad l_1 = 100,\ l_2 = 70,\ x = 15,\ y = 70.$

$\therefore \qquad\qquad\qquad\qquad C = 10225$

$\therefore \qquad\qquad\qquad$ Discriminant $= 3.6161775 \times 10^{15}$ ... a positive number,

Hence, solution is possible, the point is in reachable workspace.

For point R,

$\qquad l_1 = 100,\ l_2 = 70,\ x = 15,\ y = 170.$

$\therefore \qquad\qquad\qquad\qquad C = 34225$

$\therefore \qquad\qquad\qquad$ Discriminant $= -2.286225 \times 10^{14}$ ... a negative number,

Hence, solution is not possible, the point is not reachable. Thus, the mathematical model rejects the inverse kinematic solution automatically, when the point is not reachable.

6.6.8 (ii) Planar 3R Manipulator

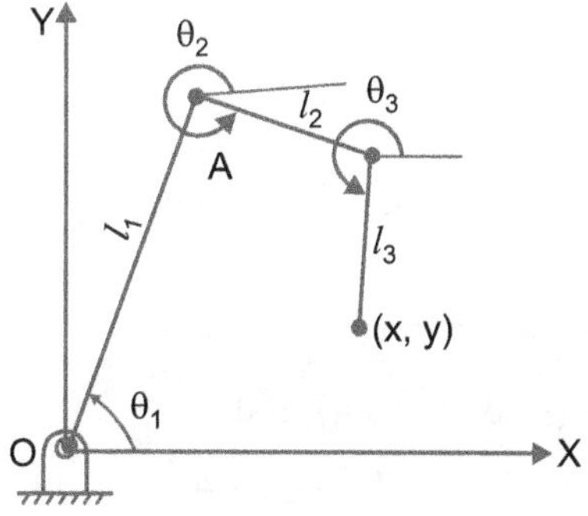

Fig. 6.46

Fig. 6.46 shows a planar 3R manipulator, which has reached a known location (x, y). By Geometric approach,

$$x = l_1\, c\theta_1 + l_2\, c\theta_2 + l_3\, c\theta_3$$
$$y = l_1\, s\theta_1 + l_2\, s\theta_2 + l_3\, s\theta_3$$

Substituting $c\theta_3 = \sqrt{1 - s^2\theta_3}$ and rearranging the terms, the above equations become,

$$\sqrt{1 - s^2\theta_3} = (x - l_1\, c\theta_1 - l_2\, c\theta_2)/l_3$$
$$s\theta_3 = (y - l_1\, s\theta_1 - l_2\, s\theta_2)/l_3 \qquad\qquad \text{... (6.44)}$$

$\therefore\quad$ Squaring and equating $s^2\theta_3$ from both the equations,

$$l_3^2 - (x - l_1\, c\theta_1 - l_2\, c\theta_2)^2 = (y - l_1\, s\theta_1 - l_2\, s\theta_2)^2$$

$\therefore\qquad$
$$x^2 + y^2 + l_1^2 + l_2^2 - l_3^2 = 2xl_1\, c\theta_1 + 2xl_2\, c\theta_2 - 2l_1l_2\, c\theta_1\, c\theta_2$$
$$+\ 2yl_1 s\theta_1 + 2yl_2\, s\theta_2 - 2l_1l_2\, s\theta_1\, s\theta_2$$

As $(x^2 + y^2 + l_1^2 + l_2^2 - l_3^2)$ is constant, denoting it by C, we get a single non-linear equation for two unknowns as,

$$2xl_1\, c\theta_1 + 2xl_2\, c\theta_2 - 2l_1l_2\, c\theta_1\, c\theta_2 + 2yl_1\, s\theta_1 + 2yl_2\, s\theta_2 - 2l_1l_2\, s\theta_1\, s\theta_2 = c$$

We know, every of these links theoretically can rotate through $360°$. Hence, assuming θ_1 to be any constant angle, the same expression may be converted into a non-linear equation for only one unknown. Thus, the terms $2xl_1\, C\theta_1$ and $2yl_1\, S\theta_1$ will now be treated as constants, hence can be transferred on right side to form another constant D, where,

$$D = C - 2xl_1\, c\theta_1 - 2yl_1\, s\theta_1$$

$\therefore\qquad$
$$D = x^2 + y^2 + l_1^2 + l_2^2 - l_3^2 - 2xl_1\, C\theta_1 - 2yl_1\, s\theta_1 \qquad\qquad \text{... (6.45)}$$

Now, substituting $C\theta_2 = \sqrt{1 - S^2\theta_2}$, the equation becomes,

$$2xl_2 \sqrt{1 - s^2\theta_2} - 2l_1l_2\, c\theta_1 \sqrt{1 - s^2\theta_2} + 2yl_2\, s\theta_2 - 2l_1l_2\, s\theta_1 s\theta_2 = D$$

$\therefore\quad$
$$(2xl_2 - 2l_1l_2\, c\theta_1) \sqrt{1 - s^2\theta_2} = D + (2l_1l_2\, s\theta_1 - 2yl_2)\, s\theta_2$$

Squaring both the sides,

$$(4x^2 l_2^2 + 4l_1^2 l_2^2\, c^2\theta_1 - 8xl_1 l_2^2\, c\theta_1) - (4x^2 l_2^2 + 4xl_1^2 l_2^2\, c^2\theta_1 - 8xl_1 l_2^2\, c\theta_1)\, s^2\theta_2$$
$$=\ D^2 + (4l_1^2 l_2^2\, s^2\theta_1 + 4y^2 l_2^2 - 8yl_1 l_2^2\, s\theta_1)\, s^2\theta_2 + 4Dl_1l_2\, s\theta_1 - 4Dyl_2)\, s\theta_2$$

This is a quadratic equation of $s\theta_2$ as follows:

$$[4l_2^2 (x^2 + y^2 + l_1^2) - 8l_1 l_2^2 (x\, c\theta_1 + y\, s\theta_1)]\, s^2\theta_2$$
$$+\ [4Dl_2 (l_1\, s\theta_1 - y)]\, s\theta_2 + [D^2 + 8xl_1 l_2^2\, C\theta_1 - 4l_1^2 l_2^2\, c^2\theta_1 - 4x^2 l_2^2)] = 0 \qquad\qquad \text{... (6.46)}$$

Thus, for given value of θ_1, two values of θ_2 may be found and corresponding values of θ_3 will be obtained.

If for certain value of θ_1 discriminant is negative, the desired location may be in reachable workspace (RWS) but not reachable with that orientation of the first link. So we will have to change numeric value of θ_1 and check its reachability.

In other words, for every point in Reachable workspace there will be at least one value of θ_1 where the discriminant is not negative. While locating a particular point, for many values of θ_1 the discriminant is not negative, one may say that dexterity of the manipulator at that point is greater.

For particular point, if it is observed that θ_1 can take absolutely any value from 0° to 360°, then the point must be part of the Dexterous Workspace (DWS).

Problem 6.19:

A planar 3R manipulator has link lengths l_1 = 100 mm, l_2 = 80 mm and l_3 = 60 mm. Determine its reachable workspace and state whether point (200, 100) is reached with θ_1 = 40°. If yes, what are the values of θ_2 and θ_3? If no, what should be minimum value of θ_1 so that the point will be reached by the manipulator?

Solution:

The reachable workspace of the manipulator is a circle of radius $(l_1 + l_2 + l_3)$ that is 240 mm. All points inside this circle including centre point will be reached by the manipulator, with different values of θ_1, θ_2 and θ_3.

The given point has

x = 200, y = 100

That means its distance from centre is

$$\sqrt{200^2 + 100^2} = 223.6068$$

This distance is less than the radius of RSW. Hence point is reachable, with certain value of θ_1. Now to check whether it is reachable by θ_1 = 40°.

We find discriminant of equation (6.45).

$$\text{Discriminant, } \Delta = [4Dl_2 (l_1 \, s\theta_1 - y)]^2$$
$$- 4 [4l_2^2 (x^2 + y^2 + l_1^2) - 8l_1 l_2^2 (x \, C\theta_1 + y \, s\theta_1)]$$
$$[D^2 + 8xl_1 l_2^2 \, C\theta_1 - 4l_1^2 \, l_2^2 \, C^2\theta_1 - 4x^2 l_2^2] \qquad \text{... (6.47)}$$

where, link lengths are l_1 = 100, l_2 = 80, l_3 = 60, end effector position is x = 200, y = 100 and $c\theta_1 = \cos 40°$, $s\theta_1 = \sin 40°$.

$$\therefore \qquad\qquad\qquad D = 19302.47$$
$$\therefore \qquad \text{Discriminant, } \Delta = 7.7769 \times 10^{16} \text{ ... a positive number}$$

Hence, the point (200, 100) is reachable with $\theta_1 = 40°$.

To find corresponding values of θ_2 and θ_3, we will find roots of the quadratic equation given by equation (6.46).

$$\therefore \qquad s\theta_2 = 0.591192 \qquad \Rightarrow \qquad \theta_2 = 36.24164°$$
$$\text{or} \qquad s\theta_2 = -0.06892 \qquad \Rightarrow \qquad \theta_2 = -3.9517°$$

Correspondingly from equation (6.43),

$$\theta_3 = -11.1222° \qquad\qquad \text{For } \theta_2 = 36.24164°$$
$$\theta_3 = 43.41212° \qquad\qquad \text{For } \theta_2 = -3.9517°$$

Problem 6.20:

State whether the manipulator of "Problem 6.19" will reach point (200, 100) with $\theta_1 = 135°$. If yes, determine corresponding values of θ_2 and θ_3. If no, determine range of θ_1 for the reachability.

Solution:

Again, we will start with discriminant of equation (6.46).

Where link lengths are $l_1 = 100$, $l_2 = 80$, $l_3 = 60$,

End effector is at x = 200, y = 100,

and $c\theta_1 = \cos 135°$, $s\theta_1 = \sin 135°$

$$\therefore \qquad\qquad\qquad D = 76942.13562$$

Using equation (6.46),

$$\text{Discriminant} = -3.018273 \times 10 \text{ ... a negative number,}$$

Hence, solution does not exist for $\theta_1 = 135°$

To find range of θ_1 for reachability, we use condition that discriminant be zero. Therefore, we write equation (6.46) with θ_1 as unknown variable, and equate it to zero.

$$\therefore \quad [24621483.4 \, (100 \, s\theta_1 - 100)]^2 = 4 \, [1536 \times 10^6 - 5.12 \times 10^6 \, (200 \, c\theta_1 + 100 \, s\theta_1)]$$
$$[4896092234 + 1024 \times 10^6 \, c\theta_1 - 256 \times 10^6 \, c^2\theta_1]$$

Solving this equation using numerical methods, range of θ_1 is found as,

$$1.17° \leq \theta_1 \leq 51.96°$$

It should be noted that the point (200, 100) may be reached in various orientations, due to various combinations of θ_1, θ_2 and θ_3. Therefore, dexterity of manipulator is high to reach this point, but not as high as one may say that the point is in Dexterous Workspace. The DWS of this particular manipulator is a circle of radius $(l_2 + l_3 - l_1) = 40$, and the given point (200, 100) lies far away from DWS, although it is inside RWS.

6.6.8 (iii) Planar 2 DoF Manipulator with a Rotary and a Prismatic Joint

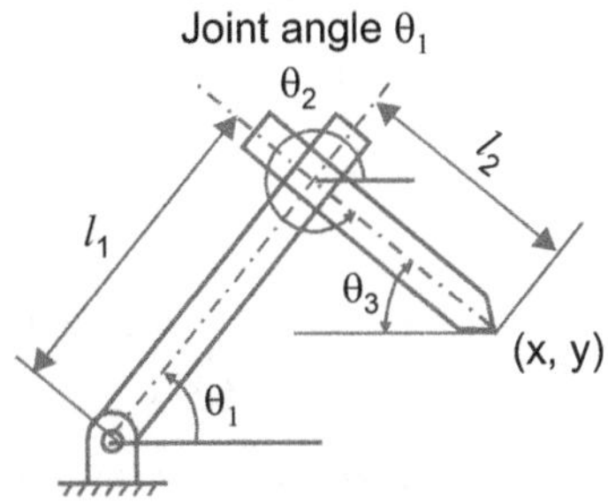

Fig. 6.47

Fig. 6.47 shows a manipulator, where link length l_1 is fixed but joint variable θ_1 is variable. Link length l_2 is variable and also joint angle θ_2 have variables. But as the joint 2 is prismatic, angle between links is not going to change. Let it be equal to 90°. (It may have any other constant value).

For our convenience, let

$$\theta_3 = 360 - \theta_2$$

Using Geometric approach, the co-ordinates may be expressed as,

$$x = l_1 \, c\theta_1 + l_2 \, c\theta_3$$
$$y = l_1 \, s\theta_1 - l_2 \, s\theta_3$$

It is observed that,

$$\theta_3 = 90 - \theta_1 = 360 - \theta_2$$

Thus, θ_2 and θ_3 are variables dependent on angle θ_1.

$\therefore \qquad\qquad c\theta_3 = s\theta_1 \qquad$ and $\qquad s\theta_3 = c\theta_1$

$\therefore \quad$ Above equations become,

$$x = l_1 \, c\theta_1 + l_2 \, s\theta_1 \qquad\qquad \text{... (6.48)}$$
$$y = l_1 \, s\theta_1 - l_2 \, c\theta_1 \qquad\qquad \text{... (6.49)}$$

where, l_2 and θ_1 are unknown variables as mentioned earlier.

Eliminating l_2 from equations (6.48) and (6.49), we get,

$$\frac{x - l_1 \, c\theta_1}{s\theta_1} = \frac{l_1 \, s\theta_1 - y}{c\theta_1}$$

$\therefore \qquad x \, c\theta_1 - l_1 \, c^2\theta_1 = l_1 \, s^2\theta_1 - y \, s\theta_1$

$\therefore \qquad x \, c\theta_1 + y \, s\theta_1 = l_1$

Substituting $c\theta_1 = \sqrt{1 - s^2\theta_1}$ and squaring, we get,

$$x^2 - x^2 s^2\theta_1 = l_1^2 - 2l_1 y\, s\theta_1 + y^2 s^2\theta_1$$

$$\therefore \quad (x^2 + y^2)\, s^2\theta_1 - 2l_1 y\, s\theta_1 + (l_1^2 - x^2) = 0$$

This is a quadratic equation of $s\theta_1$. The roots of this equation are,

$$s\theta_1 = \frac{2l_1 y \pm \sqrt{4l_1^2 y^2 - 4(x^2 + y^2)(l_1^2 - x^2)}}{2(x^2 + y^2)} \qquad \ldots (6.50)$$

Equation (6.50) is used to find two values of θ_1 and corresponding values of length l_2 may be found from either equation (6.48) or (6.49).

It is important to note that RWS of this manipulator is very small. It will be an annular ring with inner radius equal to l_1 and outer radius equal to $\sqrt{l_1^2 + l_{2max}^2}$ assuming that the links are perpendicular to each other.

If the angle between links is not 90°, but some other fixed angle, say α, then outer radius of the RWS will be given by cosine rule that is $\sqrt{l_1^2 + l_{2max}^2 - 2l_1 l_{2max} \cos \alpha}$.

Problem 6.21:

Determine length l_2 of the sliding link and angle θ_1 of the rotating link for a manipulator as shown in Fig. 6.47, if it is required to locate its end point at (50, 87) when $l_1 = 75$ mm.

Solution:

Here, $l_1 = 75$, $x = 50$, $y = 87$.

Using equation (6.49),

$$s\theta_1 = 0.979061 \quad \Rightarrow \quad \theta_1 = 78.2544°$$

or

$$s\theta_1 = 0.316996 \quad \Rightarrow \quad \theta_1 = 18.4814°$$

Using equation (6.47),

$$l_2 = 35.4753 \qquad \text{For } \theta_1 = 78.2554°$$

and

$$l_2 = -66.6633 \qquad \text{For } \theta_1 = 18.4814°$$

Angle $\theta_1 = 18.4814°$ and link length $l_2 = -66.6633$ is not a physical solution, as negative length will cause loss of joint, hence must be rejected.

Other solution i.e. Angle $\theta_1 = 78.2544°$ and link length $l_2 = 35.4753$ has a little geometrical problem. If length l_2 is determined for $\theta_1 = 78.2544°$. Using equation (6.49), it is also evaluated as –66.6633. This indicates that the first link has angle θ_1 greater than 90°, and is equal to $180 - 78.2544 = 101.7456°$.

Substituting this new value of θ_1 in equation (6.48) and equation (6.49), we get, $l_2 = 66.6633$ by both equations.

Thus, surely the point (50, 87) will be reached when $\theta_1 = 101.7456°$ and $l_2 = 66.6633$.

6.6.8 (iv) Cartesian Configuration

Though this is a spatial manipulator, the inverse kinematic analysis will be very easy, when the robot operator wishes to locate the end effector at particular location. This manipulator has three variable link lengths in three different directions. These three link lengths directly decide the x, y, z co-ordinates of the end effector.

Problem 6.22:

A Cartesian configuration robot as shown in Fig. 6.39 has the fixed distances as follows:

$$L_2 = 200 \text{ mm}$$
$$L_5 = 50 \text{ mm}$$
$$L_6 = 75 \text{ mm}$$

Determine the link lengths L_1, L_3, L_4 so that the end effector is located at (400, 350, 300).

Solution:

To determine the link lengths, the position vector of the transformation matrix (obtained earlier) may be equated to $[400\ 350\ 300]^T$.

$$\therefore \qquad L_2 + L_4 + L_5 = 400$$
$$L_3 = 350$$
$$L_1 - L_6 = 300$$

Substituting the values of the fixed lengths,

$$200 + L_4 + 50 = 400$$
$$L_3 = 350$$
$$L_1 - 75 = 300$$

Thus, every equation gives us answer for every individual link length. Therefore,

$$L_1 = 150 \text{ mm}$$
$$L_3 = 350 \text{ mm}$$
$$L_4 = 225 \text{ mm}$$

6.6.8 (v) Cylindrical Configuration

This is a spatial manipulator. Geometric approach will be difficult to use here, therefore, we will use Algebraic approach. The configuration has four unknown variables L_1, L_3, θ_1 and θ_4 as shown in Fig. 6.29 of earlier section, where it was analysed for Forward kinematics. As there are four unknowns, inverse kinematic problem must define x, y, z co-ordinates of a location to reach and orientation of any one axis with respect to the base frame. These four quantities may be equated to the corresponding elements of composite homogeneous transformation matrix and the four unknowns may be evaluated.

Problem 6.23:

A cylindrical configuration manipulator as shown in Fig. 6.29 has,

$L_1 = 250$, $L_2 = 125$, $L_4 = 75$, $L_5 = 50$.

Determine the length L_3 and the angles θ_1 and θ_4 so that the end effector is located at point (12, 325, 230).

Solution:

As the height of manipulator that is distance L_1 is given as 250 mm, the inverse kinematics problem reduces to only three unknowns, hence only three equations will be sufficient to get the solution. These three equations will be obtained by equating position vector elements to x, y, z, co-ordinates of the desired location.

The composite homogeneous transformation matrix for the cylindrical configuration is already derived in earlier section and is,

$$^0T_5 = \begin{bmatrix} -S_1 & C_1S_4 & C_1C_4 & L_5C_1C_4 - L_4S_1 + L_2C_1 - L_3S_1 \\ C_1 & S_1S_4 & S_1C_4 & L_5S_1C_4 + L_4C_1 + L_2S_1 + L_3C_1 \\ 0 & C_4 & -S_4 & L_1 - L_5S_4 \\ 0 & 0 & 0 & 1 \end{bmatrix}$$

$\therefore$ Inverse kinematics equations are,

$$L_5C_1C_4 - L_4S_1 + L_2C_1 - L_3S_1 = 12$$

$$L_5S_1C_4 + L_4C_1 + L_2S_1 + L_3C_1 = 325$$

$$L_1 - L_5S_4 = 230$$

Substituting the given values in the above equations

$$50\, c\theta_1\, c\theta_1 - 75\, s\theta_1 + L25\, c\theta_1 - L_3s\theta_1 = 12 \qquad \ldots (6.51)$$

$$50\, s\theta_1\, c\theta_4 + 75\, c\theta_1 + L25\, s\theta_1 + L_3c\theta_1 = 325 \qquad \ldots (6.52)$$

$$250 - 50\, s\theta_4 = 230 \qquad \ldots (6.53)$$

From equation (6.53),

$$\sin \theta_4 = (250 - 230)/50$$

$\therefore$ $\theta_4 = \sin^{-1} 0.4 = 23.5782°$

Substituting this value in equations (6.51) and (6.52),

$$45.8256\, c\theta_1 - 75\, s\theta_1 + 125\, c\theta_1 - L_3 s\theta_1 \quad = \quad 12 \qquad \qquad \text{... (6.54)}$$
$$\text{and} \; 45.8256\, s\theta_1 + 75\, c\theta_1 + 125\, s\theta_1 + L_3 c\theta_1 \quad = \quad 325 \qquad \qquad \text{... (6.55)}$$

Rearranging equations (6.54) and (6.55) for L_3 and equating them.

$$L_3 = \frac{(45.8256\, c\theta_1 - 75\, s\theta_1 + 125\, c\theta_1 - 12)}{s\theta_1} = \frac{(325 - 45.8256\, s\theta_1 - 75\, c\theta_1 - 125\, s\theta_1)}{c\theta_1} \qquad \text{... (6.56)}$$

$\therefore$ Eliminating L_3, we get,

$$45.8256\, c^2\theta_1 = 75\, s\theta_1 c\theta_1 + 125\, c^2\theta_1 - 12\, c\theta_1$$
$$= 325\, s\theta_1 - 45.8256\, s^2\theta_1 - 75\, s\theta_1 c\theta_1 - 125\, s^2\theta_1$$

$\therefore$ $45.8256 + 125 = 12\, c\theta_1 + 325\, s\theta_1$

Substituting $c\theta_1 = \sqrt{1 - s^2\theta_1}$, and squaring both sides after rearranging the terms,

$$(170.8256 - 325\, s\theta_1)^2 = 144 - 144\, s^2\theta_1$$

$\therefore$ $170.8256^2 - 2 \times 170.8256 \times 325\, s\theta_1 + 325^2\, s^2\theta_1 = 144 - 144\, s^2\theta_1$

$\therefore$ $(325^2 + 144)\, s^2\theta_1 - (2 \times 170.8256 \times 325)\, s\theta_1 + (170.8256^2 - 144) = 0$

Solving this quadratic equation, we get,

$$s\theta_1 = 0.5563 \qquad \Rightarrow \qquad \theta_1 = 33.8003°$$
$$\text{or} \qquad s\theta_1 = 0.4935 \qquad \Rightarrow \qquad \theta_1 = 29.5712°$$

Using equation (6.56), we get,

$$L_3 = 158.6025 \;\text{ and }\; L_3 = 201.7466 \qquad \text{For } \theta_1 = 33.8003°$$
$$\text{and} \qquad L_3 = 201.7446 \;\text{ and }\; L_3 = 201.7446 \qquad \text{For } \theta_1 = 29.5712°$$

L_3 is not matching for $\theta_1 = 33.8003°$ because of geometry problems. It must produce same answers after replacing θ_1 by $(180 - \theta_1)$.

$\therefore$ $L_3 = -351.7446 \;\text{ and }\; L_3 = -351.7446 \qquad \text{For } \theta_1 = 146.1997$

Thus, the geometrical (trigonometrical) problem is solved and we get distance L_3 which is verified by both the equations under (6.25). But physically this solution is not possible as the distance is negative. Hence, there is only one solution having,

$$L_3 = 201.7446$$
$$\theta_1 = 29.5712°$$
$$\text{and} \qquad \theta_4 = 23.5782°$$

which will locate the end effector at the desired position.

6.6.8 (iv) PUMA Robot

It is already mentioned in the earlier section that the PUMA robot has 6 DoF due to six variable angles. The transformation matrix of PUMA robot is already derived in the previous section. As the configuration has six variables, it automatically becomes compulsory to use all elements of the composite homogeneous transformation matrix.

The inverse kinematic problem for PUMA robot must provide information about all the link lengths and the orientations of axes. Then to locate end effector at desired location, one may start the inverse kinematic solution by equating axes orientations with the desired orientations, thus three equations are obtained. Then by equating the x, y, z co-ordinates three more equations are obtained. Then these six non-linear simultaneous equations are solved to get sets of solutions. This procedure involves a huge amount of rearrangements of equations and heavy numeric calculations. Hence, in next problem we will only study the approach and not the complete solution.

Problem 6.24:

It is required to locate the end effector of the PUMA robot at (450, 550, 650) with orientations of axes as,

1. X-axis of the end effector makes 60° with Z-axis of the base frame.
2. Y-axis of the end effector is parallel to and in the same directions as X-axis of the base frame.
3. Z-axis of the end effector makes 60° with Y-axis of the base frame.

Get the inverse kinematic solution, with the link lengths as,

$$L_1 = 100, \qquad L_2 = 500,$$
$$L_3 = 350, \qquad L_4 = 250,$$
$$L_5 = 50, \qquad L_6 = 75$$

and the end effector distance from the wrist is $L_7 = 60$.

Solution:

First we will get orientation matrix using the given description of axes. The description of axes may be sketched as shown in Fig. 6.48.

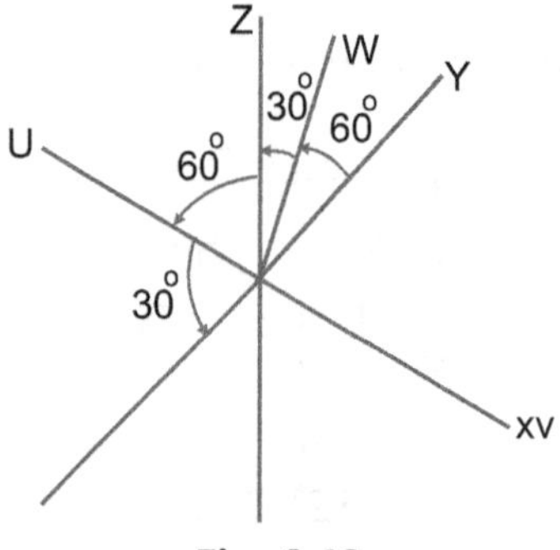

Fig. 6.48

Thus, component of U-axis along X-axis is 0.

Component of U-axis along Y-axis is –sin 60°.

Component of U-axis along Z-axis is cos 60°.

Similarly, that of V-axis along X-axis is 1.000

Similarly, that of V-axis along Y-axis is 0.

Similarly, that of V-axis along Z-axis is 0.

Similarly, that of W-axis along X-axis is 0.

Similarly, that of W-axis along Y-axis is cos 60°.

Similarly, that of W-axis along Z-axis is sin 60°.

Therefore, orientation matrix between the base frame and the end effector may be written as,

$$\begin{bmatrix} 0 & 1 & 0 \\ -s60 & 0 & c60 \\ c60 & 0 & s60 \end{bmatrix} = \begin{bmatrix} A & D & G \\ B & E & H \\ C & F & I \end{bmatrix}$$

where the terms A, B, C, D, E, F, G, H and I are the expressions mentioned in previous section.

$\therefore$ By F = 0, we get,

$$0 = -s_3c_4s_5 - s_3s_4s_5$$

$\therefore \qquad c_4 = -s_4 \qquad \Rightarrow \qquad \cos\theta_4 = -\sin\theta_4$

$\therefore \qquad \tan\theta_4 = -1 \qquad \Rightarrow \qquad \theta_4 = -45° \text{ or } 135°$

Similarly by $\qquad c = \cos 60$ we get,

$$s_3c_4c_5c_6 - s_3s_4s_5c_6 + c_3s_6 = \cos 60$$

Substituting $c_4 = -s_4$ we get,

$$c_3s_6 = \cos 60 + s_3s_4c_6 (c_5 + s_5) \qquad \qquad \text{... (6.57)}$$

Further by, $\qquad I = \sin 60$ we get,

$$s_3s_4s_5s_6 - s_3c_4c_5s_6 + c_3c_6 = \sin 60$$

Again by substituting $c_4 = -s_4$ we get,

$$c_3c_6 = \sin 60 - s_3s_4s_6 (c_5 + s_5) \qquad \qquad \text{... (6.58)}$$

The term $(c_5 + s_5)$ may be eliminated from equations (6.56) and (6.57) as,

$$(c_5 + s_5) = \frac{c_3s_6 - \cos 60}{s_3s_4c_6} = \frac{\sin 60 - c_3c_6}{s_3s_4s_6}$$

$\therefore$ The new equation becomes,

$$c_3s_6^2 = s_6 \cos 60 = c_6 \sin 60 - c_3c_6^2$$

$\therefore \qquad c_3 = c_6 \sin 60 + s_6 \cos 60 \qquad \qquad \text{... (6.59)}$

... and so on.

This way we may go on either evaluating the variables or we may eliminate them.

Further equate expressions of J, K, L with the x, y, z, co-ordinates of the desired location. Finally, we will come out with five non-linear simultaneous equations, not six equations because one of the variables is already determined ($\theta_4 = -45°$). Solving those equations, we will get only one set of solution which will locate end effector at the desired point.

If there is an extra degree of freedom, it will have one more variable introduced for the same number of equations. Thus, multiple sets of solutions will be possible, resulting in multiple orientations to reach the same location by the end effector.

6.6.8 (vii) Additional Problem on Spatial Manipulator

Consider a 3 DoF spatial manipulator as shown in Fig. 6.49. As this has 3 degrees of freedom, it has 3 variable parameters and those are the three angles, viz. angle between base frame and rotating disk at base, angle of first binary link with the horizontal plane and angle between the two binary links.

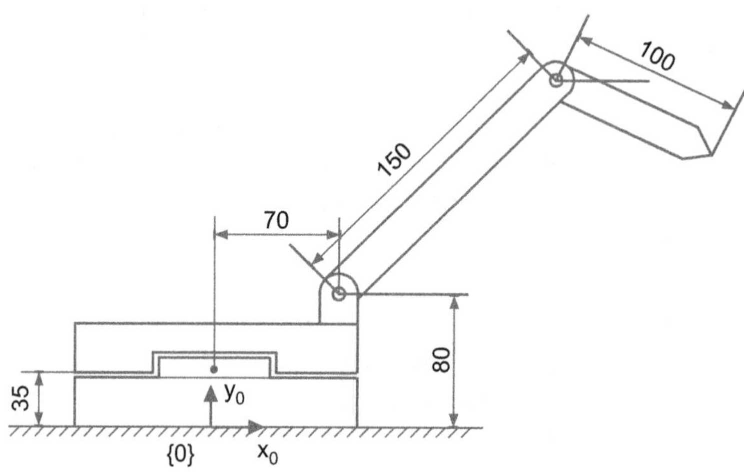

Fig. 6.49: Spatial manipulator with 3 DoF

Let it be required to find the three angles so that the end point will reach (80, 100, 120) with respect to the frame {0} shown in Fig. 6.49.

We may solve geometry problems as follows.

Visualise the manipulators view when looked through Y_0 axis. The manipulator will be seen as a straight line attached to the base circle as shown in Fig. 6.50. The figure shows the top view of manipulator, when it has located its end at (80, 100, 120).

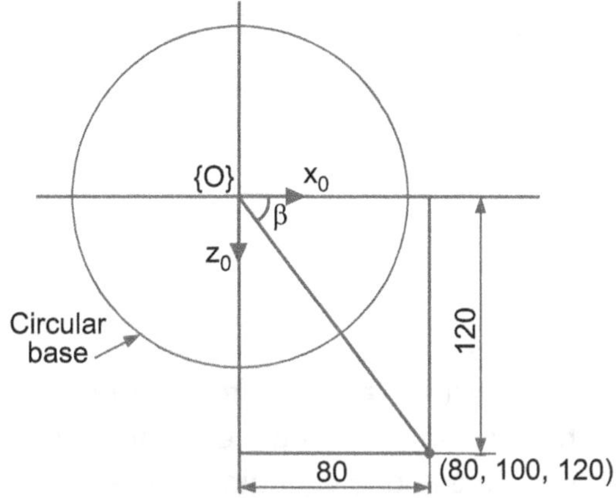

Fig. 6.50: Top view of the manipulator

From Fig. 6.50, it is clear that the base frame must be rotated by angle β, as the first step to locate the end point of manipulator at the desired location.

where,
$$\beta = \tan^{-1} \frac{120}{80}$$

$\therefore$
$$\beta = 56.3099°$$

If we visualise the manipulator in the vertical plane passing through the origin of frame {0} and the desired location then, it becomes a 2 DoF manipulator in that plane, and that may have 2 solutions for inverse kinematic analysis.

When we visualize manipulator in direction perpendicular to that vertical plane assuming X-axis parallel to the top view of line joining the origin and the desired location, Z-axis perpendicular to the same line and Y-axis with same orientation as previous, the desired point will have new x, y, z co-ordinates. This change of orientation of frame {XYZ} is shown in Fig. 6.51.

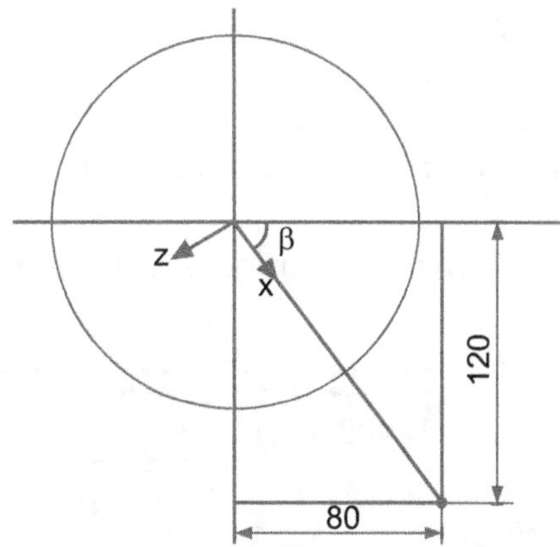

Fig. 6.51: Frame {XYZ} in new orientation

The y-co-ordinate is unaffected and hence,
$$y = 100$$

But new x-co-ordinate will be,
$$x = \sqrt{80^2 + 120^2} = 144.222$$
and new z-co-ordinate will be,
$$z = 0$$

Further, the co-ordinate system must be, now, shifted from its original location to the start of the first binary link. This shift of origin will change co-ordinates of the desired location of the end point. Fig. 6.52 shows shift and the origin. (The shift in Y-axis direction must be imagined).

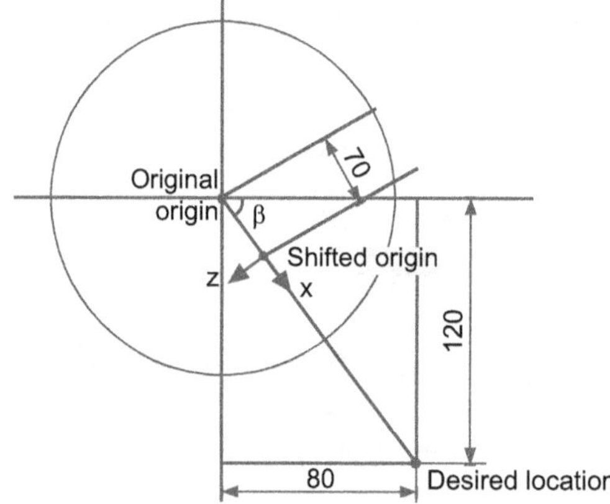

Fig. 6.52: Frame {XYZ} at new location

∴   The new co-ordinates of the desired end point location are,
$$x = 74.222$$
$$y = 20$$
$$z = 0$$

Thus, next level of decomposition is a 2 DoF planar manipulator which has link lengths 150 mm and 100 mm and is required to locate its end point at point (74.222, 20).

This situation is similar to Fig. 6.44. Therefore, using equations (6.38), (6.39) and (6.35)
$$C = x^2 + y^2 + l_1^2 - l_2^2$$
$$= 74.222^2 + 20^2 + 150^2 - 100^2$$
∴
$$C = 18408.9$$

Then,
$$s\theta_1 = \frac{4Cyl_1 \pm \sqrt{16C^2y^2l_1^2 - 16l_1^2 (x^2 + y^2)(C^2 - 4x^2l_1^2)}}{8l_1^2 (x^2 + y^2)}$$

$$\therefore \qquad s\theta_1 = 0.789245 \qquad \text{or} \qquad s\theta_1 = -0.373852$$

$$\therefore \qquad \theta_1 = 52.115° \qquad \text{or} \qquad \theta_1 = -21.9534°$$

$$\therefore \qquad \theta_2 = -79.6958° \qquad \text{for} \qquad \theta_1 = 52.115°$$

$$\text{and} \qquad \theta_2 = 49.5328° \qquad \text{for} \qquad \theta_1 = -21.9534°$$

Thus, inverse kinematic solutions are,

1. $\beta = 56.3099°, \theta_1 = 52.115°, \theta_2 = -79.6958°$

2. $\theta = 56.3099°, \theta_1 = -21.9534°, \theta_2 = 49.5328°$ **... (Ans)**

Alternatively, we may solve the problem using Algebraic approach, wherein will require transformation matrix between the frame {0} and frame at the end point.

Fig. 6.53 shows various frames attached at the base point, end point and joints. All the frames are right handed, so the reader may identify orientation of the missing axis in each frame.

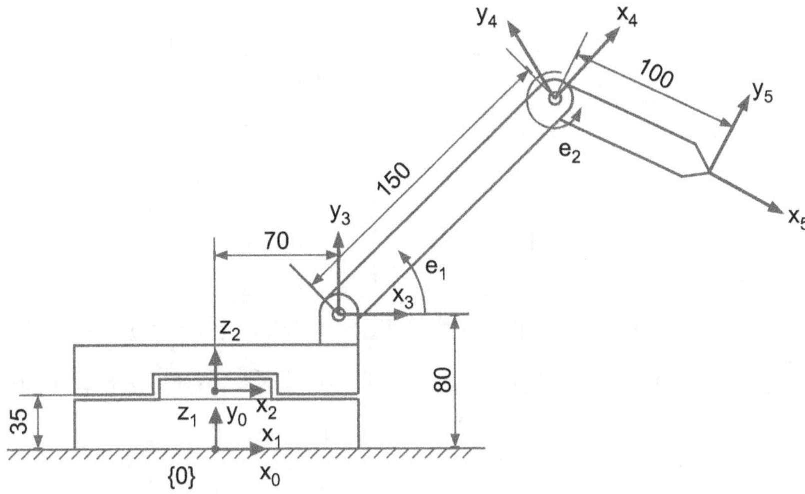

Fig. 6.53: Frame Assignments

Frame {1} is arranged at frame {0}, otherwise distance 35 mm will not be considered by DH-Parameters.

DH-Parameters:

Frame	θ	d	a	α
1	0	0	0	-90°
2	$\beta = 0$	35	0	0
3	0	45	70	90°
4	θ_1	0	150	0
5	θ_2	0	100	0

The DH Parameter θ of frame {2}, frame {4} and frame {5} will be the variable angles. For our convenience we may denote them by β, θ_1, θ_2. According to the orientations shown in Fig. 6.52, β is equal to zero.

Composite Rotation Matrix:

The transformation matrix between frame {0} and the end point may be obtained as below.

$$^0T_5 = {}^0T_1\,{}^1T_2\,{}^2T_3\,{}^3T_4\,{}^4T_5$$

Using equation (6.56),

$$^0T_5 = \begin{bmatrix} 1 & 0 & 0 & 0 \\ 0 & 0 & 1 & 0 \\ 0 & -1 & 0 & 0 \\ 0 & 0 & 0 & 1 \end{bmatrix} \begin{bmatrix} c\beta & -s\beta & 0 & 0 \\ s\beta & c\beta & 0 & 0 \\ 0 & 0 & 1 & 35 \\ 0 & 0 & 0 & 1 \end{bmatrix} \begin{bmatrix} 1 & 0 & 0 & 70 \\ 0 & 0 & -1 & 0 \\ 0 & 1 & 0 & 45 \\ 0 & 0 & 0 & 1 \end{bmatrix}$$

$$\begin{bmatrix} c\theta_1 & -s\theta_1 & 0 & 150\,c\theta_1 \\ s\theta_1 & c\theta_1 & 0 & 150\,s\theta_1 \\ 0 & 0 & 1 & 0 \\ 0 & 0 & 0 & 1 \end{bmatrix} \begin{bmatrix} c\theta_2 & -s\theta_2 & 0 & 100\,c\theta_2 \\ s\theta_2 & c\theta_2 & 0 & 100\,s\theta_2 \\ 0 & 0 & 1 & 0 \\ 0 & 0 & 0 & 1 \end{bmatrix}$$

$$= \begin{bmatrix} c\beta & -s\beta & 0 & 0 \\ 0 & 0 & 1 & 35 \\ -s\beta & -c\beta & 0 & 0 \\ 0 & 0 & 0 & 1 \end{bmatrix} \begin{bmatrix} 1 & 0 & 0 & 70 \\ 0 & 0 & -1 & 0 \\ 0 & 1 & 0 & 45 \\ 0 & 0 & 0 & 1 \end{bmatrix}$$

$$\begin{bmatrix} c(\theta_1 + \theta_2) & -s(\theta_1 + \theta_2) & 0 & 100c\,(\theta_1 + \theta_2) + 150\,c\theta_1 \\ s(\theta_1 + \theta_2) & c(\theta_1 + \theta_2) & 0 & 100s\,(\theta_1 + \theta_2) + 150\,s\theta_1 \\ 0 & 0 & 1 & 0 \\ 0 & 0 & 0 & 1 \end{bmatrix}$$

$$= \begin{bmatrix} c\beta & 0 & s\beta & 70\,c\beta \\ 0 & 1 & 0 & 80 \\ -s\beta & 0 & c\beta & -70\,s\beta \\ 0 & 0 & 0 & 1 \end{bmatrix}$$

$$\begin{bmatrix} c(\theta_1 + \theta_2) & -s(\theta_1 + \theta_2) & 0 & 100c\,(\theta_1 + \theta_2) + 150\,c\theta_1 \\ s(\theta_1 + \theta_2) & c(\theta_1 + \theta_2) & 0 & 100s\,(\theta_1 + \theta_2) + 150\,s\theta_1 \\ 0 & 0 & 1 & 0 \\ 0 & 0 & 0 & 1 \end{bmatrix}$$

$$\therefore \ ^{0}T_{5} = \begin{bmatrix} c\beta c(\theta_1 + \theta_2) & -c\beta s(\theta_1 + \theta_2) & s\beta & (100c\,(\theta_1 + \theta_2) + 150\,c\theta_1 + 70)\,c\beta \\ s(\theta_1 + \theta_2) & c(\theta_1 + \theta_2) & 0 & 100s\,(\theta_1 + \theta_2) + 150\,s\theta_1 + 80 \\ -s\beta c(\theta_1 + \theta_2) & s\beta s(\theta_1 + \theta_2) & c\beta & -(100c\,(\theta_1 + \theta_2) + 150\,c\theta_1 + 70)\,s\beta \\ 0 & 0 & 0 & 1 \end{bmatrix}$$

Now the desired x, y, z co-ordinates may be equal to elements of the position vector given by $^{0}T_{5}$.

$$\therefore \qquad (100c\,(\theta_1 + \theta_2) + 150\,c\theta_1 + 70)\,c\beta = 80 \qquad \qquad \text{... (6.60)}$$
$$100s\,(\theta_1 + \theta_2) + 150\,s\theta_1 + 80 = 100 \qquad \qquad \text{... (6.61)}$$
$$-\,(100c\,(\theta_1 + \theta_2) + 150\,c\theta_1 + 70)\,s\beta = 120 \qquad \qquad \text{... (6.62)}$$

Substituting a new angle (angle of the second binary link with the horizontal plane)
$$\gamma = \theta_1 + \theta_2 \qquad \qquad \text{... (6.63)}$$

For convenience, the above equations may be rewritten as,
$$(100\,c\gamma + 150\,c\theta_1 + 70) = 80 \qquad \qquad \text{... (6.64)}$$
$$s\gamma = 0.2 - 1.5\,s\theta_1 \qquad \qquad \text{... (6.65)}$$
$$-\,(100\,c\gamma + 150\,c\theta_1 + 70)\,s\beta = 120 \qquad \qquad \text{... (6.66)}$$

From equation (6.65),
$$c\gamma = \sqrt{1 - (0.2 - 1.5\,s\theta_1)^2}$$
$$\therefore \qquad c\gamma = \sqrt{0.96 + 0.6\,s\theta_1 - 2.25\,s^2\theta_1} \qquad \qquad \text{... (6.67)}$$

Further from equations (6.64) and (6.65), we get,
$$c\gamma + 1.5\,c\theta_1 + 0.7 = \frac{0.8}{c\beta} \qquad \qquad \text{... (6.68)}$$

and
$$c\gamma + 1.5\,c\theta_1 + 0.7 = -\frac{1.2}{s\beta} \qquad \qquad \text{... (6.69)}$$

Equating equations (6.68) and (6.69), we get,
$$\tan\beta = -1.5$$

Thus,
$$\beta = -56.3099°$$

Substituting this value of β and substituting for $c\gamma$ from equation (6.66) into equation (6.67),
$$\sqrt{0.96 + 0.65\,s\theta_1 - 2.25\,s^2\theta_1} = 1.44222 - 1.5\,c\theta_1 - 0.7$$

Squaring both the sides,

$$0.96 + 0.6\,s\theta_1 - 2.25\,s^2\theta_1 = 0.55089 - 2.22666\,c\theta_1 + 2.25\,c^2\theta_1$$

$$\therefore \quad -1.84089 + 0.6\,s\theta_1 + 2.22666\,c\theta_1 = 0$$

Substituting,

$$c\theta_1 = \sqrt{1 - s^2\theta_1}$$

$$2.22666\,\sqrt{1 - s^2\theta_1} = 1.84089 - 0.6\,s\theta_1$$

Squaring both the sides,

$$4.958 - 4.958\,s^2\theta_1 = 3.388876 - 2.209068\,s\theta_1 + 0.36\,s^2\theta_1$$

Thus, finally we get a quadratic equation of $s\theta_1$ as,

$$5.318\,s^2\theta_1 - 2.209068\,s\theta_1 - 1.569124 = 0$$

$$\therefore \quad s^2\theta_1 - 0.415395\,s\theta - 0.295059 = 0$$

The roots of this equation are,

$$s\theta_1 = \frac{0.415395 \pm \sqrt{0.415395^2 + 4 \times 0.295059}}{2}$$

$$\therefore \quad s\theta_1 = 0.789248 \qquad \text{or} \qquad s\theta_1 = -0.37385$$

$$\therefore \quad \theta_1 = 52.115° \qquad \text{or} \qquad \theta_1 = -21.9532°$$

From these two answers, we will find two values of γ using equation (6.65).

$$\therefore \quad s\gamma = -0.983872 \qquad \text{or} \qquad s\gamma = 0.760775$$

$$\therefore \quad \gamma = -79.6958° \qquad \text{or} \qquad \gamma = 49.5326°$$

Thus, the inverse kinematic solutions are,

1. $\beta = -56.3099°, \qquad \theta_1 = 52.115°, \qquad \gamma = -79.6958°$
2. $\beta = -56.3099°, \qquad \theta_1 = 21.9532°, \qquad \gamma = 49.5326°$ **... (Ans.)**

The answers for the algebraic approach tally with the answers of the geometric approach.

EXERCISES

1. What is a co-ordinate frame? Describe its orientation and location for any particular joint.

2. If {UVW} is rotated by θ about X-axis and then rotated by ϕ about U-axis, the composite rotation matrix may be obtained by

   (a) $R = R_{X,\theta}\,R_{X,\phi}$

   (b) $R = R_{X,\phi}\,R_{X,\theta}$

Select your comment from following statement and justify

(i)   Answer 'a' is right and answer 'b' is wrong.

(ii) Answer 'a' is wrong and answer 'b' is right.

(iii) Answers 'a' and 'b' both are right.

(iv) Answers 'a' and 'b' both are wrong.

3. A 2×2 rotation matrix is given as,

$$R = \begin{bmatrix} 0.78801 & 0.61566 \\ -0.61566 & 0.78801 \end{bmatrix}$$

Determine the angle and the direction of rotation if it is,

(i)   rotation about X-axis

(ii) rotation about Y-axis.

4. Determine numeric values of XXX in following rotation matrix. State the axis about which the rotation is performed and also determine the angle of rotation.

$$R = \begin{bmatrix} 0.89101 & XXX & XXX \\ XXX & XXX & 0 \\ -0.45399 & 0 & XXX \end{bmatrix}$$

5. Sketch the frames if, $^{UVW}R_{XYZ} = \begin{bmatrix} 0 & 1 & 0 \\ -1 & 0 & 0 \\ 0 & 0 & 1 \end{bmatrix}$

6. Frame {UVW} is rotated by 15° about X-axis then by −20° about V-axis and finally by 35° about Z-axis. Then it locates a point ^{UVW}P = (25, 10, 5). Map the point in {XYZ}. Similarly, map point ^{XYZ}Q = (25, 10, 5) in {UVW}.

7. Following matrix has only one incorrect element. Identify and correct that element.

$$T = \begin{bmatrix} 0.125 & 0.831925535 & 0.54062455 & -0.328 \\ 0.75 & 0.27838822 & 0.6 & 0.598 \\ 0.649519 & 0.58 & 0.5896822 & 0.7248 \\ 0 & 0 & 0 & 1 \end{bmatrix}$$

8. Determine numeric values at XXX in the following transformation matrix and also find its inverse, if distance between origins of {XYZ} and {UVW} is 2.25.

$$^{XYZ}T_{UVW} = \begin{bmatrix} XXXX & -0.3216 & XXXX & -0.3257 \\ 0.2789 & XXXX & XXXX & 0.6789 \\ XXXX & 0.7751 & -0.4107 & XXXX \\ 0 & XXXX & XXXX & XXXX \end{bmatrix}$$

9. Sketch the frames, if $^{A}T_{B} = \begin{bmatrix} 0 & 0 & -1 & 12 \\ -1 & 0 & 0 & 15 \\ 0 & 1 & 0 & 20 \\ 0 & 0 & 0 & 1 \end{bmatrix}$

10. Frame {UVW} is rotated by 75° about W-axis, then translated by 15 units and rotated by −35° with respect to X-axis, rotated by 25° and translated by then 10 units with respect to U-axis. Further, translated by 35 units along V-axis and rotated by 55° about Z-axis. Determine location of a point having x = 20, y = 35, z = 15 with respect to {UVW}.

11. Frame {A} was initially aligned with {B} and has same position as that of {B}. It is rotated by 90° about X_B. Then translated by 10 units along Y_A and then rotated by −90° about Z_B. Determine the transform $^{B}T_{A}$.

12. Fill in the blanks using proper alternatives:
    (i) θ_i is angle between ....
       (X_i and Y_i/Y_i and Y_{i-1}/Z_i and Z_{i-1}/X_i and X_{i-1}

    (ii) α_3 must be angle between ....
       (X_0 and X_3/Z_0 and Z_3/X_2 and X_3/Z_2 and Z_3

    (iii) α_4 is distance between ....
       (origin 0 and origin 4/origin 2 and origin 3/origin 3 and origin 4/origin 4 and origin 5)

    (iv) Origin of {UVW} has co-ordinates with respect to {XYZ} as,
       x = 25, y = −37, z = 43
       If U-axis is opposite to Y-axis and W-axis is parallel to X-axis and also both the frames are right handed, the numeric value of D-H Parameter 'a' of frame {UVW} with respect to {XYZ} will be ....
       (25/37/43/−25/−37/−43)

13. Obtain 4 × 4 transformation matrix $^{UVW}T_{XYZ}$ when frame {UVW} has D-H Parameters as θ, d, a and α with respect to frame {XYZ}.

14. List D-H Parameters for the frames {1} and {2} shown in Fig. 6.54.

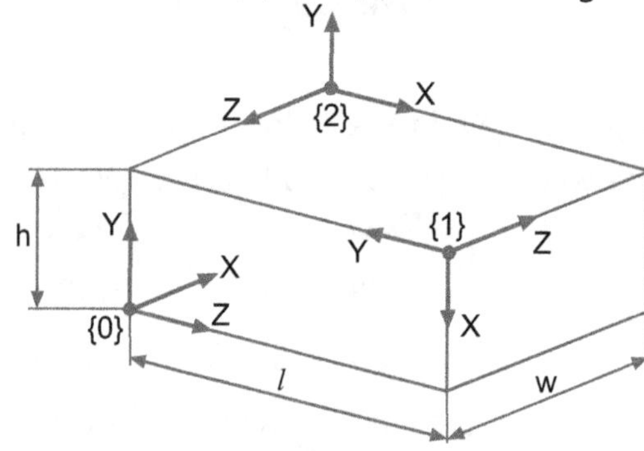

Fig. 6.54

15. State rules for assigning co-ordinate frames {i – 1} and {i} for getting D-H Parameters.

16. Write transformation between {XYZ} and {UVW} if {UVW} has emerged from {XYZ} by rotation of –90° and translation of 10 units with respect to X-axis followed by rotation of 90° about V-axis and finally translation of 15 units along Z-axis.

17. Write transformation matrix between {XYZ} and {UVW} if angle between X and U, and Y and V is 45° and that between Z and W is 0°. Also origin of {UVW} has x, y, z co-ordinates 25, 50 and 35 respectively.

18. List D-H Parameters for frames shown in Fig. 6.55.

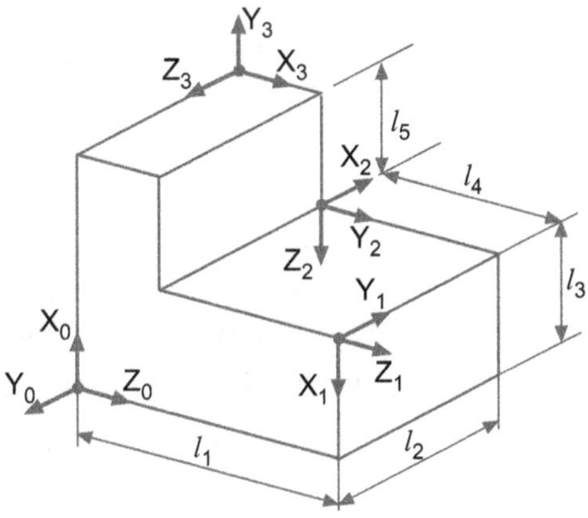

Fig. 6.55

19. Attach co-ordinate frames at 0, 1, 3 for D-H Parameters listed below. Refer Fig. 6.56.

Point	θ	d	a	α
1	–90°	0	l	180°
2	90°	0	–h	0°
3	180°	b	0	90°
4	0°	l	0	90°

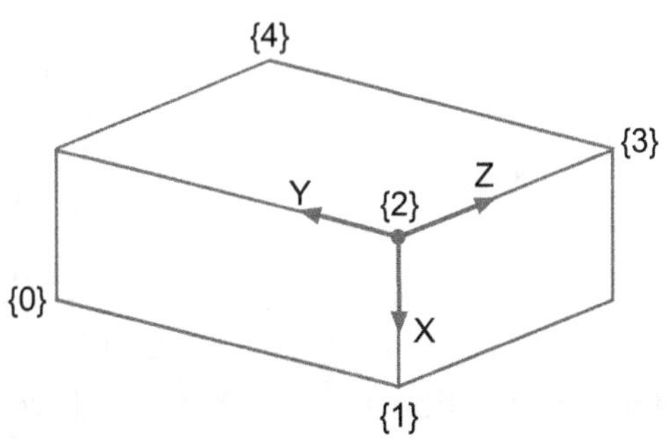

Fig. 6.56

20. Locate points B, C, D, E and attach co-ordinate frames to Fig. 6.57 according to Denavit Hartenberg Parameters listed below:

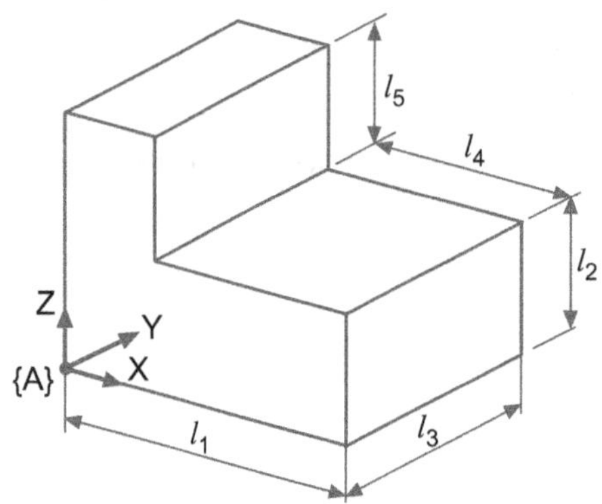

Point	θ	d	a	α
B	180°	l_2	$-l_1$	−90°
C	0°	$-l_3$	l_4	90°
D	−90°	l_5	$-l_3$	90°
E	180°	$l_4 - l_1$	$-l_3$	90°

Fig. 6.57

21. Frame {UVW} emerged from {XYZ} by translation of 15 units and rotation of 180° with respect to W followed by translation of 25 units along negative X-axis followed by rotation of 90° about V-axis. Point P has u, v, w co-ordinates as 20, −15, 35. Determine its location with respect to {XYZ}.

22. {UVW} is obtained from {XYZ} by rotation of 90° about X-axis then by translation of 5 units and rotation of 90° with respect to Y-axis followed by rotation of −90° about U-axis and lastly translation of 10 units along W-axis. What will be the position of point P with respect to {UVW} if it is located at (23, 7, −5) with respect to {XYZ}?

23. A camera locates an object and the robot base by following transformation matrices,

$$^{camera}T_{object} = \begin{bmatrix} 0 & 0 & 1 & 40 \\ 1 & 0 & 0 & -15 \\ 0 & 1 & 0 & 23 \\ 0 & 0 & 0 & 1 \end{bmatrix}$$

and

$$^{camera}T_{robot} = \begin{bmatrix} -1 & 0 & 0 & 65 \\ 0 & 0 & -1 & -25 \\ 0 & -1 & 0 & 75 \\ 0 & 0 & 0 & 1 \end{bmatrix}$$

Determine relation of the object with respect to the robot base. Also determine the transformation matrices of the object and the robot base with respect to the camera, if the camera is rotated by 90° about its own X-axis.

24. Transformation matrix of an object with respect to the robot base is given by,

$$^{base}T_{object} = \begin{bmatrix} 1 & 0 & 0 & 15 \\ 0 & 0 & 1 & -35 \\ 0 & -1 & 0 & 20 \\ 0 & 0 & 0 & 1 \end{bmatrix}$$

The gripper of the robot has its application vector parallel to X-axis of the robot base frame and the sliding vector parallel to the Y-axis of the robot base frame. Determine the 3×3 rotation matrix between the robot base and gripper; also between the object and the gripper. Further, determine the 4×4 transformation matrix between the robot base and the object if the object is moved by 10 units along Y-axis of the robot base frame and then rotated by 90° about Z-axis of the robot base frame.

25. An object and a vision system are related as below,

$$^{camera}T_{object} = \begin{bmatrix} 0 & 1 & 0 & 15 \\ -1 & 0 & 0 & -5 \\ 0 & 0 & 1 & 25 \\ 0 & 0 & 0 & 1 \end{bmatrix}$$

The object is rotated by 90° about its own Z-axis, then it is translated by 10 units along its new X-axis. Determine the relation between the vision system and the displaced object. Further, if the camera is turned by 90° about its own Y-axis, what will be the transformation matrix of the displaced object with respect to the rotated camera?

26. Assign co-ordinate frame at proper locations to the manipulator shown in Fig. 6.58. List the DH parameters and get composite homogeneous transformation matrix between the base and the end effector.

   (**Note:** Approach vector for the end effector must be always horizontal).

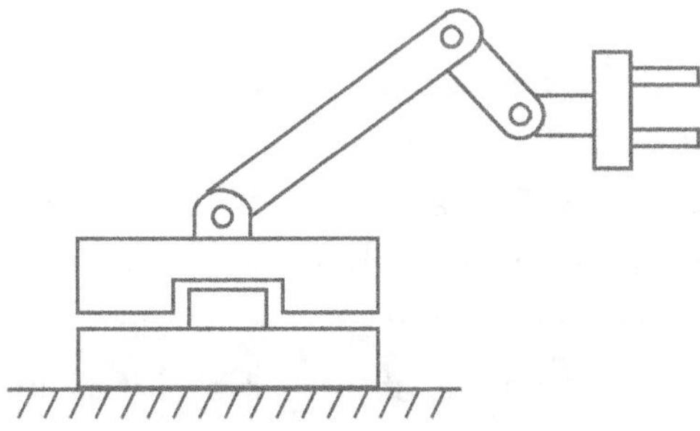

Fig. 6.58

27. List DH parameters mentioning whether they are fixed or variable by assigning co-ordinate frames to the robot configuration shown in Fig. 6.59. Get the transformation matrix between base and the gripper, if gripper orientation has no constraints.

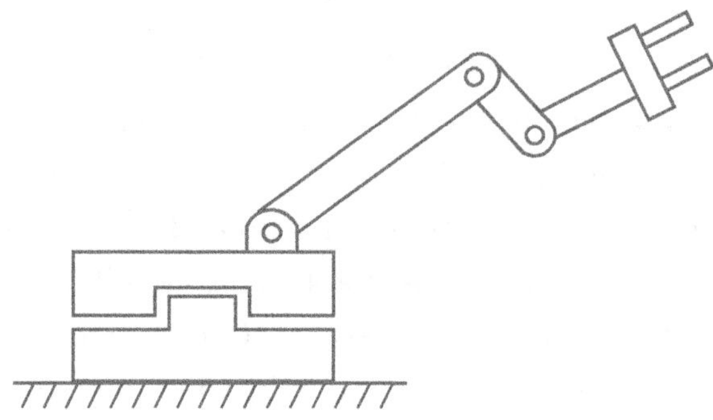

Fig. 6.59

28. List DH parameters for configuration shown in Fig. 6.60 and get the final composite homogeneous transformation matrix.

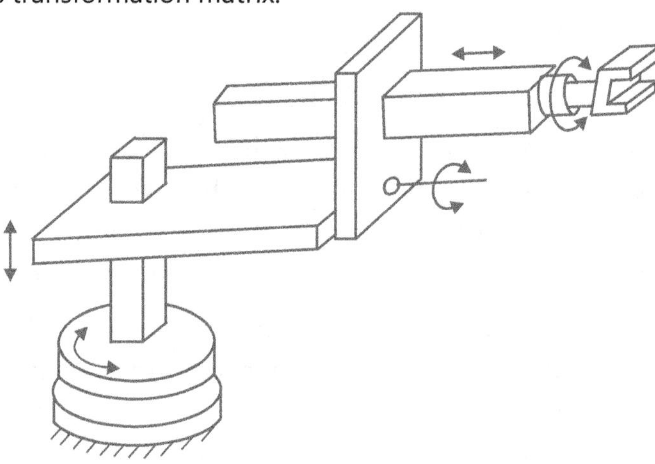

Fig. 6.60

29. Perform complete forward kinematic analysis of Standard robot. (This robot has a prismatic joint. Therefore, its 6 degrees of freedom include 1 linear and 5 angular variables. Hence, the analysis will be as big as that for PUMA robot).

30. A 5 DoF manipulator has 3 revolute joints and 2 linear joints. The manipulator is required to reach a certain known location in its workspace. State and explain whether the inverse kinematics for this manipulator is solvable if all link lengths are known.

31. An inverse kinematic analysis of a manipulator produces number of solutions. What may be the reasons to reject some of these solutions while selecting the best suitable solution?

32. Fig. 6.61 shows a manipulator.

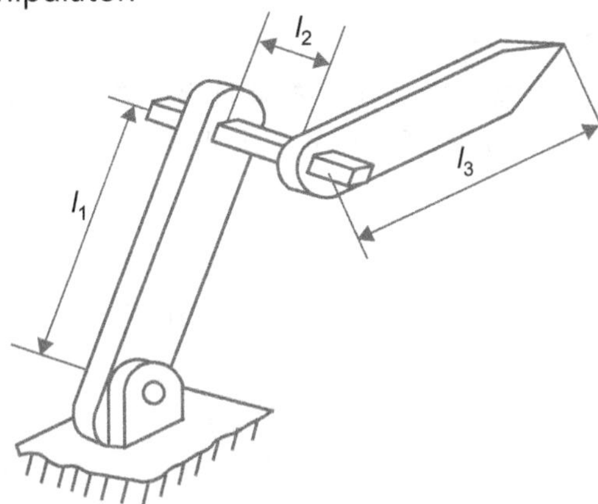

Fig. 6.61

State whether the manipulator is planar or spatial, if all the lengths are fixed. Also determine degrees of freedom of the manipulator and state which approach (algebraic or geometric) will be useful for inverse kinematic solution of such a manipulator.

33. A 2R planar manipulator has l_1 = 50 and l_2 = 75. Determine the orientations of links to locate point (75, 50).

34. A 2R manipulator has l_1 = 150 and l_2 = 55. It is required to reach point (60, 70). State whether the point is reachable. If not, what may be done to reach the point.

35. A 2R manipulator has l_1 = 200 and l_2 = 80. It is required to reach point (70, 35) in all the orientations. State whether the point is reachable atleast in any one orientation. If no, suggest always be which we can make it reach in all orientations.

36. A 2 DoF manipulator as shown in Fig. 6.47 has l_1 = 100 mm and stretch of sliding link limited to 75 mm. If the links remain always perpendicular to each other, determine angle of first link and stretch of the second link required to reach point (120, 0).

37. A 2 DoF manipulator as shown in Fig. 6.47 is required to reach (100, 70), with L_1 = 120. Determine the angle and stretching of the sliding link required if links are not at right angle but include an angle of 110°.

38. Solve inverse kinematics and get the mathematical model for a 3 DoF planar manipulator shown in Fig. 6.62.

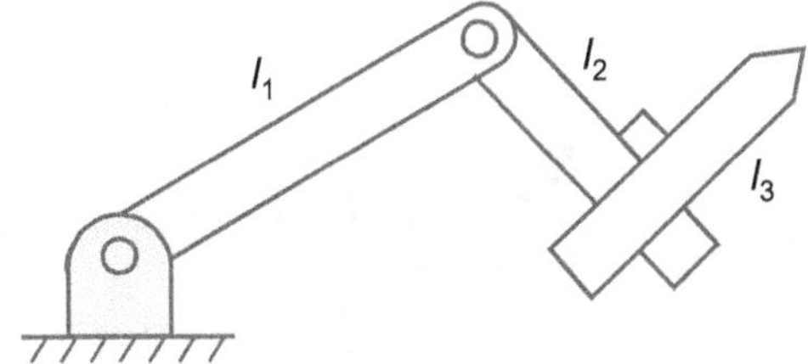

Fig. 6.62

39. A planar manipulator shown in Fig. 6.63 is required to reach point (65, 80). Solve the manipulator for inverse kinematics and get the angle of link first and extensions of link second and link third required. Link first and Link second are always perpendicular to each other. Link second and Link third make angle of 110°. Length of link first is 75 mm.

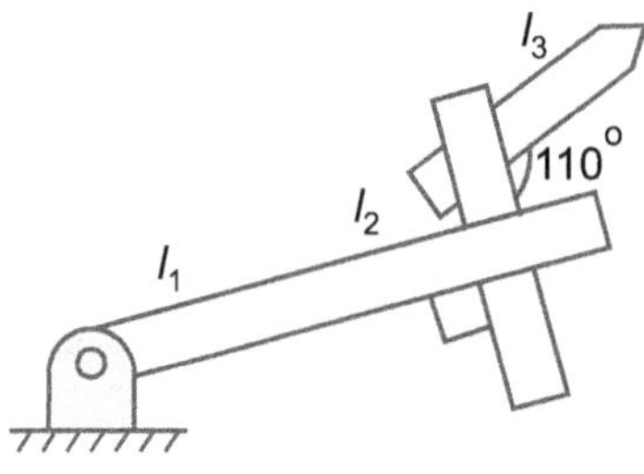

Fig. 6.63

***

Unit IV

Chapter 7: DYNAMICS

7.1 Introduction to Dynamics

Dynamics is a study where forces required to cause motion are calculated. A manipulator must move at a constant speed or accelerate or decelerate during its work cycle. This time-dependent position and orientation of a manipulator is termed as its dynamic behaviour. Time varying torques are applied at the joint, by the joint actuators, to balance the internal and external forces. Internal forces are those, which are caused due to motion i.e. velocity and acceleration. Inertial, Coriolois and frictional forces are kind of internal forces. The external forces are those exerted by the environment, like the applied load, gravitation force. Considering these forces, a mathematical model for the dynamic behaviour of the manipulator is developed. The model includes a set of "equations of motion" (EOM) that describes the dynamic response of the manipulator to the input torque applied by actuators. In simple words, the EOM gives dynamic behaviour of the manipulator, that means they give relationship between joint actuator torques and link movements. Thus, it provides useful information for execution of a typical work cycle and also for the simulation and design of control algorithm.

7.2 Methods for Formulation of Dynamic Equation

There are several methods to derive equations of motion of a manipulator. The two well-known methods are:
1.   Newton-Euler Formulation (NE).
2.   Lagrange-Euler Formulation (LE)

The NE formulation involves determining the linear and angular accelerations of each link and use the well-known concept of free body diagram for describing all forces and moments acting on the link.

The LE formulation involves computation of the scalar energies that is kinetic and potential energies of each link in terms of generalised co-ordinate system i.e. co-ordinate system of the base frame, and their derivatives with respect to time.

It should be clearly noted that, a given manipulator gives the same equations of motion by every method. We are going to discuss formulation by Lagrange-Euler method.

Balancing of a Stick :

We will take a simple example to understand what we mean by dynamic behaviour and dynamic study. Fig. 7.1 shows a very common and well-known event of balancing a stick on hand (or on a finger). Naturally, it requires skills in moving the hand with such an acceleration, and velocity for a very short duration so that disturbance, if any, causing the stick to fall down is quickly balanced. Here, the momentary disturbance is external load, which may give rise to internal forces like inertia force, and the hand movements are analogous to joint actuations.

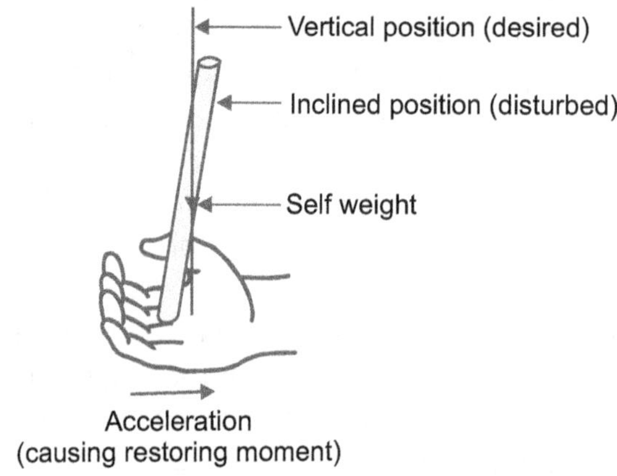

Fig. 7.1 : Balancing of a stick

In this situation, objective is to balance the forces and moments so that movement, if any, will be nullified.

In robotics, objective of dynamic study is to calculate forces, moments those will cause the desired motion.

7.3 Actuation of a Link with Single Rotary Joint

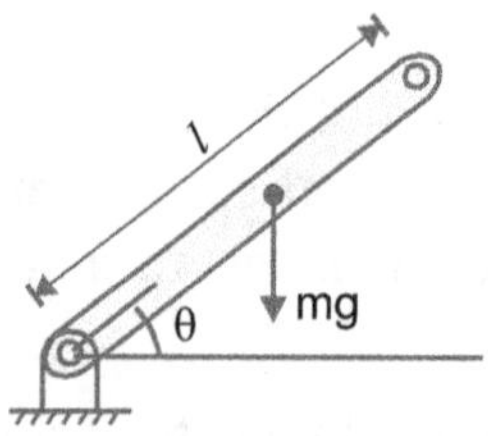

Fig. 7.2 : Single link with a rotating joint

Fig. 7.2 shows a rigid link attached to a rigid support by a rotating joint. Let the total mass 'm' be concentrated at centre of gravity (CG) of the link having length 'l'. The angular velocity of the link be '$\dot{\theta}$' and linear velocity 'v'.

The total kinetic energy possessed by the link is,

$$K \;=\; \frac{1}{2}mv^2 + \frac{1}{2}I\dot{\theta}^2 \qquad \qquad \text{... (7.1)}$$

where,   'I' = Mass moment of inertia of the slender link

$$=\; \frac{ml^2}{12}$$

Now, we know that linear velocity = radius $\times$ angular velocity.

$$\therefore \qquad v \;=\; l/2 \times \dot{\theta}$$

Substituting for 'v' and 'I' in equation (7.1), we get,

$$K \;=\; \frac{1}{2}\,m\left(\frac{l\dot{\theta}}{2}\right)^2 + \frac{1}{2}\frac{ml^2}{12}\,\dot{\theta}^2$$

$$\therefore \qquad K \;=\; \frac{ml^2\dot{\theta}^2}{8} + \frac{ml^2\dot{\theta}^2}{24}$$

$$K \;=\; \frac{ml^2\dot{\theta}^2}{6} \qquad \qquad \text{... (7.2)}$$

The potential energy produced by the link is,

$$P \;=\; mgh$$

Similarly, $$P \;=\; \frac{1}{2}\,mgl\sin\theta \qquad \qquad \text{... (7.3)}$$

A scalar function called "Lagrangian function" or "Lagrangian" L, is defined as the difference between the total kinetic energy and the total potential energy of a mechanical system. Lagrangian of the link is,

$$L \;=\; K - P$$

$$=\; \frac{ml^2\dot{\theta}^2}{6} - \frac{mgl\sin\theta}{2} \qquad \qquad \text{... (7.4)}$$

Now, according to Lagrangian-Euler formulation, partial derivative of Lagrangian with respect to joint parameters (θ in this case), and further differentiation with respect to time, helps us in finding the torque at the joint.

Thus, the torque at the joint is,

$$\tau^* = \frac{d}{dt}\left(\frac{\partial L}{\partial \dot\theta}\right) - \left(\frac{\partial L}{\partial \theta}\right) \qquad \dots (7.5)$$

∴   In case of the link under consideration, joint torque,

$$\tau = \frac{d}{dt}\left(\frac{ml^2\dot\theta}{3}\right) + \left(\frac{mgl\cos\theta}{2}\right)$$

∴

$$\tau = \frac{ml^2\ddot\theta}{2} + \frac{mgl\cos\theta}{2} \qquad \dots (7.6)$$

7.4 Dynamic Model of a 2 DoF Planar RR Manipulator (W-11)

Fig. 7.3 shows a 2 DoF planar RR manipulator with link lengths l_1 and l_2 and masses m_1 and m_2, acting through the CGs of the links C_1 and C_2.

Let K_1, K_2 be the kinetic energies of link 1 and link 2 respectively and P_1, P_2 be the potential enegries of link 1 and link 2 respectively.

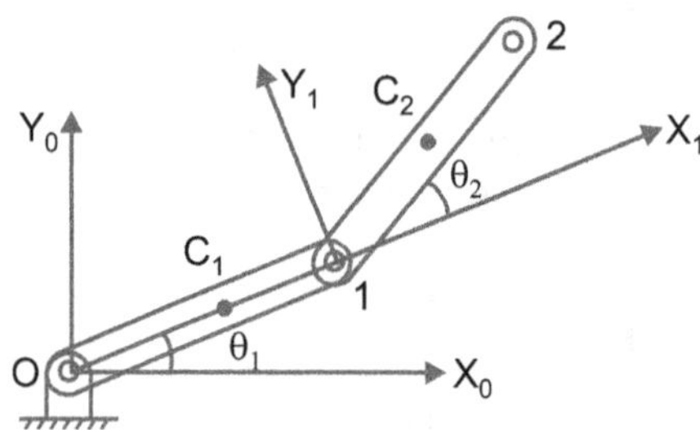

Fig. 7.3 : Planar 2 DoF RR manipulator

∴   Lagrangian, $L = K_1 + K_2 - P_1 - P_2$

From equations (7.2) and (7.3),

$$K_1 = \frac{1}{2}m_1v_1^2 + \frac{1}{2}I_1\dot\theta_1^2 = \frac{ml_1^2\dot\theta_1^2}{6} \qquad \dots (7.2\ a)$$

$$P_1 = m_1gh_1 = \frac{1}{2}m_1gl_1\sin\theta_1 \qquad \dots (7.3\ a)$$

K_2 and P_2 are energies with respect to the base co-ordinate frame. Therefore, it is needed to map the CG of link 2 in base frame. The manipulator under study is a planar manipulator,

---

hence we will use geometric approach[*] to map the CG. If manipulator under study is a spatial manipulator, geometric approach will be difficult to use. We will go for the algebraic approach in that case. The algebraic approach, maps the point by getting the composite homogeneous transformation matrix between the link frame and the base frame. In the geometric approach, we will use geometric (trignometric) expressions to locate (map) the CG of the link with respect to the base frame.

Let x and y be the co-ordinates of CG of link 2.

$\therefore$
$$x = l_1 \cos \theta_1 + \frac{1}{2} l_2 \cos (\theta_1 + \theta_2) \qquad \text{... (7.7)}$$

and
$$y = l_1 \sin \theta_1 + \frac{1}{2} l_2 \sin (\theta_1 + \theta_2) \qquad \text{... (7.8)}$$

Differentiating with respect to time, we will get linear velocities as,

$$\dot{x} = -l_1 \sin \theta_1 \, \dot{\theta}_1 - \frac{l_2}{2} \sin (\theta_1 + \theta_2) (\dot{\theta}_1 + \dot{\theta}_2) \qquad \text{... (7.9)}$$

$$\dot{y} = l_1 \cos \theta_1 \, \dot{\theta}_1 + \frac{l_2}{2} \cos (\theta_1 + \theta_2) (\dot{\theta}_1 + \dot{\theta}_2) \qquad \text{... (7.10)}$$

These are components of the total linear velocity 'v' of the point in X_0 and Y_0 directions.

$\therefore$ Total linear velocity,

$$v^2 = \dot{x}^2 + \dot{y}^2$$

$$= l_1^2 s^2 \theta_1 \, \dot{\theta}_1^2 + \frac{l_2^2}{4} s^2 (\theta_1 + \theta_2) (\dot{\theta}_1 + \dot{\theta}_2)^2 + l_1 l_2 \, s\theta_1 \, s(\theta_1 + \theta_2) \, \dot{\theta}_1 (\dot{\theta}_1 + \dot{\theta}_2)$$

$$+ l_1^2 c^2 \theta_1 \, \dot{\theta}_1^2 + \frac{l_2^2}{4} c^2 (\theta_1 + \theta_2) (\dot{\theta}_1 + \dot{\theta}_2)^2 + l_1 l_2 \, c\theta_1 \, c(\theta_1 + \theta_2) \, \dot{\theta}_1 (\dot{\theta}_1 + \dot{\theta}_2)$$

As $\cos \theta_1 \cos (\theta_1 + \theta_2) + \sin \theta_1 \sin (\theta_1 + \theta_2) = \cos \theta_2$

$$v^2 = l_1^2 \dot{\theta}_1^2 + \frac{l_2^2}{4} (\dot{\theta}_1 + \dot{\theta}_2)^2 + l_1 \, l_2 \, c\theta_2 (\dot{\theta}_1^2 + \dot{\theta}_1 \dot{\theta}_2) \qquad \text{... (7.11)}$$

Also angular velocity of link 2,

$$\omega_2 = \dot{\theta}_1 + \dot{\theta}_2$$

$\therefore$ Kinetic energy of link 2,

$$K_2 = \frac{1}{2} m_2 v_2^2 + \frac{1}{2} I_2 \omega_2^2$$

$$= \frac{1}{2} m_2 \left[l_1^2 \dot{\theta}_1^2 + \frac{l_2^2}{4} (\dot{\theta}_1 + \dot{\theta}_2)^2 + l_1 l_2 \, c\theta_2 \, (\dot{\theta}_1^2 + \dot{\theta}_1 \, \dot{\theta}_2) \right] + \frac{m_2 l_2^2}{24} (\dot{\theta}_1 + \dot{\theta}_2)^2$$

$$\therefore \qquad K_2 = \frac{1}{2} m_2 \, l_1^2 \, \dot{\theta}_1^2 + \frac{1}{6} m_2 l_2^2 (\dot{\theta}_1 + \dot{\theta}_2)^2 + \frac{1}{2} m_2 l_1 \, l_2 \, c\theta_2 \, (\dot{\theta}_1^2 + \dot{\theta}_1 \, \dot{\theta}_2) \qquad \ldots (7.12)$$

Potential energy of link 2.

$$P_2 = m_2 g h_2$$

where, $h_2 = y$

$$\therefore \qquad P_2 = m_2 g \left[l_1 \, s\theta_1 + \frac{1}{2} \, l_2 s \, (\theta_1 + \theta_2) \right] \qquad \ldots \text{from equation (7.8)}$$

$$\therefore \qquad P_2 = m_2 g l_1 \, s\theta_1 + \frac{1}{2} \, m_2 g l_2 \, s \, (\theta_1 + \theta_2) \qquad \ldots (7.13)$$

Now, Lagrangian $L = K_1 + K_2 - P_1 - P_2$

From equations (7.2a), (7.3a), (7.12) and (7.13),

$$L = \frac{1}{6} m_1 l_1^2 \, \dot{\theta}_1^2 + \frac{1}{2} m_2 l_1^2 \, \dot{\theta}_1^2 + \frac{1}{6} m_2 l_2^2 (\dot{\theta}_1 + \dot{\theta}_2)^2 + \frac{1}{2} m_2 l_1 l_2 \, c\theta_2 \, (\dot{\theta}_1^2 + \dot{\theta}_1 \, \dot{\theta}_2)$$

$$- \frac{1}{2} m_1 g l_1 \, s\theta_1 - m_2 g l_1 \, s\theta_1 - \frac{1}{2} m_2 g l_2 \, s \, (\theta_1 + \theta_2)$$

The terms required for calculation of joint torque are given in equation (7.5). Therefore, preparation for joint torque as,

At joint 1,

$$\frac{\partial L}{\partial \theta_1} = - \frac{1}{2} m_1 g l_1 \, c\theta_1 - m_2 g l_1 \, c\theta_1 - \frac{1}{2} m_2 g l_2 \, c \, (\theta_1 + \theta_2) \qquad \ldots (7.14)$$

$$\frac{\partial L}{\partial \dot{\theta}_1} = \frac{1}{3} m_1 l_1^2 \, \dot{\theta}_1 + m_2 l_1^2 \, \dot{\theta}_1 + \frac{1}{3} m_2 l_2^2 \, (\dot{\theta}_1 + \dot{\theta}_2)$$

$$+ \frac{1}{2} m_2 l_1 l_2 \, c\theta_2 \, (2 \, \dot{\theta}_1 + \dot{\theta}_2) \qquad \ldots (7.15)$$

Differentiating equation (7.15) with respect to time,

$$\frac{d}{dt} \left(\frac{\partial L}{\partial \dot{\theta}_1} \right) = \left[\frac{1}{3} m_1 l_1^2 + m_2 l_1^2 + \frac{1}{3} m_2 l_2^2 + m_2 l_1 l_2 \, c\theta_2 \right] \ddot{\theta}_1 + \left[\frac{1}{3} m_2 l_2^2 + \frac{1}{2} m_2 l_1 l_2 c\theta_2 \right] \ddot{\theta}_2$$

$$- \left[m_2 l_1 l_2 \, \dot{\theta}_1 \, \dot{\theta}_2 + \frac{1}{2} m_2 l_1 l_2 \, \dot{\theta}_2^2 \right] s\theta_2 \qquad \ldots (7.16)$$

Torque at joint 1, using equations (7.14) and (7.16), we get,

$$\tau_1 = \frac{d}{dt} \left(\frac{\partial L}{\partial \dot{\theta}_1} \right) - \left(\frac{\partial L}{\partial \theta_1} \right)$$

$$\therefore \quad \tau_1 = \left[\left(\frac{m_1}{3} + m_2\right) l_1^2 + \frac{m_2}{3} l_2^2 + m_2 l_1 l_2\, c\theta_2\right] \ddot{\theta}_1$$

$$+ m_2 \left[\frac{l_2^2}{3} + \frac{l_1 l_2}{2}\, c\theta_2\right] \ddot{\theta}_2 - m_2 l_1 l_2 s\theta_2 \left(\dot{\theta}_1 + \frac{\dot{\theta}_2}{2}\right) \dot{\theta}_2$$

$$+ \left(\frac{m_1}{2} + m_2\right) g l_1\, c\theta_1 + \frac{m_2}{2}\, g l_2\, c\,(\theta_1 + \theta_2) \qquad \dots (7.17)$$

At joint 2,

$$\frac{\partial L}{\partial \theta_2} = -\frac{1}{2} m_2 l_1 l_2\, s\theta_2\, (\dot{\theta}_1^2 + \dot{\theta}_1 \dot{\theta}_2) - \frac{1}{2} m_2 g l_2\, c\,(\theta_1 + \theta_2) \qquad \dots (7.18)$$

$$\frac{\partial L}{\partial \dot{\theta}_2} = \frac{1}{3}\, m_2 l_2^2\, (\dot{\theta}_1 + \dot{\theta}_2) + \frac{1}{2} m_2 l_1 l_2\, c\theta_2\, \dot{\theta}_1 \qquad \dots (7.19)$$

Differentiating equation (7.19) with respect to time,

$$\frac{d}{dt}\left(\frac{\partial L}{\partial \dot{\theta}_2}\right) = \left[\frac{1}{3}\, m_2 l_2^2 + \frac{1}{2} m_2 l_1 l_2\, c\theta_2\right] \ddot{\theta}_1 + \frac{1}{3}\, m_2 l_2^2\, \ddot{\theta}_2 - \frac{1}{2} m_2 l_1 l_2\, s\theta_2\, \dot{\theta}_1 \dot{\theta}_2 \quad \dots (7.20)$$

Torque at joint 2, using equations (7.18) and (7.20),

$$\tau_2 = \frac{d}{dt}\left(\frac{\partial L}{\partial \dot{\theta}_2}\right) - \frac{\partial L}{\partial \theta_2}$$

$$\therefore \quad \tau_2 = m_2 \left[\frac{l_2^2}{3} + \frac{l_1 l_2}{2}\, c\theta_2\right] \ddot{\theta}_1 + \frac{m_2}{3}\, l_2^2\, \ddot{\theta}_2$$

$$+ \frac{m_2}{2}\left[l_1 l_2\, s\theta_2\, \dot{\theta}_1^2 + g l_2\, c(\theta_1 + \theta_2)\right] \dots (7.21)$$

Equations (7.17) and (7.21) are the EOM for the 2 DoF planar RR manipulator. In other words, it is the required dynamic model.

7.5 Dynamic Model Requirements of a Spatial Manipulator

7.5.1 Velocity of a Point on a Spatial Manipulator

In case of spatial manipulator, we will have to use algebraic approach to map the required points like CGs of various links with respect to the base frame. The mapping may be represented as,

$$^0r = \,^0T_i\, ^ir$$

where,

$^i r$ is location of the desired CG with respect to frame i attached to the first end of that link.

$^0 T_i$ is transformation matrix between the base frame and the ith frame.

$^0 r$ is position of the CG of ith link with respect to the base frame.

Now, velocity of that point with respect to 0th frame,

$$^0 v_i = {}^0 \dot{r} = \left[\sum_{j=1}^{i} \frac{\partial\, {}^0 T_i}{\partial q_j}\, \dot{q}_j \right] {}^i r \qquad \text{... (7.22)}$$

where, q_j is joint parameter of jth joint that is either linear displacement 'd' or angular displacement 'θ'.

Let us develop this equation for better understanding, assuming that only n^{th} joint is allowed to perform movement, while rest of the joints are locked.

Hence,

$$\frac{\partial\, {}^0 T_i}{\partial q_n}\, \dot{q}_n = \frac{\partial}{\partial q_n} ({}^0 T_1\, {}^1 T_2\, ... \, {}^{n-1} T_n\, ... \, {}^{i-1} T_i)\, \dot{q}_n$$

$$= ({}^0 T_1\, {}^1 T_2\, ... \, {}^{n-2} T_{n-1}) \left[\frac{\partial}{\partial q_n}\, {}^{n-1} T_n \right] ({}^n T_{n+1}\, ... \, {}^{i-1} T_i)\, \dot{q}_n$$

$$\frac{\partial\, {}^0 T_i}{\partial q_n} = {}^0 T_{n-1} \frac{\partial^{n-1} T_n}{\partial q_n}\, {}^n T_i\, \dot{q}_n \qquad \text{... (7.23)}$$

where,

$$^{n-1}T_n = \begin{bmatrix} c\theta_n & -s\theta_n\, c\alpha_n & s\theta_n\, s\alpha_n & a_n\, c\theta_n \\ s\theta_n & c\theta_n\, c\alpha_n & -c\theta_n\, s\alpha_n & a_n\, s\theta_n \\ 0 & s\alpha_n & c\alpha_n & d_n \\ 0 & 0 & 0 & 1 \end{bmatrix}$$

θ_n, d_n, α_n and a_n are Denavit-Hartenberg parameters of nth joint that is, DH parameters of nth frame with respect to $(n-1)^{th}$ frame.

If the nth joint is prismatic, the movement will be linear and along z_{n-1} axis, that means there will be a change in magnitude of d_n with respect to time; whereas other DH parameters are constant. Thus, q_n is d_n and $\dot{q}_n$ is $\dot{d}_n$ (linear velocity).

$$\therefore \quad \frac{\partial}{\partial d_n}\,{}^{n-1}T_n = \frac{\partial}{\partial d_n}\begin{bmatrix} c\theta_n & -s\theta_n\,c\alpha_n & s\theta_n\,s\alpha_n & a_n\,c\theta_n \\ s\theta_n & c\theta_n\,c\alpha_n & -c\theta_n\,s\alpha_n & a_n\,s\theta_n \\ 0 & s\alpha_n & c\alpha_n & d_n \\ 0 & 0 & 0 & 1 \end{bmatrix}$$

$$\frac{\partial}{\partial d_n}\,{}^{n-1}T_n = \begin{bmatrix} 0 & 0 & 0 & 0 \\ 0 & 0 & 0 & 0 \\ 0 & 0 & 0 & 1 \\ 0 & 0 & 0 & 0 \end{bmatrix} \qquad \text{... (7.24)}$$

Equation (7.24) is valid only for prismatic joint.

If the nth joint is rotating, the movement will be angular and about axis z_{n-1}, that means there will be a change in magnitude of angle θ_n with respect to time and remaining DH parameters will be constant with respect to time. Thus, q_n is θ_n and $\dot{q}_n$ is $\dot{\theta}_n$ (angular velocity).

$$\therefore \quad \frac{\partial}{\partial \theta_n}\,{}^{n-1}T_n = \frac{\partial}{\partial n}\begin{bmatrix} c\theta_n & -s\theta_n\,c\alpha_n & s\theta_n\,s\alpha_n & a_n\,c\theta_n \\ s\theta_n & c\theta_n\,c\alpha_n & -c\theta_n\,s\alpha_n & a_n\,s\theta_n \\ 0 & s\alpha_n & c\alpha_n & d_n \\ 0 & 0 & 0 & 1 \end{bmatrix}$$

$$= \begin{bmatrix} -s\theta_n & -c\theta_n\,c\alpha_n & c\theta_n\,s\alpha_n & -a_n\,s\theta_n \\ c\theta_n & -s\theta_n\,c\alpha_n & s\theta_n\,s\alpha_n & a_n\,c\theta_n \\ 0 & 0 & 0 & 0 \\ 0 & 0 & 0 & 0 \end{bmatrix} \qquad \text{... (7.25)}$$

It is observed that if ${}^{n-1}T_n$ is premultiplied by following matrix

$$\begin{bmatrix} 0 & -1 & 0 & 0 \\ 1 & 0 & 0 & 0 \\ 0 & 0 & 0 & 0 \\ 0 & 0 & 0 & 0 \end{bmatrix}$$

the same result as given by equation (7.25) is obtained.

Let us verify,

$$
\begin{bmatrix} 0 & -1 & 0 & 0 \\ 1 & 0 & 0 & 0 \\ 0 & 0 & 0 & 0 \\ 0 & 0 & 0 & 0 \end{bmatrix}
\begin{bmatrix} c\theta_n & -s\theta_n\,c\alpha_n & s\theta_n\,s\alpha_n & a_n\,c\theta_n \\ s\theta_n & c\theta_n\,c\alpha_n & -c\theta_n\,s\alpha_n & a_n\,s\theta_n \\ 0 & s\alpha_n & c\alpha_n & d_n \\ 0 & 0 & 0 & 1 \end{bmatrix}
$$

$$
= \begin{bmatrix} -s\theta_n & -c\theta_n\,c\alpha_n & c\theta_n\,s\alpha_n & -a_n\,s\theta_n \\ c\theta_n & -s\theta_n\,c\alpha_n & s\theta_n\,s\alpha_n & a_n\,c\theta_n \\ 0 & 0 & 0 & 0 \\ 0 & 0 & 0 & 0 \end{bmatrix}
$$

Thus, verified that the result is same.

Similarly, the matrix obtained for prismatic joint and given by equation (7.24) is used as premultiplier of $^{n-1}T_n$, then,

$$
\begin{bmatrix} 0 & 0 & 0 & 0 \\ 0 & 0 & 0 & 0 \\ 0 & 0 & 0 & 1 \\ 0 & 0 & 0 & 0 \end{bmatrix}
\begin{bmatrix} c\theta_n & -s\theta_n\,c\alpha_n & s\theta_n\,s\alpha_n & a_n\,c\theta_n \\ s\theta_n & c\theta_n\,c\alpha_n & -c\theta_n\,s\alpha_n & a_n\,s\theta_n \\ 0 & s\alpha_n & c\alpha_n & d_n \\ 0 & 0 & 0 & 1 \end{bmatrix}
= \begin{bmatrix} 0 & 0 & 0 & 0 \\ 0 & 0 & 0 & 0 \\ 0 & 0 & 0 & 1 \\ 0 & 0 & 0 & 0 \end{bmatrix}
$$

It produces the required result as given by equation (7.24).

Using these matrices, we may return back to equation (7.22) and write velocity of CG of ith link in a generalised form as,

$$
^0v_i = \left[\sum_{j=1}^{i} {}^0T_{j-1}\, q_j\, {}^{j-1}T_i\, \dot{q}_j \right] {}^i r \qquad \text{... (7.26)}
$$

where,
$$
Q_j = \begin{bmatrix} 0 & 0 & 0 & 0 \\ 0 & 0 & 0 & 0 \\ 0 & 0 & 0 & 1 \\ 0 & 0 & 0 & 0 \end{bmatrix} \qquad \text{... For prismatic joints}
$$

and
$$
Q_j = \begin{bmatrix} 0 & -1 & 0 & 0 \\ 1 & 0 & 0 & 0 \\ 0 & 0 & 0 & 0 \\ 0 & 0 & 0 & 0 \end{bmatrix} \qquad \text{... For rotating joints}
$$

7.5.2 The Inertial Tensor

After calculating velocity of CG of particular link with respect to the base frame, it is now turn to get a generalised expression for moment of inertia of the ith link.

Consider a small element of mass 'dm' in generalised co-ordinate system as shown in Fig. 7.4.

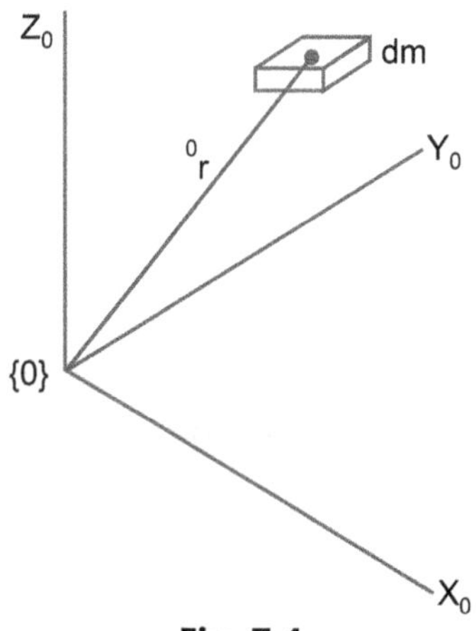

Fig. 7.4

The mass dm is located at point $^0r = \begin{bmatrix} x \\ y \\ z \\ 1 \end{bmatrix}$.

As the mass is not symmetric about any principal axis, the moment of inertia will have all possible components as product of the mass and its distances along 2 axes simultaneously, where the 2 axes are chosen as one of the principal axes combined one-by-one with all the three axes. Thus, total nine combinations as follows,

With respect to X-axis,
$$dm \cdot x \cdot x,\ dm \cdot x \cdot y,\ dm \cdot x , z$$
With respect to Y-axis,
$$dm \cdot y \cdot x,\ dm \cdot y \cdot y,\ dm \cdot y \cdot z$$

With respect to Z-axis,
$$dm \cdot z \cdot x,\ dm \cdot z \cdot y,\ dm \cdot z \cdot z$$

Additionally, these are the terms for the first moments of the body. Those are product of the mass and its distance along each axis. Thus, three terms as $dm \cdot x,\ dm \cdot y,\ dm \cdot z$.

Integration is performed to calculate each of these terms for the entire mass. If all these terms are put together in a matrix form, it gives us mass distribution of the body about each axis of the co-ordinate frame. The 4 × 4 matrix obtained by arranging the mass, the first moment of mass and the moment of inertia is termed as Inertia Tensor. Inertia tensor for i^{th} link may be written in terms of integration of a small mass of ith link and co-ordinates of that small mass as,

$$I_i \; = \; \begin{bmatrix} \int x_i^2 \, dm_i & \int x_i y_i \, dm_i & \int x_i z_i \, dm_i & \int x_i \, dm_i \\[2ex] \int x_i y_i \, dm_i & \int y_i^2 \, dm_i & \int y_i z_i \, dm_i & \int y_i dm_i \\[2ex] \int x_i z_i \, dm_i & \int y_i z_i \, dm_i & \int z_i^2 \, dm_i & \int z_i dm_i \\[2ex] \int x_i \, dm_i & \int y_i dm_i & \int z_i \, dm_i & \int dm_i \end{bmatrix} \qquad \ldots (7.27)$$

7.5.3 The Total Kinetic Energy

The kinetic energy depends on mass, velocity as well as, moment of inertia. Therefore, for a small mass of ith link,

$$dK_i \; = \; \frac{1}{2} \, dm_i \, (^0v_i)^2 \qquad \ldots (7.28)$$

As we are now considering spatial manipulators, velocity will not be a single scalar value. It will be a column matrix (i.e. column vector) representing x, y, z components of velocity.

$$^0v_i \; = \; \begin{bmatrix} v_x \\ v_y \\ v_z \\ 1 \end{bmatrix}$$

When we require square of a column vector having 4 elements, matrix multiplication will not be possible. As the rank of matrix is 4×1, it can be multiplied by a matrix having rank 1×4. Therefore,

$$(^0v_i)^2 \; = \; {}^0v_i \cdot {}^0v_i \; = \; T_r \, (^0v_i \, {}^0v_i^T)$$

i.e. $$(^0v_i)^2 \; = \; \begin{bmatrix} v_x \\ v_y \\ v_z \\ 1 \end{bmatrix} [v_x \; v_y \; v_z \; 1] \; = \; \begin{bmatrix} v_x^2 \\ v_y^2 \\ v_z^2 \\ 1 \end{bmatrix}$$

where 'T_r' is called as Tracer operator.

By substituting velocity from equation (7.26) into equation (7.28) with use of Tracer operator, we get,

$$dK_i = \frac{1}{2} T_r \left[\left(\sum_{j=1}^{i} {}^0T_{j-1} \, Q_j \, {}^{j-1}T_i \, \dot{q}_j \, {}^ir \right) \left(\sum_{k=1}^{i} {}^0T_{k-1} \, Q_k \, {}^{k-1}T_i \, \dot{q}_k \, {}^ir \right) \right] dm_i$$

$$= \frac{1}{2} T_r \left[\sum_{j=1}^{i} \sum_{k=1}^{i} ({}^0T_{j-1} \, Q_j \, {}^{j-1}T_i) \, {}^ir \, {}^ir^T \, dm_i \, ({}^0T_{k-1} \, Q_k \, {}^{k-1}T_i)^T \, \dot{q}_j \, \dot{q}_k \right]$$

Performing integration, total kinetic energy of ith link is,

$$K_i = \frac{1}{2} T_r \left[\sum_{j=1}^{i} \sum_{k=1}^{i} ({}^0T_{j-1} \, Q_j \, {}^{j-1}T_i) \int {}^ir \, {}^ir^T \, dm_i \, ({}^0T_{k-1} \, Q_k \, {}^{k-1}T_i)^T \, \dot{q}_j \, \dot{q}_k \right]$$

The integration $\int {}^ir \, {}^ir^T \, dm_i$ is Inertia Tensor I_i.

$$\therefore \qquad K_i = \frac{1}{2} T_r \left[\sum_{j=1}^{i} \sum_{k=1}^{i} ({}^0T_{j-1} \, Q_j \, {}^{j-1}T_i) \, I_i \, ({}^0T_{k-1} \, Q_k \, {}^{k-1}T_i)^T \, \dot{q}_j \, \dot{q}_k \right] \qquad \ldots (7.29)$$

If the manipulator has n DoF i.e. n-links then, total kinetic energy of the manipulator is,

$$K = \sum_{i=1}^{n} K_i$$

$$\therefore \qquad K = \frac{1}{2} \sum_{i=1}^{n} \sum_{j=1}^{i} \sum_{k=1}^{i} T_r \left[({}^0T_{j-1} \, Q_j \, {}^{j-1}T_i) \, I_i \, ({}^0T_{k-1} \, Q_k \, {}^{k-1}T_i)^T \, \dot{q}_j \, \dot{q}_k \right] \qquad \ldots (7.30)$$

7.5.4 The Total Potential Energy

The potential energy of ith link will be,

$$P_i = m_i g \, {}^0r_i \qquad \ldots (7.31)$$

where, ${}^0r_i$ is position of CG of the ith link with respect to the base frame.

$$\therefore \qquad P_i = m_i g \, {}^0T_i \, {}^ir$$

If the manipulator has n DoF that means n-links, then total potential energy will be,

$$P = \sum_{i=1}^{n} m_i \cdot g \, {}^0T_i \, {}^ir \qquad \ldots (7.32)$$

7.5.5 The Lagrangian and the Joint Torques

Now, the Lagrangian may be obtained as,

$$L = K - P$$

where, K and P are obtained using equations (7.30) and (7.32) respectively.

Further, individual joint torque may be obtained as,

$$\tau_i = \frac{d}{dt}\left(\frac{\partial L}{\partial \dot{q}_i}\right) - \left(\frac{\partial L}{\partial q_i}\right) \qquad \ldots (7.33)$$

Equation (7.33) gives set of EOM which describes the dynamic behaviour of the spatial manipulator.

7.6 Acceleration of a Rigid Body

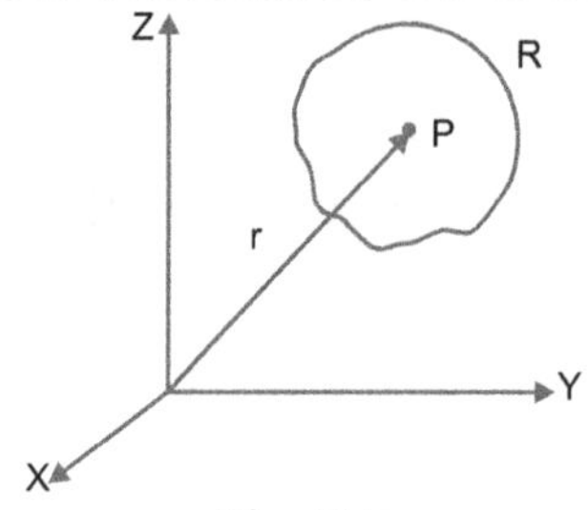

Fig. 7.5

'R' be the rigid body.

'P' is any particle of rigid body at distance 'r' from origin of co-ordinate system XYZ.

Position vector is r.

Velocity of the particle 'P' with respect to the coordinate frame

$$v(t) = \frac{dr}{dt}$$

Acceleration of a particle P is given by,

$$a(t) = \frac{d\,v(t)}{dt} = \frac{d}{dt}\left(\frac{dr}{dt}\right)$$

$$a(t) = \frac{d^2r}{dt^2}$$

7.7 Newton's Equation and Euler Equation

Newton's Equation:

The translational motion of the link in terms of the balance of forces is described by the Newton's equation. The force 'F', acting at the centre of mass of the link is given by,

$$F = m_i \cdot \dot{v}_i \qquad \ldots (i)$$

where, $\dot{v}_i$ is the linear acceleration of the link.

Euler Equation:

The Euler equation for the rotational motion of the link describes the moment balance about the centre of mass of the link. The angular velocity of the link ω_i and the moment of inertial tensor I_i relate to the total moments M_i acting on link as,

$$M_i = \frac{d}{dt}(I_i\,\omega_i)$$

$$= \underbrace{I_i \cdot \dot{\omega}_i}_{\text{[Direct torque]}} + \underbrace{\omega_i \times (I_i\,\omega_i)}_{\begin{array}{c}\text{Gyroscopic torque induced by dependence}\\\text{of } I_i \text{ on link's orientation w.r.t. the base frame}\end{array}} \qquad \dots \text{(ii)}$$

Equations (i) and (ii) are recursively applied to evaluate the inertia force and torque acting at the centre of mass of each link of the manipulator. These equations are together called as 'Newton-Euler equation'.

7.8 Newton-Euler Dynamic Formulation

The Newton-Euler (NE) formulation is based on Newton's second law and d'Alembert principle. The force balance on the link of manipulator leads to a set of equations, whose structure allows a recursive solution. The NE formulation requires two passes over the links.

7.8.1 A Forward Pass (Forward Iteration) : (FP)

It describes the kinematic relationships of a moving co-ordinate frame and is carried out to compute the velocities and accelerations of each link recursively, starting at the base and propagating forward towards the end effector.

Boundary conditions:

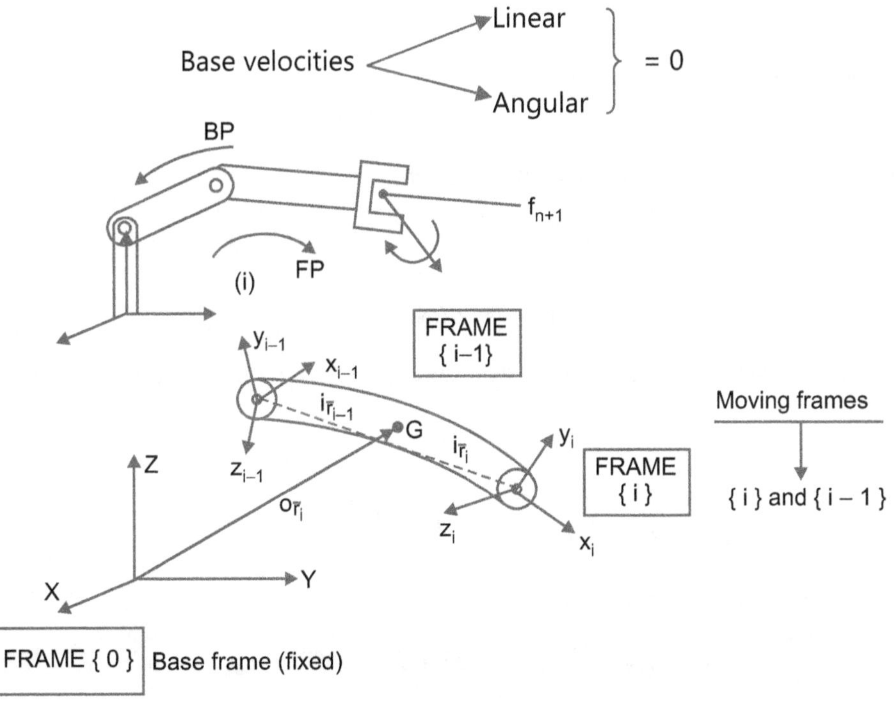

Fig. 7.6

Kinematic relationship between the links in the 3×3 rotation matrix $^{i-1}R_i$ transforms rotation of any vector with reference to frame {i} to the frame {i − 1}.

The rotation matrix $^{i-1}R_i$ is the upperleft 3×3 submatrix of $^{i-1}T_i$.

$$^{i-1}T_i = \begin{bmatrix} c\theta_i & -s\theta_i\,c\alpha_i & s\theta_i\,s\alpha_i & a_i\,c\theta_i \\ s\theta_i & c\theta_i\,c\alpha_i & -c\theta_i\,s\alpha_i & a_i\,s\theta_i \\ 0 & s\alpha_i & c\alpha_i & d_i \\ 0 & 0 & 0 & 1 \end{bmatrix}$$

$$= \begin{bmatrix} ^{i-1}R_i & ^{i-1}D_i \\ 0\ 0\ 0 & 1 \end{bmatrix}$$

We know,

$$(^{i-1}R_i)^{-1} = {}^{i}R_{i-1} = (^{i-1}R_i)^T$$

Using the rotational transformation matrices, it is possible to express the vectors related to link i with respect to link frame {i} instead of base frame {0}.

It gives constant vectors.

The linear velocity of the centre of mass of link i,

$$\bar{v}_i = v_i + \omega_i \times {}^{i}\bar{r}_i$$

The linear acceleration of the centre of mass of link i

$$\dot{\bar{v}}_i = \frac{d}{dt}(\bar{v}_i)$$

$$= \dot{v}_i + \dot{\omega}_i \times {}^{i}\bar{r}_i + \omega_i \times (\omega_i \times {}^{i}\bar{r}_i)$$

where, $^{i}\bar{r}_i$ is the position vector of centre of mass of link (i) from frame {i} with respect to base frame {0}.

For prismatic joint,

$$^{i}\omega_i = {}^{i}R_{i-1}\,^{i-1}\omega_{i-1}$$

$$^{i}\dot{\omega}_i = {}^{i}R_{i-1}\,^{i-1}\dot{\omega}_{i-1}$$

$$^{i}v_i = {}^{i}R_{i-1}[^{i-1}v_{i-1} + \hat{z}_0\,\ddot{d}_i] + 2\,^{i}\omega_i \times (^{i}R_{i-1}\,\hat{z}_0\,\dot{d}_i) + {}^{i}\omega_i \times (^{i}R_0\,^{i-1}D_i)$$

$$+ {}^{i}\omega_i \times [^{i}\omega_i \times (^{i}R_0\,^{i-1}D_i)]$$

Here $\hat{z}_0 = [0\ 0\ 1]^T$ is unit vector in z_0 direction and $(^iR_0\ ^{i-1}D_i)$ is given by,

$$^iR_{i-1}\ ^{i-1}D_i \;=\; \begin{bmatrix} c_i & s_i & 0 \\ -s_ic\alpha_i & c_ic\alpha_i & s\alpha_i \\ s_is\alpha_i & -c_ic\alpha_i & c\alpha_i \end{bmatrix} \begin{bmatrix} a_ic_i \\ a_is_i \\ d_i \end{bmatrix} = \begin{bmatrix} a_i \\ d_is\alpha_i \\ d_ic\alpha_i \end{bmatrix}$$

with $\qquad\qquad c_i \;=\; c\theta_i = \cos\theta_i$

and $\qquad\qquad s_i \;=\; s\theta_i = \sin\theta_i$

The above equation for $^i\dot{\omega}_i,\ ^i\ddot{\omega}_i,\ ^i\dot{v}_i,\ ^i\ddot{\bar{v}}_i$ give forward NE equations.

FP starts at base i.e. at $i = 0$.

Initial conditions with fixed base of manipulator are,

$$^0v_0 = 0,\ ^0\dot{v}_0 = 0,\ ^0\omega_0 = 0 \text{ and } ^0\dot{\omega}_0 = 0$$

The gravity effect can be included by considering the linear acceleration of base frame

$$^0\dot{v}_0 \;=\; g = [g_x\ g_y\ g_z]^T$$

7.8.2 Backward Pass (Backward Iteration)

Knowing the velocities and accelerations of each link, the forces and moments acting on each link can be evaluated by starting at the end effector and moving towards back-end.

Generalized torque for the joint i in the base frame {0} is,

$$\tau_i \;=\; \hat{f}_{i-1}^{\,T}\ \hat{\tau}_{i-1}$$

Using rotational transformation matrix R, the general equations (i) and (ii) i.e. NE and EE and f_i and t_i are transformed to joint link co-ordinates to give final backward recursive equation.

$$^iF_i \;=\; m_i\ ^i\dot{\bar{v}}_i$$

$$^iM_i \;=\; I_i\ ^i\dot{\omega}_i + {}^i\omega_i \times (I_i\ ^i\omega_i)$$

Joint forces and moments are

$$^if_i = {}^iF_i + {}^iR_{i+1}\,{}^{i+1}f_{i+1}$$

$$^it_i = {}^iR_{i+1}\,{}^{i+1}t_{i+1} + ({}^iR_0\,{}^{i-1}D_i) \times {}^iR_{i+1}\,{}^{i+1}f_{i+1} + ({}^iR_0\,{}^{i-1}D_i + {}^iR_0\,{}^i\bar{r}_i) \times {}^iF_i + {}^iM_i$$

$$\tau_i = {}^if_i^T\,{}^iR_{i-1}\,\hat{z}_0$$

Thus, N-E equations of motions are a set of forward and backward recursive equations with kinematics and dynamics of each link referred to link co-ordinate system.

Notations:

$$\begin{aligned}
C_i &\Rightarrow \text{Centre of mass of link}\\
{}^{i-1}\bar{r}_i &\Rightarrow \text{Position vector of } C_i \text{ from frame } \{i-1\}\\
{}^i\bar{r}_i &\Rightarrow \text{Position vector of } C_i \text{ from frame } \{i\}\\
m_i &\Rightarrow \text{Mass of link}\\
I_i &\Rightarrow \text{Inertia tensor of link w.r.t. a frame } \{C_i\}\\
\bar{v}_i &\Rightarrow \text{Linear velocity of centre of mass}\\
\dot{\bar{v}}_i &\Rightarrow \text{Linear acceleration of centre of mass}\\
\omega_i &\Rightarrow \text{Angular velocity of link}\\
\dot{\omega}_i &\Rightarrow \text{Angular acceleration of link}\\
F_i &\Rightarrow \text{Total external force acting at the centre of mass of link}\\
M_i &\Rightarrow \text{Total external moment acting on link at centre of mass of link}\\
v_{i-1} \text{ and } \omega_{i-1} &\Rightarrow \text{Linear and angular velocities of frame } \{i-1\} \text{ w.r.t. base frame } \{0\}\\
{}^{i-1}\omega_i &\Rightarrow \text{Relative angular velocity of frame } \{i\} \text{ w.r.t. frame } \{i-1\}
\end{aligned}$$

f_i and t_i $\Rightarrow$ Force and moment exerted by link $\{i-1\}$ on link $\{i\}$ at the origin of frame $\{i-1\}$ w.r.t. base frame $\{0\}$

f_{i+1} and t_{i+1} $\Rightarrow$ Force and moment exerted by link $\{i\}$ on link $\{i+1\}$ at the origin of frame $\{i\}$

Comparison of L-E and N-E Formulations:

(i) The recursive N-E formulation has a computational complexity of order $O(n)$ i.e. mathematical operations of multiplication and addition are proportional to n, the number of degrees of freedom of the manipulator.

(ii) Whereas the recursive L-E formulation has a complexity of order $O(n^4)$.

The drawback of recursive formulation is that, it is not as amenable to simple physical interpretation as the closed form LE formulation is.

EXERCISES

1. Get expression for velocity of end effector of a Cartesian configuration.

2. Get expression for velocity of CG of third link of a 3 DoF 3R planar manipulator.

3. Get a mathematical model for dynamic response of a single horizontal link, hinged perfectly to rigid support as shown in Fig. 7.7.

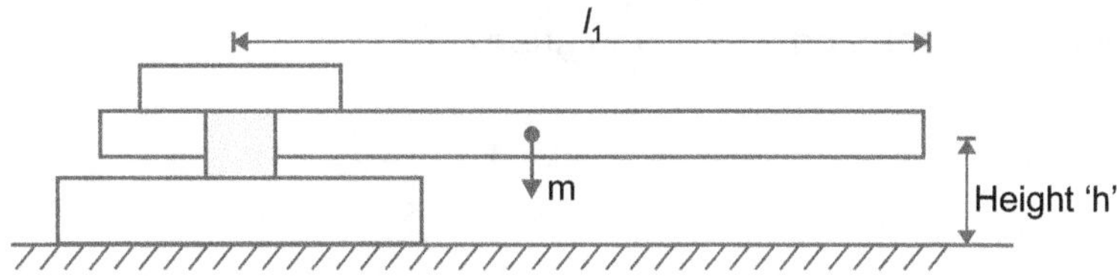

Fig. 7.7

4. Fig. 7.8 shows front view and top view of a 2R planar manipulator. Obtain dynamic model for the manipulator if the links have masses m_1 and m_2 and lengths are l_1 and l_2 respectively.

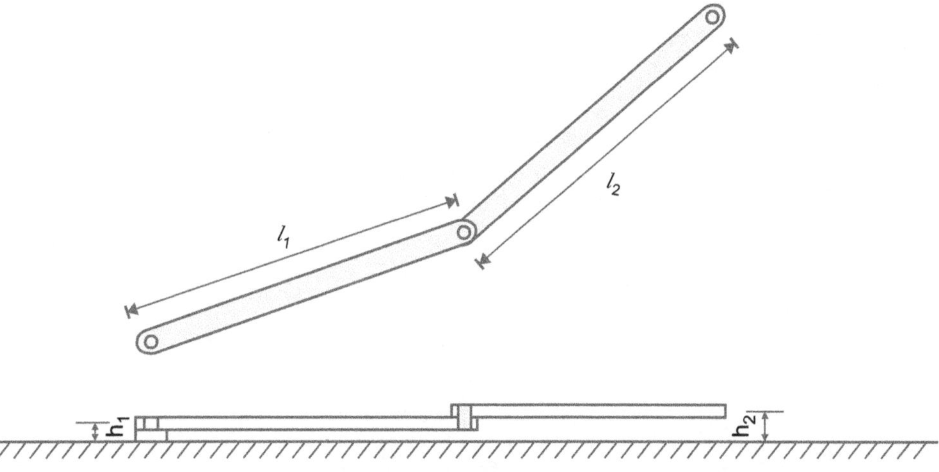

Fig. 7.8

5. Get a transformation matrix for mapping velocity of a 3 DoF manipulator having first and third joints as rotating joints and the second joint as prismatic joint.

6.   Write algorithm for LE formulation to derive EOM of a spatial manipulator.

7.   Discuss use of :

     (i)   Newton equation

     (ii)   Euler equation

     (iii) Lagrangian

8.   Explain Newton-Euler dynamic formulation.

9.   Compare L-E formulation and N-E formulation.

Unit III

Chapter 8: TRANSMISSION SYSTEMS
AND
ROBOT SIMULATION

8.1 Actuation Schemes

–   Before applying actuation schemes to the general kinematic structure of a manipulator that has been selected, we need to categorize the schemes according to the application. The actuator, reduction system and transmission system are designed together and are closed coupled. The actuation schemes can be explained with reference to –
(I)   Actuator location.
(II) Reduction and transmission systems.

8.1.1 Actuator Location

- Generally, actuator location is at or near the joint it drives.
- **Direct drive configuration:** It is an arrangement in which the actuator can produce enough torque or force, its outputs can attach directly to the joint.
  It offers the advantages:
  (i)   Simplicity in design and
  (ii)   Superior controllability i.e. without transmission or reduction elements between the actuator and the joint. The joint motions can be controlled in the same manner as the actuator itself.
- Many actuators are suitable for relatively high speed and low torque applications, thus, they need a **speed reduction system.**
- Also, the actuators tend to be heavy. If they can be located remotely from the joint and towards the base of the manipulator, the overall inertia of the manipulator can be reduced.
- Therefore, it reduces the size needed for the actuators. To get these benefits, a **transmission system** is required to transfer the motion from the actuator to the joint.
- **A remotely placed actuator:**
  –   In a joint drive system with remotely mounted actuator, the reduction system may be placed at the actuator, or at the joint. An arrangement is made which can combine with functions of transmission and reduction. Apart from added complexity, the major disadvantage of reduction and transmission systems is that they may introduce additional friction and flexibility into the mechanism.

- When reduction is associated with the joint, the transmission will be working at higher speeds and lower torques.
- Lower torque means that flexibility will be less of a problem. And if the weight of the reducer is significant, some of the advantage of remotely mounted actuators is lost.
- The optimal distribution of reduction stages throughout the transmission depends on the following factors:
  - (i) the flexibility of the transmission,
  - (ii) the weight of the reduction system,
  - (iii) the friction associated with the reduction system, and
  - (iv) the ease of incorporating these components into the overall manipulator design.

8.2 Reduction and Transmission Systems

There are different types of reduction and transmission systems, that include –

(i) Gears

(ii) Belts, cables and chains

(iii) Harmonic drives

(iv) Cyclo drives

(v) Antifriction drive

8.2.1 (i) Gears

These are the most common elements used for reduction. The most common means of torque or force transmission combines gears into a 'gear train', so that the output shaft speed and torque are a linear function of the input shaft speed and torque. The gears transmit rotary motion and torque through the pair of mating gear teeth, the profiles of which are cams acting against one another to produce the desired motion.

Gears are classified by the general configuration of the gear shaft.

- Spur gears for parallel shaft.
- Bevel gear for orthogonal intersecting shafts.
- Worm or cross helical gears for non-parallel and non-intersecting (i.e. skew shafts).
- Rack gearing.

Different types of gears have different load ratings, wear characteristics, and frictional properties.

Gear Ratio (n):

This term describes the speed reduction and torque rise effects of a gear pair.

when, $n > 1 \Rightarrow$ It indicates reduction in speed

$n = 1 \Rightarrow$ Constant speed

$n < 1 \Rightarrow$ Indicates increase in speed

The relationship between input and output speeds and torques are given by,

$$N_O = \left(\frac{1}{n}\right) n_i$$

$$T_O = n \cdot T_i$$

where, N_O and N_i are output and input speeds respectively.

T_O and T_i are output and input torques respectively.

Disadvantages:

- The major disadvantage of using gears is that of added **backlash** and **friction.**
- **Backlash** results from imperfectly meshed gears and it can be defined as the maximum angular motion of the output gear when the input gear remains fixed.
- But if the gear teeth are meshed tightly to eliminate backlash, there can be excessive amounts of friction.
- Increase in cost of drive: Very precise gears and very precise mounting minimize problem of backlash and friction but at the same time it will increase the overall cost of drive system.

8.2.2 (ii) Belts, Cables and Chains   (W-11)

- Belts, cables and chains can be used to transmit actuator position and force information, or in continuous motion as power transmitting devices.
- Some of the configurations are:
  - (a)   Flat belts
  - (b)   V-belts
  - (c)   Timing belts
  - (d)   Cables and flexible bands
  - (e)   Straps
  - (f)   Chains
- Most of these elements must be flexible enough to bend around pulleys, they also tend to be flexible in the longitudinal direction. The flexibility of these elements is proportional to their lengths.
- As these systems are flexible, there must be some kind of mechanism for preloading the loop to ensure that the belt or cable stays engaged on the pulley. Large preload can add undue strain to the flexible element and cause excessive friction.
- Cables or flexible bands can be used either in a closed loop or as single-ended elements which are always kept in tension by some form of preload.

To eliminate preload:

- In a particular joint, that is spring loaded in one direction, a single-ended cable could be used to pull against it.
- Also, two active single-ended systems can oppose each other.

  This arrangement can eliminate the problem of excessive preloads, but it will add more actuators in the system.

  - Roller chains work in similar fashion as that of flexible bands, but can bend around relatively small pulleys while retaining a high stiffness. Due to wear and heavy loads on the pins connecting the links, toothed belt systems may be more compact than roller chains for certain applications.
  - Band, cable, belt and chain drives have the ability to combine transmission with reduction. The gear ratio of the transmission system is,

$$n = \frac{r_2}{r_1}$$

where,

  n – is the gear ratio

  r_1 – Radius of input (i.e. driving pulley)

  r_2 – Radius of output (i.e. driven pulley)

It is shown in Fig. 8.1.

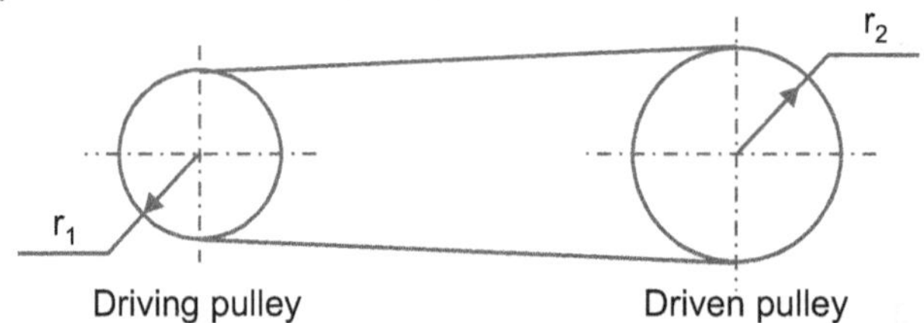

Fig. 8.1: Ability of band, cable, belt and chain drives

to combine transmission with reduction

8.2.3 (iii) Harmonic Drive

- Harmonic drives utilize toothed components in a unique manner to provide large velocity ratios and high torque capacities in a very compact space.
- The drive has three basic components:

  (a) A rigid circular spline.

  (b) A flexible circular spline, and

  (c) An elliptical wave generator.

- The flexible circular spline normally has two fewer teeth than the rigid circular spline. The wave generator deforms the flexible circular spline, thus engaging teeth at diametrically opposite points coincident with the major axis of the elliptical wave generator and disengaging points at the minor axis.

- The general equation for reduction ratio is,

$$\frac{\omega_i}{\omega_o} = \frac{N_o}{N_c - N_f}$$

where, N_o – Number of teeth on output member of flexible circular spline or rigid

N_c – Number of teeth on circular spline

N_f – Number of teeth on flexible circular spline

Fig. 8.2 shows components of harmonic drive.

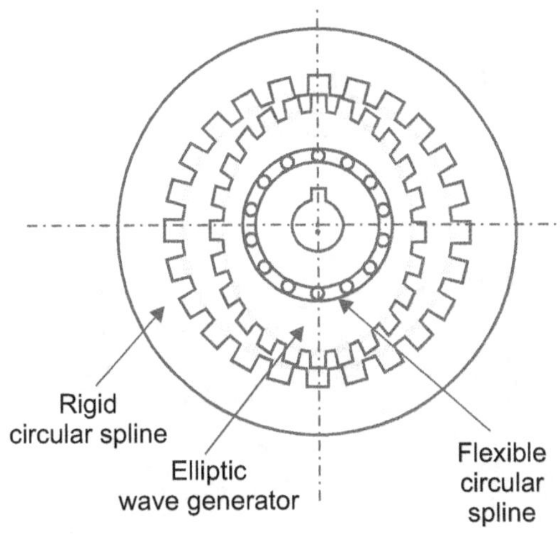

Fig. 8.2: Harmonic drive unit

- Thus, elliptical wave generator input deflects flexible circular spline to engage teeth at the major axis.

Flexible circular spline output rotates in opposite direction to input.

Rigid circular spline is rotationally fixed.

- Thus, harmonic drive provides high mechanical advantage with speed reduction.

These are available with velocity ratios from **64: 1** to **320: 1** and torque capacities upto **2.45 × 10^4 *lb/in*.**

Drawbacks:

- The motion is not perfectly smooth but has a small ripple corresponding to the drive frequency. The amount of ripple increases with the applied load. This may lead to oscillations in the manipulator system.
- The spring constant of the harmonic drive is not linear but decrease with increasing load. Variable stiffness with load is a complicating feature in the analysis of performance and design of control systems.
- **Flexibility:** The harmonic drive is more flexible than corresponding gear systems. Flexibility sometimes complicates the position and high-speed control considerations.

8.2.4 (iv) Cyclo-Drives

- It is similar to harmonic drives, but in this case, there are no deformations involved. Contact is made between carefully shaped rows by means of balls.
- The **friction** introduced is therefore, **very low** as in ball bearings, whereas **stiffness** is **very high.**

8.2.5 (v) Anti-Friction Drives

- Lead screws or ball bearing screws provide large reduction in a compact package.
- Fig. 8.3 and Fig. 8.4 shows these drives.

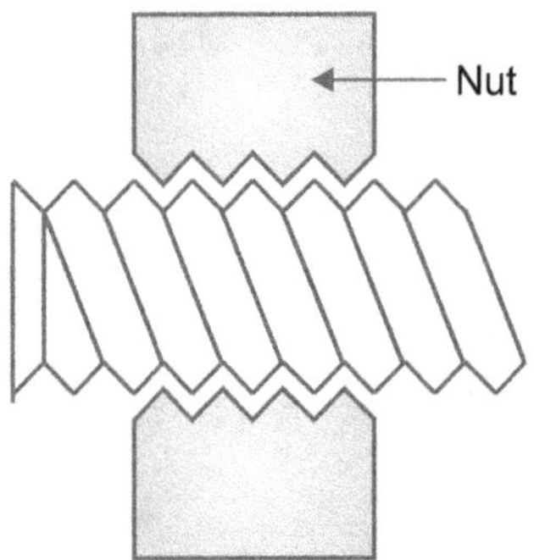

Fig. 8.3: Lead Screws

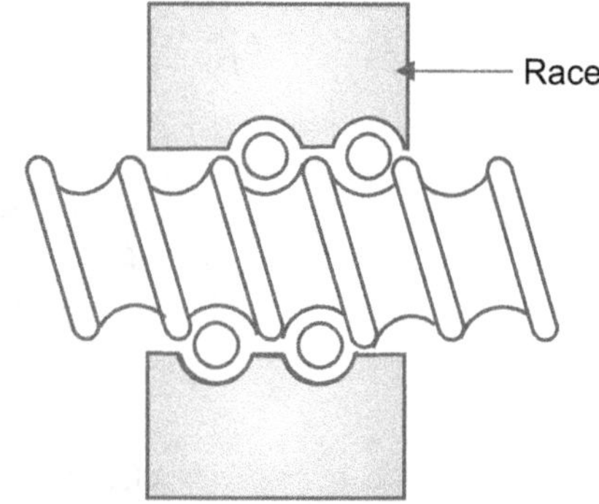

Fig. 8.4: A Ball Bearing Screw

- Lead screws are very stiff and can support very large loads, and have the property that they transform rotary motion into linear motion.
- Ball bearings are similar to lead screws, but instead of having the nut threads riding directly on the screw threads, a recirculating circuit of ball bearings rolls between the sets of threads.

  Ball bearing screws have very low friction and are generally back drivable.

8.3 Stiffness and Deflections

- For most of the manipulators, the important aspects for design are:

    - the overall stiffness of the structure and the drive system.

    - the resulting deflections under given loads.

- Stiff systems provide two advantages:

    (a) A particular manipulator does not have sensors to measure the tool frame location directly, it is estimated using the forward kinematics based on sensed joint positions. Here links cannot sag under gravity or other loads for an accurate calculation. DH-description of the linkages to remain fixed under various loading condition is required.

    (b) Flexibilities in the structure or drive train will lead to resonances which have an undesirable effect on manipulator performance.

- **Flexible elements in parallel:** The combination of two flexible members of stiffness k_1 and k_2 when connected in parallel produce the net stiffness (k_p).

$$k_p = k_1 + k_2$$

- **Flexible elements in series:** The combination of two flexible members of stiffness k_1 and k_2 when connected in series produce the net stiffness (k_s).

$$k_s = \frac{1}{k_1} + \frac{1}{k_2}$$

- For a transmission system, we often have the case of one stage of reduction or transmission in series with a following stage of reduction or transmission.

8.3.1 Torsional Stiffness of Shafts

Shafts are used for transmitting rotary motion. The torsional stiffness of a round shaft while transmitting motion can be calculated as,

$$k = \frac{\pi \cdot G \cdot d^4}{32 \cdot l}$$

where, $\quad$ k $\;-\;$ Torsional stiffness of shaft

$\quad$ G $\;-\;$ Modulus of rigidity or shear modulus of elasticity of shaft material (7.5×10^{10} N/m^2 for steel)

$\quad$ d $\;-\;$ The shaft diameter

$\quad$ l $\;-\;$ The shaft length

8.3.2 Stiffness of Gears

Though the gears have high stiffness, they introduce compliance into the drive system.

The stiffness of output gear can be estimated using the formula, assuming fixed input gear.

$$k = kg \cdot b \cdot r^2$$

where, k — is stiffness of output gear
   b — is the face width of the gear
   r — is the radius of output gear
   kg — 1.35×10^{10} N/m^2 for steel.

Relationship between the stiffness on the input side (i.e. k_i) and the stiffness on the output side (i.e. k_o):

Let k_i be the stiffness of the transmission system prior to reduction (i.e. on the input side) and k_o be the stiffness of the transmission system on the output side.

n be the gear ratio.

$\therefore$ The input torque,

$$T_i = k_i \cdot \delta \cdot \theta_i \qquad \qquad \text{... (8.1)}$$

The output torque,

$$T_o = k_o \cdot \delta \cdot \theta_o \qquad \qquad \text{... (8.2)}$$

— Assuming perfectly rigid gear pair,

and $$T_o = n \cdot T_i \qquad \qquad \text{... (8.3)}$$

Also $$\theta_o = \frac{1}{n} \theta_i \qquad \qquad \text{... (8.4)}$$

— From equation (8.2),

$$k_o = \frac{T_o}{\delta \cdot \theta_o}$$

$$= \frac{n \cdot T_i}{\delta \cdot \left(\frac{1}{n} \cdot \theta_i \right)} \qquad \qquad \text{... } (\because \text{ From equations (8.3) and (8.4))}$$

$$= \frac{n \cdot k_i \cdot \delta \cdot \theta_i}{\frac{1}{n} \cdot \delta \cdot \theta_i} \qquad \qquad \text{... (From equations (8.1) and (8.2))}$$

$$k_o = n^2 \cdot k_i$$

Hence, a gear reduction has the effect of increasing the stiffness by the square of the gear ratio.

8.3.3 Stiffness of Belts

In a belt drive system, stiffness is given by,

$$k_b = \frac{AE}{l}$$

where, k_b – is the stiffness of belt drive

A – is the cross-sectional area of the belt

E – is the modulus of elasticity of the belt

l – is the length of the free belt between pulleys and one third of

the length of the belt in contact with the pulleys

8.3.4 Stiffness of Links

Considering a single link as a cantilever beam, we can calculate the stiffness at the end point, as shown in Fig. 8.5 as follows.

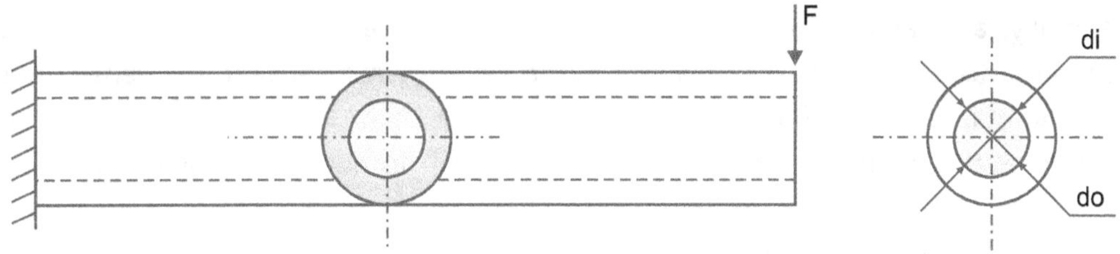

Fig. 8.5: Hollow circular cantilever beam loaded with F at its end

For a round hollow cantilever beam, the stiffness is given by,

$$k = \frac{3\pi \cdot E \cdot (d_o^4 - d_i^4)}{64 \cdot l^3}$$

where,   E – the modulus of elasticity (2.1×10^{11} N/m^2 for steel)

d_i and d_o – are the inner and outer diameters of the tubular beam

l – is the length of the beam

For a cantilever beam of square cross-section, stiffness is given by,

$$k = \frac{E(b_o^4 - b_i^4)}{4 \cdot l^3}$$

where, b_i and b_o are the outer and inner widths of the beam.

$(b_o - b_i)$ is the wall thickness

l is the length of beam.

- Above formulae for estimating stiffness of various elements like gears, shafts, belts, and links have been discussed. They provide some guidance in sizing structural members and transmissions elements.

But sometimes, many sources of flexibility are very difficult to model. As the drive train often introduces significantly more flexibility than the link of a manipulator.

The sources of flexibility such as bearing flexibility, flexibility of the actuator mounting etc. are not considered here.

Therefore, **Finite Element Techniques** can be used to find more accurately the stiffness as well as other properties of more realistic structural elements.

8.4 Position Sensing (W-11)

- Generally, all manipulators are servo-controlled mechanisms, i.e. the force or torque command to an actuator is calculated based on the error between the sensed position of the joint and the desired position.
  Therefore, this requires that each joint have some arrangement for position sensing device.
- The common approach is to locate a position sensor directly on the shaft of the actuator. If the drive train is stiff and has no backlash the true joint angles can be calculated from the actuator shaft positions.
- The popular position feedback device is –

(i) The incremental rotary optical encoder:
- It consists of a glass disk marked with alternating transparent and opaque stripes aligned radially. A phototransmitter (a light source) is located on one side of the disk, and a photoreceiver is on the other side. As the disk rotates, the light beam is alternately completed and broken. The output from photoreceiver is a pulse train whose frequency is proportional to the speed of rotation of the disk. In a typical encoder, there are two sets of phototransmitter and receivers aligned 90° out of phase. This phasing provides direction information i.e. if signal 'A' leads signal 'B' by 90°, the encoder disk is rotating in one direction, but if 'B' leads 'A', then it is going in other direction. By counting the pulses and by adding or subtracting based on the sign, it is possible to use the encoder to provide **position information** with respect to a known starting location.

Fig. 8.6 shows an arrangement of this encoder.

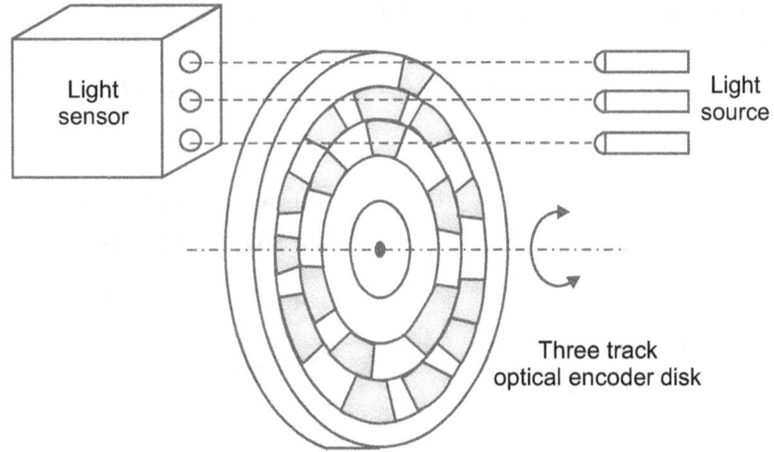

Fig. 8.6: The incremental rotary optical encoder

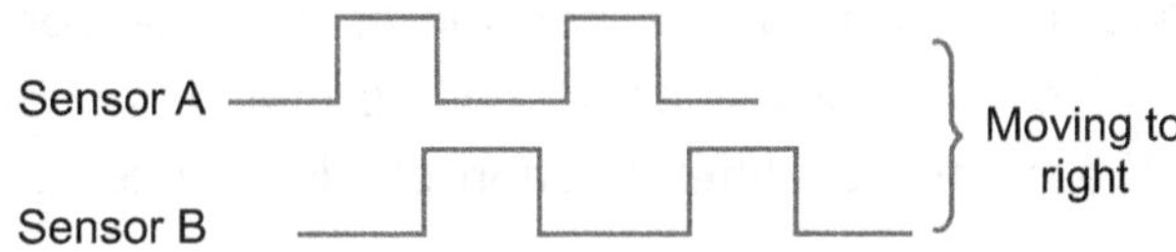

(ii) Resolvers:

- These are devices which output two analog signals - one the sine of the shaft angle and the other cosine.
- The shaft angle is determined from the relative magnitude of the two signals.
- Thus, there are only two stator windings placed 90° mechanically out of phase with each other. If the rotor is excited with a voltage $A \cdot \sin \omega t$, then the outputs on stator terminals will be,

$$V_1 = A \cdot \sin \omega t \cdot \sin \theta$$
$$V_2 = A \sin \omega t \cdot \cos \theta$$

where, θ is the angle of the rotor with respect to the stator.

- The resolution is a function of the quality of the resolver and the amount of noise picked up in the electronics sand cabling. They are more reliable than optical encoders, but the resolution is lower.
- Resolvers cannot be placed directly at the joint without additional gearing to improve the resolution.

(iii) Potentiometers:

The potentiometer is a well-known position or angle sensor. These are connected in a bridge configuration, they produce a voltage proportional to the shaft position.

Disadvantages: Difficulties with resolution, linearity, and noise susceptibility limit their use.

(iv) Tachometers:

- They are sometimes used to provide an analog signal proportional to the shaft velocity.
- Fig. 8.7 shows variation to output (voltage) vs. shaft speed (rpm).

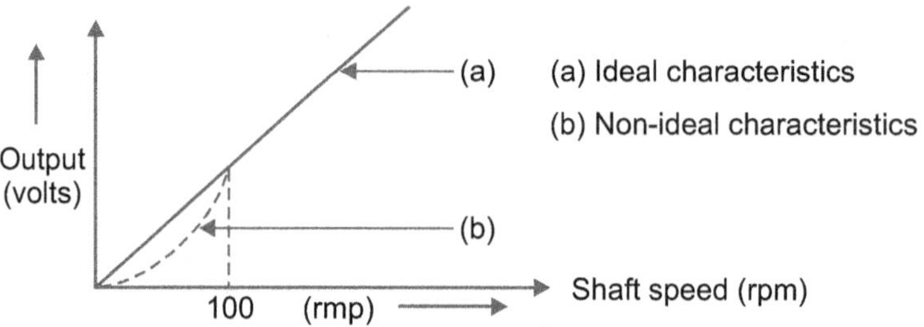

Fig. 8.7: Variation of output vs. shaft speed

- In principle, the signal from a joint position or angle sensor can be electronically differentiated to obtain joint velocity. This approach is sometimes practical, but often is not. The numerical differentiation can introduce noise, as well as a time lag.
- Several types of sensors can be used for measurement of robot joint velocity, e.g.
  - Tachometer generator
  - Tachsyn
  - Linear Velocity Transducer (LVT)

8.5 Force Sensing   (W-11)

- A variety of devices have been designed to measure forces of contact between a manipulator's end-effector and the environment which it contacts.

8.5.1 Strain Gauges

- These sensors make use of sensing elements called **strain gauges.** These are of either the semiconductor or the metal foil category.
- Strain gauges can be mounted at appropriate points on the robot structure to determine the strain at these points.

Principle of Operation:

'A mechanical deformation produces a change in resistance of the gauge, which can then be related to the applied force'.

Consider a simple strain gauge consisting of a plastic body (i.e. non-conducting body) whose top surface is coated with a thin layer of a conducting material (e.g. aluminium or copper). If the conductive coating is assumed to have a uniform cross-sectional area 'A', then the resistance of the device is given by,

$$R = \frac{L}{\sigma \cdot A}$$

where, σ is the conductivity of the conducting material.

L is the length of the gauge.

Fig. 8.8 shows the arrangement of strain gauge.

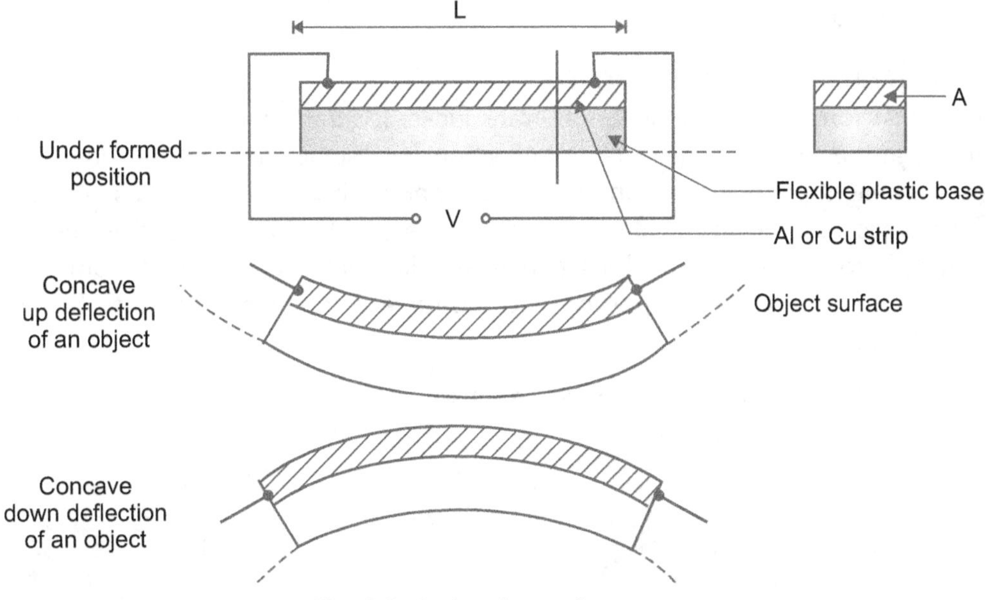

Fig. 8.8: A simple strain gauge

–   When conductive material is glued to an object, any deformation will cause the gauge to bend either concave up or concave down as shown in Fig. 8.8. The gauge length is either reduced or lengthened.

–   It is seen that such action causes a corresponding decrease or increase in the gauge resistance.

–   There are four basic types of strain gauges.

(a)   Unbonded type

(b)   Bonded metal foil type

(c)   Thin film type

(d)   Semiconductor type

–   There are three places where such sensors are usually placed on a manipulator.

(a) **At the joint actuators:** These sensors measure the torque or force output of the actuator itself. These are useful for some control schemes but usually do not provide good sensing of contact between the end-effector and the environment.

(b) **Between the end-effector and the last joint of the manipulator:** These sensors are usually referred to as wrist sensors. They are a mechanical structure instrumented with strain gauges which can measure the forces and torques acting on the end-effector. These sensors are capable of measuring from three to six components of the force or torque vector acting on the end-effector.

(c) **At the finger tips of the end-effector:** These force-sensing fingers have built-in strain gauges to measure from one to four components of force acting at each finger tip.

8.5.2 Typical Wrist Force Sensor

–   Most wrist force sensors function as transducers for transforming forces and moment exerted at the hand into measurable deflections or displacements at the wrist.

–   There are eight pairs of semiconductor strain gauges bonded to the cross-bar structure of the device, one gauge on each side of a deflection bar. The gauges on the opposite open ends of the deflection bars and wired differentially to a potentiometer circuit whose output voltage is proportional to the force component normal to the plane of the strain gauge.

Fig. 8.9 shows internal structure of wrist force sensor.

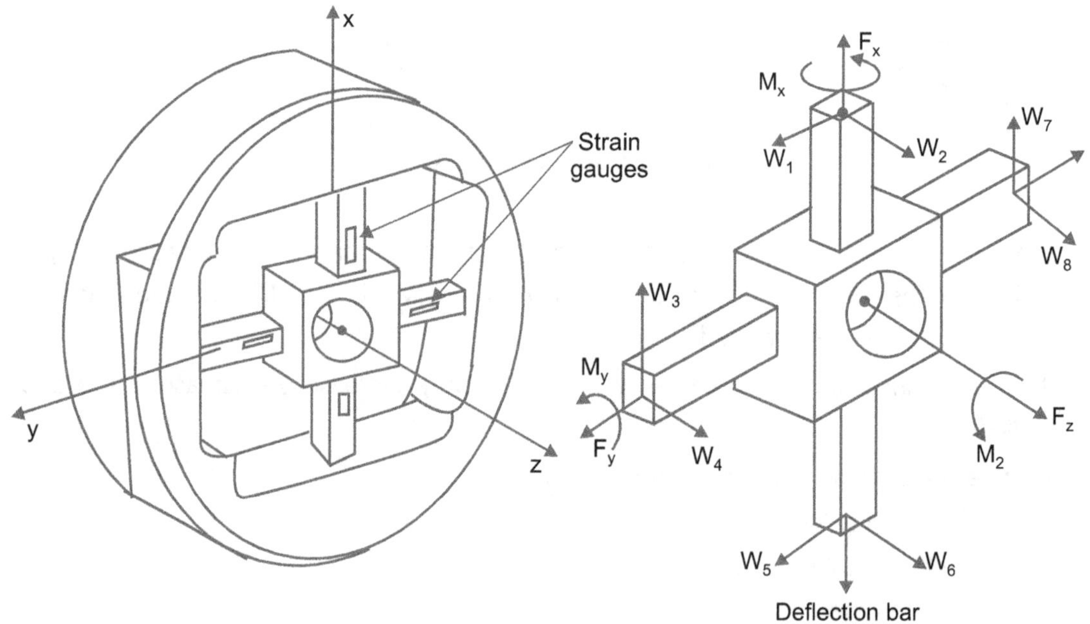

Fig. 8.9: Wrist force sensor

- The differential connection of the strain gauges provides automatic compensation for variations in temperature.
- The eight pairs of strain gauges are oriented normal to the x, y and z axes of the force co-ordinate frame, the three components of force F and three components of moment M can be determined by properly adding and subtracting the output voltages, respectively. This can be achieved by premultiplying the sensor reading by a sensor calibration matrix i.e. (M_F).
- The resolved force vector directed along the force sensor co-ordinate can be obtained as,

$$\mathbf{F} = \mathbf{M_F} \cdot \mathbf{W}$$

where, $\quad F = (\text{forces, moments})^T$

$\quad\quad\quad = (F_x, F_y, F_z, M_x, M_y, M_z)^T$

$\quad W = \text{Raw reading}$

$\quad\quad\quad = (w_1\ w_2,\ w_3,\ ...,\ w_8)^T$

and sensor calibration matrix.

$$M_F = \begin{bmatrix} r_{11} \cdots\cdots r_{18} \\ \vdots \\ \vdots \\ r_{61} \cdots\cdots r_{68} \end{bmatrix}$$

where, $r_{ij} \neq 0$

Thus, a raw matrix (W) in volts can be converted to **force/moment Newton-meters.**

8.5.3 Required Performance Specifications of Wrist Force Sensors

(i) High stiffness: The natural frequency of a mechanical device is related to its stiffness. Thus, high stiffness ensures that disturbing forces will be quickly damped out to permit accurate readings during short time intervals.

Also, it reduces the magnitude of the deflections of an applied force/moment, that may add to the positioning error of the hand.

(ii) Compact design: Compact design ensures that the device will not restrict the movement of the manipulator in a crowded workspace. It minimizes collisions between the sensor and the other objects present in the workspace. With the compact force sensor, it is important to place the sensor as close to the tool as possible to reduce positioning error as a result of the hand rotating through small angles. Also it is desirable to measure as large a hand force/moment as possible. This minimizes the distance between the hand and the sensor reduces the lever arm forces applied at the hand.

(iii) Linearity: Linearity between the response of force sensing elements and the applied force/moments permits resolving the forces and moments by simple matrix operations.

Also, the calibration of the force sensor is simplified.

(iv) Low hysteresis: It also produces hysteresis effects that do not restore the position measuring devices back to their original readings.

(v) Internal friction: Internal friction reduces the sensitivity of the force sensing elements because forces have to overcome this friction before a measurable deflection can be produced.

Problem 8.1:

A shaft with torsional stiffness of 500 N-m/rad is connected to the input side of a gear set with n = 10 and whose output gear exhibits a stiffness of 5000 Nm/rad. What is the output stiffness of the combined drive system ?

Solution:

$$\text{Gear ratio, } n = 10$$

We have the relation

$$\frac{1}{k_s} = \frac{1}{k_1} + \frac{1}{k_2}$$

Here,

$$k_1 = \text{Stiffness of output gear} = 5000 \text{ N-m/rad}$$

$$k_2 = \text{Stiffness of input gear}$$

$$= n^2 \cdot k_o$$

$$= (10)^2 \times 500 \qquad \left(\begin{array}{c}\text{... where, } k_o \text{ is torsional stiffness of a}\\ \text{input shaft}\end{array}\right)$$

$$\therefore \quad \frac{1}{k_s} = \frac{1}{5000} + \frac{1}{(10)^2\, 500}$$

$$\frac{1}{k_s} = \frac{50000 + 5000}{5000 \times 50000}$$

$$= 2.2 \times 10^{-4}$$

$$k_s = 4545.45 \text{ N·m/rad}$$

8.6   Robot Simulation for Welding Application using CAD/CAM Interface

Current welding application is prepared based on the 'Mastercam Design X5' environment. Robot simulation settings are based on Robomaster module.

(A) Geometry Creation: Create 2 D geometry & Solid model by using CAD facility of CAD/CAM software.

1.   **Press F9 to HIDE/SHOW co-ordinate axes.**

2.1   Select Create – Rectangle – 1600X1200

2.2   Select Create – Rectangle – 600X600

As shown below.

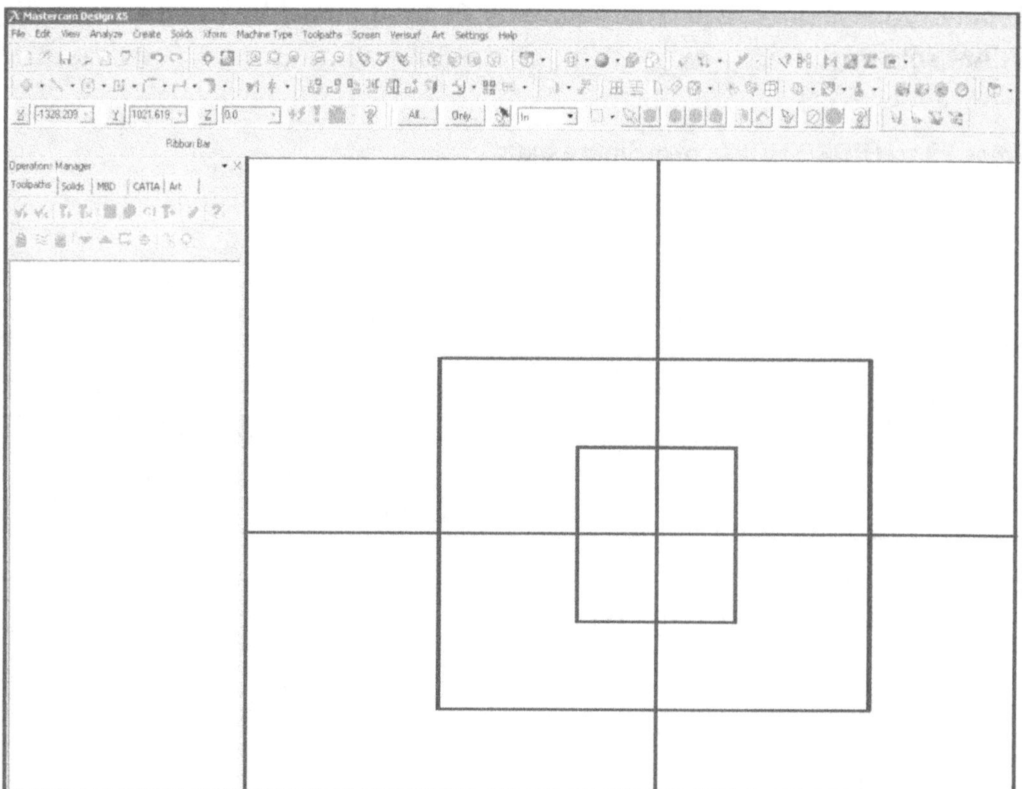

3.1   **Select Fillet: R 20 at corners (outer rectangle)**

3.2   **Select Fillet: R 100 at corners (inner rectangle)**

As shown below

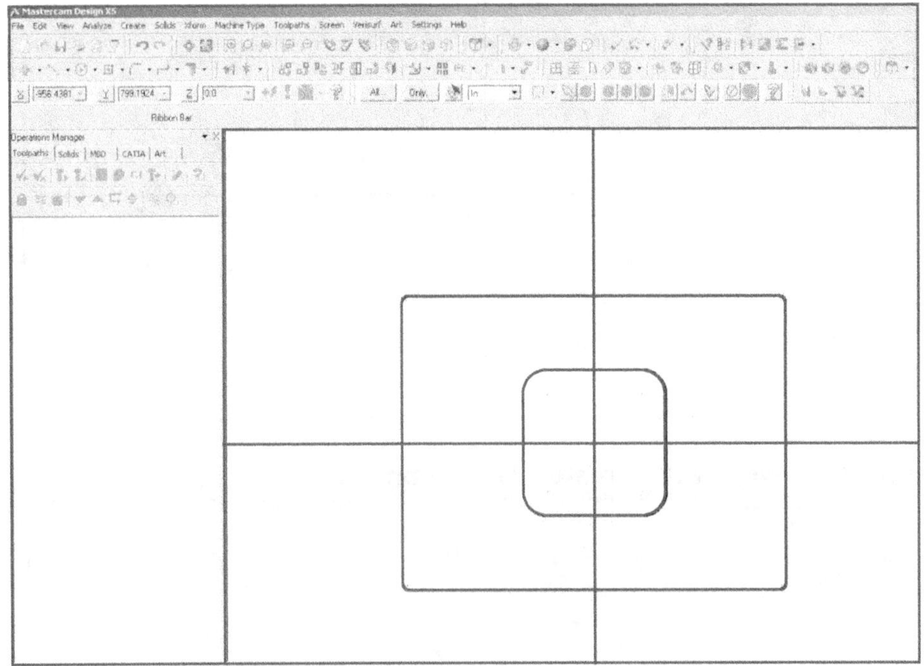

4.2 Select-Solid–Extrude–Select outer rectangle–Extrude Distance 50 mm

4.1 Select-Solid–Extrude–Select inner rectangle–Extrude Distance 200 mm

Result as shown below:

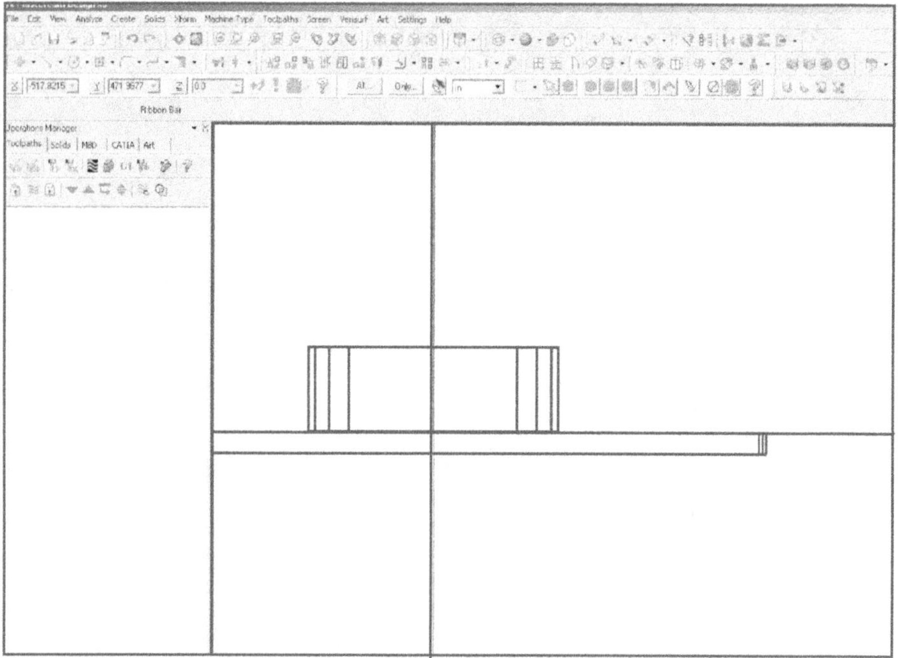

Draw triangle for wedge, with Create – Line command

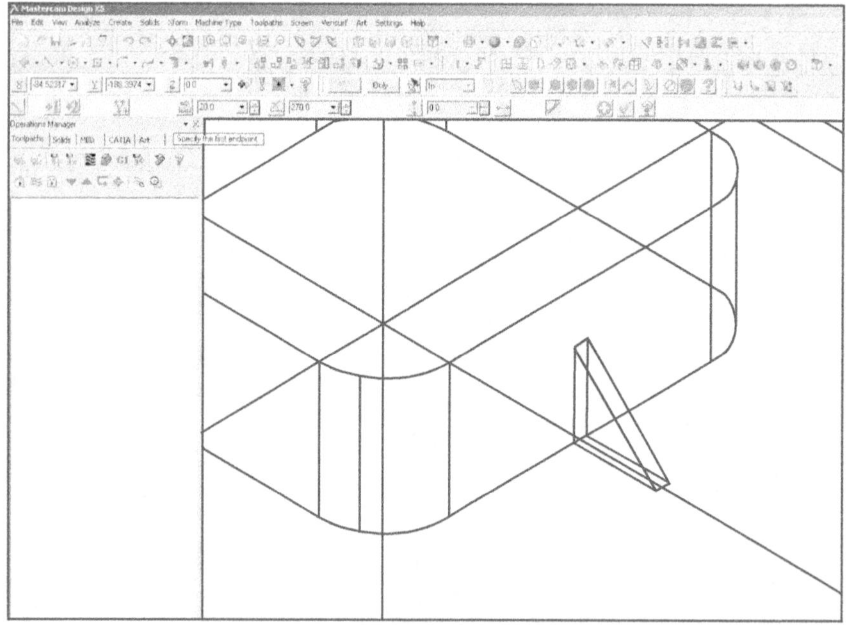

6.1 Making wedge: Solid - Extrude command

6.2 To Rotate the wedge by 90 Deg.

XFORM- Rotate – 4 items – 90 Deg.

Result as shown below:

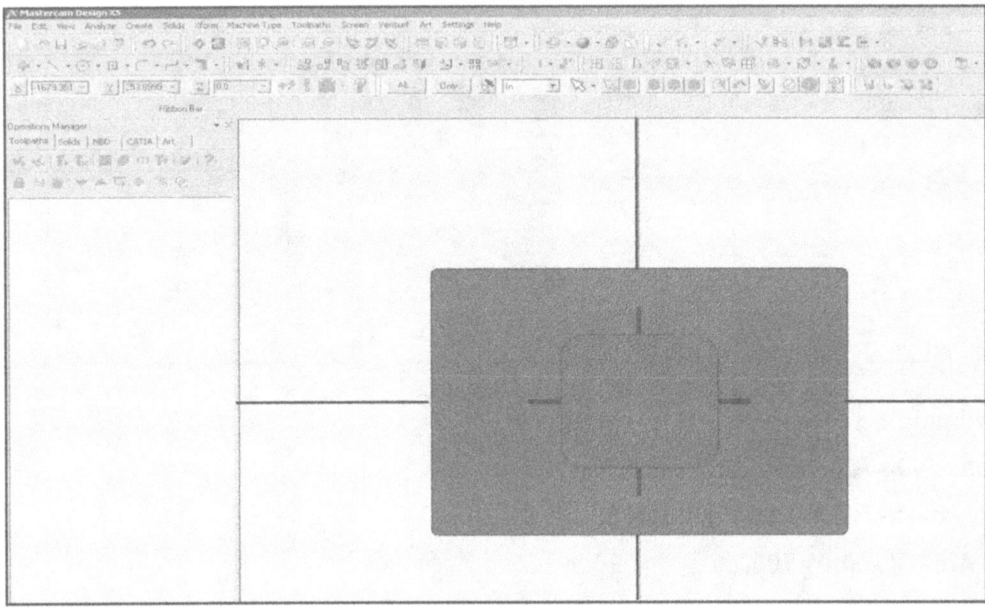

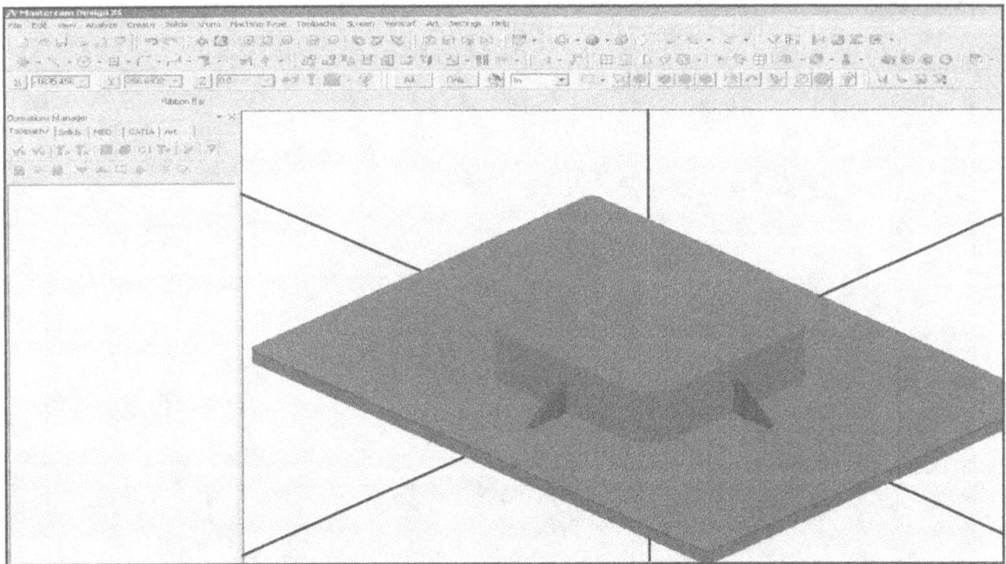

7.1 To draw Circle   - Select Arc – X700,Y500,Z0   R 50.

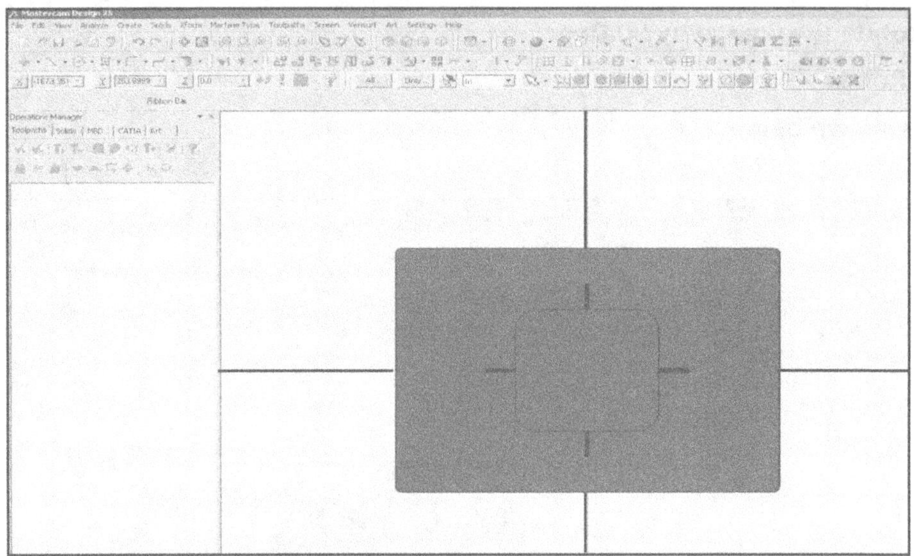

Draw remaining Circles :

Select Arc – X-700,Y500,Z0   R 50.

Select Arc – X-700,Y-500,Z0   R 50.

Select Arc – X700, Y-500,Z0   R 50.

End result:

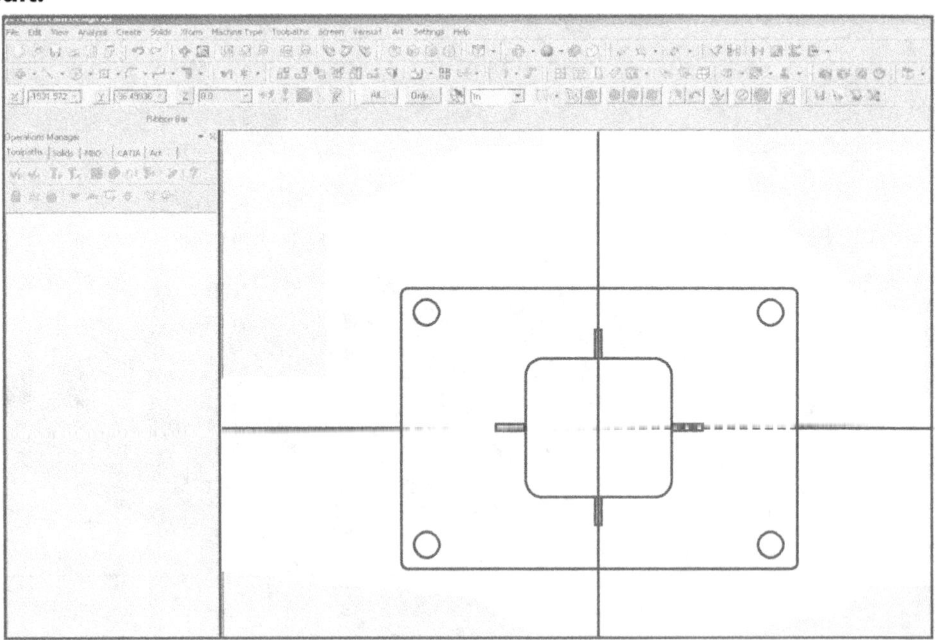

8.1 To cut Holes: Select – Solid – Extrude – Select ALL FOUR circles to cut.

Select option - Extrude Cut

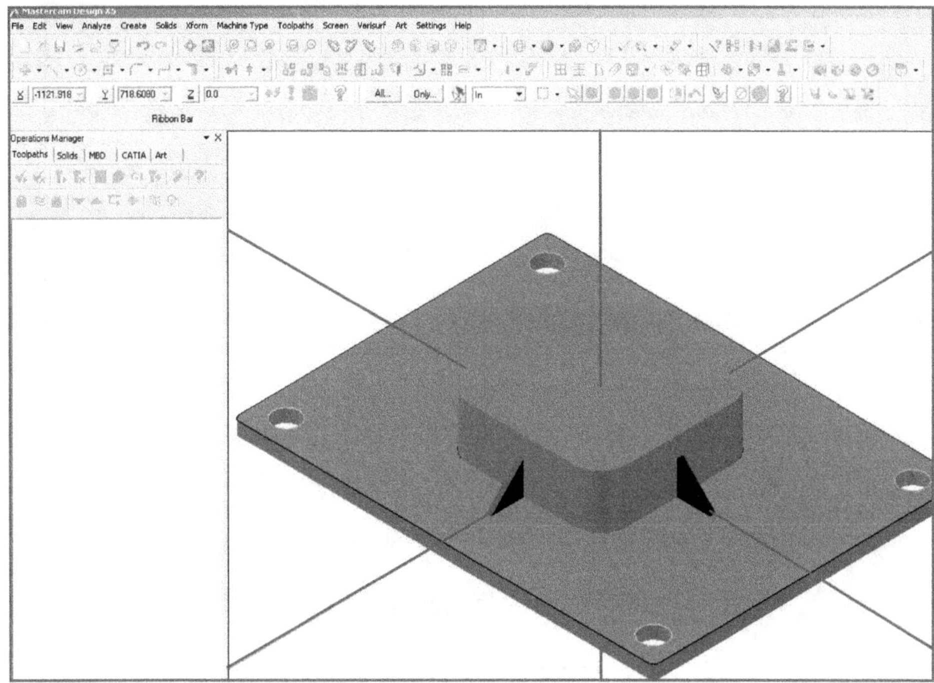

Decide profile to weld.

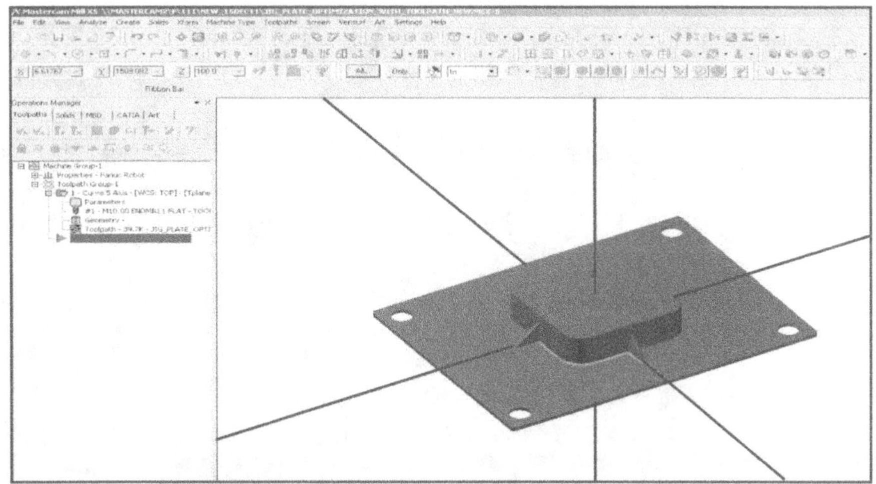

10. Generate CAM toolpath accordingly by using CAM software.

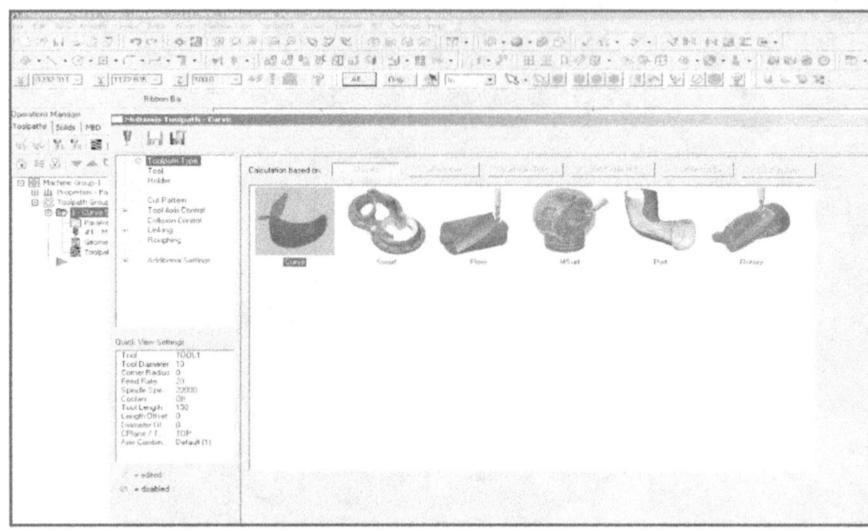

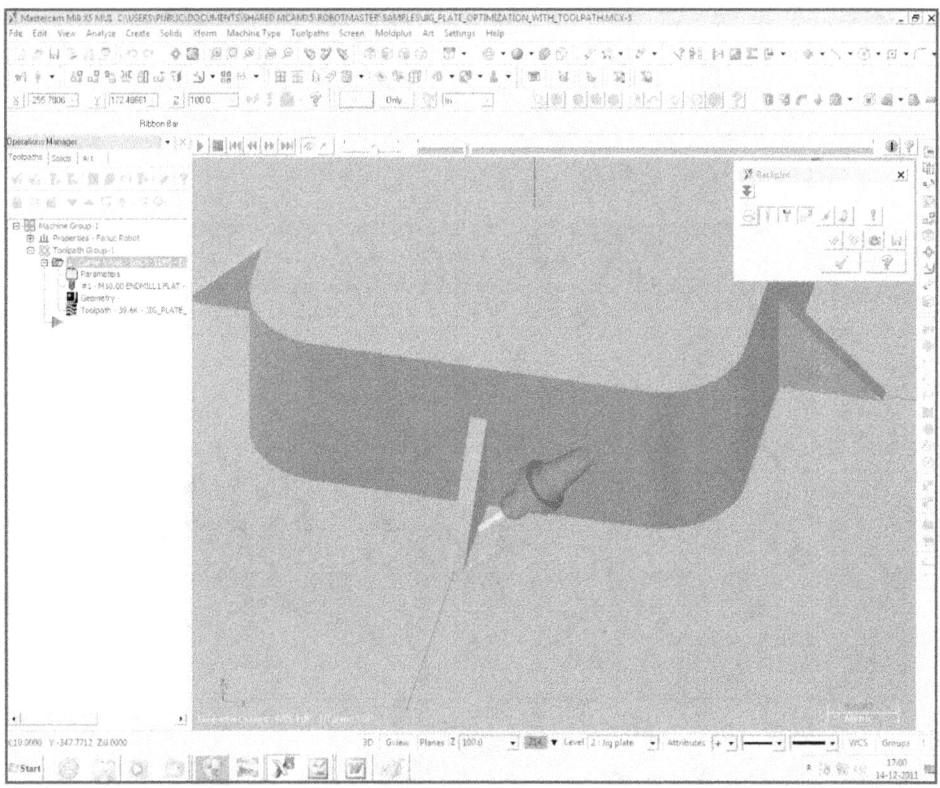

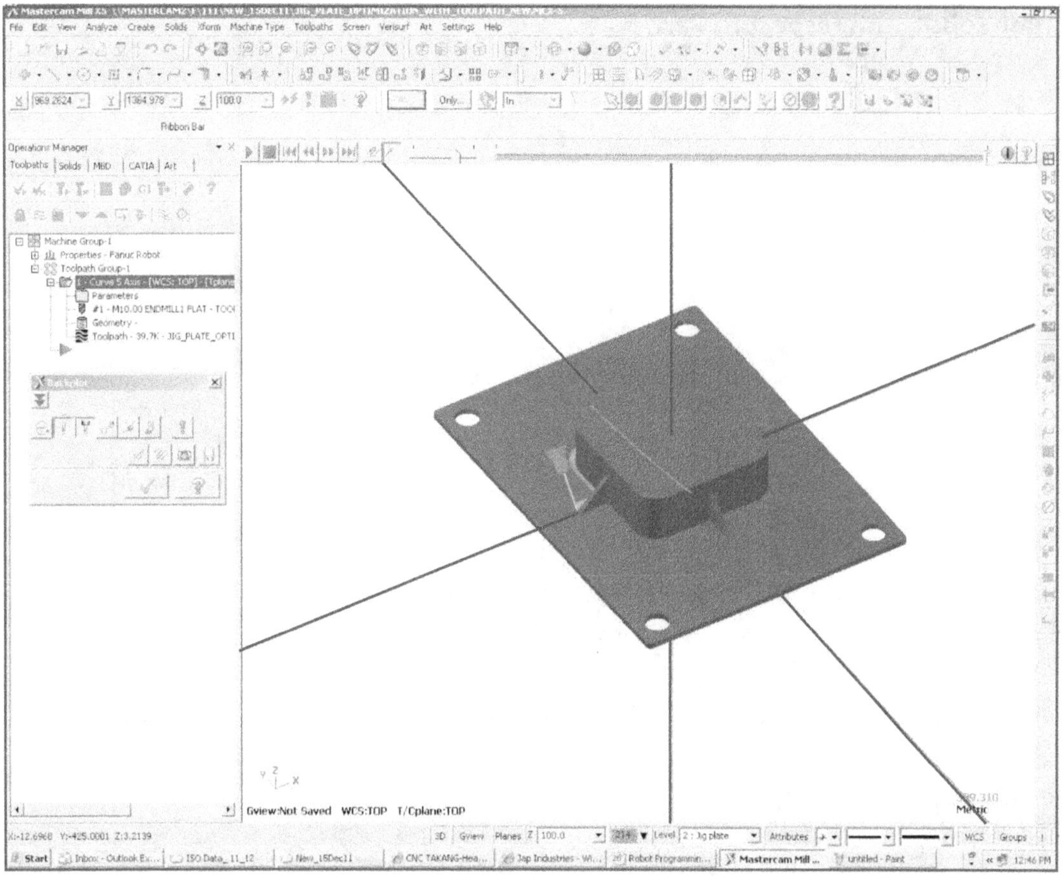

11. Assign Robot: Select robot for which you want to generate program.

12. End Effectors: Assign End Welding gun as end effector.

13. Global and Local Settings: Enter location position in Global & Local Settings to position robot with respect to Part.

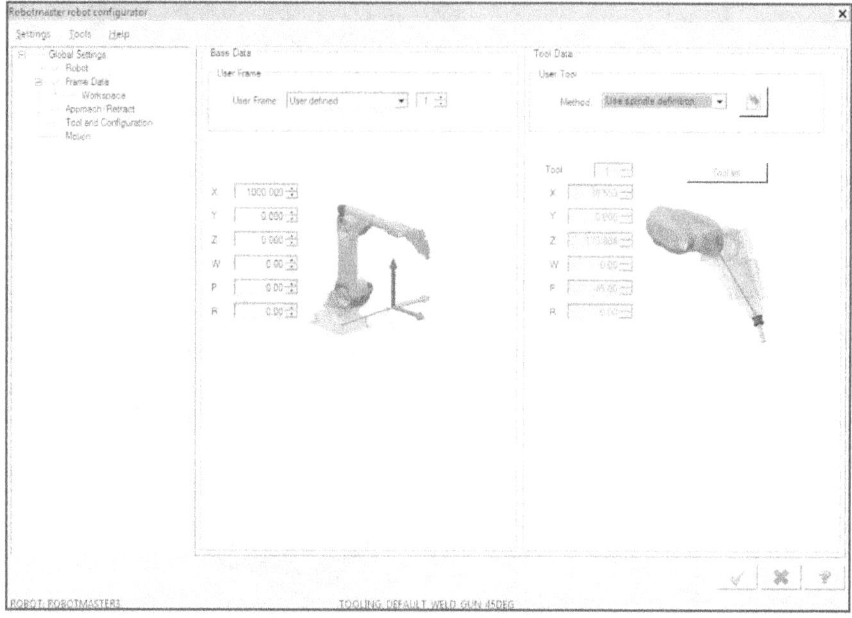

14. Assign part model : Select model from CAM environment for simulation.

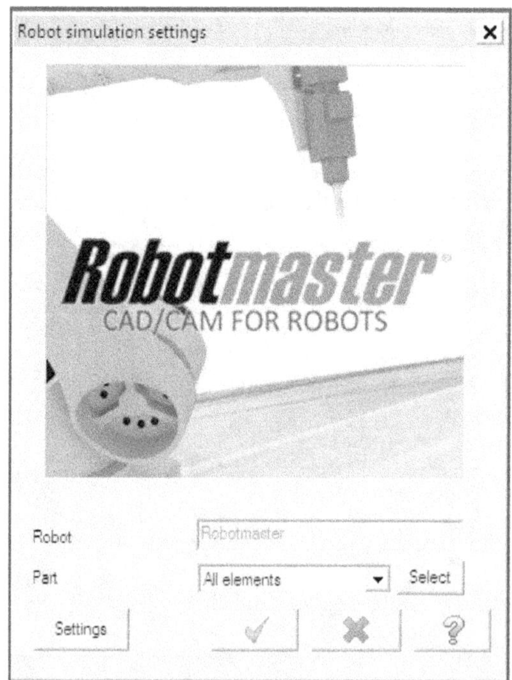

15. Add welding ON and OFF setting.

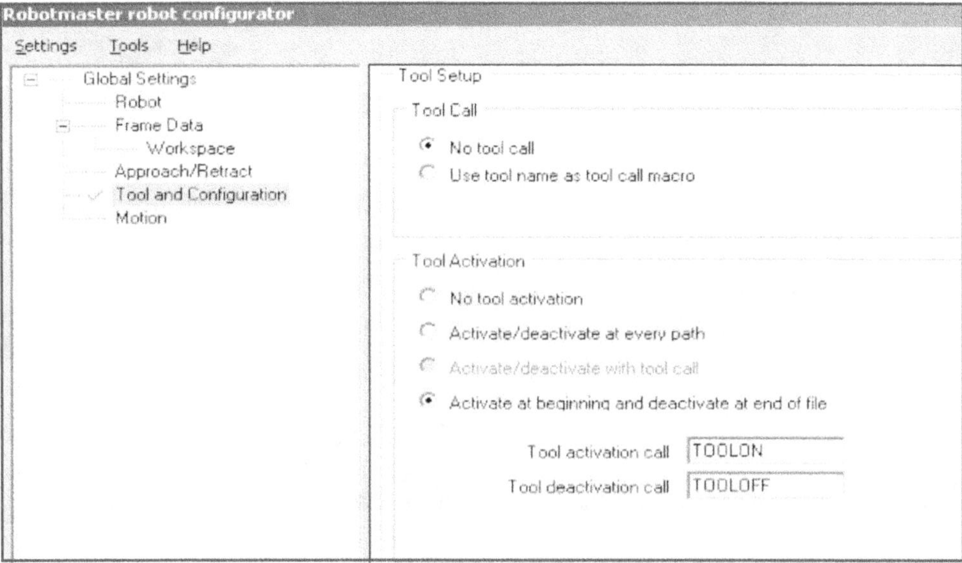

16. Check the positions of robot with respect to Job.

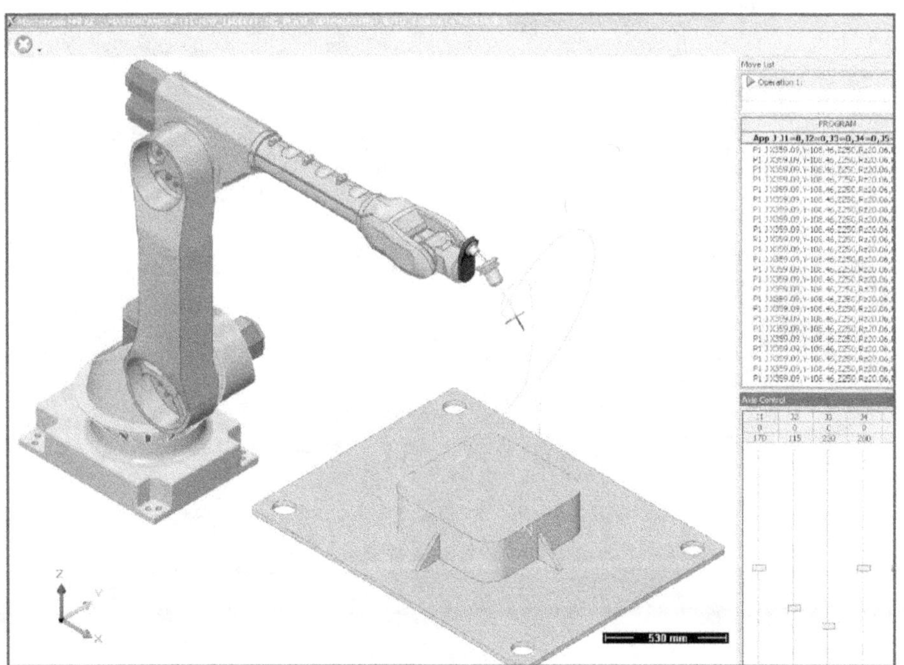

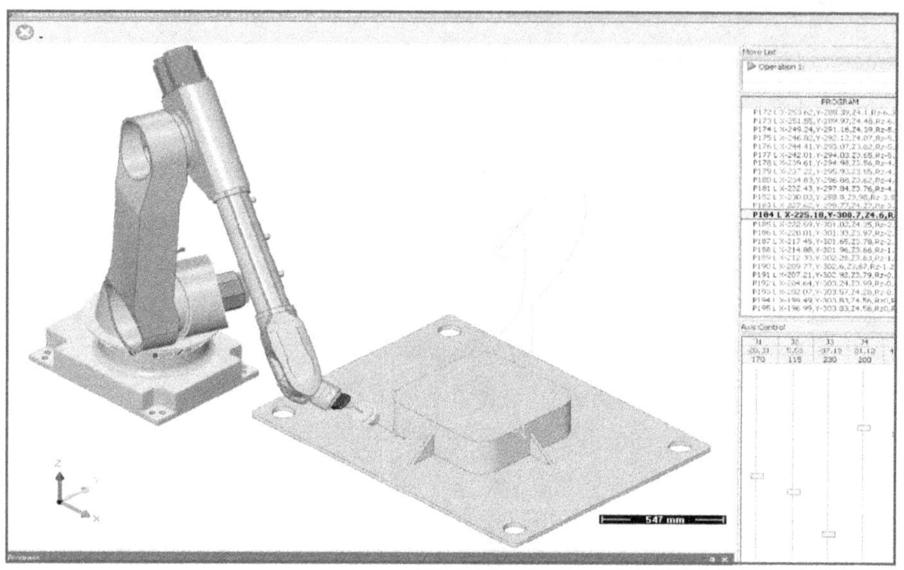

17. Understand joint movements on Virtual Robot.

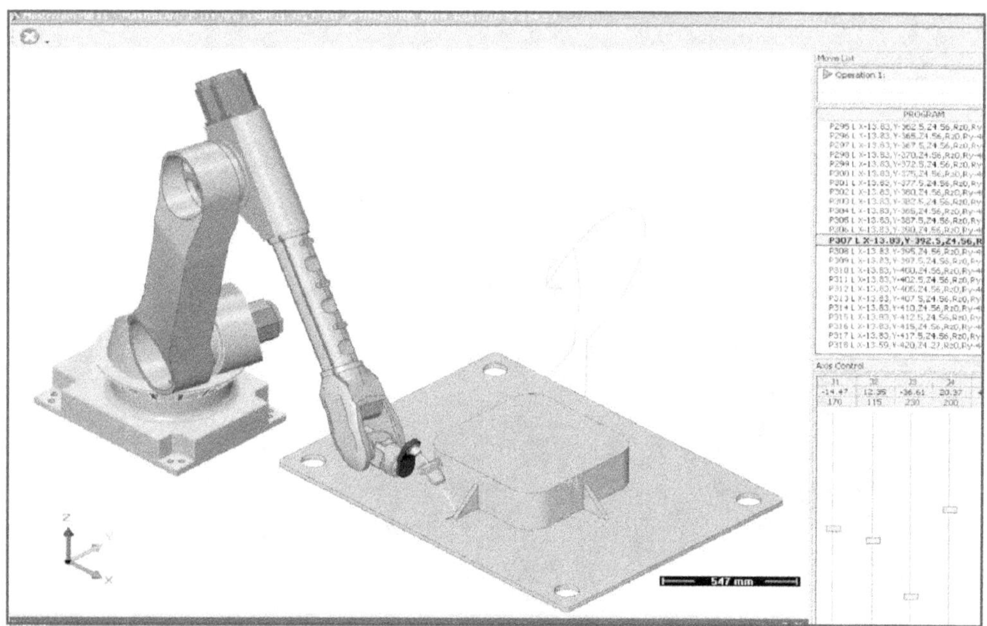

18. Simulate Welding application.

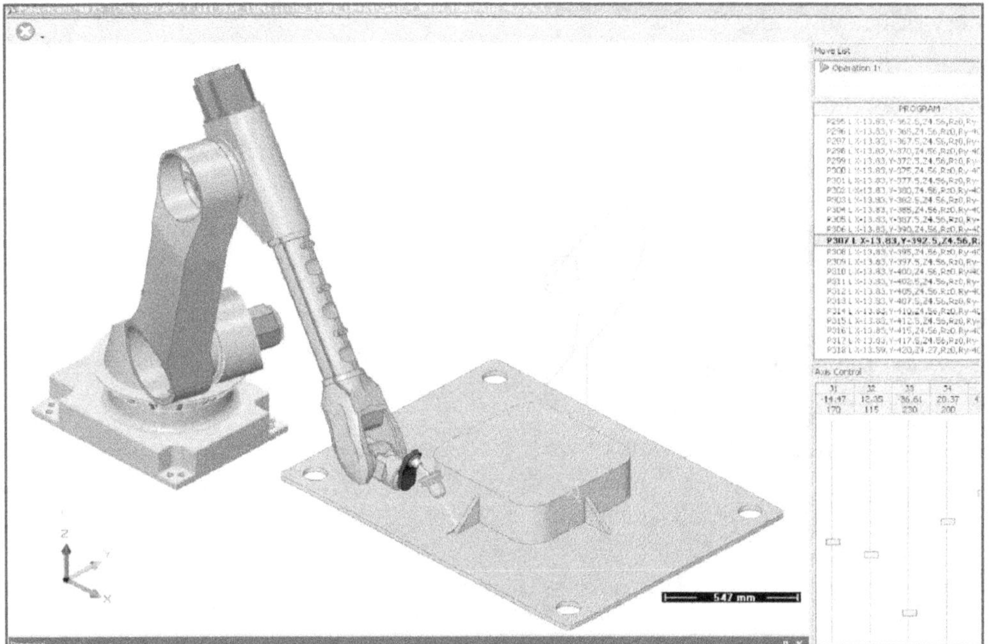

<hr>

EXERCISES

1. What are actuation schemes for a manipulator ?

2. Explain actuator location and state different types of reduction and transmission systems.

3. Explain reduction and transmission systems.

4. What are the advantages and disadvantages of –

    (i)   Gears

    (ii) Belt, cables and chains

    (iii) Harmonic drives

    (iv) Cyclo and antifriction drives

5. Explain stiffness as an important aspect for manipulator mechanism design.

6. Discuss the term stiffness with reference to the following elements:

    (i)   Gears

    (ii) Belts

    (iii) Shafts and

    (iv) Links

7. State various position sensing devices. Explain working principle of the incremental rotary optical encoder.

8. Explain force sensing with wrist force sensor.

9. Explain working of strain gauge as a force sensor.

10. Write notes on:
    (i) Actuation schemes
    (ii) Stiffness and deflection
    (iii) Position sensing
    (iv) Force sensing
    (v) A Simple strain gauge
    (vi) Typical wrist force sensor
    (vii) Performance specifications of wrist force sensors.

Unit V

Chapter 9: VISION SYSTEM FOR ROBOTICS

9.1 Introduction to Vision Systems   (W-11)

- Robot vision or computer vision or machine vision is an important sensor technology. Vision system is recognised as the most powerful of robot sensory capabilities.
- **Definitions:** "Robot vision may be defined as the process of extracting, characterizing, and interpreting information from images of a three-dimensional world".
- Vision system designed for a robot or manufacturing system must meet the following criteria:
    (i)   the need for a relatively low-cost vision system (typically under 15 lakhs).
    (ii)   the need for relatively rapid response time needed for robot or manufacturing applications, typically a fraction of a second;
    (iii) reliable operation;
    (iv)   simplicity; and
    (v)   ease of scene illumination.

9.2 Need of a Vision in a Robotic System

(i)   The vision systems are needed to perform tasks which include **selecting parts** that are randomly oriented from a bin or conveyor.

(ii)   It is also used for **parts identification**.

(iii)   Vision system is used sometimes for a limited inspection, in automation plant.

(iv)   Sometimes, it is used in traditional applications to reduce the cost of part and tool fixturing, and to allow the robot program to test for and adapt to limited variations in the environment.

(v)   Advances in vision system, enhance, the vision capabilities, to allow for vision-based guidance of robot arm.

(vi)   It is used for complex inspection for close dimensional tolerances, improved recognition, and part location capabilities.

(vii)   Advances in vision systems will permit applications not only in manufacturing, but also in photointerpretation, wave-housing, robotic operations in hazardous environments, autonomous navigation, cartography, and medical image analysis.

(viii) Therefore, vision systems can provide information about the position, orientation, identity and condition of each part in the surroundings. This data can be used to automate the manipulation of objects, plan robot motions to avoid collision with obstacles, or decide how to grasp an object.

(ix)   Use of robotic vision system makes assembly, quality control, parts handling, and classification tasks more robust.

9.3 Robot Vision System – Levels of Processing   (W-11)

Robot vision system has three broad levels of processing as –

(i)   Low level vision system;   (ii)   Medium level vision systems; and
(iii) High-level vision system.

Above three levels are subdivided into:

(i)   Low Level Vision Systems:

Low level vision systems are primitive in the sense that they may be considered as "automatic reactions" requiring no intelligence on the part of the vision system. Low level vision systems are subdivided into:

  (a)   Sensing: It is the process that yields a visual image. Special lighting techniques are frequently used to obtain an image of sufficient contrast for later processing.

  (b)   Preprocessing: It deals with techniques such as noise reduction and enhancement of details.

(ii)   Medium Level Vision System:

Medium level vision systems are those processes that extract, characterize, and label components in an image resulting from low-level vision. Medium level vision systems are subdivided into –

  (a)   Segmentation: It is the process that partitions an image into objects of interest.

  (b)   Description: It deals with the computation of features (e.g. size, shape etc.) suitable for differentiating one type of object from another.

  (c)   Recognition: It is the process that identifies the objects (e.g. wrench, bolt, engine block).

(iii) High Level Vision System:

It is the system that refers to processes that attempt to emulate cognition.
Interpretation is treated as high level vision system.

Interpretation:

It assigns meaning to an ensemble of recognized objects.

9.4 Functions of a Machine Vision Systems

Machine vision is concerned with the sensing of vision data and its interpretation by a computer. The operation of the vision system consists of three functions:

(i)   Sensing and digitizing image data.
(ii) Image processing and analysis.

  (a)   Preprocessing   – Low level vision.
  (b)   Segmentation
  (c)   Description   – Medium level vision
  (d)   Recognition
  (e)   Interpretation   – High level vision

(iii) Applications:

   (a)   Inspection of part;

   (b)   Identification of part; and

   (c)   Visual sensing and navigation.

Machine Vision is concerned with the sensing of vision data and its interpretation by a computer. The typical vision system consists of the camera and digitizing hardware, a digital computer, and hardware and software necessary to interface them. The operation of the vision system consists of three functions as illustrated.

1.   Sensing and digitizing image data

2.   Image processing and analysis

3.   Application

1.   **Sensing and digitizing image data:**

   (i)   The sensing and digitizing functions involve the input of vision data by means of a camera focused on the scene of interest. Special lighting techniques are frequently used to obtain an image of sufficient contrast for later processing. The image viewed by the camera is typically digitized and stored in computer memory.

   (ii)   The digital image is called a *frame* of vision data and is frequently captured by a hardware device called a grabber.

   (iii)   The frames consist of a matrix of data representing projections of the scene sensed by the camera. The elements of the matrix are called picture elements, or *pixels*. The number of pixels are determined by a sampling process performed on each image frame. A single pixel is a projection of a small portion of the scene which reduces that portion to a single value. The value is the measure of the light intensity for that element of the scene. Each pixel intensity is converted into a digital value.

   (iv)   The digitized image matrix for each frame is stored and then subjected to image processing and analysis functions for data reduction and interpretation of the image. These steps are required in order to permit real-time application of vision analysis required in robotic applications.

   (v)   Typically an image frame will be thresholded to produce a binary image, and then various feature measurements will further reduce the data representation of the image.

(vi)   This data reduction can change the representation of a frame from several hundred thousand bytes of raw image data to several hundred bytes of feature value data. The resultant feature data can be analyzed in the available time for action by the robot system.

2.   Image processing and analysis:

(i)   Various techniques to compute the feature values can be programmed into the computer to obtain feature descriptors of the image which are matched against previously computed values stored in the computer. These descriptors include shape and size characteristics that can be readily calculated from the thresholded image matrix.

(ii)   To accomplish image processing and analysis, the vision system must be trained frequently. In training, information is obtained on prototype objects and stored as computer models.

(iii)   The information gathered during training consists of features such as the area of the object, its perimeter length, major and minor diameters and similar features. During subsequent operation of the system, feature values computed on unknown objects viewed by the camera are compared with the computer models to determine if match has occurred.

(iv)   The final function of a machine vision system is the applications function. The current applications of machine vision in robotics include inspection, part identification, location and orientation. Research is ongoing in advanced applications of machine vision for use in complex inspection, guidance and navigation.

(v)   Many two-dimensional vision systems can operate on a binary image which is the result of a simple thresholding technique. This is based on an assumed high contrast between the object(s) and the background. Image contrast can be manipulated by using a controlled lighting system.

(vi)   Another way of classifying vision systems is according to the number of gray levels used to characterize the image. In a binary image the gray level values are divided into either of two categories, black or white. Other systems permit the classification of each pixel's gray level into various levels, the range of which is called a gray scale.

(vii)   As is true in humans, vision capabilities endow a robot with a sophisticated sensing mechanism that allows the machine to respond to its environment in an "intelligent" and flexible manner.

3.   Applications of Vision include:
  (i)   Detecting object presence or type.
  (ii)   Determining object location and orientation before grasping.
  (iii)   Feedback during grasping.
  (iv)   Feedback for path control in welding and other continuous processes.
  (v)   Feedback for fitting a part during assembly.
  (vi)   Reading identity codes.
  (vii)   Object counting.
  (viii) Inspection, example of printed circuit boards to detect incorrectly inserted components.

9.5 Image Acquisition

Visual information is converted to electrical signals by visual sensors. When sampled spatially and quantized in amplitude, these signals yield a *digital image.*

The following is of importance with regard to digital images:
1.   The principal imaging techniques used for robotic vision.
2.   The effects of sampling on spatial resolution.
3.   The effects of amplitude quantization on intensity resolution.

The principal devices used for robotic vision are television cameras, consisting either of a tube or a solid-state imaging sensor, and associated electronics.

As far as a color CCD camera is concerned, the captured image, which is made of a pixel array $I_k(x, y)$ (where $k = 1, 2, 3$; $x = 1, 2, ..., m$; $y = 1, 2, ..., n$)

where size is m × n, contains the colour information and intensity of three colour channels. This colour pixel array can be represented as

$$I_k(x, y) = \begin{bmatrix} I(1, 1) & I(1, 2) & ... & I(1, n) \\ I(2, 1) & I(2, 2) & ... & I(2, n) \\ ... & ... & ... & ... \\ I(m, 1) & I(m, 2) & ... & I(m, n) \end{bmatrix} \qquad (k = 1, 2, 3)$$

The representation of pixel varies from the purposes of image processing. RGB (red, green, and blue) method, HSB (hue, saturation, and brightness) method, and CMYK (cyan, magenta, yellow, and black) method are commonly used. In the field of machine vision, RGB method is generally employed. In this case, each pixel is represented by three channels which denote red, green, and blue intensity respectively.

Formation of a Digital Image

The imaging literature is filled with a variety of imaging devices, including dissectors, flying spot scanners, videocons, orthicons, plumbicons, CCD'c (chargecouple devices), and others. These devices differ both in the ways in which they form images and in the properties of the images so formed. However, all the devices convert light energy to voltage in similar ways.

9.6 Sampling

The sampling density, the number of sampling points per unit measure, is usually referred to as the (spatial) resolution and, since the sampling device is usually arranged as a square grid, it is measured in terms of the number of sampling elements along each orthogonal axis. This normally corresponds to the extent of the number of pixels in both the horizontal and vertical directions. Most current commercial frame-grabbers have spatial resolutions of 512×512 pixels. In summary, digital image acquisition equipment is essentially concerned with the generation of a two-dimensional array of integer values representing the reflectance function of the actual scene at discrete spatial intervals, and this is accomplished by the processes of sampling and quantization, since these are fundamentally important concepts.

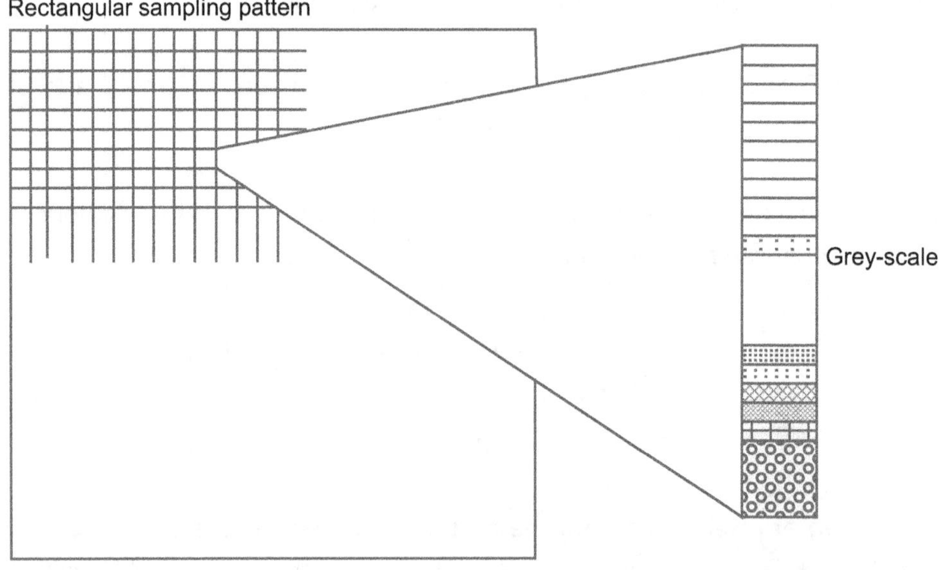

Fig. 9.1

9.7 Image Processing

Vision processing has three levels -

1. **Low-level vision [sensing and preprocessing]:** Use algorithms to compensate noise reduction and then a primitive image can be extracted.

2. **Medium-level [subdivision-segmentation, description, and recognition of individual objects]:** Refers to those processes that extract, categorize, and label components in an image resulting from low-level vision and

3. **High-level vision [interpretation]:** Refers to processes that attempt to emulate cognition.

Plenty of image preprocessing techniques are available in the field of robot vision.

The method used for image preprocessing range from spatial-domain and frequency domain.

Only a subset of them is suited for real-time image processing if the processing speed plays a predominant role in this process.

Convolution technique is one of the spatial-domain techniques used most frequently (also referred to as templates, windows, or filters). The desired image f(x, y) can be obtained by convoluting the original image i(x, y) with a convolution mask h(x, y).

$$f(x, y) \ = \ h(x, y) * i(x, y)$$

In robot vision system, the convolution masks are usually a 3×3, 5×5 or 7×7 matrices.

For computational purposes, the 3×3 matrix is widely utilized in real-time systems where system speed is required. A typical convolution mask is given as

$$H_{3\times3} \ = \ \begin{bmatrix} h_{11} & h_{12} & h_{13} \\ h_{21} & h_{22} & h_{23} \\ h_{31} & h_{32} & h_{33} \end{bmatrix}$$

The implementation of $H_{3\times3}$ convolution can be defined as

$$f(x, y) \ = \ \sum_{j=1}^{3} \sum_{k=1}^{3} i(x + j - 2, y + k - 2) \cdot h(j, k)$$

9.8 The Image Preprocessing Techniques   (W-11)

These include

1.   Smoothing

Smoothing operations are used for reducing noise and other spurious effects that may be present in an image as a result of sampling, quantization, transmission, or disturbances in the environment during image acquisition.

2.   High Pass Filtering

High pass filtering is utilized to sharpen images that are out of focus or fuzzy. Its convolution mask is

$$H_{High\text{-}pass} = \begin{bmatrix} -1 & -1 & -1 \\ -1 & 9 & -1 \\ -1 & -1 & -1 \end{bmatrix}$$

2.   Median Filtering

Median filtering ranks the current set of nine pixel intensities in order of magnitude and places the median intensity value into the destination image at the central point. The whole image is processed in turn by sliding the window over the entire image.

3.   Low Pass Filtering

Low pass filtering is exploited to smooth out a sharp image. Its convolution mask is given as:

$$H_{Low\text{-}pass} = \begin{bmatrix} 1 & 1 & 1 \\ 1 & 2 & 1 \\ 1 & 1 & 1 \end{bmatrix}$$

4.   Noise Cleaning

Noise cleaning is employed to remove random noise spikes on the captured image. Its convolution mask is given as:

$$H_{Noise\text{-}cleaning} = \begin{bmatrix} 1 & 2 & 1 \\ 2 & 4 & 2 \\ 1 & 2 & 1 \end{bmatrix}$$

5.   Averaging

Averaging can be used to remove random noise spikes and clean edge features in the image. Its convolution mask is given as:

$$H_{Averaging} = \begin{bmatrix} 1 & 1 & 1 \\ 1 & 0 & 1 \\ 1 & 1 & 1 \end{bmatrix}$$

6.   Thresholding

Digital image thresholding is a crucial process in robot vision system, which is used to manipulate the captured image. To separate and extract the object from the background in terms of an image array $f(x, y)$, a threshold of T is normally utilized.

The thresholding technique is not limited to a fixed value T. A thresholded image can be acquired by

$$g(x, y) = \begin{cases} 1 & \text{if } f(x, y) > T \\ 0 & \text{otherwise} \end{cases}$$

In the case of dark objects on a light background, thresholding takes the selected grayscale value T and compares each pixel intensity in the image. If the intensity at pixel $f(x, y) < T$ that pixel is replaced by a logic 0 value. If the intensity $f(x, y) > T$ that pixel is replaced by a logic 1 value.

In general, thresholding falls into two categories, which are manual thresholding and adaptive thresholding. Adaptive thresholding takes a histogram of all the pixel intensities in the images, detects the pixel intensity most frequent in the image and follows the histogram curve down to identify the minimum. An adaptive thresholding is capable of figuring out an optimal thresholding value.

9.9 Edge Detection

After getting the thresholded binary image, detecting edges is a fast and simple task.

Edges in images are areas with strong intensity contrasts – a jump in intensity from one pixel to the next. Edge detecting an image significantly reduces the amount of data and filters out useless information, while preserving the important structural properties in an image. This is the performance reason that edge detection has to be carried out before Hough transform.

There are many ways to perform edge detection. However, the majority of different methods may be grouped into two categories, gradient and Laplacian. The gradient method detects the edges by looking for the maximum and minimum in the first derivative of the image. The Laplacian method searches for zero crossings in the second derivative of the image to find edges.

Edge plays a central role in robot vision. Using the information from the contours means a considerable reduction in the volume of data to be processed in image analysis. In addition, using the contours obtained from the image is their relative stability under fluctuations in the lighting of the scene. The standard approaches to contour detection are implicitly based on a very simple model in which the image is regarded as ideally composed of essentially constant region separated by step edges. The classical approach to contour detection makes use of digital (finite-difference) versions of standard isotropic derivative operators, such as the gradient or *Laplacian*.

The first derivative of a contour model is zero in all regions of constant intensity. The second derivative is zero in all locations, except at the onset and termination of an intensity transition.

Laplacian Edge Detection

The Laplacian is a scalar second derivative operator for functions of two dimensions, given by:

$$\nabla f(x,\, y) \;=\; \frac{\partial^2}{\partial x^2} f(x,\, y) \;+\; \frac{\partial^2}{\partial y^2} f(x,\, y)$$

The digital Laplacian at point (x, y) can be defined as:

$$L[f(x,\, y)] \;=\; [f(x + 1,\, y) + f(x - 1,\, y) + f(x,\, y + 1) + f(x,\, y - 1)] - 4f(x,\, y)$$

9.10 A Typical Vision System for a Robot

A typical vision system for a robot is shown in Fig. 9.10. A CCD (Charge-Coupled Device) camera is placed which views the object. The image is projected by a video camera onto the CCD which detects, stores, and read out the accumulated charge generated by the light on each portion of the image. Light detection occurs through the absorption of light on a photoconductive substrate (e.g. silicon).

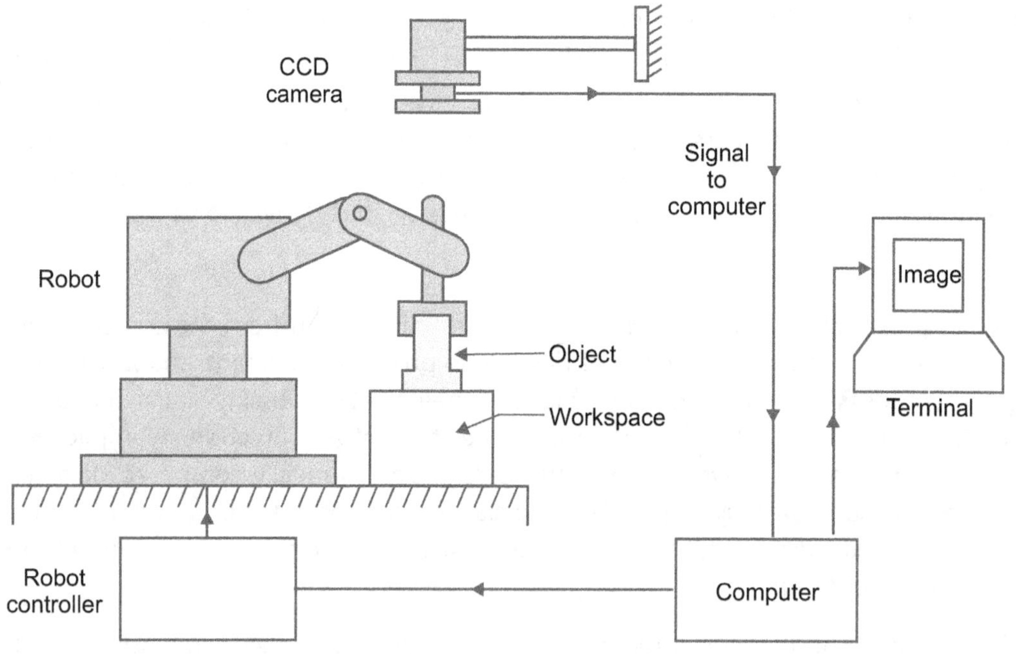

Fig. 9.2: Robot Vision System-Block Diagram

9.11 System Hardwares and Functions

Hardware	Functions	Techniques and Applications
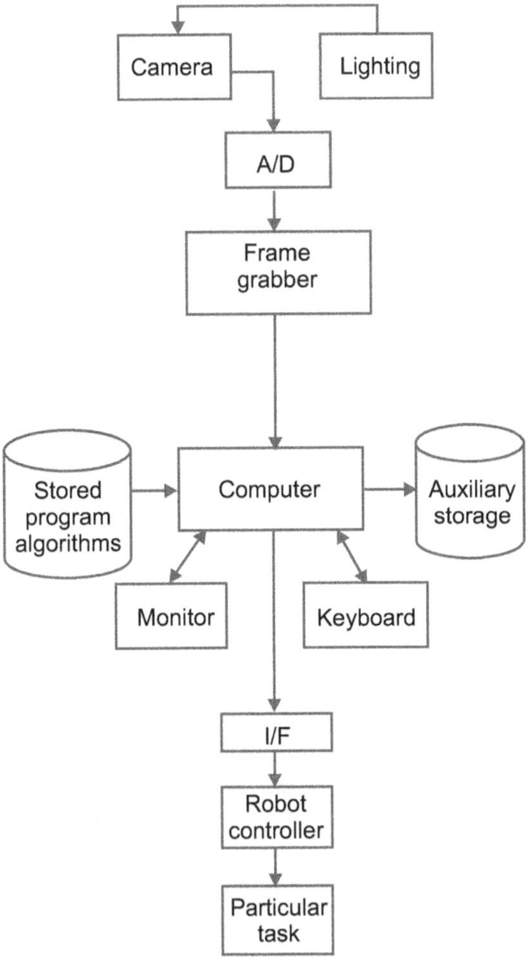 **Fig. 9.3**	(i) Sensing and digitizing image data	(a) Signal conversion: – Sampling – Quantization – Encoding (b) Image storage/frame grabbler (c) Lighting – Structured light – Back lighting – Beam splitter – Restore reflector – Specular illumination – Other techniques
	(ii) Image processing and analysis	(a) Data reduction: – Windowing – Digital conversion (b) Segmentation: – Thresholding – Region growing – Edge detection (c) Feature extraction – Descriptions (d) Object recognition – Template matching
	(iii) Applications	(a) Inspection (b) Identification (c) Visual serving and navigation.

EXERCISES

1. What is a vision system? How can vision systems be classified? Explain the categories.
2. Explain the basic need of a vision in a robotic system.
3. What are the functions of a machine vision system?
4. Explain typical vision system for a robot.
5. Explain:
   - (i) Image acquisition
   - (ii) Sampling
   - (iii) Image processing
   - (iv) Image processing techniques
   - (v) Edge detection.

Unit V
Chapter 10: ROBOT PROGRAMMING

10.1 Introduction

To operate robot, it becomes necessary to give instructions by certain ways. The robot programming is simply the design of a work pattern so that the robot may perform work without human help.

Definition:

'A robot program can be defined as a path of movements of its manipulator, combined with peripheral equipment actions to support its work cycle'.

The peripheral equipment action includes operation of the end effector, making logical decisions and communicating with other equipments in the robot work cell.

For some applications, the program needs to cover actions of the robot that must be co-ordinated with the processes of various interdependent machines. Therefore, all robot programs are a combination of specific programming commands. The program is a set of commands, arranged which control movement, position, hand-controlled instructions, read instructions, etc.

The first basic task is the preparation of the layout of the system and the sequence of moves in drive unit, then program can be written using text editors. A program writing includes –
(a)   Definition of a problem to be solved.
(b)   Preparation of flow-chart for the overall analysis of the solution.
(c)   Selecting best techniques of the solution.
(d)   Programming language coding for the problem solution.
(e)   Validation of the solution.
(f)   Some other techniques for the verification of the solution.

10.2 Programming Methods   (W-11)

Various programming commands are entered in the robots controller memory, in order to program the operation. These are the following ways to enter the commands:
1.   Manual mode of programming.
2.   Lead through mode.

(i)   Powered Lead through or Teach Pendant Lead through programming.

(ii)   Manual Lead through or Walk through mode of programming.

3.   Computer-terminal mode or textual robot language.

4.   Off-line programming mode.

10.2.1 Manual Mode of Programming

–   It is used for robots with point-to-point open loop-controller, basically with limited-sequence pick and place robots.

–   A sequencing device is used to regulate the sequence in which the motion occur. The sequencing device determines the order in which each joint is actuated to form the complete motion cycle.

–   In this method, a manual type of machine set up like setting up and adjusting the necessary end-stops, switches, cams and wiring the sequence is involved rather than actual computer programming.

   Therefore, it is categorized as first-generation programming approach.

Advantages:

(i)   It is usually simple and does not require a skilled operator.

(ii)   Capital investment and maintenance costs are low.

(iii)   Robots with this type of mode are capable of operating at high speeds.

(iv)   Robots have good positioning accuracy and repeatability.

Disadvantages:

(i)   They have limited flexibility.

(ii)   They have only 2 or 3 DoF.

(iii)   Unavailability of controlling the intermediate points along the path.

(iv)   For each axis only two positions can be programmed with this mode.

10.2.2 Lead through Mode

–   It is the first real robot program method used in most of the industries. They had initiated in 1960's.

   Requirements: The lead through methods require the programmer to move the manipulator through the specified motion path and that path be stored in the memory by the robot controller.

–   Motion of a robot manipulator through the desired path accomplishes recording the path into controller memory. Lead through programming is subdivided into –

(a) Powered Lead Through or Teach Pendant Lead Through –

–   It is the most common method used for robot programming.

–   It makes use of teach pendant for controlling the various joint motors. Teach Pendant is a small hand held device, sometimes called as control box, that contains toggle switches, dials, and buttons to regulate the physical movement and programming capabilities of robot. Teach Pendant is simple to handle and learn and suitable to program many tasks in industry. It doesn't need skilled operator. The program cannot be entered into the pendant while the robot is off-line.

–   It results in movement of robot arm and wrist through a series of points in working space wherein each point is recorded there into the memory for further playback during the work cycle, and during playback testing, the robot moves through the sequence of positions under its own power.

–   This method is limited to point-to-point motion of the manipulator, which include transfer of parts from one point to other point, machine loading and unloading through a particular sequence and spot welding operation when welding gun moves from one point to other point.

(b) Manual Lead Through or Walk-Through Programming:

–   It is suitable for playback robots continuous path.

–   Also it fulfils the irregular motion patterns, roughly locating the tool center point for some robots.

–   **Application** of walk-through programming.

It includes:

- Spray painting
- Arc welding
- Grinding
- Deburring and polishing

–   **Requirements:**

(i)   It requires the operator to physically grasp the end effector and manually move it through the motion sequence.

(ii) It also requires the recording of the path into memory. The motions are recorded as a series of closely spaced point and during actual playback the actual robot arm goes through the same sequence of points.

(iii) If the robot arm is heavy and unable to move on itself, a actual robot is replaced by a special device. This device has similar joint configuration to the robot. It is equipped with a control switch that is activated by the operator.

(iv) It requires a highly skilled operator to perform the precise motion tasks if the robot cannot be programmed off-line.

10.2.3 Computer Terminal Mode or Textual Robot Language

– They are sometimes referred as "teach by showing methods".

– It has started in 1970's.

– It is similar to computer programming, where programmer uses a program with high-level language and enters it on a CRT monitor.

– It provides greater flexibility and high efficiency.

– While writing and debugging the actual program, the robot does not have to be taken out of the operation. Thus, it will not affect productivity.

– Control function in robot is carried out by digital computers.

Disadvantage:

(i) It requires a skilled operator.

10.2.4 Off-line Programming

– It is the process by which robot programs are developed without requiring the use of robot, i.e. it permits the program to be prepared off-line and download to the robot controller for executing it.

It includes –

(i) generating point co-ordinate data,

(ii) function data and

(iii) motion cycle logic.

Advantages:

(i) Off-line programming provides the ability to create or modify a program for robot without disturbing the robot activities.

(ii) Optimization of layout and cycle time of the operation can be made possible in advance.

(iii) It is not required to redesign each operation every time it is used previously prepared procedures and routines can be incorporated in the program.

(iv) Sensors can be used for detecting external environment, where necessary action can be taken in response. It would increase the programming complexity and the robot would be considered to be in adaptive operation mode.

(v) Routine CAD and CAM information can be made to incorporate included into the control functions.

(vi) In order to have movements actually programmed, programs can be run in advance without having the risk of damage.

(vii) By utilizing previously developed routines, robots can be used to manufacture individual parts.

(viii) Change in design can be incorporated quickly indicating flexibility of off-line programming mode.

Requirements for Off-line Programming :

(i) Fundamental knowledge of the process or the task to be programmed.

(ii) It is necessary to generate geometric description of components and their relationships within the work place.

(iii) It requires knowledge regarding robot geometrical description, kinematics and dynamics.

(iv) It also needs computer based system for programming the robots using the above dates.

(v) Program produced are to be verified at specific stage.

(vi) It needs to have appropriate interfacing in order to allow communication of control data.

10.3 Motion Interpolation

– Broadly interpolation is a process used to estimate and intermediate value of any one variable (i.e. dependent variable), which is a function of second variable (i.e. independent) variable, when values of the dependent variable corresponding to several discrete values of the independent variable are known.

– **Illustration:** Consider programming a two-axis servo controlled Cartesian robot with eight number of addressable points for each axis. Therefore, in all there are total of sixty four number of addressable points that we could use in any program that might be written.

Fig. 10.1 shows work volume.

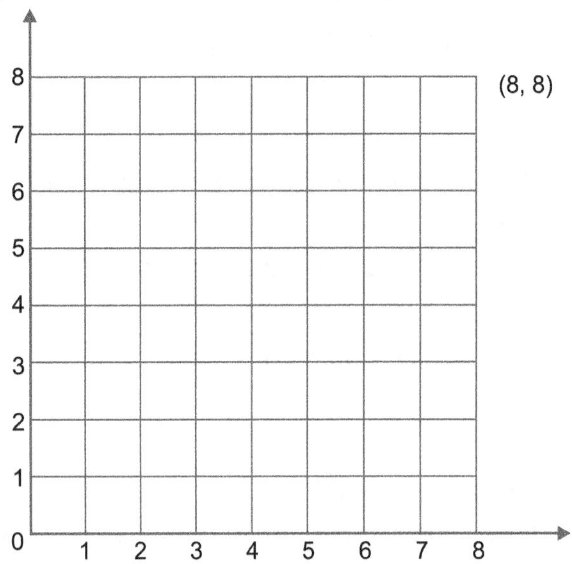

Fig. 10.1: 8 × 8 addressable points in robot work space

A program for this robot to start to with (1, 1) and traverse the perimeter of the rectangle could be given as in Table 10.1.

Table 10.1

Step	Move
1	1, 1
2	8, 1
3	8, 8
4	1, 8
5	1, 1

–   If we were to remove **step 3** in this program, the servo-controlled robot would execute **step 4** by tracing a path along the diagonal line from point (8, 1) to (1, 8). This process is called interpolation.

There are various schemes of interpolation which can be specified for the robot to get from one point to another. These are as under:

(i)   Joint-interpolation

(ii)   Straight-line interpolation

(iii)   Circular interpolation

(iv)   Manual lead through programming (Irregular smooth motions)

10.3.1 Joint-Interpolation

- Most of the commercially available robot controllers use joint-interpolation procedure as a default (i.e. the controller will follow a joint-interpolated motion between the two points unless the programmer provides some other type of interpolation.

- Controller gives the distance to be moved by each joint to get from the first point defined in the program to the next.

- After the distance has specified, it selects the joint that requires the longest time. And also determining the overall time it will take to complete the move at a given speed.

- Using this known move time, and the amount of the movement required for the other axes, the controller subdivides the total move into smaller increments so that all joints start and stop their motions at the same time.

- **Illustration:** Consider the move from point (1, 1) to point (7, 4) in the grid of Fig. 10.2 and Fig. 10.3.

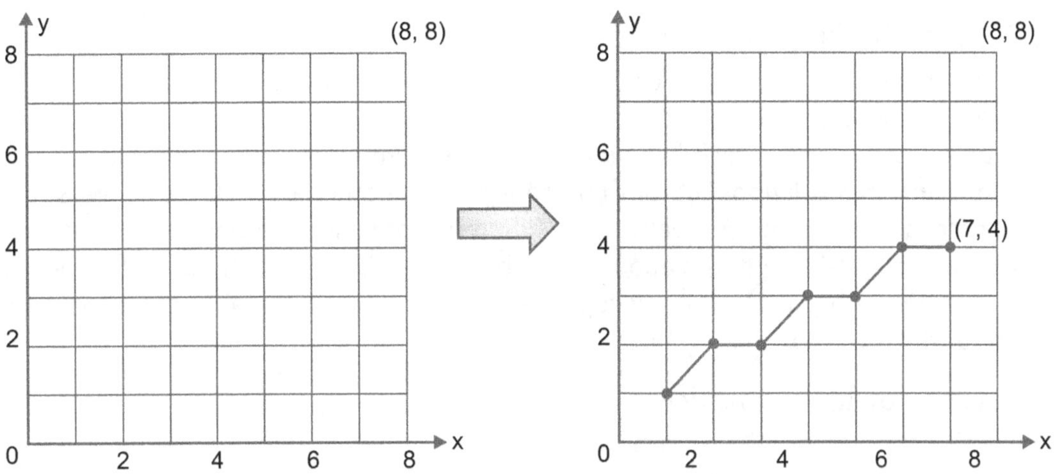

Fig. 10.2: Robot workspace   **Fig. 10.3: Robot taking interpolated path**

- Linear joint 1 must move six increments and joint 2 must move three increments.
- In order to determine the joint-interpolated path, the controller would determine a set of intermediate addressable points along the path between 1, 1 and 7, 4, which would be followed by the robot. Table 10.2 gives the process.

Table 10.2

Step	Move	Remarks
1	1, 1	User defined starting point
2	2, 2	Internally generated interpolation point
3	3, 2	Internally generated interpolation point
4	4, 3	Internally generated interpolation point
5	5, 3	Internally generated interpolation point
6	6, 4	Internally generated interpolation point
7	7, 4	User given end point

- Here, the controller alternatively moves both axes or just one axis. For each move requiring actuation of both axes, the two axes start and stop together. Such an actuation causes the robot to take a path as shown in Fig. 10.3.
- The controller gives the equivalent path as specified in program and then generates the internal points as close to that line as possible.
- The resulting path is an approximation rather than a straight line.
- In present case 64-addressable points are present which give rough approximation. But as number of addressable points increases, grid becomes more dense and the approximation would be better.

10.3.2 Straight-line Interpolation

- An interpolation procedure resulting in straight-line approximation is termed as straight-line interpolation.
- For a Cartesian robot, which has only linear axes, joint interpolation is same as that of straight-line interpolation. But for other robots with rotational and linear joints, straight line interpolation produces a path that is different from joint interpolation.
- Thus, in straight-line interpolation, the robot controller gives the straight line path between the two points and develops the sequence of addressable points along the path for the robot to pass through.

10.3.3 Circular Interpolation

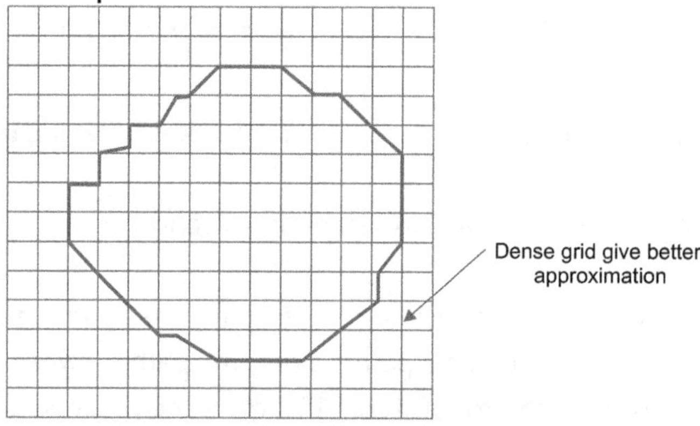

Fig. 10.4: Circular Interpolation

- In this type of interpolation, the movements that are made by the robot actually consist of short-straight-line segments, therefore, circular interpolation provides a linear approximation of the circle.
- First of all it requires the programmer to define a circle in the robot's workspace. Specifying three points that lie along the circle is a convenient way to represent it.
- The controller then constructs an approximation of the circle by selecting a series of addressable points that lie closest to the defined circle.
- If the grid of addressable point is much more dense, the linear interpolation looks like a real circle.
- Finally, the circular interpolation can be readily programmed using a textual programming language than with lead through techniques.

10.3.4 Manual Lead Through Programming or Irregular Smooth Motions

- In this method, when the programmer takes the manipulator wrist to teach spray painting or arc welding, the movements typically consist of **combinations of smooth motion segments.**
- These segmental moves are sometimes –
  - approximately straight lines.
  - curve, and
  - back and forth motions.

  Therefore, these movements are called as **irregular smooth motions**, and an interpolation process therein called as irregular smooth motion interpolation.
- Further, the motion path is divided into a sequence of closely spaced points that are recorded into the controller memory in order to approximate the irregular smooth pattern being taught by the programmer.
- These positions constitute the nearest addressable points to the path followed during programming. In this approach, the interpolated path may consist of large number of individual points that the robot must playback during subsequent program execution.

10.4 Robot Programming Languages Generation

There are various capabilities and structures of the textual robot languages. These are identified according to the generations as follows.

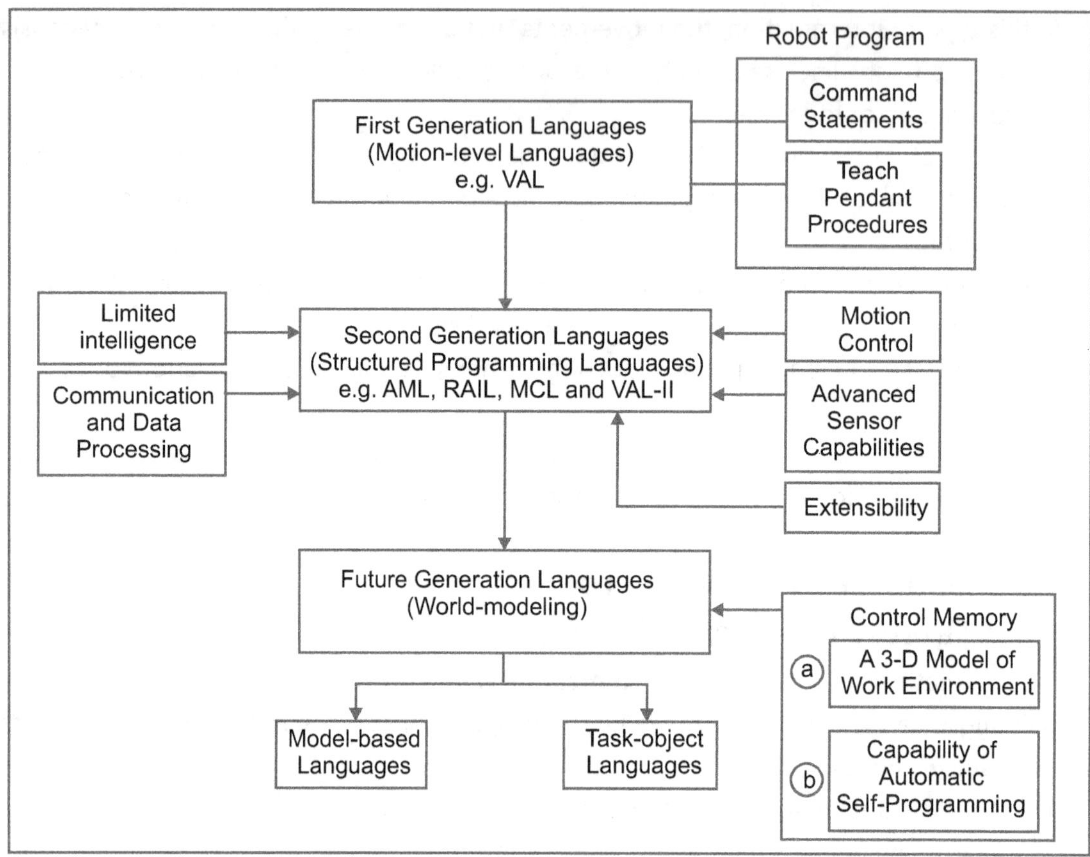

Fig. 10.5: Generation of Robot Programming Languages

(i)   First Generation Languages:

- It uses combination of:
  - command statements and
  - teach pendant procedures

  basically for robot building.

- Initially, they were developed in order to implement motion control with a textual programming language, therefore, sometimes they are called as **'motion-level languages'**.

- **Features of First Generation Language:**
  - (a)   It has ability to define manipulator motions using the statements to define the sequence of the motions and the teach pendant to define the point locations.
  - (b)   It has capability of straight-line interpolation.
  - (c)   It includes ability of branching.

(d) It also has ability to define elementary sensor commands involving binary signals.

(e) They can be used to define the motion sequence of the manipulator (i.e. MOVE command).

(f) They have input/output capabilities (e.g. WAIT, SIGNAL commands).

(g) They can be used to write subroutines (BRANCH).

- Example of first generation language is VAL.

- **Limitations:**

    (a) Inability to specify complex arithmetic computations for use during program execution.

    (b) Inability to make use of complex sensors and sensor data.

    (c) It has a limited capability to communicate with other computers.

    (d) These languages are not that much flexible to extend them for future enhancement.

(ii) Second Generation Languages:

- It involves more intelligence as compared to the first generation languages.
- It can handle more complex tasks.
- They possess structured control constructs used in computer programming languages, therefore sometimes they are referred as the **'structured programming languages'**.
- Examples of this category include languages like AML, RAIL, MCL and VAL-II.
- Programming using these languages is much similar to that of computer programming.

- **Features and Capabilities:**

    (a) They make use of **teach pendant** to define locations in the workspace.

    (b) **Motion control:** It has ability to define manipulator motions.

    (c) **Advanced sensor capabilities:** It includes the capacity to deal with more than simple binary signals, and the capability to control devices by means of the sensory data.

    (d) **Limited intelligence:** It is the ability to make use of the information about the work environment, in order to improve or modify the system's behaviour.

    (e) **Communication and data processing:** These languages have capability to interact with the computers and its data-bases for keeping records, report generation and control of activities in the workcell.

    (f)   **Extensibility:**

- This means that the language can be extended or enhanced by the user to handle the requirements of future applications, future sensing devices and future robots.
- It also means that the language can be expanded by developing commands, subroutines, and macro statements.

(iii) Future Generation Languages:

- It involves a concept of **"world-modeling"** which means **model-based languages** and **task-object languages.**
- While programming, based on world-modeling, the robot possesses knowledge of the three-dimensional world and is capable of developing its own procedure to perform a particular task.
- There are two basic aspects of a programming language based on world-modeling.

    (a)   A three-dimensional model of the work environment around the robot system is stored in its control memory.

        The model includes –

- Robot manipulator itself.
- The work table.
- Fixtures.
- Tools.
- Parts etc.

Generation of model might be possible either by providing the robot with the capacity to see the work environment or by inputing 3D geometric data into the control memory.

    (b)   The capacity for automatic self-programming.

- The robot intelligence required in world modeling includes the ability to solve problems and make decisions relying on other than preprogrammed instructions. Use of artificial intelligence is first approach to this problem and another approach is research on hierarchical control systems for robotics.
- With future generation languages, it is possible to accomplish robot programming completely off-line without the need for a teach pendant to physically show each point in the program to the robot.

10.5 Robot Programming Languages

Following section shows some of the major programming languages.

(i) Assembly Robot Language (ARL): It was developed to execute complicated tasks in assembly and inspection of high level controls.

(ii) Hitachi Assembly Robot Language (HARL): A commercial version developed for point to point assembly and handling tasks. It is based on ARL-basics.

(iii) Arm Languages (AL): This language is currently under continual development, originally developed at Stanford University for programming robots. This language made use of WAVE language.

(iv) Vic Arm Language (VAL): It is considered to be an interactive version of AL. Its hardware have been used to all Unimate robots. Now VAL-II is being tested. It is also called as Victor's Assembly Language.

(v) A Manufacturing Language (AML): It is developed and represented by IBM. Example, RS-1 which is a cartesian hydraulic robot is developed by IBM. 7535 electric robot is developed by Sankyo of Japan.

(vi) Intuitive Robot Language (IRL): This language was developed for high precision assembly robots by Microbo, a Swiss Company.

(vii) Language de Manipulation (LM): It makes use of basic concepts of AL, and is used on a microcomputer. It was developed by IMAG Robotics Laboratory at Gernable University.

(viii) MCL (Manufacturing Control Language): It is an extended version of APT, aiming to program flexible units i.e. of a set of machines controlled by one or more robots.

(ix) Programming Language for Arc Welding (PLAW): For intelligent welding which uses sensors for control, this language is suited to this application.

(x) Robot Language (ROL): It was developed in order to design a complete commercial system for computerised control applicable to any robot.

(xi) Sigma Language (SIGLA): For industrial robot, this language is most suitable. It was developed by Olivetti for the Cartesian Sigma Robots.

(xii) Robot Programming Language (RPL): It was developed by the Stanford Research Institute. It includes capabilities for interpreting video signals. It also enables robot to visually identify the parts.

(xiii) Draper Industrial Assembly Language (DIAL): It was developed at Charles Stark Drapur Laboratory. It uses electronic force feedback to duplicate human sense of touch in assembling various parts.

(xiv) Robotic Automatrix Incorporation Language (RAIL): It was developed by Automatrix Inc. in 1981.

(xv) Roboter Exapt (ROBEX): It was developed by Achen of Germany.

(xvi) Structured Robot Language (SRL): It was developed at ESPRIT; Germany in 1985.

(xvii) Virtual Machine Language (VML): It was developed by CNR, Italy.

10.6 Robot Language Structure

– The features of first generation languages and second generation languages are discussed under this. (a) The language must be designed to operate with a robot system. (b) It must be able to support the robot programming, control of the robot manipulator and interfacing with peripherals in the work cell. (c) It should also support data communications with other computer system in the industry.

Robot language structure can be explained with reference to the following points:

(I) Operating systems and

(II) Robot language elements and functions

10.6.1 Operating Systems

– With the textual languages, the programmer can use CRT monitor, an alphanumeric keyboard, and a teach pendant.

– Programs can be stored either on magnetic tape or disk. Requirement of language is that there should be some mechanism which will permit the user to –

  • determine whether to write a new program.

  • edit an existing program.

  • execute a program or

  • perform some other function.

  This type of mechanism or system is called as an **'Operating System'.**

– The purpose of the operating system is to facilitate the operation of the computer by the user and to maximize the performance and efficiency of the system and the peripheral devices.

– A robot language operating system has three basic modes of operation.

  (a) Monitor mode

  (b) Run mode and

  (c) Edit mode.

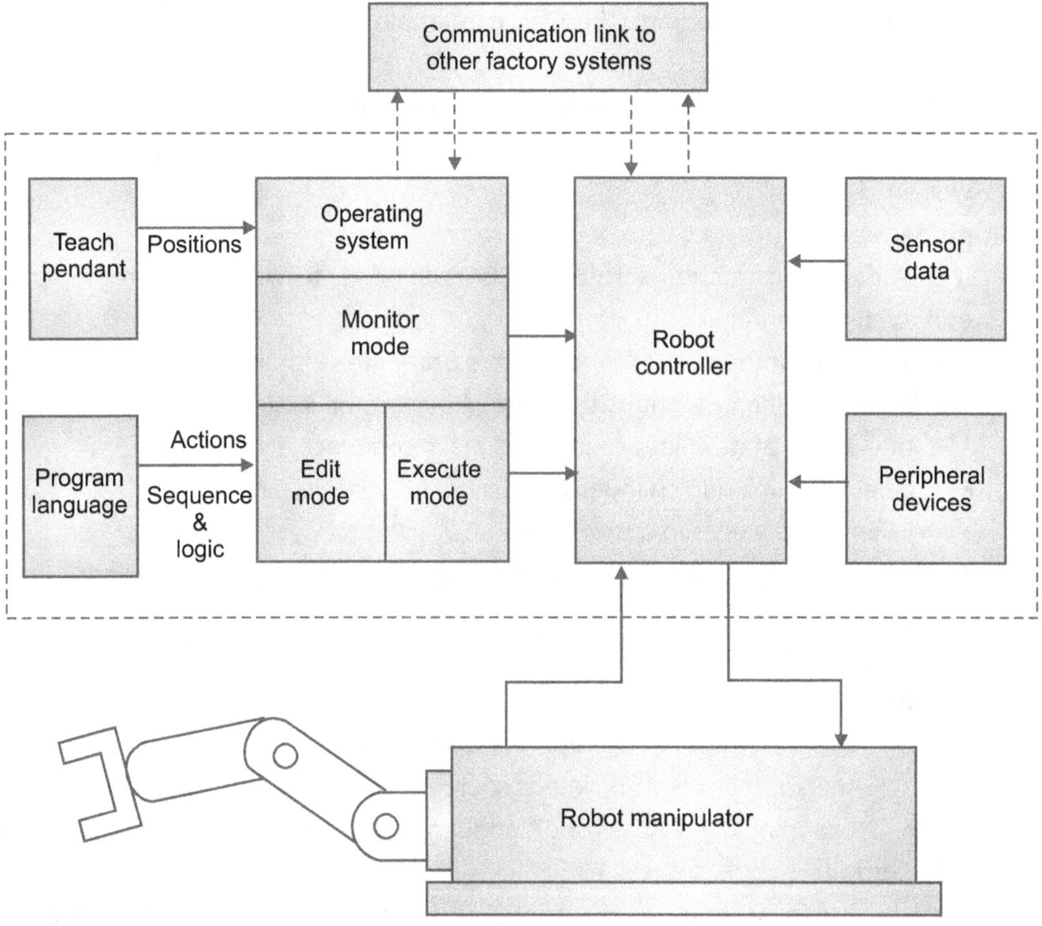

Fig. 10.6: Robot system with its components, co-ordinated by Means of the language

(a) Monitor mode:

- It is used to accomplish overall supervisory control of the system, therefore it is referred as **'Supervisory Mode'**.
- Herein user can define locations in space using the teach pendant, he can set speed control for the robot, store programs, transfer programs from storage back into control memory or move back and forth between the other modes of operation as edit or run.

(b) Run mode:

- It is used for executing a robot program i.e. in this mode robot is performing the sequence of instructions in the program.

- For correctness of program, the user can employ debugging procedures into the language.
- Some modem robot languages permit the user to cross back into the monitor or edit mode while the program is being executed, so that another program can be written.

(c) Edit mode:
- It provides an instruction set which allows the user to write new programs or to edit existing programs.
- The operation of the editing mode differs from one language system to another.
- The kind of editing operations that can be performed include –
  - the writing of new lines of instructions in sequence.
  - deleting or making changes to existing instructions, and
  - inserting new lines in a program.
- The robot language program is processed by the operating system using –
  (i) Interpreter or
  (ii) A compiler

(i) Interpreter:
- It is a program in the operating system that executes each instruction of the source program, where source program is the users robot language program. e.g. **VAL** is robot language processed by an interpreter.

(ii) Compiler:
- It is a program in the operating system that passes through the entire source program and pretranslates all of the instructions into machine level code that can be read and executed by the robot controller. e.g. **MCL** is robot language processed by a compiler.

Compiled programs result in faster execution times.

10.6.2 Robot Language Elements and Functions (W-11)

Following are the robot language elements and functions:
(a) Constants and variables.
(b) Aggregates and location variables.
(c) WAIT, DELAY, SIGNAL commands.
(d) Branching.
(e) Motion commands.
(f) End-effector and sensor commands.
(g) Computations and operations.

(h) Program sequence control.
(i) Subroutines.
(j) Communications and data processing.
(k) Monitor mode commands.

10.6.2 (a) Constants and Variables

(i) Constants:
- A constant is a value which does not change during the execution of program.
- Constant can be integers (i.e. while numbers) real numbers, containing decimal point, or strings that are enclosed in quotes.
- The range of values for numerical constants depends upon the computer system, on which the language is implemented.
- A bit capacity of the CPU gives a limit on the range of values that the computer can handle.
- Integer and real numbers can be positive or negative as indicated by a '+' or '–' sign.
- A string is a sequence of 8-bit alphanumeric character or symbols, generally having marker as e.g. 'machine'.
- The exact syntax might vary from one language to other.

(ii) Variables:
- A variable in computer programming is a symbol or symbolic name that can change in value during the execution of the program.
- Variable can be integers (i.e. whole numbers), real numbers, containing decimal point, or strings that are enclosed in quotes.
- The range of values for variables depends on the computer system; on which the language is implemented.
- Variable symbols and names are created from the alphanumeric character set
  i.e. letters a through z and
        digits 0 through 9
- For establishing variable means, there are certain rules in the various robot languages.
  (a) The variable name must begin with an alphabetic letter.
  (b) The variable name must not be identical to the language vocabulary word.
  (c) For first generation languages, the specification of integer variables might be used.
  (d) For second generation languages, variables can be specified for integers, real numbers or strings.

10.6.2 (b) Aggregates and Location Variables

- An aggregate is an ordered set of constants and variables.
- AML permits the specification of an aggregate by enclosing it with the bracketing symbols e.g. <match>, and by separating the elements in the aggregate by commas.

  e.g. (i) $\boxed{< 15.722, 220.057, 12.212, 24.092, 125.170 >}$

  This example is an aggregate consisting of five real numbers.

  The aggregate can contain elements that are all of different type. Any combination of integers, real numbers, and strings can be contained in the same aggregate.

  (ii) $\boxed{< \text{'look', 'take'} >}$

  This example consists of two strings. Therefore, it is not always necessary that the aggregate contain elements of same type.

- An aggregate can also be used to specify joint co-ordinate values of a robot's joints. Above example (a) could be used to define a five axis robot's joint co-ordinate values for a point in space, which is as follows.

  $\boxed{\text{DEFINE P1 = POINT}< 15.722, 220.057, 12.212, 24.092, 125.170 >}$

  Above statement can be illustrated as:

  General interpretation of the aggregate in above statement is that –

- The first three values (15.722, 220.057, 12.212) define the position of the robot wrist or the tool attached to the wrist, in world space (x – y – z) co-ordinates).
- The remaining two values (24.092, 125.170) define the rotations of the wrist joints in degrees relative to some neutral reference frame.

10.6.2 (c) WAIT, DELAY and SIGNAL Commands

- All industrial robots can be instructed to send signals or wait for signals during program execution.
- These signals are called as interlocks. An interlock in robotic workcell design is a method of preventing the work cycle sequence from continuing unless a certain condition or set of conditions are satisfied. Thus, it is a feature of work cell control which plays an important role in regulating the sequence in which the various elements of the cycle are carried out.

Purpose of providing Interlocks:

(i)   To make sure that a raw workpart was at the pickup location on the conveyor before the robot tried to grasp the object.

(ii) To determine when the machining cycle was completed before the robot attempts to load the part into the fixture, and

(iii) To indicate that the part has been successfully loaded so that the automatic machining cycle can begin.

Interlocks can be subdivided into two categories:

(i) Output interlocks:

An output interlock involves the use of a signal sent from the workstation controller to one of the machines or other devices in the workcell.

It corresponds to the **SIGNAL** command.

(ii) Input interlocks:

An input interlocks are usually used to determine conditions that the work part has been properly loaded and the robot gripper has been removed to a safe distance. Thus, an input interlock makes use of a signal sent from one of the components in the cell to the workstation controller.

It corresponds to the **WAIT** command. It is used to indicate that a certain condition or set of conditions have been met and that the programmed work cycle sequence can continue. An input interlock can be used in a machine loading application to signal the workstation controller that the part has been properly loaded into the fixture on the machine tool table.

Illustration:

Consider a robot for unloading a press. It is important to inhibit the robot from having its gripper enter the press before the press is open, an even more obvious, it is important that the robot remove its hand from the press before the press closes. In order to have this co-ordination, two commands that can be used during program.

(i) SIGNAL P:

It instructs the robot controller to output a signal through line P, where P is one of the several output lines available to the controller.

(ii) WAIT Q:

It indicates that the robot should wait at its current location until it receives a signal on line Q, where Q is one of several input lines available to the robot controller.

(iii) DELAY Y SEC:

The robot would be programmed to wait for a specified amount of time to ensure that the operation had taken place, thus, causing the robot to delay before proceeding to the next step. Therefore, above command indicates that the robot should wait Y seconds before proceeding to the next step in the program.

e.g. consider a two-axis robot is to be used to perform the unloading of the press. The layout is as shown in Fig. 10.7.

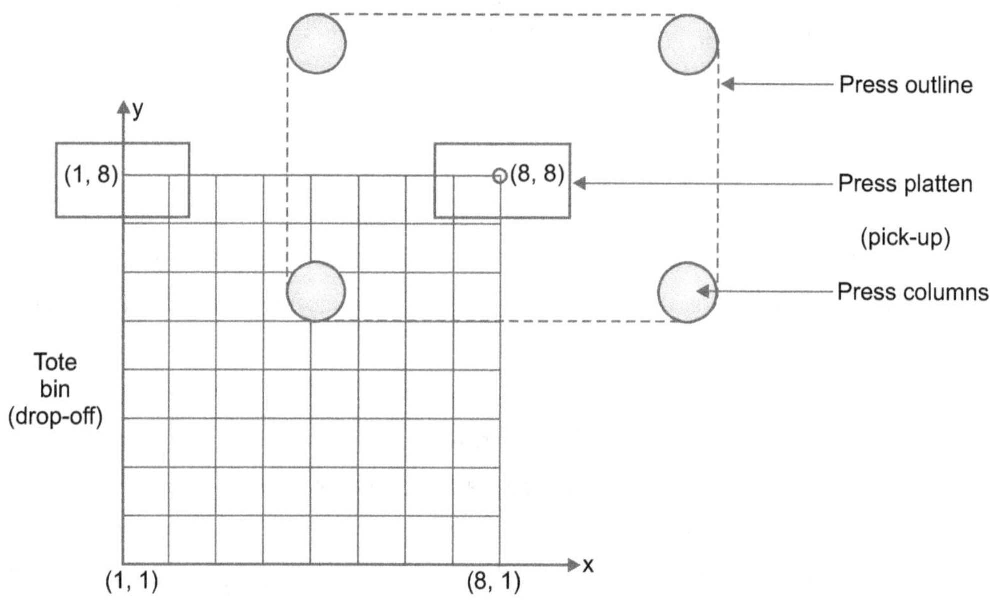

Fig. 10.7: Workspace for Robot for Press Unloading Operation

- The platten of the press where parts are to be picked-up is at the location (8, 8).
- The robot must drop the parts in a tote bin positioned at (1, 8).
- One of the columns of the press is in the way of an easy straight line move from (8, 8) to (1, 8).
- Thus, the robot must move its arm around the near side of the column in order to avoid collision with it. It can be accomplished by the use of points (8, 1) and (1, 1).
- Now point (8, 1) will be the position to wait for the press to open before entering the press to remove the part and the robot will be started from point (1, 1), a point in space known to be safe in the application.
- Thus, we can use controller ports 1 to 10 as output i.e. **SIGNAL** lines and port 11 through 20 as input lines i.e. **WAIT.**

– Generally, output line 4 will be used to actuate (i.e. SIGNAL) the press, and output lines 5 and 6 will be used to close and open the gripper respectively.

– Input line 11 will be used to receive the signal from the press indicating that it has opened (i.e. WAIT).

– Table 10.3 gives the program to complete the press unloading task.

Table 10.3

Step	Move or Signal	ϵ_0 Remarks
0	1, 1	Start at home position
1	8, 1	Move to wait position
2	WAIT 11	Wait for press to open
3	8, 8	Move to pick up point
4	SIGNAL 5	Signal gripper to close
5	8, 1	Move to safe position
6	SIGNAL 4	Signal press to actuate
7	1, 1	Move around press column
8	1, 8	Move to tote pan
9.	SIGNAL 6	Signal gripper to open
10	1, 1	Move to safe position

– Use of DELAY command is illustrated in Table 10.4 which is modification of above Table 10.3. It uses time as the means for assuming that the gripper is either opened or closed.

Table 10.4

Step	Move or Signal	ϵ_0 Remarks
0	1, 1	Start at home position
1	8, 1	Move to wait position
2	WAIT 11	Wait for press to open
3	8, 8	Move to pick up point
4	SIGNAL 5	Signal gripper to close
5	DELAY 1 SEC	Signal gripper to close
6	8, 1	Move to safe position
7	SIGNAL 4	Signal press that hand is clear
8	1, 8	Move around press column
9	1, 8	Move to tote pan
10	SIGNAL 6	Signal hand to open
11	DELAY 1 SEC	Wait for gripper to open
12	1, 1	Move to home position

10.6.2 (d) Branching

- In a industrial robot, controller provides a method of dividing a program into one or more branches, called as branching.
- Branching allows the robot program to be subdivided into convenient segments that can be executed during the program.
- A branch can be a subroutine that is called one or more times during the program.
- The subroutine can be executed either by branching to it at a particular place in the program or by testing an input signal line to branch to it.
- Most controllers allow the user to specify whether the signal should interrupt the program branch currently being executed or wait until the current branch completes. The interrupt capability is used for error branches. Depending on the event and the design of the error branch, the robot will either take some corrective action or simply terminate the robot motion and signal for human assistance.
- Branch capability has its frequent use when the robot has been programmed to perform more than one task. In this case, separate branches are used for each individual task.
- Use of branching reduces lines of code (i.e. programming lines). Also there is significant efficiency in robot programming when branches are used. There is substantial reduction in the programming effort using branching capability.

10.6.2 (e) Motion Commands

Motion commands are used for controlling the movement of the manipulator arm.

For this purpose, textual language is used. Motion commands can be illustrated with reference to –

(i)   MOVE and Related statements.
(ii) SPEED control.
(iii) Definition of point in the workspace.
(iv) Paths and frames.

(i)   MOVE and Related statements:
   MOVE P1:
- It indicates that end of the arm (end effector) to move from its present position to the point (previously defined), named P_1.
- The point is defined in terms of the robot's joint positions, and so P_1 defines the position and orientation of the end-effector.
- The **MOVE** statement causes the arm to move with a joint-interpolated motion.
- **VAL-II language** provides for a straight line move with the statement.

MOVES P1:

Here suffix s indicates straight-line interpolation. The controller evaluates a straight line trajectory from the current position to the point P_1 and causes the robot arm to follow that trajectory.

- **Via points:**

    In some cases, the trajectory must be controlled so that the end-effector passes through some intermediate points as it moves from the present position to the next position defined in the statement. This intermediate position is called as **via point.**

    The case where there is an obstacle and clearances to be considered along the motion path, there is a need of via-point. e.g. while removal of a part from a production machine, the arm trajectory would have to be planned so that no interference occurs with the machine. The move statement for this case will be as follows:

    MOVE P1 VIA P2

    This command tells the robot to move its arm to point P_1 but pass through via point P_2 making to move.

- Sometimes, a move sequence involves a approach to a point and departure from the point. This kind of situation is found in applications like material handling system, in which it is necessary for gripper to be moved to some intermediate position above the part before proceeding to it for the pick up. e.g. **According to VAL II**, suppose the robot's task is to pick up a part from a container.

    Assuming that initially gripper is open.

    Following sequence can be employed.

APPRO P_1, 50
MOVES P_1
SIGNAL (to close gripper)
DEPART 50

- **APPRO:** Command causes the end-effector to be moved to the zone of the point P_1, but offset from the point along the tool z-axis in the negative direction (above the part) by a distance of 50 mm.
- **MOVES P_1 and SIGNAL:** For this location the end-effector is moved straight to the point P_1 and closes its gripper around the part.
- **DEPART:** Statement causes the robot to move away from the pick up point along the tool z-axis to a distance equal to 50 mm.

    VAL II provides straight-line interpolation rather than joint-interpolation. These commands are APROS and DEPARTS, respectively.

Incremental moves:

In the incremental move, the direction and distance of the move must be defined. This is done by specifying the particular point or points to be moved and the distance of that move. Move distance for linear joints are defined in inches or millimeters, while rotational joint moves are specified in degrees of rotation.

AML illustrates possibilities of incremental moves

```
D MOVE (1, 10)
D MOVE (< 3, 4, 5 >, < 40, –50, 80 >)
```

D MOVE is the command for an incremental move or "Delta" move. In paranthesis the joint and the distances of the incremental move are specified.

The first statement: Moves joint 1 (which is assumed to be linear) by 10 in.

The second statement: Commands an incremental move of axes 3, 4 and 6 by 40°, –60° and 80° respectively.

AL - language provides move statement. It is designed for multiple arm control, the move statement can be used to identify which arm is to be moved.

  e.g. **MOVE ARM 1 TO P1**

The robot is instructed to move its arm number 1 from the current position to point P_1.

(ii) SPEED Control:

- The SPEED control command is used to define the velocity with which the robot's arm is moved.
- When the SPEED command is given in the monitor mode, it shows some absolute measure of velocity available for the robot.
- e.g. **SPEED 80 IPS**.
  - It indicates that the speed of the end effector during program execution shall be 80 in/sec, unless it is changed to some other value during the program.
  - If no units are given, then the speed command indicates some value relative to the robot designer's concept of 'normal' speed.

    e.g. **SPEED 80**

    indicates that the robot should operate at 75% of normal speed during program execution.

(iii) Definition of point in the workspace:

- Motion control programs have used points in the workspace. The location of these points must be defined for the program. The point location is usually defined with the help of teach pendant. The pendant is used to drive the robot arm to the desired position and orientation.

  A following command

  HERE P_1

  indicates that HERE statement is used in VAL language. The position and orientation of each joint are stored in control memory as an aggregate as,

  $< 15.722, 220.057, 12.212, 24.092, 125.170 >$

  where, first three values are x-y-z co-ordinates in world space and the rest of values are wrist rotation angles.

- Also, the points in space can be specified by designating the point and its co-ordinate values by typing them into control memory directly without using the teach pendant.

  Following statement shows the specification of points in space.

  DEFINE P_1 = POINT $< 15.722, 220.057, 12.212, 24.092, 125.170 >$

(iv) Paths and Frames:

- Path in the workspace can be defined by connecting various points together.

  e.g.

  DEFINE PATH 1 = PATH (P_1, P_2, P_3, P_4)

  The path PATH 1 shows the points P_1, P_2, P_3 and P_4 connected in series, defined relative to the robot's world-space.

  The path begins at P_1 and end of the path is the last point that is specified in the series.

  The way in which the robot moves between the points in the path is determined by the motion statement i.e.

  MOVE PATH 1

  It indicates that the robot arm would move through the sequence of positions defined in PATH 1 using a joint-interpolated motion between the points.

  Another statement

  MOVES PATH 1

  It indicates that straight line interpolation must be used to move between the points in the path.

- A frame is a Cartesian co-ordinate system that may have other points or paths defined relative to it. The following statement defines the concept of frame in robot programming.

  > DEFINE FRAME 1 = FRAME (P_1, P_2, P_3)

  - The variable name given to the frame is FRAME 1.
  - Its position in space is defined using the three points P_1, P_2 and P_3. Point P_1 becomes the origin of the frame, P_2 is a point along x-axis, and P_3 is a point in the xy plane.
  - As the separation between points is increased, the accuracy is also improved in the calculations.
  - The three points uniquely define the Cartesian co-ordinate system of the new frame.
  - The z-axis is perpendicular to the xy-plane, with its positive direction pointing to form a right-hand co-ordinate system.
  - For number of frames, a routing path, called ROUTE, can be defined relative to one of the frames as below.

    > DEFINE ROUTE : FRAME 1 = PATH (M_1, M_2, M_3, M_4, M_5)

Here, the series of points M_1 through M_5 defines the routing pattern at the first position on the part identified by FRAME 1.

Instead of the five points being defined relative to the world space co-ordinate system, they are defined relative to new co-ordinate system FRAME 1. When the robot is commanded to follow the path the statement must include the definition of the reference frame.

i.e.

> MOVES ROUTE : FRAME 1

For executing the sequence of routing operations

> MOVES ROUTE: FRAME 2
>
> :
>
> :
>
> MOVES ROUTE: FRAME 3
>
> :
>
> :
>
> MOVES ROUTE: FRAME 5

... (For 5 number of frames)

Each of the points in ROUTE is transformed into the new frame, and the straight line segment path is executed.

10.6.2 (f) End-effector and Sensor Commands

- **End-effector commands:**
  - In order to control end-effector operation, most elementary commands are used as,
    OPEN   and   CLOSE
    VAL II - differentiates between differences in the timing of the gripper action.
  - Above two commands OPEN and CLOSE cause the action to occur during execution of the next motion.
    Also,
    OPEN I   and   CLOSE I
    cause the action to occur immediately, without waiting for the next motion to begin. It results in a small time delay. These are for non-served gripper.
  - The command
    CLOSE 50 MM or **CLOSE 1.965 IN**
    When applied to a gripper that has servo control over the width of the finger opening would place the gripper to an opening of 50 mm (1.965 in).
  - For some grippers having tactile or force sensors built into fingers. These permit the robot to sense the presence of the object and to apply a measured force to the object during grasping it.
    e.g. force measurement for a gripper can be controlled to apply a certain force against the part being grasped.
    i.e.
    CLOSE 4.0 LB
    It indicates that apply a 4 *lb* gripping force against the part.
  - With proper instrumentation, AL language statement
    CENTER
    provides a fairly high level of control for tactile sensors. It causes the gripper to slowly close until contact is made with the object by one of the fingers. The CENTER statement allows the robot to center its arm around the object rather than causing the object to be moved by the gripper closure. This is useful in getting the position of an object whose location is only approximately known by the robot.
  - For end-effectors to be powered tools, rather than gripper, the robot must be able to position the tool and operate it. AL language gives a command which might be used to control the powered tool.
    i.e.

```
OPERATE TOOL (SPEED = 110 RPM)
OPERATE TOOL (TORQUE = 6 IN LB)
OPERATE TOOL (TIME = 12 SEC)
```

    Above statements apply to the operation of a powered rotational tool.

First two statements indicate that either the tool can be operated at 110 r/min or it can be operated with a torque of 6 in-*lb*. The powered tool would be operated at 110 r/min until the screw began to tighten, at which point the torque statement would take precedence. The third statement indicates that after 10 sec. the operation will terminate.

- **Sensor commands:**
  - The SIGNAL command can be used both for turning on or off an output signal. The statements

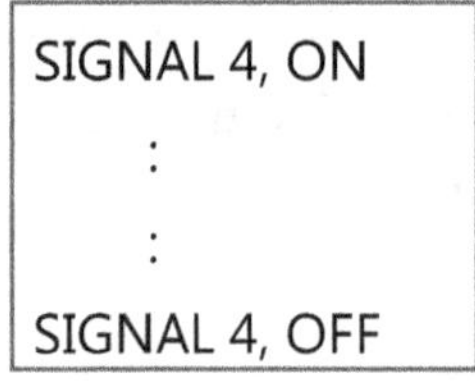

It indicates that the signal from output port 4 to be turned on at one point in the program and turned off at another point in the program. (Signal in this case is binary).

An analog output could also be controlled with the SIGNAL command.

SIGNAL 106, 5.5

It provides an output of 5.5 units within the allowable range of the output signal.

  - The WAIT command can also be used both for on or off conditions. Here the robot provides power to some external device. The WAIT is used to verify that the device has been turned on before permitting the program to continue. Further, the robot turns off the device and the device signals back that it has been turned off before the program continues. The statements are as below.

Commands	Comments
SIGNAL 4, ON	Robot turns on the device.
WAIT 12, ON	Device signals back that it is on.
:	
:	
SIGNAL 4, OFF	Robot turns off the device.
WAIT 12, OFF	Device signals back that it is off.

  - The WAIT command can be used for analog signals as well as binary digital signals as similar to SIGNAL command.
  - The variable can be defined as follows:

DEFINE MOTOR 1 = OUTPUT 4
DEFINE SENSR 2 = INPORT 12

which would permit the preceding input output statements to be written in following way.

```
SIGNAL MOTOR 1, ON
WAIT SENSR 2, ON
        :
        :
SIGNAL MOTOR 1, OFF
WAIT SENSR 2, OFF
```

- It is also possible to define an analog signal, either input or output, as a variable which is used during program execution. The statement

  DEFINE VOLT 1 = OUTPUT 104

  It specifies that the variable VOLT 1 will be used with output port 104.

  SIGNAL VOLT 1

  It is used when at some point in the program, the variable could be computed to be a particular value and that value could be sent to the designed device in the cell by above statement.

  The value of VOLT 1 would be signaled to the external device through output port 104.

- Similarly, WAIT command can be used for an analog input signal.

  DEFINE VOLT 2 = INPORT 112.

  Here, specification of the variable name and associated input port is done by above statement.

- Use of a variable can be made in a WAIT statement as,

  WAIT VOLT 2

  It indicates that the program execution should wait for the value of the signal on input port 112 to have a value that is greater than or equal to VOLT 2. The programmer must keep in mind what the normal signal level is likely to be since this may influence the logic of the program.

- **THE REACT Command:**

  It is used to continuously monitor an incoming signal and to respond to a change in the signal. A particular use of this kind of command is when some error or safety hazard has occurred in the workcell and the condition is detected by one of the sensors.

  A statement

  REACT IS, SAFETY

  indicates that the input line 15, is to be continuously monitored, and when a change in its signal value occurs, branch to a subroutine called SAFETY.

- The use of REACT statements in textual languages is to complete the current motion command before interrupting. In some cases, an intermediate reaction is required. The statement for this is,

  REACT 1, SAFETY

  This causes immediate suspension of the regular program execution, so that a transfer to SAFETY is done at once.

- Analog input-output signals can be used with REACT commands. The analog signal level at which the reaction occurs must be specified in the statement.

  REACT 115, 5.5, SAFETY (PRIORITY 2)

  It indicates that the transfer to subroutines SAFETY must occur if and when the input signal on port 115 becomes greater than or equal to 5.5 V.

- When variable names are used, the statement is,

```
DEFINE VAR 12 = INPORT 12
          ⋮

          ⋮

REACT VAR 12, SAFETY (PRIORITY 2)
```

  The REACT command facilitates the design of an 'interrupt' system in the robot program. The purpose of an interrupt system is to transfer control from one part of the program to another in response to conditions that take priority, over regular program execution.

10.6.2 (g) Computations and Operations

(i) Mathematical operators:

Symbol	Meaning
+	addition
−	subtraction
*	multiplication
/	division
**	exponentiation
=	equal to

(ii) Trignometric, logarithmic, exponential and similar functions:

Function	Remark	Function	Remark
SIN (A)	Sine of an angle A	A COT (A)	Arc cotangent of an ∠ A
COS (A)	Sine of one angle A	LOG (X)	Natural logarithm of X
TAN (A)	Tangent of an angle A	EXP (X)	Exponential function
COT (A)	Cotangent of an angle A	ABS (X)	Absolute value of X
ASIN (A)	Arc sine of an ∠ A	ABS (X)	Largest integer less than or equal
A COS (A)	Arc cosine of an ∠ A	INT (X)	to X
A TAN (A)	Arc tangent of an ∠ A	SQRT (X)	Square of root X

(iii) Relational operators:

Operators	Remarks
EQ	Equal to
NE	Not equal to
GT	Greater than
GE	Greater than or equal to
LT	Less than
LE	Less than or equal to

(iv) Logical operators:

Operators	Remark
AND	Logical AND operator
OR	Logical OR
NOT	Logical complement

Expressions:

e.g.

9 + (6 * N)	Arithmetic expression
N = N + 1	Arithmetic expression
TAN (20)	Trignometric function
COUNT GT 12	Relational expression

10.6.2 (h) Program Sequence Control

– A variety of instructions are available in the textual robot languages to control the logical flow of the program.

– Before using subroutines, the following statements are available in the second generation languages

    GOTO 15

It indicates an unconditional branch to statement 12. The GOTO statement can be used with a logical expression as under

IF (logical expression) GOTO 15

It indicates that if the logical expression is true, then the program branches to statement 15. Otherwise, it continues to the next statement in the program.

10.6.2 (i) Subroutines

The statements

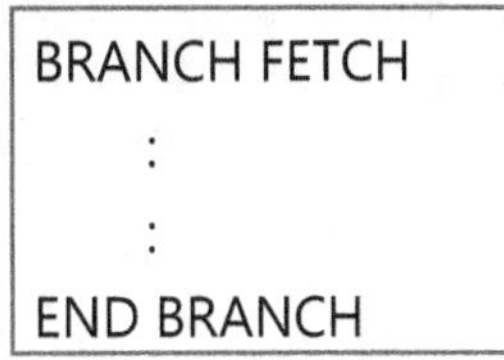

It indicates the start and the end of a branch or subroutine and to name the subroutine (FETCH). In order to call the branch during program execution,

FETCH

is used.

Here, branches will be referred by move appropriate name **SUBROUTINE.**

A subroutine with a single argument is shown as

```
SUBROUTINE PLACE (M)
    :
    :
END SUBROUTINE
```

The argument M is used during subroutine. The subroutine would be called using a statement that would identify the value of the argument.

e.g.

CALL PLACE (4)

Another statement used with subroutines is

RETURN

which results in termination of the subroutine and returns control of the program back to the statement following the call statement for the subroutine.

The effect of **RETURN** is similar to **END BRANCH** statement in the subroutine.

10.7 Robot Programming Exercises

(1) Example showing use of subroutine:

A program for palletizing operation is to be written. To review, the robot must pick up parts from an incoming chute and deposit them onto a pallet. The pallet has four rows that are 50 mm apart and six columns that are 40 mm apart. The plane of the pallet is assumed to be parallel to the xy plane. The rows of the pallet are parallel to the x-axis and the columns of the pallet are parallel to the y-axis. Fig. 10.8 shows the arrangement of the pallet. The objects are to be picked up are about 25 mm tall.

Use the following constants and variables in the program.

- **Variables:**

ROW	The row number (an integer value).
COLUMN	The column (an integer value)
X	An X-co-ordinate value
Y	A Y-co-ordinate value

- **Location constant:**
  PICKUP   The pickup point on the chute.
  CORNER   The corner starting on the pallet.
- **Location variables:**
  DROP   The dropoff point.

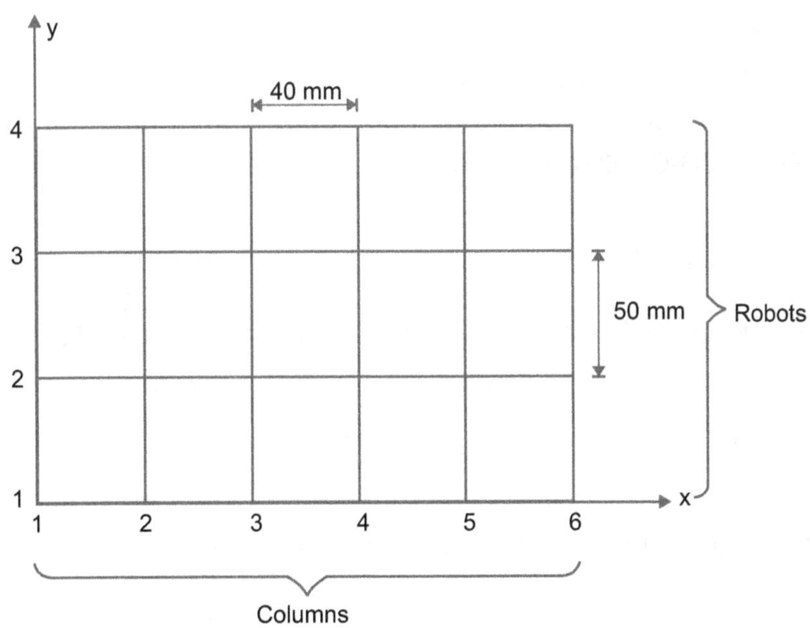

Fig. 10.8: Configuration of Pallet

- **Some additional parameters:**
  MAXCOL   –   The number of columns on the pallet
  MAXROW   –   The number of rows on the pallet
  YSPACE   –   The spacing in the Y-direction (i.e. spacing between rows)
  XSPACE   –   The spacing in the X-direction (i.e. spacing between columns)
  Subroutine   –   PALLET

The subroutine uses the above parameters as arguments that must be identified when the subroutine is called.

SIGNAL 1 (i.e. output line 1) is used to initiate the delivery of an empty pallet into the loading position.

WAIT 11 (i.e. input line 11) is used in conjunction with a sensor device to ensure that the pallet delivery has been accomplished.

SIGNAL 2 (i.e. output line 2) is used to initiate the removal of the filled pallet from the loading position.

WAIT 12 (i.e. input line 12) tests to make sure that it has been removed.

Program:

```
      PROGRAM PALLETIZE
      DEFINE PICKUP = JOINTS (1, 2, 3, 4, 5)
      DEFINE CORNER = JOINTS (1, 2, 3, 4, 5)
      DEFINE DROP = CO-ORDINATES (X, Y)
      OPEN I
5     SIGNAL 1
      WAIT 11
      CALL PALLET (MAX COL = 6, MAXROW = 4, XSPACE = 40, YSPACE = 50)
      SIGNAL 2
      WAIT 12
      GOTO 5
      END PROGRAM.
      SUBROUTINE PALLET (MAXCOL, MAXROW, XSPACE, YSPACE)
      ROW = 0
10    Y = ROW * YSPACE
      COLUMN = 0
20    X = COLUMN * XSPACE
      DROP = CORNER + <X, Y>
      APPRO PICKUP, 50
      MOVES PICKUP
      CLOSE I
      DEPART 50
      APPRO DROP, 50
      MOVES DROP
      OPEN I
      DEPART 50
      COLUMN = COLUMN + 1
      IF COLUMN LT MAXCOL GOTO 20
      ROW = ROW + 1
      IF ROW LT MAXROW GOTO 10
      END SUBROUTINE
```

– Statement needed to illustrate a subroutine that might be used in an emergency stop situation.

```
          :
          :
REACT 114, 5.0, SAFETY
          :
          :
SUBROUTINE SAFETY
STOP 2
SIGNAL 1, ON
SIGNAL 2, OFF
END SUBROUTINE
```

The REACT command indicates that the controller must measure the value of the signal on input line 114 and transfer to SUBROUTINE SAFETY if the SIGNAL ever exceeds a value of 5.0. SIGNAL 1, ON - might be used to turn on an alarm SIGNAL 2, OFF - could be used to turn off a piece of machinery that works with the robot in the cell.

(2) Example of a VAL Program:

Steps	Command Lines	Meaning
1	APPRO PART, 50	Move to a location, which is 50 mm above the location PART (which is a location to be defined).
2	MOVES PART	Move along a straight-line to PART.
3	CLOSE I	Close the gripper jaws to grip the object immediately.
4	DEPARTS 150	Withdraw 150 mm from PART along a straight-line path.
5	APPROZ BOX, 200	Approach along a straight-line to a location 200 mm above the location, BOX (which is to be defined afterwards).
6	MOVE BOX	Move to BOX.
7	OPEN I	Open the hand, and drop the object.
8	DEPART 75	Withdraw 75 mm from BOX.

Steps

1
6 are examples of **joint-interpolated motions.**
7

Steps

$$\left.\begin{array}{c} 2 \\ 4 \\ 5 \end{array}\right\}$$ are examples of **straight-line motions.**

Steps

$$\left.\begin{array}{c} 3 \\ 7 \end{array}\right\}$$ are **hand-control instructions.**

(3) Program to pick objects from a pallet:

In a pallet, objects protrude at 40 mm from the face of the pallet, and are located in a number of rows and columns. The pallet has 3 rows that are 30 mm apart and 4 columns that are 50 mm apart. The plane of pallet is parallel to xy-plane.

The rows are parallel to X-axis and the columns are parallel to Y-axis. The objects are to be picked up one after another from the pallet and placed in a location chute.

Fig. 10.9 shows the pallet.

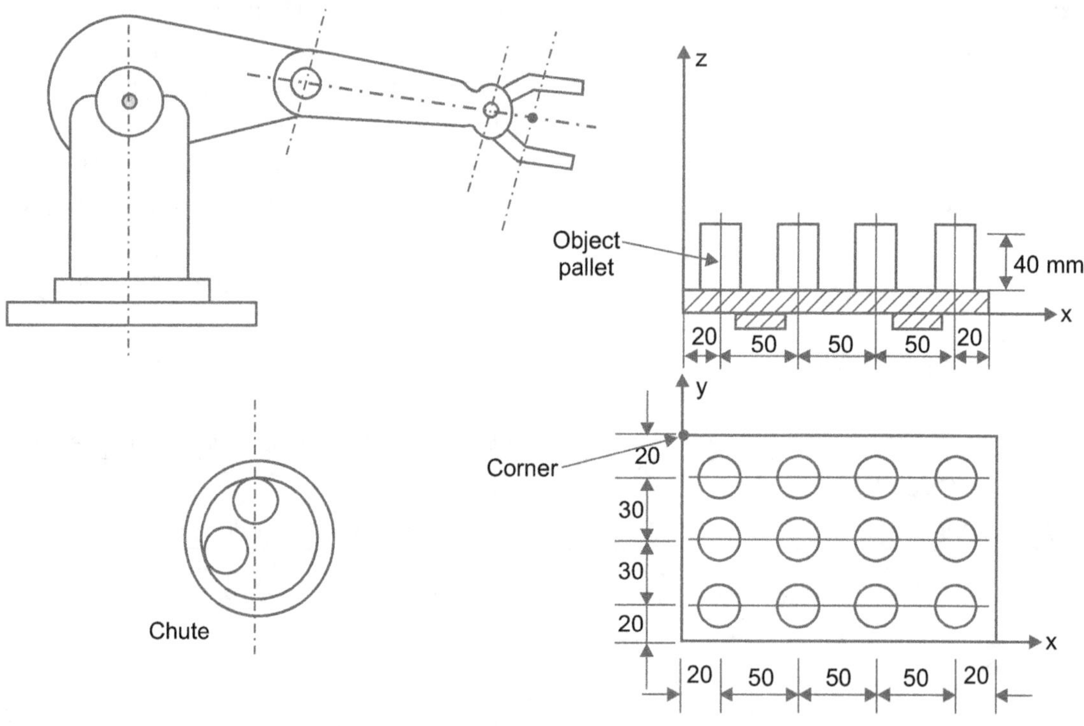

Fig. 10.9

```
PROGRAM DEPALLET 1
      REMARK PROGRAM TO PICK OBJECTS FROM A PALLET
      REMARK CORNER AND CHUTE LOCATIONS ARE TAUGHT
            SET I MAXCOL = 4
            SET I MAXROW = 3
            SET I ROW = 1
            SET I COLUMN = 1
            SET PICK = CORNER
            SHIFT PICK BY 20.00, -20.00, 60.00
            OPEN I
10    MOVE PICK
            DRAW 0, 0, -25.00
            CLOSE I
            DRAW 0, 0, 25.00
            MOVE CHUTE
            OPEN I
            GO SUB PALLET
            IF ROW LE MAXROW THEN 10
END
PROGRAM PALLET
      REMARK SUBROUTINE FOR LOCATIONS
            SET I COLUMN = COLUMN + 1
            IF COLUMN GT MAXCOL THEN 20
            SHIFT PICK BY 50.00, 0.00, 0.00
            GO TO 10
20    SET I ROW = ROW + 1
            IF ROW GT MAX ROW THEN 30
            SHIFT PICK BY -150.00, -30.00, 0.00
            SET I COLUMN = 1
30    RETURN
END
```

(4) Program for weldment:

A welding is to be done. The trajectory for weld is a continuous path arc welding.

Paths	Welding Pattern Along
$(P_2 - P_3)$	with triangular weaving.
$(P_3 - P_4)$	with straight weld.
$(P_4 - P_5 - P_6)$	with circular interpolation.
$(P_6 - P_7)$	with straight weld.
$(P_7 - P_8 - P_9)$	with circular arc.
$(P_9 - P_{10})$	with straight weld and.
$(P_{10} - P_{11})$	with five point weaving.

The weld torch starts its movement from home position P_1 and departs to location P_{12}. Craterfilling is done at the end of trapezoidal weaving. Write a VAL program for suitable arc welding.

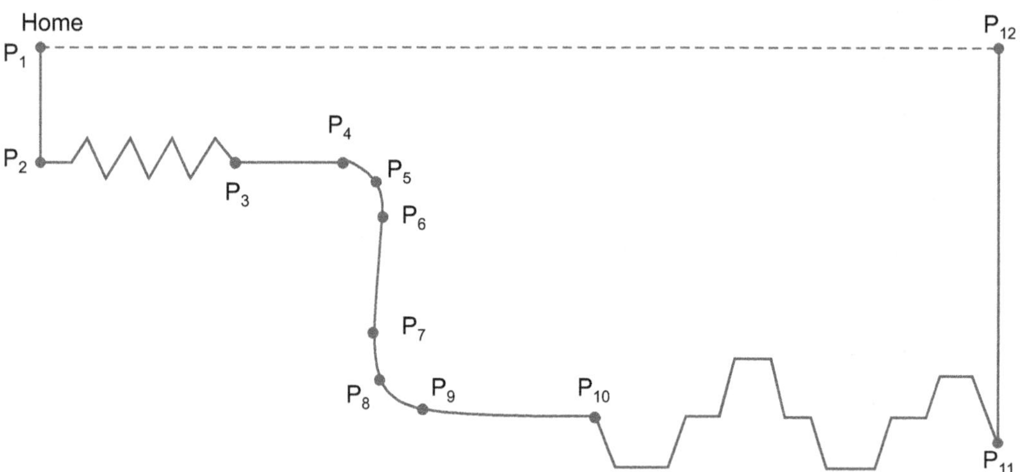

Fig. 10.10: Welding Pattern

PROGRAM WELD PATTERN

Steps	Program Lines	Remarks
1	WSET 1 = 10, 40, 50	WSET instruction sets the welding speeds
2	WSET 2 = 8, 35, 60	as 10 mm/s welding voltage 40% and
3	WSET 3 = 12, 40, 55	welding current of 50% as welding
4	WVSET 1 = 5, 5	condition 1.

Steps	Program Lines	Remarks
5	WVSET 2 = 10, 7, 2, 0, 1, 2, 0	
6	MOVE P1	
7	MOVE P2	
8	WSTART 1, 1	Starts welding under present welding conditions and weaving condition
9	MOVES P3	
10	WEND 0.5	Inactivates a welding start signal.
11	WSTART 2	
12	MOVES P4	
13	CIRCLE P4, P5, P6	
14	MOVES P7	
15	CIRCLE P7, P8, P9	
16	MOVES P10	
17	WEND 0.5	
18	WSTART 3, 2	
19	MOVES P11	
20	CRATERFILL 0.8, 3	
21	WEND 0.5	
22	MOVE P12	
END		

EXERCISES

1. What is a 'Robot Program' ? State various steps in program writing.

2. Explain various methods used to enter the programming command into the controller memory.

3. State various modes of programming.

4. Explain:

    (i)   Manual mode of programming

    (ii) Lead through mode of programming

    (iii) Textual robot language

    (iv) Off-line programming mode.

5.   Discuss various interpolation schemes.

6.   Explain in brief:
   - (i)   Joint interpolation
   - (ii)   Straight-line interpolation
   - (iii)   Circular interpolation
   - (iv)   Irregular smooth motions

7.   Explain generations of Robot Programming Languages.

8.   Discuss Robot Language Structure with reference to operating systems; robot language elements and functions.

9.   Explain basic modes of robot language operating system.

10.   State various Robot Language elements and functions.

11.   Write notes on:
   - (i)   Constants, variables, aggregates and location variables.
   - (ii)   WAIT, DELAY and SIGNAL commands.
   - (iii)   Branching
   - (iv)   Motion commands.
   - (v)   End-effector and sensor commands
   - (vi)   Subroutines

12.   Explain WAIT, DELAY and SIGNAL commands with suitable examples.

13.   State various Robot Languages. Discuss them in brief.

Unit VI

Chapter 11: ARTIFICIAL INTELLIGENCE, SIMULATION AND ASSOCIATED TOPICS IN ROBOTICS

> *Study is like the heaven's glorious sun,*
> *That will not be deep-search'd with saucy looks;*
> *Small have continual plodders ever won,*
> *Save base authority from others' books.*
> *These earthly godfathers of Heaven's lights*
> *That give a name to every fixed star,*
> *Have no more profit of their shining nights*
> *Than those that walk and wot not what they are.*
> *—William Shakespeare, Love's Labours Lost*

11.1 Introduction to Artificial Intelligence

In the most recent decades, the study of Artificial Intelligence has flourished.

Areas of particular importance include the following:

- machine learning
- multi-agent systems
- artificial life
- computer vision
- planning
- playing games (chess in particular)

Artificial intelligence is the study of systems that act in a way that to any observer would appear to be intelligent.

Artificial Intelligence techniques are used to solve relatively simple problems or complex problems that are internal to more complex systems.

Another definition of Artificial Intelligence is, *Artificial Intelligence involves using methods based on the intelligent behavior of humans and other animals to solve complex problems.*

The possibility of creating a robot with emotions and real consciousness is one that is often explored in the realms of science fiction but is rarely considered to be a goal of Artificial Intelligence.

Definitions of AI:

(1) Concerned with the dimension, thought process and reasoning measure success in terms of human performance.

    (i) "The exciting new effort to make computer think ... machines with mind, in the full and literal sense".   – By Haugeland, 1985

    (ii) "The automation of activities that we associate with human thinking, activities such as decision-making, problem solving, learning.   – By Bellman, 1978

According to definitions (i) and (ii) systems think like human.

(2) Concerned with the dimension thought process and reasoning measure success in terms of rationality.

    (iii) "The study of mental faculties through the use of computational models".

    – By Charniak and McDermott, 1985

    (iv) "The study of the computation that makes it possible to perceive, reason and act".

    – By Winston, 1992. According to definitions (iii) and (iv) systems think rationally.

(3) Concerned with the dimension behaviour, measure success in terms of human performance.

    (v) "The art of creating mics that perform functions that require intelligence when performed by people".   – By Kurzweil, 1990.

    (vi) "The study of how to make computers do things at which, at the moment, people are better".

    – By Rich and Knight, 1991. According to definitions (v) and (vi) system act like humans.

(4) Concerned with the dimension, behaviour measure success in terms of rationality.

    (vii) "A field of study that seeks to explain and emulate intelligent behaviour in terms of computational process."   – By Schalkoff, 1990

    (viii) "The branch of computer science that is concerned with the automation of intelligent behaviour".   – By Luger and Stubblefield, 1993

According to definitions (vii) and (viii) system act rationally. People may have the confusion between approaches centered.

A human centered approach must be an empirical science, involving hypothesis and experimental conformation.

A rationalist approach involves a combination of mathematics and engineering.

11.2 History of Artificial Intelligence

In 1956, the term **Artificial Intelligence** was first used by John McCarthy at a conference in Dartmouth College, in Hanover, New Hampshire.

In 1957, Newell and Simon invented the idea of the GPS, whose purpose was, as the name suggests, solving almost any logical problem. The program used a methodology known as means ends analysis, which is based on the idea of determining what needs to be done and then working out a way to do it. This works well enough for simple problems, but AI researchers soon realized that this kind of method could not be applied in such a general way - the GPS could solve some fairly specific problems for which it was ideally suited, but its name was really a misnomer.

At this time there was a great deal of optimism about Artificial Intelligence. Predictions that with hindsight appear rash were widespread. Many commentators were predicting that it would be only a few years before computers could be designed that would be at least as intelligent as real human beings and able to perform such tasks as beating the world champion at chess, translating from Russian into English, and navigating a car through a busy street. Some success has been made in the past 50 years with these problems and other similar ones, but no one has yet designed a computer that anyone would describe reasonably as being intelligent.

In 1958, McCarthy invented the LISP programming language, which is still widely used today in Artificial Intelligence research.

11.3 Artificial Intelligence Problems

In AI much of the early work focused on the formal tasks, such as:

(a) **Game playing:** Samuel wrote 'a checkers playing program that not only played games with opponents but also used its experience at those games to improve its latter performance.'

(b) Theorem proving: The logic Theorist was able to prove several theorems from the first chapter whitehead and Russell's "Principa Mathematica".

People who are able to design a system for game playing and theorem proving, are intelligent. But initially, it was thought that this process required very little knowledge and could therefore be programmed easily.

At a later stage, this assumption turned out to be false, since no computer is fast enough to overcome the combinatorial explosion generated by most problems.

The AI problems are divided into a number of tasks:

1. Mundane Task:

(a) Perception: Requires a large amount of world knowledge, it becomes a difficult problem.

   (i)   Vision
   (ii) Speech

(b) Natural language: The ability to use language to communicate a wide variety of ideas, is the most important thing that separates human from the other animals. The problem is extremely difficult.

   (i)   Understanding
   (ii) Generation
   (iii) Translation

(c) Common sense reasoning: It is a sort of problem solving, that we do everyday when we decide how to get to work in the morning.

(d) Robot control

2. Formal Task:

   (a) Games:
       (i)   Chess
       (ii) Backgammon
       (iii) Checkers GO

   (b) Mathematics:
       (i)   Geometry
       (ii) Logic
       (iii) Integral calculus
       (iv) Proving properties of programs.

3. Expert Tasks:

Requires only specialized expertise without any assistance.

- (a) Engineering:
    - (i) Design
    - (ii) Fault finding
    - (iii) Manufacturing planning
- (b) Scientific analysis
- (c) Medical diagnosis
- (d) Financial analysis.

Before embarking on the study of specific AI problems and solution techniques, it is important to discuss the following four questions:

1. What are the underlying assumptions about intelligence?
2. What kinds of techniques will be useful for solving AI problems?
3. At what level of details are we trying to model human intelligence?
4. How will we know when we have succeeded in building an intelligent program?

11.4 Foundation of Artificial Intelligence

There are various disciplines that contribute ideas, viewpoints and techniques to AI, as follows:

1. Philosophy:

Deals with

- (a) Rules used to draw valid conclusions.
- (b) Theory of how mental mind arises from a physical brain.
- (c) The source of knowledge.
- (d) How does knowledge lead to action?

2. Mathematics:

Deals with

- (a) Formal rules to draw valid conclusion.
- (b) What can be computed?
- (c) How do we reason with uncertain information?

3. Economics:

Deals with

- (a) How to make decisions to maximize payoff?
- (b) How should we do this when others may not go along?
- (c) How should we do this when the payoff may be far in future?

4. **Neuroscience:**

Deals with how brain processes information.

5. **Psychology:**

How humans and animals think and act.

6. **Computer Engineering:**

Deals with how we can build an efficient computer.

7. **Control Theory and Cybernetics:**

Deals with how artifacts can operate under their own control.

8. **Linguistics:**

Deals with how language relates to thought.

11.5 Artificial Intelligence Techniques

Artificial Intelligence problems span a very broad spectrum. They appear to have very little in common except that they are hard.

There are some techniques that are appropriate for the solution for a variety of AI problems.

AI research results that intelligence requires knowledge. Knowledge possesses some less desirable properties, including:

(a) It is voluminous.

(b) It is hard to characterize accurately.

(c) It is constantly changing.

(d) It differs from data by being organized in a way that corresponds to the ways it will be used.

AI technique is a method that exploits knowledge that should be represented in such a way that:

(a) The knowledge captures generalization. In other words, it is not necessary to represent separately each individual situation. Instead, situations that share important properties are grouped together. If knowledge does not have this property then inordinate amounts of memory and updating will be required. So, we usually call something without this property "data" rather than knowledge.

(b) It can be understood by people who must provide it.

For many programs, bulk of data can be acquired automatically. e.g. taking readings from a variety of instruments. In many AI domains, most of the knowledge a program has must be ultimately provided by the people in terms that they understand.

(c) It can be easily modified to correct errors and to reflect changes in the world and in our world view.

(d) It can be used in many situations even if it is not totally accurate or complete.

(e) It can be used to help overcome its own sheer bulk by helping to narrow the range of possibilities that must be usually considered.

Although AI techniques must be designed in keeping these constrains imposed by AI problems, there is some degree of independence between AI problems and problem solving techniques.

It is possible to solve AI problem without using AI techniques, but those solutions are not likely to be very good.

It is possible to apply AI techniques to the solution of non-AI problems. This is a good thing to do for problems that possess many of the same characteristics as the AI problems.

Advanced Techniques

11.5.1 Genetic Algorithms

Introduction

While mother nature has acted a real world laboratory for churning out existence proofs, man has constantly looked up at her to provide innovative methodologies and paradigms that can aid in solving complex problems. From systems that are modelled on biological neuronal networks to those that mimic genetic evolutions, the relentless quest for gaining insights into the techniques of controlling, regulating and adapting delicate systems has continued over time. Genetic Algorithm forms one such technique copied from nature that relies largely on the manner in which we have evolved over a period of time.

Genetic Algorithms (GAs)

Genetic Algorithms are based on the theory of natural selecting and working on generating a set of random solutions and making them compete in an arena where only the fittest survive. Each solution in the set is equivalent to chromosome. (The sperm from the father and the egg from the mother supply the **chromosomes** that make up the child). A set of such solutions (chromosomes) forms a **population**. The algorithm then uses three basic genetic operators viz.:

(a) Reproduction

(b) Crossover

(c) Mutation

Together with a fitness function to evolve a new population or the next generation starting from a random set of solutions, the algorithm uses these operators and the fitness function to guide its search for the optimal solution. It is thus based on a guided random search mechanism. The fitness function gauges how good the solution in question is and provides a measure to its adaptability on survivability. The genetic operators copy the mechanisms based on the principles of human evolution.

Here three examples that highlight how optimization and learning can be achieved using GAs (Genetic Algorithms) are discussed below.

Problem1: Optimization: Job-Shop Scheduling

The job-shop scheduling problem comprises series of zones that are capable of manufacturing products. The objective is to find out the type of schedule that optimizes the entire chain. This could be done for instance by manufacturing the right number of products, reducing the quantity or cost of production or idle time etc.

Here the basic aim is to understand the working of GA. So we just simplify the problem and redefine to suit our needs.

Assume there are three manufacturing units m_1, m_2 and m_3 each of which is capable of manufacturing a different product. A manufacturing schedule could be a set of numbers for example, 20, 35, 15 wherein each number indicates the quantity of the concerned product manufactured by m_1, m_2 and m_3 respectively. This schedule could yield a certain profit (say 40) computed by some equation. In GA terminology the function used to compute the profit is called the fitness function. The set {20, 35, 15} forms the chromosome while its members form the genes. All else are the values that these genes can assume.

Further the problem can be simplified by maintaining clarity by discarding the amount of products generated by a unit. The simplification in terms of binary numbers yields chromosomes of the type (1, 0, 1) indicating that m_1 and m_3 are manufacturing while m_2 is non-productive in this schedule. We also, simplify the fitness function by assuming that the profit of a schedule is measured by the binary number formed by the individual genes (0s and 1s) in the chromosome. Thus, the schedule {1, 0, 1} would have a fitness of $(101)_2$ or 5. Our problem now boils down to finding the best schedule to maximize the value of the number formed by the genes comprising the chromosome.

The problem appears trivial since the best solution {1, 1, 1} can be found in the first glance but our objective here is to see how the GA arrives at this.

Using GA to Solve Job-Shop Problem

The following steps make up the GA:

1. Represent a solution as a chromosome and find a suitable fitness function. Here chromosome solutions are ({1, 0, 1}, {1, 1, 0}, etc.) and also identifying a fitness function f(chromosome) = (concat (Gene 1, Gene 2, Gene 3))$_{10}$ which joins the three genes (bits) that comprise the chromosome and returns its decimal equivalent to help us evaluate the chromosome.

2. Choose a population of solution and initialize it –

   Consider here population size 4 (In practice this number is much larger).

   Let the initial population be [{0, 0, 1}, {0, 1, 0}, {1, 1, 0}, {1, 0, 1}]

   This forms the initial randomly evolved starting generation.

3. We now apply the genetic operator one-by-one. This involves the following steps :

   (a) Determine the fitness of each solution (chromosome) as also the total fitness of the population Σf_i. Following table gives these values.

Fitness and Expected Count of a Generation

Solution No.	Solution S_i	f_i = Locat (Gene 1, Gene 2, Gene 3)$_{10}$	%P_i = f/Σf_i * 100	E_c = N * % P_i
1.	{0, 0, 1}	1	7.14	28.6
2.	{0, 1, 0}	2	14.29	57.1
3.	{1, 1, 0}	6	42.86	171.4
4.	{1, 0, 1}	5	35.71	142.9
Σ		14	100	400
–	–	6	42.86	171.43

The last column gives the actual number of solutions of that type that could occur in the population and is called the expected count of the solution E_C.

(b) Reproduction: To evolve the next generation, we select a set of N chromosomes whose average distribution is equal to the expected count distribution. Simple solution to do this is given below:

– The significance of the expected count lies in the fact that if we generated 1000 sets of each chromosome (4000 in all) then about 286 would be of type {0, 0, 1} and 571 of type {0, 1, 0} and so on. If we now choose 4 chromosomes from the pool of 4000, then it is unlikely that the ones that have low fitness are all selected. Likewise in a population of 1000, we could imagine that if we choose a random number from 0-999 and obtained a number between 0-70, it means we are selecting the chromosome {0, 0, 1} since its percentage probability is about 71. Similarly, if the number falls in the range of 71-213 (143 units) it would mean selection of {0, 1, 0} and for ranges 214-642 and 643-999 (429 and 357 units apart since % probabilities are 42.86 and 35.71 respectively) it would mean selection of {1, 1, 0} and {1, 0, 1} respectively.

Mode of Selection

Values Generated	Selected Solution
265	{1, 1, 0}
301	{1, 0, 1}
515	{1, 1, 0}
85	{0, 1, 0}

The new set of four chromosomes form what is called the mating pool. It is on these that we apply the genetic operators.

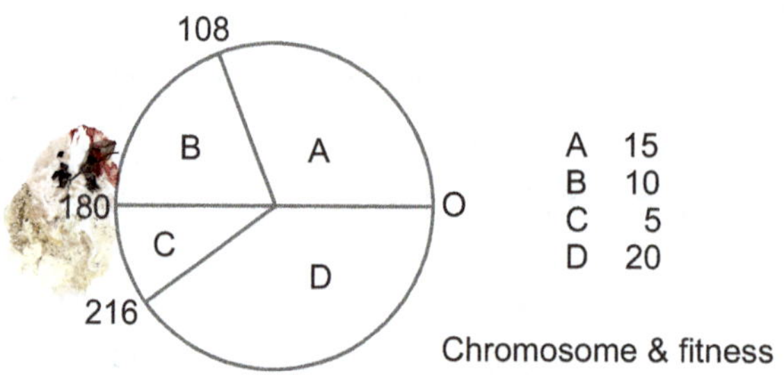

Roulette wheel

Roulette wheel depicts a typical Roulette wheel wherein the sections are partitioned based on the fitness values 20, 10, 5, 15 of some four chromosomes.

Crossover: Crossover is the process of swapping portions of the two selected chromosomes. Most often swapping occurs at gene boundaries called crossing sites or chiasma. In the present case each of the chromosomes has three genes, which means its length is 3. Thus, the chromosomes can have two crossing sites shown below by the numbered arrows.

 [Gene 1, $\downarrow$1Gene 2, $\downarrow$2Gene 3]

We now take two solutions randomly out of the mating pool and determine whether cross-over should occur or not. Cross-over need not occur in every generation. Generally, a cross-over probability or rate P_c that remains constant throughout is used. In the current case we assume that cross-over does take place to describe how it is affected. If it does not occur then the two selected solutions form two of the entities of the new generation provided they are not subjected to mutation described later.

Imagine we select two chromosomes {1, 0, 1} and {1, 1, 0} randomly for crossover. We then randomly choose either of two possible crossing sites – 1 or 2. If the crossing site numbered 2 is chosen then the resultant chromosomes would be formed as shown below.

$\downarrow_2$

{1, 0, 1}

$\downarrow_2$ $\longrightarrow$ {1, 0, 0} and {1, 1, 1}

{1, 1, 0}

Let us assume that the two of the other solutions {1, 1, 0} and {0, 1, 0} are crossed over (once again based on Pc) this time at position 1 to obtain the solutions {0, 1, 0} and {1, 1, 0}. Note that this does not generate new solutions, such things can happen in GAs.

Mutation: As in nature, mutation occurs very infrequently. Accordingly the mutation probability or rate Pm is fixed at a very low value and chances are that it takes place once in thousands of generations. Mutation is realized by flipping the value of a randomly selected gene in a chromosome. Mutation in the present case, if Pm permits, can be effected by randomly selecting one of the three bits representing the genes and flipping its state. For instance the chromosome {0, 1, 0} could mutate to any of {1, 1, 0} or {0, 0, 0} or {0, 1, 1} patterns randomly.

Since, we have not transgressed through many generations we assume mutation will not occur at the moment. Thus the resultant next generation population along with the necessary statistics is shown in the following table.

Resultant solution S_i	F_i
{0, 1, 0}	2
{1, 0, 0}	4
{1, 1, 1}	7
{1, 1, 0}	6
Σ	19
Maximum	7

As can be seen we have hit upon the maximum value of fitness for the chromosome {1, 1, 1}. The procedure has thus yielded the solution {1, 1, 1} indicating that when all units are turned ON, the resulting profit is the highest.

11.5.2 Evolving Neural Networks with GA

Neural networks suffer from some basic drawbacks. Here you see these problems and its solution with GA.

(a) Network topology selection: How do we know that a particular network configuration is the best? Most of the time the network configuration ion is decided based on thumb rule or heuristic pertaining to the problem.

In GA, the search of solution begins with some known solution. In this case, a set of network topologies which are encoded in a chromosome.

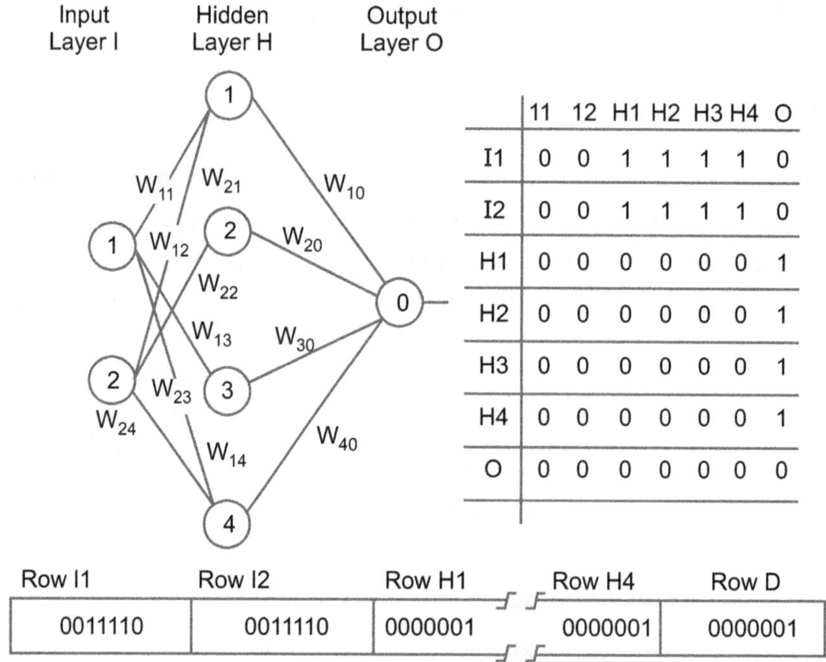

	11	12	H1	H2	H3	H4	O
I1	0	0	1	1	1	1	0
I2	0	0	1	1	1	1	0
H1	0	0	0	0	0	0	1
H2	0	0	0	0	0	0	1
H3	0	0	0	0	0	0	1
H4	0	0	0	0	0	0	1
O	0	0	0	0	0	0	0

Row I1	Row I2	Row H1	Row H4	Row D
0011110	0011110	0000001	0000001	0000001

Fig. 11.1: A typical artificial neural network and a possible method of representing its weights as a chromosome

Above Fig. 11.1 shows the manner in which various neurons in the layer are connected. A '1' indicates a connection while '0' indicates otherwise. Note that use of such a chromosome does limit the search to a finite number of neurons. One may increase the number of layers which will make the chromose to contain longer sequence more the information contained within the chromosome, the more the computational time required to complete the search. Here the chromosome is in place, we need to find a fitness function to evaluate them. A good fitness function should take into account network compactness, accuracy and learning rate. Considering all of them also contributes to computation cost. A simple and effective fitness function can be formulated using the reciprocal of the sum of squares of the errors reported after training the network for a predetermined number of epochs.

With the population size, crossover and mutation probabilities and the number of epochs fixed a priori, the GA can now run by training individual networks using small random number and training patterns. After the fixed number of epochs, the fitness of each network is found and evaluated.

(b) Finding optimal set of weight: One of the serious limitations of the most commonly used back propagation algorithm is that it cannot guarantee an optimal convergence. In quite a few cases, the algorithm manages to provide weights that lead to only a sub-optimal solution. Further there is no method to recover from some local optima. Using GA to find the set of optimal weight can help solve this problem to great extend.

The chromosome here is an ordered chain of weights. It is shown in Fig. 11.2.

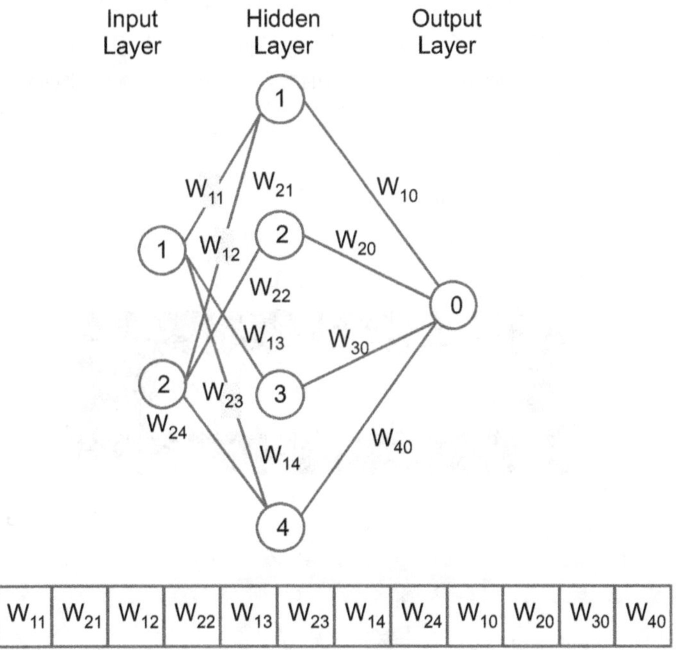

W11	W21	W12	W22	W13	W23	W14	W24	W10	W20	W30	W40

Fig. 11.2: A typical artificial neural network and its corresponding chromosome representation (The darkened lines indicate the gene boundaries)

Here too the reciprocal of the sum of the squares of the error reported after training the network for a predetermined number of epochs could depict the fitness of a set of weights. Crossover can be effected by swapping the gene mutation. It can be effected by randomly adding/subtracting a small value between 0 and 1 from the weight that comprises a randomly selected gene.

11.5.3 ANT Algorithm

Take the example of one of nature's creations-Ants. Ants can trigger our search for new algorithms. Ants are capable of navigating complex terrains in search of food. They also find their way back to the nest. Over a period of time a colony of ants are able to find the best or shortest path between the food source and the nest. So how do they achieve this? As they navigate they keep laying pheromones which tend to modify their environment and serve as a means for communication amongst them in the colony. Pheromones are chemicals that are volatile and give way over a period of time. All ants choose to move over track of high pheromone concentration. In the beginning each ants goes in search of food and as they move, the pheromone is laid along the part. When an ant finds the food source it starts its return journey along the same path and adds to the phenomenon concentration along it. Since, the colour comprises a large number of ants, a parallel search ensures. Chances are that several of them discover the food source through different paths. Naturally, the ant that found the closest path would over a period of time shuttle up and down more number of times than its counterparts. This increases the pheromone concentration of the shortest path and for other ants too to choose it. Over a period of time, only shortest path exists while other paths fade away.

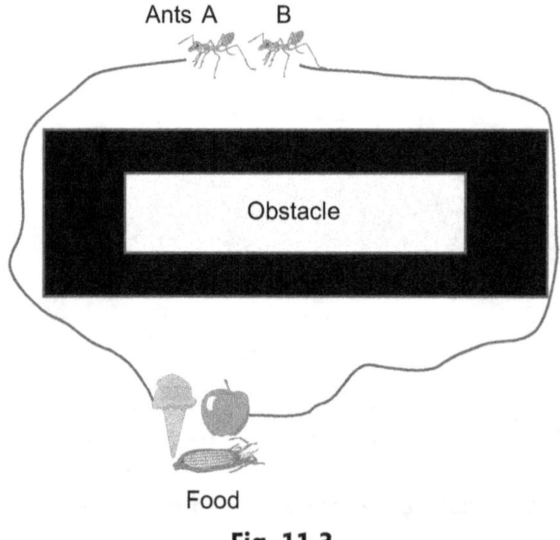

Fig. 11.3

Fig. 11.3 depicts two ants A and B. This algorithm can be easily related to the well known travelling salesman problem. Most efficient and yet simple algorithm may be formulated by looking into nature's vast repositories.

Pheromone Trail and Update

A typical Ant colony optimization algorithm can be used to find the shortest path between a pair of nodes A and B in a simple connected graph G = (N, E) with $|N|$ nodes. A certain amount of pheromone ξ_0 is associated with each arc initially. The movement of the ants is governed by the intensity of the pheromone trail which in turn is updated by the traversing ant(s). The updates done are proportional to the estimated profits gained by the ant. Gains depend on how good the solutions are from the perspective of the ant. Movement from one node to another is decided based on the information about the outgoing arcs. In its simple form the probability of an ant **a** at node **i** taking a path to its next immediate neighbour **j** is given by

O if j does not belong to the set O_i of the immediate neighbours of i

$$P_{ij}^a = \xi_{ij}/\Sigma\xi_{ij}$$

$$j \in O_i$$

Trails are updated by ants by depositing a constant value of pheromone on the arcs every time they traverse it. Thus, as ant moves from node i to node j at time t the value of ξ_{ij} changes to $\xi_{ij}(t) + \Delta\xi$. This tends to increase the probability of the arc being used by other ants to avoid overcrowding due to high pheromone concentration on the sub-optimal paths (leading to a minima in this case), the pheromone is made to evaporate at some rate. Evaporation is modelled as an exponential curve.

$\xi = (1 - r)\xi$, where r is a value chosen in the interval (0, 1).

In the real world ants update their pheromone trails on the fly. In the world of optimization this method may be changed to suit the search domain. Trails could be updated after the ant discovers a solution path. Such trails could be updated based on the fitness of the solution found. The pheromone laid along the path could be proportional to its fitness. This will face other ants to trend along such hopefully better solutions.

11.6 Need and Applications of Artificial Intelligence

The two most fundamental concerns of AI researchers are knowledge representation and search like most sciences. AI is decomposed into a number of subdisciplines that, while sharing an essential approach to problem solving, have concerned themselves with different application.

The following are major application areas of AI:

1. Game Playing:

Most of the early research in state space search was done using common board games such as checkers, chess and the 8-puzzle.

Most games played use well-defined set of rules, this makes it easy to generate the search space and frees the researcher from many ambiguities and complexities inherent in the less structured problem.

The board configuration used in playing these games are easily represented on a computer, requiring none of the complex formalisms needed to capture the semantic subtleties of more complex problem domain.

Game-playing programs, inspite of their simplicity, offer their own challenges, including an opponent moves may not be reliably anticipated.

2. Automated Reasoning and Theorem Proving:

Automatic theorem proving is the oldest branch of artificial intelligence. A wide variety of problems can be attacked by representing the problem description and relevant background information as logical axioms and treating problem instances as theorems to be proved. Automatic theorem systems are not capable of solving extremely complex problems independently without human assistance.

3. Expert Systems:

Expert knowledge is a combination of a theoretical understanding of the problem and a collection of heuristic problem-solving rules that experience has shown to be effective in the domain.

Expert systems are constructed by obtaining this knowledge from a human expert and coding it into a form that a computer may apply to similar problems.

This reliance on the knowledge of a human domain expert for the system's problem-solving strategies is a major feature of the expert systems.

4. Natural Language Understanding and Semantic Modeling:

One of the long-standing goals of artificial intelligence is the creation of programs that are capable of understanding human language. Not only the ability to understand natural language seems to be one of the most fundamental aspects of human intelligence, but also its successful automation would have an incredible impact on the usability and effectiveness of computer themselves. Much efforts has been put into writing programs that understand natural language. Although these programs have achieved success within restricted contexts, systems that can use natural language with the flexibility and generality that characterize human speech are beyond current methodologies.

5. Modelling Human Performance:

The design of systems that explicitly model some aspects of human solving has been the fertile area of research in both artificial intelligence and psychology. Human performance modelling, in addition to providing AI with much of its basic methodology, has proved to be a powerful tool for formulating and testing theories of human cognition.

11.7 SIMULATION

11.7.1 Definitions

(1) A method for implementing a model over time.

(2) A technique for testing, analysis, or training in which real-world systems are used, or where real-world and conceptual systems are reproduced by a model.

(3) An unobtrusive scientific method of inquiry involving experiments with a model, rather than with the portion of reality that the model represents.

(4) A methodology for extracting information from a model by observing the behavior of the model as it is executed.

(5) A non-technical term meaning not real, imitation In sum, simulation is an applied methodology that can describe the behavior of that system using either a mathematical model or a symbolic model. It can be the imitation of the operation of a real-world process or system over a period of time.

11.7.2 Need of Simulation

- Simulation, simulation model, or software model is also used to refer to the software implementation of a model.

- The conduct of a simulation study results in the generation of system performance data, most often in large quantities. These data are stored in a computer system as large arrays of numbers. The process of converting the data into meaningful information that describes the behavior of the system is called analysis. There are numerous techniques and approaches to conducting analysis. The development and use of these techniques and approaches are a function of the branch of mathematics and systems engineering called *operations research*.

- Simulation is often used to identify the better of two alternatives or the best of several alternatives. In such studies, the alternatives are simulated to determine estimated performance, and then the different estimated performances are compared. Since performance is described with samples from a distribution, comparison of performance is not as simple as comparing two numbers. Very sophisticated statistical procedures exist for comparing twosystems and for comparing multiple systems

- Simulation is often used to optimize system performance.

The simulation study includes a number of function:

(1) Design of experiments: The design of a set of simulation experiments suitable for addressing a specific system performance question;

(2) Performance evaluation: The evaluation of system performance, measurement of how it approaches a desired performance level;

(3) Sensitivity analysis: System sensitivity to a set of input parameters;

(4) System comparison: Comparison of two or more system alternatives to derive best system performance with given conditions;

(5) Constrained optimization: Determination of optimum parameters to derive system performance objective.

11.7.3 Tools and Techniques of Simulation

(i) Monte Carlo simulation

It is also called the Monte Carlo method, which randomly samples values from each input variable distribution and uses that sample to calculate the model's output. This process of random sampling is repeated until there is a sense of how the output varies given the random input values. Monte Carlo simulation models system behavior using probabilities.

When setting up a Monte Carlo simulation or employing the Monte Carlo Method, one follows a four-step process. These four steps are:

Step 1   Define a distribution of possible inputs for each input random variable.

Step 2   Generate inputs randomly from those distributions.

Step 3   Perform a deterministic computation using that set of inputs.

Step 4   Aggregate the results of the individual computations into the final result.

While these steps may seem overly simplistic, they are necessary to capture the essence of how Monte Carlo simulations are set up and run.

This four-step method requires having the necessary components in place to achieve the final result. These components may include:

(1)   *Probability distribution functions* (pdfs) for each random variable.

(2)   *A random number generator.*

(3)   *A sampling rule:* A prescription for sampling from the pdfs.

(4)   *Scoring:* A method for combining the results of each run into the final result.

(5)   *Error estimation:* An estimate of the statistical error of the simulation output as a function of the number of simulation runs and other parameters.

(ii) Continuous simulation whereby the system variables are continuous functions of time. Time is the independent variable and the system variables evolve as time progresses. Continuous simulations systems make use of differential equations in developing the model.

(iii) Discrete-event Simulation

It is the simulation tool in which the system variables are discrete functions in time. These discrete functions in time result in system variables that change only at distinct instants of time. The changes are associated with an occurence of a system event. Discrete-event simulations advance time from one event to the next event. This simulation paradigm adheres to queuing theory models. Continuous and discrete-event simulations are dynamic systems with variables changing over time.

(iv) Deterministic Simulation

It takes place when a given set of inputs produce a determined, unique set of outputs. Thus, these simulations include no uncertainty and no variability. Physics-based simulations and engineering simulations can be deterministic simulations. For both deterministic and stochastic simulations, output is determined by input.

(v) Stochastic simulation

It accepts random variables as inputs, which logically lead to random outputs. This type of simulation is more difficult to represent and analyze because appropriate statistical techniques must be used. Thus, these simulations do include uncertainty and variability. Stochastic simulations are common in models for discrete-event systems.

11.7.4 Attributes or Defining Properties / Characteristics of the Simulation

There are three primary descriptors applied to simulation that serve as attributes or defining properties/characteristics of the simulation. These are:

- fidelity,
- resolution, and
- scale.

(i) Fidelity

It is a term used to describe how the model or the simulation closely matches reality. The simulation that closely matches or behaves like the real system it is representing has a high fidelity. Attaining high fidelity is not easy because models can never capture every aspect of a system. Models are built to characterize only the aspects of a system that are to be investigated.

A great degree of effort is made to achieve high fidelity. A low fidelity is tolerated with regard to the components of the system that are not important to the investigation. Similarly, different applications might call for different levels of fidelity. The simulation of the system for thesis research and development may require higher levels of fidelity than a model that is to be used for training.

Often, the term fidelity is used incorrectly with *validity* to express the accuracy of the representation. Only validity conveys three constructs of accuracy of the model:

    (1) **Reality:** How the model closely matches reality
    (2) **Representation:** Some aspects are represented, some are not
    (3) **Requirements:** Different levels of fidelity required for different applications.

(ii) Resolution

It is also known as granularity, is the degree of detail with which the real world is simulated. The more detail included in the simulation, the higher the resolution. A simple illustration would be the simulation of an orange tree. A simulation that represents an entire grove would prove to have a much lower resolution of the trees than a simulation of a single tree. Simulations can go from low to high resolution. Return to the example of the tree: The model can begin with a representation of the entire forest, then a model of an individual tree, then a model of that individual tree ' s fruit, with a separate model of each piece of fruit in varying stages of maturity.

(iii) Scale

It is the size of the overall scenario or event the simulation represents; this is also known as level. Logically, the larger the system or scenario, the larger the scale of the simulation. Take for example a clothing factory. The simulation of a single sewing machine on the factory floor would consist of a few simulation components, and it would require the representation of only a few square feet of the entire factory. Conversely, a simulation of the entire factory would require representations of all machines, perhaps hundreds of simulation components, spread out over several hundred thousand square feet of factory space. Obviously, the simulation of the single sewing machine would have a much smaller scale than the simulation of the entire factory.

ASSOCIATED TOPICS IN ROBOTICS

11.8 Maintenance and Safety

Introduction:

In automated production, to a greater extent than before a contribution of maintenance is being required by a new design solutions involving robotics in order to increase availability and reliability of manufacturing system. Characteristic features of new manufacturing techniques are increasing interrelation of workstations by means of handling and storage, incorporation of robots into handling and production operations including assembly. Analysis have shown that both the degree of complexity of machines and plants and the degree of linkage lead to increasing downtimes. If this tendency is not counteracted by new and more comprehensive measures of maintenance, degradation will continue and will ultimately affect the efficiency and productivity of the robotized production system.

Industrial robots have high power movement and are freely programmable with regard to routes and speed of movement. Accident hazards arise because even when behaving as planned, it is not usually possible for an outsider or predict the next movement. Errors, for example, in the position control or in the speed monitoring can produce completely unpredictable movements with undefined speed within the kinematically possible range of movement, with conventions machines movement usually take place within the machine whereas with industrial robots working space and maximum range of movement are not immediately recognizable. Therefore, precautions must be taken to safeguard the hazardous zone.

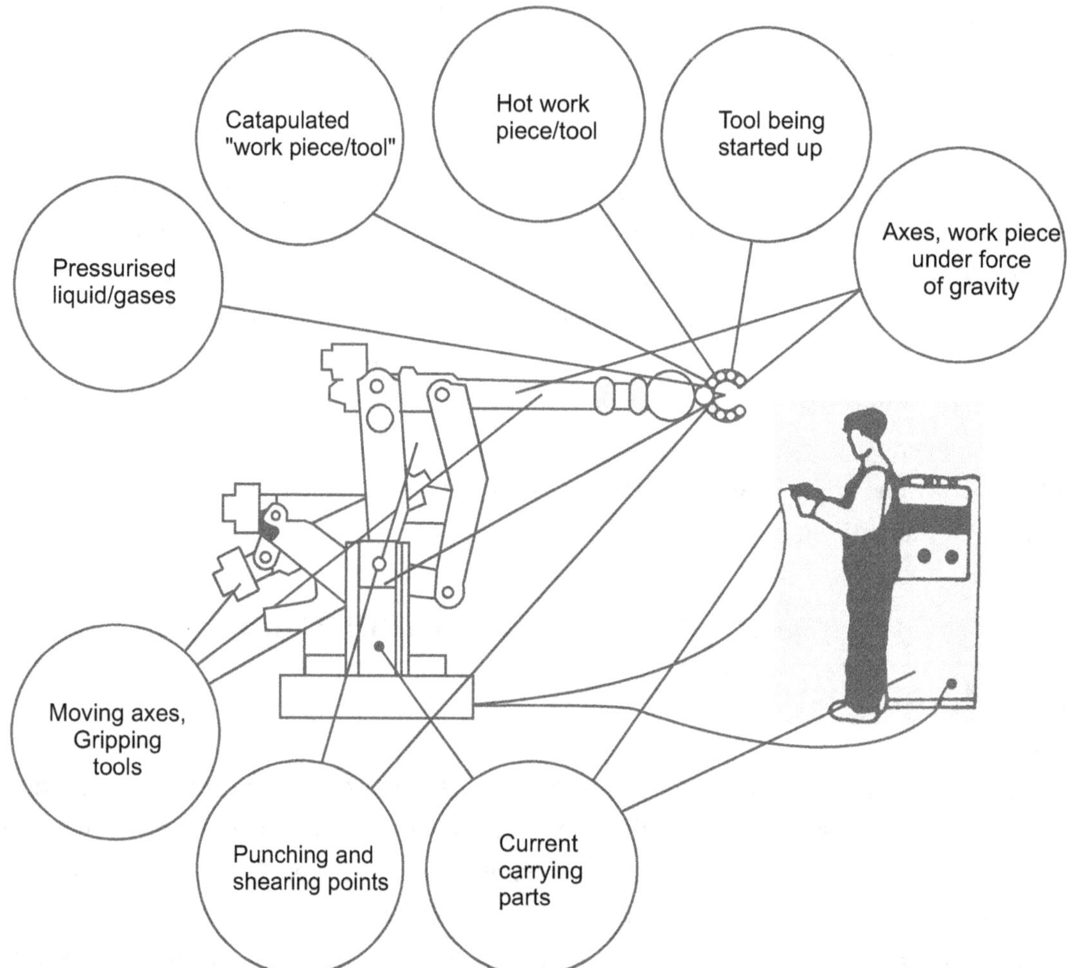

Fig. 11.4: Type and location of hazards when robots are used

Risks Specific to Robots :

These can be classified as:

(i)   Collision between man and robot.

(ii)   Danger from projecting components.

(iii)   Wedging, jamming.

(iv)   Unforeseen commencement of motion.

(v)   Others, such as burns, type of radiation (laser source), electric arcs etc.

Some of the sources for the above risks may include:
(i)   Bad design of man/machine system.
(ii)   Necessary entry into a non-authorised area.
(iii)   Deliberate neutralizing of safety mechanisms.
(iv)   The guards fail to fulfil their safety functions.
(v)   The emergency stop is not sufficiently rapid for safety purposes.

Robot Maintenance:

Perhaps no other single factor in manufacturing operation has been neglected, misunderstood and mismanaged as maintenance. If you intend to have the best system available, then see that you have the best maintenance programme. Poorly maintained equipments/systems results in poor quality products, disrupted production schedules, delayed deliveries and lost customers etc. Degradation can only be minimized by proper maintenance.

Most robots required relatively little maintenance but what is specified is essential to continue performance and longevity. From maintenance point of view, a robot can be looked upon as being made up of three major elements/parts.

(a) Manipulator:

It is the functional structure that physically performs the task and is a jointed mechanical device driven by some source of power. These are made up of linkages and gears, drive belts or chains, various typse of bearings etc. Some of the points that require consideration include:
(i)   Periodic visual and/for operational checks for required adjustment needed, if any.
(ii)   Sign of undue wear and part replacement as per manufacturers check list and corrective instructions.
(iii)   Extreme care to avoid contamination in the fluid media.
(iv)   Adequate means for water separation e.g. water separator directly at the inlet to the machine.
(v)   Regular attention for lubrication points.

(b) Controls:

The controls are either electrical, electronic or pneumatic. The required maintenance procedures for control and memory will vary widely depending on the particular design and complexity. In general, maintenance will involve:
(i)   Functional checks for manual controls and switches.
(ii)   Electrical/electronic adjustments.
(iii)   Observations regarding potential fraying of wires and cables and the condition of connections and connectors.
(iv)   Servo control setting regarding acceleration, deceleration and velocity parameters.

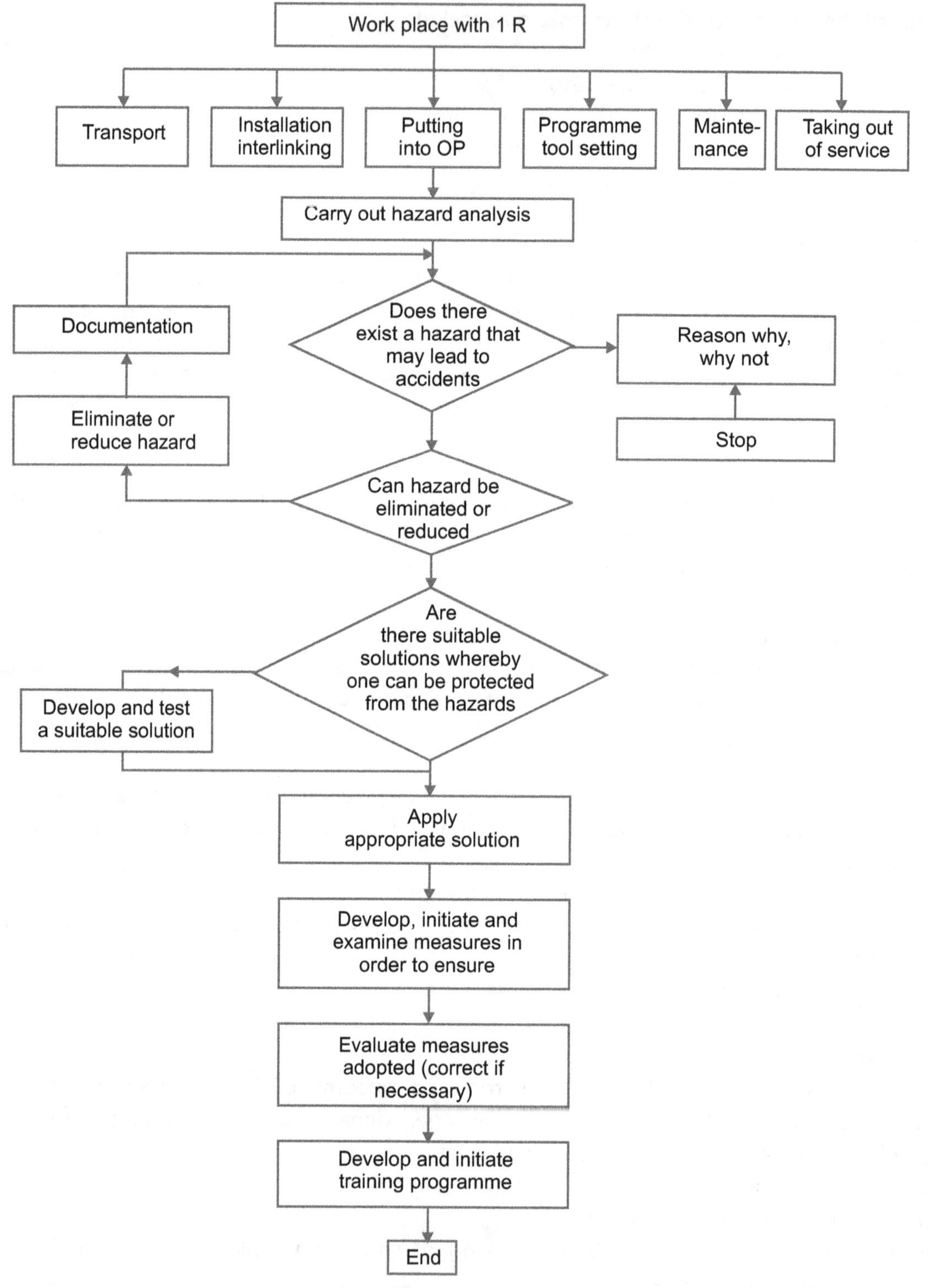

Fig. 11.5: Accident prevention procedure

(c) End of arm toolings:

It is critical element in the reliability chain and these toolings vary from application to application. In all cases, design should provide dependability for robots reliability and performance. Regular maintenance is critical, the nature of which will depend on the particular tool. Worn parts should be replaced. Regular lubrication may be required.

Maintenance is a business and should run like a business. See Table 11.1. Available data indicate that an annual maintenance cost is about 10 to 12% of their acquisition cost for industrial robots. Lack of understanding about robot maintenance programmes creates a threatening atmosphere. For upper management it is the threat of a bad investment for manufacturing engineers, it is the threat of technological complexities, for production managers, it is the threat of lost production and delayed shipments and so on.

These threats can be substantially eliminated by good communication regarding what is being planned and why it is needed.

Table 11.1: Indicate a plan for maintenance check list

Sr. No.	Description	Check : Yes/No
1.	Get involved with the project at start.	
2.	Plan for training.	
3.	Identify required skills.	
4.	Execute training plan.	
5.	Involve personnel at installation.	
6.	Develop and co-ordinate the plan.	
7.	Provision for spare parts, tools etc.	
8.	Develop work documentation plan.	

Robot Safety Systems:

With reference to Fig. 11.6, levels of safety zones are:

Level 1:   Workstation perimeter penetration.

Level 2A: Area within the workstation but outside the reach of the robot.

Level 2B: Area within the workstation but within the reach of the robot.

Level 3:   A small volume surrounding the robot arm which moves with the arm.

Level 1: Protection is often obtained by the case of wire fencing which not only keeps out unauthorized personal but also protects personal from flying projectiles if the robot should loss its grip on an object or a part should break into pieces, safety at level 2 and 3 has been much harder to implement and still are being developed.

In order to have an idea of risk zone concept of three zone could be identified in desending order of risk-red, orange, yellow. Operting zone of the robot being the highest risk becomes the red zone. The area covered by the MRE but outside the OZ becomes orange. All other areas within the perimeter guarding of the installation will then be designated as yellow. Refer Fig. 11.6.

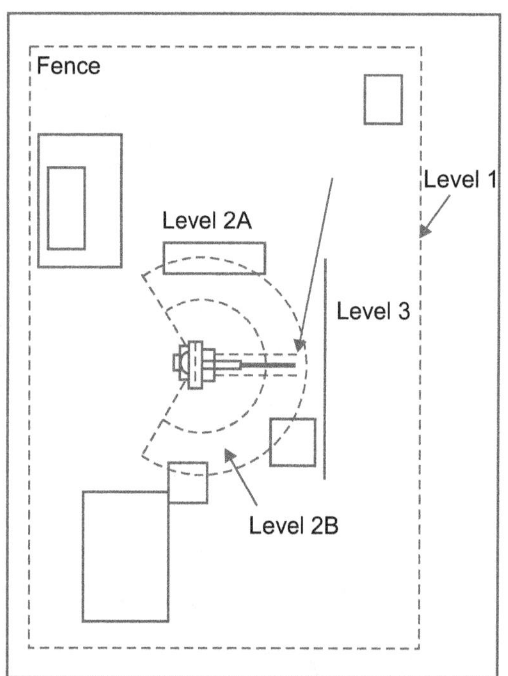

Fig. 11.6: Safety zones and levels

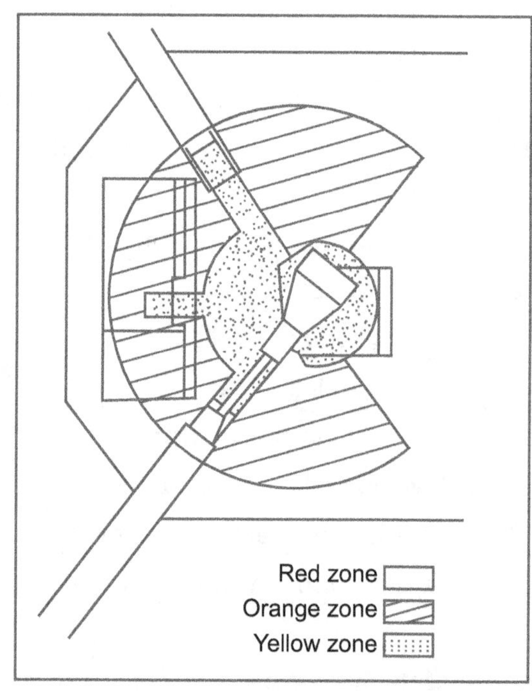

Fig. 11.7: Risk zones in robotic cells

Present State of Safety Technology:

So far, inspite of differently oriented problems, conventional safety technology has been used. Some of the techniques or technologies used are:

(a) Fencing:

It is by far the most widely used safety device and will continue to be used in near future, because,

    (i)   It is usually simple to produce.

    (ii)   It provides inexpensive protection outside the fencing.

    (iii)   It provides protection against thrown away parts.

For most installation this type of guarding fence should be a minimum of 2.0 m high with a mesh of maximum 50 mm square to prevent hand from entering the robot area. The general construction of perimeter fences usually consists of regular sized panels made up of a box section or angle section with either weldmesh or solid screen panels in between. The panels are usually fixed in place between suitably mounted pillars. This type of guarding allows for easy construction and layout of access doors. When using this type of barrier the following considerations may be taken into account.

(i)   It may be difficult to transport parts of components into the robot cell. e.g. car bodies or engine sub-frames for welding, front and rear windscreen for assembly into the car aperture.

(ii)   Sliding doors and work loading hatches are needed to provide adequate access for equipment, materials and maintenance requirement.

(iii)   Door safety interlocking systems are required to stop or hold the robot whenever the doors or hatches are accessed. There are many different types of interlocking switches available varying from magnetic to microswitch operation.

(iv)   Wire mesh is difficult to see through, particularly for long periods of time. If the operator is required to implement many visual checks, it may be necessary to replace the mesh with toughered perpex window.

(v)   Fixed fencing does not provide the ultimate in ensuring the safety of workers. To be commercially viable, sophisticated and expensive robot installation must function to their fullest production capacity and to achieve this they must be provided with equally sophisticated and efficient safety systems geared to this objective.

(b) Photoelectric guarding:

With development in technology and the need to remain competitive, the invisible safeguards commonly known as light barriers, light curtains or photo-electric cells can be used.

Light barriers are defined as electro-sensitive means which may be used as:

(i)   A trip device which stops moving machinery when the beam is broken.

(ii) A presence sensing device to detect the presence of a person or object in the restricted area by interrupting the beam.

Depending on the restricted or danger area to be guarded, PE cells be positioned vertically, horizontally at an angle or in any combination of these modes. They may be installed on machinery where danger to persons will not arise from interruption of the beam i.e. all dangerous movements are stopped before contact can be made with the dangerous parts. Fig. 11.8 shows a safety light curtain.

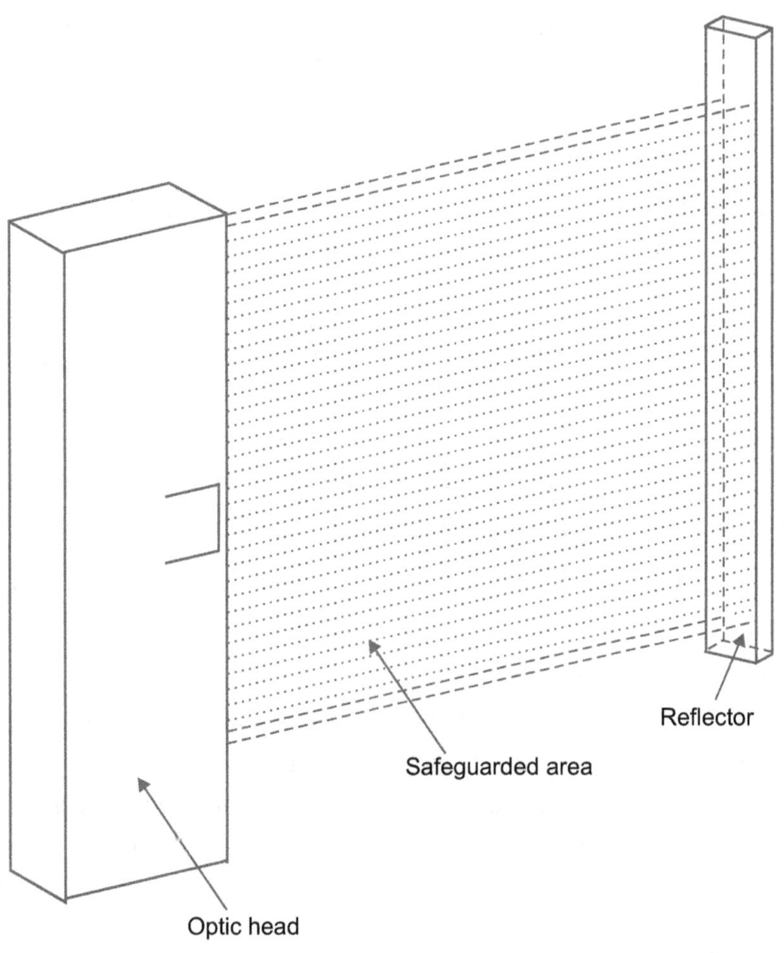

Fig. 11.8: Safety light curtain consisting of optic head and reflector

Fig. 11.9 shows the complete track of car spot welding station covered by light curtains.

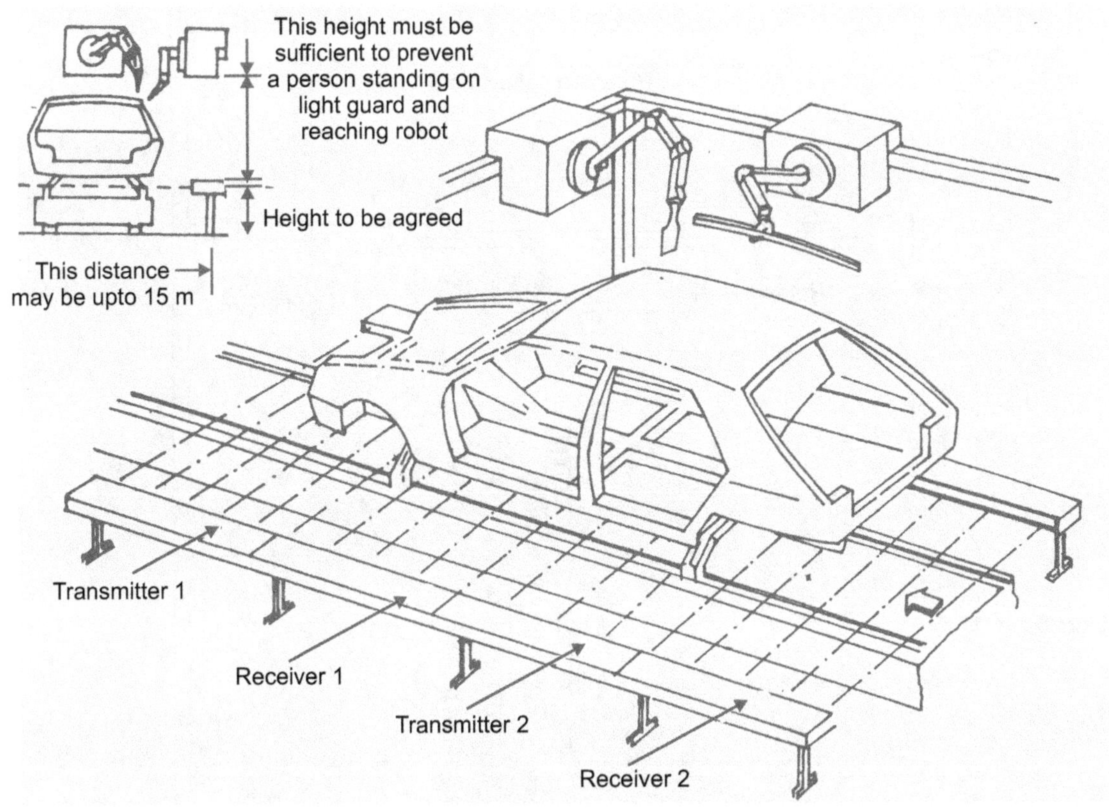

Fig. 11.9: Light curtains covering the complete track of car spot welding station

(c) Safety mats:

The guarding of dangerous machinery with mechanical guards is not always possible or practical. In some processes, such guards can severely limit accessibility to the machine, and can often restrict visibility. They can also reduce production rates.

One solution therefore, is to use safety mats placed in dangerous access ways, which will switch off the machine when some one steps into those areas.

Fig. 11.10 shows the arrangement of robot welding station comprising a welding robot and a rotary table to allow components to be fed into the cell along with typical safety barriers.

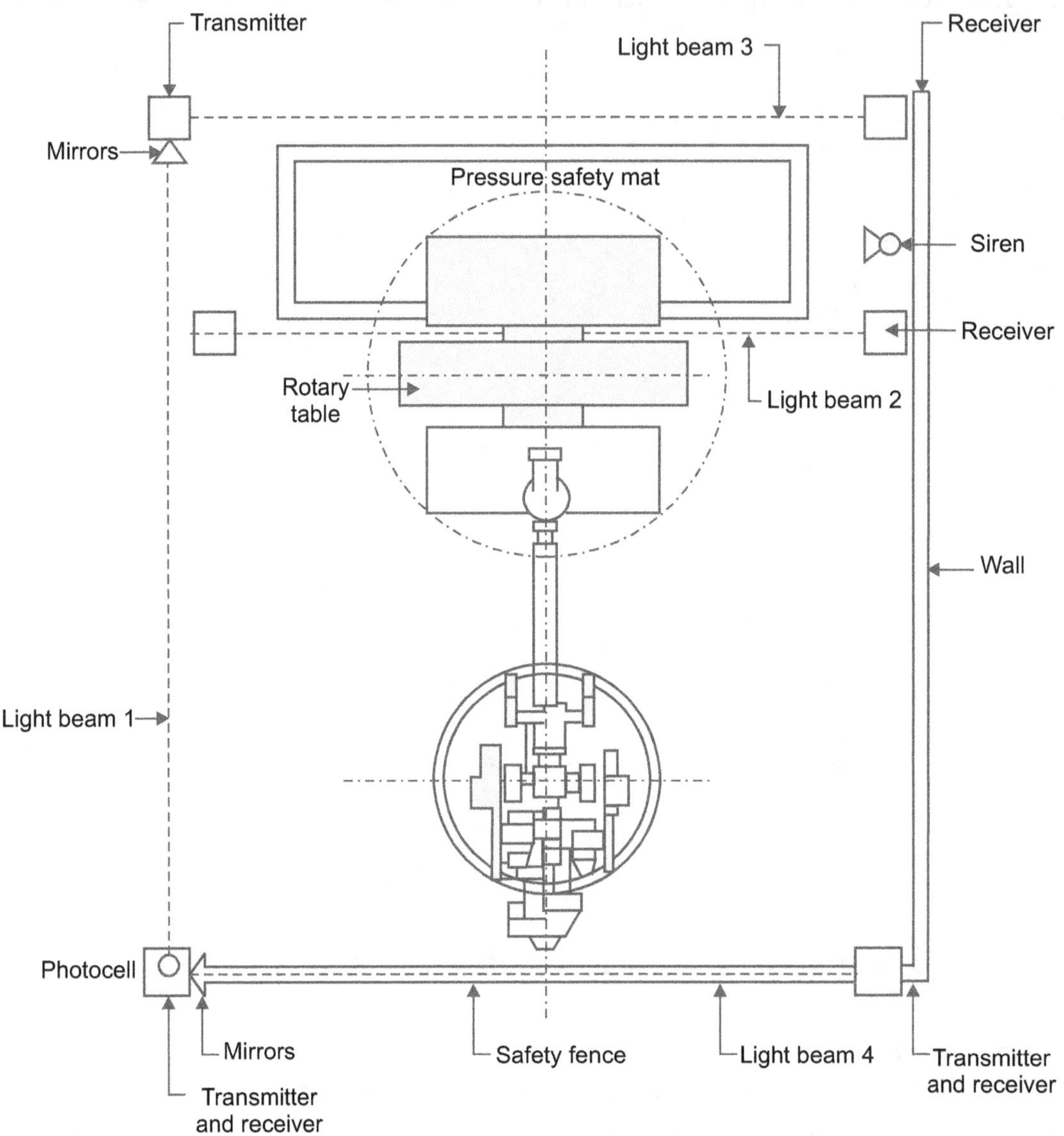

Fig. 11.10: Safety barriers for robot welding station

11.9 New Trends and Recent Updates in Robotics

Intelligent robots will offer novel chances in various ways and for different areas. The subsequent selection of applications gives some comments on the chances offered:

(i) Robots for the extension of the human work range are being used in areas such as space, underwater, and the micro- and nano- world.

(ii)   Robots for the alleviation of humans from hard or dangerous work will be used as intelligent tools in complex environments. Examples are machinery for construction work, in tunnelling, sewage channeling and cleaning, waste disposal, de-mining, de-construction of nuclear power-plants.

(iii)   Service robots, serving humans for making life easier, will be built for delivery services in office environments and hospitals, cleaning, or lawn mowing. An economic profit is difficult to assess, as they are most often directly competing with relatively cheap and still somewhat attractive human labor.

(iv)   Edutainment-robots (for education and entertainment) will probably be the first ones to introduce advanced concepts of "intelligence". They have the advantage that malfunctions usually do not endanger the user and are of no serious economic consequences, and that they are therefore very suitable to try out novel ideas, even in mass production. Playing football with robots is just one of the most popular topics in this field. It is typical that computer games are increasingly integrating artificial intelligence into their programmes as demonstrated for example by the game "Republic – The Revolution".

(v)   Medical techniques are a dominant research area in robotics today. It includes prostheses for limbs and hands, artificial organs for audio and vision sensing, other techno-implants, surgery robot assistants, in particular for endoscopic surgery, robot helping assistants for handicapped, for rehabilitation, or for the aged to enable them to stay in their familiar environment as long as possible.

Embedded robotics is an extension of machine-oriented robotics to systems. Applications range from 'cartronics', 'domotronics', to medical systems, and to advanced man-machine-interfaces making use of wearable computing equipment.

Robotics is a key science of this century. The development of robots into "intelligent" machines and systems will offer chances, however, challenges will have to be overcome. Intelligent robots should be able to communicate with users and work as intelligent tools in a co-operative way in the same work-space. The paper presents some aspects and results discussed by a study group on robotics, consisting of experts from engineering and natural sciences, philosophy, medicine, and legal science on "Perspectives on human ways of acting in future society". It will comment on robot intelligence, on expected benefits of future robot technology, as well as on socio-economic, legal and ethical constraints.

Here, "intelligence", and in particular the intelligence of robots, has been defined in a rather anthropocentric way, according to the needs of humans co-operating with such robots and using them as intelligent tools. Subsequently, trends and expected benefits of such intelligent robots are addressed.

Technology related to and growing from robotics has been discussed. It includes areas such as mechatronics, automotive concepts, micro- and nanotechniques, smart machine technology, soft computing, embedded robotics, and dynamics and control of complex, bio-inspired motion systems.

Relations to biology and neuro-science play an important role in defining robotics trends, and in giving an answer to the question: will humans be replaced by robots some day? The arguments converge to the conclusion that humans will make use of advanced robotics tools in an evolutionary way.

The relation between man and machine will be a most important issue. It will require efforts in the technology of communication, and in the discussion of socio-economic, legal and ethical issues.

On one side, communication will make use of the progress of classical tools for communicating with computers. In addition, the non-linguistic communication, the information transfer through motion and gesture, through emotional expressions and the phenomenology of humanoids, will support the information flow between man and machine and lead to some kind of "understanding". Progress will come through edutainment robots.

Socio-economic aspects will come up in allocating work between man and machine. Suggestions are being made for the simultaneous optimization of "Man, Techniques and Organization". Examples for allocating authority, the decision making, in joint tasks of man and machine are shown.

The classical objective of robotics, to build a robot which can work autonomously and which can do the work of man, is undergoing a change of paradigm: Instead of building machines that can do the work of humans, we should build machines that can do the work which humans cannot do, or do not want to do. A robot definition which considers this trend to intelligent machinery is given.

In such a complex, far reaching and promising area as robotics it is unavoidable that ethical and legal constraints have to be set. Ideas and suggestions are briefly presented, including some philosophical comments on the indiscriminate use of anthropological terms such as 'conscience', 'autonomy', 'behaviour', which can lead to a failure of appreciation of basic differences between man and machine and to problematic lines of reasoning.

A classification of potential applications for intelligent robots and the chances offered by them is listed. The actual state of the art is shown e.g. by some examples, referring to nano-manipulation, a human leg prosthesis, and by looking at developments in the medical area.

11.10 Economical Justification of Robot Design

With the basic knowledge of industrial applications of robots in mind, it is important that each robot application be evaluated, both technically and economically. This section provides a checklist to aid in the technical evaluation along with a strategy for economic justification of the application of a robot. In addition, since the decision to use or not to use a robot also requires non-monetary factors, a "qualitative" justification section is included.

1. Technical justification for potential applications

Though robots are capable of performing many tasks, the complexity involved with using a robot for a specific application may require considerable time and effort in the setup stages to justify deployment of the robot. Each application should be evaluated on a case by case basis, based on the complexity of the application, the run length and the costs involved.

To evaluate the use of robot for a particular application a checklist is given in Table 1.1. The checklist is based on factors such as requirements for the application, the physical environment for the application and the operational strategies that influence the application.

To use the checklist in Table 11.2, read the propositions and then grade the answer to each question in terms of a five point scale with 1 for 'strongly disagree' to 5 for 'strongly disagree'. Based on the grade points awarded to the questions in the checklist compute an overall score. This overall score can be an indicator for making the decision.

Table 11.2: Checklist for evaluating robot applications

	Application Requirements	
A.1	Monotonous/Repetitive operation.
A.2	Medium complex operation (based on required positioning and orientation moves which must be done to complete operation).
A.3	No complex judgement or decision-making required.
A.4	Cycle time is greater than 3 seconds.
A.5	Need to position and orient part or tool.
A.6	Shape, size or features change from piece to piece.
A.7	Require high positioning repeatability/accuracy.
A.8	Large payloads.
A.9	Need to move to multiple positions or through points which are path developed.
	Physical Environment	
B.1	Work station is well organized (orderly and repeatable).
B.2	Production volume 7,20,000 and 10,00,000 pieces/year.
B.3	Hazardous environment.
B.4	Motion of robot need not be co-ordinated with other machines.
B.5	Machines in workstation can receive parts automatically.
B.6	Machines in workstation need not communicate with robot.

An overall score greater than 50 out of a maximum of 75 clearly favours the application of robot for the task. It is also possible to give weight to various propositions and a weighted overall score can be computed. Also some propositions may be very vital for the application and a score of 1 or 2 in them may be a deciding factor for the Yes/No answer. For example, if the answer to proposition "No complex judgement or decision-making required" is "strongly disagree" (a grade point score 1), the decision may be not to go for use of robot for the application. Similarly, if the user finds that many of the scores associated with the answer are 3 or less the use of robots for the application should be reconsidered. A cost analysis should precede the decision in favour of robot use.

2. Economic Aspects

Cost is a single parameter commonly used for quantitative justification because it is possible to convert most of the quantifiable parameters into costs. The savings that accrue as a result of application of robots in manufacturing processes are the negative costs. When trying to cost justify the deployment of a robot, it is important to calculate the costs and savings over the lifetime of the robot. Typically, it is not possible to justify a robot to replace a human worker based purely on cost comparisons for one operation. Instead, cost justifying the robot requires evaluating the return on investment of the robot over the life of the robot and how quickly the robot would payback the investment. Note that much of the "savings" is in non-traditional areas such as quality improvement. As a guide, Table 11.3 contains many of the costs and savings involved in the use of a robot.

Table 11.3: Significant costs and savings involved in the deployment of robot

Costs involved
Robot and its peripherals
Tooling
Installation
Layout changes
Equipment modifications
Maintenance
Safety equipment
Training
Application engineering
Potential Savings Areas
Labour
Increase in production
Reduced scrap, raw material
Manual tooling
Supervision
Worker training costs
Energy savings
Supplies and materials needed by operator
Increase in production capacity
In-process and finished inventories.

The cost justification process must take into consideration additional costs such as:

- Cost of maintaining the robot system.
- Cost of redesigning the product so that it can be robotically worked on.
- Cost of redesigning the manufacturing system.
- Cost of adding other support equipment that would be used by the robot to perform the application.

Standard methods of economic analysis like break-even analysis, present worth, return on investment etc. can be used for detailed economic analysis and arriving at an answer.

3. Qualitative Justification

To justify a robot for a manufacturing application, many factors come into play. Several of these are not traditionally economically based, but instead apply to issues such as quality and safety. The justification for applications of robots should also consider these qualitative factors to arrive at a conclusion. Some of the qualitative factors that must be evaluated when deciding whether or not to use a robot for a particular application are the following.

Quality:

Consistency of quality is one of the main reasons for deployment of robots in manufacturing process. It is difficult but possible to quantify quality and cost of quality. For example, in applications where the robot is applying adhesives, paint or lubricants etc. robot can consistently apply the same amount of material on each part. The increase in quality can be measured in terms of lower scrap rates, less raw material use and more consistent parts.

Productivity:
A robot may not be better than a human operator in performing the task once but the robot can maintain a constant speed and quality when performing the task repetitively. A robot never gets sick or needs to rest. It can work tirelessly 24 hours a day – 7 days a week or 365 days a year. It is called 24/7 or 24/365 worker. This results in productivity increase that may be directly measurable through increased production quantities. Use of robots also reduces dependency on human labour and gives better delivery schedules, improved customer relations and goodwill. These benefits are difficult to quantify.

Hazards:
Using a robot for certain application eliminates the need for a human operator to interact with dangerous material, hazardous environment or hazardous conditions such as radioactive materials, hot workpieces, heavy loads, excessive noise, or toxic gases. The cost of hazard for a human operator is difficult to quantify.

Flexibility:
Deployment of robots increases the flexibility of the product mix, production schedule and production volume that can be processed in a workcell. The increased flexibility is a definite advantage but is difficult to quantify.

4. Robot Safety

A robotic system is an integration of robots, machines, computerized information channels and human beings, where no element can be considered perfect or immune from eventual failure and malfunction. Since the humans work rather close to the robots, this increases the risk of mutual damage. All these factors necessitate the formulation of safety guidelines that indicate how the conditions of conflict can be minimized. Only when all the system components are functioning safely and reliably, the high productivity levels associated with the robotic systems can be realized.

The humans can be divided into 5 groups that are at risk of direct injury from a robot.

1. **Workers:** A robot is deployed in the industry for specific application. There will be human workers in close vicinity of the robot for doing tasks invariably overshooting into the work space of the robot. These workers are at the greatest risk of getting injured.

2. **Programmers:** A robot programmer using online programming method is in direct contact with the robot. This closeness with the robot's work envelops has its inherent danger of injury.

3. **Maintenance Engineers:** A maintenance engineer is also in direct contact and is at risk from the same dangers as programmers. Additionally, because maintenance procedures often require that safety interlocks be disconnected, the inherent risk is greater for the maintenance engineer.

4. **Casual Observers:** The casual observer is inquisitive, if the robot is not rigidly guarded, then a casual observer may move towards a robot that looks stationary and be injured when it continues or resumes its operation.

5. **Others outside the assumed danger zone:** Components manipulated by robot can slip or flyout the grippers and strike persons well outside the assumed danger zone of the robot if the surrounding area is not properly secured.

In a practical sense, safety procedures and devices allow the authorized entry of humans into a robot's working envelope with minimum risk of injury. Hardware devices and sensors would monitor all anticipated reasonable access to a robot's work envelope, safety devices make use of physical safeguards available in a variety of forms. Some of them are:

- Some contact microswitches.
- Restrained keys to the access doors.
- Pressure mats.
- Infrared light beams or light barriers.
- Vision systems.

11.11 Future Scope for Robotisation

The advances in robotics technology are not directed only for its use in industries. There has been almost a parallel growth of robotics technology in non-industrial environments. Robots are finding their way into research laboratories, energy plants, agriculture, hospitals, space, homes, textiles, services, education etc. It may be sometimes difficult to classify a particular application into whether it is industrial or non-industrial.

The applications of robots are only limited by the need and imagination of the developer and the user. Robots have almost invaded in every walk of life. Different applications of robots in some diverse segments are listed below. This list is in no way exhaustive.

Home Sector:

Science fiction stories always considered robots as domestic slaves. This is going to be a reality in near future, though many of the current domestic applications are not much more than expensive toys. Some of the domestic applications possible are:

- Sweeping and cleaning.
- Cooking.
- Entertainment.
- Replacing pets.
- Garden maintenance.
- Security.

Health Care:

The use of robots in human health care has a wide scope. Robotic technology is in use and is going to expand in health care for:

- Patient care and monitoring.
- Surgery.
- Rehabilitation: Prosthetic limbs and robotic wheel chairs.

Micro-robots can be injected into the human body to perform microsurgery.

Service Sector:

Service sector can carry out diverse functions like:

- Traffic control.
- Fire fighting.
- Drive a vehicle.
- Sweep office rug, classrooms, streets.
- Manage shopping malls.
- Serve food in restaurant.
- Maintenance and repair.
- Disaster recovery.

Agriculture and Farms:

Robot's use in agriculture and farming sector is very much limited today but is going to increase. They can be used to

- plough fields, sow seeds and transplant sapling etc.
- pluck, sort and pack fruits.
- breed livestock.
- animal shearing.

Research and Exploration:

With the help of robots, research in many inaccessible areas have been possible because of their greater capabilities to face hazardous environments and remote handling capabilities.

These include:

- Space exploration.
- Under sea exploration.
- Nuclear research.
- Geological exploration.

The list of tasks given above for different sectors can be explained further to include following. A robot should:

- Play football, cricket, etc.
- Knit a sweater.
- Change a tire, repair a puncture.
- Dispense gasoline.
- Dance.
- Play musical instruments.
- Polish diamonds.
- Make paintings.
- Talk and listen.

Robots have many potential applications other than material handling, assembly, etc. in

- Pharmaceutical industry.
- Textile industry.
- Chemical industry.
- Mining industry.
- Construction industry.
- Energy sector.

EXERCISES

1. Define Artificial Intelligence. Explain the areas of particular importance of Artificial Intelligence.

2. Discuss in brief various techniques of Artificial Intelligence.

3. Explain need of Artificial Intelligence in the present scenario.

4. Discuss in brief role of Artificial Intelligence with reference to various applications.

5. Define simulation. Explain need of simulation.

6. State various functions of simulation study.

7. Discuss tools and techniques of simulation.

8. Explain maintenance and safety aspects of robots.

9. Discuss recent trends in robotics.

10. Explain "Economical justification of robot design" in brief.

11. Discuss future scope for robotisation.

12. Write short notes on :

    (i)   AI Problems

    (ii)   Genetic algorithm

    (iii) Artificial neural network

    (iv)   ANT algorithm

    (v)   Simulation techniques

    (vi)   Characteristics of simulation.

APPENDIX
ROBOTMASTER (ROBOT PROGRAMMING & SIMULATION)

Robotmaster is a software which is seamlessly integrates robot programming, simulation and code generation inside Mastercam, delivering quicker robot programming.

Getting the most out of robots

Using Robots for Manufacturing

With Robotmaster, manufacturers can program robots quickly and efficiently, using Mastercam's industry proven CAD/CAM software technology. Driven by the growing trend towards lean and flexible manufacturing, robots are progressively replacing conventional dedicated manufacturing units, such as CNC milling machines. Robots, once typically perceived as only positioning devices have advanced in accuracy and rigidity, and are now being used increasingly for manufacturing and material removal. Using robots, manufacturers are producing higher quality products at lower cost, and are achieving the speed and flexibility they need to challenge their competitors throughout the world.

According to the International Federation of Robotics, as of 2007 over 950,000 robots have been installed for industrial applications worldwide, and an additional 100,000 are being sold every year. While many companies currently using CNC machines have been exploring the opportunity of manufacturing with the use of robots, they have been limited by a lack of time and cost-effective programming tools. Currently less than 1% of robots are programmed using CAD/CAM (computer aided design and manufacturing) software because of a lack of mature robot programming solutions. Robotmaster eliminates this barrier.

Robotmaster delivers:
- Cost-efficiency and flexibility of robots coupled with the ease of programming of Mastercam.
- Programming of robots from CAD/CAM software as easy as CNC machine programming.
- A sure way to beat the competition – worldwide – on cost, flexibility and response time.

Revolutionary CAD/CAM Approach to Robot Programming Robotmasters strong background in CAM (Computer Aided Manufacturing) software has enabled it to bring a revolutionary approach to robot programming. Unlike the wide range of software claiming to offer off-line programming for robots that are truly only simulation tools with very limited programming capability. Robotmaster delivers easy programming of precise tool motion control and quick generation of long tool path trajectories with minimal programmer intervention.

Robotmaster uses mature CAD/CAM software technologies to program robots with the same flexibility and speed as software used for programming CNC machine tools. Conventional off-line programming solutions are based on either a very cumbersome and tedious point to point programming approach or a post-processor solution that offers very little flexibility and functionality.

Robotmaster CAD/CAM Programming:

- Generates more profit with your robot. Robotmaster generates programs off-line and eliminates lost production time during programming.
- Enables your robot for short production runs. Robotmaster shrinks programming time from day to hours by generating robot control code directly from CAD/CAM tools.
- Delivers closest conformance to design. Robotmaster creates simple or complex robot trajectories accurately without teaching points.

Integrated Programming Solution

Robotmaster seamlessly integrates programming, simulation and code generation inside the Mastercam platform. The multi-software approach of conventional off-line programming solutions forces the use of one software for CAD/CAM programming, another for converting trajectories to robot positions and finally a third to simulate and validate the programmed trajectories.

Robotmaster Integrated Solution

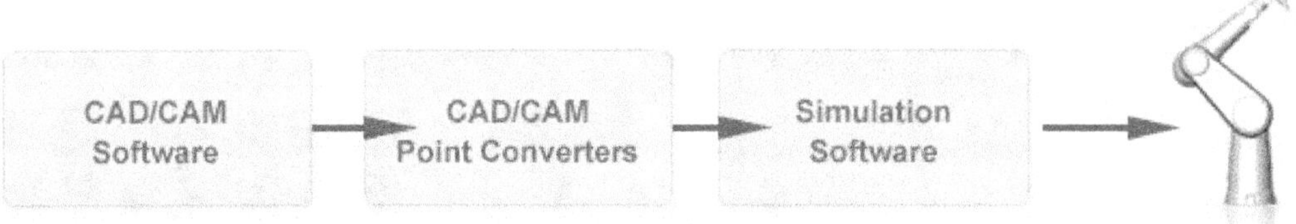

CAD/CAM Interface

Powerful Part Modeling

Streamlined CAD engine makes design work easier than ever before. Each piece of geometry you create is "live", letting you quickly modify it until it's exactly what you want. Traditional functions are consolidated into a few simple clicks to simplify the creation of even the most complex parts.

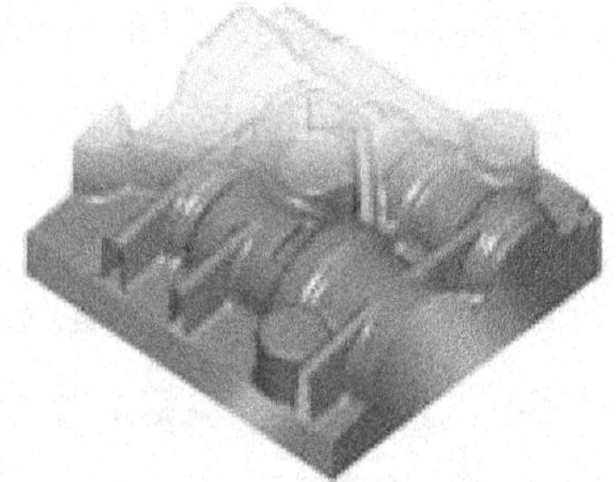

Wireframe, surface and solid modeling

OR Import CAD model

Alternatively the part may be created using other CAD software and the model may be imported either directly in your choice of native or neutral file formats. Data translators are available for IGES, Parasolid®, SAT (ACIS solids), AutoCAD® (DXF, DWG, and Inventor TM files), SolidWorks®, Solid Edge®, STEP, EPS, CADL, STL, VDA, and ASCII, CATIA®, Pro/E®, and more.

CAD/CAM Based Programming

Create simple or complex robot trajectories accurately without teaching points using Mastercam Mill or Router. The programming of the robot trajectory is done graphically using the same process and tools used for CNC machines, by selecting geometry (lines, arcs, part edges and/or 3D part). Once the geometry is selected, parameter boxes guide the user in making the proper selection of process information. The software automatically generates the robot trajectory based on the above information.

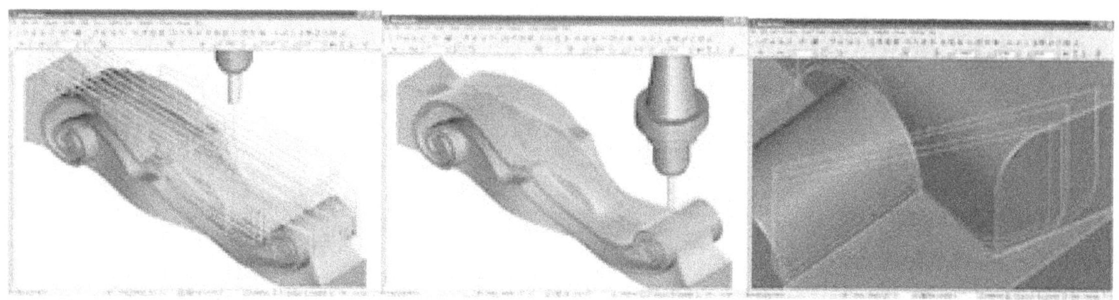

Flexible finishing   **Automated material removal**   **Leftover re-machining**

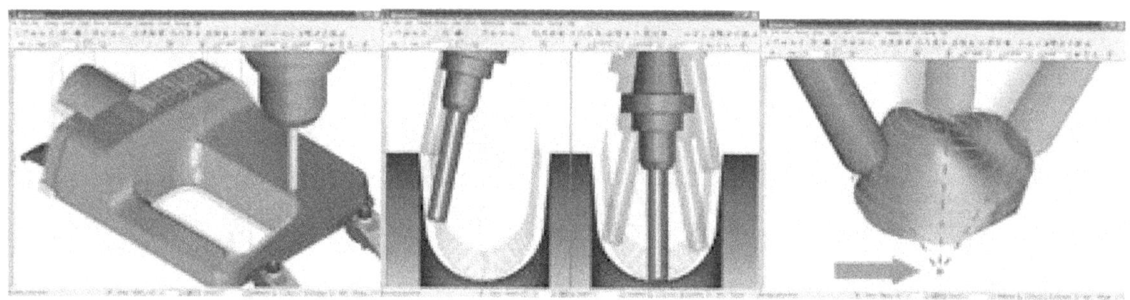

Optimized finishing   **Precise tool axis control**   **Flexible tool orientation**

Robot Configuration Libraries

Use Robotmaster's extensive configuration library to easily select your Robot and End-of-arm Tooling and convert CAD/CAM toolpaths for your specific hardware requirements and setup.

- Choose from FANUC, ABB, MOTOMAN, KUKA, STAUBLI and more.
- Enter robot operating parameters like:
- Entire robotic cell setup.
- End of arm tooling.
- Setup (user frame and tool center point data).
- Tool changer information.
- Motion parameters.
- Linear rail and/or rotary table configuration.

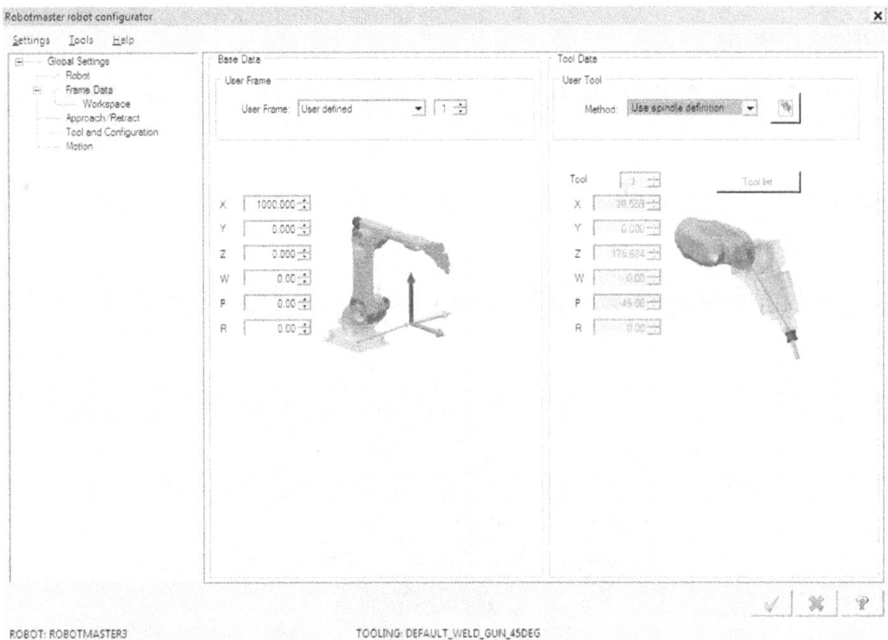

Manage user frame and tool center point data

Robot specific motion parameters settings

(a) Linear rail and rotary axis paramaters control

(b) End of arm tooling selection

Convert CAD/CAM Data to 6-axis Robot Output

Use the graphical interface to fine-tune the parameters by which Robotmaster will translate the 2 to 5 axis CNC toolpath data into a 6-axis robot toolpath.

-   Set robot configuration for optimal robot posture.
-   Manage motion between operations.

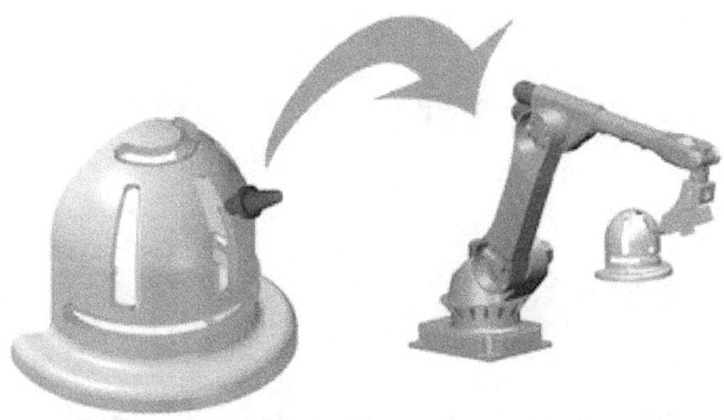

Convert CAD/CAM toolpaths to robot positions.

Optimization of Programs

Use automated settings to quickly optimize robot motion and precise control of rotation around tool for:

- Avoiding singularity and joint limits.

- Maximizing robot dexterity.

- Optimizing joint speeds and ensuring smooth robot playback.

Maintain fixed tool orientation

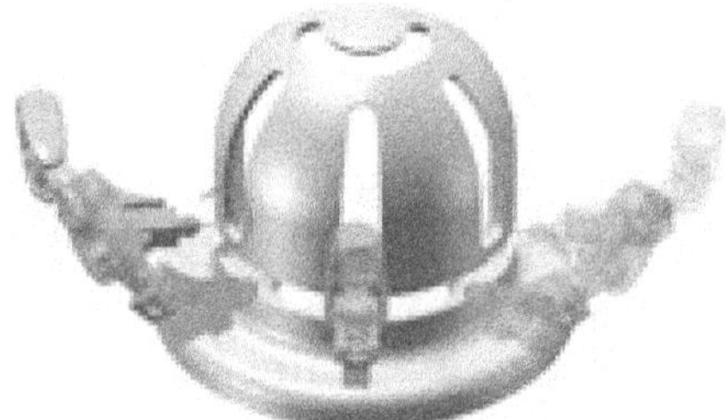

Vary tool orientation by rotation

Follow a relative orientation along a trajectory

Rotate tool across the trajectory

Robot Simulation

Validate the programs by using Robotmaster's robot simulator.

- View robot motion in continuous or step mode, by individual operation or complete toolgroup.
- Automatic detection of collisions.
- View either robot only or entire manufacturing cell.

Simulate entire cell with housing

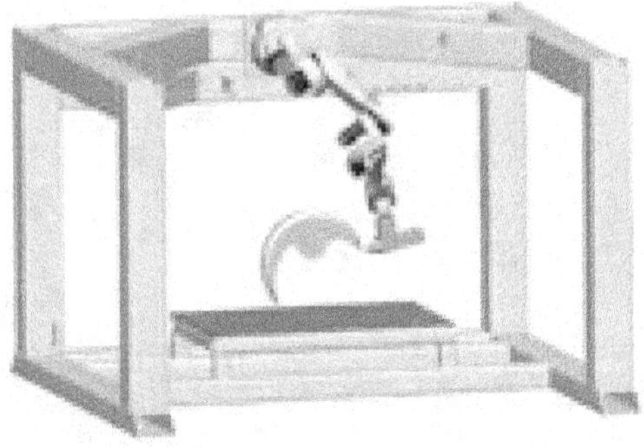

Hide housing during simulation

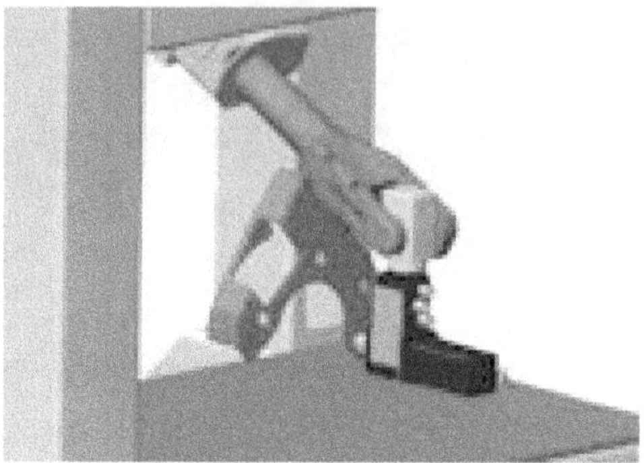

Detection of robot to part collision

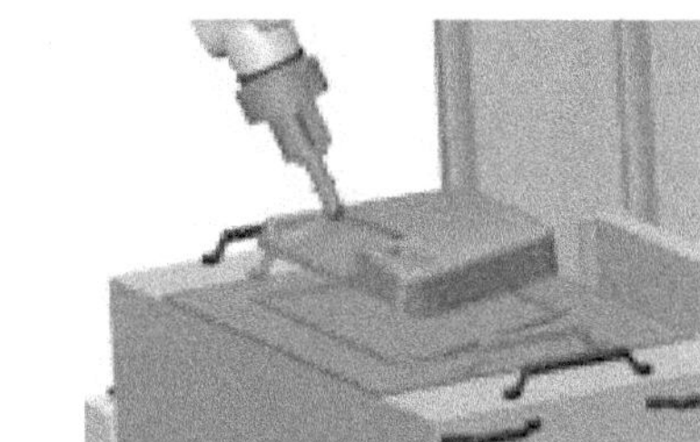

Detection of tolling to part collision

Code Generator

Robotmaster's post-processor generates the robot-ready program file.

- Generate programs in robot native language.
- Customizable robot code output.
- Multi-file output for managing long programs with limited robot memory.

Robot specific code file output will be generated.

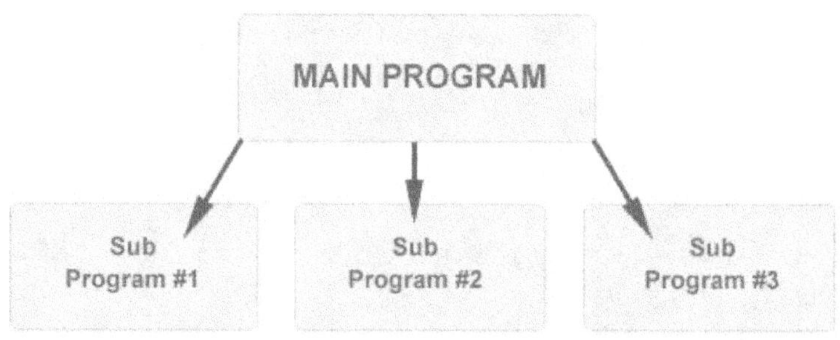

Multi-file output for managing long programs

ROBOTMASTER V5

Robotmaster Version 5 provides innovative new tools to effortlessly program and optimize robot tasks producing error-free robot paths. Expanding on powerful optimizing tools Robotmaster Version 5 has set a new standard for programming robots with the same ease and functionality as CNC machines. Below is a preview of some of the powerful enhancements of Robotmaster Version 5.

Workspace Analysis

The new Workspace Analysis (WSA) is designed to make the part placement experience simple and easy. When presented with the task of programming a part with a robot, it is often difficult and time consuming to determine where to properly position and orient the part. The WSA feature takes away most of the time and headache that is involved in figuring out the appropriate position and orientation of a part to be located in the workspace of the robot.

This feature is also useful for designing fixtures for the part or validating the choice of robot, tooling and overall setup. The WSA allows the user to visualize what used to be an unknown challenge, requiring lengthy manually trial and error, finding the optimal setup in mere minutes.

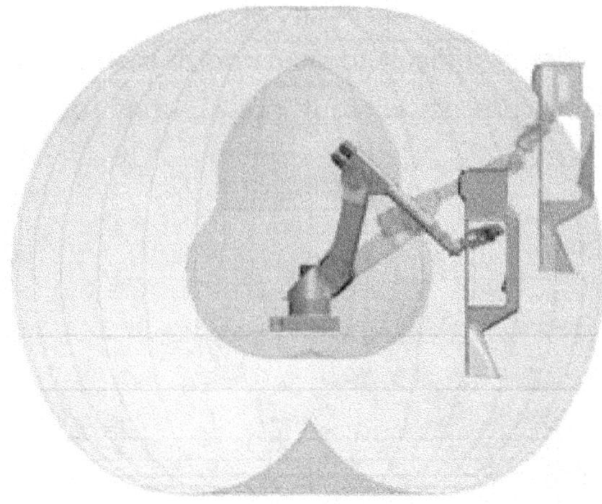

Tool Tilt Optimization

The new Tool Tilt Optimization (TTO) provides the user with increased flexibility when it comes to avoiding collisions and optimizing robot motion. The TTO feature allows a programmer to manage tool tilt angles easily and quickly always ensuring smooth robot motion. The user is now in full control of the tilt direction with visual tools that will help a programmer find solutions to challenges that would otherwise be difficult or impossible to resolve.

Rail Optimization

The new Rail Optimization provides an easy tool to program rails more effectively. The rail position can be controlled with great flexibility ensuring proper robot posture, maximizing the entire workspace and easily exploiting the full potential of a robot mounted on rails. It is no longer difficult to synchronize the rail and robot motion ensuring an optimized and continuous process without interruptions to reposition the robot on the rail.

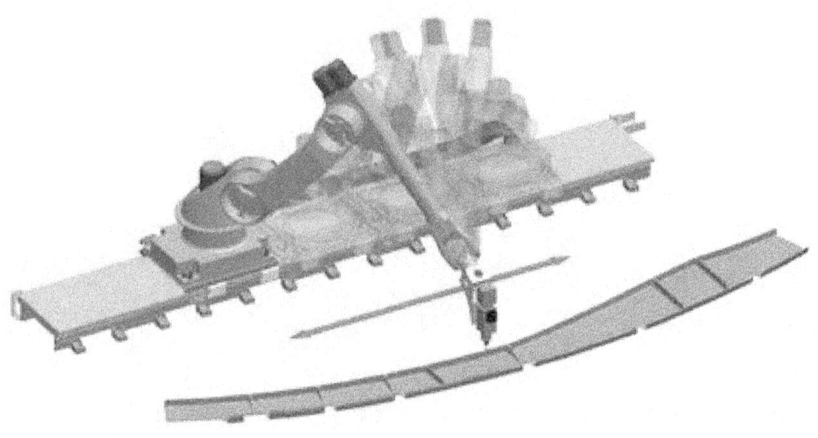

Optimization Enhancements

Optimization has been enhanced with the addition of Advanced Layers. Gradient maps provide the robot joint angles as well as the robot's elbow posture. These enhancements offer powerful tools to adequately manage the robot's posture as well as optimize for any specific robot joint.

Additional enhancements to optimization include:

- Ability to optimize up to three parameters: tool rotation, tool tilt and rail position.
- Errors on the path are displayed with a red ruler and hovering the mouse over this band displays information about the error;
- The path between program points can be checked during optimization, ensuring enhanced error detection.
- A new mapping technique is used to display multi-turn joints, this tool is very useful to de-bug issues typical to joints 4 and 6 on a standard 6-axis robot.

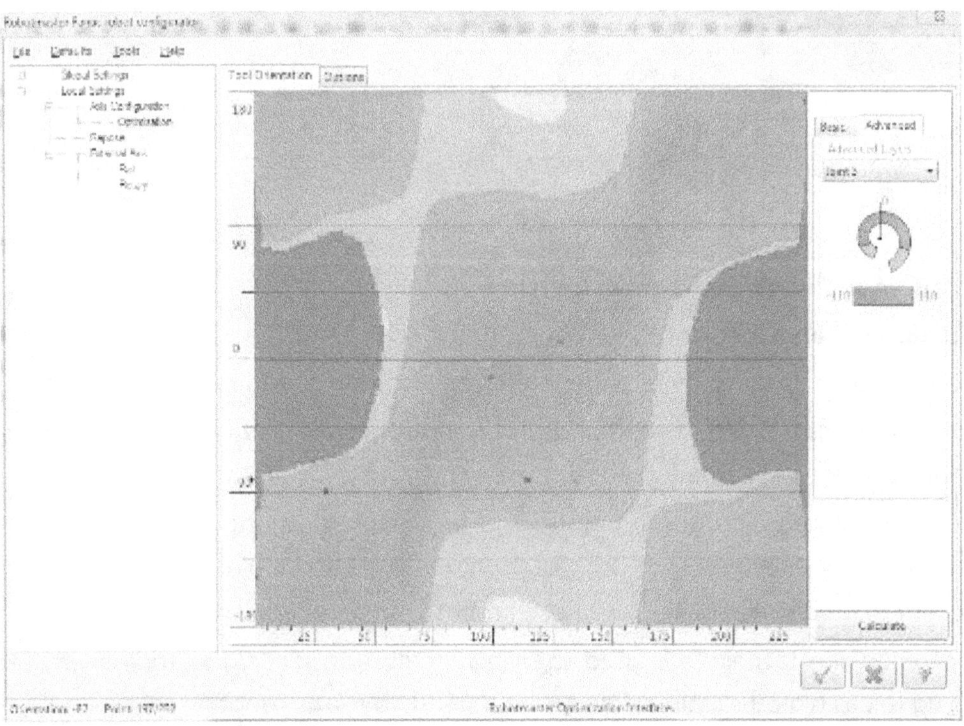

Post Processor Graphical Configurator

A new post processor configurator allows the user to quickly set appropriate settings for ultimate control of program codes. Extensive configuration parameters are available for each specific robot brand providing for flexible code output that fully exploits the language syntax and robot features.

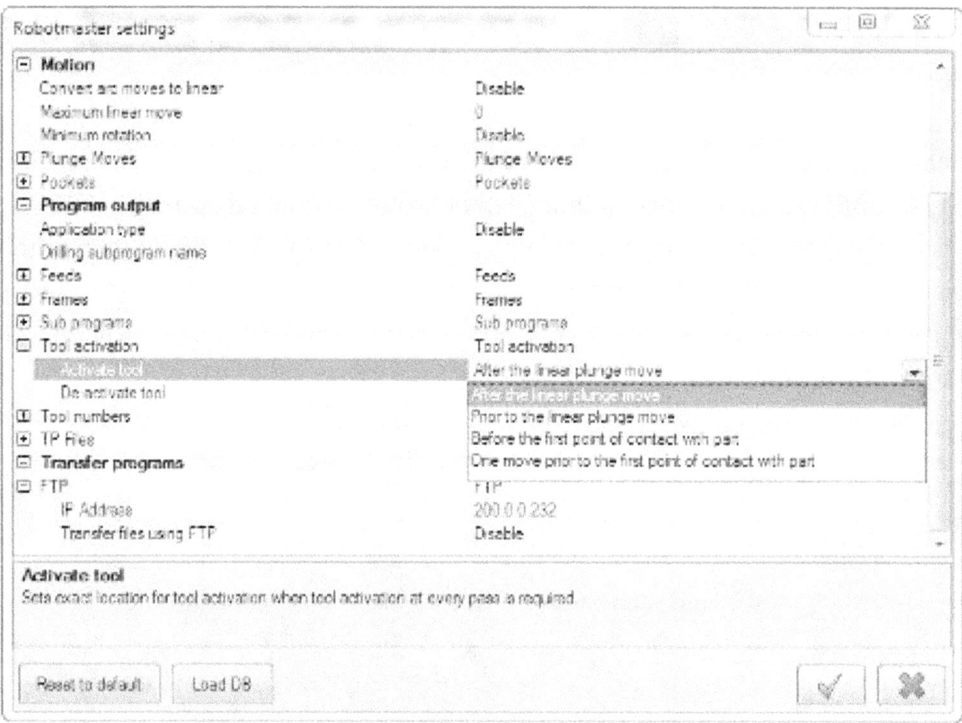

New features and enhancements at a glance

Optimization enhancements:

- Ability to optimize up to three parameters: tool rotation, tool tilt and rail position.
- Errors are displayed with a red band on the bottom ruler and hovering the mouse over this band displays information about the error.
- The path between program points can be checked during optimization, ensuring enhanced error detection
- Gradient maps display the values of each robot joint or external axes.

  A new mapping technique is used to display multi-turn joints, this tool is very useful to de-bug issues typical to joints 4 and 6 on a standard 6-axis robot.
- The elbow angle of the robot can be displayed as a gradient map, allowing the ability to manage the robot posture.
- An observation zone can be set on any robot joint to monitor its values.

Productivity enhancements:
- Workspace analysis tool.
- Ability to use the simulator to set repose values.
- Motion settings and robot configuration which are global parameters can be set as local settings for a specific operation.
- Converting joint moves to linear is now available for all robot brands.
- New settings dialog enabling flexible user preferences.
- Ability to set default preferences for local settings.
- Enhanced saving and reading of global and local settings.
- Ability to check prior operations during simulation and optimization.
- Enhanced control of rotary axes.

Performance enhancements:
- Maximum program size has been increased to 2 million points.
- New database with enhanced performance and future flexibility.
- Operation synchronization for synchronizing modified operations for quicker processing.
- Memory caching for increased performance during optimization and simulation.
- Automatic data management on RAM or disk for optimal performance for small and large programs.
- Faster calculation time for simulation and optimization.

Interface enhancements:
- Global and local settings have been separated.
- Global and local settings can be accessed using buttons on the main interface.
- New settings interface provides increased user preferences.
- New post processor configuration interface.

Simulator enhancements:
- Increased performance for simulating large programs.
- Improvements to graphics and rendering.
- Ability to jog parallel link robots and robots having joint 3 values from horizontal.
- Full screen simulation with larger graphics area.
- Ability to by-pass robot joint limitations for simulation providing for an easy way to de-bug programs.

Post Processor enhancements:

- Faster post processing.
- Graphical post configuration interface for easily setting program output preferences.

ROBOTS SUPPORTED

1. **FANUC**
2. **KUKA**
3. **ABB**
4. **YASKAWA**

1. FANUC

FANUC Robotics industrial robots and automated systems cover a wide range of applications for the aerospace, automotive, consumer goods, food, metal fabrication, medical, pharmaceutical, solar panel, and many other industries.

Advantage : Improve quality, maximize productivity, reduce costs, and increase your competitive edge without outsourcing,

2. KUKA

Compared with other technical innovations, the robot is still relatively young. The world's first industrial robot was not installed until the middle of the 20th century. The first electrically driven robot – controlled by a microprocessor – was launched on the market in 1974. In 1996, KUKA Robot Group achieved a quantum leap in industrial robot development. That year saw the launch of the first PC-based controller, developed by KUKA. This marked the dawn of a new era of "real" mechatronics, characterized by the precise interaction of software, controller and mechanical systems.

This means that the use of robot technology ensures consistently high quality for capital goods and consumer products from a vast range of different sectors. For robots can be used in practically any application: handling, stacking, inspecting, polishing or grinding. In combination with new gripper and sensor technologies, previously unimaginable robotic applications become possible.

Creativity, dynamism and innovation are required to implement these versatile and technologically demanding applications. These attributes are the key to economic success and market leadership. KUKA Robot Group knows the challenges facing both people and machines, understands its customers' requirements and is developing ideas to meet them – Working Ideas.

Everything that moves in automation comes from KUKA Robot Group

The continuous on-going development of robot and control technology is enabling robotics to establish itself across a broad spectrum of different markets. Cooperating robots are playing their part to optimize production processes and make them more flexible, not just in the automotive industry. In this development, several robots work together to machine the same parts at the same time, for example, thereby reducing cycle times, or they jointly handle heavy parts to share the payload. An additional new concept is focusing on improving the cooperation between robots and human operators with overlapping workspaces in order to achieve an optimal degree of automation. Well-thought-out function packages play an increasingly important role.

In General Industry, i.e. business in the non-automotive sector, the primary objective of development work is to tap into new markets, particularly in the fields of logistics, plastics, metalworking, foundry, medical technology and the entertainment industry. New function packages enable KUKA robot technology to penetrate into additional fields of application. The focus here is on logistics (palletizing, depalletizing), baggage handling at airports, handling tasks in bending processes and the seat-testing robot "Occubot".

3. ABB :

ABB is a global leader in power and automation technologies that enable utility and industry customers to improve their performance while lowering environmental impact.

Technology plays a key role for ABB. We have activities all over the world working to develop unique technologies that make our customers more competitive, while minimizing environmental impact.

Sustainability is integral to all aspects of our business. We strive to balance economic, environmental and social objectives and integrate them into our daily business decisions

4. YASKAWA :

Motoman industrial robots for: assembly, handling, machine tending, packaging, palletizing, painting, welding, and more.

✳✳✳

University Question Paper

DECEMBER 2011

Time : 3 Hours   **Max. Marks. : 100**

SECTION - I

Q. 1 (a) Sketch and explain the concept of work envelope (or work volume) with reference to **[6]**

  (i)   Cartesian robot.

  (ii) Polar robot.

(b) Explain the terms: **[6]**

  (i)   Accuracy.

  (ii) Precision.

  (iii) Resolution-as used in Robotics.

Ans. (i) Accuracy: Please refer to Section 1.10 (iii) on page 1.33.

(ii) Precision: Please refer to Section 3.4 (ii) on page 3.3.

(iii) Resolution-as used in Robotics: Please refer to Section 1.10 (ii) on page 1.32.

(c) Compare the advantages and disadvantages of hydraulic and electric drives. **[6]**

Ans. Please refer to Section 4.5 on page 4.22.

Q. 2 (a) State three laws of robotics. Explain the importance of third law. **[8]**

Ans. Please refer to Section 1.2 on page 1.1.

(b) Explain any four important parameters used for evaluating robot performance. **[8]**

Ans. Please refer to Section 1.10 on page 1.30.

OR

Q. 3 (a) Explain the method of classification of Robots based on geometric configuration. Write in brief about the characteristics of these robots. **[8]**

Ans. Please refer to Section 1.9 on page 1.22.

(b) Explain with neat sketches different joints used in Robots. **[8]**

Ans. Please refer to Section 1.8 (b) on page 1.13.

Q. 4 (a) Explain with neat sketch one type each of **[8]**

  (i)   Position sensor.

  (ii) Force sensor.

Ans. (i) Position sensor: Please refer to Section 8.5 on page 8.11.

   (ii) Force sensor: Please refer to Section 8.6 on page 8.13.

(b) State any four types of grippers. What are different factors to be considered in selection and design of grippers?						**[8]**

Ans. Please refer to Section 2.3 on page 2.5. Also refer to Section 2.2.4 on page 2.4.

OR

Q. 5 (a) "Selection of appropriate sensors is an important step in Robot design". Elaborate this with reference to						**[8]**

   (i)   A pick and place Cartesian robot for handling cartings-wt 10 kg.

   (ii)   A spot welding jointed arm robot with a reach of 1.5 m radius.

(b) Compare vacuum grippers Vs mechanical grippers.				**[8]**

SECTION - II

Q. 6 (a) Explain Denavit-Hartenberg parameters for assigning frames to links and identifying joint-link parameters and explain their limitations.		**[10]**

Ans. Please refer to Sections 6.3, 6.3.1, 6.3.2 and 6.3.3 on page 6.37 to 6.39.

(b) A planar 3R manipulator as shown in Fig. 1, has link lengths l_1 = 100 mm, l_2 = 80 mm and l_3 = 60 mm. Determine it's reachable workspace and state whether point (200, 100) is reached with θ_1 = 40°. If yes, what are the values of θ_2 and θ_3? If no, what should be the minimum value of θ_1 so that the point will be reached by the manipulator?						**[6]**

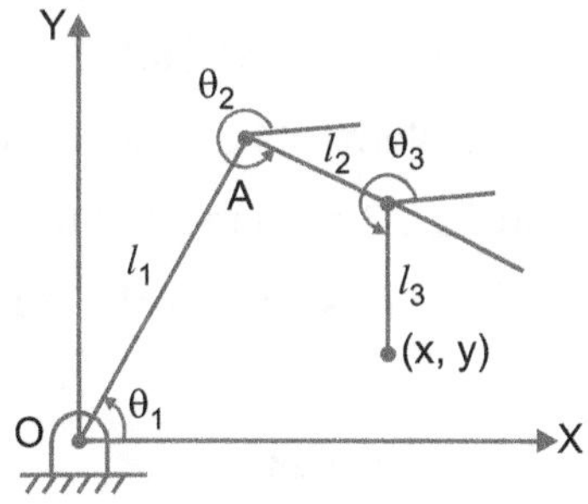

Fig. 1

OR

Q. 7 (a) Explain dynamic model of a 2 DoF planar RR manipulator and get expressions for EOM of the same.						**[10]**

Ans. Please refer to Section 7.4 on page 7.4.

(b) A camera locates an object by **[6]**

$$^{Camera}T_{Object} = \begin{bmatrix} 0 & -1 & 0 & 50 \\ 1 & 0 & 0 & -75 \\ 0 & 0 & 1 & 20 \\ 0 & 0 & 0 & 1 \end{bmatrix}$$

The camera is then translated by 15 units along Z-axis of the object, then rotated about its own X-axis by −90°. Determine the new relation between camera and object.

Q. 8 (a) What is a vision system? How can vision systems be classified? Explain the categories. **[8]**

Ans. Please refer to Sections 9.1 and 9.3 on pages 9.1 and 9.2.

(b) Explain in brief various power transmitting devices in robots with advantages of each. **[8]**

OR

Q. 9 (a) Describe imaging devices and image processing techniques used in a robot.

[10]

Ans. Please refer to Section 9.8 on page 9.8.

(b) Explain how belts, cables and chains are used for power transmission and how can preload be eliminated. **[6]**

Ans. Please refer to Section 8.3.2 (ii) on page 8.4.

Q. 10 (a) Write short note on methods of robot programming. **[6]**

Ans. Please refer to Section 10.2 on page 10.1.

(b) Describe robot language elements and their functions. **[6]**

Ans. Please refer to Section 10.6.2 on page 10.16.

(c) Explain in brief three different search techniques with respect to AI in robots.

[6]

✱✱✱